FAR FROM THE MADDING CROWD

THOMAS HARDY was born in a cottage in Higher Bockhampton, near Dorchester, on 2 June 1840. He was educated locally and at sixteen was articled to a Dorchester architect, John Hicks. In 1862 he moved to London, found employment with another architect, Arthur Blomfield, began to write poetry and published an essay. By 1867 he had returned to Dorset to work as Hicks's assistant and began his first (unpublished) novel, *The Poor Man and the Lady*.

On an architectural visit to St Juliot in Cornwall in 1870 he met his first wife, Emma Gifford. Before their marriage in 1874 he had published four novels and was earning his living as a writer. More novels followed and in 1878 the Hardys moved from Dorset to the London literary scene. But in 1885, after building his house at Max Gate near Dorchester, Hardy again returned to Dorset. He then produced most of his major novels: *The Mayor of Casterbridge* (1886), *The Woodlanders* (1887), *Tess of the D'Urbervilles* (1891), *The Pursuit of the Well-Beloved* (1892) and *Jude the Obscure* (1895). Amidst the controversy caused by *Jude the Obscure*, he turned to the poetry he had been writing all his life. In the next thirty years he published over nine hundred poems and his epic drama in verse, *The Dynasts*.

After a long and bitter estrangement, Emma Hardy died at Max Gate in 1912. Paradoxically, the event triggered some of Hardy's finest love poetry. In 1914, however, he married Florence Dugdale, a close friend for several years. In 1910 he had been awarded the Order of Merit and was recognized, even revered, as the major literary figure of the time. He died on 11 January 1928. His ashes were buried in Westminster Abbey and his heart at Stinsford in Dorset.

ROSEMARIE MORGAN teaches at Yale University and has also held Visiting Distinguished Professorships at the University of British Columbia, Canada, and Kansai University, Japan. She made her mark on Hardy studies with *Women and Sexuality in the Novels of Thomas Hardy*, followed by *Cancelled Words: Rediscovering Thomas Hardy*. Her extensive publications include articles on Charlotte Brontë, Toni

Morrison, Mary Chesnut and women writers of the American frontier. She is currently working on a study of childhood in Victorian literature and culture, and has recently completed articles on 'women' and 'marriage' for *The Oxford Reader's Companion to Hardy*. In 1995 she became Honorary Vice-President of the Thomas Hardy Society, and in 1997 President of the Thomas Hardy Association; she was appointed to the Consulting Board of Victorian Studies in Italy.

SHANNON RUSSELL holds a post doctoral Fellowship specializing in nineteenth- and twentieth-century literature at Oxford. She has published on the Victorian period and most recently co-edited *Letters of a Hindoo Rajah*. Her current work includes acting as head of research for the Yale edition of Tennessee Williams's *Journals* and editing Forster's *Life of Charles Dickens* for Penguin Classics.

PATRICIA INGHAM is General Editor of all Hardy's fiction in the Penguin Classics Edition. She is a Fellow of St Anne's College, Reader in English and *The Times* Lecturer in English Language, University of Oxford. She has written extensively on the Victorian novel and on Hardy in particular. Her most recent publications include *Dickens, Women and Language* (1992) and *The Language of Gender and Class: Transformation in the Victorian Novel* (1996). She has also edited Charles Dickens's *American Notes for General Circulation* and *Martin Chuzzlewit*, Elizabeth Gaskell's *North and South*, and Thomas Hardy's *The Pursuit of the Well-Beloved and The Well-Beloved* and *The Woodlanders* for Penguin Classics.

THOMAS HARDY

Far From the Madding Crowd

Edited with an Introduction and Notes by
ROSEMARIE MORGAN
with SHANNON RUSSELL

PENGUIN BOOKS

PENGUIN BOOKS

Published by the Penguin Group
Penguin Books Ltd, 80 Strand, London WC2R 0RL, England
Penguin Putnam Inc., 375 Hudson Street, New York, New York 10014, USA
Penguin Books Australia Ltd, 250 Camberwell Road, Camberwell, Victoria 3124, Australia
Penguin Books Canada Ltd, 10 Alcorn Avenue, Toronto, Ontario, Canada M4V 3B2
Penguin Books India (P) Ltd, 11 Community Centre, Panchsheel Park, New Delhi – 110 017, India
Penguin Books (NZ) Ltd, Cnr Rosedale and Airborne Roads, Albany, Auckland, New Zealand
Penguin Books (South Africa) (Pty) Ltd, 24 Sturdee Avenue, Rosebank 2196, South Africa

Penguin Books Ltd, Registered Offices: 80 Strand, London WC2R 0RL, England

www.penguin.com

First published 1874
This edition published in Penguin Classics 2000
Reprinted 2003

028

Set in 10/12.5pt Monotype Baskerville
Typeset by Rowland Phototypesetting Ltd, Bury St Edmunds, Suffolk
Printed in England by Clays Ltd, St Ives plc

ISBN-13: 978–0–141–43965–5

CONTENTS

ACKNOWLEDGEMENTS

My appreciation and warmest thanks go to the staff of the Beinecke Rare Book and Manuscript Library at Yale University who not only gave me unlimited access to Hardy's holograph manuscript of *Far From the Madding Crowd* but also provided a constant flow of friendly assistance and goodwill. To Patricia Ingham I wish to express my gratitude for her unfailing patience in what she rather ruefully called her 'Leslie Stephen' role – which was, in truth, never less than excellent editorial advice.

R. M.

GENERAL EDITOR'S PREFACE

This edition uses, with one exception, the first edition in *volume* form of each of Hardy's novels and therefore offers something not generally available. Their dates range from 1871 to 1897. The purpose behind this choice is to present each novel as the creation of its own period and without revisions of later times, since these versions have an integrity and value of their own. The outline of textual history that follows is designed to expand on this statement.

All of Hardy's fourteen novels, except *Jude the Obscure* (1895) which first appeared as a volume in the Wessex Novels, were published individually as he wrote them (from 1871 onwards). Apart from *Desperate Remedies* (1871) and *Under the Greenwood Tree* (1872), all were published first as serials in periodicals, where they were subjected to varying degrees of editorial interference and censorship. *Desperate Remedies* and *Under the Greenwood Tree* appeared directly in volume form from Tinsley Brothers. By 1895 ten more novels had been published in volumes by six different publishers.

By 1895 Hardy was sufficiently well-established to negotiate with Osgood, McIlvaine a collected edition of all earlier novels and short story collections plus the volume edition of *Jude the Obscure. The Well-Beloved* (radically changed from its serialized version) was added in 1897, completing the appearance of all Hardy's novels in volume form. Significantly this collection was called the 'Wessex Novels' and contained a map of 'The Wessex of the Novels' and authorial prefaces, as well as frontispieces by Macbeth-Raeburn of a scene from the novel sketched 'on the spot'. The texts were heavily revised by Hardy, amongst other things, in relation to topography, to strengthen the 'Wessex' element so as to suggest that this half-real half-imagined location had been coherently conceived from the beginning, though of course he knew that this was not so. In practice 'Wessex' had an uncertain and ambiguous development in the earlier editions. To trace the growth of Wessex in the novels as they appeared it is necessary to read them in their original pre-1895 form, for the 1895–6 edition represents a substantial layer of reworking.

Similarly in the last fully revised and collected edition of 1912–13, the Wessex Edition, further alterations were made to topographical detail and photographs of Dorset were included. In the more open climate of opinion then prevailing, sexual and religious references were sometimes (though not always) made bolder. In both collected editions there were also many changes of other kinds. In addition novels and short story volumes were grouped thematically as 'Novels of Character and Environment', 'Romances and Fantasies' and 'Novels of Ingenuity' in a way suggesting a unifying master plan underlying all texts. A few revisions were made for the Mellstock Edition of 1919–20, but to only some texts.

It is various versions of the 1912–13 edition which are generally available today, incorporating these layers of alteration and shaped in part by the critical climate when the alterations were made. Therefore the present edition offers the texts as Hardy's readers first encountered them, in a form of which he in general approved, the version that his early critics reacted to. It reveals Hardy as he first dawned upon the public and shows how his writing (including the creation of Wessex) developed, partly in response to differing climates of opinion in the 1870s, 1880s and early 1890s. In keeping with these general aims, the edition will reproduce all contemporary illustrations where the originals were line drawings. In addition for all texts which were illustrated, individual volumes will provide an appendix discussing the artist and the illustrations.

The exception to the use of the first volume editions is *Far From the Madding Crowd*, for which Hardy's holograph manuscript will be used. That edition will demonstrate in detail just how the text is 'the creation of its own period': by relating the manuscript to the serial version and to the first volume edition. The heavy editorial censoring by Leslie Stephen for the serial and the subsequent revision for the volume provide an extreme example of the processes that in many cases precede and produce the first book versions. In addition, the complete serial version (1892) of *The Well-Beloved* will be printed alongside the volume edition, since it is arguably a different novel from the latter.

To complete the picture of how the texts developed later, editors trace in their Notes on the History of the Text the major changes in 1895–6 and 1912–13. They quote significant alterations in their explanatory notes and include the authorial prefaces of 1895–6 and 1912–13. They also indicate something of the pre-history of the texts in manuscripts where these are available. The editing of the short stories will be separately dealt with in the two volumes containing them.

Patricia Ingham
St Anne's College, Oxford

CHRONOLOGY: HARDY'S LIFE AND WORKS

1840 2 June: Thomas Hardy born, Higher Bockhampton, Dorset, eldest child of a builder, Thomas Hardy, and Jemima Hand, who had been married for less than six months. Younger siblings: Mary, Henry, Katharine (Kate), to whom he remained close.

1848–56 Schooling in Dorset.

1856 Hardy watched the hanging of Martha Browne for the murder of her husband. (Thought to be remembered in the death of Tess Durbeyfield.)

1856–60 Articled to Dorchester architect, John Hicks; later his assistant.

late 1850s Important friendship with Horace Moule (eight years older, middle-class and well-educated), who became his intellectual mentor and encouraged his self-education.

1862 London architect, Arthur Blomfield, employed him as a draughtsman. Self-education continued.

1867 Returned to Dorset as a jobbing architect. He worked for Hicks on church restoration.

1868 Completed his first novel *The Poor Man and the Lady* but it was rejected for publication (see 1878).

1869 Worked for the architect Crickmay in Weymouth, again on church restoration.

1870 After many youthful infatuations thought to be referred to in early poems, met his first wife, Emma Lavinia Gifford, on a professional visit to St Juliot in north Cornwall.

1871 *Desperate Remedies* published in volume form by Tinsley Brothers.

1872 *Under the Greenwood Tree* published in volume form by Tinsley Brothers.

1873 *A Pair of Blue Eyes* (previously serialized in *Tinsleys' Magazine*). Horace Moule committed suicide.

1874 *Far from the Madding Crowd* (previously serialized in the *Cornhill Magazine*). Hardy married Emma and set up house in London (Surbiton).

They had no children, to Hardy's regret; and she never got on with his family.

1875 The Hardys returned to Dorset (Swanage).

1876 *The Hand of Ethelberta* (previously serialized in the *Cornhill Magazine*).

1878 *The Return of the Native* (previously serialized in *Belgravia*). The Hardys moved back to London (Tooting). Serialized version of part of first unpublished novel appeared in *Harper's Weekly* in New York as *An Indiscretion in the Life of an Heiress*. It was never included in his collected works.

1880 *The Trumpet-Major* (previously serialized in *Good Words*). Hardy ill for many months.

1881 *A Laodicean* (previously serialized in *Harper's New Monthly Magazine*). The Hardys returned to Dorset.

1882 *Two on a Tower* (previously serialized in the *Atlantic Monthly*).

1885 The Hardys moved for the last time to a house, Max Gate, outside Dorchester, designed by Hardy and built by his brother.

1886 *The Mayor of Casterbridge* (previously serialized in the *Graphic*).

1887 *The Woodlanders* (previously serialized in *Macmillan's Magazine*).

1888 *Wessex Tales*.

1891 *A Group of Noble Dames* (tales). *Tess of the D'Urbervilles* (previously serialized in censored form in the *Graphic*). It simultaneously enhanced his reputation as a novelist and caused a scandal because of its advanced views on sexual conduct.

1892 Hardy's father, Thomas, died. Serialized version of *The Well-Beloved*, entitled *The Pursuit of the Well-Beloved*, in the *Illustrated London News*. Growing estrangement from Emma.

1892–3 *Our Exploits at West Poley*, a long tale for boys, published in an American periodical, the *Household*.

1893 Met Florence Henniker, one of several society women with whom he had intense friendships. Collaborated with her on *The Spectre of the Real* (published 1894).

1894 *Life's Little Ironies* (tales).

1895 *Jude the Obscure*, a savage attack on marriage which worsened relations with Emma. Serialized previously in *Harper's New Monthly Magazine*. It received both eulogistic and vitriolic reviews. The latter were a factor in his ceasing to write novels.

1895–6 First Collected Edition of novels: Wessex Novels (16 volumes), published by Osgood, McIlvaine. This included the first book edition of *Jude the Obscure.*

1897 *The Well-Beloved* (rewritten) published as a book; added to the Wessex Novels as vol. XVII. From now on he published only the poetry he had been writing since the 1860s. **No more novels.**

1898 *Wessex Poems and Other Verses.* Hardy and Emma continued to live at Max Gate but were now estranged and 'kept separate'.

1901 *Poems of the Past and the Present.*

1902 Macmillan became his publishers.

1904 Part I of *The Dynasts* (epic-drama in verse on Napoleon). Hardy's mother, Jemima, 'the single most important influence in his life', died.

1905 Met Florence Emily Dugdale, his future second wife, then aged 26. Soon a friend and secretary.

1906 Part 2 of *The Dynasts.*

1908 Part 3 of *The Dynasts.*

1909 *Time's Laughingstocks and Other Verses.*

1910 Awarded Order of Merit, having previously refused a knighthood.

1912–13 Major collected edition of novels and verse, revised by Hardy: The Wessex Edition (24 volumes). 27 November: Emma died still estranged. This triggered the writing of Hardy's finest love-lyrics about their early time in Cornwall.

1913 *A Changed Man and Other Tales.*

1914 10 February: married Florence Dugdale (already hurt by his poetic reaction to Emma's death). *Satires of Circumstance. The Dynasts: Prologue and Epilogue.*

1915 Mary, Hardy's sister, died. His distant young cousin, Frank, killed at Gallipoli.

1916 *Selected Poems.*

1917 *Moments of Vision and Miscellaneous Verses.*

1919–20 Mellstock Edition of novels and verse (37 volumes).

1922 *Late Lyrics and Earlier with Many Other Verses.*

1923 *The Famous Tragedy of the Queen of Cornwall* (drama).

1924 Dramatized *Tess* performed at Dorchester. Hardy infatuated with the local woman, Gertrude Bugler, who played Tess.

1925 *Human Shows, Far Phantasies, Songs and Trifles.*

1928 Hardy died on 11 January. His heart was buried in Emma's grave at Stinsford, his ashes in Westminster Abbey. *Winter Words in Various Moods and Metres* published posthumously. Hardy's brother, Henry, died.

1928–30 Hardy's autobiography published (on his instructions) under his second wife's name.

1937 Florence Hardy (his second wife) died.

1940 Hardy's last sibling, Kate, died.

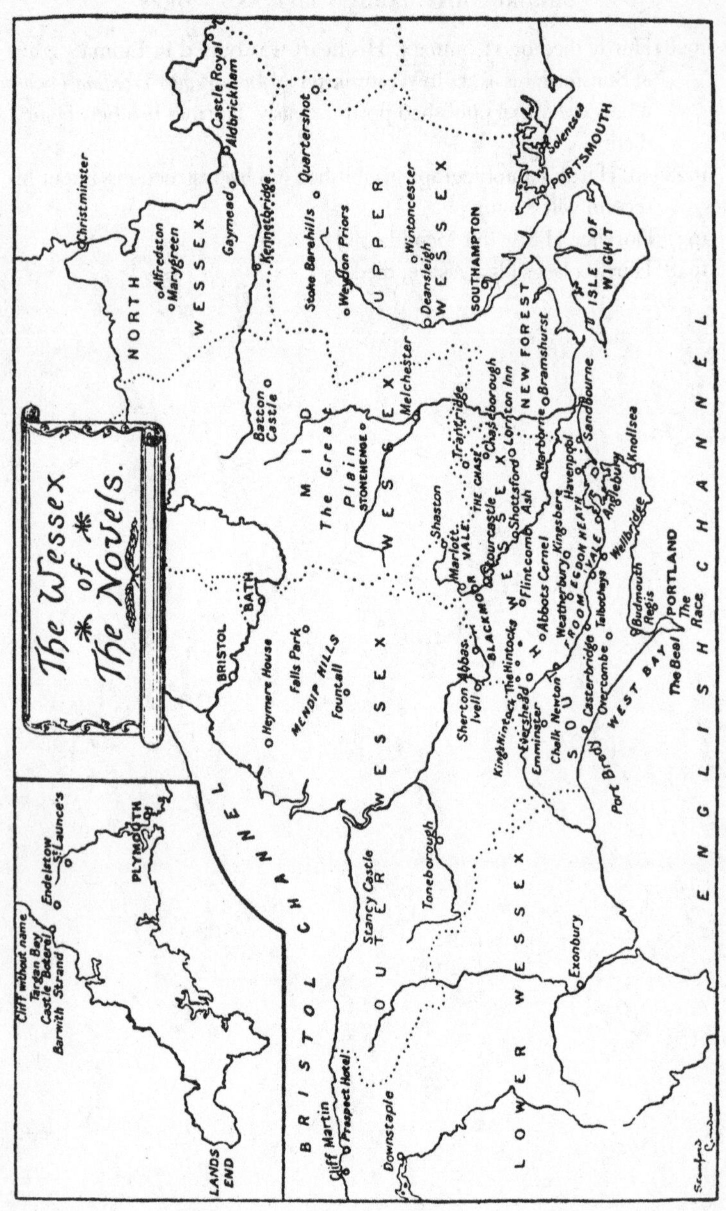

This map is from the Wessex Novels Edition, 1895–6

BIBLIOGRAPHICAL NOTE

The following abbreviations are used for texts frequently cited throughout the edition:

Collected Letters	R. L. Purdy and M. Millgate (eds.), *The Collected Letters of Thomas Hardy*, 7 vols. (Oxford: Clarendon Press, 1978–88)
Cornhill	*The Cornhill Magazine*, 1874, edited by Leslie Stephen. (London: Macmillan, 1962)
Life	Florence Emily Hardy, *The Life of Thomas Hardy, 1840–1928* (London: Macmillan, 1962)
Literary Notebooks	L. Bjork (ed.), *The Literary Notebooks of Thomas Hardy* (London: Macmillan, 1985)
Biography	Michael Millgate, *Thomas Hardy: A Biography* (Oxford: Clarendon Press, 1982)
Personal Writings	Harold Orel (ed.), *Thomas Hardy's Personal Writings: Prefaces, Literary Opinions, Reminiscences* (New York: St Martin's Press, 1966)
Purdy	Richard Little Purdy, *Thomas Hardy: A Bibliographical Study* (Oxford: Clarendon Press, 1968)
Seymour-Smith	Martin Seymour-Smith, *Hardy* (London: Bloomsbury, 1994)
Works	Michael Millgate (ed.), *The Life and Works of Thomas Hardy* (Athens, Georgia: 1985)

INTRODUCTION

Hardy never saw his manuscript version of *Far From the Madding Crowd* in print. Nor have his readers, until today. This edition brings into publication for the very first time Hardy's own original words just as they left his pen – just as they appeared on his editor's desk, prior to alteration and serialization in the *Cornhill Magazine* in 1874.

Customarily, manuscripts were not returned from publishing houses to such obscure authors as the anonymous creator of *Far From the Madding Crowd* of 1874. Consequently, it may have been inconvenient for Hardy not to have recovered his original text for making revisions to post-*Cornhill* editions but it was by no means unusual. What did strike Hardy as extraordinary was that it turned up, many decades later, in 1918, in the London offices of his former *Cornhill* publishers, Smith, Elder & Co. 'How surprising that you should have found the MS,' he wrote to Mrs Reginald Smith, 'I thought it "pulped" ages ago. And what a good thought of yours, to send it to the Red Cross, if anybody will buy it.'[1]

But no such dignity of disinterestedness unhanded the creative act itself. Hardy was still applying revisions to the 'Wessex' topography of *Far From the Madding Crowd* as late as 1912. And despite a certain collapse of vision in re-viewing a world now remote in memory and imagination – a collapse most noticeable in the inconsistency of his revisions to the progressive indirection of Gabriel Oak's stature and centrality[2] – and despite the fact that he never had his original work to hand over the years, Hardy did endeavour to restore something of his first intentions, his initial integrity and candour, to volume editions of the novel.

The 'restoration' was itself a matter of integrity. The original manuscript version, submitted for serialization in the *Cornhill* – which subsequently provided the copy-text for all later editions of *Far From the Madding Crowd* up until the present day – had, after all, been severely compromised. And although he had learned much about publication politics from his editor, Leslie Stephen, in the month-by-month process of editorial criticism and censorship, Hardy never lost his fierce contempt for all forms of 'tampering with natural truth', as he put it some fourteen years later in 'The Profitable Reading of Fiction'.[3] Indeed, the focus of his post-*Cornhill* revisionary work says as much: whereas his late-century topographical revisions were purely pragmatic, now that 'Wessex' had begun to emerge, by the 1890s, as a fully unified microcosmic construct, in his earlier revisions he sought, primarily, to recover the 'natural truth' of his original text. His later typological revisions were largely what I would call 'prophylactic', notably in the case of adjustments to Oak's loss of authority and stature (manly authority was closely associated with virility in the Victorian mind), which shrinks rather inconveniently towards the end of the novel in line with his diminishing centrality. But Hardy's very first attempts had been to restore something of *Far From the Madding Crowd*'s original candour. It was imperative that the 'things which everybody is thinking but nobody is saying . . . be taken up and treated frankly' – and for Hardy this included such unmentionable 'things' as female sexuality, illegitimacy and, in the case of Fanny Robbin, the moral innocence of the unmarried mother commonly outcast as a fallen woman in the world of the Victorian reader.

Leslie Stephen's first reaction to Hardy's work had been one of sheer delight. He knew nothing of Hardy's experimental if somewhat graceless polemic on class privilege entitled '*The Poor Man and the Lady*, A Story with no plot: containing some original verses' (1868: rejected for publication by Macmillan). Nor had he heard of the melodramatic, plot-driven *Desperate Remedies* (1871) which Hardy had undertaken on the advice of well-meaning publishers who had not overlooked the unquestionable literary promise in *The Poor Man and the Lady* while deploring its highly questionable disdain of audience, readership and market. But in coming across Hardy's second published novel, *Under the Greenwood Tree* (1872), Stephen was utterly charmed. Without further ado he sought out the name of its anonymous author and wrote to say he had been filled with 'great pleasure' by the 'admirable' descriptions of country life – surely such writing would please the readers of the *Cornhill Magazine* as much as it had pleased him? Hardy was, at that time, in the throes of completing *A Pair of Blue Eyes* (1873), his third published novel. He responded, even so, to Stephen's invitation to submit a story for serial publication by sketching an outline of a 'pastoral tale' comprising 'a young woman-farmer, a shepherd, and a sergeant of cavalry'[4] – a rural tale most eminently suitable, in Stephen's opinion, to a popular periodical of the *Cornhill*'s high cultural and literary standing.

Thus, with but a few rough chapters in hand, Stephen commissioned *Far From the Madding Crowd*, Hardy's fourth published novel, virtually sight unseen.

Hardy was first and foremost a poet. Coventry Patmore, one of the most popular poets of the Victorian era, genuinely regretted that *A Pair of Blue Eyes* had not been written in verse, that 'such unequalled beauty and power should not have assured themselves the immortality which would have been impressed upon them by the form of verse'.[5] The devices of rhythmical, figurative and metaphorical language, together with the strategies of symbolic action, embodiment, metonymy and so on, all came naturally to Hardy. Equally, his usages were innovative and his ideas nonconformist. Heedful of practicalities he placed himself dutifully in Stephen's hands fully prepared to meet editorial demands for more generally accepted literary forms. And where the demands related to chapter organization, story-plotting or the special needs of serialization, Hardy was more or less compliant; but where they conflicted with what he called his 'higher aims' or his deep-seated iconoclasm he was apt to pay lip service to convention and a considerably heavier debt to repression. Yet, despite this spirit of compromise, his continuing and often unwitting transgression of social and moral boundaries eventually taxed his editor's patience so sorely that he simply cut and deleted as and when he saw fit, with or without the author's permission.

The transgressions were sometimes as minor as the naming of an unmentionable item of anatomy ('buttocks'), or the casual touching of bodies (Bathsheba's hand on Oak's waist), or too free a use of the Lord's name, or even a neologism here and there ('emotional', 'feminality') – which Hardy's Victorian critics were to scorn as cheap and nasty and the *Oxford English Dictionary* was to enter into its lexicon. Less innocuous, and more systematically purged from the manuscript by the slashing editorial pencil, were Hardy's insouciant references to female sexual desire, whether they were made lightheartedly by the rustics or in earnest by Bathsheba – as in discussing her 'wantonness' (in modern parlance, sexual playfulness) in conversation with Oak. Without the benefit of hindsight, in these instances, Stephen inferred a simple ignorance of the proprieties in this new and inexperienced novelist.

Certainly Hardy was lax, given the literary conventions of the day which insisted on the presence of a censorious voice, or a moralizing narrator, to assist in the acceptance and preservation of prevailing socio-sexual codes and values. Inclusion of these internal 'censors' seems to have been anathema to Hardy. At any rate he included them on occasions too infrequent or too slight for the purposes of the novel's edification – a moral edification that was still of paramount importance to people in high places in the 1870s. Thus it was that in a final exasperated editorial swoop Stephen excised *Far From the Madding Crowd*'s most flagrant of all transgressions: Hardy's poignantly tender delineation in the manuscript of Fanny's last sleep with her stillborn babe in her arms.

Far From the Madding Crowd is, in many respects, the precursor to *Tess of the D'Urbervilles* (1891), with the role of Tess split between the trusting homespun girl (Fanny) seduced by the untrustworthy 'blue-blood' (Troy), and the courageous, self-determined girl struggling to make her way in a world made by men for men, played by Bathsheba. Unlike Tess, however, Bathsheba is by birth middle class, by education accomplished, by inclination innovative, daring and adventurous – conversely, vulnerable, unguarded and rash. And unlike Tess, she is a farmer – farming being the province of men, according to Oak and his compeers. Thus she is repeatedly subjected to judgemental views, to public scrutiny of her private life, to superstitious belief and sexual prejudice, as also to the prevailing laws of matrimony which deprive her of her property and the entitlements she had earned in her own right which are now assigned to her (thriftless) husband upon marriage. And in her complexity, in her youthful contradictory impulses, in her self-protective hauteur born of fear and insecurity, in her sexually challenging excitement and self-unseeing recklessness, she is rarely free of male censure both within and beyond the novel.

Yet, as literary tradition has it, to be put on trial-of-conscience in this manner is the test of a monolithic consciousness. Hardy's major heroines invariably find themselves up against the trial and judgement of the dominant class in this way – emotionally and psychologically endangered in a representative Victorian world in which the skills of self-preservation (physical, mental, intellectual, political) are devalued in women; in which premarital sexual experience ends in a woman's ruin or in compulsory marriage; in which class and sexual dominance combine to consolidate a formidable male power-threshold on which man's superior social status turns – the power that inevitably galvanizes the erotic.

Victorian women did not of course lack sexual power. But in contrast to men, social codes and practices gave recognition either to their sexual power *or* to their class power but very rarely both in tandem. Culturally speaking, the one was doomed to arrest the other. It is not simply, though, that the male 'wolf' is a creature of superior class in Hardy's world. It is also that, despite being doubly empowered by virtue of class privilege and masculine authority, he still hungers after the female life-force – the woman's secret energy and vital intelligence – to the ugly point of feeding upon it and mutilating it.

A Pair of Blue Eyes was the first of the Wessex novels to introduce this dissonant element into a pastoral domain traditionally associated with birth and renewal – the regenerative world of nature. Undoubtedly a vital force and, moreover, a supreme agent of that strange enchantment which inspirits the Wessex universe, Hardy's pastoral world remains, primarily, a place apart into which characters enter as if by magnetization and depart as if by expulsion, hurt and hurting, angry, injured and sad. Disillusion, deep disturbance and often irretrievable loss follow re-entry into this particular ancestral village. For many returning natives, notably Frank Troy, Clym Yeobright, Grace Melbury, Jocelyn Pierston and even (symbolically) the 'pretender' Alec D'Urberville, such re-entry enacts a physical return to the place of origins where, in some way or another, they no longer belong.

This process of relocation and dislocation parallels, in turn, Hardy's own imaginative 'return' over the years, which, in psychoanalytic terms, serves to 'integrate' his own belonging, whether it be his own loss of the past, his haunted sense of untraceable origins, or his unconscious yearning for the irrecoverable maternal abode of infancy. The interiorization by 'covering' or 'inwrapping' of so many of his more significant dwellings in *Far From the Madding Crowd* reinforces the idea that his Wessex construct, as a reconstruction of the world of his birthplace, imaginatively resurrects the vanished world of natal origins – the maternal space or 'enwombed' (his word) abodes from the long-lost distant past. Bathsheba's own 'homestead' (IX), for example, is not only covered by velvety-soft mosses and (architecturally) faced with finely detailed features but is also actually spoken of as a 'body' almost in the same breath that it is 'effaced as a distinct property'. In this sense, Hardy's unerring imaginative 'return' to his reconstructed place of origins renews the attempt to recreate and complete – thus to integrate – the configured original native state. Aesthetically and psychologically this configuration shapes the body-construct of Wessex, which itself undergoes constant expansion and revision continuously throughout the twenty years of Hardy's growth as a novelist and loss of youth as a man.

But if *A Pair of Blue Eyes* introduces the first of many variations on the fraught theme of relational inequity and dissonance in Hardy's novels, *Far From the Madding Crowd* breaks this ground fully with Wessex and all that it connotes in terms of a 'partly real, partly dream-country'[6] – a country abounding with natural harmonies and riven with incongruent, disparate elements. Almost by chance, it seems, and arriving oddly late in the novel's composition during the penultimate serial instalment for November 1874, Wessex[7] is invoked for the very first time (derived from ancient Anglo-Saxon kingdoms), just at the point when all the principal characters are about to converge on the very same prehistoric spot, at Greenhill, but will converge as disparate entities. They will do little more, by way of connection, than graze each other's consciousnesses. That is to say, what will become the great unifying construct of Wessex is inaugurated in this early novel at the very point when the central characters are most disunited.

Inadvertently or otherwise, the disparities are apposite. At one level *Far From the Madding Crowd* follows the relatively simple folkloric plot of an unconventional young woman's struggle as a farmer whose fortunes are complicated by the passions of three very different men: the loyal, dependable, straitlaced Shepherd Oak; the ascetic, repressed, obsessively ardent Farmer Boldwood; and the 'fallen' aristocrat turned rogue male, Sergeant Troy. But at another level this multilayered text offers 'a high intellectual treat', as R. H. Hutton described it[8] – albeit, in the context, simply, of the book's learned wisdom.

Hutton was looking for enlightenment, or what Victorians would have called edification. And if Hardy's dissident moral universe did not always provide this particular philosophical comfort, his abundant array of literary, classical and biblical allusions almost certainly did. These were 'high intellectual treats' indeed. Invariably thought-provoking, frequently ironized and often delightfully picturesque, it was not necessarily the aptness of the allusion or the brilliance of the literary analogue so much as its familiarity as part of a shared cultural heritage which excited the interest and pleasure of Victorian readers. The more esoteric the allusion, the more intense the reader's bright moment of recognition; the more ironic the implications, the greater the reader's satisfaction and pleasure – even the unschooled were familiar with Bible stories and classical mythology. Therefore, at a very fundamental level of cultural familiarity, when Cainy Ball's 'pore mother' – being neither a 'Scripture-read woman' nor a churchgoer – makes a mistake at his christening and wrongly names her infant son 'Cain' because she had thought ''twas Abel killed Cain' (from the Genesis story, 4:1–15), Hardy's readers would have been thoroughly entertained. Humour depends very largely upon an audience's sense of its own prior knowledge.

Such biblical allusions by unlettered folk would, in life, have been garnered from religious sermons, the rubric of Christian church services, Sunday schools and the (current) popular Bible-reading gatherings that took place in private homes. Within the Weatherbury world, Hardy's rustics mediate these dialogues at several levels, but primarily by invoking the biblical text in a seemingly knowing and edifying manner while remaining unaware that their allusions are either misbegotten or utterly irrelevant. It follows, not infrequently, that while they provide an unstoppable flow of irony and amusement within and beyond the novel, the humorous implications of these disorderly allusions cannot but help extend into the realms of satire. Cainy Ball's Genesis story, for example, touches subtly on what will later become an aspect of Hardy's radical iconoclasm: his satirical attack upon the rituals of organized religion. For just as Cainy's heretical name 'could never be got rid of in the parish', and henceforth enforces its own mythic potency and 'mother-right', and just as the village parson, who, try as he might, remains powerless to alter the consequences of his own baptismal rites, and is thus powerless to enforce Christianity's mythic potency, so a quietly subversive point emerges: it is no longer Cainy Ball's insouciant 'heathen' mother who seems absurd in her beliefs but the self-righteous Christian pastor himself.

The allusion thus works on several levels. There is the 'recognition' level: this invites readers familiar with the Genesis myth to participate in the story-telling process, to enjoy a pleasurable moment of shared assumptions, to give a nod and a wink to inside knowledge. Born of this, there is the satisfying experience of cultural fellowship. Then, at the 'intellectual' level, there is the 'treat', for those who are looking in that direction, of challenging those shared assumptions (notably the manner in which the Genesis story influences church dogma) which are now restored to their original narrative base not in sacred writings but in folk-culture, in oral history: the Cain story is retold as another Cain story and becomes a paradigm of the story-telling process.

This manner of assimilating religious doctrine to folk-culture, of implicitly devaluing the former in favour of the latter, of subverting Christian belief systems to pagan mythologies, and of pointing a critical finger at the Judaeo-Christian God, may be a theme which later develops more forcefully in Hardy's poetry but it remains, nevertheless, an important philosophical route to such mature Wessex novels as *Tess* and *Jude*. In *Far From the Madding Crowd* Hardy's allusive approaches to this theme are made, more often, with a quieter irony. A good example is Levi Everdene's rather unorthodox invocation of the seventh commandment (VIII), which allows him the fantasy and illicit sexual pleasure of committing adultery with his own wife (see also note 16 to VIII). Alternatively, there is Hardy's direct allusion to Exodus 17:6: here the Lord's command to Moses to strike a rock on Mount Horeb from which water will stream for the Israelites to drink intersects, narratorially, with the intensely erotic moment of Bathsheba's first kiss with Troy which brings 'upon her a stroke resulting, as did that of Moses in Horeb, in a liquid stream – here a stream of tears' (see note 4 to XXVII).

In both cases, irony is implicit in the misapplication of sacred writings to secular matters, in the misalignment of judgemental moral decree and human sexual passion, in the clash of religious orthodoxy and cultural heterodoxy. And the remedial function of the allusion, in that it may also serve to straitjacket transgressive erotica with the strong arm of 'The Word of God', remains no less ironic for the fact that it legitimizes, by means of a palimpsestic reading of sacred script, the very thing it affects to indict. In effect, erotica enters through the (textual) back door, so to speak – yet another high intellectual treat.

At another level of allusive implication, the absurdity of the comparison, most apparent in Hardy's use of mock-heroic allusions, often serves to draw the reader into a complicit relationship with the narrator and, in turn, into sympathy and affection for the character currently under scrutiny. When, for instance, the new, young mistress of the Everdene estate rather nervously and a little imperiously begins her payroll activities for the very first time, and when 'the remarkable coolness of her manner' takes on the 'proportionate increase of arrogance and reserve' shown by 'Jove and his family' when they moved from 'their cramped quarters on the peak of Olympus into the wide sky above it' (x), so the light mockery of this allusion invites the reader's indulgent smile. There is something delightfully absurd in the comparison – the young woman-farmer rising up the social scale/the mighty Jove ascending to the stars. And the absurdity amuses, in this instance, because the twinned images fascinate by virtue of being not quite identical. Unlike the purposefully inapt relation set between Moses on Mount Horeb and Bathsheba in the Hollow of Ferns, which possesses no bewitching twinning effect, the Jovian allusion provides a recognizable analogy: the act of exaggeration makes the analogue possible.

Any form of irony which apprises its audience of circumstances, events and situations unknown to the character, tends to empower readers to a sense of omnipotence and, consequently, to an emotional generosity and a compassion for the human struggle in perspective. Thus, where the light mockery invites a smile it also invites complicity – not least because this is a smile Bathsheba might also laughingly share with us, in regarding her self-importance at this moment. The same could also be true of Gabriel Oak, when caught in a similar situation of petty pride. When, for example, he decides never to play the flute in Bathsheba's presence because it distorts his features – his 'eyes a-staring out like a strangled man's' – he is aligned, at this moment, with 'the divine Minerva herself' who, according to mythology, invented the flute but discarded it because it distorted her features (see note 23 to VIII). Although this allusion lacks Hardy's customary wit in conjuring delightfully absurd comparisons, it does halt the reader for a brief moment to focus upon Oak's conceit. This, in turn, prompts the recollection that in his first view of Bathsheba, in the looking-glass sequence, Oak had judged vanity to be an innate fault in women. Thus readers are apprised of his sexual double-standard which he could, perhaps, regard in a passing moment of good-humoured self-mockery as an innate fault in men. 'Perhaps' is the key word here. And in raising a doubt or two in the reader's mind, the allusion serves the added purpose of contributing a breadth and depth of understanding to individual human characters and their situations.

Hardy's allusions, then, operate at several different levels, sometimes leavening the effect of the narrator's stance in deflating the heroic, sometimes reconciling apparent contradictions or conveying, by indirection, an incongruity of meaning, while at other times attracting readers into a complicit relation with the narrator and character in view, or simply adding a new dimension to characterization, and at all times inviting readers into the story-telling process. But there is one further aspect worth mentioning here. This is the pictorial aspect. Very many of Hardy's allusions are, in fact, quite clearly and simply pictorial enhancers designed specifically to address the interest of the educated reader.

When, for example, in the shears-grinding scene (XIX), Oak is said to stand 'somewhat as Eros is represented when in the act of sharpening his arrows', the implications, aside from the sexual symbolism attached to Eros, are purely iconic, in terms of their function as visual intensifiers. It happens thus. Eros (otherwise Cupid), the boy-god of love and young son of Venus, is traditionally depicted with bow and arrow; he is said to wet with blood the grindstone on which he sharpens his arrows. This is the image depicted in a host of art works. And one of the most popular of these, in Hardy's time, was Raphael's suite of thirty-two pictures illustrating the adventures of Psyche – the beautiful maiden loved by the boy Eros, but visited by him only at night; forbidden to seek out his identity, Psyche one night steals a look at him while sleeping; he awakens and flees; she is then enslaved by Venus and treated most cruelly; when these trials end the lovers are wed.

So it was that from Shakespeare's *Midsummer Night's Dream* (which calls up 'Cupid's strongest bow'), to Rafael Mengs's painting, 'Cupid Sharpening His Arrows', to the statue of Cupid stringing his bow (at the Louvre), or sleeping (Rome), or mounted on a tiger (Negroni), to the array of Cupids in literature (Horace, Ovid, Apuleius, Molière), and to the designer-saturation of Cupids on Victorian mantelpieces, drapes, and even tableware, Hardy was, pictorially speaking, drawing upon a shared cultural heritage of unquestionable familiarity, interest and pleasure to his Victorian contemporaries.

The same pictorial effect occurs with his allusion to 'Flaxman's . . . Mercury' (XXXVII). This invokes the painter John Flaxman, whose engraved line-drawing entitled 'Mercury Conducting the Souls of the Suitors to the Infernal Region' depicts a scene from Homer's *Odyssey* where Mercury (messenger of the gods) is leading Penelope's suitors off to Hades. While Odysseus was absent during the Trojan War, Penelope was besieged by many suitors; upon his return, with the help of his son, Odysseus killed them. Flaxman's drawings, engraved by William Blake, were widely admired in Hardy's day (equally, Homer), and thus provided him with a source of vivid serial images which could be instantly evoked in the minds of his contemporary readers at the drop of one brief allusion. Precursors of cinematographic images, they had the effect of 'stills'. In their allusive capacity they rely for their effect upon their imagistic pervasiveness within the culture – just as, say, the Mona Lisa (from Da Vinci's painting in the Louvre to the lyrics of folk-rock to the cinematography of Monty Python) figures pervasively in twentieth-century Western culture.

As in the Eros allusion where no apt analogue exists (Oak is not a boy-lover furtively pursuing sensual pleasure in the woods at night), the Flaxman set of 'stills' bears only the loosest relation to Hardy's story which focuses, at this point, upon the abashed workfolk emerging from their night-drinking with Troy. The bathos inherent in the comparison introduces a mildly comic aspect, but ultimately the allusion functions in common with all others as a form of extratextual dialogue conjoining the reader to the actual process of story-making by virtue of recognizing and sharing a common cultural ancestry.

In an important iconoclastic sense, then, Hardy draws upon the disparities between folklore and intellectual history, between oral and literary culture (the two 'Cain' stories/the tale of Everdene's 'seventh'), in order to accentuate their historical confluence and their mutual ancestry, born not of mortal or divine events in the real world but of the human imagination. When R. H. Hutton spoke of 'a high intellectual treat' he was not to know, at that early point in Hardy's career, quite how intellectually inventive, or quite how iconoclastic the Wessex novels were going to become. Although, in terms of stylistics, he might well have perceived that Hardy's experimental modes of stylistic incongruity, genre-crossing and indeterminacy – modes now commonly regarded as typical of his intellectual challenge to traditional narrative form – were already taking shape in *Far From the Madding Crowd.* And among them, the newly invented Wessex construct – itself the embodiment of the clash between the traditional and the experimental – was not only taking shape in this early novel but also proving to be, even in its period of gestation, conspicuously central to Hardy's pluralistic organization.

Encompassing the fresh and verdant charm so keenly sought by Leslie Stephen, and so rhapsodized as 'idyllic' by those contemporary critics looking in the same direction, Wessex provides a dual correspondence not only to the myth and magic of a Golden Age world but also to the 'strife' which is absented from Hardy's title but represented in the story proper. Here, in thematic dislocation from its Golden Age origins in Thomas Gray's poem, 'Elegy Written in a Country Churchyard', which begins: 'Far from the madding crowd's ignoble strife',[9] Hardy's representation of strife shapes his Wessex construct in several ways. For instance, the degree to which the human dilemma of, say, relational discord makes its impact upon the reader depends in part upon its manifestation in non-human (natural world) forms. And if these dissonant non-human forms remain, at first sight, relatively hidden – the lambing season arrives late, the bee-swarming (for honey-making) is irregular and unruly – their ultimate emergency lays bare the symbiosis between human and non-human disorder in no uncertain terms. In the event, the least hidden of these emergencies coincides with the most public of 'strife' manifestations in Bathsheba's personal life: as late summer storms, in the outside world, wreak havoc on her crops, so there is chaos on the inside as her husband wreaks havoc with her work-force, driving them drunk and insensible.

And at a broader symbolic level Hardy also places his Wessex construct at the centre of a purposeful anomaly (or anti-pastoralism), as when the verdant pastures where sheep may safely graze transform into grotesque death-traps. In effect, the deadly temptation to which nature's creatures are susceptible provides a close correspondence to the grotesque incongruity of conflicting passions in human affairs and humanity's collisions of desire and self-destruction.

By implication rather than by direct correspondence, 'ignoble strife' also shapes the novel's underlying philosophical forms: the irrationalism underlying human consciousness, the surreal nature of human imagination and the absurdity of the human condition[10] (later to feature importantly in the ontological direction of Hardy's *œuvre*). The agency of this implicit correspondence is frequently the 'rustic chorus', the working community at the hub of Hardy's 'partly real, partly dream-country'. Personifying, at the evolutionary level, the incoherence and indeterminacy of the natural world and, at the existential level, the collision between the meaninglessness of existence and the needs of the human spirit, Hardy's rustics subscribe to a lopsided form of philosophical determinism as a kind of spiritual anodyne. Drawing upon belief systems from the outside world, as much to give significance to all that is incomprehensible as to give a semblance of order to all that is disorderly, they not only spout biblical sayings with all the studious piety of a Watch Committee and all the inexactitude of a Mrs Malaprop but also invoke pagan beliefs in almost the same breath. Thus local superstitions, traditional omens and ancient portents intersect with Ecclesiastes and Job, providing a delightfully incongruous series of signs pointing the way, quite arbitrarily, towards Destiny – or, at any rate, towards some kind of incoherent but controlling power to which humanity can attribute the absurdity of the world and the folly of its own actions.

In line with these exchanges Hardy also adopts a stylistic collision of modes not altogether uncommon in non-literary areas of Victorian cultural inscription. To cite a popular example: when the specific curvature of a piano leg is matched to the erotic body and correspondingly adorned with lacy fripperies, we (if not Victorians) might well speak of incongruity, an outright collision of modes (public/private; esoteric/exoteric), made all the more emphatic by a contemporary fashion which de-emphasized the female leg (not to mention female undergarments) virtually to the point of disappearance. Less titillatingly, a comparable collision of modes appears with the inscription of Gothic design upon technologically advanced works of engineering, or delicate filigree work upon hulking iron manufactures, or the festooning of the new sewage-disposal system of the 1860s, the innovative water-closet which, unlike the earlier earth-closet, sported rosebuds and lilies within its recesses.

Genre-crossing of this kind came naturally to Victorians – possibly reflecting, in aesthetic forms, their consciousness of living in what was popularly known as the 'Age of Transition' – caught between an age already dead and another not yet born, as one contemporary put it. At any rate, in the literary sphere such genre-crossing attracted no special attention: melodrama could intersect with psychological verisimilitude within a single narrative event, extravagant symbolism could enter a naturalistic alignment, and naive sentimentality could coexist with sophisticated brutality and violence.

Even so, Hardy's own style of genre-breaking did attract negative attention. It was not his breaking of 'pastoral' conventions, most noticeable in the first part of the novel where 'shepherd' and 'milkmaid' disappear from their original setting and reappear in different permutations of themselves (somewhat anticipating the theme of *The Well-Beloved*, 1897). Nor was it the incongruity of his mock-heroic touches – that Oak, in the disagreeable and unheroic event of losing an argument with Bathsheba, might be aligned with Moses leaving the presence of Pharaoh, or that in the mundane arrangement of her payroll activities Bathsheba might be aligned with the auspicious 'thesmothetes', or lawmakers, of ancient Athens. These incongruities, being but the stuff of irony and amusement, delighted readers from all walks of life willing to indulge an obvious absurdity. Rather, it was, once more, a question of decorum. Class boundaries were not properly observed: Oak and the rustics got too much above themselves in the quality of their material belongings, powers of articulacy and 'profane-minded familiarity with the Bible'.[11] Sexual boundaries were not observed: the 'good shepherd' of traditional pastorals and biblical mythologies, which Hardy subtly juxtaposes with Oak's alternative role of the ambitious, industrious 'self-improver' of modern times, proved too much for some Victorians for whom the marriage of 'pastoral virtue' with insubordinate womanhood of the upcoming liberation era clashed uncomfortably with prescribed roles and cultural forms. Bathsheba was, for Henry James, unpleasantly 'coarse',[12] for others, a shameless 'hussy' and Gabriel Oak should have known better than to marry her.

The genre-crossing at this point reflects, in part, Hardy's lifelong attempt to break with the prescribed literary tradition of the happy ending and to embrace instead the indeterminism of its dissolution. The crossing may seem one of romance and realism, but these terminologies, being both generic and loose, are themselves already crossed. It may be more precise to speak of the kind of abstention Hardy himself understood as passing beyond, or breaking with, prevailing concepts of coherency, consonance and even consciousness itself. To his way of thinking notions of a coherent universe, or of consonance in sexual relationships, or that consciousness operates as the prime agency of understanding and knowledge, all these collapse in the face of a presuppositionless philosophy. Presupposing, in this instance, that immemorial love culminates in getting-married-and-living-happily-ever-after, presupposes a consonance in sexual relationships. It also presupposes a coherency of forms, ideas, ideologies, conventions and, of course, human institutions. Moreover, in Victorian terms, it also presupposes a coherent universe. For, from the most personal and private of forms (sexual relationships), through the most public and social of forms (matrimony), to the eschatological coherency of forms essential to the presupposition that (earthly) marriages are made in a (divine) heaven, the last call is necessarily upon a fundamentally coherent universe.

Hardy abstains from framing his world with such presuppositions. And in this sense alone he crosses from traditional narrative form to something approaching the surrealistic forms of the twentieth century in which the imagination is freed from such conscious controls. In the case of breaking with the novel's 'happy ending' this becomes a freeing from the conscious controls of literary influence. Given this framework, neither the pastoral genre, even at its most idyllic and harmonious, nor the anticipated 'happy ending' romance of traditional literary genres succeeds in overriding the dissonant voices at the close of *Far From the Madding Crowd*. Imagistically the 'happy ending' disappears in any case from the reader's perspective. All the attentive reader is left with is a shadowy configuration of two blurred figures setting out for matrimonials obscured in gloomy mist – and this crowns the story's end in a concluding 'wedding' chapter entitled 'A Foggy Night and Morning'. Likewise, as far as the narrative voice goes, the same purported 'happy ending' disappears under the incongruity of utterances. The first of these intones a biblical verse speaking of a 'love as strong as death' – itself a travesty of the original which celebrates, in the Song of Solomon, a woman's lust for the male body – while the second mocks the entire performance with Joseph Poorgrass's comically irrelevant biblical quotation from Hosea which declares it all 'might have been worse'.

Thus, the controls of influence are artfully abused. And, correspondingly, the incongruity of the convention, both literary and matrimonial (as 'happy ending'), comes full circle with its recovery of the novel's most uncompromising comment, voiced most uncompromisingly by Frank Troy. These are the words that will later form the foundation of an important theme, for Hardy, on the denaturing, by institutionalization, of human love relationships. But for the moment, only his non-compliant 'wicked soldier-hero'[13] may openly frame the words – that 'All romances end at marriage.'

R. M.

Notes

1. See *Collected Letters*, V, 243–4. The manuscript was sold through Christie's of London on 22 April 1918 to a New York dealer, and subsequently purchased by A. Edward Newton of Pennsylvania.
2. Some of these late revisions are recorded in the Notes section at the end of this book.
3. 'The Profitable Reading of Fiction', reprinted in *Personal Writings*, was originally published in the New York journal *Forum* in March 1888.
4. *Life*, 95.
5. *Life*, 104–5.
6. Hardy's words in his Preface to *Far From the Madding Crowd* (see Appendix I).
7. Chapter XLIX: the Greenhill sheep fair scene.
8. See the *Spectator*, 3 January 1874.
9. See also note 2 to Preface on Gray's 'Elegy'.
10. Hardy called himself an 'irrationalist', and although absurdist elements remain subtle and implicit in this early work they clearly anticipate the more explicit treatment he gives them in the later novels which, in turn, anticipates the concept of the absurd as later employed by Cocteau in the 1920s, Albert Camus in the 1940s, Samuel Beckett, Eugene Ionesco, Harold Pinter in the post-war years and, of course, in its rejection of rational, analytical processes, the great international modern movement of Surrealism.
11. See, for example, R. H. Hutton's article in the *Spectator*, 19 December 1874, 1597–9. See also Andrew Lang in the *Academy*, 2 January 1875, who complains that Hardy misleads his reader by presenting 'shepherds and rural people with the eye of a philosopher who understands all about them, though he is not of them, and who can express their dim efforts at rendering what they think and feel in language like that of Mr Herbert Spencer'. Herbert Spencer (1820–1903), author of a vast work entitled *Synthetic Philosophy*, was an eminent philosopher who, together with Charles Darwin and Thomas Henry Huxley, was responsible for popularizing the theory of evolution. Spencer coined the phrase 'survival of the fittest', later attributed to Darwin, and pioneered psychology and sociology as scholarly disciplines.
12. See the *Nation*, 24 December 1874. See also Andrew Lang: 'there are passages where the manner and the matter jar, and are out of keeping' (*Academy*, 2 January 1875).
13. Hardy described Troy thus to Leslie Stephen.

A NOTE ON THE HISTORY OF THE TEXT

HISTORY OF THE TEXT

This text publishes for the very first time the holograph manuscript of *Far From the Madding Crowd*, commissioned in 1873 by Leslie Stephen, editor of the *Cornhill Magazine*, and issued in twelve monthly instalments running from January to December 1874. The manuscript was begun tentatively in September 1873 and completed in August 1874. Hardy never set eyes on it again. As his work in progress appeared in print, month by month, so his manuscript vanished, month by month, into the vaults of Smith, Elder & Co. It was only recovered by chance in 1918 when, with Hardy's permission, it was sold to raise funds for the Red Cross and the war effort (see Introduction).

The number of manuscript chapters submitted for each *Cornhill* instalment fell between three and five, most of unequal length. Hardy did not number his chapters, presumably anticipating editorial changes and advice on instalment length. Nor did he attempt any kind of coherent numeration until all the various textual portions pertaining to the chapters in progress had been properly compiled; in fact, many manuscript leaves bear the deleted markings of an earlier pagination. Nor did he necessarily adhere to his original chapter titles. He frequently modified these, in interlinear revision, to accommodate his own changes in chapter content – as and when people and events veered off in a direction hitherto unforeseen in his first conception of things.

A close study of the manuscript suggests that Hardy did not, in fact, feel strictly bound by any particular serial structure, such as creating a cliff-hanger, or small crisis, or an unresolved conflict, or even a knotty misunderstanding or two, at the close of each instalment. Initially, for example, he wrote Oak's early marriage proposal into a chapter entitled 'Short account of Gabriel Oak's love affair till a crisis came' (IV), but when the proposal scene turned out to be something of a *divertissement* rather than a dramatic 'crisis' he changed the chapter title to 'Gabriel's resolve:

The visit: The mistake'. Whereupon, now feeling his way towards a more auspicious turning-point, he then devised the 'pastoral tragedy' chapter (v), and it was this 'crisis' that Leslie Stephen finally used to conclude the first January number. But even in this instance the 'tragedy' chapter shows a certain indeterminacy of direction (see notes to v), whereas the 'fire' chapter (vi) which follows it actually provides the most dramatic crisis of all. How better to conclude an instalment if not with a valiant firefighter's sudden and unexpected confrontation with the beloved woman he thought he had lost – with Bathsheba's slow unveiling and Oak's abashed voice saying, 'Do you want a shepherd, ma'am?' But, as it happened, the 'fire' episode did not end the first number but rather opened the second.

Evidently instalment length rather than intensity of crisis-point determined the choice of concluding chapter in this instance. But the most important consideration here – as far as the composition process was concerned – is that the internal stresses and dramatic conflicts of the story seem to have determined their own periods of irresolution and their own points of crisis; they appear to be less bound by serialization structures than by their own natural rhythms. The exception to this might be the denouement which suffers the familiar fate of having to be buckled into shape, and there was certainly an occasional incompatibility between the flow of the manuscript text and the demands of periodical form. But on the whole, each instalment's closing chapter depended primarily upon the overall length of the monthly number and not upon a plotted series of textual knots.

Accordingly, for presentation purposes, this edition notes the 1874 serial arrangement of chapter clusters, but does not include Helen Paterson's woodcut illustrations as designed for each *Cornhill* number with the illustrated plate facing the new instalment's title page.[1] This edition does not follow the serial in one other respect: the extraneous, two-page, 'All Saints' and All Souls'' chapter (xvi) featuring Fanny's and Troy's aborted attempt at marriage is omitted. Although this insert may seem intrinsic to Hardy's original text, it was grafted on to the story on proofsheets and does not represent an extant part of the holograph manuscript. (Following Stephen's advice on pace and plot, Hardy also shortened the lengthy and rather meandering Chapter xv featuring the 'malthouse' garrulous gossipers, and inserted the 'All Saints'' piece to tighten up the slack midpoint section of the April issue.) To omit this chapter simply to preserve the integrity of this manuscript-based edition may seem overly scrupulous given that there are probably some invisible ways in which its inclusion shaped Hardy's creation of all that followed thereafter in the novel's ultimate development. It is included as Appendix III, so that readers may judge for themselves.

The *Cornhill* edition has, up to the present day, provided the copy-text for all other editions. The first of these was published by Smith, Elder & Co. on 23 November 1874, a few days before the final December issue appeared. With the book's instant success and rapid sell-out George Smith printed a slightly revised second impression in late February 1875 (erroneously dated 1874). This two-volume edition, being costly at twenty-one shillings, was succeeded by a less expensive, one-volume edition in 1877. This, too, was basically a resetting of the *Cornhill* text, although Hardy had made one or two substantive revisions in the meantime, in response to outside criticism.

To R. H. Hutton's complaint in the *Spectator*[2] that Jan Coggan carries in his waistcoat pocket a repeater watch ill-befitting his station in life, which 'seems to suggest a totally different world of physical belongings', Hardy promptly responded by adding a justifying phrase: 'which he had inherited from some genius in his family' (see note 5 to XXXI). Hutton's class assumptions notwithstanding, inherited watches do reflect a strong ancestral tradition in Hardy's tale. Equally they function symbolically (notably in Oak's case) or as the agency of the plot (Troy), and Coggan himself not only tracks Bathsheba with the aid of his hour-striking watch but is also one of the first to trace Fanny Robbin's whereabouts and to blurt out undisclosed information.

Alternatively, with Hutton's suggestion of textual imitation in Chapter XVII – 'The following passage strikes us as a study almost in the nature of a careful caricature of George Eliot' – Hardy not only deleted the offending piece in a description of Boldwood but also abbreviated the entire passage for the 1877 revised edition.[3]

Of greater significance were those revisions Hardy made at this time accentuating Troy's blue-blood lineage and illegitimate birth. These are significant first of all because, as the manuscript's interlinear and proof revisions show, Troy had from the outset attracted Hardy's continuing interest more than any other male character in *Far From the Madding Crowd.*

And second, because this particularly keen focus on the intersection of class dominance and sexual exploitation was later to develop into an important theme in several of his works.

In the meantime the *Cornhill* text had been serialized in the United States in *Every Saturday* (although this ceased publication in October 1874), *Littell's Living Age, Eclectic Magazine* and *New York Semi-Weekly Tribune* from 1874 to 1875. The first American book edition was published in November 1874 by Henry Holt. Although this was based on the *Cornhill* text the resetting is unreliable and, in the final instalments, noticeably incompatible with both the manuscript and *Cornhill* versions. The large German publishing house of Tauchnitz was fully reliable. In 1878 Tauchnitz brought out a two-volume edition (no significant revisions) based on the Smith, Elder 1877 text. Unlike several of his American counterparts, and notwithstanding the lack of international copyright laws, Baron von Tauchnitz neither pirated nor bowdlerized the works of foreign authors, and willingly paid for their intellectual property. In Hardy's case this clearly paid off: after numerous reprintings *Far From the Madding Crowd* still featured on Tauchnitz's '500 Best Titles' list in 1939.

In 1894–5 Hardy set out to revise all his novels, on proofsheets, in preparation for the first complete collection of his works to be published by Osgood, McIlvaine and to be based on the text first typeset for Macmillan's Colonial Library edition of 1894. *Far From the Madding Crowd* was then published as the second of sixteen volumes in this Wessex Novels series, complete with a Preface and a new frontispiece etching by H. Macbeth-Raeburn. It was also complete with a newly co-ordinated Wessex topography. Specific locations, directions and distances were now standardized (in conformity with the other Wessex novels), but not always in significant proportions and, unfortunately, not always in keeping with the world in view. For example, in extending to a quarter of a mile the original 100 yards distance between Bathsheba's house and Weatherbury church, Hardy may have satisfied his desire for precise and accurate topography, given the growth and importance of his Wessex world which, by the 1890s, had taken on the mythic proportions of a Homeric universe, but the extra distance does not, in fact, fully cohere with his original conception of things, and now puts a considerable strain on Bathsheba's vision, so to speak. As she gazes out of her attic window at sundown to where the village boys are playing fives[4] in the churchyard, she can plainly see –

despite the obscuring trees and fading evening light – the brown-haired as distinct from the black-haired lads, and can plainly hear their peals of hearty laughter (XLIII). Unfortunately, the specific details of this scene would not be plainly visible or plainly audible at a distance of a quarter of a mile. Bathsheba would not only need a pair of binoculars in order to be able to distinguish the tonal shades of the boys' hair but would also need the acoustic assistance of a strong, steady easterly wind to carry the laughter in her direction. In addition, the extended distance makes it highly unlikely that she would now be able to hear, from inside her bedroom at night and through the sound of heavy rain pounding down outside, the 'strange noise' of water pouring from the mouth of the 'gurgoyle' into the pool of water it had created on the earth beneath (XLV).

Alternative problems of textual distortion also arise with Hardy's amendment of the distance between Weatherbury and Bath, but, on the other hand, little damage is done in changing place-names to conform to the topography of later Wessex novels: 'Windleton', for instance, simply becomes 'Yalbury Bottom', as in *The Mayor of Casterbridge* (1886), and 'Kingsbere' is tagged on to a list of place-names signifying nothing in particular other than a topographical connection between *Far From the Madding Crowd* and, say, *The Trumpet-Major* (1889) or *Tess of the D'Urbervilles* (1891).

Hardy continued to work along these lines subsequently, although a significant proportion of his postscriptive topographical changes, notably those made to the *Harper* 1901 edition, were abandoned at the end of the day and not incorporated into the so-called 'definitive' Wessex edition of 1912. In the meantime, he also continued to work on minute details of dialect, changing *you* to *ye* and *ye* to *'ee* and vice versa, much as he had done in the first manuscript writing, never fully satisfied that he had achieved precisely the right balance between standard and dialectal forms – the subtle balance required to preserve both a very necessary textual fluency or intelligibility and the rich, salt-of-the-earth expressiveness of his Wessex workfolk.

Some of these changes did appear in Macmillan & Co.'s first publication of *Far From the Madding Crowd* in 1902, based on the Osgood, McIlvaine text and commonly known as the Uniform Edition. A greater impact on the 1902 text was made, however, by Hardy's substantive revisions concerning Bathsheba's doubts about Troy's drowning. In so far as it was possible to include these revisions in the cheap Macmillan edition without affecting the typesetting, this was done, though with some damage to characterization and textual integrity. Bathsheba's reiterated doubts do not, in fact, greatly undermine the irony that arises when readers have knowledge of a situation of which the characters remain unaware (in this case all but Bathsheba remain convinced of Troy's death). And, on an equally positive note, her fierce resistance to the news of his death most sensitively represents a psychologically apt reaction to feelings of bereavement and loss which are frequently accompanied by acts of denial and negation. However, the one glaring inconsistency this particular late revision does enforce upon the 1902 text is that, because Gabriel Oak's role is not modified accordingly, since he pays little heed to these (newly stressed) anguished denials in the woman he loves, his charge that she should marry Boldwood out of duty strikes far more shockingly upon the reader's ears than hitherto. Oak's emotional deafness to her plight, in the original version, could after all be taken by sympathetic readers as a self-protective mechanism, which his accompanying moral sternness aptly buttresses – the moral and emotional characteristics being but the opposite sides of the same coin. But since this newly reinforced anguish on her part accentuates the unresponsiveness on his, readers are confronted with a blatantly ugly fall from grace in a man who, at this point, has recovered his chances of running for husband selection and should therefore be gaining the approval of readers.

It was to the 1912 Macmillan edition, commonly known as the Wessex edition, that Hardy made his last significant revisions to *Far From the Madding Crowd*: continuing to accentuate Bathsheba's doubts, stressing the issue of Boldwood's insanity, attempting to enhance Oak's stature and authority, and adding some modifications to accidentals – although, in truth, he never ceased to make minor adjustments to his novels up until the end of his life. His long-hoped-for de luxe edition, the Mellstock limited edition of 500 sets, shows that he was still balancing dialectal forms, adding stresses here and there, altering topographical details as late as 1919 – markings that are also visible on his own copy of the Wessex edition. The 'good hand'[5] never ceased making new tracings upon the old.

All *Cornhill*-based editions published during the twentieth century have incorporated variants from the Osgood, McIlvaine/Wessex editions; some have also included other selected variants from the *Harper* 1901 edition. The most significant of these, as they appear in successive editions over the years, are recorded in the Notes, but *none* has been incorporated into this manuscript edition which remains completely free of editorial practices of this nature.

The most questionable of all are the Henry Holt variants which Hardy in fact declined to sanction. Holt had requested, in November 1874, an advance copy of the last chapters of *Far From the Madding Crowd* for American book publication. But since Hardy had lost sight of his manuscript earlier in the summer and had completed the November proofs the previous August, he had nothing especially presageful to offer. Some critics have tried to explain the Holt variants by claiming an alternative draft – that Hardy sent him a different version of the final chapters. This seems highly unlikely for several reasons. The first is that Hardy barely had time, writing against deadlines, to complete the manuscript pieces required for the *Cornhill* publication, let alone time for composing an alternative version for Holt. The second is that although he did sketch out rough fragments in notebooks and on bits of tree bark and woodland leaves (he says), he not only reserved these fragments for occasional set pieces which he inserted into the manuscript proper, but also abandoned this practice as soon as he got into his stride with serial writing. By the time he had reached the June issue (XXIV), and Bathsheba's entanglement with Troy, he was no longer integrating extraneous material, aside from a fragment on 'Sheep-rot' which he further fragmented and dispersed among the several chapters in progress (see Appendix II). Third: since Hardy had completed revisions to *Far From the Madding Crowd* the previous August and was now proofreading for the Smith, Elder book publication in November 1874, it seems implausible that he would have prepared an alternative version for Holt during this busy period, although there would have been nothing to stop Holt from resurrecting deleted phrases from the proofsheets. And finally, Hardy's marriage. Leaving his maternal home at Bockhampton for the first time in his life, with a new bride (September 1874), with a new winter home to set up for six months in Surbiton, and with new ideas already brimming for his next novel,[6] Hardy would not have been in the least inclined to make special exceptions for a publisher he was already beginning to distrust.

As it happened, Holt was already making 'adaptations' to *Far From the Madding Crowd* for American readers. Long accustomed to editorial interference Hardy seems to have been bemused, maybe even nonplussed, by this informality, but not for long. If he passed no comment on Holt's clumsy substitution of 'the Mediterranean' for 'South America' when, in all his fastidiousness, Boldwood is said to attach 'as much importance to a crease in the coat as to an earthquake in South America' (LI), or if he remained silent about Gabriel's transformation into a church-warden, which may have given Oak a much-needed boost of manly virtue towards the end of the novel (LVI), Hardy nevertheless remained uneasy about Holt's cavalier attitude to matters literary and linguistic, and did eventually cut off business relations with him altogether in 1878.

Bowdlerization was to remain a lifelong problem for Hardy. So too were the vexed copyright laws which gave authors very little protection against unscrupulous publishers. By contrast, compositorial errors seemed, simply, to be a state-of-the-art hazard which Hardy took in his stride. He corrected and revised only the most blatantly erroneous of those originating in the *Cornhill*, omitting many that have subsequently passed through the hands of successive editors to the present day – while collecting several more along the way. Minor as these errors may be they do not belong in Hardy's text – whether they put 'lancelote' where Hardy has 'lanceolate' in manuscript (XXI), or whether they give Fanny the name 'Robin' instead of 'Robbin'.

Unfortunately, in the case of misspelled names, once they were in print Hardy had no choice but to adopt the same spelling. When 'Robin' appeared on the bookstands with the opening *Cornhill* instalment he could do nothing save apply the same misspelled name to his own composition in progress (see Appendix II). Thus the manuscript bears the two spellings.[7] It opens with 'Robbin' and changes to 'Robin' in the chapters Hardy was then preparing for the May instalment (XX–XXIII), when he had just discovered the opening number with its unauthorized spelling of 'Robin'.

TRANSCRIPTION OF THE MANUSCRIPT

In this edition we have endeavoured to keep strictly to what Hardy himself originally wrote, as extant in the holograph manuscript of *Far From the Madding Crowd*,[8] now at the Beinecke Rare Book and Manuscript Library, Yale University. Thus we have restored the original usage, 'Robbin', as Hardy first conceived the name, and have followed the same principle with all names, chapter headings and titles. Hardy began with 'Mary-ann', not 'Maryann' as later editions have it, so 'Mary-ann' it stays; likewise his original use of upper-case letters in his title, '*Far From the Madding Crowd*', later to become '*Far from the Madding Crowd*'.

Working on the principle that Hardy, like Shakespeare, might be deemed exempt from prevailing fashions in grammar, spelling and conventional usages of all kinds, we have kept strictly to all substantives as they appear in the manuscript, despite the occasional grammatical oddity. Thus, for example, we have retained Hardy's 'ize' suffixes, 'emphasize', 'harmonize', where the *Cornhill* puts 'ise' – alternatively his 'recognise' where the *Cornhill* puts 'ize' – and we have respected his occasional 'American' spellings, as in 'tranquility', and even his misspellings like 'boddice', 'terrestial' and 'trochar'. However, in the very rare instance where sense would be obscured by the retention of an obvious error in the manuscript, we have made a silent correction. Where Hardy is careless in his hyphens in words, for instance, we have standardized the text based on his dominant tendency.

We have not noted every textual change in the *Cornhill*, which prefers, for instance, 'Oh' over Hardy's 'O', 'an ewe' over his 'a ewe', and is frequently prone to change 'that' to 'which'. Nor have we listed individually his copious manuscript and proof revisions to dialect words. These tend to remain inferential rather than substantive: 'you' or 'ye' might replace 'ee', and vice versa; 'en' might alternate with conventional pronouns of every gender and kind, and so on. With these, and such regional usages as 'chiel' (child) and 'nater' (nature), Hardy sought a confluence of the vernacular and the literary and persisted in this work to the very end of his days.

In keeping with the prevailing publication practice at the time Hardy left the final punctuation of his text to the *Cornhill* compositors who were instructed in the house-style of Smith, Elder & Co. Even if he had had a decided preference for a particular style there would have been little point in asserting it within the manuscript in any consistent way, since, as he learned from the very first serial instalment onwards, house compositors exercised a free hand over every aspect of his own application of accidentals, from putting apostrophes in 'baint' ('bain't') to imposing the prevailing house-style on his spellings and grammatical constructions.

Hardy genuinely deplored 'having to write against time',[9] but although the manuscript shows occasional signs of careless writing the main body is perfectly coherent, with or without standard, consistent accidentals – with or without the long stretches of unmarked dialogue and the decidedly 'open' style of punctuation. Whether this 'open' style indicates his preference at that time for minimal punctuation or simply a willing adherence to house-style requirements, one thing is clear: later accidentals personally revised by Hardy some twenty years afterwards do show his decided predilection for the former. So, aside from filling out abbreviated forms (such as '&'), inserting possessives, marking the unmarked dialogues with the double quotation-marks preferred (over single) by Hardy in the manuscript, or, on rare occasions, furnishing accidentals for clarity (e.g. a full stop if there is no end punctuation, including the occasional omission of the full stop in chapter titles), we have kept to his minimalist style. We have also observed his preference for dashes over commas, colons over semi-colons, exclamation marks or full stops in place of question marks and his slightly eccentric manner of not italicizing Frenchisms and of omitting hyphens in compound constructions – 'tenderly shaped', for example, where the *Cornhill* prefers 'tenderly-shaped'. If Hardy occasionally omits hyphens in words that he usually hyphenates, they have been inserted. Where he is inconsistent in his positioning of accidentals in relation to quotation-marks, or in his use of capitalization (including Shepherd, Sergeant and Miss), we have made the occasional change to reflect his preferred style.

Thus, the present edition restores the original work as first created by Hardy throughout the twelve-month period of composition which also happened to be a twelve-month period of suppressed opposition to editorial pressures or direct editorial intervention, and all that that means in terms of intensified artistic creativity. In later years, writing with the nonchalant diffidence of fame, he is reported to have said that what Stephen excised from the serial version he himself would not bother to restore to the book version. But of course he did bother – for the rest of his entire life. The underlying truth of the 'bother' was, however, the loss of inspiration, of recovering the original vision and first stretch of the imagination – that inexpectation of the moment's sudden thought and instant flash of feeling, that budding idea ushered in by an inchoate phrase. This much – and it is a good deal too much – Hardy sensed he had lost when, looking back on *Far From the Madding Crowd* from a long distance in later life, he knew it to be the work of a far younger man.

R. M.

Notes

1. See Appendix IV.
2. Reprinted in R. G. Cox, ed., *Thomas Hardy: The Critical Heritage* (London: Routledge & Kegan Paul, 1970), pp. 23–4.
3. ibid, pp. 24–6. R. H. Hutton had been one of the first to proclaim, in his initial review of *Far From the Madding Crowd* (*Spectator*, 3 January 1874), that George Eliot was probably its author. However, Hardy's name appeared (by his own modest request) in the announcement of the first two-volume edition of the book in November, whereupon Hutton did not openly admit his mistake but instead levelled accusations of imitation – that 'Mr Hardy' adopts 'a style of remark on his own imaginative creations which is an exaggeration of George Eliot's', and so on (*Spectator*, 19 December 1874). Hardy promptly set about writing a city-based novel, *The Hand of Ethelberta* (1875), to prove he could create a world as remote from Eliot's regional settings as its metropolitan life was from 'sheep and shepherds' (*Life*, 103).
4. Later (1895) 'prisoner's base' – a rougher game of touch and capture.
5. See Hardy's famous words written to Leslie Stephen, dated 18 February (1874?): 'Perhaps I may have higher aims some day, and be a great stickler for the proper artistic balance of the completed work, but for the present circumstances lead me to wish to be considered a good hand at a serial' (*Life*, 100).
6. See note 3 above.
7. The existence, in the manuscript, of the two different spellings should not be confused with Hardy's personally authorized name changes such as 'Frank' instead of 'Alfred' (deleted: ms leaf 1–123), 'Oak' instead of 'Strong', 'Poorgrass' instead of 'Poorhead', and so on.

8. When the manuscript was later discovered, in 1918, in the offices of Hardy's publishers, Smith, Elder & Co., one page was missing. Hardy copied the missing page from the *Cornhill* so that the entire manuscript could be bound and sold to raise funds for the Red Cross. See also notes and references to the extraneous 'All Saints' and All Souls'' chapter (XVI in *Cornhill*) (Appendix III).

9. See *Life*, 101.

FAR FROM THE MADDING CROWD

CHAPTER I

Description of Farmer Oak: An incident.

When Farmer Oak smiled, the corners of his mouth spread, till they were within an unimportant distance of his ears, his eyes were reduced to mere chinks, and diverging wrinkles appeared round them, extending upon his countenance like the rays in a rudimentary sketch of the rising sun.

His Christian name was Gabriel,[1] and on working days he was a young man of sound judgment, easy motions, proper dress and general good character. On Sundays he was a man of misty views, rather given to a postponing treatment of things, whose best clothes and seven-and-six-penny umbrella were always hampering him: upon the whole one who felt himself to occupy morally that vast middle space of Laodicean[2] neutrality which lay between the Sacrament[3] people of the parish and the drunken division of its inhabitants – that is, he went to church, but yawned privately by the time the congregation reached the Nicene[4] creed, and thought of what there was for dinner when he meant to be listening to the sermon. Or, to state his character as it stood in the scale of public opinion, when his friends and critics were in tantrums he was considered rather a bad man; when they were pleased he was rather a good man; when they were neither he was a man whose moral colour was a kind of pepper and salt mixture.

As he lived six times as many working days as Sundays, his appearance in his old clothes was most peculiarly his own – the neighbours' mental picture of him always presenting him as dressed in that way when their imaginations answered to the thought "Gabriel Oak". He wore a low crowned felt hat, spread out at the base by tight jamming upon the head for security in high winds, and a coat like Doctor Johnson's,[5] his lower extremities being encased in ordinary leather leggings, and boots emphatically large, affording to each foot a roomy apartment so constructed that any wearer might stand in a river all day long and know nothing about it – their maker being a conscientious man who always endeavoured to compensate for any weakness in his cut by unstinted dimension and solidity.

Mr Oak carried about with him by way of watch what may be called a small silver clock: in other words it was a watch as to shape and intention, and a small clock as to size. This instrument, being several years older than Oak's grandfather, had the peculiarity of going either too fast or not at all: the smaller of its hands, too, occasionally slipped round on the pivot, and thus, though the minutes were told with the greatest precision, nobody could be quite certain of the hour they belonged to. The stopping peculiarity of his watch Oak remedied by thumps and shakes, when it always went on again immediately, and he escaped any evil consequences from the other two defects by constant comparisons with and observations of the sun and stars, and by pressing his face close to the glass of his neighbours' windows when passing by their houses, till he could discern the hour marked by the green-faced timekeepers within. It may be mentioned that Oak's fob, being painfully difficult of access by reason of its somewhat high situation in the waistband of his trousers (which also lay at a remote height under his waistcoat) the watch was as a necessity pulled out by throwing the body extremely to one side, compressing the mouth and face to a mere mass of wrinkles on account of the exertion required, and drawing up the watch by its chain, like a bucket from a well.

But some thoughtful persons, who had seen him walking across one of his fields on a certain December morning – sunny, and exceptionally mild – might have regarded Gabriel Oak in other aspects than these. In his face one might notice that many of the hues and curves of youth had tarried on to manhood: there even remained in his remoter crannies some relics of the boy. His height and breadth would have been sufficient to make his presence imposing had they been exhibited with due consideration. But there is a way some men have, rural and urban alike – for which the mind is more responsible than flesh or sinew – a way of curtailing their dimensions by their manner of showing them; and from a quiet modesty that would have become a vestal,[6] which seemed continually to impress upon him that he had no great claim on the world's room, Oak walked unassumingly, and with a faintly perceptible bend, quite distinct from a bowing of the shoulders. This may be said to be a defect in an individual if he depends for his valuation as a total more upon his appearance than upon his capacity to wear well, which Oak did not. He had just reached the time of life at which "young" is ceasing to be the prefix of "man" in speaking of one. He was at the brightest period of masculine life, for his intellect and emotions were clearly separate: he had passed the time during which the influence of youth indiscriminately mingles them in the character of impulse, and he had not yet arrived at the state wherein they become united again, in the character of prejudice, by the influence of a wife and family. In short he was twenty-eight and a bachelor.

The field he was in sloped steeply to a ridge called Norcombe Hill, through an adjunct of which ran the highway from Norcombe to Casterbridge, sunk in a deep cutting.[7] Casually glancing over the hedge, Oak saw coming down the hill towards him an ornamental spring waggon painted yellow and gaily marked, drawn by two horses, a waggoner walking alongside, bearing a whip perpendicularly. The waggon was laden with household goods and window plants, and on the apex of the whole sat a woman, young and attractive. Gabriel had not beheld the sight for more than half a minute when the vehicle was brought to a standstill just beneath his eyes.

"The tailboard of the waggon is gone, Miss," said the waggoner.

"Then I heard it fall," said the girl in a soft though not particularly low voice. "I heard a noise I could not account for when we were coming up the hill."

"I'll run back."

"Do," she answered.

The sensible horses stood perfectly still, and the waggoner's steps sank fainter and fainter in the distance.

The girl on the summit of the load sat motionless, surrounded by tables and chairs with their legs upwards, backed by an oak settle and ornamented in front by pots of geraniums, myrtles and cactuses, together with a caged canary – all probably from the windows of the house just vacated. There was also a cat in a willow basket, from the partly opened lid of which the animal gazed with half-closed eyes, and smilingly surveyed the small birds around.

The handsome girl waited for some time idly in her place, and the only sound heard in the stillness was the hopping of the canary up and down the perches of its prison. Then she looked attentively downwards: it was not at the bird, nor at the cat: it was at an oblong package tied in paper, and lying between them. She turned her head to learn if the waggoner were coming; he was not yet in sight; and then her eyes crept back to the package, her thoughts seeming to run upon what was inside it. At length she drew the article into her lap and untied the paper covering; a small swing looking-glass was disclosed, in which she proceeded to survey herself attentively. Then she parted her lips, and smiled.

It was a fine morning, and the sun lighted up to a scarlet glow the crimson jacket she wore, and painted a soft lustre upon her bright face and black hair. The myrtles geraniums and cactuses packed around her were fresh and green, and at such a leafless season they invested the whole concern of horses, waggon, furniture, and girl with the peculiar charm of rarity. What possessed the girl to indulge in such a performance in the sight of the sparrows, blackbirds and unperceived farmer, who were alone its spectators – whether the smile began as a factitious one to test her capacity in that art – nobody knows: it ended certainly in a real smile; she blushed at herself, and seeing her reflection blush, blushed the more.

The change from the customary spot and necessary occasion of such an act – from the dressing hour in a bedroom to a time of travelling out of doors – lent to the idle deed a novelty it certainly did not intrinsically possess. The picture was a delicate one. Woman's prescriptive infirmity had stalked into the sunlight, which had invested it with the freshness of an originality. A cynical inference was irresistible by Gabriel Oak as he regarded the scene, generous though he fain would have been –: there was no necessity whatever for her looking in the glass. She did not adjust her hat, or pat her hair, or press a dimple into shape, or do one thing to signify that any such intention had been her motive in taking up the glass. She simply observed herself as a fair product of Nature in a feminine direction – her expression seeming to glide into far-off though likely dramas in which men would play a part – vistas of probable triumphs – the smiles being of a phase suggesting that hearts were imagined as lost and won. Still, this was but conjecture, and the whole series of actions were so idly put forth as to make it rash to assert that intention had any part in them at all.

The waggoner's steps were heard returning: she put the glass in the paper, and the whole again in its place.

When the waggon had passed on Gabriel withdrew from his point of espial, and descending into the road followed the vehicle to the turnpike gate at the bottom of the hill, where the object of his contemplation now halted for the payment of toll. About twenty steps still remained between him and the gate when he heard a dispute. It was a difference concerning two pence between the persons with the waggon and the man at the toll-bar.

"Mis'ess's niece is upon the top of the things, and she says that's enough that I've offered ye, you grate miser, and she won't pay any more." These were the waggoner's words.

"Very well, then mis'ess's niece can't pass," said the turnpike keeper, closing the gate.

Oak looked from one to the other of the disputants, and fell into a reverie. There was something in the tone of two pence remarkably insignificant: three pence had a definite value as money – it was an appreciable infringement on a day's wages,[8] and, as such, a haggling matter; but two pence – "Here," he said stepping forward and handing two pence to the gatekeeper; "let the young woman pass." He looked up at her then: she heard his words, and looked down.

Gabriel's features adhered throughout their form so exactly to the middle line between the beauty of Saint John and the ugliness of Judas Iscariot[9] as represented in a window of the church he attended, that not a single lineament could be selected and called worthy either of distinction or notoriety. The red jacketed and dark haired maiden probably thought so too, for she carelessly glanced over him and told her man to drive on. She might have looked her thanks to Gabriel on a minute scale, but she did not speak them: more probably she felt none, for in gaining her a passage he had lost her her point, and we know how women take a favour of that kind.

The gate-keeper surveyed the retreating vehicle. "That's a handsome maid," he said to Oak.

"But she has her faults," said Gabriel.

"True, farmer."

"And the greatest of them is – well, what it is always."

"Beating people down two pence: ay, 'tis true."

"O no."

"What, then?"

Gabriel, perhaps a little piqued by the comely traveller's indifference, glanced back to where he had witnessed her performance over the hedge, and said "Vanity."

CHAPTER II

Night. – The flock – An interior – Another interior.

It was nearly midnight on the eve of St Thomas:[1] the shortest day in the year. A desolating wind wandered from the north over the hill whereon Oak had watched the yellow waggon and its occupant in the sunshine of a few days earlier.

Norcombe Hill – forming part of Norcombe Ewelease – was one of the spots which suggest to a passer-by that he is in the presence of a shape approaching the indestructible as nearly as any to be found on earth. It was a featureless convexity of chalk and soil – an ordinary specimen of those smoothly outlined protuberances of the globe which may remain undisturbed on some great day of confusion when far grander heights and dizzy granite precipices topple down.

The hill was covered on its northern side by an ancient and decaying plantation of beeches, whose upper verge formed a line over the crest fringing its arched curve against the sky, like a mane. To-night, these trees sheltered the southern slope from the keenest blasts, which smote the wood and floundered through it with a sound as of grumbling, or gushed over its crowning boughs in a weakened moan. The dry leaves in the ditch simmered and boiled in the same breezes, a tongue of air occasionally ferretting out a few, and sending them spinning across the grass. A group or two of the latest in date among this dead multitude had remained on the twigs which bore them till this very mid-winter time,[2] and in falling rattled against the trunks with smart taps.

Between this half-wooded, half-naked hill and the vague still horizon its summit indistinctly commanded was a mysterious sheet of fathomless shade – the sounds only from which suggested that what it concealed bore some humble resemblance to features here. The thin grasses, more or less coating the hill, were touched by the wind in breezes of differing powers, and almost differing natures – one rubbing the blades heavily, another raking them piercingly, another brushing them like a soft broom. The instinctive act of human-kind here was to stand, and listen, and learn how the trees on the right and the trees on the left wailed or chanted to each other in the regular antiphonies of a cathedral choir; how hedges and other shapes to leeward then caught the note, lowering it to the tenderest sob; and how the hurrying gust then plunged into the south to be heard no more.

The sky was clear – remarkably clear – and the twinkling of all the stars seemed to be but throbs of one body, timed by a common pulse. The north star was directly in the wind's eye, and since evening the Bear had revolved round it outwardly to the east, till it was now at a right angle with the meridian. A difference of colour in the stars – oftener read of than seen in England – was really perceptible here. The kingly brilliancy of Sirius pierced the eye with a steely glitter, the star called Capella was yellow, Aldebaran and Betelgueux shone with a fiery red.[3]

To persons standing alone on a hill during a clear midnight such as this – the roll of the world eastward is almost a palpable movement. The sensation may be caused by the panoramic glide of the stars past earthly objects, which is perceptible in a few minutes of stillness; or by a fancy that the better outlook upon space afforded by a hill emphasizes terrestial revolution; or by the wind; or by the solitude; but whatever be its origin the impression of riding along is vivid and abiding. The poetry of motion is a phrase much in use, and to enjoy the epic form of that gratification it is necessary to stand on a hill at a small hour of the night, and, first enlarging the consciousness with a sense of difference from the mass of civilized mankind, who are horizontal and disregardful of all such proceedings at this time, long and quietly watch your stately progress through the stars. After such a nocturnal reconnoitre among these astral clusters, aloft from the customary haunts of thought and vision, some men may feel raised to a capability for eternity at once.

Suddenly an unexpected series of sounds began to be heard in this place up against the sky. They had a clearness which was to be found nowhere in the wind, and a sequence which was to be found nowhere in nature. They were the notes of Farmer Oak's flute.

The tune was not floating unhindered into the open air, but it seemed muffled in some way, and was altogether too curtailed in power to spread high or wide. It came from the direction of a small dark object under the plantation hedge – a shepherd's hut now presenting an outline to which an uninitiated person might have been puzzled to attach either meaning or use. The image as a whole was that of a small Noah's Ark[4] on a small

Ararat, allowing the traditionary outlines and general form of the Ark which are followed by toy makers, and by these means are established in men's imaginations among the firmest because the earliest impressions, to pass as an approximate pattern. The hut stood on small wheels which raised its floor about a foot from the ground. Such shepherd's huts are dragged into the fields when the lambing season comes on, to shelter the shepherd in his enforced nightly attendance.

It was only latterly that people had begun to call Gabriel "Farmer" Oak. During the twelvemonth preceding this time he had been enabled by sustained efforts of industry and chronic good spirits to lease the small sheep farm of which Norcombe Hill was a portion, and stock it with two hundred sheep. Previously he had been a bailiff[5] for a short time, and earlier still a shepherd only, tending the flocks of large proprietors from his childhood with his father, till old Gabriel sank to rest.

This venture, unaided and alone, into the paths of farming as master and not as man, with an advance of sheep not yet paid for, was a critical juncture with Gabriel Oak, and he recognised his position clearly. The first movement in his new progress was the lambing of his ewes, and sheep having been his speciality from his youth, he wisely refrained from deputing the task of tending them at this season to a hireling or a novice.

The wind continued to beat about the corners of the hut, but the flute-playing ceased. A rectangular space of light appeared in the side of the hut, and in the opening the outline of Farmer Oak's figure. He carried a lantern in his hand, and closing the door behind him came forward and busied himself about this nook of the field for nearly twenty minutes, the lantern light appearing and disappearing here and there, and brightening him or darkening him as he stood before or behind it.

Oak's motions, though they had a quiet energy, were slow, and their deliberateness accorded well with his occupation. Fitness being the basis of all beauty, nobody could have denied that his steady swings and turns in and about the flock had elements of grace. Yet, although if occasion demanded he could do or think a thing with as mercurial[6] a dash as can the men of towns who are more to the manner born, his special power, morally, physically, and mentally, was static, owing little or nothing to momentum in any case, as a rule.

A close examination of the ground hereabout, even by the wan starlight only, revealed how a portion of what would have been casually called a wild slope had been appropriated by Farmer Oak for his great purpose this winter. Detached hurdles thatched with straw were stuck into the ground at various scattered points, amid and under which the whitish forms of his meek ewes moved and rustled. The ring of the sheep-bell, which had been silent during his absence, recommenced, in tones which had more mellowness than clearness, owing to an increasing growth of surrounding wool, and continued till Oak withdrew again from the flock. He returned to the hut, bringing in his arms a new-born lamb, consisting of four legs large enough for a full-grown sheep united by an unimportant membrane about half the substance of the legs collectively, which constituted the animal's entire body just at present.

The little speck of life he placed on a wisp of hay before the small stove, over which simmered a can of milk. Oak extinguished the lantern by blowing into it with pouted lips and then pinching out the snuff, the cot being lighted by a candle suspended from a nail by a twisted wire. A rather hard couch, formed of a few corn-sacks thrown carelessly down covered half the floor of this little habitation, and here the young man stretched himself along, loosened his woollen cravat, and closed his eyes. In about the time a person unaccustomed to bodily labour would have decided upon which side to lie, Farmer Oak was asleep.

The inside of this hut as it now presented itself, was cosy and even alluring, and the scarlet handful of fire, in addition to the candle, reflecting its own genial colour upon whatever it could reach, flung associations of enjoyment even over utensils and tools. In the corner stood the sheep-crook, and along a shelf at one side were ranged bottles and cannisters of the simple preparations pertaining to ovine surgery and physic – Spirits of wine, turpentine, tar, magnesia, ginger, and castor oil being the chief. On a triangular shelf across the corner stood bread, bacon, cheese, and a cup for ale or cider, the source of which was a flagon beneath. Beside the provisions lay the flute, the notes of which had lately been called forth by the lonely watcher to beguile a tedious hour. The house was ventilated by two round holes, like the lights of a cabin, with wood slides.

The lamb, revived by the warmth, began to bleat, and the sound entered Gabriel's ears and brain with an instant meaning, as expected sounds will. Passing from the profoundest sleep to the most alert wakefulness with the same ease that had accompanied the reverse operation, he looked at his watch, found that the hour hand had shifted again, put on his hat, took the lamb in his arms, and carried it into the darkness. After placing the little creature with its mother he stood and carefully examined the sky to ascertain the time of night from the altitudes of the stars.

The Dog-star[7] and Aldebaran, pointing to the restless Pleiades were half way up the southern sky, and beneath them hung Orion[8] which gorgeous constellation never burnt more vividly than now as it swung itself high above the rim of the landscape. Castor and Pollux with their quiet shine almost rested on the ground: the barren and gloomy Square of Pegasus was creeping round to the north-west; far away through the plantation Vega sparkled like a lamp suspended amid the leafless trees; and Cassiopeia's Chair[9] stood daintily poised on the uppermost boughs.

"One o'clock," said Gabriel.

Being a man not without a frequent consciousness that there was some beauty in this life he led, he stood still after looking at the sky as a useful instrument, and regarded it in an appreciative spirit, as a work of art superlatively beautiful. For a moment he seemed impressed with the speaking loneliness of the scene, or rather with the complete abstraction from all its compass of the sights and sounds of man. Human shapes, interferences, troubles, and joys were all as if they were not, and there seemed to be on the shaded hemisphere of the globe no sentient being save himself: he could fancy them all gone round to the sunny side.

Occupied thus, with eyes stretched afar, Oak gradually perceived that what he had previously taken to be a star low down behind the outskirts of the plantation was in reality no such thing. It was an artificial light not fifty yards off.

To find themselves utterly alone at night where company is desirable and expected makes some people fearful; but a case more trying by far to the nerves is to discover some mysterious companionship when intuition, sensation, memory, analogy, testimony, probability, induction – every kind of evidence in the logician's list – have united to persuade consciousness that it is quite alone.

Farmer Oak went towards the plantation and pushed through its lower boughs to the windy side. A dim mass under the slope reminded him that a shed occupied a place here – the site being a cutting into the slope of the hill, so that at its back-part the roof was almost level with the ground. In front it was formed of boards nailed to posts and covered with tar as a preservative. Through crevices in the roof and side spread streaks and dots of light, a combination of which made up the radiance that had attracted him. Oak stepped up behind, where, leaning down upon the roof and putting his eye close to a crack he could see into the interior clearly.

The place contained two women and two cows. By the side of the latter a steaming bran mash stood in a bucket. One of the women was past middle age. Her companion was apparently young and graceful: he could form no decided opinion upon her looks, her position being almost beneath his eye, so that he saw her in a bird's eye aerial view, as Satan first saw Paradise.[10] She wore no bonnet or hat, but had enveloped herself in a large cloak, which was carelessly flung over her head as a covering.

"There, now we'll go home," said the elder of the two, resting her knuckles upon her hips and looking at their goings-on as a whole. "I do hope Daisy will fetch round again now. I have never been more frightened in my life, but I don't mind breaking my rest if she recovers."

The young woman, whose eyelids were apparently inclined to fall together on the smallest provocation of silence, yawned without parting her lips to any inconvenient extent, whereupon Gabriel caught the infection and slightly yawned in sympathy. "I wish we were rich enough to pay a man to do these things," she said.

"As we are not we must do them ourselves," said the other. "For you must help me if you stay."

"Well – my hat is gone, however," continued the younger. "It went over the hedge, I think. The idea of such a slight wind catching it."

The cow standing erect was of the Devon breed, and was encased in a tight warm hide of rich Indian red, as absolutely uniform from eyes to tail as if the animal had been dipped in a dye of that colour, her long back being mathematically level. The other was spotted – grey and white. Beside her Oak now noticed a little calf about a day old, looking idiotically at the two women, which showed it had not long been accustomed to the phenomenon of eyesight, and often turning to the lantern, which it apparently mistook for the moon, inherited instinct having as yet had little time for correction by experience. Between the sheep and the cows, Lucina[11] had been busy on Norcombe Hill lately.

"I think we had better send for some oatmeal," said the elder woman. "There's no more bran."

"Yes, aunt. And I'll ride over for it as soon as it is light."

"But there's no side saddle."[12]

"I can ride on the other: trust me."

Oak, upon hearing these remarks became more curious to observe her features, but this prospect being denied him by the hooding effect of the cloak, and by her forehead coming in the way of what the cloak did not cover, he felt himself drawing upon his fancy for their details. – In making even horizontal and clear inspections we colour and mould according to the wants within us whatever our eyes bring in: had Gabriel been able from the first to get a distinct view of her countenance his estimate of it as very handsome or slightly so would have been as his soul required a divinity at the moment or was ready supplied with one. Having then for some time known the want of a satisfactory form to fill an increasing void within him, his position moreover affording the widest scope for his fancy, he straightway painted her a beauty.

By one of those whimsical coincidences in which Nature, like a busy mother, seems to spare a moment from her unremitting labours to turn and make her children smile, the girl now dropped the cloak, and forth tumbled ropes of black hair over a red jacket. Oak knew her instantly as the heroine of the yellow waggon, myrtles and looking-glass: prosily, as the woman who owed him twopence.

They placed the calf beside its mother again, took up the lantern, and went out, the light sinking down the hill till it was no more than a nebula. Gabriel Oak returned to his flock.

CHAPTER III

A girl on horseback: conversation.

The sluggish day began to break. Even its position terrestially is one of the elements of a new interest, and for no particular reason save that the incident of the night had occurred there Oak went again into the plantation. Lingering and musing here he heard the steps of a horse at the foot of the hill, and soon there appeared in view an auburn pony with a girl on its back, ascending by the path leading past the cattle shed: she was the young woman of the night before. Gabriel instantly thought of the hat she had mentioned as having lost in the wind: possibly she had come to look for it. He hastily scanned the ditch, and after walking about ten yards along it, found the hat among the leaves. Gabriel took it in his hand and returned to his hut. Here he ensconced himself, and looked through the loophole in the direction of the rider's approach.

She came up and looked around – then on the other side of the hedge. Gabriel was about to advance and restore the missing article, when an unexpected performance induced him to suspend the action for the present. The path after passing the cow-shed bisected the plantation. It was not a bridle-path – merely a pedestrian's track, and the boughs spread horizontally at a height not greater than seven feet above the ground, which made it impossible to ride erect beneath them. The girl, who wore no riding-habit, looked around for a moment as if to assure herself that all humanity was out of view, then dexterously dropped backwards flat upon the pony's back, her head over its tail, her feet against its shoulder and her eyes to the sky. The rapidity of her glide into this position was that of a kingfisher – its noiselessness that of a hawk: Gabriel's eyes had scarcely been able to follow her. The tall lank pony seemed used to such phenomena, and ambled along unconcerned. Thus she passed under the level boughs.

The performer seemed quite at home anywhere between a horse's head and its tail, and the necessity for this abnormal attitude having ceased with the passage of the plantation, she began to adopt another, even more obviously convenient than the first. She had no side-saddle, and it was very apparent that a firm seat upon the smooth leather beneath her was unattainable sideways. Springing to her accustomed perpendicular like a bowed sapling, and satisfying herself that nobody was in sight, she seated herself in the manner demanded by the saddle, though hardly expected of the woman, and trotted off in the direction of Tewnell Mill.

Oak was amused – perhaps a little astonished, and hanging up the hat in his hut, went again among his ewes. An hour passed, the girl returned, properly seated now, with a bag of bran in front of her. On nearing the cattle shed she was met by a boy bringing a milking pail, who held the reins of the pony whilst she slid off. The boy led away the animal, leaving the pail with the young woman.

Soon a soft spirt alternating with a loud spirt came in regular succession from within the shed. They were the sounds of a person milking a cow.[1]

Gabriel took the lost hat in his hand, and waited beside the path she would follow in leaving the hill.

She came, the pail in one hand, hanging against her knee. The left arm was extended as a balance, enough of it being shown bare to make Oak wish that the event had happened in summer when the whole would have been revealed. There was a bright air and manner about her now, by which she seemed to imply that the desirability of her existence could not be questioned; and this rather saucy assumption failed in being offensive because a beholder felt it to be, upon the whole, true. Like exceptional emphasis in the tone of a genius, that which would have made mediocrity ridiculous was an addition to recognised power. It was with some surprise that she saw Gabriel's face rising like the moon, behind the hedge.

The adjustment of the farmer's hazy conceptions of her charms to the portrait of herself she now presented him with was less a diminution than a difference. The starting-point selected by the judgment was her height. She seemed tall, but the pail was a small one, and the hedge diminutive; hence making allowance for error by comparison with these, she could have been not above the height to be chosen by women as best. All features of consequence were severe and regular. It may have been observed by persons who go about the shires with eyes for beauty that in English women a classically formed face is seldom found united with a figure of the same pattern, the highly finished features being generally too large for the remainder of the frame; that a graceful and proportionate figure of eight heads[2] usually goes off into random facial curves. Without throwing a Nymphean[3] tissue over a milkmaid it may be said that criticism checked itself in examining details to return to where it began, and looked at her proportions with a long consciousness of pleasure. From the contours of her figure in its upper part, she must have had a beautiful neck and shoulders, but it may be stated that since her infancy nobody had ever seen them. Had she been put into a low dress, she would have run and thrust her head into a bush. Yet she was not a shy girl by any means; it was merely her instinct to draw the line dividing the seen from the unseen higher than they do it in towns.

That the girl's thoughts hovered about her face and form as soon as she caught Oak's eyes conning the same page was natural, and almost certain. The self-consciousness shown would have been vanity if a little more pronounced, and dignity if a little less. Rays of male vision seem to have a tickling effect upon virgin faces in rural districts: she hastily brushed hers with her hand, as if Gabriel had been irritating its pink surface with a long straw, and the free air of her previous movements was reduced at the same time to a chastened phase of itself. Yet it was the man who blushed, the maid not at all.

"I found a hat," said Oak.

"It is mine," said she, and, from a sense of proportion kept down to a small smile an inclination to laugh distinctly – "It flew away last night."

"One o'clock this morning."

"Well – it was." She was surprised. "How did you know?" she said.

"I was here."

"You are Farmer Oak, are you not?"

"That or thereabouts. I'm lately come to this place."

"A large farm?" she inquired, casting her eyes around, and swinging back her hair, which was black in the shaded hollows of its mass; but it being now an hour past sunrise the rays touched its prominent curves with a colour of their own.

"No: not large. About a hundred." (In speaking of farms the word "acres" is omitted by the natives by analogy with such old expressions as "a stag of ten").

"I wanted my hat this morning," she went on. "I had to ride to Tewnell Mill."

"Yes: you had."

"How do you know?"

"I saw you."

"Where?" she inquired, a misgiving bringing every muscle of her lineaments and frame to a standstill.

"Here – going through the plantation, and all down the hill," said Farmer Oak, with an aspect excessively knowing with regard to some matter in his mind, as he gazed at a remote point in the direction named, and then turned back to meet his colloquist's eyes.

A perception caused him to withdraw his own from hers as suddenly as if he had been caught in a theft. Recollection of the strange antics she had indulged in when passing through the trees, was succeeded in the girl by a nettled palpitation, and that by a hot face. It was a time to see a woman redden who was not given to reddening as a rule: not a point in the milkmaid but was of the deepest rose colour. From the Maiden's Blush through all varieties of the Provence down to the Crimson Tuscany[4] the countenance of Oak's acquaintance quickly graduated; whereupon he, in considerateness, had turned away his head.

The sympathetic man still looked the other way, and wondered when she would recover whiteness sufficient to justify him in facing her again. He heard what seemed to be the flitting by of a dead leaf upon the breeze, and looked. She had gone away.

With an air between that of Tragedy and Comedy Gabriel returned to his work.

Five mornings and evenings passed. The young woman came regularly to milk the healthy cow or attend to the sick one, but never allowed her vision to stray in the direction of Oak's person. His want of tact had deeply offended her – not by seeing what he could not help, but by letting her know that he had seen it. For, as without law there is no sin, so without eyes there is no immodesty, and she appeared to feel that Gabriel's espial had made her an indecorous woman without her own connivance. It was food for great regret with him: it was also a contretemps which touched into life a latent heat he had experienced in that direction.

The acquaintanceship might however have ended in a slow forgetting, but for an incident which occurred at the end of the same week. One afternoon it began to freeze, and the frost increased with evening, which drew on like a stealthy tightening of bonds. It was a time when in cottages the breath of the sleepers freezes to the sheets, when round the drawing room fire of a thick-walled mansion the sitters' backs are cold even whilst their faces are all aglow. Many a small bird went to bed supperless that night among the bare boughs.

As the milking hour drew near Oak kept his usual watch upon the cow-shed. At last he felt cold, and shaking an extra quantity of bedding round the yeaning ewes, he entered the hut and heaped more fuel upon the stove. The wind came in at the bottom of the door, to prevent which Oak wheeled the cot round, a little more to the south. Then the wind spouted in at a ventilating hole – of which there was one on each side of the hut.

Gabriel had always known that when the fire was lighted and the door closed one of these must be kept open – that chosen being always on the side away from the wind. Closing the slide to windward he turned to open the other: on second thoughts the farmer considered he would first sit down, leaving both closed for a minute or two till the temperature of the hut was a little raised. He sat down.

His head began to ache in an unwonted manner, and, fancying himself weary by reason of the broken rests of the preceding nights, Oak decided to get up, open the slide, and then allow himself to fall asleep. He fell asleep without having performed the necessary preliminary.

How long he remained unconscious Gabriel never knew. During the first stages of his return to perception peculiar deeds seemed to be in course of enactment. His dog was howling, his head was aching fearfully – somebody was pulling him about, hands were loosening his neckerchief.

On opening his eyes he found that evening had sunk to dusk in a strange phase of unexpectedness. The young girl with the remarkably pleasant lips and white teeth was beside him. More than this – astonishingly more – his head was upon her lap, his face and neck were disagreeably wet, and her fingers were unbuttoning his collar.

"Whatever is the matter?" said Oak, vacantly.

She seemed to experience a sensation of mirth, but of too insignificant a kind to start the capacity of enjoyment.

"Nothing now," she answered, "since you are not dead. It was a wonder you were not suffocated in this hut of yours."

"Ah – the hut!" murmured Gabriel. "I gave ten pounds for that hut. But I'll sell it and sit under thatched hurdles as they did in old times, and curl up to sleep in a lock of straw. It played me nearly the same trick the other day!" Gabriel by way of emphasis, brought down his fist upon the frozen ground.

"It was not exactly the fault of the hut," she observed, speaking in a tone which showed her to be that novelty among women – one who finished a thought before beginning the sentence which was to convey it. "You should I think have considered and not have been so foolish as to leave the slides closed."

"Yes – I suppose I should," said Oak, absently. He was endeavouring to catch and appreciate the sensation of being thus with her – his head upon her dress – before the event passed on into the heap of bygone things. He wished she knew his impressions; but he would as soon have thought of carrying an odour in a net as of attempting to convey the intangibilities of his feeling in the coarse meshes of language. So he remained silent.

She made him sit up, and then Oak began wiping his face and shaking himself like a Samson.[5] "How can I thank ye," he said at last gratefully, some of the natural rusty red having returned to his face.

"O never mind that," said the girl smiling, and allowing her smile to hold good for Gabriel's next remark, whatever that might prove to be.

"How did you find me?"

"I heard your dog howling and scratching at the door of the hut, when I came to the milking – (it was so lucky – Daisy's milking is almost over for the season, and I shall not come here after this week or the next). The dog saw me, and jumped over to me, and laid hold of my dress. I came across and looked round the hut the very first thing to see if the slides were closed. My uncle has a hut like this one, and I have heard him tell his shepherd not to go to sleep without leaving a slide open. I opened the door and there you were like dead: I threw the milk over you as there was no water – forgetting it was warm, and no use."

"I wonder if I should have died," Gabriel said in a low voice which was rather meant to travel back to himself than on to her.

"O no," the girl replied. She seemed to prefer a less tragic probability: to have saved a man from death involved talk that should harmonize with the dignity of such a deed – and she shunned it.

"I believe you saved my life, Miss – I don't know your name. I know your aunt's, but not yours."

"I would just as soon not tell it – rather not. There is no reason either why I should, as you probably will never have much to do with me."

"Still, I should like –"

"You can inquire at my aunt's – she will tell you."

"My name is Gabriel Oak."

"And mine isn't. You seem fond of you in speaking it so decisively Gabriel Oak."

"You see, it is the only one I shall ever have, and I must make the most of it."

"I always think mine sounds odd and disagreeable."

"I should think you might soon get a new one."

"Mercy – how many opinions you keep about you concerning other people, Gabriel Oak."

"Well, Miss – excuse the words – I thought you would like them. But I can't match you, I know, in mapping out my mind upon my tongue as I may say. I never was very clever in my inside. But I thank you. Come, give me your hand!"

She hesitated, somewhat disconcerted at Oak's old-fashioned earnest conclusion to a dialogue lightly carried on. "Very well," she said and gave him her hand, compressing her lips to a demure impassivity. He held it but an instant, and in his fear of being too demonstrative swerved to the opposite extreme, touching her fingers with the lightness of a small-hearted person.

"I am sorry," he said the instant after, regretfully.

"What for?"

"Letting your hand go so quickly."

"You may have me again if you like: there it is." She gave him her hand again.

Oak held it longer this time – indeed, remarkably long. "How soft it is – being winter-time, too – not chapped or rough or anything!" he said.

"There – that's long enough," said she, though without pulling it away. "But I suppose you are thinking you would like to kiss it? You may if you want to."

"I wasn't thinking of any such thing," said Gabriel simply: "but I will –"

"That you won't!" she exclaimed, snatching her hand back.

Gabriel felt himself guilty of another want of tact.

"Now find out my name," she said teasingly; and withdrew.

CHAPTER IV

Gabriel's resolve: The visit: The mistake.

The only superiority tolerable in women,[1] as a rule, is that of the unconscious kind, but a superiority which recognises itself may sometimes please by suggesting at the same time possibilities of impropriation to the subordinated man.

This well-favoured and comely girl soon made appreciable inroads upon the emotional constitution of young Farmer Oak. Love, being an extremely exacting usurer (a sense of exorbitant profit, spiritually, by an exchange of hearts, being at the bottom of pure passions, as that of exorbitant profit bodily or materially is at the bottom of those of lower atmosphere) every morning his feelings were as sensitive as the Money Market in calculations upon his chances. His dog waited for his meals in a way so like that in which Oak waited for the girl's presence that the farmer was quite struck with the resemblance, felt it lowering, and would not look at the dog. However he continued to watch through the hedge at her regular coming, and thus his sentiments towards her were deepened without any corresponding effect being produced upon herself. Oak had nothing finished and ready to say as yet, and not being able to frame love-phrases which end where they begin; passionate tales,

> "– Full of sound and fury
> Signifying nothing,"[2]

he said no word at all.

By making enquiries he found that the girl's name was Bathsheba[3] Everdene, and that the cow would go dry in about seven days. He dreaded the eighth day.

At last the seventh day came. The cow had ceased to give milk for that year, and Bathsheba Everdene came up the hill no more. Gabriel had reached a pitch of existence he never could have anticipated a short time before. He liked saying "Bathsheba" as a private enjoyment instead of whistling, turned over his taste to black hair, though he had sworn by brown ever since he was a boy, isolated himself till the space he filled in the public eye was contemptibly small. Love is a possible strength in an actual weakness. Marriage transforms a distraction into a support the power of which should be, and happily often is, in direct proportion to the degree of imbecility it supplants. Oak began now to see light in this direction, and said to himself, "I'll make her my wife, or upon my soul I shall be good for nothing." All this while he was perplexing himself as to an errand on which he might consistently visit the cottage of Bathsheba's aunt.

He found his opportunity in the death of a ewe, mother of a living lamb. On a day which had a summer face and a winter constitution – a fine January morning when there was just enough blue sky visible to make cheerfully disposed people wish for more, and an occasional sunshiny gleam of silvery whiteness, Oak put the lamb into a respectable Sunday basket, and stalked across the fields to the house of Mrs Hurst the aunt – George the dog walking behind with a countenance of great concern at the serious turn pastoral affairs seemed to be taking.

Gabriel had watched the blue wood-smoke curling from the chimney with strange meditation. At evening he had fancifully traced it down the chimney to the spot of its origin – seen the hearth and Bathsheba beside it, but in her outdoor dress; for the clothes she had worn on the hill were by association equally with her person included in the compass of his affection: they seemed at this early time of his love a necessary ingredient of the sweet mixture called Bathsheba Everdene.

He had made a toilet of a nicely adjusted kind – of a nature between the carefully neat and the carelessly ornate – of a degree between fine-market-day and wet-Sunday selection. He thoroughly cleaned his silver watch-chain with whiting, put new lacing-straps to his boots, looked to the brass eyelet holes, went to the inmost heart of the plantation for a new walking-stick and trimmed it vigorously on his way back, took a new handkerchief from the bottom of his clothes-box, put on the light waistcoat patterned all over with sprigs of an elegant flower uniting the beauties of both rose and lily, without the defects of either, and used all the hair-oil he possessed upon his usually dry, sandy and inextricably curly hair till he had deepened it to a splendidly novel colour between that of guano and Roman cement, making it stick to his head like mace round a nutmeg, or wet seaweed round a boulder after the ebb.

Nothing disturbed the stillness of the cottage save the chatter of a knot of sparrows on the eaves: one might fancy scandal and *tracasseries*[4] to be no less the staple subject of these little coteries on roofs than of those under them. It seemed the omen was an unpropitious one, for, as the rather untoward commencement of Oak's overtures, just as he arrived by the garden gate he saw a small cat inside, going into various arched shapes and fiendish convulsions at the sight of his dog George. The dog took no notice, for he had arrived at an age at which all superfluous barking was cynically avoided as a waste of breath – in fact he never barked even at the sheep except to order, when it was done with an absolutely neutral countenance, as a liturgical form of commination-service[5] which though offensive had to be gone through once now and then just to frighten the flock for their own good.

A voice came from behind some laurel bushes, into which the cat had run:

"Poor dear! Did a nasty brute of a dog want to kill it! – did he, poor dear!"

"I beg yer pardon," said Oak to the voice, "but George was walking on behind me with a temper as mild as milk."

Almost before he had ceased speaking Oak was seized with a misgiving as to whose ear was the recipient of his answer. Nobody appeared, and he heard the person retreat among the bushes.

Gabriel meditated, and so deeply that he brought small furrows into his forehead by sheer force of reverie. Where the issue of an interview is as likely to be a vast change for the worse as for the better, any initial difference from expectation causes nipping sensations of failure. Oak went up to the door a little abashed: his marital rehearsal and the reality had had no common grounds of opening.

Bathsheba's aunt was indoors. "Will you tell Miss Everdene that somebody would be glad to speak to her?" said Mr Oak. (Calling yourself merely Somebody, and not giving a name, is not by any means to be taken as an example of the ill-breeding of the rural world: it springs from a refined sense of modesty of which townspeople with their cards and announcements have no notion whatever).

Bathsheba was out. The voice had evidently been hers.

"Will you come in, Mr Oak?"

"O thank ye," said Gabriel, following her to the fireplace. "I've brought a lamb for Miss Everdene. I thought she might like one to rear: girls do."

"She might," said Mrs Hurst musingly: "though she's only a visitor here. If you will wait a minute Bathsheba will be in."

"Yes, I will wait," said Gabriel sitting down. "The lamb isn't really the business I came about, Mrs Hurst. In short I was going to ask her if she'd like to be married."

"And were you indeed."

"Yes. Because if she would I should be very glad to marry her. D'ye know if she's got any other young man hanging about her at all?"

"Let me think," said Mrs Hurst, poking the fire superfluously. . . . . . "Yes – bless you, ever so many young men. You see Farmer Oak, she's so good-looking and an excellent scholar besides – she was going to be a governess once, you know, only she was too wild. Not that her young men ever come here – but, Lord, in the nature of women she must have a dozen!"

"That's unfortunate," said Farmer Oak contemplating a crack in the stone floor with sorrow. "I'm only an everyday sort of man, and my only chance was in being the first comer . . . Well, there's no use in my waiting, for that was all I came about: so I'll take myself off home-along, Mrs Hurst."

When Gabriel had gone about two hundred yards along the down he heard a "hoi-hoi!" uttered behind him in a piping note of more treble quality than that in which the exclamation usually embodies itself when shouted across a field. He looked round and saw a girl racing after him, waving a white handkerchief.

Oak stood still – and the runner drew nearer. It was Bathsheba Everdene. Gabriel's colour deepened: hers was already deep, not as it appeared from emotion, but from running.

"Farmer Oak – I –" she said, pausing for want of breath, pulling up in front of him with a slanted face, and putting her hand to her side.

"I have just called to see you," said Gabriel, pending her further speech.

"Yes – I know that," she said panting like a robin, her face red and moist from her exertions, like a peony[6] petal before the sun dries off the dew. "I didn't know you had come (pant) to ask to have me, or I should have come in from the garden instantly. I ran after you to say (pant) that my aunt made a mistake in sending you away from courting me (pant) –"

Gabriel expanded. "I'm sorry to have made you run so fast, my honey," he said, with a grateful sense of favours to come. "Wait a bit till you've found your breath."

"– It was quite a mistake – aunt's telling you I had a young man already," Bathsheba went on. "I haven't a sweetheart at all (pant) and I never had one, and I thought that, as times go with women, it was *such* a pity to send you away thinking that I had several."

"Really and trewly I am glad to hear that!" said Farmer Oak, smiling one of his long special smiles, and blushing with gladness. He held out his hand to take hers, which, when she had eased her side by pressing it there, was prettily extended upon her bosom to still her loud-beating heart. Directly he seized it she put it behind her, so that it slipped through his fingers like an eel.

"I have a nice snug little farm," said Gabriel with half a degree less assurance than when he had seized her hand.

"Yes: you have."

"A man has advanced me money to begin with, but still, it will soon be paid off, and though I am only an everyday sort of man I have got on a little since I was a boy." Gabriel uttered "a little" in a tone to show her that it was the complacent form of "a great deal." He continued: "when we are married, I am quite sure I can work twice as hard as I do now."

He went forward and stretched out his arm again. Bathsheba had overtaken him at a point beside which stood a low, stunted holly bush, now laden with red berries. Seeing his advance take the form of an attitude threatening a possible enclosure if not compression of her person, she edged off round the bush.

"Why Farmer Oak," she said, over the top, looking at him with rounded eyes, "I never said I was going to marry you."

"Well – that *is* a tale!" said Oak, with dismay. "To run after anybody like this – and then say you don't want me!"

"What I meant to tell you was only this," she said eagerly, and yet half-conscious of the absurdity of the position she had made for herself: "that nobody has got me yet as a sweetheart, instead of my having a dozen as my aunt said; I *hate* to be thought men's property in that way – though possibly I shall be to be had some day. Why, if I'd wanted you I shouldn't have run after you like this; t'would have been the *forwardest* thing! But there was no harm in hurrying to correct a piece of false news that had been told you."

"O no – no harm at all."

But there is such a thing as being too generous in expressing a judgment impulsively, and Oak added with a more appreciative sense of all the circumstances – "Well I am not quite certain it was no harm."

"Indeed, I hadn't time to think before starting whether I wanted to marry you or not, for you'd have been gone over the hill."

"Come," said Gabriel, freshening again; "think a minute or two. I'll wait awhile, Miss Everdene. Will you marry me? Do Bathsheba. I love you far more than common!"

"I'll try to think," she observed rather more timorously: "if I can think out of doors; but my mind spreads away so."

"But you can give a guess."

"Then give me time." Bathsheba looked thoughtfully into the distance away from the direction in which Gabriel stood.

"I can make you happy," said he to the back of her head across the bush. "You shall have a piano in a year or two – farmers' wives are getting to have pianos now, and I'll practise up the flute right well to play with you in the evenings."

"Yes: I should like that."

"And have one of those little ten-pound gigs for market – and nice flowers, and birds – cocks and hens I mean, because they are useful," continued Gabriel, feeling balanced between prose and verse.

"I should like it very much."

"And a frame for cucumbers – like a gentleman and lady."

"Yes."

"And when the wedding was over, we'd have it put in the newspaper list of marriages."

"Dearly I should like that."

"And the babies in the Births – every man-jack of 'em!"

"Don't talk so!"

"And at home by the fire, whenever you look up there I shall be – and whenever I look up there will be you."

Her countenance fell, and she was silent awhile. He contemplated the red berries between them over and over again to such an extent that holly seemed in his after life to be a cypher signifying a proposal of marriage. Bathsheba decisively turned to him.

"No: 'tis no use," she said. "I don't want to marry you."

"Try!"

"I have tried hard all the time I've been thinking; for a marriage would be very nice in one sense. People would talk about me, and think I had won my battle, and I should feel triumphant, and all that. But a husband –"

"Well!"

"Why, he'd always be there, as you say: whenever I looked up, there he'd be."

"Of course he would – I, that is."

"Well, what I mean is that I shouldn't mind being a bride at a wedding if I could be one without having a husband. But since a woman can't show off in that way by herself I shan't marry – at least yet."

"That's a terrible wooden story."

At this elegant criticism of her statement Bathsheba made an addition to her dignity by a slight sweep away from him.

"Upon my heart and soul, I don't know what a maid can say stupider than that," said Oak. "But dearest," he continued in a palliative voice, "don't be like it!" Oak sighed a deep honest sigh – none the less so in that, being like the sigh of a pine plantation, it was rather noticeable as a disturbance of the atmosphere. "Why won't you have me?" he said, appealingly, creeping round the holly to reach her side.

"I cannot," she said retreating.

"But why?" he persisted, standing still at last in despair of ever reaching her, and facing her over the bush.

"Because I don't love you."

"Yes, but –"

She contracted a yawn to an inoffensive smallness so that it was hardly ill-mannered at all. "I don't love you," she said.

"But I love you – and as for myself, I'm content to be liked."

"O Mr Oak – that's very fine! You'd get to despise me."

"Never," said Mr Oak, so earnestly that he seemed to be coming by the force of his words straight through the bush and into her arms. "I shall do one thing in this life – one thing certain – that is, love you, and long for you, and *keep wanting you* till I die." His voice had a genuine pathos now, and his large brown hands trembled a quarter of an inch each way.

"It seems dreadfully wrong not to have you when you feel so much," she said with a little distress, and looking hopelessly around for some means of escape from her moral dilemma. "I wish I hadn't run after you." However she seemed to have a short cut for getting back to cheerfulness, and set her face to signify archness. "It wouldn't do, Mr Oak. I want somebody to tame me: I am too independent: and you would never be able to, I know."

Oak cast his eyes down the field in a way implying that it was useless to attempt argument.

"Mr Oak," she said with luminous distinctness and common sense: "You are better off than I. I have hardly a penny in the world – I am staying with my aunt for my bare sustenance – I am better educated than you – and I don't love you a bit: that's my side of the case. Now yours: you are a farmer just beginning, and you ought in common prudence if you marry at all (which you should certainly not think of doing at present) to marry a woman with money, who would stock a larger farm for you than you have now."

Gabriel looked at her with a little surprise and much admiration.

"That's the very thing I had been thinking myself!" he naively said.

Farmer Oak had one-and-a-half Christian characteristics too many to succeed with Bathsheba at present: his humility, and a superfluous moiety of honesty. Bathsheba was decidedly disconcerted.

"Well then, why did you come and disturb me!" she said, almost angrily if not quite, an enlarging red spot arising in each cheek.

"I can't do what I think would be . . . would be . . ."

"Right?"

"No: wise."

"You have made an admission *now*, Mr Oak," she exclaimed, with even more hauteur, and rocking her head disdainfully. "After that, do you think I could marry you? Not if I know it."

He broke in, passionately. "But don't mistake me like that. Because I am open enough to own what every man in my position would ha' thought of, you make your colours come up your face and get crabbed with me. That about your not being good enough for me is nonsense. You speak like a lady – all the parish notice it, and your uncle in Weatherbury is, I have heard, a large farmer – much larger than ever I shall be. May I call in the evening – or will you walk along wi' me on Sundays? I don't want you to make up your mind at once, if you'd rather not."

"No – no – I cannot. Don't press me any more – don't. I don't love you – so 'twould be ridiculous!" she said, with a laugh.

No man likes to see his emotions the sport of a merry-go-round of skittishness. "Very well," said Oak, firmly, with the bearing of one who was going to give his days and nights to Ecclesiastes[7] for ever. "Then I'll ask you no more."

CHAPTER V

Departure of Bathsheba: A pastoral tragedy.

The news which one day reached Gabriel, that Bathsheba Everdene had left the neighbourhood, had an influence upon him which might have surprised any who never had suspected that the more emphatic the renunciation the less absolute its character as a rule.

It may have been observed that there is no regular path for getting out of love as there is for getting in. Some people look upon marriage as a short cut that way, but it has been known to fail. Separation, which was the means that chance offered to Gabriel Oak by Bathsheba's disappearance, though effectual with people of certain humours, is apt to idealize the removed object with others – notably those whose affection, placid and regular as it may be, flows deep and long. Oak belonged to the even-tempered order of humanity, and felt the secret fusion of himself in Bathsheba to be burning with a finer flame now that she was gone – that was all.

His incipient friendship with her aunt had been nipped by the failure of his suit and all that Oak learnt of Bathsheba's movements was done indirectly. It appeared that she had gone to a place called Weatherbury, more than twenty miles off, but in what capacity – whether as a visitor, or permanently, he could not discover.

Gabriel had two dogs. George the elder exhibited an ebony-tipped nose surrounded by a narrow margin of pink flesh, and a coat marked in random splotches approximating in colour to white and slaty grey; but the grey, after years of sun and rain, had been scorched and washed out of the more prominent locks, leaving them of a reddish brown, as if the blue component of the grey had faded, like the indigo from the same kind of colour in Turner's[1] pictures. In substance it had originally been hair, but long contact with sheep seemed to be turning it by degrees into wool of a poor quality and staple.

This dog had originally belonged to a shepherd of inferior morals and dreadful temper, and the result was that George knew the exact degree of condemnation signified by cursing and swearing of all descriptions better than the wickedest old man in the neighbourhood. Long experience had so precisely taught the animal the difference between such exclamations as "Come in!" and "D— ye, come in!" that he knew to a hair's breadth the rate of trotting back from the ewes' tails that each call involved, if a staggerer with the sheep-crook was to be escaped. Though old, he was clever and trustworthy still.

The young dog, George's son, might possibly have been the image of his mother, for there was not much resemblance between him and George. He was learning the sheep-keeping business, so as to follow on at the flock when the other should die, but had got no further than the rudiments as yet – still finding an insuperable difficulty in distinguishing between doing a thing well enough and doing it too well. So earnest and yet so wrong-headed was this young dog (he had no name in particular and answered with perfect readiness to any pleasant interjection) that, if sent behind the flock to help them on, he did it so thoroughly that he would have chased them across the county with the greatest pleasure if not called off, or reminded when to stop by the example of old George.

Thus much for the dogs. On the further side of Norcombe Hill was a chalk pit, from which chalk had been drawn for generations and spread over adjacent farms. Two hedges converged upon it in the form of a V, but without quite meeting. The narrow opening left, which was immediately over the brow of the pit, was protected by a rough railing.

One night when Farmer Oak had returned to his house, believing there would be no further necessity for his attendance on the down, he called as usual to the dogs, previously to shutting them up in the outhouse till next morning. Only one responded – old George. The other could not be found – either in the house, lane, or garden. Gabriel then remembered that he had left the two dogs on the hill eating a dead lamb (a kind of meat he usually kept from them, except when other food ran short) and concluding that the young one had not finished his meal, he went indoors to the luxury of a bed, which latterly he had only enjoyed on Sundays.

It was a still, moist night. Just before dawn he was assisted in waking by the abnormal reverberation of familiar music. To the shepherd, the note of the sheep-bell, like the ticking of the clock to other people, is a chronic sound that only makes itself noticed by ceasing or altering in some unusual manner from the well-known idle tinkle which signifies to the accustomed ear, however distant, that all is well in the fold. In the solemn calm of the awakening morn that note was heard by Gabriel beating with unusual violence and rapidity. This exceptional ringing may be caused in two ways – by the rapid feeding of the sheep bearing the bell, as when the flock breaks into new pasture, which gives it an intermittent rapidity, or by the sheep starting off in a run, when the sound has a regular palpitation. The experienced ear of Oak knew the sound he now heard to be caused by the running of the flock with great velocity.

He jumped out of bed, dressed, tore down the lane through a foggy dawn, and ascended the hill. The forward ewes were kept apart from those among which the fall of lambs would be later, there being two hundred of the latter class in Gabriel's flock. These two-hundred seemed to have absolutely vanished from the hill. There were the fifty with their lambs, enclosed at the other end as he had left them, but the rest forming the bulk of the flock were nowhere. Gabriel called at the top of his voice the shepherd's call.

"Ovey, ovey, ovey!"[2]

Not a single baa. He went to the hedge – a gap had been broken through it, and in the gap were the footprints of the sheep. Rather surprised to find them break fence at this season, yet putting it down instantly to their great fondness for ivy in winter-time, of which a great deal grew in the plantation, he followed through the hedge. They were not in the plantation. He called again: the valleys and furthest hills resounded as when the sailors invoked the lost Hylas on the Mysian shore;[3] but no sheep. He passed through the trees and along the ridge of the hill. On the extreme summit, where the ends of the two converging hedges of which we have spoken were stopped short by meeting the brow of the chalk pit, he saw the younger dog, standing against the sky – dark and motionless as Napoleon at St Helena.[4]

A horrible conviction darted through Oak. With a sensation of bodily faintness he advanced: at one point the rails were broken through, and there he saw the footprints of his ewes. The dog came up, licked his hand, and made signals implying that he expected some great reward for signal services rendered. Oak looked over the precipice. The ewes lay dead at its foot – a heap of two hundred mangled carcases, representing in their then condition at least 200 more.

Oak was an intensely humane man: indeed, his humanity often tore in pieces any politic intentions of his bordering on strategy, and carried him on as by gravitation. A shadow in his life had always been that his flock ended in mutton – that a day came and found every shepherd an arrant traitor to his defenceless sheep. His first feeling now was one of pity for the untimely fate of these gentle ewes and their unborn lambs.

It was a second to remember another phase of the matter. The sheep were not insured. – All the savings of a frugal life had been dispersed at a blow: his hopes of being an independent farmer were laid low – possibly for ever. Gabriel's energies patience and industry had been so severely taxed, during the years of his life between eighteen and eight and twenty, to reach his present stage of progress that no more seemed to be left in him. He leant down upon a rail, and covered his face with his hands.

Stupors however do not last for ever, and Farmer Oak recovered from his. It was as remarkable as it was characteristic that the one sentence he uttered was in thankfulness:

"Thank God I am not married: what would *she* have done in the poverty now coming upon me!"

Oak raised his head, and wondering what he could do, listlessly surveyed the scene. By the outer margin of the pit was an oval pond, and over it hung the attenuated skeleton of a chrome-yellow moon, which had only a few days to last – the morning star[5] dogging her on the right hand. The pool glittered like a dead man's eye, and as the world awoke a breeze blew, shaking and elongating the reflection of the moon without breaking it, and turning the image of the star to a phosphoric streak upon the water. All this Oak saw and remembered.

As far as could be learnt it appeared that the poor young dog, still under the impression that, as he was kept for running after sheep, the more he ran after them the better, had at the end of his meal off the dead lamb, which may have given him additional energy and spirits collected all the ewes into a corner, driven the timid creatures through the hedge, across the upper field, and by main force of worrying had given them momentum enough to break down a portion of the rotten railing, and so hurled them over the edge.

George's son had done his work so thoroughly that he was considered too good a workman to live – and was, in fact, taken and tragically shot at twelve o'clock that same day – another instance of the untoward fate which so often attends dogs and other philosophers who follow out a train of reasoning to its logical conclusion, and attempt perfectly consistent conduct in a world made up so largely of compromise.

Gabriel's farm had been stocked by a dealer – on the strength of Oak's promising look and character – who was receiving a per-centage from the farmer till such time as the advance should be cleared off. Oak found that the value of stock, plant and implements which were really his own would be about sufficient to pay his debts, leaving himself a free man with the clothes he stood up in, and nothing more.

CHAPTER VI[1]

The fair: the journey: the fire.

Two months passed away. We are brought on to a day in February on which was held the yearly statute or hiring fair[2] in the town of Casterbridge.

At one end of the street stood from two to three hundred farm and other labourers waiting to be hired – all men of the stamp to whom Labour suggests nothing else than a wrestle with Gravitation, and Pleasure nothing more than a renunciation of the same. Among these, carters and waggoners were distinguished by having a piece of whip-cord twisted round their hats; thatchers wore a fragment of woven straw; shepherds held their sheep-crooks in their hands; and thus the situation required was known to the hirers at a glance.

In the crowd was an athletic young fellow of somewhat superior appearance to the rest – in fact, his superiority was enough marked to lead several labourers standing by to speak to him enquiringly as to a farmer, and to use "Sir" as a terminational word. His answer always was:

"I am looking for a place myself – a bailiff's. Do you know of anybody who wants one?"

Gabriel was paler now. His eyes were more meditative and his expression was more sad. He had passed through an ordeal of wretchedness which had given him more than it had taken away. He had lost all he possessed of worldly property: he had sunk from his modest elevation down to a lower ditch than that from which he had started; but he had[3] now a dignified calm he had never before known and that indifference to fate which, though it often makes a villain of a man is the basis of his sublimity when it does not. And thus the abasement had been exaltation and the loss gain.

In the morning a regiment of cavalry had left the town, and a sergeant and his party had been beating up for recruits through the four streets. As the end of the day drew on, and he found himself not hired, Gabriel almost wished that he had joined them, and gone off to serve his country, then on the brink of a war.[4] Weary of standing in the market-place, and not much minding the kind of work he turned his hand to, he decided to offer himself in some other capacity than that of bailiff.

All the farmers seemed to be wanting shepherds. Sheep-tending was Gabriel's speciality. Turning down an obscure street and entering an obscurer lane he went up to a smith's shop.

"How long would it take you to make a shepherd's crook?"

"Twenty minutes."

"How much?"

"Two shillings."

He sat on a bench and the crook was made, a stem being given him into the bargain.

He then went to a ready-made clothes shop, the owner of which had a large rural connection. As the crook had absorbed most of Gabriel's money he attempted, and carried out, an exchange of his overcoat for a regulation shepherd's smockfrock.

This transaction having been completed, he again hurried off to the centre of the town, and stood on the kerb of the pavement as a shepherd, crook in hand.

Now that Oak had turned himself into a shepherd it seemed that bailiffs were most in demand. However, two or three farmers noticed him and drew near. Dialogues followed, more or less in the subjoined form.

"Where do you come from?"

"Norcombe."

"That's a long way."

"Twenty miles."

"Whose farm were you upon last?"

"My own."

This reply invariably operated like a rumour of cholera: the enquiring farmer would edge away, and shake his head dubiously. Gabriel like his dog, was too good to be trustworthy, and he never made any advance beyond this point.

It is better to accept any chance that offers itself, and then extemporise a procedure to fit it, than to get a good plan matured, and wait for a chance of using it. Gabriel wished he had not nailed up his colours as a shepherd, but had rather laid himself out for anything in the whole cycle of labour that had been required in the fair. It grew dusk. Some merry men were whistling and singing by the corn-exchange: Gabriel's hand, which had lain for some time idle in his smockfrock pocket, touched his flute, which he carried there. Here was an opportunity for putting his dearly bought wisdom into practice.

He drew out his flute and began to play "Jocky to the Fair"[5] in the style of a man who had never known a moment's sorrow. Oak could pipe with Arcadian[6] sweetness, and the sound of the well-known notes cheered his own heart as well as those of the loungers. He played on with spirit, and in half an hour had two or three shillings' worth of coppers.[7]

By making enquiries he learnt that there was another fair at Shottsford, the next day.

"Where is Shottsford?"

"Eight miles t'other side of Weatherbury."

Weatherbury. It was where Bathsheba had gone two months before. This information was like coming from night into noon.

"How far is it to Weatherbury?"

"Five or six miles."

Bathsheba had probably left Weatherbury long before this time, but the place had enough interest attaching to it to lead Oak to choose Shottsford Fair as his next field of enquiry. He resolved to walk half the distance overnight, sleeping at Weatherbury. Making a hasty meal, and with a portion of his bread and cheese still under his arm he struck out into the country by a footpath, which had been recommended as a short cut to the village in question.[8] Although Bathsheba thus acted as an inducement to him to travel that way, Oak resolutely determined to keep out of her sight – a familiar contradiction.

The path wended through water meadows traversed by little brooks, whose quivering surfaces were braided along their centres and folded into creases at the sides, or where the flow was more rapid, the stream was marked with spots of white froth, which rode on in undisturbed serenity. On the high road the dead and dry carcases of leaves tapped the ground as they went along helter-skelter upon the shoulders of the wind, and little birds in the hedges were rustling their feathers and tucking themselves in comfortably for the night, retaining their places if Oak kept moving, but flying away if he stopped to look at them. He passed through a wood when the game-birds were rising to their roosts, and heard the crack-voiced cock-pheasants' "cu-uck, cuck", and the wheezy whistle of the hens.

By the time he had walked half a dozen miles every shape on the landscape had assumed a uniform hue of blackness. He ascended a hill, and could just discern ahead of him a waggon, drawn up under a great overhanging tree on the roadside.

On coming close he found there were no horses attached to it, the spot being apparently quite deserted. The waggon from its position seemed to have been left there for the night, for beyond about half a truss of hay which was heaped in the bottom, it was quite empty. Gabriel sat down on the shafts of the vehicle and considered his position. He calculated that he had walked at least eight or nine miles of the journey, and having been on foot since daybreak he felt tempted to lie down upon the hay in the waggon instead of pushing on to the village of Weatherbury and having to pay for a lodging.

Eating his last slices of bread and cheese, and drinking from the bottle of cider he had taken the precaution to bring with him, he got into the lonely waggon. Here he spread half of the hay as a bed, and, as well as he could in the darkness, pulled the other half over him by way of bed-clothes, covering himself entirely, and feeling physically as comfortable as ever he had in his life. Inward melancholy it was impossible for a man like Oak, introspective far beyond his neighbours, to banish, whilst conning the present untoward page of his history. So, thinking of his misfortunes, amorous and pastoral he fell asleep, shepherds enjoying, in common with sailors, the privilege of being able to summon the god instead of having to wait for him.

On somewhat suddenly awakening, after a sleep of whose length he had no idea, Oak found that the waggon was in motion. He was being carried along the road at a rate rather considerable for a vehicle without springs, and under circumstances of physical uneasiness, his head being dandled up and down on the bed of the waggon like a kettle-drumstick. He then distinguished voices in conversation, coming from the forepart of the waggon. His concern at this dilemma – (which would have been alarm had he been a thriving man; but misfortune is a fine opiate to personal terror) – led him to peer cautiously from the hay, and the first sight he saw were the stars above him. Charles's Wain[9] was getting towards a right angle with the Pole Star, and Gabriel concluded that it must be about nine o'clock – in other words, that he had slept two hours. This small astronomical calculation was made without any positive effort, and whilst he was stealthily turning to discover if possible into whose hands he had fallen.

Two figures were dimly visible in front, sitting with their legs outside the waggon, one of whom was driving. Gabriel soon found that this was the waggoner, and it appeared they had come from Casterbridge fair like himself.

A conversation was in progress, which continued thus: –

"Be as 'twill she's a fine handsome body as far's looks be concerned."[10]

This was enunciated in the tone of a man who consulted oracles between every sentence he spoke.[11]

"Ay – so 'a seem, Billy Smallbury – so 'a seem." This utterance was very shaky by nature, and more so by circumstance, the jolting of the waggon not being without its effect upon the speaker's larynx. It came from the man who held the reins.

"She's a very vain feymell – so 'tis said here and there."

"Ah now. If so be 'tis like that, I can't look her in the face. Lord no: not I! – heh-heh-heh! Such a shy man as I be!"

"Yes – she's very vain. 'Tis said that every night at going to bed she looks in the glass to put on her nightcap properly."

"And not a married woman: O the world!"

"And 'a can play the peanner, so 'tis said. Can play so clever that 'a can make a psalm tune sound as well as the merriest working-day song a man can wish for."

"D'ye tell o't! A happy mercy for us, and I feel quite unspeakable! And how do she pay?"

"That I don't know, Joseph Poorgrass."[12]

On hearing these and other similar remarks a wild thought flashed into Gabriel's mind that they might be speaking of Bathsheba. There were however no grounds for retaining such a supposition, for the waggon, though going in the direction of Weatherbury might be going beyond it, and the woman alluded to seemed to be the mistress of some estate. They were now apparently close to Weatherbury, and not to alarm the speakers unnecessarily Gabriel slipped out of the waggon unseen.

He turned to an opening in the hedge, which he found to be a stile, and mounting thereon he sat meditating whether to seek a cheap lodging in the village, or to ensure a cheaper one by lying under some hay or corn-stack. The crunching jangle of the waggon died upon his ear. He was about to walk on when he noticed on his left hand an unusual light – appearing about half a mile distant. Oak watched it, and the glow increased. Something was on fire.

Gabriel again mounted the stile, and leaping down on the other side upon what he found to be ploughed soil, made across the field in the exact direction of the fire. The blaze, enlarging in a double ratio by his approach and its own increase, showed him as he drew nearer the outlines of ricks beside it, lighted up to great distinctness. A rickyard was the source of the fire. His weary face now began to be painted over with a rich orange glow, and the whole front of his smockfrock and gaiters was covered with a dancing shadow pattern of thorn twigs – the light reaching him through a leafless intervening hedge – and the metallic curve of his sheep-crook shone silver-bright in the same abounding rays. He came up to the boundary fence, and stood to regain breath. It seemed as if the spot was unoccupied by a living soul.

The fire was issuing from a long straw rick, which was so far gone as to preclude any possibility of saving it. A rick burns differently from a house. As the wind blows the fire inwards, the portion in flames completely disappears like melting sugar, and the outline is lost to the eye. However, a hay or a wheat rick, well put together, will resist combustion for a length of time, if it begins on the outside.

This before Gabriel's eyes was a rick of straw, loosely put together, and the flames darted into it with lightning swiftness. It glowed on the windward side, rising and falling in intensity like the end of a cigar. Then a superincumbent bundle rolled down, with a whisking noise, flames elongated and bent themselves about with a quiet roar, but no crackle. Banks of smoke went off horizontally at the back like passing clouds, and behind these burned hidden flames, illuminating the semi-transparent sheet of smoke to a lustrous yellow uniformity. Individual straws in the foreground were consumed in a creeping movement of ruddy heat, as if they were knots of red worms, and above shone imaginary fiery faces, tongues hanging from lips, glaring eyes, and other fancied forms, from which at intervals sparks flew in clusters like birds from a nest.

Oak suddenly ceased from being a mere spectator by discovering the case to be more serious than he had at first imagined. A scroll of smoke blew aside and revealed to him a wheat rick in startling juxtaposition with the decaying one, and behind this a series of others, composing the main corn produce of the farm; so that instead of the straw rick standing, as he had imagined, comparatively isolated, there was a regular connection between it and the remaining ricks of the group.

Gabriel leapt over the hedge, and saw that he was not alone. The first man he came to was running about in a great hurry as if his thoughts were several yards in advance of his body, which they could never drag on fast enough.

"O, man – fire, fire! A good master and a bad servant is fire fire – I mane a bad servant and a good master: O Mark Clark come! and you Billy Smallbury – and you Mary-ann Money – and you Joseph Poorgrass, and Matthew there, for his mercy endureth forever!" Other figures now appeared behind this shouting man and among the smoke, and Gabriel found that far from being alone he was in a great company – whose shadows danced merrily up and down, timed by the jigging of the flames, and not at all by their owners' movements. The assemblage – belonging to that class of society which casts its thoughts into the form of feeling, and its feelings into the form of commotion – set to work with a remarkable confusion of purpose.

"Stop the draught under the wheat-rick!" cried Gabriel to those nearest to him. The corn stood on stone staddles, and between these, tongues of yellow hues from the burning straw licked and darted playfully. If the fire once got *under* this stack, all would be lost.

"Get a tarpaulin – quick!" said Gabriel.

A rick-cloth was brought, and they hung it like a curtain across the channel. The flames immediately ceased to go under the bottom of the corn stack, and stood up vertical.

"Stand here with a bucket of water and keep the cloth wet," said Gabriel again.

The flames, now driven upwards, began to attack the angles of the huge roof covering the wheat stack.

"A ladder!" cried Gabriel.

"The ladder was against the straw rick and is burnt to a cinder," said a spectre-like form in the smoke.

Oak seized the cut ends of the sheaves, as if he were going to engage in the operation of "reed-drawing", and digging in his feet and occasionally sticking in the stem of his sheep-crook he clambered up the beetling face. He at once sat astride the very apex, and began with his crook to beat off the fiery fragments which had lodged thereon, shouting to the others to get him a bough, and a ladder, and some water.

Billy Smallbury – one of the men who had been on the waggon – by this time had found a ladder, which Mark Clark ascended, holding on beside Oak upon the thatch. The smoke at this corner was stifling, and Clark a nimble fellow, having been handed a bucket of water bathed Oak's face and sprinkled him generally, whilst Gabriel, with a long beech bough in one hand and his crook in the other kept beating the stack and dislodging all fiery particles.

On the ground the group of villagers were still occupied in doing all they could to keep down the conflagration – which was not much. They were all tinged orange, and backed up by shadows as tall as fir trees. Round the corner of the largest stack, out of the direct rays of the fire, stood a pony, bearing a young woman on its back. By her side was another female on foot. These two seemed to keep at a distance from the fire, that the horse might not become restive.

"He's a shepherd," said the woman on foot. "Yes – he is. See how his crook shines as he beats the rick with it. And his smockfrock is burnt in two holes, I declare. A fine young shepherd he is too, ma'am."

"Whose shepherd is he?" said the equestrian in a clear voice.

"Don't know ma'am."

"Don't any of the others know?"

"Nobody at all – I've asked 'em. Quite a stranger, they say."

The young woman on the pony rode out from the shade and looked anxiously around.

"Do you think the barn is safe?" she said.

"D'ye think the barn is safe, Jan Coggan?" said the woman on foot, passing on the question to the nearest man in that direction.

"Safe now – leastwise I think so. If this rick had gone the barn would hev followed. 'Tis that shepherd up there that have done the most good – he sitting on the top o' rick, whizzing his great long arms about like a windmill."

"He does work hard," said the young woman on horseback looking up at Gabriel through her thick woollen veil. "I wish he was shepherd here. Don't any of you know his name?"

"Never heard the man's name in my life, or seed his form afore."

The fire began to get worsted, and Gabriel's elevated position being no longer required of him, he made as if to descend.

"Mary-ann," said the girl on horseback, "go to him as he comes down, and say that the farmer wishes to thank him for the great service he has done."

Mary-ann stalked off towards the rick and met Oak at the foot of the ladder. She delivered her message.

"Where is your master the farmer?" asked Gabriel, kindling with the idea of getting employment, that seemed to strike him now.

"'Tisn't a master; 'tis a mistress, Shepherd."

"A woman-farmer?"

"Ay 'a b'lieve, and a rich one too," said a bystander. "Lately a come here from a distance. Took on her uncle's farm, who died suddenly. Used to measure his money in half-pint cups. They say now that she've business in five Bank of Englands,[13] and thinks no more of playing pitch-and-toss-sovereign than you and I do of pitch-halfpenny[14] – not a bit in the world, shepherd."

"That's she back there upon the pony," said Mary-ann; "wi' her face a covered up wi' a black cloth with holes in 'en."

Oak, his features black, grimy, and undiscoverable from the smoke and heat, his smockfrock burnt into holes, dripping with water, the ash stem of his sheep-crook charred six inches shorter than it had been, advanced with the humility stern adversity had thrust upon him up to the slight female form in the saddle. He lifted his hat with respect, and not without gallantry: stepping close to her hanging feet he said in a hesitating voice,

"Do you happen to want a shepherd, ma'am?"

She lifted the Shetland veil tied round her face, and looked all astonishment. Gabriel and his cold-hearted darling Bathsheba Everdene were face to face.

She did not speak, and he mechanically repeated in an abashed and sad voice,

"Do you want a shepherd, ma'am?"

CHAPTER VII

Recognition: a timid girl.

Bathsheba withdrew into the shade. She scarcely knew whether most to be amused at the singularity of the meeting or to be concerned at its awkwardness. There was room for a little pity, also for a little exultation; the former at his position, the latter at her own. Embarrassed she was not, and she remembered Gabriel's declaration of love to her at Norcombe only to think she had nearly forgotten it.

"Yes," she murmured putting on her role of dignity and turning again to him with a little warmth of cheek: "I do want a shepherd. But. . . . ."

"He's the very man, ma'am," said one of the villagers, quietly.

Conviction breeds conviction. "Ay that 'a is," said a second, decisively.

"The man truly!" said a third with heartiness.

"He's all there!" said number four, fervidly.

"Then will you tell him to speak to the bailiff," said Bathsheba in a practical tone, for deep love,[1] a summer eve, and loneliness, would have been necessary to give the meeting its proper fulness of romance.

The bailiff was pointed out to Gabriel who, checking the palpitation within his breast at discovering that this Ashtoreth[2] of strange report was only a modification of Venus the well-known and admired, retired with him to talk over the necessary preliminaries of hiring.

The fire before them wasted away. "Men," said Bathsheba, "you shall take a little refreshment after this extra work. Will you come to the house, or shall I send out something?"

"Send it out please ma'am, to Warren's Malthouse," they replied, almost as one man.

Bathsheba then rode off into the darkness, and the men straggled on to the village in twos and threes – Oak and the bailiff being left by the rick alone.

"And now," said the bailiff finally, "all is settled I think about yer coming, and I am going home-along. Good night to ye, Shepherd."

"Can you get me a lodging?" inquired Gabriel.

"Than I can't indeed," he said moving past Oak as a Christian edges past an offertory plate when he does not mean to contribute. "If you follow on the road till you come to Warren's Malthouse where they are all gone to have their bit and drop I dare say some of 'em will tell you of a place. Good night to ye, Shepherd."

The bailiff who showed this nervous dread of loving his neighbour as himself[3] went up the hill, and Oak walked on to the village, still astonished at the rencounter with Bathsheba, glad of his nearness to her, and perplexed at the rapidity with which the unpractised girl of Norcombe had developed into the supervising and cool woman here. But some women only require an emergency to make them fit for one.

Obliged to some extent to forgo dreaming in order to find the way he reached the churchyard, and passed round it under the wall where several old chestnuts grew. There was a wide margin of grass along here, and Gabriel's footsteps were deadened by its softness even at this indurating period of the year. When abreast of a trunk which appeared to be the oldest of the old he became aware that a figure was standing behind it on the other side. Gabriel did not pause in his walk, and in another moment he accidentally kicked a loose stone. The noise was enough to disturb the motionless stranger who started, and assumed a careless position.

It was a slim girl, rather thinly clad.

"Good night to you," said Gabriel, heartily.

"Good night," said the girl to Gabriel.

The voice was unexpectedly attractive: it was the low and dulcet note suggestive of romance; common in descriptions, rare in experience.

"I'll thank you to tell me if I'm in the way for Warren's Malthouse?" Gabriel resumed, primarily to gain the information, indirectly to get more of the music.

"Quite right. It's at the bottom of the hill. And do you know" – The girl hesitated, and then went on again. "Do you know how late they keep open the Buck's Head Inn?" She seemed to be won by Gabriel's heartiness, as Gabriel had been won by her modulations.

"I don't know where the Buck's Head is, or anything about it. Do you think of going there tonight."

"Yes –" The female again paused. There was no necessity for any continuance of speech, and the fact that she did add more seemed to proceed from an unconscious desire to show unconcern by making a remark, which is noticeable in the ingenuous when they are acting by stealth. "You are not a Weatherbury man?" she said.

"I am not. I am the new shepherd – just arrived."

"Only a shepherd – and you seem almost a farmer by your ways."

"Only a shepherd," Gabriel repeated, in a dull cadence of finality. His eyes were directed to the feet of the girl as he spoke, and for the first time he saw lying there a bundle of some sort. She may have perceived the direction of his face, for she said, coaxingly,

"You won't say anything in the parish about having seen me here – will you? At least not for a day or two."

"I won't if you wish me not to," said Oak.

"Thank you indeed," the other replied. "I am rather poor and I don't want people to know anything about me." Then she was silent, and shivered.

"You ought to have a cloak on such a cold night," Gabriel observed. "I would advise you to get indoors."

"O no – Would you mind going on and leaving me?" she asked. "I thank you much for what you have told me."

"I will go on," he said, adding hesitatingly – "Since you are not very well off perhaps you would accept this trifle from me. It is only a shilling, but it is all I have to spare."

"Yes – I will take it," said the stranger, gratefully.

She extended her hand: Gabriel his. In feeling for each other's palms in the gloom before the money could be passed a minute incident occurred which told much. Gabriel's fingers alighted on the young woman's wrist. It was beating with a throb of tragic intensity. He had frequently felt the same quick hard beat in the femoral artery of his lambs when overdriven. It suggested a consumption too great of a vitality, which, to judge from her figure and magnitude, was already too little.

"What is the matter?"

"Nothing."

"But there is?"

"No, no, no! Let your having seen me be a secret?"

"Very well – I will. Good night again."

"Good night."

The young girl remained motionless by the tree, and Gabriel descended into the village. He fancied that he had felt himself in the penumbra of a very deep sadness when touching that slight and fragile creature. But wisdom lies in moderating mere impressions, and Gabriel endeavoured to think little of this.

CHAPTER VIII

The malthouse: the chat: news.

Warren's Malthouse was enclosed by an old wall covered with ivy, and though not much of the exterior was visible at this hour, the character and purposes of the building were clearly enough shown by its outline upon the sky. From the walls an overhanging thatched roof sloped up to a point in the centre, upon which rose a small wooden lantern, filled with louvre-boards on all the four sides, and from these openings a mist was dimly perceived to be escaping into the night air. There was no window in front, but a square hole in the door was glazed with a single pane, through which red comfortable rays now stretched out upon the ivied wall in front. Voices were to be heard inside.

Oak's hands skimmed the surface of the door with fingers extended to an Elymas-the-sorcerer[1] pattern, till he found a leather strap, which he pulled. This lifted a wooden latch and the door swung open.

The room inside was lighted only by the ruddy glow from the kiln mouth, which shone over the floor with the streaming horizontality of the setting sun, and threw upwards the shadows of all facial irregularities in those assembled around, with the effect of the footlights upon the features of Her Majesty's Servants[2] when they approach too near. The stone-flag floor was worn into a path from the doorway to the kiln mouth, and into undulations everywhere. A curved settle of unplaned oak stretched along one side, and in a remote corner was a small bed and bedstead, the owner and frequent occupier of which was themaltster.

This aged man was now sitting opposite the fire, his frosty white hair and beard overgrowing his gnarled figure like the grey moss and lichen upon an old appletree. He wore breeches and the laced up shoes called ankle-jacks; he kept his eyes fixed upon the fire.

Gabriel's nose was greeted by an atmosphere laden with the sweet smell of new malt. The conversation (which seemed to have been concerning the origin of the fire) immediately ceased, and every one ocularly criticised him to the degree expressed by looking at him with narrowed eyelids and contracting the flesh of their foreheads, as if he had been a light too strong for their sight. Several exclaimed meditatively after this operation had been completed.

"O, 'tis the new shepherd, 'a b'lieve."

"We thought we heard a hand pawing about the door for the bobbin, but weren't sure 'twere not a dead leaf blowed across," said another. "Come in Shepherd: sure ye be welcome, though we don't know yer name."

"Gabriel Oak – that's my name, neighbours."

The ancient maltster sitting in the midst turned at this – his turning being as the turning of a rusty crane.

"That's never Gable Oak's grandson over at Norcombe – never!" he said as a formula expressive of surprise, which nobody was supposed for a moment to take literally.

"My father and my grandfather were old men of the name of Gabriel," said the shepherd placidly.

"Thought I knowed the man's face as I seed him on the rick! – thought I did! And where be ye trading o't to now, Shepherd?"

"I'm thinking of biding here," said Mr Oak.

"Knowed yer grandfather for years and years!" continued the maltster, the words coming forth of their own accord as if the momentum previously imparted had been sufficient.

"Ah – and did you!"

"Knowed yer grandmother."

"And her too!"

"Knowed yer father when he was a chiel. Why my boy Jacob there and your father were sworn brothers – that they were sure – weren't ye, Jacob?"

"Ay, sure," said his son, a young man about sixty-five, with a semi-bald head and one tooth in the left centre of his upper jaw, which made much of itself by standing prominent, like a milestone[3] in a bank. "But 'twas

Joe had most to do with him. However, my son William must have knowed the very man afore us – didn't ye Billy, afore ye left Norcombe?"

"No, 'twas Andrew," said Jacob's son Billy, a child of forty or thereabouts, who exhibited the peculiarity of possessing a cheerful soul in a gloomy body, and whose whiskers were assuming a chinchilla shade here and there.

"I remember Andrew," said Oak, "as being a man in the place when I was quite a child."

"Ay – the other day I and my youngest daughter Liddy were over at my grandson's christening," continued Billy. "We were talking about this very family, and 'twas only last Purification Day[4] in this very world, when the use-money[5] is gied away to the second best poor folk, you know Shepherd, and I can mind the day because they all had to traypse up to the Vestry – yes, this very man's family."

"Come Shepherd and drink. 'Tis gape and swaller with us – a drap of sommit, but not of much account," said the maltster removing from the fire his eyes, which were vermilion red and bleared by gazing into it for so many years. "Take up the God-forgive-me, Jacob. See if 'tis warm Jacob."

Jacob stooped to the God-forgive-me, which was a two-handled tall mug standing in the ashes, cracked and charred with heat, rather furred with extraneous matter about the outside, especially in the crevices of the handles, the innermost curves of which may not have seen daylight for several years by reason of this encrustation thereon – formed of ashes accidentally wetted with cider and baked hard; but to the mind of any sensible drinker, the cup was no worse for that, being incontestably clean on the inside and about the rim. It may be observed that such a class of mug is called a God-forgive-me in Weatherbury and its vicinity for uncertain reasons; probably because its size makes any given toper feel ashamed of himself when he sees its bottom in drinking it empty: this idea is, however, a mere guess.

Jacob on receiving the order to see if the liquor was warm enough, placidly dipped his forefinger into it by way of thermometer, and having pronounced it nearly of the proper degree, raised the cup and very civilly attempted to dust some of the ashes from the bottom with the skirt of his smockfrock, because Shepherd Oak was a stranger.

"A clane cup for the shepherd," said the maltster commandingly.

"No – not at all," said Gabriel in a reproving tone of considerateness. "I never care about dirt in its natural state and when I know what sort it is." Taking the mug he drank an inch or more from the depth of its contents, and duly passed it to the next man. "I wouldn't think of giving such trouble to neighbours in washing up, when there's so much work to be done in the world already –" continued Oak, in a moister tone, after recovering from the stoppage of breath ever occasioned by serious pulls at large mugs.

"A right sensible man," said Jacob.

"True, true, as the old woman said," observed a brisk young man – Mark Clark by name, a genial and pleasant gentleman whom to meet was to know, to know was to drink with, and to drink with was to pay for.[6]

"And here's a mouthful of bread and bacon that Mis'ess have sent, Shepherd. The cider will go down better with a bit of victuals. Don't ye chaw quite close, Shepherd, for I let the bacon fall in the road outside as I was bringing it along, and may be 'tis rather gritty. There 'tis clane dirt, and we all know what that is, as you say, and you baint a particular man we see, Shepherd."

"True true – not at all," said the friendly Oak.

"Don't let yer teeth quite meet, and you won't feel the sandiness at all. Ah, 'tis wonderful what can be done by contrivance!"

"My own mind exactly, neighbour."

"Ah, he's his grandfer's own grandson! – his grandfer were just such a nice unparticular man!" said the maltster.

"Drink Henry Fray – drink," magnanimously said Jan Coggan – a person who held Saint-Simonian notions[7] of share and share alike where liquor was concerned, – as the vessel showed signs of approaching him in its gradual revolution among them.

Having at this moment reached the end of a wistful gaze into mid-air Henry did not refuse. He was a man of more than middle age with eyebrows high up in his forehead – who laid it down that the law of the world was bad, with a long-suffering look through his listeners, at the world alluded to – as it presented itself to his imagination. He always signed his name "Henery" – strenuously insisting upon that spelling, and if any passing schoolmaster ventured to remark that the second "e" was superfluous and old fashioned he received the reply that H,e,n,e,r,y, was the name he was christened and the name he would stick to – in the tone of one to whom orthographical differences were matters which had a great deal to do with personal character.

Mr Jan Coggan, who had passed the cup to Henery was a crimson man with a spacious countenance, and private glimmer in his eye, whose name had appeared on the marriage register of Weatherbury and neighbouring parishes as best man and chief witness in countless unions of the previous twenty years: he also very frequently filled the post of head godfather in baptisms of the subtly-jovial kind.

"Come Mark Clark – come. There's plenty more in the barrel," said Jan.

"Ay – that I will as the doctor said," replied Mr Clark who twenty years younger than Jan Coggan revolved in the same orbit. He secreted mirth on all occasions for special discharge at popular parties – his productions of this class being more noticeably advanced than Coggan's, inflicting a faint sense of reduplication and similitude upon the elder members of such companies.

"Why, Joseph Poorgrass, ye ha'n't had a drop!" said Mr Coggan to a very shrinking man in the background, thrusting the cup towards him.

"Such a shy man as he is!" said Jacob Smallbury. "Why, ye've hardly had strength of eye enough to look in our young mis'ess's face, so I hear, Joseph?"

All looked at Joseph Poorgrass with pitying reproach.

"No – I've hardly looked at her at all," faltered Joseph, reducing his body smaller whilst talking, apparently from a meek sense of undue prominence. "And when I seed her, 'twas nothing but blushes with me."

"Poor feller," said Mark Clark.

"'Tis a curious nature for a man," said Jan Coggan.

"Yes," continued Joseph Poorgrass – his shyness, which was so painful as a defect, just beginning to fill him with a little complacency now that it was regarded in the light of an interesting study. "'Twere 'er blush, blush, blush with me every minute of the time, when she were speaking to me."

"I believe ye, Joseph Poorgrass, for we all know ye to be a very bashful man."

"'Tis terrible bad for a man, poor soul," said the maltster. "And how long have ye suffered from it Joseph?"

"O, ever since I was a boy. Yes – mother was concerned to her heart about it – yes. But 'twas all nought."

"Did ye ever take anything to try and stop it, Joseph Poorgrass?"

"O ay, tried all sorts. They took me to Greenhill Fair, and into a grate large jerry-go-nimble show,[8] where there were women-folk riding round – standing upon horses, with hardly anything on but their smocks, but it didn't cure me a morsel – no not a morsel. And then I was put errand-man at the Woman's Skittle Alley[9] at the back of the Tailor's Arms in Casterbridge. 'Twas a horrible gross situation, and altogether a very curious place for a good man. I had to stand and look wicked people in the face from morning till night; but 'twas no use – I was just as bad as ever after all. Blushes hev been in the family for generations. There, 'tis a happy providence that I be no worse, so to speak it – yes, a happy thing, and I feel real thanksgiving."[10]

"True," said Jacob Smallbury, deepening his thoughts to a profounder view of the subject. "'Tis a thought to look at, that ye might have been worse, but even as you be 'tis a very bad affliction for ye, Joseph. For you see, Shepherd though 'tis very well for a woman, dang it all, 'tis awkward for a man like him, poor feller?" He appealed to the shepherd by a heart-feeling glance.

"'Tis – 'tis," said Gabriel recovering from a meditation as to whether the saving to a man's soul in the run of a twelvemonth by saying Dang instead of what it stood for made it worth while to use the word.[11] "Yes – very awkward for the man."

"Ay – and he's very timid too," observed Jan Coggan. "Once he had been working late at Windleton, and had had a drap of drink, and lost his way as he was coming home-along through Yalbury Wood – didn't ye, Joseph?"

"No, no, no – not that story," expostulated the modest man, forcing a laugh to bury his concern, and forcing out too much for the purpose – laughing over the greater part of his skin, round to his ears, and up among his hair, insomuch that Shepherd Oak, who was rather sensitive himself, was surfeited, and felt he would never adopt that plan for hiding trepidation any more.[12]

"And so 'a lost himself quite," continued Mr Coggan with an impassive face implying that a true narrative, like time and tide, must run its course and would wait for no man. "And as he was coming along in the middle of the night, much afeard, and not able to find his way out of the trees no-how, 'a cried out, 'Man-a-lost! man-a-lost!' A owl in a tree happened to be crying Whoo-whoo-whoo! as owls do you know, Shepherd (Gabriel nodded) and Joseph, all in a tremble, said 'Joseph Poorgrass of Weatherbury, sir!' "

"No, no, now – that's too much," said the timid man, becoming a man of brazen courage all of a sudden. "I didn't say *Sir* – I'll take my oath I didn't say 'Joseph Poorgrass o' Weatherbury, *Sir*' – no, no, what's right is right, and I never said Sir to the bird, knowing very well that no person of a gentleman's rank would be hollering there at that time o' night. 'Joseph Poorgrass of Weatherbury' – that's every word I said, and I shouldn't 'a said that if 't hadn't been for Keeper Day's[13] metheglin. . . . . There, t'was a happy providence it were no worse, as I may say," continued Joseph, swallowing his breath in content.

The question of which was right being tacitly waived by the company, Jan went on meditatively.

"And he's the fearfullest man – baint ye Joseph? Ay, another time ye were lost by Lambing-Down gate – weren't ye Joseph."

"I was," replied Poorgrass, as if there were some matters too serious even for modesty to remember itself under, and this was one.

"Yes – that were the middle of the night too. The gate would not open, try how he would, and knowing there was the devil's hand in it, he kneeled down."

"Ay," said Joseph, acquiring confidence from the warmth of the fire, the cider, and a growing perception of the artistic capabilities of the experience alluded to. "My heart died within me that time; but I kneeled down and said the Lord's Prayer, and then the Belief right through, and then the Ten Commandments, in earnest prayer. But no, the gate wouldn't open; and then I went on with Dearly Beloved Brethren, and thinks I, this makes four, and 'tis all I know out of book, and if this don't do it nothing will, and I'm a lost man. Well, when I got to Saying After Me I rose from my knees and found the gate would open – yes, neighbours, the gate opened the same as ever."

A meditation on the obvious inference was indulged in by all, during which each directed his vision into the ashpit which glowed like a desert in the tropics under a vertical sun; shaping their eyes long and liny, partly because of the light, partly from the depth of the subject discussed – each man severally drawing upon the tablet of his imagination a clear and correct picture of Joseph Poorgrass under the remarkable conditions he had related, and surveying the position in all its bearings with critical exactness.

Gabriel broke the silence. "What sort of a place is this to live at – and what sort of a miss'ess is she to work under?" Gabriel's bosom thrilled gently as he thus slipped under the notice of the assembly the innermost subject of his heart.

"We d'know little of her – nothing. She only showed herself a few days ago. Her uncle was took bad, and the doctor was called with his world-wide skill, but he couldn't save the man. As I take it, she's going to keep on the farm."

"That's about the shape o't, 'a b'lieve," said Jan Coggan. "Ay 'tis a very good family. I'd as soon be under 'em as under one here and there. Her uncle was a very fair sort of man. Did ye know en Shepherd – a bachelor-man?"

"Not at all."

The enquirer paused a moment and then continued his relation, which, as did every remark he made, instead of being casual, seemed the result of a slow convergence of forces that had commenced their operation in times far remote.

"I used to go to his house a-courting my first wife Charlotte who was his dairy maid. Well, a very good hearted man were Farmer Everdene,[14] and I being a respectable young fellow was allowed to call and see her and drink as much ale as I liked, but not to carry away any – outside my skin I mane of course."

"Ay, ay, Jan Coggan. We know yer maning."

"And so you see 'twas beautiful ale, and I wished to value his kindness as much as I could, and not to be so ill-mannered as to drink only a thimbleful, which would have been insulting the man's generosity."

"True, Master Coggan – 'twould so," corroborated Mark Clark.

"– And so I used to eat a lot of salt afore going, and then by the time I got there I were as dry as a lime basket – so thorough dry that that ale would slip down – ah, 'twould slip down sweet! Happy times – heavenly times! Ay, 'twere like drinking blessedness itself. Pints and Pints! Such lovely drunks as I used to have at that house. You can mind Jacob? You used to go wi' me sometimes."

"I can – I can," said Jacob. "That one too, that we had at Buck's Head on a White Monday, was a pretty tipple – a very pretty tipple indeed."

"'Twas. But for a drunk of really a noble class – and on the highest principles, that brought you no nearer to the dark man than you were afore you begun – there was none like those in Farmer Everdene's kitchen. Not a single damn allowed: no, not a bare poor one, even at the most cheerful moment when all were blindest; though the good old word of sin thrown in here and there would have been a great relief to a merry soul."

"True," said the maltster. "Nature requires her swearing at the regular times, or she's not herself; and unholy exclamations is a necessity of life."

"But Charlotte," continued Coggan, " – not a word of the sort would Charlotte allow, nor the smallest item of taking in vain. . . . . Ay, poor Charlotte – I wonder if she had the good fortune to get into Heaven when 'a died! But 'a was never much in luck's way, and perhaps 'a went downwards after all poor soul."

"And did any of you know Miss Everdene's father or mother?" inquired the shepherd, who found some difficulty in keeping the conversation in the desired channel.

"I knew them a little," said Jacob Smallbury. "But they were town folk, and didn't live here. They've been dead for years. Father, what sort of people were Miss'ess's father and mother?"

"Well," said the maltster, "he wasn't much to look at, but she was a lovely woman. He was fond enough of her as his sweetheart."

"Used to kiss her in scores and long hundreds – so 'twas said here and there," observed Coggan.

"He was very proud of her too when they were married, as I've been told," said the maltster.

"Ay," said Coggan. "He admired her[15] so much that he used to light the candle three times every night to look at her."

"Boundless love – I shouldn't have supposed it in the world's universe!" murmured Joseph Poorgrass, who habitually spoke on a large scale in his moral reflections.

"Well to be sure," said Gabriel.

"O 'tis true enough – I knowed the man and woman both well – Levi Everdene – that was the man's name sure enough. 'Man' saith I in my hurry but he were of a higher circle in life than that – 'a was a gentleman-tailor really, worth scores of pounds. And he became a very celebrated bankrupt two or three times."

"O I thought he was quite a common man!" said Joseph.

"O no no! That man failed for heaps of money – hundreds in gold, and Bank of England notes – handfuls of them."

The maltster being rather short of breath, Mr Coggan, after absently scrutinizing a coal which had fallen among the ashes, took up the narrative, with a private twirl of his eye:

"Well now, you'd hardly believe it but that man – our Miss Everdene's father – was one of the ficklest husbands alive, after a while. Understand, 'a didn't want to be fickle, but he couldn't help it. The pore feller were faithful and true enough to her in his wish, but his heart would rove, do what 'a would. Ay – 'a spoke to me in real tribulation about it once. 'Coggan,' he said 'I could never wish for a handsomer woman than I've got; but feeling she's ticketed as my lawful wife I can't help my wicked heart wandering, do what I will.' But at last I believe he cured it by making her take off her wedding ring and calling her by her maiden name as they sat together after the shop was shut, and so 'a would get to fancy she were only his sweetheart, and not married to en at all. And so as soon as he could thoroughly fancy he was doing wrong and committing the seventh,[16] 'a got to like her as well as ever, and they lived on a perfect example of mutel love."

"Ah, 'twas a blessed[17] remedy," murmured Joseph Poorgrass, "and we ought to feel deep cheerfulness, as I may say, that a happy providence kept it from being any worse –. You see he might have gone the bad road and given his eyes to unlawfulness entirely – yes, gross unlawfulness – so to say it."

"You see," said Billy Smallbury, with testimonial emphasis, "the man's will was to do right, sure enough, but his heart didn't chime in."

"He got so much better that he was quite religious in his later years, wasn't he Jan?" said Joseph Poorgrass. "He got himself confirmed over again in a more serious way, and took to saying Amen almost as loud as a clerk, and he liked to copy comforting verses from the tombstones. He used, too, to hold the holy money plate at Let Your Light so Shine,[18] and stand godfather to poor little come-by-chance children that had no father at all in the eye of matrimony, and keep a missionary-box upon his table to nab folks unawares when they called; Yes and he would box the boys' ears, if they laughed in church, till they could hardly stand upright, and do other deeds of piety common to the saintly inclined."

"Ay – at that time he thought of nothing but righteousness," added Billy Smallbury. "One day Parson Thirdly[19] met him and said, 'Good Morning, Mister Everdene; 'tis a fine day.' 'Amen' said Everdene, quite absent-like, thinking only of religion when he seed a parson. Yes, he was a very Christian man."

"His second cousin John was the most religious of the family however," said the old maltster. "None of the others were so pious as he, for they never went past we church people in their Christianity, but John's feelings growed as strong as a chapel-member's. 'A was a watch and clock maker by trade and thought of nothing but godliness, poor man. 'I judge every clock according to his works,' he used to say when he were in his holy frame of mind. Ay – he was a very Christian man."

"Their daughter was not at all a pretty chiel at that time," said Henery Fray. "Never should have thought she'd have growed up such a handsome body as she is."

"'Tis to be hoped her temper is as good as her face."

"Well yes – but the baily will have most to do with the business and ourselves. Ah!" Henery shook his head, gazed into the ash-pit, and smiled volumes of ironical knowledge.

"A queer Christian, as the d— said of the owl,"[20] volunteered Mark Clark.

"He is," said Henery, with a manner implying that irony must necessarily cease at a certain point. "Between we two, man and man, I believe that man would as soon tell a lie Sundays as working days – that I do so."

"Good faith, you do talk," said Gabriel, with apprehension.

"True enough," said the man of bitter moods, looking round upon the company with the antithetic laughter that comes from a keener appreciation of the untold miseries of life than ordinary men are capable of. "Ah, there's people of one sort, and people of another but that man – Bless your souls!"

The company suspended consideration of whether they wanted their souls blessed that moment, as the shortest way to the end of the story.

"I believe that if so be that Baily Pennyways's heart were put inside a nutshell he'd rattle," continued Henery. "He'll strain for money as a salmon will strain for the river's head. 'Tis a thief and a robber – that's what 'tis."

"You must be a very aged man, maltster, to have sons growed up so old and ancient," remarked Gabriel, changing the subject.

"Father's so old that 'a can't mind his age; can ye, father?" interposed Jacob. "And he's growed terrible crooked too lately," Jacob continued, surveying his father's figure, which was rather more bowed than his own. "Really one may say that father there is three-double."

"Crooked folk will last a long while," said the maltster grimly, and not in the best humour.

"Shepherd would like to hear the pedigree of yer life father – wouldn't ye, Shepherd?"

"Ay, that I should," said Gabriel, with the heartiness of a man who had longed to hear it for several months. "What may your age be, maltster?"

The maltster cleared his throat in an exaggerated form for emphasis, and elongating his gaze to the remotest point of the ashpit, said in the slow speech justifiable when the importance of a subject is so generally felt that any mannerism must be tolerated in getting at it, "Well I don't mind the year I were born in; but perhaps I can reckon up the places I've lived at, and so get it that way. I bode at Juddle Farm across there" (nodding to the north) "till I were eleven. I bode seven at Lower Twifford" (nodding to the east) "where I took to malting. Then I went to Norcombe and malted there two and twenty years, and two and twenty years I was there turnip-hoeing and harvesting. Ah, I knowed that old place Norcombe years afore you were thought of, Master Oak" (Oak smiled a corroboration of the fact). "Then I malted at Snoodly under Drool four year, and four year turnip-hoeing; and I was fourteen times eleven months at Moreford Saint Jude's (nodding north-west-by-north). Old Twills wouldn't hire me for more than eleven months at a time, to keep me from being chargeable to the parish if so be I was disabled. Then I was three year at Mellstock, and I've been here one and thirty year come Candlemas. How much is that?"

"Hundred and seventeen," chuckled another old gentleman, given to mental arithmetic and little conversation, who had hitherto sat unobserved in a corner.

"Well then, that's my age," said the maltster, emphatically.

"O no, father!" Jacob remonstrated. "Your turnip-hoeing were in the summer and your malting in the winter of the same years, and ye don't ought to count both halves, father."

"Chok' it all! – I lived through the summers, didn't I? That's my question. I suppose ye'll say next I be no age at all to speak of?"

"Sure we shan't," said Gabriel, soothingly.

"Ye be a very old aged person, maltster," attested Jan Coggan, also soothingly. "We all know that, and you must have a wonderful talented constitution to be able to live so long. Mustn't he neighbours?"

"True, true – ye must, maltster – a wonderful talented constitution," said the meeting, unanimously.

The maltster, being now pacified, was even generous enough to voluntarily disparage in a slight degree the virtue of having lived a great many years by mentioning that the cup they were drinking out of was three years older than he.

While the cup was being examined the end of Gabriel Oak's flute became visible over his smock-frock pocket, and Henery Fray exclaimed, "Surely Shepherd, I seed you blowing into a grate flute by-now at Casterbridge?"

"You did," said Gabriel, blushing faintly. "I've been in great trouble, neighbours, and was driven to it. I used not to be so poor as I be now."

"Never mind, heart!" said Mark Clark. "You should take it careless-like, Shepherd, and your time will come. But we could thank ye for a tune, if ye baint too tired?"

"Neither drum nor trumpet have I heard this Christmas," said Jan Coggan. "Come, raise a tune, Master Oak!"

"Ay that I will," said Gabriel readily, pulling out his flute and putting it together. "A poor tool, neighbours; an everyday chap; but such as I can do ye shall have and welcome."

Oak then struck up "Jocky to the Fair", and played that sparkling melody three times through, accenting the notes in the third round in a most artistic and lively manner by bending his body in small jerks and tapping with his foot to beat time.

"He can blow the flute very well – that 'a can," said a young married man who having no individuality worth mentioning was known as "Susan Tall's husband"; He continued admiringly, "I'd as lief as not be able to blow into a flute as well as that."

"He's a clever man, and 'tis a true comfort for us to have such a shepherd," murmured Joseph Poorgrass in a shy though complacent cadence. "We ought to feel real thanksgiving that he's not a player of loose songs instead of these merry tunes; for t'would have been just as easy for God to have made the shepherd a lewd low[21] man – a man of iniquity, so to speak it – as what he is. Yes, for our wives' and daughters' sakes we should feel real thanksgiving."

"True, true, as the old woman said," dashed in Mark Clark conclusively, not feeling it to be of any consequence to his opinion that he had only heard about a word and threequarters of what Joseph had said.

"Yes," added Joseph, beginning to feel like a man in the Bible: "for evil does thrive so in these times that ye may be as much deceived in the clanest shaved and whitest shirted man as in the raggedest tramp upon the turnpike, if I may speak it so."

"Ay, I can mind yer face now Shepherd," said Henery Fray, criticising Gabriel with misty eyes as he entered upon his second tune. "Yes – now I see ye blowing into the flute I know ye to be the same man I see play at Casterbridge, for yer mouth were scrimped up and yer eyes a-staring out like a strangled man's – just as they be now."

"'Tis a pity that playing the flute should make a man look such a scarecrow." observed Mr Mark Clark, with additional criticism of Gabriel's countenance, the latter person jerking out unconcernedly, with the ghastly grimace required by the instrument, the chorus of "Dame Durden": –[22]

'Twas Moll' and Bet' and Doll' and Kate'
And Dor'-othy Drag'-gle Tail'.

"I hope you don't mind that young man Mark Clark's bad manners?" whispered Joseph to Gabriel privately.

"Not at all," said Mr Oak.

" – For by nature ye be a very handsome man, Shepherd," continued Joseph Poorgrass, with winning suavity.

"Ay, that ye be, Shepherd," said the company.

"Thank you very much," said Oak in the modest tone good manners demanded, privately thinking, however, that he would never let Bathsheba see him playing the flute; in this resolve showing a discretion similar to that related of its sagacious inventress, the divine Minerva[23] herself.

"Ah, when I and my wife were married at Norcombe Church," said the old maltster, not pleased at finding himself left out of the subject, "we were called the handsomest couple in the neighbourhood – everybody said so."

"Danged if ye baint altered now, maltster," said a voice, with the vigour natural to the enunciation of a remarkably evident truism. It came from the old man in the background, whose general offensiveness and spiteful ways may prevent his being introduced to the reader.

"O no, no," said Gabriel.

"Don't ye play no more! Shepherd," said Susan Tall's husband, the young married man who had spoken once before. "I must be moving, and when there's tunes going on I seem as if hung in wires. If I thought after I'd left that music was still playing and I not there, I should be quite melancholy-like."

"What's yer hurry then Laban?" enquired Coggan: "You used to bide as late as the latest."

"Well, ye see neighbours, I was lately married to a woman, and she's my vocation now, and so ye see . . ." The young man halted lamely.

"New lords new laws as the saying is, I suppose," remarked Coggan, with a very compressed countenance, that the frigidity implied by this arrangement of facial muscles was not the true mood of his soul being only discernible from a private glimmer in the outer corner of one of his eyes – this eye being nearly closed, and the other only half open.

"Ay, 'a b'lieve – ha, ha!" said Susan Tall's husband, in a tone intended to imply his habitual reception of jokes without minding them at all. The young man then wished them Good Night and withdrew.

Henery Fray was the first to follow. Then Gabriel arose and went off with Jan Coggan, who had offered him a lodging. A few minutes later when the remaining ones were on their legs and about to depart Fray came back again in a hurry. He flourished his finger and threw a gaze teeming with tidings just where his glance alighted by accident, which happened to be in Joseph Poorgrass's eye.

"O – what's the matter, what's the matter Henery!" said Joseph.

"What's a-brewing, Henery?" asked Jacob and Mark Clark, in a breath.

"Baily Pennyways – Baily Pennyways – I said so: yes I said so."

"What – found out stealing anything?"

"Stealing it is. The news is that after Miss Everdene got home she went out again to see all was safe as she usually do, and coming in found Baily Pennyways creeping down the granary steps with half a bushel of barley. She flewed at him like a cat – never such a tom-boy as she is – of course I speak with closed doors?"

"You do – you do, Henery."

"She flewed at him, and to cut a long story short he owned to having carried off five sack altogether, upon her promising not to persecute en. Well, he's turned out neck and crop, and my question is, who's going to be baily now?"

The question was such a profound one that Henery was obliged to drink there and then from the large cup till the bottom was distinctly visible inside. Before he had replaced it on the table in came the young man Susan Tall's husband, in a still greater hurry.

"Have ye heard the news that's all over parish?"

"About Baily Pennyways?"

"Ah – but besides that?"

"No – not a morsel of it!" they all replied, looking into the very midst of Laban Tall and as it were advancing their intelligence to meet his words half way down his throat.

"What a night of horrors!" murmured Joseph Poorgrass waving his hands spasmodically. "I've had the new's bell[24] ringing in my left ear quite bad enough for a murder, and I've seed a magpie all alone!"[25]

"Fanny Robbin[26] – Miss Everdene's youngest servant – can't be found. They've been wanting to lock up the door these two hours, but she isn't come in. And they don't know what to do about going to bed for fear of locking her out. They wouldn't be so concerned if she hadn't been noticed in such low spirits these last few days, and Mary-ann d' think the beginning of a crowner's inquest has happened to the pore girl!"

"O – 'tis burned – 'tis burned!" said Joseph Poorgrass with dry lips.

"No – 'tis drowned!" said Tall.

"Or 'tis her father's razor!" suggested Billy Smallbury, with a vivid sense of detail.

"Well – Miss Everdene wants to speak to one or two of us afore we go to bed. What with this trouble about the baily, and now about the girl, mis'ess is almost wild."

They all hastened up the rise to the farm house, excepting the old maltster, whom neither news, fire, rain, nor thunder, could draw from his hole. There, as the others' footsteps died away, he sat down again, and continued gazing as usual into the furnace with his red bleared eyes.

From the bedroom window above their heads Bathsheba's head and shoulders, robed in mystic white, were dimly seen extended into the air.

"Are any of my men among you?" she said anxiously.

"Yes, ma'am; several," said Susan Tall's husband.

"To-morrow morning I wish two or three of you to make enquiries in the villages round if they have seen such a person as Fanny Robbin. Do it quietly: there is no reason for alarm as yet. She must have left whilst we were all at the fire."

"I beg yer pardon, but had she any young man courting her in the parish, ma'am?" asked Jacob Smallbury.

"I don't know," said Bathsheba.

"I've never heard of any such thing ma'am," said two or three.

"It is hardly likely either," continued Bathsheba. "For any lover of hers might have come to the house if he had been a respectable lad. The most mysterious matter connected with her absence – indeed the only thing which gives me serious alarm – is that she was seen to go out of the house by Mary-ann with only her in-door working gown on – not even a bonnet."

"And you mean, ma'am, excusing my words, that a young woman would hardly go to see her young man without dressing up," said Jacob, turning his mental vision upon past experiences. "That's true – she would not, ma'am."

"She had, I think, a bundle, though I couldn't see very well," said a female voice from another window, which seemed to belong to Mary-ann. "But she had no young man about here. Hers lives in Casterbridge, and I believe he's a soldier."

"Do you know his name?" Bathsheba said.

"No, miss: she was very close about it."

"Perhaps I might be able to find out if I went to Casterbridge Barracks," said William Smallbury.

"Very well: if she doesn't return to-morrow, mind you go there and try to discover which man it is and see him. I feel more responsible than I should if she had had any friends or relations alive. I do hope she has come to no harm through a man of that kind. . . . And then there's this disgraceful affair of the bailiff – but I can't speak of him now."

Bathsheba had so many reasons for uneasiness that it seemed she did not think it worth while to dwell upon any particular one. "Do as I told you, then," she said in conclusion, closing the casement.

"Ay, ay, ma'am: we will," they replied, and moved away.

That night at Coggan's, Gabriel Oak, beneath the screen of closed eyelids, was very busy with fancies and full of movement, like a river flowing rapidly under its ice. Night had always been the time at which he saw Bathsheba most vividly, and through the slow hours of shadow he tenderly regarded her image now. It is rarely that the pleasures of the imagination will compensate for the pain of sleeplessness, but they possibly did with Oak to-night, for the delight of merely seeing effaced for the time his perception of the great difference between that and possessing.

He also thought of plans for fetching his few utensils and books from Norcombe. The Young Man's Best Companion, The Farrier's Sure Guide, The Veterinary Surgeon, Paradise Lost, The Pilgrim's Progress, Robinson Crusoe, Ash's Dictionary, and Walkingame's Arithmetic, constituted his library;[27] and though a limited series it was one from which he had acquired more sound information by diligent perusal than many a man of opportunities has done from yards of laden shelves.

CHAPTER IX[1]

The homestead: a visitor: half-confidences.

By daylight the farm house now occupied by Bathsheba Everdene presented itself as a stone building of the Jacobean stage of Classic Renaissance[2] as regards its architecture, and of a proportion which told at a glance that, as is so frequently the case, it had once been the manorial residence upon a small estate around it, now altogether effaced as a distinct property and merged in the vast tract of a non-resident landlord which comprised several such modest demesnes.

Fluted pilasters, worked from the solid stone, decorated its front, and above the roof pairs of chimneys were here and there linked by an arch, some gables and other unmanageable features still retaining traces of their Gothic extraction. Soft brown mosses like faded velveteen formed patches upon the stone tiling, and tufts of the house-leek or sengreen sprouted from the eaves of the low surrounding buildings. A gravel walk leading from the door to the road in front was encrusted at the sides with more moss – but of a silver-green variety – the surface of the gravel being visible to the width of only a foot or two in the centre. This circumstance, and the generally sleepy air of the whole prospect here, together with the animated state of the reverse facade as a rule, suggested to the imagination that on the adaptation of the building for farming purposes the vital principle of the house had turned round inside its body to face the other way. Reversals of this kind, strange deformities, tremendous paralyses, are often seen to be inflicted by trade upon edifices – either individual or in the aggregate as streets and towns – which were originally planned for pleasure alone.

Lively voices were heard this morning in the upper rooms, the main staircase to which was of hard oak, the ballusters being turned and moulded in the fashion of heavy bed posts, the handrail as stout as a parapet-top, and the stairs themselves continually twisting round like a person trying to look over his shoulder. Going up we find the floors above to have a very irregular surface, rising to hillocks, sinking into valleys, ascending in slopes, and being uncarpeted the face of the boards is shown to be eaten into innumerable vermiculations. Every window replies by a clang to the opening and shutting of every door, a tremble follows every bustling movement, and a creak accompanies a walker about the house like a spirit, wherever he goes.

In the room from which the conversation proceeded Bathsheba and her servant-companion Liddy Smallbury were to be discovered sitting upon the floor and sorting a complication of papers, books, bottles and rubbish spread out thereon – remnants from the household stores of the late occupier. Liddy, the maltster's great-granddaughter, was about Bathsheba's equal in age, and her face was a prominent advertisement of the lighthearted English country-girl. The beauty her features might have lacked in form was amply compensated for by perfection of hue, which at this winter time was the softened ruddiness on a surface of high rotundity that we meet with in a Terburg or a Gerard Douw,[3] and like their presentations, it was a face which always kept on the natural side of the boundary between itself and the ideal. Though elastic in bearing she was less daring than Bathsheba, and occasionally showed some earnestness, which consisted half of genuine feeling, and half of factitious mannerliness superadded by way of duty.

Through a half open door the noise of a scrubbing brush led up to the char-woman, Mary-ann Money, a person who for a face had a circular disk, furrowed less by age than by long gazes of perplexity at distant objects. To think of her was to get good-humoured; to speak of her was to raise the image of a dried Normandy pippin.

"Stop your scrubbing a moment," said Bathsheba through the door to her. "I hear something."

Mary-ann suspended the brush.

The tramp of a horse was apparent, approaching the front of the building. The paces slackened, turned in at the wicket, and what was most unusual came up the mossy path close to the door. The door was tapped with the end of a whip or stick.

"What impertinence," said Liddy in a low voice. "To ride up the footpath like that. Why didn't he stop at the gate. Lord! 'Tis a gentleman! I see the top of his hat."

"Be quiet!" said Bathsheba.

The further expression of Liddy's concern was continued by exhibition instead of relation.

"Why doesn't Mrs Coggan go to the door!" Bathsheba continued.

Rat-tat-tat-tat, resounded more decisively from Bathsheba's oak.

"Mary-ann, you go!" said she, fluttering under the onset of a crowd of romantic possibilities.

"O ma'am – see here's a mess!"

The argument was unanswerable after a glance at Mary-ann.

"Liddy – you must," said Bathsheba.

Liddy held up her hands and arms, coated with dust from the rubbish they were sorting, and looked imploringly at her mistress.

"There – Mrs Coggan is going!" said Bathsheba, exhaling her relief in the form of a long breath which had lain in her bosom a minute or more.

The door opened, and a deep voice said,

"Is Miss Everdene at home?"

"I'll see, sir," said Mrs Coggan, and in a minute appeared in the room.

"Dear, dear, what a universe this world is!" continued Mrs Coggan (a wholesome looking lady who had a voice for each class of remark according to the emotion involved: who could toss a pancake or twirl a mop with the accuracy of pure mathematics, and who appeared at this moment with hands shaggy with fragments of dough and arms encrusted with flour). "I am never up to my elbows, Miss, in making a pudding but one of two things happens – either my nose must needs begin tickling and I can't live without scratching it or somebody knocks at the door. Here's Mr Boldwood[4] wanting to see you, Miss Everdene."

A woman's dress being a part of her countenance and any disorder in the one being of the same nature with a malformation or wound in the other, Bathsheba said at once:

"I can't see him in this state. Whatever shall I do?"

Not-at-homes were hardly naturalized in Weatherbury farm houses, so Liddy suggested, "Say you're a fright with dust, and can't come down."

"Yes – that sounds very well," said Mrs Coggan critically.

"Say I can't see him – that will do."

Mrs Coggan went downstairs, and returned the answer as requested, adding however on her own responsibility, "Miss is dusting bottles, Sir, and is quite a object – that's why 'tis."

"O very well," said the deep voice, indifferently. "All I wanted to ask was if anything had been heard of Fanny Robbin?"

"Nothing Sir – but we may know to-night. William Smallbury is gone to Casterbridge where her young man lives as is supposed, and the other men be enquiring about everywhere."

The horse's tramp then re-commenced and retreated – and the door closed.

"Who is Mr Boldwood?" said Bathsheba.

"A gentleman-farmer at Upper Weatherbury."

"Married?"

"No, Miss."

"How old is he?"

"Forty I should say – very handsome – rather stern looking."[5]

"What a bother this dusting is! I am always in some unfortunate plight or other," Bathsheba said complainingly. "Why should he enquire about Fanny?"

"O because, as she had no friends in her childhood, he took her and put her to school, and got her her place here under your uncle. He's a very kind man that way, but Lord – there!"

"What?"

"Never was such a hopeless man for a woman! He's been courted by sixes and sevens – all the girls gentle and simple for miles round have tried him. Jane Perkins worked at him for two months like a slave, and the two Miss Taylors spent a year upon him, and he cost Farmer Ives's daughter nights of tears and twenty pounds worth of new clothes, but Lord – the money might as well have been thrown out of the window."

A little boy came up at this moment and looked in upon them. This child was one of the Coggans, (Smallburys and Coggans were as common among the families of this district as the Avons and Derwents among our rivers), and he always had a loosened tooth or a cut finger to show to particular friends, which he did with a complacent air of being thereby elevated above the common herd of afflictionless humanity – to which exhibition people were expected to say "Poor child" with a dash of congratulation as well as pity.

"I've got a pen-nee!" said Master Coggan in a scanning tone.

"Well – who gave it you Teddy?" said Liddy.

"Mis-terr Bold-wood! He gave it to me for opening the gate."

"What did he say?"

"He said, where are you going my little man, and I said, to Miss Everdene's, please, and he said, she is an old woman, isn't she, my little man? and I said yes."

"You naughty child! What did you say that for?"

"'Cause he gave me the penny!"

"What a pucker[6] everything is in!" said Bathsheba, discontentedly when the child had gone. "Get away Mary-ann, or go on with your scrubbing, or do something! You ought to be married by this time, and not here troubling me."

"Ay Miss – so I did. But what between the poor men I won't have, and the rich men who won't have me, I stand forlorn as a pelican in the wilderness.[7] Ah, poor soul of me!"

"Did anybody ever want to marry you, Miss?" Liddy ventured to ask when they were again alone. "Lots of 'em I dare say?"

Bathsheba paused as if about to refuse a reply, but the temptation to say Yes since it really was in her power, was irresistible by "Sweet-and-twenty".[8]

"A man wanted to once," she said in a highly experienced tone, and the image of Gabriel Oak (as the farmer) rose before her.

"How nice it must seem!" said Liddy, with the fixed features of mental realization. "And you wouldn't have him?"

"He wasn't quite good enough for me."

"How sweet to be able to do disdain when most of us are glad to say Thank you! I seem I hear it. 'No Sir – I'm your better,' or, 'Kiss my foot, Sir; my face is for mouths of consequence.' And did you love him, Miss?"

"Oh, no. But I rather liked him."

"Do you now?"

"Of course not – what footsteps are those I hear?"

Liddy looked from a back-window into the court-yard behind, which was now getting low-toned and dim with the earliest films of night. A crooked file of men was approaching the back door. The whole string of trailing individuals advanced in the completest balance of intention, like the remarkable creatures known as Chain Salpae, which, distinctly organized in other respects, have one will common to a whole family. Some were, as usual, in snow-white smockfrocks of Russia duck, and some in whitey-brown ones of drabbet – marked on the wrists, breasts, backs, and sleeves with honeycomb work. Two or three women in pattens brought up the rear.

"The Philistines[9] are upon us," said Liddy, making her nose white against the glass.

"Oh, very well. Mary-ann, go down and keep them in the kitchen till I am dressed, and then show them in to me in the hall."

CHAPTER X

Mistress and men: inquiries.

Half an hour later Bathsheba, in finished dress and followed by Liddy, entered the upper end of the kitchen to find that her men had all deposited themselves on a long form and a settle at the lower extremity. She sat down at a table and opened the time-book, pen in hand, and a canvas money-bag beside her. From this she poured a small heap of coin. Liddy took up a position at her elbow, and began to sew, sometimes pausing and looking round, or, with the air of a privileged person, taking up one of the half sovereigns lying before her, and admiringly surveying it as a work of art merely, strictly preventing her countenance from expressing any wish to possess it as money.

"Now, before I begin, men," said Bathsheba, "I have two matters to speak of. The first is that the bailiff is dismissed for thieving, and that I have formed a resolution to have no bailiff at all, but to manage everything with my own head and hands."

The men expired an audible breath of amazement.

"The next matter is, have you heard anything of Fanny?"

"Nothing ma'am."

"Have you done anything?"

"I met Farmer Boldwood," said Jacob Smallbury, "and I went with him and two of his men, and dragged Wood Pond, but we found nothing."

"And the new shepherd have been to Buck's Head, thinking she had gone there, but nobody had seed her," said Laban Tall.

"Hasn't William Smallbury been to Casterbridge?"

"Yes, ma'am, but he's not yet come home. He promised to be back by six."

"It wants a quarter to six at present," said Bathsheba looking at her watch. "I dare say he'll be in directly. Well now then –" she looked into the book, "Joseph Poorgrass – are you there?"

"Yes Sir – ma'am I mane," said the person of that name, advancing to the table with his right side forward, dragging the left after him as a sort of useless encumbrance, and with a countenance between prayer and praise.

"What do you do on the farm?"

"I does jineral things all the year and in seedtime I shoots the rooks and sparrows, and helps at pig-killing, Sir."

"How much to you?"

"Please seven and ninepence and a good halfpenny where 'twas a bad one Sir – ma'am I mane."

"Quite correct. Now here are ten shillings in addition as a small present, as I am a new comer."

Bathsheba blushed slightly as she spoke at the sense of being generous in public, and Henery Fray, who had drawn up towards her chair lifted his eyebrows and fingers to express amazement on a small scale.

"How much do I owe you – that man in the corner – what's your name?" continued Bathsheba.

"Matthew Moon, ma'am," said a singular framework of clothes with nothing of any consequence inside them, which advanced with the toes in no definite direction forwards, but turned in or out as they chanced to swing.

"Matthew Mark did you say? – speak out – I shall not hurt you," enquired the young farmer, kindly.

"Matthew Moon, mem," said Henery Fray correctingly from behind her chair, to which point he had edged himself.

"Matthew Moon," murmured Bathsheba turning her bright eyes to the book. "Ten and two-pence halfpenny is the sum put down to you I see."

"Yes, miss'ess," said Matthew, as the rustle of wind among dead leaves.

"Here it is, and ten shillings. Now the next – Andrew Candle, you are a new man I hear. How came you to leave your last farm?"

"P-p-p-p-p-pl-pl-pl-pl-l-l-l-ease, ma'am, p-p-p-p-pl-pl-pl-pl-please ma'am – please'm – please'm – please'm – "

"'A's a stammering man, mem," said Henery Fray in an under tone, "and they turned him away because the only time he ever did speak plain he said his soul was his own and other iniquities.[1] 'A can cuss, mem, as well as you or I, but 'a can't speak a common speech to save his life."

"Andrew Candle here's yours – finish thanking me in day or two. Temperance Winkler – oh, here's another, Soberness, – both women I suppose."

"Yes'm. Here we be, a b'lieve," said a shrill chorus.

"What have you been doing?"

"Tending threshing machine, and wimbling haybonds, and saying Hoosh! to the cocks and hens when they go upon yer seeds and planting Early Flourballs and Thompson's Wonderfuls with a dibble."

"Yes – I see. Are they satisfactory women?" she enquired softly of Henery Fray.

"O mem – don't ask me! Yielding women – as scarlet a pair as ever was!" groaned Henery under his breath.

"Sit down."

"Who? mem."

"Sit down!"

Joseph Poorgrass in the background blushed and his lips became dry with fear of some terrible consequences as he saw Bathsheba summarily speaking, and Henery slinking off to a corner.

"Now for the next. Laban Tall. You'll stay on working for me?"

"For you or anybody that pays me well, ma'am," replied the young married man.

"True – the man must live," said a woman in the back quarter, who had just entered with clicking pattens.

"What woman is that?" Bathsheba asked.

"I be his lawful wife!" continued the voice with greater prominence of manner and tone. This lady called herself five and twenty, looked thirty, passed as thirty-five and was forty; she was a woman who never, like some newly married, showed conjugal tenderness in public, because she had none to show.

"Oh, you are," said Bathsheba. "Well Laban, will you stay on?"

"Yes, he'll stay ma'am!" said again the shrill tongue of Laban's lawful wife.

"Well, he can speak for himself, I suppose?"

"O Lord no, ma'am! A simple tool. Well enough, but a poor gawk-hammer mortel," the wife replied.

"Heh-heh-heh!" laughed the married man with a hideous effort of appreciation, for he was as irrepressibly good-humoured under ghastly snubs as a parliamentary candidate on the hustings.

The names remaining were called in the same manner.

"Now I think I have done with you," said Bathsheba, closing the book and shaking back the black twines of hair. "Has William Smallbury returned?"

"No, ma'am."

"The new shepherd will want a man under him," suggested Henery Fray, trying to make himself official again by a sideway approach towards her chair.

"Oh – he will. Who can he have?"

"Young Cain Ball is a very good lad," Henery said. "And Shepherd Oak don't mind his name," he added turning with an apologetic smile to the shepherd who had just appeared on the scene, and was now leaning against the doorpost with his arms folded.

"O I don't mind names," said Gabriel.

"How did Cain come by such a name?" asked Bathsheba.

"O you see, mem, his pore mother, not being a Scripture-read woman made a mistake at his christening, thinking 'twas Abel killed Cain,[2] and called en Cain meaning Abel all the time. She didn't find it out till 'twas too late, and the chiel was handed back to his godmother. 'Tis very unfortunate for the pore boy."

"It is rather unfortunate."

"Yes. However we soften it down as much as we can and call him Cainy. Ah, pore widow woman! she cried her heart out about it almost. She were brought up by a very heathen father and mother who never sent her to church or school, and it shows how the sins of the parents are visited upon the children,[3] mem."

Mr Fray here drew up his features to the degree of melancholy required when the persons involved in the given misfortune do not belong to your own family.

"Very well, then, Cainy Ball to be under shepherd. And you quite understand your duties? – you I mean, Gabriel Oak."

"Quite well, I thank you Miss Everdene," said Shepherd Oak, from the doorpost. "If I don't I'll enquire." Gabriel was rather staggered by the remarkable coolness of her manner. Certainly nobody without previous information would ever have dreamt that Oak and the handsome woman before whom he stood had ever been other than strangers. But perhaps her air was the inevitable result of the social rise which had advanced her from a cottage to a large house and fields. The case is not unexampled in high places. When, in the writings of later poets, Jove and his family were found to have moved from their cramped quarters on the peak of Olympus[4] into the wide sky above it, their words showed a proportionate increase of arrogance and reserve.

Footsteps were heard in the passage, combining in their character the qualities both of weight and measure, rather at the expense of velocity.

(All). "Here's Billy Smallbury come from Casterbridge."

"And what's the news?" said Bathsheba as Billy, after marching to the middle of the kitchen, took a handkerchief from his hat and wiped his forehead from its centre to its remoter boundaries.

"I should have been sooner Miss," he said, "if it hadn't been for the weather." He then stamped with each foot severally and on looking down his boots were perceived to be clogged with snow.

"Come at last is it." said Henery.

"Well, what about Fanny?" said Bathsheba.

"Well, ma'am, speaking in round numbers, she's run away with the soldiers," said William.

"No – not a steady girl like Fanny!"

"I'll tell ye all particulars. When I got to Casterbridge Barracks they said, 'the eleventh Dragoon Guards be gone away and new troops have come.' The Eleventh left last week for Melchester. The Route came from Government like a thief in the night,[5] as is his nature to, and afore the Eleventh knew it almost, they were on the march."

Gabriel had listened with interest. "I saw them go," he said.

"Yes," continued William, "they pranced down the street playing 'The Girl I Left Behind Me', so 'tis said, in glorious notes of triumph. Every man's inside shook with the blows of the grate drum to his deepest vitals, and there was not a dry eye throughout the town among the public-house people and the nameless women."

"But they're not gone to the war?"[6]

"No ma'am; but they be gone to take the places of them who have, which is very close connected. And so I said to myself Fanny's young man was one of the regiment, and she's gone after him. There ma'am that's it in black and white."

"Did you find out his name?"

"No. Nobody knew it. I believe he was higher in rank than a private."

Gabriel remained musing and said nothing, for he was in doubt.

"Well, we are not likely to know more tonight, at any rate," said Bathsheba. "But one of you had better run across to Farmer Boldwood's and tell him that much."

She then rose, but before retiring addressed a few words to them with a pretty dignity to which her morning dress added a soberness that was hardly to be found in the words themselves.

"Now mind you have a mistress instead of a master. I don't yet know my powers or my talents in farming, but I shall do my best, and if you serve me well, so shall I serve you. Don't any unfair ones among you (if there are any such, but I hope not) suppose that because I'm a woman I don't understand the difference between bad goings-on and good."

(All) "No'm!"

(Liddy) "Excellent well said."

"I shall be up before you are awake, I shall be afield before you are up, and I shall have breakfasted before you are afield. In short I shall astonish you all."

(All) "Yes'm!"

"And so good night."

(All) "Good night ma'am."

Then this small thesmothete stepped from the table and surged out of the kitchen,[7] her black silk dress licking up a few straws and dragging them along with a scratching noise upon the stone floor. Liddy, elevating her feelings to the occasion from a sense of grandeur, floated off behind Bathsheba with a milder dignity not entirely free from travesty, and the door was closed.

CHAPTER XI

Melchester Moor: snow: a meeting.

For dreariness nothing could surpass a prospect in the outskirts of the city of Melchester at a later hour on this same snowy evening – if that may be called a prospect of which the chief constituent was darkness.

It was a night when sorrow may come to the brightest without causing any great sense of incongruity: when, with impressible persons, love becomes solicitousness; hope sinks to misgiving; and faith to hope: the exercise of memory does not stir feelings of regret at opportunities for ambition that have been passed by, and that of anticipation does not prompt to enterprise.

The scene was a public path, bordered on the left hand by a river, behind which rose a high wall. On the right was a tract of land, partly meadow and partly moor, reaching, at its remote verge to a wide undulating heath.

The changes of the seasons are less obtrusive on spots of this kind than amid woodland scenery. Still, to a close observer, they are just as perceptible; the difference is that their media of manifestation are less trite and familiar than such well known ones as the bursting of the buds or the fall of a leaf. Many are not so stealthy and gradual as we may be apt to imagine in considering the general torpidity of a moor or heath. Winter, in coming to the place under notice advanced in some such well marked stages as the following:

The retreat of the snakes.
The transformation of the ferns.
The filling of the pools.
The rising of fog from the same.
The embrowning by frost.
The collapse of the fungi.
The permanence of the snow.

This climax of the series had been reached to night on Melchester Moor, and for the first time in the season its irregularities were forms without features; suggestive of anything, proclaiming nothing, and without more character than that of being the limit of something else – the under surface of a firmament of snow. From this chaotic sky-full of crowding flakes the heath and moor momentarily received additional clothing, only to appear momentarily more naked thereby. The vast dome of cloud above was strangely low, and formed as it were the roof of a large dark cavern, gradually sinking in upon its floor, for the instinctive thought was that the snow lining the heavens and that encrusting the earth would soon unite into one mass without any intervening stratum of air at all.

We turn our attention to the left-hand characteristics. They were flatness as regards the river, verticality as regards the wall behind it, and darkness as regards both. These features made up the mass. If anything could be darker than the sky it was the wall; if anything could be darker than the wall it was the river beneath. The indistinct summit of the facade was notched and pronged by chimneys here and there, and upon its face were faintly signified the oblong shapes of windows, though only in the upper part. Below, down to the water's edge the flat was unbroken by hole or projection.

An indescribable succession of dull blows perplexing in their regularity – sent their sound with difficulty through the thick atmosphere. It was a neighbouring clock striking ten. The bell was in the open air, and being overlaid with several inches of muffling snow had lost its voice for the time.

CHAPTER XI

About this hour the snow abated: ten flakes fell where twenty had fallen, then one had the room of ten. Not long after a form moved by the brink of the river.

By its outline upon the colourless background a close observer might have seen that it was small. This was all that was positively discoverable. Human it seemed.

The shape went slowly along, but without much difficulty, for the snow, though sudden, was not as yet more than two inches deep. At this time these words were spoken aloud.

"One. Two. Three. Four. Five."

Between each utterance the little shape advanced about half a dozen yards. It was evident now that the windows high in the wall were being counted. The word "Five" represented the fifth window from the end of the wall.

Here the spot stopped, and dwindled small. The figure was stooping. Then a morsel of snow flew across the river towards the fifth window. It smacked against the wall at a point several yards from its mark. The throw was the idea of a man conjoined with the execution of a woman. No man who had ever seen bird, rabbit, or squirrel in his childhood, could possibly have thrown with such utter imbecility as was shown here.

Another attempt, and another; till by degrees the wall must have become pimpled with the adhering lumps of snow. At last one fragment struck the fifth window.

The river would have been seen by day to be of that deep smooth sort which races middle and sides with the same gliding precision, any irregularities of speed being immediately corrected by a small whirlpool. Nothing was heard in the reply to the signal but the gurgle and cluck of one of these invisible wheels, together with a few small sounds which a sad man would have called moans, and a happy man laughter – caused by the striking of the waters against trifling objects in other parts of the stream.

The window was struck again in the same manner.

Then a noise was heard, apparently produced by the opening of the window. This was followed by a voice from the same quarter.

"Who's there?"

The tones were masculine, and not those of surprise. The high wall being that of a barrack, and marriage being looked upon with disfavour in the army, assignments and communications had probably been made across the river before tonight.

"Is it Sergeant Troy?"[1] said the little spot in the snow, tremulously.

This person was so much like a mere shade upon the earth, and the other speaker so much a part of the building that one would have said the wall was holding converse with the snow.

"Yes," came suspiciously from the shadow. "What girl are you?"

"O Frank – don't you know me!" said the spot. "Your wife, Fanny Robbin."

"Fanny!" said the wall, in utter astonishment.

"Yes," said the girl, with a half-suppressed gasp of emotion.

There was a tone in the woman which is not that of the wife, and there was a manner in the man which is rarely a husband's. The dialogue went on.

"How did you come here?"

"I asked which was your window. Forgive me!"

"I did not expect you to night. Indeed I did not think you would come at all. It was a wonder you found me here. I am orderly to-morrow."

"You said I was to come."

"Well – I said that you might."

"Yes, I mean that I might. You are glad to see me, Frank."

"O yes – of course."

"Can you – come to me?"

"My dear Fan, no! The bugle has sounded, the barrack gates are closed, and I have no leave. We are all of us as good as in Melchester Gaol till to-morrow morning."

"Then I shan't see you till then!" The words were in a faltering tone of disappointment.

"How did you get here from Weatherbury?"

"I walked – some part of the way – the rest by the carrier."

"I am surprised."

"Yes – so am I. And Frank, when will it be?"

"What?"

"That you promised."

"I don't quite recollect."

"O you do! Don't speak like that. It weighs me to the earth. It makes me say what ought to be said first by you."

"Never mind – say it."

"O, must I – it is, when shall we be married Frank?"

"O I see. Well – you have to get proper clothes."

"I have money. Will it be by banns or license?"

"Banns I should think."

"And we live in two parishes."

"Do we? What then?"

"My lodgings are in St Mary's, and this is not. So they will have to be published in both."

"Is that the law?"

"Yes. O Frank – you think me forward I am afraid! Don't dear Frank – will you – for I love you so. And you said lots of times you would marry me, and – and – I – I – I –"

"Don't cry, now! It is foolish. If I said so of course I will."

"And shall I put in the banns in my parish, and will you in yours."

"Yes."

"To-morrow?"

"Not to-morrow. We'll settle in a few days."

"You have the permission of the officers?"

"No – not yet."

"O – how is it! You said you almost had before you left Casterbridge."

"The fact is I forgot to ask. Your coming like this is so sudden and unexpected."

"Yes – yes – it is. It was wrong of me to worry you. I'll go away now. Will you come and see me to-morrow at Mrs Twills's in North Street? I don't like to come to the Barracks. There are bad women about, and they think me one."

"Quite so. I'll come to you my dear. Good night."

"Good night, Frank – good night!"

And the noise was again heard of a window closing. The little spot moved away. When she had passed the corner a subdued exclamation was heard inside the wall.

"Ho-ho – Sergeant – ho-ho!" More words followed, but they were indistinct; and they concluded amid a low peal of laughter, which was hardly distinguishable from the gurgle of the tiny whirlpools outside.

CHAPTER XII

Farmers: A rule: an exception.

The first public evidence of Bathsheba's decision to be a farmer in her own person and by proxy no more was her appearance the following market day in the corn-market at Casterbridge.

The low though extensive hall supported by wood pillars and latterly dignified by the name of Corn Exchange was thronged with burly men who talked among each other in twos and threes, the speaker of the minute looking sideways into his auditor's face and concentrating his argument by a contraction of one eyelid during delivery. The greater number carried in their hands ground-ash saplings, using them partly as walking-sticks and partly for poking up pigs, sheep, neighbours with their backs turned, and restful things in general which seemed to require such treatment in the course of their peregrinations. During conversations each subjected his sapling to great varieties of usage – bending it round his back, forming an arch of it between his two hands, overweighting it on the ground till it reached nearly a semicircle; or perhaps it was hastily tucked under the arm whilst the sample-bag was pulled forth and a handful of corn poured into the palm, which, after criticism was flung upon the floor – an issue of events perfectly well-known to half a dozen acute cocks and hens which had as usual crept into the building unobserved and waited the fulfilment of their anticipation with a high-stretched neck and oblique eye.

Among these heavy yeomen a feminine figure glided – the single one of her sex that the room contained. She moved between them as a chaise between carts, was heard after them as a romance after sermons, and was felt among them like a breeze among furnaces. It had required a little determination – far more than she had at first imagined – to take up a position here, for at her first entry the lumbering dialogues had ceased, nearly every face had been turned towards her, and those that were already turned rigidly fixed there.

Two or three only of the farmers were personally known to Bathsheba, and to these she had made her way. But if she was to be the practical woman she had intended to be, business must be carried on, introductions or none, and she ultimately acquired confidence enough to speak and reply boldly to men merely known to her by hearsay. Bathsheba too had her sample-bags, and by degrees adopted the professional pour into the hand – holding up the grains in her narrow palm for inspection, in perfect Casterbridge manner.

Something in the exact arch of her upper unbroken row of teeth, and in the keenly pointed corners of her red mouth when, with parted lips, she somewhat defiantly turned up her face to argue a point with a tall man, suggested that there was depth enough in that lithe piece of humanity for alarming potentialities of exploit, and daring enough to carry them out. But her eyes had a softness – invariably a softness – which, had they not been dark, would have seemed mistiness: as they were, it lowered an expression that might have been piercing to simple clearness.

Strange to say of a female in full bloom and vigour, she always allowed her interlocutors to finish their statements before rejoining with hers. In arguing on prices, she held to her own firmly, as was natural in a dealer, and reduced theirs persistently, as was inevitable in a woman. But there was an elasticity in her firmness which removed it from obstinacy, as there was a naïvete in her cheapening which saved it from meanness.

Those of the farmers with whom she had no dealings (by far the greater part) were continually asking each other, "Who is she?" The reply would be

"Farmer Everdene's niece: took on Weatherbury Lower Farm; turned away the baily; and swears she'll do everything herself."

The other man would then shake his head.

"Yes, 'tis a pity she's so headstrong," the first would say, "But we ought to be proud of her here – she lightens up the old place. 'Tis a handsome maid, however, and she'll soon get picked up."

It would be ungallant to suggest that the novelty of her engagement in such an occupation had almost as much to do with the magnetism as had the beauty of her face and movements. However the interest was general, and this Saturday's debut in the forum, whatever it may have been to Bathsheba as the buying and selling farmer, was unquestionably a triumph to her as the maiden. Indeed the sensation was so pronounced that her instinct on two or three occasions was to merely walk as a queen among these gods of the fallow, like a little sister of a little Jove,[1] and to neglect closing prices altogether.

The numerous evidences of her power to attract were only thrown into greater relief by a marked exception. Women seem to have eyes in their ribbons for such matters as these. Bathsheba, without looking within a right angle of him, was conscious of a black sheep among the flock.

It perplexed her first. If there had been a respectable minority on either side, the case would have been most natural. If nobody had regarded her, she would have taken the matter indifferently: such cases had occurred. If everybody, this man included, she would have taken it as a matter of course: people had done so before. But the exception, added to its smallness made the mystery – just as it was the difference between the state of an insignificant fleece and the state of all around it, rather than any novelty in the states themselves, which arrested the attention of Gideon.

She soon knew thus much of the recusant's appearance. He had full[2] and distinctly outlined Roman features, the prominences of which glowed in the sun with a bronze-like richness of tone. He was erect in attitude, and quiet in demeanour. One characteristic pre-eminently marked him: dignity.

Apparently he had some time ago reached that entrance to middle age at which a man's aspect naturally ceases to alter for the term of a dozen years or so, and, artificially, a woman's does likewise. Thirty-five and fifty were his limits of variation: he might have been either, or anywhere between the two.

It may be said that married men of forty are usually ready and generous enough to fling passing glances at any specimen of moderate beauty they may discern by the way. Probably, as with persons playing whist for love, the consciousness of a certain immunity under any circumstances from that worst possible ultimate, the having to pay, makes them unduly speculative. Bathsheba was convinced that this unmoved person was not a married man.

When marketing was over, she rushed off to Liddy, who was waiting for her beside the yellow gig in which they had driven to town. The horse was put in, and on they trotted – Bathsheba's sugar, tea, and drapery parcels being packed behind, and expressing, in some indescribable manner, by their colour, shape, and general lineaments, that they were that young lady-farmer's property, and the grocer's and draper's no more.

"I've been through it, Liddy, and it is over. I shan't mind it again, for they will all have grown accustomed to seeing me there. But this morning it was as bad as being married: eyes everywhere!"

"I knowed it would be," Liddy said. "Men be such a terrible class of society to look at a body."

"But there was one man who had more sense than to waste his time upon me." The information was put in this form that Liddy might not for a moment suppose her mistress was at all piqued. "A very good-looking man:" she continued, "upright: about forty, I should think. Do you know at all who he could be?"

Liddy couldn't think.

"Can't you guess at all?" said Bathsheba, with some disappointment.

"I haven't a notion. Besides 'tis no difference, since he took less notice of you than any of the rest. Now if he'd taken more, it would have mattered a great deal."

Bathsheba was suffering from the reverse feeling just then, and they bowled along in silence. Another gig, bowling along still more rapidly,[3] overtook and passed them.

"Why there he is!" she said.

Liddy looked. "That? That's Farmer Boldwood – of course 'tis: the man you couldn't see the other day when he called."

"O, Farmer Boldwood," murmured Bathsheba, and looked at him as he outstripped them. The farmer had never turned his head once, but with eyes fixed on the most advanced point along the road, passed as unconsciously and abstractedly as if Bathsheba and her charms had been thin air.

"He's an interesting man: don't you think so?" she remarked.

"O yes, *very*. Everybody owns it," replied Liddy.

"I wonder why he's so wrapt up and indifferent, and seemingly so far away from all he sees around him."

"It is said – but not known for certain – that he met with some bitter disappointment when he was a young man and merry. A woman jilted him they say."

"People always say that – and we know very well women scarcely ever jilt men; 'tis the men who jilt us. I expect it is simply his nature to be so reserved."

"Simply his nature – I expect so, Miss – nothing else in the world."

"Still, 'tis more romantic to think he has been served cruelly, poor thing! Perhaps after all he has."

"Depend upon it he has. O yes, Miss, he has. I feel he must have."

"However, we are very apt to think extremes of people – I shouldn't wonder after all if it wasn't a little of both – just between the two: rather cruelly used and rather reserved."

"O dear no, Miss: not between the two!"

"That's most likely."

"Yes, so it is: I am convinced it is most likely. You may take my word, Miss, that that's what's the matter with him."

CHAPTER XIII

Sortes Sanctorum:[1] *the valentine.*

It was Sunday afternoon in the farm house, on the thirteenth of February. Dinner being over, Bathsheba, for want of a better companion, had asked Liddy to come and sit with her. The old house was dreary in winter-time before the candles were lighted and the shutters closed; the atmosphere of the place seemed as old as the walls, every nook behind the furniture had a temperature of its own, for the fire was not kindled in this part of the house early in the day; and Bathsheba's new piano, which was an old one in other annals, looked particularly sloping and out of level on the warped floor before night threw a shade over its less prominent portions, and hid the unpleasantness. Liddy, like a little brook, though shallow, was always rippling; her presence had not so much weight as to task thought, and yet enough to exercise it.

On the table lay an old quarto bible, bound in leather. Liddy, looking at it said,

"Did you ever find out, Miss, who you are going to marry by means of the Bible and Key?"[2]

"Don't be so foolish Liddy. As if such things could be."

"Well – there's a good deal in it all the same."

"Nonsense, child."

"And it makes your heart beat fearfully! Some believe in it: some don't. I do."

"Very well – let's try it," said Bathsheba bounding from her seat with that total disregard of consistency which can be indulged in towards a dependent, and entering into the spirit of divination at once. "Go and get the front door key."

Liddy fetched it. "I wish it wasn't Sunday," she said on returning. "Perhaps 'tis wrong."

"What's right week days is right Sundays," replied her companion in a tone which was a proof in itself.

The book was opened – the leaves, drab with age, being quite worn away at much-read verses by the forefingers of unpractised readers in former days where they were moved along under the line as an aid to the vision. The special verse in the book of Ruth was sought out by Bathsheba, and the sublime words met her eye. They slightly thrilled and abashed her. It was Wisdom in the abstract facing Folly in the concrete. Folly in the concrete blushed, persisted in her intention, and placed the key on the book. A rusty patch immediately upon the verse, caused by previous pressure of an iron substance thereon, told that this was not the first time the old volume had been used for the purpose.

"Now keep steady and be silent," said Bathsheba.

The verse was repeated: the book turned round. Bathsheba blushed guiltily.

"Who did you try?" said Liddy curiously.

"I shall not tell you."

"Did you notice Mr Boldwood's doings in church this morning, Miss?" Liddy continued, adumbrating by the remark the track her thoughts had taken.

"No, indeed," said Bathsheba, with serene indifference.

"His pew[3] is exactly opposite yours, Miss."

"I know it."

"And you didn't see his goings on?"

"Certainly I did not. I tell you!"

Liddy assumed a smaller physiognomy, and shut her lips decisively.

This move was unexpected, and proportionately disconcerting. "What did he do?" Bathsheba said perforce.

"Didn't turn his head to look at you once all the service."

"Why should he?" again demanded her mistress, wearing a nettled look. "I didn't ask him to."

"O no. But everybody else was noticing you – and it was odd he didn't. There, 'tis like him."[4]

Bathsheba dropped into a silence intended to express that she had opinions on the matter too abstruse for Liddy's comprehension rather than that she had nothing to say.

"Dear me – I had nearly forgotten the Valentine I bought yesterday," she exclaimed at length.

"Valentine? Who for, Miss?" said Liddy. "Farmer Boldwood?"

It was the single name among all possible wrong ones that just at this moment seemed to Bathsheba more pertinent than the right.

"Well, no. It is only for little Teddy Coggan. I have promised him something, and this will be a pretty surprise for him. Liddy, you may as well bring me my desk and I'll direct it at once."

Bathsheba took from her desk a gorgeously illuminated and embossed design in post octavo which had been bought on the previous market-day at the chief stationer's in Casterbridge. In the centre was a small oval enclosure: this was left blank, that the sender might insert tender words more appropriate to the special occasion than any generalities by a printer could possibly be.

"Here is a place for writing," said Bathsheba. "What shall I put?"

"Something of this sort, I should think," returned Liddy promptly.

The rose is red
The violet blue
Carnations sweet
And so are you.

"Yes – that shall be it. It just suits itself to a chubby-faced child like him," said Bathsheba. She inserted the words in a small though legible handwriting, enclosed the sheet in an envelope, and dipped her pen for the direction.

"What fun it would be to send it to the stupid old Boldwood, and how he would wonder!" said the irrepressible Liddy, lifting her eyebrows, and indulging in awful mirth on the verge of fear as she thought of the moral and social magnitude of the man contemplated.

Bathsheba paused to regard the idea at full length. Boldwood's had begun to be a troublesome image – species of Daniel[5] in her kingdom who persisted in kneeling eastward when reason and common sense said that he might just as well follow suit with the rest and afford her the official glance of admiration which cost nothing at all. She was far from being seriously concerned about his nonconformity. Still it was faintly depressing that the most dignified and valuable man in the parish should withhold his eyes, and that a girl like Liddy should talk about it. So Liddy's idea was at first rather harassing than piquant.

"No – I won't do that. He wouldn't see any humour in it."

"He'd worry to death," said the persistent Liddy.

"Really, I don't care particularly to send it to Teddy," remarked her mistress. "He's rather a naughty child sometimes."

"Yes – that he is."

"Let's toss, as men do," said Bathsheba, idly. "Now then, head Boldwood: tail Teddy. No we won't toss money on a Sunday – that would be tempting the devil indeed."

"Toss this hymn book: there can't be no sinfulness in that miss."

"Very well. Open Boldwood – shut Teddy: no it's more likely to fall open. Open Teddy – shut Boldwood."

The book went fluttering in the air, and came down shut.

Bathsheba, a small yawn upon her mouth, took the pen, and with off-hand serenity directed the missive to Boldwood.

"Now light a candle Liddy: which seal shall we use? Here's a unicorn's head – there's nothing in that. What's this – two doves – no. It ought to be something extraordinary, ought it not, Lidd. Here's one with a motto – I remember it is some funny one, but I can't read it. We'll try this, and if it doesn't do we'll have another."

A large red seal was duly affixed. Bathsheba looked closely at the hot wax to discover the words.

"Capital!" she exclaimed, throwing down the letter frolicsomely: "'Twould upset the solemnity of a parson and clerk too."

Liddy looked at the words of the seal, and read

CHAPTER XIV

"MARRY ME."

The same evening the letter was sent, and was duly sorted in Casterbridge post office that night to be returned to Weatherbury again in the morning.

So very idly and unreflectingly was this deed done. Of love, as a spectacle Bathsheba had a fair knowledge; but of love subjectively she knew nothing.

CHAPTER XIV

Effect of the letter: Sunrise.

At dusk on the evening of Valentine's day[1] Boldwood sat down to supper as usual after coming in from the farm.[2] Upon the mantel-shelf before him was a time-piece surmounted by a spread eagle, and upon the eagle's wings was the letter Bathsheba had sent. Here his gaze was continually fastening itself, till the large red seal became as a blot on the retina of his eye;[3] and as he eat and drank he still read in fancy the words thereon, although they were too remote for his sight.

MARRY ME

The injunction was like those crystal substances which, colourless themselves, assume the tone of objects about them. Here in the quiet of Boldwood's parlour, where everything that was not grave was extraneous, and where the atmosphere was that of a Puritan Sunday[4] lasting all the week, the letter and its dictum changed their tenor from the thoughtlessness of their origin to a deep solemnity, imbibed from their accessories now.

Since the receipt of the missive in the morning, Boldwood had felt the spherical completeness of his existence heretofore to be slowly spreading into an abnormal distortion in the particular direction of an ideal passion. The disturbance was as the first floating weed to Columbus[5] – the contemptibly little suggesting possibilities of the infinitely great.

The letter must have had an origin and a motive. That the latter was of the smallest magnitude compatible with its existence at all, Boldwood of course did not know. And such an explanation did not strike him as a possibility even. It is foreign to a mystified condition of mind to realise of the mystifier that the very dissimilar processes of approving a course suggested by circumstance, and striking out onto a course from inner impulse and intention only, would look the same in the result. The vast difference between starting a train of events and directing into a particular groove a series already started, is rarely apparent to the person confounded by the issue.

When Boldwood went to bed he placed the valentine in the corner of the looking glass. He was conscious of its presence even when his back was turned upon it. It was the first time in Boldwood's life that such an event had occurred. The same feeling that caused him to think it an act which had a deliberate motive prevented him from regarding it as an impertinence. He looked again at the direction. The mysterious influences of night invested the writing with the presence of the unknown writer. Somebody's – some *woman*'s – hand had travelled softly over the paper bearing his name: her unrevealed eyes had watched every curve as she formed it: her brain had seen him in imagination the while. Why should she have imagined him? Her mouth – were the lips red or pale, plump or creased? – had curved itself to a certain expression as the pen went on – the corners had moved with all their natural tremulousness: what had been the expression?

The vision of the woman writing, as a supplement to the words written, had no individuality. She was a misty shape, and well she might be, considering that her original was at that moment sound asleep and oblivious of all love and letter-writing whatsoever. Whenever Boldwood dozed she took a form, and comparatively ceased to be a vision: when he awoke there was the letter justifying the dream.

The moon shone to-night, and its light was not of a customary kind. His window only admitted a reflection of its rays, and the pale sheen had that reversed direction which snow gives, coming upward and lighting up his ceiling in a phenomenal way, casting shadows in strange places and putting lights where shadows had used to be.

The substance of the epistle had occupied him but little in comparison with the fact of its arrival. He suddenly wondered if anything more might be found in the envelope than what he had withdrawn. He jumped out of bed in the weird light, took the letter, pulled out the flimsy sheet, shook the envelope – searched it. Nothing more was there. Boldwood looked as he had a hundred times the preceding day at the insistent red seal: "Marry me," he said aloud.

The solemn and reserved yeoman again closed the letter, and stuck it in the frame of the glass. In doing so he caught sight of his reflected features, wan in expression, and insubstantial in form. He saw how closely compressed was his mouth, and that his eyes were wide-spread and vacant. Feeling uneasy and dissatisfied with himself for this nervous excitability, he returned to bed.

Then the dawn drew on. The full power of the clear heaven was not equal to that of a cloudy sky at noon, when Boldwood arose and dressed himself. He descended the stairs and went out towards the gate of a field to the east, leaning over which he paused and looked around.

It was one of the usual slow sunrises of this time of the year, and the sky, clear over its greater surface, was leaden to the northward, and murky to the east, where, over the snowy down or ewe-lease on Weatherbury Upper Farm, and apparently resting upon the ridge, the only half of the sun yet visible burnt incandescent and rayless, like a clear and flameless fire shining over a white hearthstone. The whole effect resembled a sunset as childhood resembles age.

In other directions the fields and sky were so much of one colour by the snow that it was difficult in a hasty glance to tell whereabouts the horizon occurred; and in general there was here too that before mentioned preternatural inversion of light and shade which attends the prospect when the garish brightness commonly in the sky is found on the earth and the shades of earth are in the sky. Over the west hung the wasting moon, now dull and greenish-yellow, like tarnished brass.

Boldwood was noticing how the frost had hardened and glazed the surface of the snow till it shone in the red eastern light with the polish of marble, how, in some portions of the slope withered grass-bents, encased in icicles, stood above the smooth white face in the twisted and curved shapes of old Venetian glass, and how the footprints of a few birds, which had hopped over the snow whilst it lay in the state of a soft fleece, were now frozen to a short permanency. A half muffled noise of light wheels interrupted him. Boldwood turned back into the road. It was the mail cart – a crazy two-wheeled vehicle, hardly heavy enough to resist a puff of wind. The driver held out a letter. Boldwood took it and opened it, expecting another anonymous one. So greatly are people's ideas of probability a mere sense that precedent will repeat itself, that they often do not stop to think whether the fact of an event having once occurred is not in many cases the very circumstance which makes its repetition unlikely.

"I don't think it is for you sir," said the man, when he saw Boldwood's action. "Though there is no name, I think it is for your shepherd."

Boldwood looked then at the address.

To the new Shepherd,
Weatherbury Farm,
Near Casterbridge.

"O – what a mistake – it is not mine. Nor is it for my shepherd. It is for Miss Everdene's. You had better take it on to him – Gabriel Oak – and say I opened it in mistake."

At this moment, on the ridge, up against the flaming sky a figure was visible, like the black snuff in the midst of a candle-flame. Then it moved and began to bustle about vigorously from place to place, carrying square skeleton masses which were riddled by the same rays. A small figure on all fours followed behind. The tall form was that of Gabriel Oak: the small one that of George: the articles in course of transit were hurdles.

"Wait," said Boldwood. "That's the man on the hill. I'll take the letter to him myself."

To Boldwood it was now no longer merely a letter to another man. It was an opportunity. With a face pregnant with intention he entered the snowy field.

Gabriel at that minute descended the hill towards the right. The glow stretched down in this direction now, and touched the distant roof of Warren's Malthouse – whither the shepherd was apparently bent. Boldwood followed at a distance.

CHAPTER XV[1]

A morning meeting: the letter: a question.

The scarlet and orange light outside the malt-house did not penetrate to its interior, which was as usual lighted by a rival glow of a similar hue, radiating from the hearth.

The maltster, after having lain down in his clothes for a few hours, was now sitting beside a three legged table, breakfasting off bread and bacon. This was eaten on the plateless system, which is performed by placing a slice of bread upon the table, the meat flat upon the bread, a mustard plaster upon the meat, and a pinch of salt upon the whole; then cutting them vertically downwards with a large pocket-knife till wood is reached, when the severed lump is impaled on the knife, elevated, and sent the proper way of food. The maltster's lack of teeth appeared not to sensibly diminish his powers as a mill: he had been without them for so many years that toothlessness was felt less to be a defect than hard gums an acquisition. Indeed, he seemed to approach the grave as a parabolic[2] curve approaches a line – sheering off as he got nearer till it was doubtful if he would ever reach it at all.

In the ashpit was a heap of potatoes roasting, and a boiling pipkin of charred bread, called "coffee" – for the benefit of whomsoever should call; for Warren's Malthouse was a sort of village club – there being no inn in the place.

"I say – says I, we get a fine day and then down comes a snapper at night," was a remark now suddenly heard spreading into the malthouse from the door, which had been opened the previous moment, and the form of Henery Fray advanced to the fire, stamping the snow from his boots when about half way there. The speech and entry had not seemed to be at all an abrupt beginning to the maltster – introductory matter being often omitted in this neighbourhood, both from word and deed – and the maltster, having the same latitude allowed him, did not hurry to reply. He picked up a fragment of cheese by pecking upon it with his knife, as a butcher picks up skewers.

Henery appeared in a drab kerseymere great-coat, buttoned over his smockfrock – the brown skirts of the latter being visible to the distance of about a foot below the coat-tails, which, when you got used to the style of dress, looked natural enough, and even ornamental: it certainly was comfortable.

Matthew Moon, Joseph Poorgrass, and other carters and waggoners, followed at his heels, with great lanterns dangling from their hands, which showed that they had just come from the cart-horse stables, where they had been busily engaged since four o'clock[3] that morning.

"I be as feeble as a thrush," said Joseph Poorgrass. "A straw-mote would throw me down. Maltster, I'll have a thimbleful of cider before going any further."

"I beant much to boast of, neither," sighed Matthew. "Such a pain as I've got in the small of my back and round my lines, words don't know – really they do not. My back seems to open and shut – that 'a do. I'll have a drap of summit too, maltster: coffee will do."

The maltster pointed to a small barrel in the corner, and to the pipkin in the ashes. "Whichever ye be a-minded to," he said. "And here's a few taties [raking them out of the ashes]. Come have one – they be clane."

"Morn' t'ye, old blades! and how is it this morning?" said another person in the doorway. "And how is it yer back is so much worse Matthew Moon?" The speaker stalked in, and proved to be Mark Clark.

"O I've been sitting up with poor Pleasant, you know. I don't know what to make of her, I'm sure. The poor thing were very tranquil in the early part of the night, and had a little sleep, but 'a got restless again and quite light headed towards the morning."

"Five and thirty pound – that's what mis'ess will lose if that horse should die," said Mark Clark.

"And how is she getting on without a baily?" the maltster enquired.

Henery shook his head and smiled one of the bitter smiles, dragging all the flesh of his forehead into a corrugated heap in the centre.

"She'll rue it – surely, surely!" he said. "Benjy Pennyways were not a true man or an honest baily – as big a betrayer as Joey Iscariot[4] himself. But to think she can manage herself!" He allowed his head to swing laterally three or four times in silence. "Never in all my creeping up – never!"

This was recognised by all as the conclusion of some awful speech, which had been expressed in thought alone during the shake of the head.

Henery meanwhile retained several marks of despair upon his face, to imply that they would be required for use again directly he should go on speaking.

"All will be ruined and ourselves too, or there's no meat in gentlemen's houses!" said Mark Clark in the manner of a man ready to burst all links of habit and rear his dusky race at the shortest notice.[5]

"Ay – there's some sorrow going to happen," said Matthew Moon. "I've had three very bad dreams lately; and Sally put the bellows upon table twice following last week."

"A sure sign that sommat wrong is coming," said Joseph Poorgrass. "I had a white cat come in to me yesterday breakfast-time. And there was a coffin-handle upon my sister-law's candle last night."

"And I've seed the new moon two months following through glass. I was told, too, that Gammer Ball dreamed of bees stinging her."[6]

"Horrible. O depend upon it there's something in all this," said Joseph Poorgrass, drawing his breath fearfully, with a sense that he lived in a tragedy.

"Our mis'ess will bring us all to the bad," said Henery. "Ye may depend upon that – with her new farming ways. And her ignorance is terrible to hear. Why only yesterday she cut a rasher of bacon the longways of the flitch!"

"Ho-ho-ho!" said the assembly, the maltster's feeble note being heard amid the rest as that of a different instrument: "heu-heu-heu!"

"A head-strong maid – that's what she is – and won't listen to no advice at all. Pride and vanity have ruined many a cobbler's dog. Dear, dear, when I think of it I sorrows like a man in travel!"[7]

"True Henery – you do – I've heard ye," said Joseph Poorgrass, in a voice of thorough attestation, and with a wire-drawn smile of misery.

"What, and do she dress so high?" inquired the maltster.

"Well – not dress altogether," resumed Henery, listening attentively to the wisdom of his own words; "though 'tis that too – a sort of spiritual dress as it were. 'Tis the toss of the head, the sweep of the shoulder, and the dare of the woman in general. 'Tis a word and a blow with her, and the blow first, and 'tis got about that she said a man's Damn to Liddy when the pantry shelf fell down with all the jam-pots upon it. Only yesterday in this round world she rode all of a sudden up to me, and watched how fast or how slow I worked, rode away again and never said a friendly word. Yes, neighbours – in cold blood, without a moment's warning."

"'Twould do a martel man no harm to have what's under her bonnet," said Billy Smallbury, who had just entered bearing his one tooth before him. "She can spaik real language, and must have some sense somewhere. Do ye conceive me?"

"I do – I do; but no baily – I deserved that place," wailed Henery, signifying wasted genius by gazing blankly at visions of a high destiny apparently visible to him on Billy Smallbury's smockfrock. "There, 'twas to be, I suppose. Your lot is your lot, and Scripture is nothing; for if you do good you don't get rewarded according to your works, but are cheated in some mean way out of your recompense."

"No, no; I don't agree with 'ee there," said Mark Clark decisively. "God's a perfect gentleman in that respect."

"Good works good pay, so to speak it," attested Joseph Poorgrass.

A short pause ensued, and as a sort of entr'acte Henery turned and blew out the lanterns, which the increase of daylight rendered no longer necessary even in the malt-house with its one pane of glass.

"I wonder what a farmer-woman can want with a harpsichord, dulcimer, pianner or whatever 'tis they d'call it," said the maltster. "Liddy saith she've a new one."

"Got a pianner?"

"Ay. Seems her old uncle's things were not good enough for her. She've bought all but everything new. There's heavy chairs for the stout, weak and wiry ones for the slender; grate watches getting on to the size of clocks, to stand upon the chimbley-piece."

"Pictures for the most part wonderful frames."

"Long horse-hair settles for the drunk with horse-hair pillers at each end," said Matthew Moon.

"Looking-glasses for the pretty," said Mark Clark.

"Lying books for the wicked," said Joseph Poorgrass.

"Yes," said Henery Fray. "Then the next thing 'twill be as 'tis always with these toppermost farmers as they grow grand; the parlour will have to be a drawing room, the kitchen must then forsooth be a parlour. The wash-house is wanted then for the kitchen, and the pigs-styes is turned into a wash-house. Then says they to the landlord, if ye'll believe me my poor pigs haven't a roof between their heads and the sky, and 'tis shameful of ye! Up springs a row of outhouses – and so they get lifted up like. . . . ." Lacking a comparison Henery cast his eyes around, seemingly under the impression that one might be found somewhere against the walls.

"That's the right's o't, as the maid said," cried Mark Clark.

Henery allowed his wrinkles of irony and despair to remain a few moments longer – then, as he could think of nothing further to say that might require them, he smoothed his face and sat down.

A firm loud tread was now heard stamping outside, the door was opened about six inches and somebody on the other side exclaimed, "Neighbours, have ye got room for a few new-born lambs?"

"Ay, sure, shepherd," said the conclave.

The door was flung back till it kicked the wall and trembled from top to bottom with the blow. Mr Oak appeared in the entry with a steaming face, hay-bonds wound about his ankles to keep out the snow, a leather strap round his waist outside the smockfrock, and looking altogether an epitome of the world's health and vigour. Four lambs hung in various embarrassing attitudes over his shoulders, and the dog George, which Gabriel had contrived to fetch from Norcombe, stalked solemnly behind.

"Well, Shepherd Oak, and how's lambing this year, if I may say it?" enquired Joseph Poorgrass.

"Terrible trying," said Oak, "I've been wet through twice a day, either in snow or rain, this last fortnight. Cainy and I haven't tined our eyes to-night."

"A good few twins too, I hear, so to speak it?"

"Too many by half. Yes, 'tis a very queer lambing this year. We shan't have done by Lady Day."

"And last year 'twer all over by Sexajessamine Sunday," Joseph remarked.

"Bring on the rest, Cain," said Gabriel, "and then run back to the ewes. I'll follow you soon."

Cainy Ball – a cherry-faced young lad, with a small circular orifice by way of mouth, advanced and deposited two others and retired as he was bidden. Oak lowered the lambs from their unnatural elevation, wrapped them in hay and placed them round the fire.

"We've no lambing-hut here as I used to have at Norcombe," said Gabriel, "and 'tis such a plague to bring the weakly ones to a house. If 'twasn't for your place here, maltster, I don't know what I should do this keen weather. And how is it with you to-day maltster?"

"O neither sick nor sorry, shepherd. But no younger."

"Ay – I understand 'ee."

"Sit down Shepherd Oak," continued the ancient man of malt. "And how was the old place at Norcombe when ye went for your dog? I should like to see the old familiar spot, but faith, I shouldn't know a soul there now."

"I suppose you wouldn't. 'Tis altered very much."

"Is it true that Dicky Hill's wooden cider-house is pulled down?"

"O yes – years ago. And Dicky's cottage just above it."

"Well to be sure!"

"Yes; and Tompkins's old apple tree is rooted that used to bear two hogsheads of cider with its own apples and no help from other trees."

"Rooted – you don't say it. Ah, stirring times we live in – stirring times."

"And you can mind the old well that used to be in the middle of the place? That's turned into a solid iron pump, with a large stone trough and all complete."

"Dear, dear – how the face of nations alter, and what great changes we live to see now-a-days! Yes – and 'tis the same here. They've been talking but now of the mis'ess's strange doings."

"What have you been saying about her?" inquired Oak, sharply turning to the rest, and getting very warm.

"These middle-aged men have been pulling her over the coals for pride and vanity," said Mark Clark. "But I say, let her have rope enough. Bless her pretty face – shouldn't I like to do so – upon her cherry lips!" The gallant Mark Clark here made a peculiar and well-known sound with his own.

"Mark," said Gabriel, sternly, "now you mind this: none of that dalliance-talk – that philandering way – that dandle-smack-and-coddle style of yours – about Miss Everdene. I don't allow it. Do you hear?"

"With all my heart, as the old woman said," replied Mr Clark heartily.

"I suppose you've been speaking against her?" said Oak turning to Joseph Poorgrass with a very grim look.

"No, no – not a word I – 'tis a real joyful thing that she's no worse that's what I say," said Joseph, trembling and blushing with terror. "Matthew just said – "

"Matthew Moon – what have you been saying?" asked Oak.

"I? Why ye know I wouldn't harm a worm – no, not one underground worm," said Matthew Moon looking very uneasy.

"Well, somebody has – and look here, neighbours." Gabriel, though one of the quietest and most gentle men on earth, rose to the occasion, though in the greatest good humour. "That's my fist." Here he placed his fist, rather smaller in size than a common loaf, in the mathematical centre of the maltster's little table, and with it gave a bump or two thereon, as if to ensure that their eyes all thoroughly took in the idea of fistiness before he went further. "Now – the first man in the parish that I hear prophesying bad of our mistress, why – " (here the fist was raised and let fall, as Thor[8] might have done with his hammer in assaying it), "– he'll smell and taste that – or I'm a Dutchman."

All earnestly expressed by their features that their minds did not wander to Holland for a moment on account of this statement, well knowing it was but a powerful form of speech; but were deploring the difference which gave rise to the figure; and Mark Clark cried "Hear, hear, as the undertaker said." The dog George looked up at the same time after the shepherd's menace, and though he understood English but imperfectly, began to growl.

"Now, don't ye take on so, Shepherd, and sit down!" said Henery, with a deprecating peacefulness equal to anything of the kind in Christianity.

"We hear that ye be a extraordinary good and clever man Shepherd," said Joseph Poorgrass with considerable anxiety from behind the maltster's bedstead, whither he had retired for safety. "'Tis a great thing to be clever I'm sure," he added, making uneasy movements associated with states of mind rather than body. "We wish we were, don't we, neighbours?"

"Ay, that we do sure," said Matthew Moon, with a small anxious laugh towards Oak to show how very friendly disposed he was likewise.

"Who's been telling you I'm clever?" said Oak.

"'Tis blowed about from pillar to post quite common," said Matthew. "We hear that ye can tell the time as well by the stars as we can by the sun and moon, Shepherd."

"Yes, I can do a little that way," said Gabriel, as a man of medium sentiments on the subject.

"And that ye can make sun-dials, and prent folks' names upon their waggons almost like copper-plate, with beautiful flourishes, and great long tails. A excellent fine thing for ye to be such a clever man, Shepherd. Joseph Poorgrass used to prent to Farmer James Everdene's waggons before you came, and 'a could never mind which way to turn the J's and S's – could ye Joseph." [Joseph shook his head to express how absolute was the fact that he couldn't]. "And so you used to do 'em the wrong way like this, didn't ye Joseph." Matthew marked on the dusty floor with his whip-handle

JAMES

"And how Farmer James would cuss and call thee a fool, wouldn't he, Joseph, when 'a seed his name looking so inside-out-like!" continued Matthew Moon, with feeling.

"Ay – 'a would," said Joseph, meekly. "But you see, I wasn't so much to blame, for them J's and S's are such trying sons of dogs for the memory to mind whether they face backward or forward; and I always had such a forgetful memory too."

"'Tis a very bad affliction for ye, Joseph Poorgrass – being such a man of calamity in other ways."

"Well 'tis; but a happy providence ordered that it should be no worse, and I feel my thanks. As to Shepherd there, I'm sure mis'ess ought to have made ye her baily – such a fitting man for't as you be."

"I don't mind owning that I expected it," said Oak, frankly. "Indeed, I hoped for the place. At the same time Miss Everdene has a right to be her own baily if she chooses – and to keep me down to be a common shepherd only." Oak drew a slow breath, looked sadly into the bright ashpit, and seemed lost in thoughts not of the most hopeful hue.

The genial warmth of the fire now began to stimulate the nearly lifeless lambs to bleat and move their limbs briskly upon the hay – and to recognize for the first time the fact that they were born. Their noise increased to a chorus of baas upon which Oak pulled the milk can from before the fire, and taking a small teapot from the pocket of his smockfrock, filled it with milk, and taught those of the helpless creatures which were not to be restored to their dams how to drink from the spout – a trick they acquired with astonishing aptitude.

"And she don't even let ye have the skins of the dead lambs, I hear?"

resumed Joseph Poorgrass, his eyes lingering on the operations of Oak with the necessary melancholy.

"I don't have them," said Gabriel. "How used it to be when her uncle was here?"

"If they died afore marking," said Henery, "the skin was the shepherd's – if afterwards, the farmer's. And every live lamb of a twin the shepherd sold to his own profit – yes, every immortal one to his own profit at a shilling a-piece, if so be there were no ewes that had lost their own and wanted 'em."

"Ye be very badly used Shepherd," hazarded Joseph Poorgrass, in the hope of getting Oak as an ally in lamentation after all. "I think she's took against ye – that I do so."

"O no – not at all," replied Gabriel, hastily, and a sigh escaped him, which the deprivation of lamb skins could hardly have caused.

Before any further remark had been added a shade darkened the door, and Boldwood entered the malthouse, bestowing around upon each a nod, of a quality between friendliness and condescension.

"Ah – Oak, I thought you were here," he said. "I met the mail-cart ten minutes ago, and a letter was put into my hand which I opened, without reading the address. I believe it is yours. You must excuse the accident please."

"O yes – not a bit of difference, Mr Boldwood – not a bit," said Gabriel readily. He had not a correspondent on earth, nor was there a possible letter coming to him, whose contents the whole parish would not have been welcome to read.

Oak stepped aside and read the following in an unknown hand:

Dear Friend,

I do not know your name, but I think these few lines will reach you, which I write to thank you for your kindness to me the night I left Weatherbury in a reckless way. I also return the money I owe you, which you will excuse my not keeping as a gift. All has ended well, and I am happy to say I am going to be married to the young man who has courted me for some time – Sergeant Troy, of the 11th Dragoon Guards, now quartered in Melchester.[9] He would I know object to my having received anything except as a loan, being a man of great respectability and high honour.[10]

I should be much obliged to you if you would keep the contents of this letter a secret for the present, dear friend. We mean to surprise Weatherbury by coming there soon as husband and wife, though I blush to state it to one nearly a stranger. The sergeant is a native of Weatherbury. Thanking you again for your kindness I am

Your sincere well-wisher

Fanny Robbin.

"Have you read it Mr Boldwood?" said Gabriel. "If not you had better do so. I know you are interested in Fanny Robbin."

Boldwood read the letter and looked grieved.

"Fanny – poor Fanny! The end she is so confident of has not yet come she should remember – and may never come."

"What sort of a man is this Sergeant Troy?" said Gabriel.

"H'm – I am afraid not one to build much hope upon in such a case as this," the farmer murmured. "Though he's a clever fellow, and up to everything. Strange to say his father was a medical man who settled here several years ago because he preferred country to town – a taste which if indulged in means ruin to any professional man. He failed to scrape a connection together, and went away in debt leaving this son – a bright taking lad at that time – in a situation as copying clerk at a lawyer's in Casterbridge.[11] He stayed there for some time, and might have worked himself into a decent livelihood of some sort had he not indulged in the wild freak of enlisting. I have much doubt if ever little Fanny will surprise us in the way she mentions – very much doubt. A silly girl – silly girl! She has now lost her character – he will never marry her – and what will she do?"[12]

The door was hurriedly burst open again and in came running Cainy Ball out of breath, mouth red and open like the bell of a penny trumpet and coughing with noisy vigour and great distension of face.

"Now Cain Ball," said Oak sternly, "why will you run so fast and lose your breath so! I am always telling you of it."

"O – I – A puff of mee breath – went – the wrong way, please Mister Oak, and made me cough – hok-hok-hok!"

"Well – what have you come for?"

"I've run to tell ye," said the junior shepherd, supporting his exhausted youthful frame against the doorpost – that you must come directly. Two more ewes have twinned – that's what's the matter, Shepherd Oak."

"O that's it," said Oak jumping up, and dismissing for the present his thoughts on poor Fanny. "You are a good boy to run and tell me Cain, and you shall smell a large plum pudding some day as a treat. But before we go Cainy bring the tarpot, and we'll mark this lot and have done with 'em."

Oak took from his illimitable pockets a marking iron, dipped it into the pot and imprinted on the buttocks of the infant sheep the initials of her he delighted to muse on – "B.E.", which signified to all the region round that thenceforth the lambs belonged to Farmer Bathsheba Everdene, and to no one else.

"Now Cainy, shoulder your two, and off. Good morning Mr Boldwood." The shepherd lifted the sixteen large legs, and four small bodies, he had himself brought, and vanished with them in the direction of the lambing field hard by – their frames being now in a sleek and hopeful state pleasantly contrasting with their death's-door plight of half an hour before.

Boldwood followed him a little way up the field, hesitated, and turned back. He followed him again with a last resolve annihilating return. On approaching the nook in which the fold was constructed the farmer drew out his pocket book, unfastened it, and allowed it to lie open on his hand. A letter was revealed.

"I was going to ask you Oak," he said with unreal carelessness, "if you know whose writing this is?"

Oak glanced into the book, and replied instantly, with a flushed face, "Miss Everdene's."

Oak had coloured simply at the consciousness of sounding her name. He now felt a strangely distressing qualm from a new thought. The letter could of course be no other than anonymous; or the enquiry would not have been necessary.

Boldwood mistook his confusion: sensitive persons are always ready with their "Is it I?" in preference to objective reasoning.

"The question was perfectly fair," he returned – and there was something incongruous in the serious earnestness with which he applied himself to an argument on a valentine. "– You know it is always expected that privy inquiries will be made: that's where the – fun lies." If the word "fun" had been "torture" it could not have been uttered with a more constrained and restless countenance than was Boldwood's then.

Soon parting from Gabriel, the lonely and reserved man returned to his house to breakfast – feeling a sense of shame and regret at having so far exposed his mood now that the question had been put: He again placed the letter on the mantelpiece, and sat down to think of the circumstances attending it by the light of Gabriel's information.

CHAPTER XVI

In the market-place.

On Saturday Boldwood was in the market-house as usual, when the disturber of his dreams entered and became visible to him. Adam had awakened from his deep sleep, and behold, there was Eve.[1] The farmer took courage, and for the first time really looked at her.

Emotional causes and effects are not proportionable equations at all. The result from capital employed in the production of any movement of a mental nature is sometimes as tremendous as the cause itself is absurdly minute. When women are in a freakish mood their usual intuition, either from carelessness or inherent defect, seemingly fails to teach them this, and hence it was that Bathsheba was fated to be astonished to-day.

Boldwood looked at her – not slily, critically or understandingly, but blankly at gaze, in the way a reaper looks up at a passing train – as something foreign to his element, and but dimly understood. To Boldwood women had been remote phenomena rather than necessary complements: comets of such uncertain aspect, movement and permanence that whether their orbits were as geometrical, unchangeable, and as subject to laws as his own, or as absolutely erratic as they superficially appeared, he had not deemed it his duty to consider.

He saw her black hair, her correct facial curves and profile, and the roundness of her chin and throat. He saw then the side of her eyelids, eyes, and lashes, and the shape of her ear. Next he noticed her figure, her skirt, and the very soles of her shoes.

Boldwood thought her beautiful, but wondered whether he was right in his thought, for it seemed impossible that this romance in the flesh, if so sweet as he imagined, could have been going on long without creating a commotion of delight among men, or at least without causing more enquiry than Bathsheba had caused to be made. To the best of his judgment neither nature nor art could improve this perfect one of an imperfect many. His heart began to move within him. Boldwood, it must be remembered, though forty years of age, had never before inspected a woman with the very centre and force of his glance; they had struck upon all his senses at wide angles.

Was she really beautiful? He could not assure himself that his opinion was true even now. He furtively said to a neighbour, "Is Miss Everdene considered handsome?"

"O yes – she was a good deal noticed the first time she came if you remember. A very handsome girl indeed."

A man is never more credulous than in receiving favourable opinions on the beauty of a woman he is half or quite in love with; a mere child's word on the point has the weight of an R. A.'s. Boldwood was satisfied now.

And this charming woman had in effect said to him, "Marry me." Why should she have done that strange thing? Boldwood's blindness to the difference between approving of what circumstance suggests, and originating what it does not, was well matched by Bathsheba's insensibility to the possibly great issues of little beginnings.

She was at this moment coolly dealing with a dashing young farmer: adding up accounts with him as indifferently as if his face had been the pages of a ledger. It was evident that such a nature as his had no attraction for a woman of Bathsheba's taste. But Boldwood grew hot down to his hands with an incipient jealousy: he trod for the first time the threshold of "the injured lover's hell".[2] His first impulse was to go and thrust himself between them. This could be done, but only in one way – by asking to see a sample of her corn. Boldwood renounced the idea. He could not make the request: it was debasing Loveliness to ask it to buy and sell, and jarred with his conceptions of her.

All this time Bathsheba was conscious of having broken into that dignified stronghold at last. His eyes, she knew, were following her everywhere. This was a triumph, and had it come naturally such a triumph would have been the sweeter to her for having been delayed. But it had been brought about by misdirected ingenuity, and she valued it only in the sense in which she valued an artificial flower or a wax fruit.

Being a woman with some good sense in reasoning on subjects wherein her heart was not involved Bathsheba genuinely repented that a freak which had owed its existence as much to Liddy as to herself should ever have been undertaken, to disturb the placidity of a man she respected too highly to deliberately tease.

She nearly that day formed the intention of begging his pardon on the very next occasion of their meeting. The worst feature of this arrangement was that if he thought she ridiculed him an apology would increase the offence by being disbelieved, and if he thought she wanted him, it would read like additional evidence of her forwardness.

CHAPTER XVII

Boldwood in meditation: a visit.

Boldwood was tenant of what was called the Lower Farm, and his person was the nearest approach to aristocracy that this remoter quarter of Weatherbury could boast of. Genteel strangers, whose god was their town, who might happen to be compelled to linger about this nook for a day, heard the sound of light wheels, and prayed to see good society to the degree of a parson or squire at the very least, but it was only Mr Boldwood going out for the day. They heard the sound of wheels yet once more, and were re-animated to expectancy: it was only Mr Boldwood coming home again.

His house stood recessed from the road, and the stables, which are to a farm what a fireplace is to a house, were behind, their lower portions being lost amid bushes of laurel. Inside the blue door, open half way down, were to be seen at this time the buttocks and tails[1] of half a dozen warm and contented horses standing in their stalls; and thus viewed presenting alternations of roan and bay in shapes like a Moorish arch, the tail being a streak down the midst of each. Over these, and lost to the eye gazing in from the outer light, the mouths of the same animals could be heard busily sustaining the above-named warmth and plumpness by quantities of oats and hay. The restless and shadowy figure of a colt wandered up and down a loose-box at the end, whilst the steady grind of all the eaters was occasionally diversified by the rattle of a rope, or the stamp of a foot.

Pacing up and down at the heels of the animals was Farmer Boldwood himself. This place was his almonry and cloister[2] in one: here after looking to the feeding of his four-footed dependents, the celibate would walk and meditate of an evening till the moon's rays streamed in through the cobwebbed windows or total darkness enveloped the scene.

His square-framed perpendicularity showed more fully now than in the crowd and bustle of the market-house. In this meditative walk his foot met the floor with heel and toe simultaneously, and his fine, reddish-fleshed face was bent downward just enough to render obscure the still mouth and the well-rounded though rather prominent and broad chin. A few clear and thread-like horizontal lines were the only interruption to the otherwise smooth surface of his large forehead.

The phases of Boldwood's life were ordinary enough, but his was not an ordinary nature. Emotionally[3] and mentally, no less than socially, a commonplace condition, by itself affords no clue whatever to the potentialities of a nature.

In all cases this state may be either the mediocrity of inadequacy, as was Oak's, or what we will venture to call the mediocrity of counterpoise, as was Boldwood's. The quiet mean to which we originally found him adhering, and in which with few exceptions he had continually moved, was that of neutralization: it was not structural at all.[4] That stillness which struck casual observers more than anything else in his character and habit, and seemed so precisely like the rest of inanition, was the perfect balance of enormous antagonistic forces – positives and negatives in fine adjustment. His equilibrium disturbed, he was in extremity at once.

Boldwood was thus either hot or cold. If an emotion possessed him at all, it ruled him: a feeling not mastering him was entirely latent. Stagnant or rapid it was never slow. He was always hit mortally, or he was missed. The shallows in the characters of ordinary men were sterile strands in his, but his depths were so profound as to be practically bottomless.[5]

He had no light and careless touches in his constitution, either for good or for evil. Stern in the outlines of action, mild in the details, he was serious throughout all. He saw no absurd side to the follies of life, and thus, though not quite companionable in the eyes of merry men and scoffers, and those to whom all things show life as a jest, he was not intolerable to the earnest and those acquainted with grief. Being in this manner a man who read all the dramas of life seriously, if he failed to please when they were comedies, there was no frivolous treatment to reproach him for when they chanced to end tragically.

Bathsheba was far from dreaming that the dark and silent shape upon which she had so carelessly thrown a seed was a hotbed of tropic intensity. Had she known Boldwood's moods her blame would have been fearful, and the stain upon her heart ineradicable. Moreover had she known her present power for good and evil over this man she would have trembled at her responsibility. Luckily for her present, unluckily for her future tranquility, her understanding had not yet told her what Boldwood was. Nobody knew entirely: for though it was possible to form guesses concerning his emotional[6] capabilities from old flood-marks faintly visible, he had never been seen at the high tides which caused them.

Farmer Boldwood came to the stable door, and looked forth across the level fields. Beyond the first enclosure was a hedge, and on the other side of this a meadow, belonging to Bathsheba's farm.

It was now early spring – the time of going to grass with the sheep, when they have the first feed of the meadows, before these are laid up for mowing. The wind, which had been blowing east for several weeks, had veered to the southward, and the middle of spring had come abruptly – almost without a beginning. It was that period in the vernal quarter when we may suppose the Dryads to be waking for the season – The vegetable world begins to move and swell and the saps to rise, till in the completest silences of lone gardens and trackless plantations, where everything seemed helpless and still after the bond and slavery of frost, there are bustlings, strainings, united thrusts and pulls – altogether, in comparison with which the powerful tug of cranes and pulleys in a noisy city are but pigmy efforts.

Boldwood looking into the distant meadow saw there three figures. They were those of Miss Everdene, Shepherd Oak, and Cainy Ball.

When Bathsheba's figure shone upon the farmer's eyes it lighted him up as a little moon lights up a great tower. A man's body is the shell or the tablet of his soul as he is reserved or ingenuous, overflowing or self-contained. There was a change in Boldwood's exterior from its former impassableness: his face showed that he was now living outside his defences for the first time, and with a fearful sense of exposure. It is the usual experience of strong natures when they love.

At last he arrived at a conclusion. It was to go across and speak to her.

The insulation of his heart by his reserve during these many years, without a duct of any kind for disposable emotion, had worked its effect. It has been observed more than once that the causes of love are chiefly subjective, and Boldwood was a living testimony to the truth of the proposition. No mother existed to absorb his devotion, no sister for his tenderness, no idle ties for sense. He became supercharged with the compound, which was genuine lover's love.

He approached the gate of the meadow. Beyond it the ground was melodious with ripples, and the sky with larks, the low bleating of the flock mingling with both. Mistress and man were engaged in the operation of making a lamb "take", which is performed whenever an ewe has lost her own offspring, one of the twins of another ewe being given her as a substitute. Gabriel had skinned the dead lamb, and was tying the skin over the body of the live lamb in the customary manner, whilst Bathsheba was holding open a little pen of four hurdles, into which the mother and foisted lamb were driven, where they would remain till the old sheep conceived an affection for the young one.

Bathsheba looked up at the completion of the manoeuvre and saw the farmer by the gate, where he was overhung by a willow tree in full bloom. Gabriel, to whom her face was as the uncertain glory of an April day,[7] ever regardful of its faintest change, instantly discerned thereon the mark of some influence from without, in the form of a keenly self-conscious reddening. He also turned, and beheld Boldwood.

At once connecting these signs with the letter Boldwood had shown him, Gabriel suspected her of some coquettish procedure begun by that means, and carried on since he knew not how.

Farmer Boldwood had read the pantomime denoting that they were conscious of his presence, and the perception was as too much light turned on upon his new sensibility. He was still in the road, and by moving on he hoped that neither would recognise that he had originally intended to enter the field. He passed by, with an utter and overwhelming sensation of ignorance, shyness, and doubt. Perhaps in her manner there were signs that she wished to see him: perhaps not: he could not read a woman. The cabala of this strange philosophy seemed to be full of the subtlest meanings, expressed in the commonest ways. Every turn, look, word, and accent, contained a mystery quite distinct from its obvious import, and not one of these had ever been pondered by him until now.

As for Bathsheba, she was not deceived into the belief that Farmer Boldwood had walked by on business or in idleness. She collected the probabilities of the case, and concluded that she was herself responsible for Boldwood's appearance there. It troubled her much to see what a great flame a little wildfire was likely to kindle. Bathsheba was no schemer for marriage, nor was she deliberately a trifler with the affections of men, and a censor's experience on seeing an actual flirt after observing her would have been a feeling of surprise that Bathsheba could be so different from such a one, and yet so like what a flirt is supposed to be.

She resolved never again to look or by sign to interrupt the steady flow of this man's life. But a resolution to avoid an evil is seldom framed till the evil is so far advanced as to make avoidance impossible.

CHAPTER XVIII

The sheep-washing: the offer.

Boldwood did eventually call upon her. She was not at home. "Of course not," he murmured. In contemplating Bathsheba as a woman he had forgotten the accidents of her position as an agriculturist: that being as much of a farmer and as extensive a farmer as himself, her probable whereabouts was out-of-doors at this time of the year. This and the other oversights Boldwood was guilty of were natural to the mood and still more natural to the circumstances. The great aids to idealization in love were present here: occasional observation of her from a distance, and the absence of social intercourse with her – visual familiarity, oral strangeness. The smaller human elements were kept out of sight: the pettinesses that enter so largely into all earthly living and doing were disguised by the accident of lover and loved not being on visiting terms, and there was hardly awakened a thought in Boldwood that sorry household realities appertained to her or that she like all others had moments of commonplace when to be least plainly seen was to be most prettily remembered.

Thus a mild sort of apotheosis of her took place in his fancy whilst she still lived and breathed within his own horizon a troubled creature like himself.

It was the end of May when the farmer determined to be no longer repulsed by trivialities or distracted by suspense. He had by this time grown used to being in love: the passion now startled him less even when it tortured him more, and he felt himself adequate to the situation. On enquiring for her at her house they had told him she was at the sheepwashing, and he went off to seek her there.

The sheepwashing pool was a perfectly circular basin of stonework in the meadows, full of the clearest water. To birds on the wing its glassy surface, reflecting the light sky, must have been visible for miles round as a glistening Cyclops' eye[1] in a green face. The grass about the margin at this season was a sight to remember long – in a minor sort of way. Its activity in sucking the moisture from the rich damp sod was almost a process observable by the eye. The outskirts of this level water-meadow were diversified by rounded and hollow pastures where, just now, everything that was not a buttercup was a daisy, losing their character somewhat as they sank to the verge of the intervening river. This slid along noiselessly as a shade – the swelling reeds and sedge forming a flexible palisade along its moist brink. To the north of the mead were trees, the leaves of which were new, soft, moist and flexible, not having been stiffened or darkened by summer sun and drought, their colour being yellow beside anything green, green beside anything yellow. From the recesses of this knot of foliage the loud notes of three cuckoos were at the present moment resounding through the still air.

Boldwood went meditatively down the slopes with his eyes on his boots, which the yellow pollen from the buttercups had bronzed in artistic gradations. A tributary of the main stream flowed through the basin of the pool by means of an inlet and outlet at opposite points of its diameter. Shepherd Oak, Jan Coggan, Moon, Poorgrass, Cain Ball and several others, were assembled here, all dripping wet to the very roots of their hair – and Bathsheba was standing by in a new brown riding-habit – the first she had ever worn – the bridle of her horse being looped over her arm. Flagons of cider were rolling about upon the green. The meek sheep were pushed into the pool by Coggan and Matthew Moon, who stood by the lower hatch immersed to their waists: then Gabriel, who stood on the brink, thrust them under as they swam along with an instrument like a crutch formed for the purpose, and also for assisting the exhausted animals when their wool became saturated and they began to sink. They were then let out against the stream and through the upper opening, all impurities thus flowing away below – Cainy Ball and Joseph who performed this latter operation being if possible wetter than the rest, and resembling dolphins under a fountain, every protuberance and angle of their clothes dribbling forth a small rill.

Boldwood came close and bid her good morning with such constraint that she could not but think he had stepped across to the washing for its own sake, hoping not to find her there: more, she fancied his brow severe and his eye slighting. Bathsheba immediately contrived to withdraw, and glided along by the river till she was a stone's throw off. She heard footsteps brushing the grass, and had a consciousness that love was encircling her like a perfume. Instead of turning or waiting Bathsheba went further among the high sedges, but Boldwood seemed determined and pressed on, till they were completely past the bend of the river. Here, without being seen they could still hear the splashing and shouts of the washers above.

"Miss Everdene!" said the farmer.

She trembled, turned and said "Good morning." His tone was so utterly removed from all she had expected as a beginning. It was lowness and quiet accented: an emphasis of deep meanings, their form at the same time being scarcely expressed. Silence has sometimes a remarkable power of showing itself as the disembodied soul of feeling wandering without its carcase, and it is then more emphatic than speech. In the same way to say a little is often to tell more than to say a great deal. Boldwood told everything in that word.

As the consciousness expands on learning that what was fancied to be the rumble of wheels is the reverberation of thunder so did Bathsheba's at her intuitive conviction.

"I feel – almost – too much – to think," he said with a solemn simplicity. "I have come to speak to you without preface. My life is not my own since I have beheld you clearly. Miss Everdene – I come to make you an offer of marriage."

Bathsheba tried to preserve an absolutely neutral countenance, and all the motion she made was that of closing her lips, which had previously been a little parted.

"I am now forty one years old," he went on. "I may have been called a confirmed bachelor, and I was a confirmed bachelor. I had never any views of myself as a husband in my earlier days, nor have I made any calculation on the subject since I have been older. But we all change, and my change, in this matter, came with seeing you. I have felt lately, more and more, that my present way of living is bad in every respect. Beyond all things, I want you as my wife."

"I feel, Mr Boldwood, that, though I respect you much, I do not feel – what would justify me to – in accepting your offer," she stammered.

This giving back of dignity for dignity seemed to open the sluices of feeling that Boldwood had as yet kept closed. "My life is a burden without you," he exclaimed in a low voice – "I want you – I want you to let me say I love you again and again!"

Bathsheba answered nothing, and the horse upon her arm seemed so impressed that instead of cropping the herbage it looked up.

"I think and hope you care enough for me to listen to what I have to tell!"

Bathsheba's momentary impulse at hearing this was to ask why he thought that, till she remembered that, far from being a conceited assumption on Boldwood's part, it was but the natural conclusion of serious reflection based on deceptive premisses of her own offering.

"I wish I could say courteous flatteries to you," the farmer continued in an easier tone, "and put my rugged feeling into a graceful shape; but I have neither power nor patience to learn such things. I want you for my wife – so wildly that no other feeling can abide in me; but I should not have spoken out had I not been led to hope."

"The valentine again! O that valentine!" she said to herself, but not a word to him.

"If you can love me, say so, Miss Everdene. If not – don't say no."

"Mr Boldwood, it is painful to have to say I am surprised, so that I don't know how to answer you with propriety and respect – but am only just able to speak out my feeling – I mean my meaning; that I am afraid I can't marry you, much as I respect you. You are too dignified for me to suit you, Sir."

"But Miss Everdene!"

"I – I didn't – I know I ought never to have dreamt of sending that valentine – Forgive me Sir – it was a wanton thing which no woman with any self respect should have done. If you will only pardon my thoughtlessness, I promise never to –"

"No, no, no. Don't say thoughtlessness! Make me think it was something more – that it was a sort of prophetic instinct – the beginning of a feeling that you would like me. You torture me to say it was done in thoughtlessness – I never thought of it in that light, and I can't endure it. Ah, I wish I knew how to win you! but that I can't do – I can only ask if I have already got you. If I have not, and it is not true that you have come unwittingly to me as I have to you, I can say no more."

"I have not fallen in love with you Mr Boldwood – certainly I may say that." She allowed a very small smile to creep for the first time over her serious face in saying this, and the white row of upper teeth, and keenly cut lips already noticed, suggested an idea of heartlessness, which was immediately contradicted by the pleasant eyes.

"But you will just think – in kindness and condescension think – if you cannot bear with me as a husband! I fear I am too old for you, but believe me I will take more care of you than would many a man of your own age. I will protect and cherish you with all my strength – I will indeed. You shall have no cares – be worried by no household affairs, and live quite at ease, Miss Everdene. The dairy superintendence shall be done by a man – I can afford it well – you shall never have so much as to look out of doors at hay making time – or to think of weather in the harvest. I rather cling to the gig,[2] because it is the same my poor father and mother drove, but if you don't like it I will sell it and you shall have a pony-carriage of your own. I cannot say how far above every other idea and object on earth you seem to me – Nobody knows – God only knows – how much you are to me!"

Bathsheba's heart was young, and it swelled with sympathy for the deep-natured man who spoke so simply.

"Don't say it: don't! I cannot bear you to feel so much, and me to feel nothing. And I am afraid they will notice us, Mr Boldwood. Will you let the matter rest now? I cannot think collectedly. I did not know you were going to say this to me. O I am wicked to have made you suffer so!" She was frightened as well as agitated at his vehemence.

"Say then, that you don't absolutely refuse. Do not quite refuse!"

"I can do nothing. I cannot answer."

"I may speak to you again on the subject?"

"Yes."

"I may think of you?"

"Yes, I suppose you may think of me."

"And hope to obtain you?"

"No – do not hope! Let us go on."

"I will call upon you again to-morrow."

"No – please not. Give me time."

"Yes – I will give you any time," he said earnestly and gratefully. "I am happier now."

"No – I beg you! Don't be happier if happiness only comes from my agreeing: Be neutral Mr Boldwood! I must think."

"I will wait," he said.

And then she turned away. Boldwood dropped his eyes to the ground and stood long like a man who did not know where he was. Realities then returned upon him like the pain of a wound received in an excitement which eclipses it, and he too then went on.

CHAPTER XIX

Perplexity: grinding the shears: a quarrel.

"He is so disinterested and kind to offer me all that I can desire," Bathsheba said, musingly.

Yet Farmer Boldwood, whether by nature kind or the reverse to kind, did not exercise kindness here. The rarest offerings of the purest loves are but a self-indulgence, and no generosity at all.

Bathsheba, not being the least bit in love with him, was eventually able to look calmly at his offer. It was one which many women of her own station in the neighbourhood, and not a few of higher rank, would have been wild to accept and proud to publish. In every point of view ranging from politic to solicitous it was desirable that she, a lonely girl, should marry, and marry this earnest, well to do, and respected man. He was close to her doors: his standing was sufficient: his qualities were even supererogatory. Had she felt, which she did not, any wish whatever for the married state in the abstract, she could not reasonably have rejected him as a woman who frequently appealed to her understanding for deliverance from her whims. Boldwood as a means to marriage was unexceptionable; she esteemed and liked him: yet she did not want him. It appears that men take wives because possession is not possible without marriage, and that women accept husbands because marriage is not possible without men:[1] with totally differing aims the method is the same on both sides. But the understood incentive on the woman's part was wanting here. Besides, Bathsheba's position as absolute mistress of a farm and house was a novel one, and the novelty had not yet begun to wear off.

But a disquiet filled her which was somewhat to her credit, for it would have affected few. Beyond the mentioned reasons with which she combatted her objections, she had a strong feeling that having been the one who began the game she ought in honesty to accept the consequences. Still the reluctance remained. She said in the same breath that it would be ungenerous not to marry Boldwood, and that she couldn't do it to save her life.

Bathsheba's was an impulsive nature under a deliberative aspect. An Elizabeth in flesh[2] and a Mary Stuart in spirit, she often performed actions of the greatest temerity with a manner of extreme discretion. Many of her thoughts were perfect syllogisms; unluckily they always remained thoughts: only a few were irrational assumptions; but unfortunately they were the ones which most frequently grew into deeds.

The next day to that of the declaration she found Gabriel Oak at the bottom of her garden, grinding his shears for the sheep shearing. All the surrounding cottages were more or less scenes of the same operation: the scurr of whetting spread into the sky from all parts of the village as from an armoury previous to a campaign. Peace and war kiss each other at their hours of preparation, sickles, scythes, shears and pruning-hooks mingling with swords, bayonets and lances in their common necessity for an edge.

Cainy Ball turned the handle of Gabriel's grindstone his head performing a melancholy see-saw up and down with each turn of the wheel. Oak stood somewhat as Eros[3] is represented when in the act of sharpening his arrows; his figure slightly bent, the weight of his body thrown over on the shears, and his head balanced sideways; with a critical compression of the lip and contraction of the eyelid, to crown the attitude.

His mistress came up and looked upon them in silence for a minute or two: then she said,

"Cain, go to the lower mead to catch the bay mare. I'll turn the winch of the grindstone. I want to speak to you Gabriel."

Cain departed, and Bathsheba took the handle. Gabriel had glanced up in intense surprise, quelled its expression, and looked down again. Bathsheba turned the winch, and Gabriel applied the shears.

The peculiar motion involved in turning a wheel has a wonderful tendency to benumb the mind. It is a sort of attenuated variety of Ixion's punishment,[4] and contributes a dismal chapter to the history of gaols. The brain gets muddled, the head grows heavy, and the body's centre of gravity seems to settle by degrees in a leaden lump somewhere between the eyebrows and the crown. Bathsheba felt the unpleasant symptoms after two or three dozen turns.

"Will you turn Gabriel, and let me hold the shears," she said. "My head is in a whirl, and I can't talk."

Gabriel turned. Bathsheba then began with some awkwardness (allowing her thoughts to stray occasionally from the story to attend to the shears, which required a little nicety in sharpening).

"I wanted to ask you if the men made any observations on my going behind the sedge with Mr Boldwood yesterday."

"Yes they did," said Gabriel . . . . "You don't hold the shears right, Miss – I knew you wouldn't know the way – hold like this."

He relinquished the winch, and enclosing her two hands completely in his own (taking each as we sometimes clasp a child's hand in teaching him to write) grasped the shears with her. "Incline the edge so," he said.

Hands and shears were inclined to suit the words, and held so with noticeable firmness by the instructor as he spoke.

"That will do!" exclaimed Bathsheba. "Loosen my hands. I won't have them held! Turn the winch."

Gabriel freed her hands, quietly retired to his handle, and the grinding went on.

"Did the men think it odd?" she said again.

"Odd was not the idea, Miss."

"What did they say?"

"That Farmer Boldwood's name and your own were likely to be flung over pulpit together before the year was out."

"I thought so by the look of them! Why there's nothing in it. A more foolish remark was never made. And I want you to contradict it: that's what I came for."

Gabriel looked incredulous and sad, but between his moments of incredulity, relieved.

"They must have heard our conversation," she continued.

"Well then, Bathsheba!" said Oak, stopping the handle, and gazing into her face with astonishment.

"Miss Everdene you mean," she said with dignity.

"I mean this, that if Mr Boldwood really spoke of marriage I am not going to tell a story and say he didn't to please you. I have already tried to please you too much for my own good."

Bathsheba regarded him with round-eyed perplexity. She did not know whether to pity him for disappointed love of her, or to be angry with him for having got over it – his tone being ambiguous.

"I said I wanted you just to mention that it was not true I was going to be married to him," she said, with a slight decline in her assurance.

"I can say that to them if you wish, Miss Everdene. And I could likewise give an opinion to you on what you have done."

"I dare say. But I don't want your opinion."

"I suppose not," said Gabriel bitterly, and going on with his turning, his words rising and falling in a regular swell and cadence as he stooped or rose with the winch, which directed them according to his position, perpendicularly into the earth or horizontally along the garden, his eyes being fixed on a leaf upon the ground in which he seemed to see an imaginary representation of the narrated subject.

With Bathsheba a hastened act was a rash act, but, as does not always happen, time gained was prudence ensured. It must be added however, that time was very seldom gained. At this period the single opinion in the parish on herself and her doings that she valued as sounder than her own was Gabriel Oak's. And the outspoken honesty of his character was such that on any subject, even that of her love for or marriage with another man – the same disinterestedness of opinion might be calculated on, and be had for the asking. Thoroughly convinced of the impossibility of his own suit, a high resolve constrained him not to injure that of another.

This is a lover's most stoical virtue, as the lack of it is a lover's most venial sin. Knowing he would reply truly, she asked the question, painful as she must have known the subject would be. Such is the selfishness of some charming women. Perhaps it was some excuse for her thus torturing honesty to her own advantage that she had absolutely no other sound judgment within easy reach.

"Well, what is your opinion of my conduct," she said quietly.

"That it is unworthy of any thoughtful and meek and comely woman."

In an instant Bathsheba's face coloured with the angry crimson of a Danby sunset.[5] But she forbore to utter her feeling, and this reticence of her tongue only made the loquacity of her face the more noticeable.

The next thing Gabriel did was make a mistake.

"Perhaps you don't like the rudeness of my reprimanding you, for I know it is rudeness; but I thought it would do you good."

She instantly replied, sarcastically: "On the contrary my opinion of you is so low that I see in your abuse the praise of discerning people."

"I am glad you don't mind it, for I said it honestly, and with every serious meaning."

"I see. But unfortunately when you try not to speak in jest you are amusing – just as when you wish to avoid seriousness you sometimes say a sensible word."

In spite of all this, Bathsheba had unmistakeably lost her temper, and on that account Gabriel had never in his life kept his own better. He said nothing: she then broke out,

"I may ask, I suppose, where in particular my unworthiness lies? In my not marrying you, perhaps!"

"Not by any means," said Gabriel quietly. "I have long given up thinking of that matter."

"Or wishing it, I suppose," she said, and it was apparent that she expected an unhesitating denial of this supposition.

Whatever Gabriel felt, he coolly echoed her words,

"Or wishing it, either."

A woman may be treated with a bitterness which is sweet to her, and with a rudeness which is not offensive. Bathsheba would have submitted to an indignant chastisement for her levity had Gabriel protested that he was loving her at the same time: the impetuosity of passion unrequited is bearable, even if it stings and anathematizes; there is a triumph in the humiliation and a tenderness in the strife. This was what she had been expecting, and what she had not got. To be lectured because the lecturer saw her in the cold morning light of open-shuttered disillusion was exasperating. He had not finished either. He continued in a more agitated voice:

"My opinion is (since you ask it) that you are greatly to blame for playing pranks upon a man like Mr Boldwood, merely as a pastime. Leading on a man you don't care for is not a praiseworthy action. And even Miss Everdene if you seriously inclined towards him you might have let him discover it in some way of true loving-kindness, and not by sending him a valentine's letter."

Bathsheba laid down the shears.

"I cannot allow any man to – to criticise my private conduct!" she exclaimed. "Nor will I for a minute. So you'll please leave the farm at the end of the week!"

It may have been a peculiarity – at any rate it was a fact – that when Bathsheba was swayed by an emotion of an earthly sort her lower lip trembled: when by a refined emotion her upper or heavenward one. Her nether lip quivered now.

"Very well, so I will," said Gabriel, calmly. He had been held to her by a beautiful thread which it pained him to spoil by breaking rather than by a chain he could not break. "I should be even better pleased to go at once," he added.

"Go at once then, in Heaven's name!" said she, her eyes flashing at his, though never meeting them. "Don't let me see your face any more."

"Very well, Miss Everdene – so it shall be."

And he took his shears and went away from her in placid dignity, as Moses left the presence of Pharaoh previous to the departure from Egypt.[6]

CHAPTER XX[1]

Troubles in the fold: a message: return.

Gabriel Oak had ceased to feed the Weatherbury flock for about four and twenty hours when on Sunday afternoon the elderly gentlemen Joseph Poorgrass, Matthew Moon, Fray, and half a dozen others came running up to the house of the mistress of the Upper Farm.

"Whatever *is* the matter, men!" she said meeting them at the door just as she was on the point of coming out on her way to church, and ceasing in a moment from the close compression of her two red lips with which she had accompanied the exertion of pulling on a tight glove.

"Sixty!" said Joseph Poorgrass.

"Seventy," said Moon.

"Fifty-nine," said Susan Tall's husband.

"– Sheep have broken fence," said Fray.

"– And got into a field of young clover," said Tall.

"– Young clover," said Moon.

"– Clover!" said Joseph Poorgrass.

"And they be getting blasted," said Henery Fray.

"That they be," said Joseph.

"And all will die as dead as nits if they baint got out and cured," said Tall.

Joseph's countenance was drawn into lines and puckers by his concern. Fray's forehead was wrinkled both perpendicularly and crosswise, after the pattern of a portcullis, expressive of a double despair. Laban Tall's lips were thin and his face rigid. Matthew's jaws sank and his eyes turned whichever way the strongest muscle happened to pull them.

"Yes," said Joseph. "And I was sitting at home looking for Ephesians and says I to myself ''tis nothing but Corinthians and Thessalonians[2] in this danged Testament,' when who should come in but Henery there: 'Joseph,' he said, 'the sheep have blasted theirselves –.' "

With Bathsheba it was a moment when thought was speech and speech exclamation. Moreover she had hardly recovered her equanimity since the disturbance she had suffered from Oak's remarks.

"That's enough – that's enough! – O you fools!" she cried throwing her parasol and prayer book back into the passage, and running out of doors in the direction signified. "To come to me, and not go and get them out directly. O the stupid stumpoles!"[3]

Her eyes were at their darkest and brightest now. Bathsheba's beauty, belonging rather to the redeemed-demonian than to the blemished-angelic school, she never looked so well as when she was angry – and particularly when the effect was heightened by a rather dashing Sunday dress, carefully put on before a glass.

All the poor men ran in a jumbled throng after her to the clover field, Joseph sinking down in the midst when about half way, like an individual withering in a world which got more and more. Having once received the stimulus her presence always gave them they went round among the sheep with a will. The majority of the afflicted animals were lying down and could not be stirred. These were bodily lifted out, and the others driven into the adjoining field. Here after the lapse of a few minutes several more fell down and lay helpless and livid as the rest.

Bathsheba, with a sad, bursting heart looked at these primest specimens of her prime flock as they rolled there,

> "Swoln with wind and the rank mist they drew."[4]

Many of them foamed at the mouth, their breathing being quick and short, whilst the bodies of all were fearfully distended.

"Oh, what can I do, what can I do!" said Bathsheba helplessly. "Sheep are such unfortunate animals! – there's always something happening to them! I never knew a flock pass a year without getting into some scrape or other."

"There's only one way of saving their lives," said Tall.

"What way? Tell me quick!"

"They must be pierced in the side with a thing made on purpose."

"Can you do it? Can I?"

"No, ma'am. We can't – nor you neither. It must be done in a particular spot – if ye go to the right or left but an inch you stab the ewe and kill her. Not even a shepherd can do it as a rule."

"Then they must die," she said in a resigned tone.

"Only one man in the neighbourhood knows the way," said Joseph, now just come up. "He could cure 'em all if he were here."

"Who is he – let's get him!"

"Shepherd Oak," said Matthew. "Ah he's a clever man in talents!"

"Ah, that he is so!" said Joseph Poorgrass.

"True – he's the man," said Laban Tall.

"How dare you name that man in my presence!" she said excitedly. "I've told you never to allude to him, nor shall you if you stay with me. Ah!" she added brightening; "Farmer Boldwood knows!"

"O no, ma'am," said Matthew. "Two of his store ewes got into some vetches t'other day, and were just like these. He sent a man on horseback here posthaste for Gable, and Gable went and saved 'em. Farmer Boldwood hev not got the thing they do it with. 'Tis a holler pipe, with a sharp pricker inside – isn't it, Joseph?"

"Ay – a holler pipe," echoed Joseph. "That's what 'tis."

"Ay – sure – that's the machine," chimed in Henery Fray reflectively, with an Oriental[5] indifference to the flight of time.

"Well –," burst out Bathsheba, "don't stand there with your ays and your sures, talking at me! Get somebody to cure the sheep – instantly!"

All then stalked off in consternation to get somebody as directed, without any idea of who it was to be. In a minute they had vanished through the gate, and she stood alone with the dying flock.

"Never will I send for him – never!" she said firmly.

One of the ewes here contracted its muscles horribly, extended itself and jumped high into the air. The leap was an astonishing one. The ewe fell heavily, and lay still.

Bathsheba went up to it. The sheep was dead.

"O what shall I do – what shall I do!" she again exclaimed, wringing her hands. "I won't send for him: no, I won't!"

The most vigorous expression of a resolution does not always coincide with the greatest vigour of the resolution itself: it is often flung out as a sort of prop to support a decaying conviction which, whilst strong, required no enunciation to prove it so. The "no I won't" of Bathsheba meant virtually "I think I must."

She followed her assistants through the gate, and lifted her hand to one of them. Laban answered to her signal.

"Where is Oak staying?"

"Across the valley at Nest Cottage."

"Jump on the bay mare, and ride across, and say he must return instantly: that I say so."

Tall scrambled off to the field, and in two minutes was on Poll the bay, bare-backed, and with only a halter by way of rein. He diminished down the hill.

Bathsheba watched: so did all the rest. Tall cantered along the bridle-path through Sixteen Acres, Sheeplands, Middle Field, The Flats, Cappel's Piece, shrank almost to a point, crossed the bridge, and ascended from the valley through Springmead and Whitepits on the other side. The cottage to which Gabriel had retired before taking his final departure from the locality was visible as a white spot on the opposing hill, backed by blue firs. Bathsheba walked up and down. The men entered the field, and endeavoured to ease the anguish of the dumb creatures by rubbing them. Nothing availed.

Bathsheba continued walking. The horse was seen descending the hill, and the wearisome series had to be repeated in reverse order: Whitepits, Springmead, Cappel's Piece, The Flats, Middle Field, Sheeplands, Sixteen Acres. She hoped Tall had had presence of mind enough to give the mare up to Gabriel, and return himself on foot. The rider neared them. It was Tall.

"O what folly!" said Bathsheba.

Gabriel was not visible anywhere.

"Perhaps he is already gone!" she said.

Tall came into the enclosure, and leapt off – his face tragic as Morton's after the Battle of Shrewsbury.[6]

"Well?" said Bathsheba, unwilling to believe that her verbal lettre-de-cachet[7] could possibly have miscarried.

"He says beggars mustn't be choosers,"[8] said Laban.

"What?" said the young farmer, opening her eyes, and drawing in her breath for an outburst. Joseph Poorgrass retired a few steps behind a hurdle.

"He says he shall not come unless you request him to come civilly in a proper manner, as becomes any person begging a favour."

"O – ho – that's his answer! Where does he get his airs? Who am I, then, to be treated like that? Shall I beg to a man who has begged to me!"

Another of the flock sprang into the air, and fell dead.

The men looked grave, as if they suppressed opinion.

Bathsheba turned aside, her eyes full of tears. The strait she was in through pride and shrewishness could not be disguised longer: she burst out crying bitterly: they all saw it, and she attempted no further concealment.

"I wouldn't cry about it, Miss," said William Smallbury, compassionately. "Why not ask him softer-like? I'm sure he'd come then. Gable is a true man in that way."

Bathsheba checked her grief and wiped her eyes. "O it is a wicked cruelty to me – it is – it is!" she murmured. "And he drives me to do what I wouldn't: yes he does! . . . . Tall, come indoors."

After this collapse, not very dignified for the head of an establishment, she went into the house, Tall at her heels. Here she sat down and hastily scribbled a note between the small convulsive sobs of convalescence which follow a fit of crying as a ground swell follows a storm. The note was none the less polite for being written in a hurry. She held it at a distance, was about to fold it, then added these words at the bottom:

"*Do not desert me, Gabriel!*"

She looked a little redder in refolding it, and closed her lips as if thereby to suspend till too late the action of conscience in examining whether such strategy was justifiable. The note was dispatched as the message had been, and Bathsheba waited indoors for the result.

It was an anxious quarter of an hour that intervened between the messenger's departure, and the sound of the horse's tramp again outside. She could not watch this time, but leaning over the old bureau at which she had written the letter, closed her eyes as if to keep out both hope and fear.

The case, however, was a promising one. Gabriel was not angry: he was simply neutral, although her first command had been so haughty. Such pertness would have damned a little less beauty, and on the other hand, such beauty would have redeemed a little less pertness.

She went out when the horse was heard and looked up. A mounted figure passed between her and the sky, and went on towards the field of sheep, the rider turning his face in receding. Gabriel looked at her. It was a moment when a woman's eyes and tongue tell distinctly opposite tales. Bathsheba looked full of gratitude, and she said,

"O Gabriel, how could you serve me so unkindly!"

Such a tenderly shaped reproach for his previous delay was the one speech in the language that he could pardon for not being commendation of his readiness now.

Gabriel murmured a confused reply, and hastened on. She knew from the look which sentence in her note had brought him. Bathsheba followed to the field.

Gabriel was already among the turgid prostrate forms. He had flung off his coat, rolled up his shirt-sleeves, and taken from his pocket the instrument of salvation. It was a small tube or trochar, with a lance passing down the inside, and Gabriel began to use it with a dexterity that would have graced a hospital surgeon. Passing his hand over the sheep's left flank, and selecting the proper point, he punctured the skin and rumen with the lance as it stood in the tube; then he suddenly withdrew the lance, retaining the tube in its place. A current of air rushed up the tube forcibly enough to have extinguished a candle held at the orifice.

It has been said that mere ease after torment is delight for a time:[9] and the countenance of these poor creatures expressed it now. Forty-nine operations were successfully performed. Owing to the great hurry necessitated by the far-gone state of some of the flock, Gabriel missed his aim in one case, and in only one – striking wide of the mark, and inflicting a mortal blow at once upon the suffering ewe. Four had died. Three recovered without an operation. The total number of sheep which had thus strayed and injured themselves so dangerously, was fifty-seven.

When the love-led man had ceased from his labours, Bathsheba came and looked him in the face.

"Gabriel, will you stay on with me?" she said, smiling winningly, and not troubling to bring her lips quite together again at the end, because there was going to be another smile soon.

"I will," said Gabriel.

And she smiled on him again.

CHAPTER XXI

The Great Barn and the sheep-shearers.

Men thin away to insignificance and oblivion quite as often by not making the most of good spirits when they have them as by lacking good spirits when they are indispensable. Gabriel lately, for the first time since his prostration by misfortune, had been independent in thought and vigorous in action to a marked extent, conditions which, powerless without an opportunity, as an opportunity without them is barren, would have given him a sure and certain lift upwards when the favourable conjunction should have occurred. But this incurable loitering beside Bathsheba Everdene stole his time ruinously. The spring tides were going by without floating him off, and the neap might soon come, which could not.[1]

It was the first day of June, and the sheep-shearing season culminated, the landscape, even to the leanest pasture, being all health and colour. Every green was young, every pore was open, and every stalk was swollen with crowding currents of juice. God was palpably present in the country, and the devil had gone with the world to town. Flossy catkins of the later kinds, fern-fronds like bishops' crosiers, the square headed moschatelle, the odd cuckoo-pint – like an apoplectic saint in a niche of malachite – clean white lady's-smocks, the toothwort, approximating to human flesh, the enchanter's nightshade, and the black-petaled doleful-bells were among the quainter objects of the vegetable world in and about Weatherbury at this teeming time,[2] and of the animal, the metamorphosed figures of Mr Jan Coggan, the master shearer, the second and third shearers who travelled in the exercise of their calling and do not require definition by name, Henery Fray the fourth shearer, Susan Tall's husband the fifth, Joseph Poorgrass the sixth, young Cain Ball as assistant shearer, and Gabriel Oak as general supervisor. None of these were clothed to any extent worth mentioning, each appearing to have hit in the matter of raiment the decent mean between a high and low caste Hindu. An angularity of lineament and a fixity of facial machinery in general, proclaimed that serious work was the order of the day.

They sheared in the great barn, called for the nonce the Shearing Barn, which on ground plan resembled a church with transepts. It not only emulated the form of the neighbouring church of the parish, but vied with it in antiquity. Whether the barn had ever formed one of a group of conventual buildings nobody seemed to be aware: no trace of such surroundings remained. The vast porches at the sides, lofty enough to admit a waggon laden to its highest with corn in the sheaf, were spanned by heavy pointed arches of stone, broadly and boldly cut, whose very simplicity was the origin of a grandeur not apparent in erections where more ornament has been attempted. The dusky, filmed, chestnut roof, braced and tied in by huge collars, curves, and diagonals, was far nobler in design because more wealthy in material than nine-tenths of those in our modern churches. Along each side wall was a range of striding buttresses, throwing deep shadows on the spaces between them, which were perforated by lancet openings combining in their proportions the precise requirements both of beauty and ventilation.

One could say about this barn, what could hardly be said of either the church or the castle, its kindred in age and style, that the purpose which had dictated its original erection was the same with that to which it was still applied. Unlike and superior to either of those two typical remnants of mediaevalism, the old barn embodied practices which had suffered no mutilation at the hands of time. Here at least the spirit of the builders then was at one with the spirit of the beholder now. Standing before this abraded pile the eye regarded its present usage, the mind dwelt upon its past history, with a satisfied sense of functional continuity throughout, a feeling almost of gratitude, and quite of pride, at the permanence of the idea which had heaped it up. The fact that four centuries had neither proved it to be founded on a mistake, inspired any hatred of its purpose, nor given rise to any reaction that had battered it down, invested this simple grey effort of old minds with a repose if not a grandeur which a too curious reflection was apt to disturb in its ecclesiastical and military compeers. For once mediaevalism and modernism had a common standpoint. The lanceolate windows, the time-eaten arch stones and chamfers, the orientation of the axis, the misty chestnut-work of the rafters, referred to no exploded fortifying art or worn out religious creed. The defence and salvation of the body by daily bread is still a study, a religion, and a desire.

To-day the large side doors were thrown open towards the sun to admit a bountiful light to the immediate spot of the shearers' operations, which was the wood threshing-floor in the centre, formed of thick oak, black with age and polished by the beating of flails for many generations till it had grown as slippery and as rich in hue as the state-room floors of an Elizabethan mansion. Here the shearers knelt, the sun slanting in upon their bleached shirts, tanned arms, and the polished shears they flourished, causing these to bristle with a thousand rays, strong enough to blind a weak-eyed man. Beneath them a captive sheep lay panting, increasing the rapidity of its pants as misgiving merged in terror, till it quivered like the hot landscape outside.

This picture of to-day in its frame of four hundred years ago did not produce that marked contrast between Ancient and Modern which is implied by the contrast of date. In comparison with cities, Weatherbury was immutable. The citizen's *Then* is the rustic's *Now*. In London twenty or thirty years ago are old times: In Paris ten years or five. In Weatherbury three- or four-score years were included in the mere present, and nothing less than a century set a mark on its face or tone. Five decades hardly modified the cut of a gaiter, the embroidery of a smockfrock, by the breadth of a hair. Ten generations failed to alter the turn of a single phrase. In these nooks the busy outsider's ancient times are only old, his old times are still new; his present is futurity.

So the barn was natural to the shearers, and the shearers in harmony with the barn.

The spacious ends of the building, answering ecclesiastically to nave and chancel extremities, were fenced off with hurdles, the sheep being all collected in a crowd within these two enclosures, and in one angle a catching-pen was formed, in which three or four sheep were continuously kept ready for the shearers to seize without loss of time. In the background, mellowed by tawny shade, were the three women Mary-ann Money, and Temperance and Soberness Miller, gathering up the fleeces and twisting ropes of wool with a wimble, for tying them with. They were indifferently well assisted by the old maltster, who when the malting season from October to April had passed, made himself useful upon any of the bordering farmsteads.

Behind all was Bathsheba, carefully watching the men to see that there was no cutting or wounding through carelessness, and that the animals were shorn close. Gabriel, who flitted and hovered under her bright eyes like a moth, did not shear continuously, half his time being spent in attending to the others, and selecting the sheep for them. At the present moment he was engaged in handing round a mug of mild liquor, supplied from a barrel in the corner, and cut pieces of bread and cheese.

Bathsheba, after throwing a glance here, a caution there, and lecturing one of the younger operators who had allowed his last finished sheep to go off among the flock without re-stamping it with her initials, came again to Gabriel, as he put down the luncheon to drag a frightened ewe to his shearing-station – flinging it over upon its buttocks[3] with a dexterous twist of the arm. He lopped off the tresses about its head, and opened up the neck and collar, his mistress quietly looking on.

"She blushes at the insult," murmured Bathsheba, watching the pink flush which arose and overspread the neck and shoulders of the ewe where they were left bare by the clapping shears – a flush which was enviable, for its delicacy, by many queens of the coteries, and would have been creditable, for its promptness, to any woman in the world.

Poor Gabriel's soul was fed with a luxury of content by having her over him, her eyes critically regarding his skilful shears, which apparently were going to gather up a piece of the flesh at every close and yet never did so. Like Guildenstern, Oak was happy in that he was not over happy.[4] He had no wish to converse with her: that his bright lady and himself formed one group, exclusively their own, and containing no others in the world, was enough.

So the chatter was all on her side. There is a loquacity which tells nothing, which was Bathsheba's; and there is a silence which says much: that was Gabriel's. Full of this dim and temperate bliss he went on to fling the ewe over upon her other side, covering her head with his knee, gradually running the shears line after line round her front part, thence about her flank and back, and finishing over the tail.

"Well done, and done quickly!" said Bathsheba looking at her watch as the last snip resounded.

"How long Miss?" said Gabriel, wiping his brow.

"Three-and-twenty minutes and a half since you took the first lock from its forehead. It is the first time that I have ever seen one done in less than half an hour."

The clean sleek creature arose from its fleece – how perfectly like Aphrodite rising from the foam[5] should have been seen to be realized –

looking startled and shy at the loss of its garment which lay on the floor in one soft cloud, united throughout, the portion visible being the inner surface only, which never before exposed, was white as snow and without flaw or blemish of minutest kind.

"Cain Ball!"

"Yes Mister Oak: here I be!"

Cainy now runs forward with the tar-pot, "B. E." is newly stamped upon the shorn skin,[6] and away the simple dam leaps panting over the board into the shirtless flock outside. Then up comes Mary-ann, throws the loose locks into the middle of the fleece, rolls it up and carries it into the background as three-and-a-half pounds of unadulterated warmth for the winter enjoyment of persons unknown and far away, who will, however, never experience the superlative comfort derivable from the wool as it here exists new and pure – before the unctuousness of its nature whilst in a living state has dried, stiffened, and been washed out – rendering it just now as superior to anything *woollen* as cream is superior to milk and water.

But heartless circumstance could not leave entire Gabriel's happiness of this morning. The rams, old ewes, and two-shear ewes had duly undergone their stripping, and the men were proceeding with the shearlings and hogs when Oak's belief that she was going to stand pleasantly by and time him through another performance was painfully interrupted by Farmer Boldwood's appearance in the extremest corner of the barn. Nobody seemed to have perceived his entry, but there he certainly was. Boldwood always carried with him a social atmosphere of his own, which everybody felt who came near him; and the talk, which Bathsheba's presence had somewhat repressed, was now totally suspended.

He crossed over towards Bathsheba, who turned to greet him with a carriage of perfect ease. He spoke to her in low tones, and she instinctively modulated her own to the same pitch, and her voice ultimately even caught the inflection of his. She was far from having a wish to appear mysteriously connected with him, but woman at the impressible age gravitates to the larger body not only in her choice of words, which is apparent every day, but even in her shades of tone and humour, when the influence is great.

What they conversed about was not audible to Gabriel who was too independent to get near though too concerned to disregard. The issue of their dialogue was the taking of her hand by the courteous farmer to help her over the spreading-board into the bright May sunlight outside. Standing beside the sheep already shorn they went on talking again. Concerning the flock? Apparently not. Gabriel theorised, not without truth, that in quiet discussion of any matter within reach of the speakers' eyes, these are usually fixed upon it: Bathsheba demurely regarded a contemptible straw lying upon the ground, in a way which suggested less ovine criticism[7] than womanly embarrassment. She became more or less red in the cheek, the blood wavering in uncertain flux and reflux over the sensitive space between ebb and flood. Gabriel sheared on, constrained and sad.

She left Boldwood's side, and he walked up and down alone for nearly a quarter of an hour. Then she reappeared, in a new riding habit of myrtle green which fitted her to the waist as a rind fits its fruit, and young Bob Coggan led on her mare, Boldwood fetching his own horse from the tree under which it had been tied. Oak's eyes could not forsake them, and in endeavouring to continue his shearing at the same time that he watched Boldwood's manner he snipped the sheep in the groin. The animal plunged; Bathsheba instantly gazed towards it, and saw the blood.

"O Gabriel!" she exclaimed with severe remonstrance. "You who are so strict with the other men – see what you are doing yourself!"

To an outsider there was not much to complain of in this remark, but to Oak, who knew Bathsheba to be well aware that she herself was the cause of the poor ewe's wound because she had wounded the ewe's shearer in a still more vital part, it had a sting which the abiding sense of his inferiority to both herself and Boldwood was not calculated to heal. But a manly resolve to recognise boldly that he had no longer a lover's interest in her helped him occasionally to conceal a feeling.

"Bottle!" he shouted in an unmoved voice of routine. Cainy Ball ran up, the wound was anointed, and the shearing continued.

Boldwood gently tossed Bathsheba into the saddle, and before they turned away she again spoke out to Oak with the same dominative and tantalizing graciousness:

"I am going now to see Mr Boldwood's Leicesters. Take my place in the barn, Gabriel, and keep the men carefully to their work."

The horses' heads were put about, and they trotted away.

Boldwood's deep attachment was a matter of great interest among all around him, but after having been pointed out for so many years as the perfect exemplar of thriving bachelorship, his lapse was an anticlimax, somewhat resembling that of St John Long's death by consumption, in the midst of his proofs that it was not a fatal disease.[8]

"That means matrimony," said Temperance Miller, following them out of sight with her eyes.

"I reckon that's the size o't," said Coggan working along without looking up.

"Well, better wed over the mixen than over the moor,"[9] said Laban Tall, turning his sheep.

Henery Fray spoke, exhibiting miserable eyes at the same time: –

"I don't see why a maid should take a husband when she's bold enough to fight her own battles, and don't want a home; for 'tis keeping another woman out. But let it be, for 'tis a pity he and she should trouble two houses."

As usual with decided characters, Bathsheba invariably provoked the criticism of individuals like Henery Fray. Her emblazoned fault was to be too pronounced in her objections, and not sufficiently overt in her likings. We learn that it is not the rays which bodies absorb, but those which they reject that give them the colours they are known by, and in the same way people are specialized by their dislikes and antagonisms whilst their goodwill is looked upon as no attribute at all.

Henery continued, in a more complaisant mood, "I once hinted my mind to her on a few things, as nearly as a battered frame dared to do so to such a froward piece. – You all know, neighbours, what a man I be, and how I come down with my powerful words when my pride is boiling with indignation?"

"We do, we do, Henery."

"So I said, 'Mistress Everdene, there's places empty, and there's clever men willing, but the spite' – no, not the spite – I didn't say spite – 'but the villainy of the contrarikind,' I said, (meaning womankind), – 'keeps 'em out.' That wasn't too strong for her, say?"

"Passably well put."

"Yes; and I would have said it, had death and salvation overtook me for it. Such is my spirit when I have a mind!"

"A true man, and proud as a lucifer."

"You see the artfulness? Why 'twas about being baily really, but I didn't put it so plain that she could understand my meaning, so I could lay it on all the stronger. That was my depth. . . . However let her marry an she will. Perhaps 'tis high time. I believe Farmer Boldwood kissed her behind the spear-bed at the sheep-washing t'other day – that I do."

"What a lie!" said Gabriel.

"Ah, neighbour Oak – how'st know?" said Henery mildly.

"Because she told me all that passed," said Oak with a Pharisaical sense that he was not as other shearers in this matter.[10]

"Ye have a right to believe it," said Henery with dudgeon, "a very true right. But I may see a little distance into things. To be long-headed enough for a baily's place is a poor mere trifle – yet a trifle more than nothing. However I look round upon life quite promiscuous. Do you conceive me, neighbours? My words though, made as simple as I can, may be rather deep for some heads."

"O yes Henery: we quite conceive ye."

"A strange old piece goodmen – whirled about from here to yonder as if I were nothing worth. A little warped, too. But I have my depths, ha, and even my great depths! I might close with[11] a certain shepherd, brain to brain. But no – O no!"

"A strange old piece, ye say!" interposed the maltster in a querulous voice, "At the same time ye be no old man worth naming – no old man at all. Yer teeth baint half gone yet, and what's a old man's standing if so be his teeth baint gone? Weren't I stale in wedlock afore ye were out of arms? 'Tis a poor thing to be sixty when there's people far past fourscore – a boast weak as water."

It was the unvarying custom in Weatherbury to sink minor differences when the maltster had to be pacified.

"Weak as water, yes," said Jan Coggan. "Maltster, we feel ye to be a wonderful old veteran man, and nobody can gainsay it."

"Nobody," said Joseph Poorgrass. "Ye are a very honourable spectacle, Maltster, and we all respect ye for that gift."

"Ay, and as a young man, when my senses were in prosperity, I was likewise liked by a good-few who knowed me," said the maltster.

"'Ithout doubt you was – 'ithout doubt."

The bent and hoary man was satisfied and so apparently was Henery Fray. That matters should continue pleasant Mary-ann spoke, who, what with her brown complexion, and the working wrapper of rusty linsey, had at present the mellow hue of an old sketch in oils – notably some of Nicholas Poussin's.[12]

"Do anybody know of a crooked man or a lame, or any second-hand fellow at all that would do for poor me?" said Mary-ann. "A perfect article I don't expect to get at my time of life. If I could hear of such a thing 'twould do me more good than toast and ale."

Coggan furnished a suitable reply. Oak went on with his shearing, and said not another word. Pestilent moods had come, and teased away his quiet. Bathsheba had shown indications of anointing him above his fellows by installing him as the bailiff that the farm imperatively required. He did not covet the post relatively to the farm: in relation to herself, as beloved by him and unmarried to another, he had coveted it. His readings of her seemed now to be vapoury and indistinct. His lecture to her was, he thought, one of the absurdest mistakes. Far from coquetting with Boldwood, she had trifled with himself in thus feigning that she had trifled with another. He was inwardly convinced that, in accordance with the anticipations of his easy-going and worse educated comrades, that day would see Boldwood the accepted husband of Miss Everdene. Gabriel at this time of his life had outgrown the instinctive dislike which every Christian boy has to reading the bible, perusing it now quite frequently, and he inwardly said "I find more bitter than death the woman whose heart is snares and nets!"[13] This was mere exclamation – the froth of the storm. He adored Bathsheba just the same.

"We workfolk shall have some lordly junketing to-night," said Cainy Ball, casting forth his thoughts in a new direction. "This morning I see 'em making the great puddens in the milking-pails – lumps of fat as big as yer thumb, Mister Oak! I've never seed such splendid large knobs of fat before in the days of my life – they never used to be bigger than a horse-bean. And there was a great black crock upon the brandise with his legs a sticking out, but I don't know what was in within."

"And there's two bushels of biffins for apple-pies," said Mary-ann.

"Well, I hope to do my duty by it all," said Joseph Poorgrass in a pleasant masticating manner of anticipation. "Yes: victuals and drink is a cheerful thing, and gives nerves to the nerveless, if the form of words may be used. 'Tis the gospel of the body, without which he perish, so to speak it."[14]

CHAPTER XXII

A pleasant time: a second declaration.

For the shearing-supper a long table was placed on the grass-plot beside the house, the end of the table being thrust over the sill of the wide parlour-window and a foot or two into the room. Miss Everdene sat inside the window, facing down the table: she was thus at the head, without mingling with the men.

This evening Bathsheba was unusually excited, her red cheeks and lips contrasting lustrously with the mazy skeins of her shadowy hair. She seemed to expect assistance, and the seat at the bottom of the table was at her request left vacant until after they had begun the meal. She then asked Gabriel to take the place and the duties appertaining to that end, which he did with great readiness.

At this moment Mr Boldwood came in at the gate, and crossed the green to Bathsheba at the window. He apologised for his lateness: his arrival was evidently by arrangement.

"Gabriel," said she, "will you move again please, and let Mr Boldwood come there?" Oak moved in silence back to his original seat.

The gentleman-farmer was dressed in cheerful style, in a new coat and white waistcoat, quite contrasting with his usual sober suits of gray. Inwardly too he was blithe, and consequently chatty to an exceptional degree. So also was Bathsheba now that he had come, though the uninvited presence of Pennyways, the bailiff who had been dismissed for theft, disturbed her equanimity for a while.

Supper being ended, Coggan began on his own private account, without reference to listeners: –

I've lost my love and I care not,
I've lost my love and I care not;
I shall soon have another
That's better than t'other
I've lost my love and I care not.

This melody when concluded was received with a silently appreciative gaze at the table, implying that the performance, like a work by those established authors who are independent of notices in the papers, was a well-known delight which required no applause.

"Now, Master Poorgrass, your song," said Coggan.

"I be all but a shadder, and the gift is wanting in me," said Joseph diminishing himself.

"Nonsense: wou'st never be so ungrateful Joseph – never!" said Coggan, expressing hurt feelings by an inflection of voice. "And mistress is looking hard at ye as much as to say, 'Sing at once, Joseph Poorgrass.'"

"Faith, so she is: well, I must suffer it!. . . . . How do I bear her gaze? Do I blush prodigally? Just eye my features, and see if the tell-tale blood overpowers me much, neighbours?"

"No, yer blushes be quite reasonable," said Coggan.

"A very reasonable depth indeed," testified Oak.

"I always tries to keep my colours from rising when a beauty's eyes get fixed on me," said Joseph diffidently. "But if so be 'tis willed they do, they must."

"Now, Joseph, your song please," said Bathsheba from the window.

"Well really ma'am," he replied in a yielding tone, "I don't know what to say. It would be a poor plain ballet of my own composure."[1]

"Hear hear!" said the supper-party.

Poorgrass thus assured, trilled forth a flickering yet commendable piece of sentiment, the tune of which consisted of the key-note and another, the latter being the sound chiefly dwelt upon. This was so successful that he rashly plunged into a second in the same breath after a few false starts:

I sow'-ed the'-e. . . . .
I sow'-ed . . . . .
I sow'-ed the'-e seeds' of' love',
  I-it was' all' i'-in the'-e spring',
I-in A'-pril' Ma'-ay a'-nd sun'-ny' June',
  When sma'-all bi'-irds they' do' sing'.

"Well put out of hand," said Coggan. "'They do sing' was a very taking paragraph."

"Ay; and there was a pretty place at 'seeds of love,' and 'twas well rehearsed. Though 'love' is a nasty high corner when a man's voice is getting crazed. Next verse Master Poorgrass."

But during this rendering young Bob Coggan evinced one of those anomalies which will afflict little people when other persons are particularly serious, and in trying to check his laughter pushed down his throat as much of the table cloth as he could get hold of, when, after continuing hermetically sealed for a short time, his mirth ultimately burst out through his nose. Joseph perceived it and with hectic cheeks of indignation instantly ceased singing. Coggan boxed Bob's ears immediately.

"Go on Joseph – go on, and never mind the young scamp," said Coggan. "'Tis a very catching ballet. Now then again – the next bar: I'll help ye to flourish up the shrill notes where yer wind is rather wheezy: –

> O the wi'-il-lo'-ow tree' will' twist'
> And the wil'-low' tre'-ee wi'-ill twine'.

But the singer could not be set going again. Bob Coggan was sent home for his ill manners, and tranquility was restored by Jacob Smallbury, who volunteered a ballad as inclusive and interminable as that with which the worthy toper old Silenus amused on a similar occasion the swains Chromis and Mnasylus,[2] and other jolly dogs of his day.

It was still the beaming time of evening, though night was stealthily making itself visible low down upon the ground, the western lines of light raking the earth without alighting upon it to any extent, or illuminating the dead levels at all. The sun had crept round the tree as a last effort before death, and then began to sink, the shearers' lower parts becoming steeped in embrowning twilight whilst their heads and shoulders were still enjoying day – lacquered with a yellow of self-sustained brilliancy that seemed inherent rather than acquired.

The sun went down in an ochreous mist; but they sat, and talked on, and grew as merry as the gods in Homer's heaven. Bathsheba still remained enthroned inside the window, and occupied herself in knitting, from which she sometimes looked up to view the fading scene outside. The slow twilight expanded and enveloped them completely before the signs of moving were shown.

Gabriel suddenly missed Farmer Boldwood from his place at the bottom of the table. How long he had been gone Oak did not know, but he had apparently withdrawn into the encircling dusk. Whilst he was thinking of this Liddy brought candles into the back part of the room overlooking the shearers, and their lively new flames shone down the table and over the men, and dispersed among the green shadows behind. Bathsheba's form, still in its original position, was now again distinct between their eyes and the light, which revealed that Boldwood had gone inside the room, and was now sitting near her.

Next came the question of the evening. Would Miss Everdene sing to them the song she always sang so charmingly – "The Banks of Allan Water"[3] – before they went home?

After a moment's consideration Bathsheba assented, beckoning to Gabriel, who hastened up into the charmed atmosphere at once.

"Have you brought your flute?" she whispered.

"Yes, Miss."

"Play to my singing then."

She stood up in the window-opening, facing the men, the candles behind her, and Gabriel on her right hand, immediately outside the sash-frame. Boldwood had drawn up on her left, within the room. Her singing was soft and rather tremulous at first, but it soon swelled to a steady clearness. Subsequent events caused one of the verses to be remembered for many months, and even years, by more than one of those who were gathered there: –

For his bride a soldier sought her
  And a winning tongue had he:
On the banks of Allan Water
  None was gay as she.

In addition to the dulcet piping of Gabriel's flute, Boldwood supplied a bass in his customary profound voice, uttering his notes so softly however, as to abstain entirely from making anything like an ordinary duet of the song: they rather formed a rich unexplored shadow, which threw her tones into relief. The shearers reclined against each other as in early ages, and so silent and absorbed were they that her breathing could almost be heard between the bars, and at the end of the ballad, when the last tone loitered on to an inexpressible close, there arose that buzz of pleasure which is the attar of applause.

It is scarcely necessary to state that Gabriel could not avoid noting the farmer's bearing to-night towards their entertainer. Yet there was nothing exceptional in his actions beyond what appertained to his time of performing them. It was when the rest were all looking away that Boldwood observed her: when they regarded her he turned aside. When they thanked or praised her he was silent: when they were inattentive he murmured his thanks. The meaning lay in the difference between actions none of which had any meaning of themselves; and the necessity of being jealous, which lovers are troubled with, did not lead Oak to underestimate these signs.

Bathsheba then wished them good night, withdrew from the window, and retired to the back part of the room, Boldwood thereupon closing the sash and the shutters, and shutting himself inside with her. Oak wandered away under the quiet and scented trees. Recovering from the softer impressions produced by Bathsheba's voice, the shearers rose to leave. Coggan turning to Pennyways as he pushed back the bench to pass out: –

"I like to give praise where praise is due, and the man deserves it – that 'a do so," he remarked, looking at the worthy thief comprehensively, as if he were the masterpiece of some world-renowned artist.

"I'm sure I should never have believed it if we hadn't proved it, so to allude," said Joseph Poorgrass, "that every cup, every one of the best knives and forks, and every empty bottle, be in their place as perfect now as at the beginning, and not one stole at all."

"I'm sure I don't deserve half the praise you give me," said the virtuous thief, grimly.

"Well, I'll say this for Pennyways," added Coggan, "that whenever he d'really make up his mind to do a noble thing in the shape of an honest action, as I could see by his face he did to-night afore sitting down, he's generally able to carry it out. Yes I'm proud to say neighbours that he's stole nothing at all."

"Well, 'tis a good deed, and we thank ye for it, Pennyways," said Joseph, to which opinion the remainder of the company subscribed unanimously.

At this time of departure when nothing more was visible of the inside of the parlour than a thin and still chink of light between the shutters, a passionate scene was in course of enactment there.

Miss Everdene and Boldwood were alone. Her cheeks had lost a great deal of their healthful fire from the very seriousness of her position, but her eye was bright with the excitement of a triumph – though it was a triumph which had rather been contemplated than desired.

She was standing behind a low arm-chair, from which she had just risen, and he was kneeling in it – inclining himself over its back towards her, and holding her hand in both his own. His body moved restlessly – and it was with a too happy happiness.[4] This unwonted abstraction by love of all dignity from a man of whom it had ever seemed the chief component, was, in its distressing incongruity, a pain to her which quenched much of the pleasure she derived from the proof that she was idolized.

"I will try to love you," she was saying in a trembling voice quite unlike her usual self-confidence. "And if I can believe in any way that I shall make you a good wife I shall indeed be willing to marry you. But, Mr Boldwood, hesitation on so high a matter is honourable in any woman, and I don't want to give a solemn promise to-night; I would rather ask you to wait a few weeks till I can see my situation better."

"But you have every reason to believe that *then*. . . . . ."

"I have every reason to hope that at the end o' the five or six weeks between this time and harvest that you say you are going to be away from home I shall be able to promise to be your wife," she said firmly. "But remember this distinctly, I don't promise yet."

"It is enough: I don't ask more. I can wait on those dear words. And now, Miss Everdene, good-night!"

"Good-night," she said graciously – almost tenderly – and Boldwood withdrew with a serene smile.

Bathsheba knew more of him now: he had entirely bared his heart before her, even until he had almost worn in her eyes the sorry look of a grand bird without the feathers that make it grand. She had been awe-struck at her past temerity, and was struggling to make amends, without thinking whether the sin quite deserved the penalty she was schooling herself to pay. To have brought all this about her ears was terrible; but after a while the situation was not without a fearful joy.[5] The facility with which even the most timid women sometimes acquire a relish for the dreadful when that is amalgamated with a little triumph, is marvellous.

CHAPTER XXIII

The same night in the fir plantation.

Among the multifarious duties which Bathsheba had voluntarily imposed upon herself by dispensing with the services of a bailiff, was the particular one of looking round the homestead before going to bed, to see that all was right and safe for the night. Gabriel had almost constantly preceded her in this tour every evening, watching her affairs as carefully as any specially appointed officer of surveillance could have done; but this tender devotion was to a great extent unknown to his mistress, and as much as was known was somewhat thanklessly received. Women are never tired of bewailing man's fickleness in love, but they only seem to snub his constancy.

As watching is best done invisibly, she usually carried a dark lantern in her hand, and every now and then turned on the light to examine nooks and corners with the coolness of a metropolitan policeman. This coolness may have owed its existence not so much to her fearlessness of expected danger as to her freedom from the suspicion of any; her worst anticipated discovery being that a horse might not be well bedded, the fowls not all in, or a door not closed.

This night the buildings were inspected as usual, and she went round to the farm paddock. Here the only sounds disturbing the stillness were steady munchings of many mouths, and stentorian breathings from all but invisible noses, ending in snores and puffs like the blowing of bellows slowly. Then the munching would re-commence, when the lively imagination might assist the eye to discern a group of pink-white nostrils, large as caverns, and very clammy and humid on their surfaces, not exactly pleasant to the touch until one got used to them. The mouths beneath them having a great partiality for closing upon any fragment of Bathsheba's apparel which came within reach of their tongues. Above each of these a still keener vision suggested a brown forehead and two staring though not unfriendly eyes; and above all a pair of whitish crescent-shaped horns like two particularly new moons, an occasional stolid "mu!" proclaiming beyond the shade of a doubt that these phenomena were the features and persons of Daisy, Whitefoot, Bonnylass, Jolly-O, Spot, Twinkle-eye, &c.,

&c. – the respectable dairy of Devon cows belonging to Bathsheba aforesaid.

Her way back to the house was by a path through a young plantation of tapering firs, which had been planted some years earlier to shelter the premises from the north wind. By reason of the density overhead of the inwoven foliage it was gloomy there at cloudless noontide, twilight in the evening, dark as midnight at dusk, and black as the ninth plague of Egypt[1] at midnight. To describe the spot is to call it a vast, low, naturally formed hall, the plumy ceiling of which was supported by slender pillars of living wood, the floor being covered with a soft dun carpet of dead spikelets and mildewed cones, with a tuft of grass blades here and there.

This bit of the path was always the crux of the night's ramble, though, before starting, her apprehensions of danger were not vivid enough to lead her to take a companion. Slipping along here covertly as Time, Bathsheba fancied she could hear footsteps entering the track at the opposite end. It was certainly a rustle of footsteps. Her own instantly fell as gently as snow flakes. She re-assured herself by a remembrance that the path was public and that the traveller was probably some villager returning home, regretting at the same time, that the meeting should be about to occur in the darkest point of her route, even though only just outside her own door.

The noise approached, came close, and a figure was apparently on the point of gliding past her when something tugged at her skirt and pinned it forcibly to the ground. The instantaneous check nearly threw Bathsheba off her balance. In recovering she struck against warm clothes and buttons.

"A rum start upon my soul!" said a masculine voice a foot or so above her head. "Have I hurt you, mate?"

"No," said Bathsheba, attempting to shrink away.

"We have got hitched together somehow, I think."

"Yes."

"Are you a woman?"

"Yes."

"A lady I should have said."

"It doesn't matter."

"I am a man."

"Oh."

Bathsheba softly tugged again, but to no purpose.

"Is that a dark lantern you have: I fancy so," said the man.

"Yes."

"If you'll allow me I'll open it and set you free."

A hand seized the lantern, the door was opened, the rays burst out from their prison, and Bathsheba beheld her position with astonishment.

The man to whom she was hooked was brilliant in brass and scarlet. He was a soldier. His sudden appearance was to darkness what the sound of a trumpet is to silence. Gloom, the *genius loci* at all times hitherto, was now totally overthrown, less by the lantern light than by what the lantern lighted. The contrast of this revelation with her anticipations of some sinister figure in sombre garb was so great that it had upon her the effect of a fairy transformation.

It was immediately apparent that the military man's spur had become entangled in the gimp which decorated the skirt of her dress. He caught a view of her face.

"I'll unfasten you in one moment Miss," he said with new-born gallantry.

"O no – I can do it thank you," she hastily replied, and stooped for the performance.

The unfastening was not such a trifling affair. The rowel of the spur had so wound itself among the gimp cords in those few moments that separation was likely to be a matter of time.

He too stooped, and the lantern standing on the ground betwixt them threw the gleam from its open side among the fir-tree debris and the blades of long damp grass with the effect of a large glowworm. It radiated upwards into their faces and sent over half the plantation gigantic shadows of both man and woman, each dusky shape becoming distorted and mangled upon the tree-trunks till it wasted to nothing.

He looked hard into her eyes when she raised them for a moment: Bathsheba looked down again, for his gaze was too strong for her to receive pointblank with her own. But she had obliquely noticed that he was young and slim, and that he wore three chevrons upon his sleeve.

Bathsheba pulled again.

"You are a prisoner Miss: it is no use blinking the matter," said the soldier drily. "I must cut your dress if you are in such a hurry."

"Yes – please do," she exclaimed helplessly.

"It wouldn't be necessary if you could wait a moment." And he unwound a cord from the little wheel. She withdrew her own hand, but, whether by accident or design, he touched it. Bathsheba was vexed she hardly knew why.

His unravelling went on, but it nevertheless seemed coming to no end. She looked at him again.

"Thank you for the sight of such a beautiful face!" said the young sergeant, without ceremony.

She coloured with indignation. "'Twas unwillingly shown," she replied stiffly, and with as much dignity – which was very little – as she could infuse into a position of utter captivity.

"I like you the better for that incivility, Miss," he said.

"I should have liked – I wish you had never shown yourself to me by intruding here!" She pulled again, and the gathers of her dress began to give way like lilliputian musketry.[2]

"I deserve such a chastisement as your words give me. But why should such a fair and dutiful girl have such an aversion to her father's sex?"

"Go on your way, please."

"What, Beauty, and drag you after me? Do but look – I never saw such a tangle."

"O 'tis shameful of you – you have been making it worse on purpose to keep me here – you have!"

"Indeed I don't think so," said the sergeant with a merry twinkle.

"I tell you you have!" she exclaimed in high temper. "I insist upon undoing it. Now allow me."

"Certainly Miss: I am not of steel." He added a sigh which had as much archness in it as a sigh could possess without losing its nature altogether. "I am thankful for beauty even when 'tis thrown to me like a bone to a dog. These moments will be over too soon!"

"Not for my pleasure," she said.

Bathsheba was revolving in her mind whether by a bold and desperate rush she could free herself at the risk of leaving a portion of her skirt bodily behind her. The thought was too dreadful. The dress – which she had put on to appear stately at the supper – was the head and front of her wardrobe, not another in her stock became her so well.[3] What woman in Bathsheba's position, not naturally timid and within call of her retainers would have bought escape from a dashing soldier at so dear a price?

"All in good time – it will soon be done I perceive."

"This trifling provokes and – and –"

"Not too cruel!"

"– Insults me!"

"It is done in order that I may have the pleasure of apologising to so charming a woman, which I straightway do most humbly madam," he said bowing low.

Bathsheba really knew not what to say.

"I've seen a good many women in my time," continued the young man in a murmur and more thoughtfully than hitherto, critically regarding her bent head at the same time; "but I've never seen a woman so beautiful as you. Take it or leave it – be offended or like it – I don't care."

"Who are you, then, who can so well afford to despise opinion?"

"No stranger. Sergeant Troy. I am staying in this place. – There it is undone at last you see. Your light fingers were more eager than mine. I wish it had been the knot of knots, which there's no untying."[4]

This was worse and worse. She started up, and so did he. How to decently get away from him – that was her difficulty now. She sidled off inch by inch, the lantern in her hand, till she could see the redness of his coat no longer.

"Ah, Beauty: good-bye!" he said.

She made no reply and, reaching a distance of twenty or thirty yards, turned about and ran indoors.

Liddy had just retired to rest. In ascending to her own chamber Bathsheba opened the girl's door an inch or two and said,

"Liddy, is any soldier staying in the village – Sergeant Somebody – rather gentlemanly for a sergeant, and good looking: a red coat with blue facings?"

"No Miss. . . . No I say, but really it might be Sergeant Troy home on furlough, though I have not seen him. He was here once in that way when the regiment was at Casterbridge."

"Yes – that's the name. Had he a moustache – no whiskers or beard?"

"He had."

"What kind of a person is he?"

"O Miss – I blush to name it – a gay man – a walking ruin to honest girls, so some people say.[5] But I know him to be very quick and trim, who might have made his thousands like a squire. Such a clever young dand[6] as he is! A doctor's son, brought up so well, and sent to Casterbridge Grammar School for years and years. Learnt all languages while he was there, and it was said he got on so far that he could take down Chinese in shorthand but that I don't answer for, as it was only reported. However he wasted his gifted lot and listed a soldier, but even then he rose to be a sergeant without trying at all. Ah – such a blessing it is to be high born: nobility of blood will shine out even in the ranks and files. And is he really come home Miss?"

"I believe so. Good night, Liddy."

After all how could a cheerful wearer of skirts be permanently offended with the man? There are occasions when girls like Bathsheba will put up with a great deal of unconventional behaviour. When they want to be praised, which is often; when they want to be mastered, which is sometimes, and when they want no nonsense, which is seldom. Just now the first feeling was in the ascendant with Bathsheba, with a dash of the second. Moreover, by chance or by devilry, the ministrant was antecedently made interesting by being a handsome stranger who had evidently seen better days.

So she could not permanently decide whether it was her opinion that he had insulted her or not.

"Was ever anything so odd!" she at last exclaimed to herself in her own room. "And was ever anything so meanly done as what I did – to skulk away like that, from a man who was only civil and kind!" Clearly she did not think his barefaced praise of her person an insult now.

It was a fatal omission of Boldwood's that he had never once told her she was beautiful.

CHAPTER XXIV[1]

The new acquaintance described.

Idiosyncrasy and vicissitude had combined to stamp Sergeant Troy as an exceptional being.

He was a man to whom memories were an encumbrance and anticipations a superfluity. Simply feeling, considering and caring for what was before his eyes he was vulnerable only in the present. His outlook upon time was as a transient flash of the eye now and then: that projection of consciousness into days gone by and to come, which makes the past a synonym for the pathetic and the future a word for circumspection, was foreign to Troy. With him the past was yesterday; the future, to-morrow; never, the day after.

On this account he might, in certain lights, have been regarded as one of the most fortunate of his order. For it may be argued with great plausibility that reminiscence is less an endowment than a disease, and that expectation in its only comfortable form – that of absolute faith – is practically an impossibility; whilst in the form of hope and the secondary compounds, patience, impatience, resolve, curiosity, it is a constant fluctuation between pleasure and pain.

Sergeant Troy being entirely innocent of the practice of expectation was never disappointed. To set against this negative gain there may have been some positive losses from a certain narrowing of the higher tastes and sensations which it entailed. But limitation of the capacity is never recognised as a loss by the loser therefrom: in this attribute moral or aesthetic poverty contrasts plausibly with material, since those who suffer do not see it, whilst those who see it do not suffer. It is not a denial of anything to have been always without it, and what Troy had never enjoyed he did not miss; but being fully conscious that what sober people missed he enjoyed, his capacity, though really less, seemed greater than theirs.

He was perfectly truthful towards men, but to women lied like a Cretan,[2] a system of ethics, above all others, calculated to win popularity at the first flush of admission into lively society, and the possibility of the favour gained being but transient had reference only to the future.

In his sacrifices to Venus he retained the ancient doctrines of the groves,[3] and introduced vice, not as a lapse, but as a necessary part of the ceremony. But he never passed the line which divides the spruce vices from the ugly, and hence, though his morals had never been applauded, disapproval of them frequently had been tempered with a smile. This treatment had led to his becoming a sort of forestaller and regrater[4] of other men's experiences of the glorious class, to his own aggrandizement as a Corinthian[5] rather than to the moral profit of his hearers.

His reason and his propensities had seldom any reciprocating influence, having separated by mutual consent long ago: thence it sometimes happened that, while his intentions were as honourable as could be wished, any particular deed formed a dark background which threw them into fine relief. The sergeant's vicious phases being the offspring of impulse and his virtuous phases of cool meditation, the latter had a modest tendency to be oftener heard of than seen.

Troy was full of activity, but his activities were less of a locomotive than a vegetative nature, and never being based upon any original choice of foundation or direction, they were exercised on whatever chance might place in their way. Hence, whilst he sometimes reached the brilliant in speech, because that was spontaneous, he fell below the commonplace in action, from inability to guide incipient effort. He had a quick comprehension and considerable force of character, but being without the power to combine them, the comprehension became engaged with trivialities whilst waiting for the will to direct it, and the force wasted itself in useless grooves whilst unheeding the comprehension.

He was a fairly well educated man for one of middle class – exceptionally well educated for a common soldier. He spoke fluently and unceasingly. He could in this way be one thing and seem another: for instance, he could speak of love and think of dinner; call on the husband to look at the wife; be eager to pay and intend to owe.

The wondrous power of flattery in passados[6] at woman is a perception so universal as to be remarked upon by many people almost as automatically as they repeat a proverb, or say that they are Christians and the like, without thinking much of the enormous corollaries which spring from the proposition. Still less is it acted upon for the good of the complemental being alluded to. With the majority such an opinion is shelved with all those trite aphorisms which require some catastrophe to bring their tremendous meanings thoroughly home. When expressed with some amount of reflectiveness it seems co-ordinate with a belief that this flattery must be reasonable to be effective. It is to the credit of men that few attempt to settle the question by experiment, and it is for their happiness, perhaps, that accident has never settled it for them. Nevertheless, that the power of a male dissembler, who by the simple process of deluging her with untenable fictions charms the female wisely, becomes limitless and absolute to the extremity of perdition, is a truth taught to many by unsought and wringing occurrences. And some – frequently those who are as definable as middle-aged youths – though not always – profess to have attained the same knowledge by other and converse experiences, and jauntily continue their indulgence in such experiences with terrific effect. Sergeant Troy was one.

He had been known to observe casually that in dealing with womankind the only alternative to flattery was cursing and swearing. There was no third method. "Treat them fairly and you are a lost man," he would say.

This person's public appearance in Weatherbury promptly followed his arrival there. A week or two after the shearing Bathsheba, feeling a nameless relief of spirits on account of Boldwood's absence, approached her hayfields and looked over the hedge towards the haymakers. They consisted in about equal proportions of gnarled and flexuous forms, the former being the men, the latter the women, who wore tilt bonnets covered with nankeen,[7] which hung in a curtain upon their shoulders. Coggan and Mark Clark were mowing in a less forward meadow, Clark humming a tune to the strokes of his scythe, to which Jan made no attempt to keep time with his. In the first mead they were already loading hay, the women raking it into cocks and windrows, and the men tossing it upon the waggon.

From behind the waggon a bright scarlet spot emerged, and went on loading unconcernedly with the rest. It was the gallant sergeant, who had come haymaking for pleasure; and nobody could deny that he was doing the mistress of the farm real knight-service[8] by this voluntary contribution of his labour at a busy time.

As soon as she had entered the field Troy saw her, and sticking his pitchfork into the ground and picking up his walking-cane, he came forward. Bathsheba blushed with half-angry embarrassment, and adjusted her eyes as well as her feet to the direct line of her path.

CHAPTER XXV

Scene on the verge of the hay-mead.

"Ah Miss Everdene!" said the sergeant, lifting his diminutive cap. "Little did I think it was you I was speaking to the other night. And yet, if I had reflected, the 'Queen of the Corn-market' (truth is truth at any hour of the day or night, and I heard you so named in Casterbridge yesterday) – the 'Queen of the Corn-market', I say, could be no other woman. I step across now to beg your forgiveness a thousand times for having been led by my feelings to express myself too strongly for a stranger. To be sure I am no stranger to the place – I am Sergeant Troy as I told you, and I have assisted your uncle in these fields no end of times when I was a lad. I have been doing the same for you to-day."

"I suppose I must thank you for that, Sergeant Troy," said the Queen of the Corn-market in an indifferently grateful tone.

The sergeant looked hurt and sad. "Indeed you must not, Miss Everdene," he said. "Why could you think such a thing necessary?"

"I am glad it is not."

"Why, if I may ask without offence."

"Because I don't much want to thank you for anything."

"I am afraid I have made a hole with my tongue that my heart will never mend. O these infernal[1] times: that ill luck should follow a man for honestly telling a woman she is beautiful! 'Twas the most I said – you must own that; and the least I could say – that I own myself."

"There is some talk I could do without more easily than money."

"H'm. That remark is somewhat digressive."

"It means that I would rather have your room than your company."

"And I would rather have curses from you than kisses from any other woman; so I'll stay here."

Bathsheba was absolutely speechless. And yet she could not help giving an interested side thought to the sergeant's ingenuity.

"Well," continued Troy, "I suppose there is a praise which is rudeness, and that may be mine. At the same time there is a treatment which is injustice, and that may be yours. Because a plain blunt man,[2] who has never been taught concealment, speaks out his mind without exactly intending it, he's to be snapped of like a son of a sinner."

"Indeed there's no such case between us," she said, turning away. "I don't allow strangers to be bold and impudent – even in praise of me."

"Ah – it is not the fact but the method which offends you," he said sorrowfully. "But I have the sad satisfaction of knowing that my words, whether pleasing or offensive, are unmistakably true. Would you have had me look at you, and tell my acquaintance that you are quite a commonplace woman, to save you the embarrassment of being stared at if they come near you? Not I. I couldn't tell any such ridiculous lie about a beauty to encourage a single woman in England in too excessive a modesty."

"It is all pretence – what you are saying!" exclaimed Bathsheba, laughing in spite of herself at the sergeant's palpable method. "You have a rare invention, Sergeant Troy. Why couldn't you have passed by me that night, and said nothing? – that was all I meant to reproach you for."

"Because I wasn't going to," he said smiling. "Half the pleasure of a feeling lies in being able to express it on the spur of the moment, and I let out mine. It would have been just the same if you had been the reverse person – ugly and old – I should have exclaimed about it in the same way."

"How long is it since you have been so afflicted with strong feeling then?"

"Oh, ever since I was big enough to know loveliness from deformity."

"'Tis to be hoped your sense of the difference you speak of doesn't stop at faces, but extends to morals as well."

"I won't speak of morals or religion – my own or anybody else's. Though perhaps I should have been a very good Christian if you pretty women hadn't made me an idolator."

Bathsheba moved on to hide the irrepressible dimplings of merriment. Troy followed entreatingly.

"But – Miss Everdene – you do forgive me?"

"I don't."

"Why?"

"You say such things."

"I said you were beautiful, and I'll say so still, for, by G—,[3] so you are! The most beautiful ever I saw, or may I fall dead this instant! Why, upon my –"

"Don't – don't! I won't listen to you – You are so profane!" she said, in a restless state between distress at hearing him and a *penchant* to hear more.

"I again say you are a most fascinating woman. There's nothing remarkable in my saying so, is there? – I'm sure the fact is evident enough. Miss Everdene, my opinion may be too forcibly let out to please you, and for the matter of that, too insignificant to convince you, but surely it is honest, and why can't it be excused?"

"Because it – it isn't a correct one," she femininely murmured.

"O fie-fie! Am I any worse for breaking the third of that Terrible Ten than you for breaking the ninth!"[4]

"Well – it doesn't seem *quite* true to me that I am fascinating," she replied evasively.

"Not so to you: then I say with all respect that, if so, it is owing to your modesty, Miss Everdene. But surely you must have been told by everybody of what everybody notices? – and you should take their words for it."

"They don't say so, exactly –"

"O yes, they must!"

"Well I mean, to my face, as you do," she went on, allowing herself to be further lured into a conversation that intention had rigorously forbidden.

"But you know they think so."

"No – that is – I certainly have heard Liddy say they do, but. . . . ." She paused.

Capitulation – that was the purport of the simple reply – guarded as it was – capitulation, unknown to herself. Never did a fragile tailless sentence convey a more perfect meaning. The careless sergeant smiled within himself, and probably the devil smiled too from a loophole in Tophet,[5] for the moment was the turning-point of a career. Her tone and mien signified beyond mistake that the seed which was to lift the foundation had taken root in the chink: the remainder was a mere question of time and natural seriate changes.[6]

"There the truth comes out!" said the soldier in reply. "Never tell me that a young lady can live in a buzz of admiration without knowing something about it. Ah, well, Miss Everdene, you are – pardon my blunt way – you are rather an injury to our race than otherwise."

"How – indeed?" she said opening her eyes.

"Oh, it is true enough. I may as well be hung for a sheep as a lamb (an old country saying, not of much account, but it will do for a rough soldier), and so I will speak my mind regardless of your pleasure, and without hoping or intending to get your pardon. Why, Miss Everdene it is in this manner that your good looks may do more harm than good in the world." [The sergeant looked down the mead in pained abstraction]. "Probably some one man on an average falls in love with each ordinary woman. She can marry him: he is content, and leads a useful life. Such women as you a hundred men always covet – your eyes will bewitch scores on scores into an unavailing fancy for you – you can only marry one of that many. Out of them say twenty will endeavour to drown the bitterness of despised love in drink: twenty more will mope away their lives without a wish or attempt to make a mark in the world, because they have no ambition apart from their attachment to you: twenty more – the susceptible person myself possibly among them – will be always draggling after you, getting where they may just see you, doing desperate things: men are such fools. The rest may try to get over their passion with more or less success. But all these men will be saddened. And not only those ninety-nine men but the ninety-nine women they might have married are saddened with them. There's my tale. That's why I say that a woman of such loveliness as yourself Miss Everdene, is hardly a blessing to her race."

The handsome sergeant's features were during this speech as rigid and stern as John Knox's in addressing his gay young queen.[7]

Seeing she made no reply, he said, "Do you read French?"

"No: I began, but when I got to the verbs father died," she said, simply.

"I do – when I have an opportunity, which latterly has not been often[8] – and there's a proverb they have, Qui aime bien, châtie bien – he chastens that loves well. Do you understand me?"

"Ah!" she replied, and there was even a little tremulousness in the usually cool girl's voice, "if you can only fight half as winningly as you can talk, you are able to make a pleasure of a bayonet wound!" And then poor Bathsheba instantly perceived her slip in making this admission: in hastily trying to retrieve it, she went from bad to worse. "Don't however suppose that *I* derive any pleasure from what you tell me."

"I know you do not – I know it perfectly," said Troy, with much hearty conviction on the exterior of his face: and altering the expression to moodiness; "when a dozen men are ready to speak tenderly to you, and give the admiration you deserve without adding the warning you need, it stands to reason that my poor rough-and-ready mixture of praise and blame cannot convey much pleasure. Fool as I may be, I am not so conceited as to suppose that."

"I think you – are conceited, nevertheless," said Bathsheba hesitatingly, and looking askance at a reed she was fitfully pulling with one hand, having lately grown feverish under the soldier's system of procedure –

not because the nature of his cajolery was entirely unperceived, but because its vigour was overwhelming.

"I would not own it to anybody else – nor do I exactly to you. Still, there might have been some self conceit in my foolish supposition the other night. I knew that what I said in admiration might be an opinion too often forced upon you to give any pleasure, but I certainly did think that the kindness of your nature might prevent your judging an uncontrolled tongue harshly – which you have done – and thinking badly of me, and wounding me this morning, when I am working hard to save your hay."

"Well, you need not think more of that: perhaps you did not mean to be rude to me by speaking out your mind; indeed, I believe you did not," said the shrewd woman in painfully innocent earnest. "And I thank you for giving help here. But – but mind you don't speak to me again in that way, or in any other, unless I speak to you."

"O Miss Bathsheba! That is too hard!"

"No it isn't. Why is it?"

"You will *never* speak to me; for I shall not be here long. I am soon going back again to the miserable monotony of drill – and perhaps our regiment will be ordered out soon. And yet you take away the one little ewe-lamb[9] of pleasure that I have in this dull life of mine. Well, perhaps generosity is not a woman's most marked characteristic."

"When are you going from here?" she asked with some interest.

"In a month."

"But how can it give you pleasure to speak to me?"

"Can you ask, Miss Everdene – knowing as you do what my offence is based on!"

"If you do care so much for a silly trifle of that kind, then, I don't mind doing it," she uncertainly and doubtingly answered. "But you can't really care for a word from me: you only say so – I think you only say so."

"That's unjust – but I won't repeat the remark. I am too gratified to get such a mark of your friendship at any price to cavil at the tone. I *do* Miss Everdene care for it. You may think a man foolish to want a mere word – just a good morning. Perhaps he is – I don't know. But you have never been a man looking upon a woman, and that woman yourself."

"I have not."

"Then you know nothing of what such an experience is like – and Heaven forbid that you ever should."

"Nonsense, flatterer! What is it like? I am interested in knowing."

"Put shortly it is not being able to think, hear, or look in any direction except one without wretchedness, nor there without torture."

"Ah, Sergeant, it won't do – you are pretending," she said, shaking her head dubiously. "Your words are too dashing to be true."

"I am not, upon the honour of a soldier."

"But *why* is it so? – Of course I ask for mere pastime."

"Because you are so distracting – and I am so distracted."

"You look like it."

"I am indeed."

"Why you only saw me the other night, you stupid man."

"That makes no difference. The lightning works instantaneously. I loved you then, at once – as I do now."

Bathsheba surveyed him curiously from the feet upward as high as she liked to venture her glance, which was not quite so high as his eyes.

"You cannot and you don't," she said demurely. "There is no such sudden feeling in people. I won't listen to you any longer. Dear me I wish I knew what o'clock it is – I am going – I have wasted too much time here already."

The sergeant looked at his watch and told her. "What haven't you a watch Miss?" he enquired.

"I have not just at present – I am about to get a new one."

"No. You shall be given one. Yes – you shall! A gift Miss Everdene – a gift."

And before she knew what the young man was intending a heavy gold watch was in her hand.

"It is an unusually good one for a man like me to possess," he quietly said. "It was my poor father's. He was a medical man and always used it among his patients. The tick of that watch has run races with a thousand illustrious pulses in its time. It was all the fortune he left me."[10]

"But Sergeant Troy – I cannot take this – I cannot!" she exclaimed with round-eyed wonder. "A gold watch – what are you doing! Don't be such a dissembler!"

The sergeant retreated to avoid receiving back his gift, which she held out persistently towards him. Bathsheba followed as he retired.

"Keep it – do, Miss Everdene – keep it!" said the erratic child of impulse. "The fact of your possessing it makes it worth ten times as much to me. A silver one[11] will answer my purpose just as well, and the pleasure of knowing whose heart my old one beats against – well, I won't speak of that. It is in far worthier hands than ever it has been in before."

"But indeed I can't have it!" she said, in a perfect simmer of distress. "O how can you do such a thing – that is, if you really mean it. – Give me your dead father's watch, and such a valuable one! You should not be so reckless, indeed, Sergeant Troy."

"I loved my father: good; but better, I love you more. That's how I can do it," said the sergeant with an intonation of such exquisite fidelity to nature that it was evidently not all acted now. Her beauty, which, whilst it had been quiescent, he had praised in jest, had in its animated phases moved him to earnest, and though his seriousness was less than she imagined, it was probably more than he imagined himself.

Bathsheba was brimming with agitated bewilderment and she said in half suspicious accents of feeling, "Can it be – Oh how can it be – that you care for me, and so suddenly! You have seen so little of me: I may not be really so – so nice-looking as I seem to you. Please do take it – O do! I cannot and will not have it. Believe me your generosity is too great. I have never done you a single kindness, and why should you be so kind to me!"

A factitious reply had been again upon his lips, but it was again suspended, and he looked at her with an arrested eye. The truth was that as she now stood excited, wild, and honest as the day, her alluring beauty bore out so fully the epithets he had bestowed upon it that he was quite startled at his temerity in advancing them as false. He said mechanically "Ah, why," and continued to look at her.

"And my workfolk see me following you about the field, and are wondering – O this is dreadful!" she went on, unconscious of the transmutation she was effecting.

"I didn't quite mean you to accept it at first,"[12] he broke out, bluntly, "but upon my soul I wish you would now. Without any shamming – come! Don't deny me the happiness of wearing it for my sake? But you are too lovely even to care to be kind as others are."

"No, no – don't say so. I have reasons for reserve which I cannot explain."

"Let it be then, let it be," he said receiving back the watch at last. I must be leaving you now. And will you speak to me for these few weeks of my stay?"

"Indeed I will. Yet I don't know if I will. O why did you come and disturb me so!"

"Perhaps in setting a gin I have caught myself. Such things have happened. Well, will you let me work in your fields?" he coaxed.

"Yes, I suppose so – if it is any pleasure to you."

"Miss Everdene, I thank you."

"No, no."

"Good-bye!"

The sergeant lifted his cap from the slope of his head, bowed, replaced it, and returned to the distant group of haymakers.

Bathsheba could not face the haymakers now. Her heart erratically flitting hither and thither from perplexed excitement, hot, and almost tearful, she retreated homewards murmuring, "O what have I done – what does it mean – I wish I knew how much of it was true!"

CHAPTER XXVI

Hiving the bees.

The Weatherbury bees were late in their swarming this year. It was in the latter part of June, and the day after the interview with Troy in the hayfield, that Bathsheba was standing in her garden, watching a swarm in the air, and guessing their probable settling-place. Not only were they late this year, but unruly. Sometimes throughout a whole season all the swarms would alight on the lowest attainable bough, such as part of a currant bush or espalier apple tree. Next year they would, with just the same unanimity, make straight off to the uppermost member of some tall gaunt Costard or Quarrington, and there defy all invaders, who did not come armed with ladders and staves to take them.

This was the case at present. Bathsheba's eyes, shaded by one hand, were following the ascending multitude against the unexplored stretch of blue, till they ultimately halted by one of the unwieldly trees spoken of.

A process was observable exactly analogous to that of alleged formations of the universe,[1] time and times ago. The bustling swarm had swept the sky in a scattered and uniform haze, which now thickened to a nebulous centre: this glided on to a bough, and grew still denser, till it formed a solid black spot upon the light.

The men and women being all busily engaged in saving the hay – even Liddy had left the house for the purpose of lending a hand – Bathsheba resolved to hive the bees herself if possible. She had dressed the hive with herbs and honey, fetched a ladder, brush and crook, made herself impregnable with an armour of leather gloves, straw hat, and large gauze veil – once green but faded to snuff colour – and ascended a dozen rungs of the ladder. At once she heard not ten yards off a voice that was beginning to have a strange power in agitating her.

"Miss Everdene, let me assist you. You should not attempt such a feat alone!"

Troy was just opening the garden gate.

Bathsheba flung down the brush, crook, and empty hive, pulled the skirt of her dress tightly round her ankles in a tremendous flurry, and, as well as she could, slid down the ladder. By the time she reached the bottom Troy was there also, and he stooped to pick up the hive.

"How fortunate I am to have dropped in at this moment!" exclaimed the sergeant.

She found her voice in a minute. "What and will you shake them in for me?" she asked, in what, for a defiant girl, was a faltering way, though for a timid girl it would have seemed a brave way enough.

"Will I!" said Troy. "Why of course I will. How blooming you are to-day!" Troy flung down his cane and put his foot on the ladder to ascend.

"But you must have on the veil and gloves, or you'll be stung fearfully!"

"Ah yes. I must put on the veil and gloves. Will you kindly show me how to fix them properly?"

"And you must have the broadbrimmed hat too, for your cap has no brim to keep the veil off, and they'd reach your face."

"The broadbrimmed hat too, by all means."

So a whimsical fate ordered that her hat should be taken off, veil and all attached, and placed upon his head, Troy tossing his own into a gooseberry bush. Then the veil had to be tied at its lower edge round his collar, and the gloves put on him.

He looked such an extraordinary object in this guise that, flurried as she was, she could not avoid laughing outright. It was the removal of yet another stake from the palisade of cold manners which had kept him off.

Bathsheba looked on from the ground whilst he was busy sweeping and shaking the bees from the tree, holding up the hive with the other hand for them to fall into. She made use of an unobserved minute whilst his attention was absorbed in the operation to arrange her plumes a little. He came down holding the hive at arm's length, behind which trailed a cloud of bees.

"Upon my life," said Troy through the veil, "holding up this hive makes one's arm ache worse than a week of sword-exercise." When the manoeuvre was complete he approached her. "Would you be good enough to untie me and let me out? I am nearly stifled inside this silk cage."

To hide her embarrassment during the unwonted process of untying the string about his neck, she said,

"I have never seen that."

"What?"

"The sword-exercise."

"Ah. – Would you like to?" said Troy.

Bathsheba hesitated. She had heard wondrous reports from time to time by dwellers in Weatherbury, who had by chance sojourned awhile in Casterbridge near the barracks, of this strange and glorious performance the sword-exercise. Men and boys who had peeped through chinks or over walls into the barrack-yard returned with accounts of it being the most flashing affair conceivable; accoutrements and weapons glistening like stars, here, there, around, yet all by rule and compass. So she said mildly what she felt strongly,

"Yes, I should like to see it very much."

"And so you shall. You shall see me go through it."

"No! How?"

"Let me consider."

"Not with a walkingstick – I don't care to see that. It must be a real sword."

"Yes, I know – and I have no sword here. But I think I could get one by the evening. Now will you do this."

Troy bent over her and murmured some suggestion in a low voice.

"O no indeed," said Bathsheba blushing. "Thank you very much, but I couldn't on any account."

"Surely you might? Nobody would know."

She shook her head, but with a weakened negation. "If I were to," she said, "I must bring Liddy too. Might I not?"

Troy looked far away. "I don't see why you want to bring her," he said coldly.

An unconscious look of assent in Bathsheba betrayed that something more than his coldness had made her also feel that Liddy would be superfluous in the suggested scene. She had felt it even whilst making the proposal.

"Well, I won't bring Liddy – and I'll come. But only for a very short time," she added; "a very short time."

"It will not take five minutes," said Troy.

CHAPTER XXVII

The hollow amid the ferns.

The hill opposite one end of Bathsheba's dwelling extended into an uncultivated tract of land covered at this season with tall thickets of brake fern, plump and succulent[1] from recent rapid growth, and radiant in hues of clean and untainted green.

At eight o'clock this midsummer evening, whilst the bristling ball of gold in the west still swept the tips of the ferns with its long luxuriant rays, a soft brushing by of garments might have been heard among them, and Bathsheba appeared in their midst, their soft feathery arms caressing her up to her shoulders. She paused, turned, went back over the hill and down again to her own door, whence she cast a farewell glance upon the spot she had just left, having resolved not to remain near the place after all.

She saw a dim spot of orange red moving round the shoulder of the rise. It disappeared on the other side.

She waited one minute – two minutes – thought of Troy's disappointment at her non-fulfilment of a promised engagement, tossed on her hat again, ran up the garden, clambered over the bank and followed the original direction. She was now literally trembling and panting at this her temerity in such an errant undertaking: her breath came and went quickly and her eyes shone with an infrequent light. Yet go she must. She reached the verge of a pit in the middle of the ferns. Troy stood in the bottom, looking up towards her.

"I heard your rustling through the ferns before I saw you," he said, coming up and giving her his hand to help her down the slope.

The pit was a hemispherical concave, naturally formed, with a top diameter of about thirty feet, and shallow enough to allow the sunshine to reach their heads. Standing in the centre the sky overhead was met by a circular horizon of fern: this grew nearly to the bottom of the slope and then abruptly ceased. The middle, within the belt of verdure was floored with an impressible carpet of moss and grass intermingled, so yielding that the foot was half buried within it.

"Now," said Troy, producing the sword which as he raised it into the sunlight, gleamed a sort of greeting, like a living thing, "First we have four right and four left cuts: four right and four left thrusts.[2] Infantry cuts and guards are more interesting than ours, to my mind, but they are not so swashing. They have seven cuts and three thrusts. So much as a preliminary. Well, next, our cut one is as if you were sowing your corn – so." Bathsheba saw a sort of rainbow upside down in the air, and Troy's arm was still again. "Cut two, as if you were hedging – so. Three, as if you were reaping – so. Four, as if you were threshing – in that way. Then the same on the left. The thrusts are these: one; two; three; four; right: one; two; three; four; left." He repeated them. "Have 'em again?" he said. "One, two –"

"I'd rather not. Though I don't mind your twos and fours; but your ones and threes are terrible!"

"Very well – I'll let you off the ones and threes. Next, cuts, points, and guards altogether." He exhibited them. "Then there's pursuing practice in this way." He gave the movements as before. "There, those are the stereotyped forms. The infantry have two most diabolical upward cuts, which we are too humane to use. Like this – three, four."

"How murderous and bloodthirsty!"

"They are rather deathy. Now I'll be more interesting, and let you see some loose play – giving all the cuts and points, infantry and cavalry, quicker than lightning, and as promiscuously – with just enough rule to regulate instinct and yet not to fetter it. You are my antagonist, with this difference from real warfare, that I shall miss you every time by one hair's breadth, or perhaps two. Mind you don't flinch, whatever you do."

"I'll be sure not to!" she said invincibly.

He pointed to about a yard in front of him.

Bathsheba's adventurous spirit was beginning to find some grains of relish in these highly novel proceedings. She took up her position as directed, facing Troy.

"Now just to learn whether you have pluck enough to let me do what I wish, I'll give a preliminary test."

He flourished the sword by way of introduction number two, and the next thing of which she was conscious was that the point and blade of the sword were darting with a gleam towards her left side just above her hip; then of their reappearance on her right side, emerging as it were from between her ribs, having apparently passed through her body. The third item of consciousness was that of seeing the same sword, perfectly clean and free from blood held vertically in Troy's hand (in the position technically called "recover swords"). All was as quick as electricity.

"Oh!" she cried out in affright, pressing her hand to her side. "Have you run me through? – no, you have not! Whatever have you done!"

"I have not touched you," said Troy quietly. "It was mere sleight of hand. The sword passed behind you. Now you are not afraid, are you? Because if you are I can't perform. I give my word that I will not only not hurt you, but not once touch you."

"I don't think I am afraid. You are quite sure you will not hurt me?"

"Quite sure."

"Is the sword very sharp?"

"O no – only stand as still as a statue. Now!"

In an instant the atmosphere was transformed to Bathsheba's eyes. Beams of light caught from the low sun's rays, above, around, in front of her, well-nigh shut out earth and heaven – all emitted in the marvellous evolutions of Troy's reflecting blade, which seemed everywhere at once, and yet nowhere specially. These circumambient gleams were accompanied by a keen sibilation that was almost a whistling – also springing from all sides of her at once. In short, she was enclosed in a firmament of lights and sharp hisses, resembling a sky-full of meteors close at hand.

Never since the sword became the national weapon had there been more dexterity shown in its management than by the hands of Sergeant Troy, and never had he been in such splendid temper for the performance as now in the evening sunshine among the ferns with Bathsheba. It may safely be asserted with respect to the closeness of his cuts, that had it been possible for the edge of the sword to leave in the air a permanent substance wherever it flew past, the space left untouched would have been a complete mould of Bathsheba's figure.

Behind the luminous streams of this *aurora militaris*,[3] she could see the hue of Troy's sword-arm, spread in a scarlet haze over the space covered by its motions, like a twanged bowstring, and behind all Troy himself, mostly facing her, sometimes, to show the rear cuts, half-turned away, his eye nevertheless always keenly measuring her breadth and outline, and his lips tightly closed in sustained effort. Next, his movements lapsed slower, and she could see them individually. The hissing of the sword had ceased, and he stopped entirely.

"That outer loose lock of hair wants tidying," he said, before she had moved or spoken. "Wait: I'll do it for you."

An arc of silver shone on her right side: the sword had descended. The lock dropped to the ground.

"Bravely borne!" said Troy. "You didn't flinch a shade's thickness. Wonderful in a woman!"

"It was because I didn't expect it. O you have spoilt my hair!"

"Only once more."

"No – no! I am afraid of you – indeed I am!" she cried.

"I won't touch you at all – not even your hair. I am only going to kill that caterpillar settling on you. Now: still!"

It appeared that a caterpillar had come from the fern and chosen the front of her boddice as his resting place. She saw the point glisten towards her bosom and seemingly enter it. Bathsheba closed her eyes in the full persuasion that she was killed at last. However, feeling just as usual, she opened them again.

"There it is, look," said the sergeant holding his sword before her eyes.

The caterpillar was spitted upon its point.

"Why it is magic!" said Bathsheba, amazed.

"O no – dexterity. I merely gave point to your bosom where the caterpillar was and instead of running you through checked the extension a thousandth of an inch short of your surface."

"But how could you chop off a curl of my hair with a sword that has no edge?"

"No edge! This sword will shave like a razor. Look here."

He touched the palm of his hand with the blade, and then, lifting it, showed her a thin shaving of scarf-skin dangling therefrom.

"But you said before beginning that it was blunt and couldn't cut me!"

"That was to get you to stand still, and so ensure your safety. The risk of injuring you through your moving was too great not to compel me to tell you an untruth to obviate it."

She shuddered. "I have been within an inch of my life, and didn't know it!"

"More precisely speaking you have been within half an inch of being pared alive two hundred and ninety-five times."

"Cruel, cruel 'tis of you!"

"You have been perfectly safe nevertheless. My sword never errs." And Troy returned the weapon to the scabbard.

Bathsheba overcome by a hundred tumultuous feelings resulting from the scene, abstractedly sat down on a tuft of heather.

"I must leave you now," said Troy softly. "And I'll venture to take and keep this in remembrance of you."

She saw him stoop to the grass, pick up the winding lock which he had severed from her manifold tresses, twist it round his fingers, unfasten a button in the breast of his coat, and carefully put it inside. She felt powerless to withstand or deny him. He was altogether too much for her, and Bathsheba seemed as one who, facing a reviving wind, finds it to blow so strongly that it stops the breath.

He drew near and said, "I must be leaving you." He drew nearer still. A minute later and she saw his scarlet form disappear amid the ferny thicket, almost in a flash, like a brand swiftly waved.

That minute's interval had brought the blood beating to her face, set her stinging as if aflame to the very hollows of her feet, and enlarged emotion to a compass which quite swamped thought. It had brought upon her a stroke resulting, as did that of Moses in Horeb,[4] in a liquid stream – here a stream of tears. She felt like one who has sinned a great sin.

The circumstance had been the gentle dip of Troy's mouth downwards upon her own. He had kissed her.

CHAPTER XXVIII

Particulars of a twilight walk.

We now see the element of folly distinctly mingling with the many varying particulars which made up the character of Bathsheba Everdene. It was almost foreign to her intrinsic nature. It was introduced as lymph on the dart of Eros,[1] and eventually permeated and coloured her whole constitution. Bathsheba, though she had too much understanding to be entirely governed by her womanliness had too much womanliness to use her understanding to the best advantage. Perhaps in no minor point does woman astonish her helpmate more than in the strange power she possesses of believing cajoleries that she knows all the time to be false – except indeed in that of being utterly sceptical on strictures that she knows all the time to be true.

Bathsheba loved Troy in the way that only self-reliant women love when they abandon their self-reliance. When a strong woman recklessly throws away her strength she is worse than a weak woman who has never had any strength to throw away. One source of her inadequacy is the novelty of the occasion. She has never had practice in making the best of such a condition. Weakness is doubly weak by being new.

Bathsheba was not conscious of guile in this matter. Though in one sense a woman of the world it was, after all, that world of daylight coteries, and green carpets, wherein cattle form the passing crowd and winds the busy hum; where a quiet family of rabbits or hares lives on the other side of your party-wall, where your neighbour is everybody in the tything, and where calculation is confined to market days. Of the fabricated tastes of good fashionable society she knew but little, and of the formulated self-indulgence of bad, nothing at all. Had her utmost thoughts in this direction been distinctly worded (and by herself they never were) they would only have amounted to such a matter as that she felt her impulses to be pleasanter guides than her discretion. Her love was entire as a child's, and though warm as summer it was fresh as spring. Her culpability lay in her making no attempt to control feeling by subtle and careful inquiry into consequences. She could show others the steep and thorny way, but "reck'd not her own rede".[2]

And Troy's deformities lay deep down from a woman's vision, whilst his embellishments were upon the very surface: thus contrasting with homely Oak, whose defects were patent to the blindest, and whose virtues were as metals in a mine.

The difference between love and respect was markedly shown in her conduct. Bathsheba had spoken of her interest in Boldwood with the greatest freedom to Liddy, but she had only communed with her own heart concerning Troy.

All this infatuation Gabriel saw and was troubled thereby from the time of his daily journey afield to the time of his return, and on to the small hours of many a night. That he was not beloved had hitherto been his great sorrow: that Bathsheba was getting into the toils was now a sorrow greater than the first, and one which nearly obscured it. It was a result which paralleled the oft-quoted observation of Hippocrates concerning physical pains.[3]

That is a noble though perhaps an unpromising love which not even the fear of breeding aversion in the bosom of the one beloved can deter from combating his or her errors. Oak determined to speak to his mistress. He would base his appeal on what he considered her unfair treatment of Farmer Boldwood, now absent from home.

An opportunity occurred one evening when she had gone for a short walk by a path through the neighbouring cornfields. It was dusk when Oak, who had not been far afield that day, took the same path and met her returning, quite pensively, as he thought.

The wheat was now tall, and the path was narrow: thus the way was quite a sunken groove between the embrowning thicket on either side. Two persons could not walk abreast without damaging the crop, and Oak stood aside to let her pass.

"O is it Gabriel?" she said. "You are taking a walk too. Good night."

"I thought I would come to meet you, as it is rather late," said Oak, turning and following at her heels when she had brushed somewhat quickly by him.

"Thank you indeed. But I am not very fearful."

"O no. But there are bad characters about."

"I never meet them."

Now Oak, with marvellous ingenuity, had been going to introduce the gallant sergeant through the channel of "bad characters". But all at once the scheme broke down, it suddenly occurring to him that this was rather a clumsy way, and too barefaced to begin with. He tried another preamble.

"And as the man who would naturally come to meet you is away from home, too – I mean Farmer Boldwood – why, thinks I, I'll go," he said.

"Ah, yes." She walked on without turning her head, and for many steps nothing further was heard from her quarter than the rustle of the dress against the heavy corn-ears. Then she resumed rather tartly,

"I don't quite understand what you meant by saying that Mr Boldwood would naturally come to meet me."

"I meant on account of the wedding which they say is likely to take place between you and him, Miss. Forgive my speaking plainly."

"They say what is not true," she returned quickly. "No marriage is likely to take place between us."

Gabriel now put forth his unobscured opinion, for the moment had come. "Well, Miss Everdene," he said, "putting aside what people say, I never in my life saw any courting if his is not a courting of you."

Bathsheba would probably have terminated the conversation there and then by flatly forbidding the subject had not her conscious weakness of position allured her to palter and argue in endeavours to better it.

"Since this subject has been mentioned," she said very emphatically, "I am glad of the opportunity of clearing up a mistake which is very common and very provoking. I didn't definitely promise Mr Boldwood anything. I have never cared for him. I respect him, and he has urged me to marry him. But I have given him no distinct answer. As soon as he returns I shall do so. And the answer will be that I cannot think of marrying him."

"People are full of mistakes, seemingly."

"They are."

"The other day they said you were trifling with him, and you almost proved that you were not. Lately they have said that you are not, and you straightway begin to show. . . . ."

"That I am, I suppose you mean."

"Well – I hope they speak the truth."

"They do, but wrongly applied. I don't trifle with him, but then, I have nothing to do with him."

Oak was unfortunately led on to speak of Boldwood's rival in a wrong tone to her after all. "I wish you had never met that young Sergeant Troy, Miss," he sighed.

Bathsheba's steps became faintly spasmodic. "Why?" she asked.

"He is not good enough for you."

"Did anyone tell you to speak to me like this?"

"Nobody at all."

"Then it appears to me that Sergeant Troy does not concern us here," she said intractably. "Yet I must say that Sergeant Troy is an educated man and quite worthy of any woman. He is well born."

"His being higher in learning and birth than the ruck of soldiers is anything but a proof of his worth. It shows his course to be downward."

"I cannot see what this has to do with our conversation. Mr Troy's course is not by any means downward; and his superiority *is* a proof of his worth."

"I believe him to have no conscience at all. And I cannot help begging you, Miss, to have nothing to do with him. Listen to me this once – only this once! I don't say he's such a bad man as I have fancied – I pray to God he is not. But since we don't exactly know what he is, why not behave as if he *might* be bad, simply for your own safety? Don't trust him, mistress; I ask you not to trust him so."

"Why, pray?"

"I like soldiers, but this one I do not like," he said sturdily. "The nature of his calling may have tempted him astray, and what is mirth to the neighbours is ruin to the woman. When he tries to talk to you again, why not turn away with a short 'Good-day'; and when you see him coming one way, turn the other. When he says anything laughable, fail to see the point and don't smile, and speak of him before those who will report your talk as 'That fantastical man,' or 'That Sergeant What's-his-name' – 'That man of a family that has come to the dogs.' Don't be unmannerly towards him, but harmless-uncivil, and so get rid of the man."

No Christmas robin detained by a window-pane ever pulsed as did Bathsheba now.

"I say – I say again – that it doesn't become you to talk about him –

why he should be mentioned passes me quite!" she exclaimed desperately. I know this, th-th-that he is a thoroughly conscientious man – blunt sometimes even to rudeness – but always speaking his mind about you plain to your face!"

"Oh."

"He is as good as anybody in this parish! He is very particular too, about going to church – yes he is!"

"I am afeard nobody ever saw him there. I never did certainly."

"The reason of that is," she said eagerly, "that he goes in privately by the old tower door, just when the service commences and sits at the back of the gallery. He told me so."

This supreme instance of Troy's goodness fell upon Gabriel's ears like the thirteenth stroke of a crazy clock. It was not only received with utter incredulity as regarded itself but threw a doubt on all the assurances that had preceded it.

Oak was grieved to find how entirely she trusted him. He brimmed with deep feeling as he replied in a steady voice, the steadiness of which was spoilt by the palpableness of his great effort to keep it so: –

"You know, mistress, that I love you, and shall love you always. I only mention this to bring to your mind that at any rate I would wish to do you no harm: beyond that I put it aside. I have lost in the race for money and good things, and I am not such a fool as to pretend to you now I am poor, and you have got altogether above me. But Bathsheba, dear mistress, this I beg you – consider that both to keep yourself well honoured among the workfolk, and in common generosity to an honourable man who loves you as well as I, you should be more discreet in your bearing towards this soldier."

"Don't, don't, don't!" she exclaimed in a choking voice.

"Are you not more to me than my own light and life?" he went on – "Come listen to me! I am six years older than you, and Mr Boldwood is ten years older than I, and consider – I do beg you to consider before it is too late – how safe you would be in his hands!"

Oak's allusion to his own love for her to some extent lessened her anger at his interference; but she could not really forgive him, neither for letting his wish to marry her be eclipsed by his wish to do her good, nor for his slighting treatment of Troy.

"I wish you to go elsewhere," she said, a paleness of face invisible to the eye being suggested by the trembling words. "Do not remain on this farm any longer. I don't want you – I beg you to go!"

"That's nonsense," said Oak calmly. "This is the second time you have pretended to dismiss me, and what's the use of it?"

"Pretended! You shall go sir – your lecturing I will not hear. I am mistress here."

"'Go' indeed – what folly will you say next. Treating me like Dick Tom and Harry when you know that a short time ago my position was as good as yours. Upon my life Bathsheba it is too barefaced. You know too that I can't go without putting things in such a strait as you wouldn't get out of I can't tell when. – Unless, indeed, you'll promise to have an understanding man as bailiff, or manager, or something. I'll go at once if you promise that."

"I shall have no bailiff: I shall continue to be my own manager," she said decisively.

"Very well then; you should be thankful to me for staying. How would the farm go on with nobody to mind it but a woman? But mind this, I don't wish you to feel you owe me anything – Not I. What I do, I do. Sometimes I say I should be as glad as a bird to leave the place – for don't suppose I'm content to be a nobody. I was made for better things. However I don't like to see your concerns going to ruin, as they must if you keep in this mind. I hate taking my own measure so plainly, but upon my life your provoking ways make a man say what he wouldn't dream of at other times. I own to being rather interfering. But you know well enough how it is, and who she is that I like too well, and feel too much like a fool about to be civil to her."

It is more than probable that she privately and unconsciously respected him a little for this grim fidelity, which had been shown in his tone even more than in his words. At any rate she murmured something to the effect that he might stay if he wished. She said more distinctly, "Will you leave me alone now? I don't order it as a mistress – I ask it as a woman, and I expect you not to be so uncourteous as to refuse."

"Certainly I will Miss Everdene," said Gabriel gently. He wondered that the request should have come at this moment, for the strife was over, and they were on a most desolate hill far from every human habitation, and the hour was getting late. He stood still and allowed her to get as far ahead of him till he could only see her form upon the sky.

A distressing explanation of this anxiety to be rid of him at that point now ensued. A figure apparently rose from the earth beside her. The shape beyond all doubt was Troy's. Oak would not be even a possible listener, and at once turned back till a good two hundred yards were between the lovers and himself.

Gabriel went home by way of the church-yard. In passing the tower he thought of what she had said about the sergeant's virtuous habit of entering the church unperceived at the beginning of service. Believing that the little gallery door alluded to was quite disused, he ascended the external flight of steps at the top of which it stood, and examined it. The pale lustre yet hanging in the north-western heaven was sufficient to show that a sprig of ivy had grown from the wall across the door to a length of more than a foot, delicately tying the panel to the stone jamb. It was a decisive proof that the door had not been opened at least since Troy came back to Weatherbury.

CHAPTER XXIX[1]

Hot cheeks: tearful eyes.

Half an hour later Bathsheba entered her own house. There burnt upon her when she met the light of the candles the flush and excitement which were little less than chronic with her now. The farewell words of Troy, who had accompanied her to the very door, still hung in her ears. He had bidden her adieu for two days which were, so he stated, to be spent at Bath in visiting some friends. He had also kissed her a second time.

It is only fair to Bathsheba to explain here a little fact which did not come to light until a long time afterwards: that Troy's presentation of himself so aptly at the wayside this evening was not by any distinctly preconcerted arrangement. He had hinted – she had forbidden, and it was only on the chance of his still coming that she had dismissed Oak, fearing a meeting between them just then.

She now sank down in a chair, wild and perturbed by all these new and fevering sequences. Then she jumped up with a manner of decision, and fetched her desk from a side table.

In three minutes, without pause or modification she had written a letter to Boldwood at his address beyond Casterbridge, saying kindly but firmly that she had well considered the whole subject he had brought before her and kindly given her time to decide upon; that her final decision was that she could not marry him. She had expressed to Oak an intention to wait till Boldwood came home before communicating with him and giving the final reply. But Bathsheba could not wait.

It was impossible to send this letter till the next day; yet to quell her uneasiness by getting it out of her hands and so, as it were, setting the act in motion at once, she arose to take it to any one of the women who might be in the kitchen.

She paused in the passage. A dialogue was going on in the kitchen, and Bathsheba and Troy were the subject of it.

"If he marry her, she'll gie up farming."

"'Twill be a gallant life, but may bring some trouble between the mirth – so say I."

"Well, I wish I had half such a husband."

Bathsheba had too much sense to mind seriously what her servitors said about her, but too much womanly redundance of speech to leave alone what was said till it died the natural death of unminded things. She burst in.

"Who are you speaking of?" she asked.

There was a pause before anybody replied. At last Liddy said frankly, "What was passing was a bit of a word about yourself Miss."

"I thought so. Mary-ann, and Liddy and Temperance – now I forbid you to suppose such things. You know I don't care the least for Mr Troy – not I. Everybody knows how much I hate him – yes *hate* him!" said the froward young person.

"We know you do, Miss," said Liddy, "and so do we all."

"I hate him too," said Mary-ann.

"Mary-ann – O you perjured woman! How can you speak that wicked story!" said Bathsheba excitedly. "You admired him from your heart only this morning in the very world – you did – Yes, Mary-ann, you know it!"

"Yes Miss, but so did you. He's a wild scamp now, and you are right to hate him."

"He's *not* a wild scamp! How dare you to my face! I have no right to hate him – nor you – nor anybody. But I am a silly woman. What is it to me what he is – you know it is nothing. I don't care for him – I don't mean to defend his good name – not I. Mind this, if any of you say a word against him you'll be dismissed instantly!"

She flung down the letter and surged back into the parlour with a big heart and tearful eyes – Liddy following her.

"O Miss," said mild Liddy, looking pitifully into Bathsheba's face. "I am sorry we mistook you so! I did think you cared for him, but I see you don't now."

"Shut the door Liddy."

Liddy closed the door, and went on: "People always says such foolery, miss. I'll make answer hencefor'ard, 'Of course a lady like Miss Everdene can't love him' – I'll say it out in plain black and white."

Bathsheba burst out: "O Liddy, are you such a fool![2] Can't you read riddles – can't you see! Are you a woman yourself!"

Liddy's clear eyes rounded with wonderment.

"Yes, you must be a blind thing Liddy!" she said in reckless abandonment and grief. "O I love him to very distraction, and misery and agony. Don't be frightened at me, though perhaps I am enough to frighten any innocent woman. Come close – closer." She put her arms round Liddy's neck. "I must let it out to somebody – it is wearing me away. Don't you yet know enough of me to see through that miserable denial of mine. O God what a lie it was! Heaven and my Love forgive me. And don't you know that a woman who loves at all thinks nothing of perjury when it is balanced against her love? – There, go out of the room. I want to be quite alone."

Liddy went towards the door.

"Liddy come here. Solemnly swear to me that he's not a bad man – that it is all lies they say about him!"

"But, Miss, how can I say he is not if – "

"You graceless girl![3] – how can you have the cruel heart to repeat what they say? Unfeeling thing that you are. . . . . . . But *I'll* see if you or anybody else in the village, or town either, dare do such a thing!" She started off pacing from fire-place to door and back again.

"No, Miss, I don't – I know it is not true," said Liddy frightened at Bathsheba's unwonted vehemence.

"I suppose you only agree with me like that to please me. But Liddy, he *cannot be* bad, as is said. Do you hear?"

"Yes Miss, yes."

"And you don't believe he is?"

"I don't know what to say Miss," said Liddy beginning to cry. "If I say No you don't believe me, and if I say Yes, you rage at me!"

"Say you don't believe it – say you don't!"

"I don't believe him to be so bad as they make out."

"He is not bad at all. . . . . Ha, my poor life and heart – how weak I am!" she moaned in a relaxed, desultory way. "O how I wish I had never seen him! Loving is misery for women always. I shall never forgive my Maker for making me a woman, and dearly am I beginning to pay for the honour of owning a pretty face." She freshened and turned to Liddy suddenly. "Mind this, Lydia Smallbury. If you repeat anywhere a single word of what I have said to you inside this closed door I'll never trust you, or love you, or have you with me a moment longer – not a moment."

"I don't want to repeat anything," said Liddy with womanly dignity of a diminutive order. "But I don't wish to stay with you. And, if you please, I'll go at the end of the harvest, or this week, or to-day. . . . . I don't see that I deserve to be put upon and stormed at for nothing!" concluded the small woman bigly.

"No, no Liddy – you must stay!" said Bathsheba dropping from haughtiness to entreaty with capricious inconsequence. "You must not notice my being in a taking just now. You are not as a servant – you are a companion to me. Dear dear – I don't know what I am doing since this miserable ache o'my heart has weighted and worn upon me so. What shall I come to! I suppose I shall die quite young, yes – I know I shall. I wonder sometimes if I am doomed to die in the Union.[4] I am friendless enough, God knows."

"I won't notice anything, nor will I leave you!" sobbed Liddy, impulsively putting up her lips to Bathsheba's, and kissing her.

Then Bathsheba kissed Liddy, and all was smooth again. "I don't often cry, do I Lidd, but you have made tears come into my eyes," she said, a smile shining through the moisture. "Try to think him a good man, won't you dear Liddy?"

"I will Miss indeed."

"He is a sort of steady man in a wild way you know. That's better than to be as some are, wild in a steady way. I am afraid that's how I am. And promise me to keep my secret – do, Liddy dear! And do not let them know that I have been crying about him, because it will be dreadful for me, and no good to him, poor thing!"

"Death's head himself shan't wring it from me, Mistress, if I've a mind to keep anything, and I'll always be your friend," replied Liddy emphatically, and at the same time bringing a few more tears into her own eyes – not from any particular necessity, but from the artistic sense of making herself in keeping with the remainder of the picture which seems to influence women at such times. "I think God likes us to be good friends, don't you?"

"Indeed I do."

"And dear Miss, you won't harry me and storm at me, will you, because you seem to swell so tall as a lion then, and it frightens me. Do you know, I fancy you would be a match for any man when you are in one o' your takings."

"Never – do you?" said Bathsheba, slightly laughing, though somewhat seriously alarmed by this Amazonian[5] picture of herself. "I hope I am not a bold sort of maid – mannish?" she continued with some anxiety.

"O no – not mannish; but so almighty womanish that 'tis getting on that way sometimes. . . . Ah, Miss," she said, after having drawn her breath very sadly in and sent it very sadly out. "I wish I had half your failing that way. 'Tis a great protection to a poor maid[6] in these days!"

CHAPTER XXX

Blame: fury.

The next evening Bathsheba, with the idea of getting out of the way of Mr Boldwood in the event of his returning to answer her note in person, proceeded to fulfil an engagement made with Liddy some few hours earlier. Bathsheba's companion, as a gage of their reconciliation, had been granted a week's holiday to visit her sister who was married to a thriving hurdler and crib-maker living in a delightful labyrinth of hazel copse not far from Yalbury. The arrangement was that Miss Everdene should honour them by coming there for a day or two to inspect some ingenious contrivances which this man of the woods had introduced into his wares.

Leaving her instructions with Gabriel and Mary-ann that they were to see everything carefully locked up for the night, she went out of the house just at the close of a timely thunder-shower, which had refined the air, and daintily bathed the mere coat of the land, all beneath being dry as ever. Freshness was exhaled in an essence from the varied contours of bank and hollow, as if the earth breathed maiden breath, and the pleased birds were hymning to the scene. Before her among the clouds there was a contrast in the shape of lairs of fierce light which showed themselves in the neighbourhood of a hidden sun, lingering on to the farthest north-west corner of the heavens that this midsummer season allowed.

She had walked nearly three miles of her journey, watching how the day was retreating, and thinking how the time of deeds was quietly melting into the time of thought, to give place in its turn to the time of prayer and sleep, when she beheld advancing over the hill the very man she sought so anxiously to elude. Boldwood was stepping on, not with that quiet tread of reserved strength which was his customary gait, when he always seemed to be balancing two thoughts. His manner was stunned and sluggish now.

Boldwood had for the first time been awakened to woman's privileges in the practice of tergiversation without regard to another's distraction, and, maybe, blight. That Bathsheba was a firm and positive girl, far less inconsequent than her fellows had been the very lung of his hope; for he had held that these qualities would lead her to adhere to a straight course for consistency's sake, and accept him, though her fancy might not flood him with the iridescent hues of uncritical love. But the argument now came back as sorry gleams from a broken mirror. The discovery was no less a scourge than a surprise.

He came on looking upon the ground, and did not see Bathsheba till they were less than a stone's throw apart. He looked up at the sound of her pit-pat, and his changed appearance sufficiently denoted to her the depth and strength of the feelings paralysed by her letter.

"O – is it you, Mr Boldwood," she faltered, a guilty warmth pulsing in her face.

Those who have the power of reproaching in silence may find it a means more effective than words. There are accents in the eye which are not on the tongue, and more tales from pale lips than can enter an ear. It is both the grandeur and the pain of the remoter moods that they avoid the pathway of sound. Boldwood's look was unanswerable.

Seeing she turned a little aside he said, "What, are you afraid of me?"

"Why should you say that?" said Bathsheba.

"I fancied you looked so," said he. "And it is most strange, because of its contrast with my feeling for you."

She regained self possession, fixed her eyes calmly, and waited.

"You know what that feeling is," continued Boldwood deliberately. "A thing strong as death. No dismissal by a hasty letter affects that."

"I wish you did not feel so strongly about me. It is generous of you, and more than I deserve, but I must not hear it now."

"Hear it? What do you think I have to say, then? I am not to marry you, and that's enough. Your letter was excellently plain. I want you to hear nothing – not I."

Bathsheba was unable to direct her will into any definite groove for freeing herself from this fearfully awkward position. She confusedly said "Good evening", and was moving on. Boldwood walked up to her, heavily and dully.

"Bathsheba – darling – is it final indeed?"

"Indeed it is."

"O Bathsheba – have pity upon me!" Boldwood burst out. "God's sake, yes – I am come to that low, lowest stage – to ask a woman for pity! Still, she is you – she is you."

Bathsheba commanded herself well. But she could hardly get a clear voice for what came instinctively to her lips: "There is little honour to the woman in that speech." It was only whispered, for something unutterably mournful no less than distressing in this spectacle of a man showing himself to be so entirely the vane of a passion enervated the instinct for punctilio.

"I am beyond myself about this, and am mad," said he. "I am no stoic at all to be supplicating here; but I do supplicate you. I wish you knew what is in me of devotion to you – but it is impossible, that. In bare human mercy to a lonely man don't throw me off now!"

"I don't throw you off – indeed, how can I? – I never had you." In her noon-clear sense that she had never loved him she forgot for a moment her thoughtless angle on that day in February.

"But there was a time when you turned to me, before I thought of you.

I don't reproach you, for even now I feel that the ignorant and cold darkness that I should have lived in if you had not attracted me by that letter – valentine you call it – would have been worse than my knowledge of you, though it has brought this misery. But, I say, there was a time when I knew nothing of you, and cared nothing for you, and yet you drew me on. And if you say you gave me no encouragement I cannot but contradict you."

"What you call encouragement was the childish game of an idle minute. I have bitterly repented of it – ay, bitterly, and in tears. Can you still go on reminding me?"

"I don't accuse you of it – I deplore it. I took for earnest what you insist was jest, and now this that I pray to be jest you say is awful wretched earnest. Our moods meet at wrong places. I wish your feeling was more like mine, or my feeling more like yours! O could I but have forseen the torture that trifling trick was going to lead me into – how I should have cursed you; but only having been able to see it since I cannot do that, for I love you too well! But it is weak idle driveling to go on like this. – Though, Bathsheba, you are the first woman of any shade or nature that I have ever looked at to love. It is the having been so near claiming you for my own that makes this denial so hard to bear. How nearly you promised me! But I don't speak now to move your heart, and make you grieve because of my pain; it is no use, that. I must bear it: my pain would get no less by paining you."

"But I do pity you – deeply – O so deeply!" she earnestly insisted.

"Do no such thing – do no such thing. Your dear love, Bathsheba, is such a great thing beside your pity that the loss of your pity as well as your love is no great addition to my sorrow, nor does the gain of your pity make it sensibly less. O sweet – how dearly you spoke to me behind the spear-bed at the washing-pool, and in the barn at the shearing, and that dearest last time in the evening at your home! Where are your pleasant words all gone – your earnest hope to be able to love me? Where is your firm conviction that you would get to care for me very much? Really forgotten? – really?"

She checked emotion, looked him quietly and clearly in the face and said in her low firm voice, "Mr Boldwood, I promised you nothing. Would you have had me a woman of clay when you paid me that furthest, highest compliment a man can pay a woman – telling her he loves her? I was bound to show some feeling, if I would not be a graceless shrew. Yet each of those pleasures was just for the day – the day just for the pleasure. How was I to know that what is a pastime to all other men was death to you. Have reason, do, and think more kindly of me!"

"Well, never mind arguing – never mind. One thing is sure: you were all but mine, and now you are not nearly mine. Everything is changed, and that by you alone, remember. You were nothing to me once, and I was contented; you are now nothing to me again, and O my soul, how different the second nothing is from the first! Would to God you had never taken me up, since it was only to throw me down!"

Bathsheba, in spite of her mettle began to feel unmistakable signs that she was inherently the weaker vessel. She strove miserably against this feminality[1] which would insist upon supplying unbidden emotions in stronger and stronger current. She had tried to elude agitation by fixing her mind on the trees, sky, any trivial object before her eyes, whilst his reproaches fell, but ingenuity could not save her now.

"I did not take you up – surely I did not!" she answered as heroically as she could. "But don't be in this mood with me. I can endure being told I am in the wrong, if you will only tell it me gently! O Sir, will you not kindly forgive me, and look at it cheerfully –"

"Cheerfully! Can a man fooled to utter heartburning find a reason for being merry? If I have lost, how can I be as if I had won? Heavens, you must be heartless quite! Had I known what a fearfully bitter sweet this was to be, how I would have avoided you, and never seen you, and been deaf to you. – I tell you all this, but what do you care! You don't care."

She returned silent and weak negatives, and swayed her head desperately as if to thrust away the words as they came showering about her ears from the lips of this trembling man in the climax of life with his bronzed Roman face and fine frame.

"Dearest, dearest, I am wavering even now between the two opposites of recklessly renouncing you, and labouring humbly for you again. Forget that you have said No and let it be as it was. Say, my love, Bathsheba, that you only wrote that refusal to me in fun – say it to me!"

"It would be useless, and painful to both of us. You overrate my capacity for love. I don't possess half the warmth of nature you believe me to have. An unprotected childhood in a cold world has beaten gentleness out of me."

He immediately said with more resentment: "That may be true, somewhat: but ah, Miss Everdene, it won't do as a reason. You are not the cold woman you would have me believe. No, no. It isn't because you have no feeling in you that you don't love me. You naturally would have me think so – you would hide from me that you have a burning heart like mine. You have love enough, but it is turned into a new channel. I know where."

The swift music of her heart became hubbub now, and she throbbed to extremity. He was coming to Troy. He did then know what had transpired! And the name fell from his lips the next moment.

"Why did Troy not leave my treasure alone?" he asked fiercely. "When I had no thought of injuring him why did he force himself upon your notice? Before he worried you your inclination was to have me: when next I should have come to you your answer would have been Yes. Can you deny it – I ask, can you deny it?"

"I cannot."

"I know you cannot. But he stole in in my absence and robbed me. Why didn't he win you away before, when nobody would have been grieved? – when nobody would have been set talebearing – Now the people sneer at me – the very hills and sky seem to laugh at me till I blush shamefully for my folly. I have lost my respect – my good name – my standing – lost it, never to get it again. Go and marry your man – go on!"

"O Sir – Mr Boldwood!"

"You may as well. I have no further claim upon you. As for me, I had better go somewhere alone, and hide, – and pray. I loved a woman once. I am now ashamed. When I am dead they'll say, miserable lovesick man that he was. Heaven – Heaven – if I had got jilted secretly, and the dishonour not known, and my position kept! But no matter – it is gone, and the woman not gained. Shame upon him – Shame!"

His unreasonable anger terrified her, and she glided from him, without obviously moving. "I am only a girl, – do not speak to me so!"

"All the time you knew – how very well you knew – that your new freak was my misery. Dazzled by brass and scarlet – O Bathsheba – this is woman's folly indeed!"

"You are taking too much upon yourself!" she said vehemently. "Everybody is upon me – everybody. It is unmanly to attack a woman so! I have nobody in the world to fight my battles for me, but no mercy is shown. Yet if a thousand of you sneer and say things against me, I *will not* be put down!"

"You'll chatter with him doubtless about me. Say to him, 'Boldwood would have died for me.' Yes, and you have given way to him knowing him to be not the man for you. He has kissed you – claimed you as his. Do you hear – he has kissed you. Deny it!"

The most tragic woman is cowed by a tragic man, and although Boldwood was, in vehemence and glow nearly her own self rendered into another sex, Bathsheba's cheek quivered. She gasped, "Leave me Sir – leave me! I am nothing to you. Let me go on!"

"Deny that he has kissed you."

"I shall not."

"Ha – then he has!" came hoarsely from the farmer.

"He has," she said slowly, and in spite of her fear, defiantly. "I am not ashamed to speak the truth."

"Then curse him; and curse him!" said Boldwood breaking into a whispered fury. "Whilst I would have given worlds to touch your hand you have let a rake come in without right or ceremony and – kiss you! Aha – a time of his life shall come when he will have to repent – and think wretchedly of the pain he has caused another man; and then may he ache, and wish, and curse, and yearn – as I do now!"

"Don't, don't, O don't pray down evil upon him!" she implored in a miserable cry. "Anything but that – anything. O be kind to him, Sir, for I love him true!"

Boldwood's ideas had reached that point of fusion at which outline and consistency entirely disappear. The impending night appeared to concentrate in his eye. He did not hear her at all now.

"I'll punish him – by my soul that will I! I'll meet him, soldier or no, and I'll horsewhip the untimely stripling for this reckless theft of my property. If he were a hundred men I'd horsewhip him . . ." He dropped his voice suddenly and unnaturally. "Bathsheba, sweet lost coquette, pardon me. I've been blaming you – threatening you – behaving like a churl to you – when he's the greater sinner. He stole your dear heart away with his unfathomable lies! . . . . . It is a fortunate thing for him that he's gone back to his regiment – that he's in Melchester and not here! I hope he may not return here just yet. I pray God he may not come into my sight, for I may be tempted beyond myself. O Bathsheba, keep him away – yes keep him away from me!"

For a minute Boldwood stood so inertly after this that his soul seemed to have been entirely exhaled with the breath of his passionate words. He turned his face away, and withdrew, and his form was soon covered over by the twilight as his footsteps mixed in with the low hiss of the leafy trees.

Bathsheba who had been standing motionless as a model all this latter time, flung her hands to her face, and wildly attempted to ponder on the exhibition which had just passed away. Such astounding wells of fevered feeling in a still man like Mr Boldwood were incomprehensible, dreadful. Instead of being a man trained to repression he was – what she had seen him.

The force of the farmer's threats lay in their relation to a circumstance known at present only to herself: her lover was coming back to Weatherbury the very next day. Troy had not returned to Melchester Barracks as Boldwood and others supposed, but had merely gone for a day or two to visit some acquaintance in Bath, and had yet a week or more remaining to his furlough.

She felt wretchedly certain that if he revisited her just at this nick of time, and came into contact with Boldwood, a fierce quarrel would be the consequence. She panted with solicitude when she thought of possible injury to Troy. The least spark would kindle the farmer's swift feelings of rage and jealousy; he would lose his self-mastery as he had this evening; Troy's blitheness might become aggressive; it might take the direction of derision, and Boldwood's anger might then take the direction of revenge.

With almost a morbid dread of being thought a gushing girl, this guideless woman too well concealed from the world under a manner of carelessness the warm depths of her strong emotions. But now there was no reserve. In her distraction, instead of advancing further, she walked up and down, beating the air with her fingers, pressing her brow, and murmuring brokenly to herself. Then she sat down on a heap of stones by the wayside to think. There she remained long. The dark rotundity of the earth eclipsed the foreshores and promontories of coppery cloud which bounded some green and pellucid expanses in the western sky. Amaranthine glosses came over them then, and the unresting world wheeled her round to a contrasting prospect eastward, in the shape of indecisive and palpitating stars. She gazed upon their silent throes amid the shades of space, but realised none at all. Her troubled spirit was far away with Troy.

CHAPTER XXXI

Night: horses tramping.

The village of Weatherbury was quiet as the graveyard in its midst, and the living were lying well-nigh as still as the dead. The church clock struck eleven. The air was so empty of other sounds that the whirr of the clockwork immediately before the strokes was distinct, and so was also the click of the same at their close. The notes flew forth with the usual blind obtuseness of inanimate things – flapping and rebounding among walls, undulating against the scattered clouds, spreading through their interstices into bottomless space.

Bathsheba's crannied and mouldy halls were to-night occupied only by Mary-ann, Liddy being, as was stated, with her sister whom Bathsheba had set out to visit. A few minutes after eleven had struck, Mary-ann turned in her bed with a sense of being disturbed. She was totally unconscious of the nature of the interruption to her sleep. It led to a dream, and the dream to an awakening, with an uneasy sensation that something had happened. She left her bed and looked out of the window. The paddock abutted on this end of the building, and in the paddock she could just discern by the uncertain gray a moving figure, approaching the horse that was feeding there. The figure seized the horse by the forelock, and led it to the corner of the field. Here she could see some object which circumstances proved to be a vehicle, for after a few minutes spent apparently in harnessing she heard the trot of the horse down the road, mingled with the sound of light wheels.

Two varieties only of humanity could have entered the paddock with the ghostlike glide of that mysterious figure. They were a woman, and a gipsy man. A woman was out of the question in such an occupation at this hour, and the comer could be no less than a thief, who might probably have known the weakness of the household on this particular night, and have chosen it on that account for his daring attempt. Moreover, to raise suspicion to conviction itself, there were gipsies in Weatherbury Bottom.

Mary-ann, who had been afraid to shout in the robber's presence, having seen him depart had no fear. She hastily slipped on her clothes, stumped down the unjointed[1] staircase with its hundred creaks, ran to Coggan's, the nearest house, and raised an alarm. Coggan called Gabriel, who now again lodged in his house as at first, and together they went to the paddock. Beyond all doubt the horse was gone.

"Listen!" said Gabriel.

They listened. Distinct upon the stagnant air came the sound of a trotting horse passing over Weatherbury Hill – just beyond the gipsies' encampment in Weatherbury Bottom.

"That's our Dainty – I'll swear to her step!" said Jan.

"Mighty me! Won't miss'ess storm and call us fools[2] when she comes back!" moaned Mary-ann. "How I wish it had happened when she was at home, and none of us had been answerable!"

"We must ride after." said Gabriel decisively. "I'll be responsible to Miss Everdene for what we do. Yes, we'll follow."

"Faith, I don't see how," said Coggan. "All our horses are too heavy for that trick except little Poppet, and what's she between two of us. . . . If we only had that pair over the hedge we might do something."

"Which pair?"

"Mr Boldwood's Tidy and Moll."

"Then wait here till I come hither again!" said Gabriel. He ran down the hill towards Farmer Boldwood's.

"Farmer Boldwood is not at home," said Mary-ann.

"All the better," said Coggan. "I know what he's gone for."

Less than five minutes brought up Oak again, running at the same pace, with two halters dangling from his hand.

"Where did you find 'em?" said Coggan turning round and leaping upon the hedge without waiting for an answer.

"Under the eaves – I knew where they were kept," said Gabriel following him. "Coggan you can ride bare-backed? There is no time to look for saddles."

"Like a hero!" said Jan.

"Mary-ann, you go to bed," Gabriel shouted to her from the top of the hedge.

Springing down into Boldwood's pastures each pocketed his halter to hide it from the horses, who, seeing the men empty handed, docilely allowed themselves to be seized by the mane, when the halters were dexterously slipped on. Having neither bit nor bridle Oak and Coggan extemporized the former by passing the rope through the animal's mouths and looping it on the other side. Oak vaulted astride and Coggan clambered up by aid of the bank, when they ascended to the gate and galloped off in the direction taken by Bathsheba's horse and the robber. Whether the horse was harnessed to a trap or not was a matter of some uncertainty.

Weatherbury Bottom was reached in three or four minutes. They scanned the shady green patch by the roadside. The gipsies were gone.

"The devils!"[3] said Oak. "Which way have they gone I wonder?"

"Straight on, as sure as God made little apples," said Jan.

"Very well, we are better mounted and must overtake 'em," said Oak. "Now on at full speed."

No sound of the rider in their van could now be discovered. The road-metal grew softer and more clayey as Weatherbury was left behind, and the late rain had left its surface in a somewhat plastic, but not muddy state. They came to cross-roads. Coggan suddenly pulled up Moll and slipped off.

"What's the matter?" said Gabriel.

"We must try to track 'em since we can't hear 'em," said Jan fumbling in his pockets. He struck a light, and held the match to the ground. The rain had been heavier here, and all foot and horse tracks made previous to the storm had been abraded and blurred by the drops, and they were now so many little scoops of water which reflected the flame of the match like eyes. One set of tracks was fresh and had no water in them: one pair of ruts was also dry, and not small canals like the others. The footprints forming this recent impression were full of information as to pace: being difficult to describe in words they are given in the following diagram: – [4]

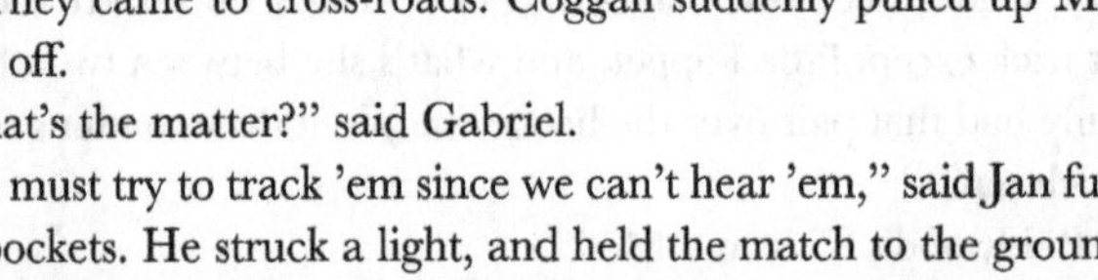

"Straight on!" Jan exclaimed. "Tracks like that mean a stiff gallop. No wonder we don't hear him. And the horse is harnessed – look at the ruts. Ay, that's our mare sure enough!"

"How do you know?"

"Old Jimmy Harris only shoed her last week, and I'd swear to his make among ten thousand."

"The rest of the gipsies must have gone on earlier, or some other way," said Oak. "You saw there were no other tracks?"

"Trew." They rode along silently for a long weary time. Coggan's watch struck one.[5] He lighted another match and examined the ground again:

"'Tis a canter now," he said throwing away the light. "A twisty rickety pace for a gig. The fact is, they overdrove her at starting; we shall catch them yet."

Again they hastened on. Coggan's watch struck two. When they looked again the hoof marks were as follows:

"That's a trot, I know," said Gabriel.

"Only a trot now," said Coggan cheerfully. "We shall overtake him in time."

They pushed rapidly on for yet two or three miles. "Ah – a moment," said Jan. "Let's see how she was driven up this hill. 'Twill help us." A light was promptly struck upon his gaiters as before, and the examination made.

"Hurrah!" said Coggan. "She walked up here – and well she might. We shall get them in two miles for a crown."

They rode three, and listened. No sound was to be heard save a mill-pond trickling hoarsely through a hatch, and suggesting gloomy possibilities of drowning by jumping in. Gabriel dismounted when they came to a turning. The tracks were absolutely the only guide as to direction that they now had, and great caution was necessary to avoid confusing them with some others which had made their appearance lately.

"What does this mean? – though I guess," said Gabriel, looking up at Coggan as he moved the match over the ground about the turning. Coggan, who no less than the panting horses had latterly shown signs of weariness, again scrutinized the mystic charactery.

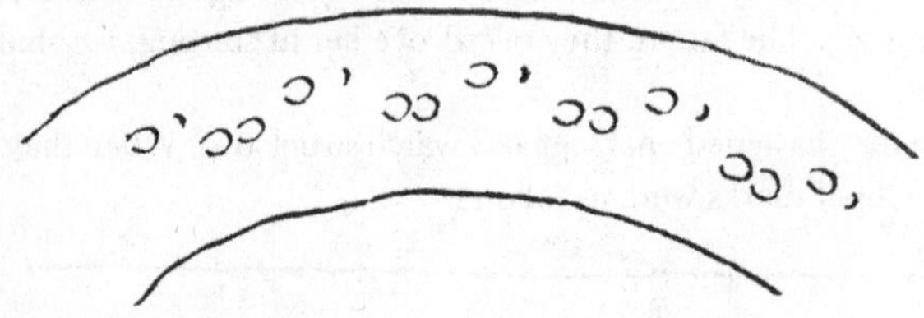

He screwed up his face and emitted a long "whew-w-w!"

"Lame," said Oak.

"Yes. Dainty is lamed: the near-foot-afore," said Coggan slowly, staring still at the footprints.

"We'll push on," said Gabriel remounting his humid steed.

Although the road along its greater part had been as good as any turnpike-road in the country it was technically only a byway. The last turning had brought them into the high road leading to Bath. Coggan recollected himself.

"We shall have him now!" he exclaimed.

"Where?"

"Pettiton Turnpike. The keeper of that gate is the sleepiest man between here and London – Dan Randall, that's his name – knowed 'en for years when he was at Casterbridge Gate. Between the lameness and the gate 'tis a done job."

They now advanced with extreme caution. Nothing was said until, against a shady background of foliage five white bars were visible, crossing their front a little way ahead.

"Hush – we are almost close!" said Gabriel.

"Amble on upon the grass," said Coggan.

The white bars were blotted out in their midst by a dark shape in front of them. The silence of this still time was pierced by an exclamation from that quarter.

"Hoy-a-hoy! Gate!"

It appeared that there had been a previous call which they had not noticed, for on their close approach, the door of the turnpike-house opened, and the keeper came out half-dressed, with a candle in his hand. The rays illumined the whole group.

"Keep the gate close!" shouted Gabriel. "He has stolen the horse."

"Who?" said the turnpike man.

Gabriel looked at the driver of the gig, and saw a woman – Bathsheba, his mistress.

On hearing his voice she had turned her face away from the light. Coggan had however caught sight of her in the meanwhile.

"Why 'tis mistress, I'll take my oath!" he said, amazed.

Bathsheba it certainly was, and she had by this time done the trick she could do so well, namely, mask a surprise by coolness of manner. "Well Gabriel," she enquired quietly. "Where are you going?"

"We thought – " began Gabriel.

"I am driving to Bath," she said, taking for her own use the assurance that Gabriel lacked. "An important matter made it necessary for me to give up my visit to Liddy, and go off at once. What, then, were you following me?"

"We thought the horse was stolen."

"Well – what a thing! . . . How very foolish of you not to know that I had taken the trap and horse. I could neither wake Mary-ann nor get into the house, though I hammered for ten minutes against her window-sill. Fortunately I could get the key of the coach-house, so I troubled no one further. Didn't you think it might be me?"

"Should we, Miss?"

"Perhaps not. Why, those are never Farmer Boldwood's horses! – Goodness mercy – what have you been doing – bringing trouble upon me in this way! What, musn't a lady move an inch from her own door without being dogged like a thief?"

"But how were we to know if you left no account of your doings Miss?" expostulated Coggan. "And ladies don't drive at these hours as a jineral rule of society."

"I did leave an account – and you would have seen it in the morning – I wrote in chalk on the coach-house doors that I had come back for the horse and gig and driven off: that I could arouse nobody, and should return soon."

"But you'll consider, ma'am, that we couldn't see that till it got daylight?"

"True," she said, and though angry at first, she had too much sense to blame them long or seriously for a devotion to her that was as valuable as it was rare. She added with a very pretty grace,

"Well, I really thank you heartily for taking all this trouble. But I wish you had borrowed anybody's horses but Mr Boldwood's."

"Dainty is lame, Miss," said Coggan. "Can ye go on?"

"It was only a stone in her shoe. I dismounted and pulled it out a hundred yards back. I can manage very well, thank you. I shall be in Bath by daylight. Will you now return please?"

She turned her head – the gateman's candle shimmering upon her quick clear eyes as she did so – passed through the gate, and was soon wrapped in the embowering shades of mysterious summer boughs. Coggan and Gabriel put about their horses, and fanned by the velvety air of this July night retraced the road by which they had come.

"A strange vagary this of hers, isn't it Oak?" said Coggan, curiously.

"Yes," said Gabriel shortly.[6] "Coggan, suppose we keep this night's work as quiet as we can?"

"I am of one and the same mind, Gable."

"Very well. We shall be home by three o'clock or so, and can creep into the parish like lambs."

Bathsheba's perturbed meditation by the roadside had ultimately evolved a conclusion that there were only two remedies for the present desperate state of affairs. The first was merely to keep Troy away from

Weatherbury till Boldwood's indignation had cooled; the second, to listen to Oak's entreaties and Boldwood's denunciations, and give up Troy altogether.

Alas – could she give up this new love – induce him to renounce her by saying she did not like him, could no more speak to him, and beg him for her good to end his furlough in Bath and see her and Weatherbury no more?

It was a picture full of misery, but for a while she contemplated it firmly, allowing herself nevertheless, as girls will, to dwell upon the happy life she would have enjoyed had Troy been Boldwood, and the path of love the path of duty – inflicting upon herself gratuitous tortures by imagining him the lover of another woman after forgetting her; for she had penetrated Troy's nature so far as to estimate his tendencies pretty accurately, but unfortunately loved him no less in thinking that he might soon cease to love her – indeed, considerably more.

She jumped to her feet. She would see him at once: yes, she would implore him by word of mouth to assist her in this dilemma. A letter to keep him away could not now reach him in time, even if he should be disposed to listen to it.

Was Bathsheba altogether blind to the obvious fact that the support of a lover's arms is not of a kind best calculated to assist a resolve to renounce him? Or was she sophistically sensible, with a thrill of pleasure, that by adopting this course for getting rid of him she was ensuring a meeting with him at any rate once more?

It was now dark and the hour must have been nearly ten. The only way to accomplish her purpose was to give up the idea of visiting Liddy at Yalbury, return to Weatherbury Farm, put the horse into the gig, and drive at once to Bath. The scheme seemed at first impossible: the journey was a fearfully heavy one, even for a strong horse; it was most venturesome for a woman at night and alone.

But could she go on to Liddy's and leave things to take their course? No, no, anything but that. Bathsheba was full of a stimulating turbulence, beside which caution vainly prayed for a hearing. She turned back towards the village.

Her walk was slow for she wished not to enter Weatherbury till the cottagers were in bed, and, particularly, till Boldwood was secure. Her plan was now to drive to Bath during the night, see Sergeant Troy in the morning before he set out to come to her, bid him farewell, and dismiss him: then to rest the horse all day (herself to weep the while, she thought), starting early the next morning on her return journey. By this arrangement she could trot the horse gently all the day, reach Liddy at Yalbury in the evening, and come home to Weatherbury with her whenever they chose: so nobody would know she had been to Bath at all.

This idea she proceeded to carry out, with what success we have already seen.

CHAPTER XXXII

In the sun: a harbinger.

A week passed, and there were no tidings of Bathsheba, nor was there any explanation of her Gilpin's rig.[1]

Then a note came for Mary-ann, stating that the business which had called her mistress to Bath still detained her there, but that she hoped to return in the course of another week.

Another week passed. The oat-harvest began, and all the men were afield under a monochromatic Lammas sky, amid the trembling air and short shadows of noon. Indoors nothing was to be heard save the droning of blue-bottle flies: out of doors the whetting of scythes and the hiss of tressy oat-ears rubbing together as their perpendicular stalks of amber yellow fell heavily to each swath. Every drop of moisture not in the men's bottles and flagons in the form of cider was raining as perspiration from their foreheads and cheeks. Drought was everywhere else.

They were about to withdraw for a while into the charitable shade of a tree in the fence, when Coggan saw a figure in a blue coat and brass buttons running to them across the field. "I wonder who that is?" he said.

"I hope nothing is wrong about mistress," said Mary-ann, who with some other women were tying the bundles (oats being always sheaved on this farm). "But an unlucky token came to me indoors this morning. I went to unlock the door, and dropped the key, and it fell upon the stone floor and broke into two pieces. Breaking a key is a dreadful bodement. I wish mis'ess was home."

"'Tis Cain Ball," said Gabriel, pausing from whetting his reap-hook. Oak was not bound by his agreement to assist in the cornfield; but the harvest month is an anxious time for a farmer, and the corn was Bathsheba's, so he lent a hand.

"He's dressed up in his best clothes," said Matthew Moon. "He hev been away from home for a few days, since he's had that felon upon his finger, for 'a said, since I can't work I'll have a hollerday."

"A good time for one – an excellent time," said Joseph Poorgrass, straightening his back, for he like some of the others had a way of resting for a few minutes on such hot days for reasons preternaturally small – of which Cain Ball's advent on a week day in his Sunday clothes was one of the first magnitude. "'Twas a bad leg allowed me to read the Pilgrim's Progress. And Mark Clark learnt All Fours in a whitlow."

"Ay, and my father put his arm out of joint to have time to go courting," said Jan Coggan in an eclipsing tone, wiping his face with his shirt-sleeve, and thrusting back his hat upon the nape of his neck.

By this time Cainy was nearing the group of harvesters, and was perceived to be carrying a large slice of bread and ham in one hand, from which he took mouthfuls as he ran, the other hand being wrapped in a bandage. When he came close his mouth assumed the bell shape and he began to cough violently.

"Now Cainy!" said Gabriel, sternly. "How many more times must I tell you to keep from running so fast when you are eating. You'll choke yourself some day – that's what you'll do, Cain Ball."

"Hok-hok-hok!" replied Cain. "A crumb of my victuals went the wrong way – hok-hok! That's what 'tis, Mister Oak! And I've been visiting Bath because I had a felon on my thumb – yes, and I've seen – ahok-hok!"

Directly Cain mentioned Bath, they all threw down their hooks and forks, and drew round him. Unfortunately the erratic crumb did not improve his narrative powers, and a supplementary hindrance was that of a sneeze, jerking from his pocket his rather large watch, which dangled in front of the young man pendulum-wise.

"Yes," he continued, directing his thoughts to Bath and letting his eyes follow; "I've seed the world at last – yes – and I've seed our mis'ess – ahok-hok-hok!"

"Bother the boy!" said Gabriel. "Something is always going the wrong way down your throat so that you can't tell what's necessary to be told."

"Ahok! – there! – please Mister Oak a gnat have just flewed into my stomach, and brought the cough on again!"

"Yes – that's just it. Your mouth is always open, you young rascal."

"'Tis terrible bad to have a gnat fly down yer throat, pore boy!" said Matthew Moon.

"Well, at Bath you saw –" prompted Gabriel.

"I saw our mistress," continued the junior shepherd, "and a soldier, walking along. And bymeby they got closer and closer, and then they went arm in crook, like courting complete – hok-hok! – like courting complete – hok! – courting complete –" Cain seemed to have coughed away the thread of his narrative at this point, and pending his recovery of breath looked up and down the field, apparently for some clue to it. "Well, I see our mis'ess and a soldier – a-ha-a-wk!"

"D— the boy!" said Gabriel.

"'Tis only my manner, Mister Oak, if ye'll excuse it!" said Cain Ball, looking reproachfully at Oak with eyes drenched in their own dew.

"Here's some cider for him – that'll cure his throat," said Jan Coggan, lifting a flagon of cider, pulling out the cork, and applying the hole to Cainy's mouth, Joseph Poorgrass in the meantime beginning to think apprehensively of the serious consequences that would follow Cainy Ball's strangulations in his cough, and the history of his Bath adventures dying with him.

"For my poor self, I always say 'Please God' afore I do anything," said Joseph in an unboastful voice; "and so should you, Cain Ball. 'Tis a great safeguard, and might perhaps save you from being choked to death some day."

Mr Coggan poured the liquor with unstinted liberality at the suffering Cain's circular mouth, half of it running down the side of the flagon, and half of what reached his mouth running down outside his throat, and half of what ran in going the wrong way, and being coughed and sneezed around the persons of the gathered reapers in the form of a rarefied cider fog, which for a moment hung in the sunny air like a small exhalation.

"There's a great clumsy sneeze! Why can't ye have better manners, you young dog!" said Coggan withdrawing the flagon.

"The cider went up my nose!" cried Cainy as soon as he could speak – "and now 'tis gone down my neck, and into my poor dumb felon, and over my shiny buttons and all my best cloze!"

"The pore lad's cough is terrible unfortunate," said Matthew Moon. "And a great history on hand too! Bump his back, shepherd."

"'Tis my nater," mourned Cain. "Mother says I always was so excitable when my feelings were worked up to a point."

"True, true," said Joseph Poorgrass. "The Balls were always a very excitable family. I knowed the boy's grandfather – a truly nervous and modest man, even to genteel refinement. 'Twas blush blush with him almost as much as 'tis with me – not but that 'tis a fault in me."

"Not at all Master Poorgrass," said Coggan. "'Tis a very noble quality in ye."

"Heh-heh, well – I wish to noise nothing abroad – nothing at all," murmured Poorgrass diffidently. "But we are born to things – that's true. Yet I would rather my trifle were hid – though perhaps a high nature is a little high, and at my birth all things were possible to my maker, and he may have begrudged no gifts. . . . But under your bushel, Joseph! – under your bushel with you.[2] – A strange desire, neighbours – this desire to hide, and no praise due. Yet there is a Sermon on the Mount with a calendar of the blessed at the head, and certain meek men may be named therein."[3]

"Cainy's grandfather was a very clever man," said Matthew Moon. "Invented a' apple tree out of his own head, which is called by his name to this day – the Early Ball – you know 'em Jan? A Quarrington grafted on a Tom-Putt, and a Rathe-ripe upon top o' that again. 'Tis trew 'a used to bide about in a public house in a way he had no business to by rights – but there – 'a were a clever man in the sense of the term."

"Now then," said Gabriel impatiently, "what did you see, Cain?"

"I seed our mis'ess go into a sort of a park place where there's seats and shrubs and flowers, arm in crook with a soldier," continued Cainy firmly, and with a dim sense that his words were very effective as regarded Gabriel's emotions. "And I think the soldier was Sergeant Troy. And they sat there together for more than half an hour, talking moving things, and she once was crying almost to death. And when they came out her eyes were shining and she was as white as a lily; and they looked into one another's faces as desperately friendly as a man and woman can be."

Gabriel's features seemed to get thinner. "Well, what did you see besides?"

"Oh – all sorts."

"White as a lily? – you are sure 'twas she?"

"Yes."

"Well, what besides?"

"Great glass windows to the shops, and great clouds in the sky full of rain, and old wooden trees in the country round."

"You stun-poll – what will ye say next!" said Coggan.

"Let en alone," interposed Joseph Poorgrass. "The boy's maning is that the sky and the earth in the kingdom of Bath is not altogether different from ours here. 'Tis for our good to gain knowledge of strange countries, and as such the boy's words should be suffered, so to speak it."

"And the people of Bath," continued Cain, "never need to light their fires except as a luxery, for the water springs up out of the earth ready boiled for use."[4]

"'Tis true as the light," testified Matthew Moon. "I've heard other navigators say the same thing."

"They drink nothing else there," said Cain, "and seem to enjoy it, to see how they swaller it down."

"Well, it seems a barbarous practice enough to us, but I daresay the natives think nothing of it," said Matthew.

"And don't victuals spring up as well as drink?" asked Coggan, twirling his eye.

"No – I own to a blot there in Bath – a true blot. God didn't provide 'em with victuals as well as drink, and 'twas a drawback I couldn't get over at all."

"Well 'tis a curious country to say the least," observed Moon; "and it must be a curious people that live therein."

"Miss Everdene and the soldier were walking about together, you say?" said Gabriel, returning to the group.

"Ay; and she wore a beautiful gold-colour silk gown, trimmed with black lace, that would have stood alone without legs inside if required. 'Twas a very winsome sight. And her hair was brushed splendid. And when the sun shone upon the bright gown and his red coat – my! how handsome they looked. You could see 'em all the length of the street."

"And what then?" murmured Gabriel.

"And then I went into Griffins to have my boots hobbed, and then I went to Rigg's batty-cake shop and asked 'em for a penneth of the cheapest and nicest stales, that were all but blue-mouldy but not quite. And whilst I was chawing 'em down I walked on and seed a clock – with a face as big as a baking-trendle – "

"But that's nothing to do with mistress!"

"I'm coming to that, if you'll leave me alone, Mister Oak!" remonstrated Cainy. "If you excites me, perhaps you'll bring on my cough, and then I shan't be able to tell ye nothing."

"Yes – let him tell it his own way," said Coggan.

Gabriel settled into a despairing attitude of patience, and Cainy went on:

"And there were great large houses, and more people all the week long than at Weatherbury Club-walking[5] on White Tuesdays. And I went to grand churches and chapels. And how the parson would pray! Yes, he would kneel down, and put up his hands together, and there were the holy gold rings on his fingers a-twinkling in yer eyes, that he'd earned by praying so excellent well! Ah yes, I wish I lived there!"

"Our poor Parson Thirdly can't get no money to buy holy rings," said Matthew Moon, thoughtfully. "And as good a man as ever walked. I don't believe poor Thirdly have a single one, even of humblest tin or copper. Such a great ornament as they'd be to him on a dull afternoon, when he's up in the pulpit lighted by the wax candles. But 'tis impossible poor man. Ah, to think how unequal things be!"

"Perhaps he's made of different stuff than to wear 'em," said Gabriel grimly. "Well, that's enough of this. Go on Cainy – quick."

"O – and the new style of parsons wear moustaches and long beards," continued the illustrious traveller; "and look like Moses and Aaron complete, and make we fokes in the congregation feel all over like the children of Israel."[6]

"A very right feeling – very," said Joseph Poorgrass.

"And there's two religions going on in the nation now – High Church and High Chapel. And, thinks I, I'll play fair: so I went to High Church in the morning, and High Chapel in the afternoon."

"A right and proper boy," said Joseph Poorgrass.

"Well, at High Church they pray singing and believe in all the colours of the rainbow; and at High Chapel they pray preaching and believe in drab and whitewash only. And then – I didn't see no more of Miss Everdene at all."

"Why didn't you say so before, then!" exclaimed Oak, with much disappointment.

"Ah," said Matthew Moon, "she'll wish her cake dough[7] if so be she's over intimate with that man."

"She's not over intimate with him," said Gabriel, indignantly.

"She would know better," said Coggan. "Our mis'ess has too much sense under those knots of black hair to do such a mad thing."

"You see, he's not a coarse ignorant man, for he was well brought up," said Matthew dubiously. "'Twas only wildness that made him a soldier, and maids – little rascals![8] – maids rather like your man of sin."

"Now Cain Ball," said Gabriel restlessly, "can you swear in the most awful form that the woman you saw was Miss Everdene?"

"Cain Ball, you are no longer a babe and suckling," said Joseph, in the sepulchral tone the circumstances demanded, "and you know what taking an oath is. 'Tis a horrible testament, mind ye, which you say and seal with your blood-stone, and the prophet Matthew tells us that on whomsoever it shall fall it will grind him to powder.[9] Now before all the workfolk here assembled can you swear to your words as the shepherd asks ye?"

"Please no, Mister Oak!" said Cainy looking from one to the other with great uneasiness at the spiritual magnitude of the position. "I don't mind saying 'tis true, but I don't like to say 'tis d— true, if that's what you mane."

"Cain, Cain, how can you!" said Joseph sternly. "You are asked to swear in a holy manner, and you swear like wicked Shimei the son of Gera, who cursed as he came.[10] Young man, fie!"

"No, I don't! 'Tis you want to squander a pore boy's soul Joseph Poorgrass – that's what 'tis!" said Cain, beginning to cry. "All I mane is that in common truth 'twas Miss Everdene and Sergeant Troy, but in the horrible so-help-me truth that ye want to make of it perhaps 'twas somebody else."

"There's no getting at the rights of it," said Gabriel, turning to his work.

"Cain Ball, you'll come to a bit of bread!" groaned Joseph Poorgrass.

Then the reapers' hooks were flourished again, and the old sounds went on. Gabriel, without making any pretence of being lively, did nothing to show that he was particularly dull. However Coggan knew pretty nearly how the land lay, and when they were in a nook together he said,

"Don't take on about her Gabriel. What difference does it make whose sweetheart she is, since she can't be yours?"

"That's the very thing I say to myself," said Gabriel.

CHAPTER XXXIII[1]

Home again: a juggler.

That same evening at dusk Gabriel was leaning over Coggan's garden-gate, taking an up-and-down survey before retiring to rest.

A vehicle of some kind was softly creeping along the grassy margin of the lane. From it came the tones of two women talking. The tones were natural and not at all repressed. Oak instantly knew the voices to be those of Bathsheba and Liddy.

The carriage came opposite and passed by. It was Miss Everdene's gig, and Liddy and her mistress were the only occupants of the seat. Liddy was asking questions about the city of Bath, and her companion was answering them listlessly and unconcernedly. Both Bathsheba and the horse seemed weary.

The exquisite relief of finding that she was here again, safe and sound overpowered all reflection, and Oak could only luxuriate in the sense of it. All grave reports were forgotten.

He lingered and lingered on, till there was no difference between the eastern and western expanses of sky, and the timid hares began to skip courageously round the dim hillocks. Gabriel might have been there an additional half hour when a dark form walked slowly by. "Good night Gabriel," the passer said.

It was Boldwood. "Good night sir," said Gabriel.

Boldwood likewise vanished up the road, and Oak shortly afterwards turned indoors to bed.

Farmer Boldwood went on towards Miss Everdene's house. He reached the front, and approaching the door, saw a light in the parlour. The blind was not drawn down, and inside the room was Bathsheba, looking over some papers or letters. Her back was towards Boldwood. He went to the door, knocked, and waited with tense muscles and an aching brow.

Boldwood had not been outside his garden since his meeting with Bathsheba in the road to Yalbury. Silent and alone, he had remained in moody meditation on woman's ways, deeming as essentials of the whole sex the accidents of the single one of their number he had ever closely beheld. By degrees a more charitable temper had pervaded him, and this was the reason of his sally to-night. He had come to apologise and beg forgiveness of Bathsheba with something like a sense of shame at his violence, having but just now learnt that she had returned – from a visit to Liddy as he supposed.

He enquired for Miss Everdene. Liddy's manner was odd, but he did not notice it. She went in, leaving him standing there, and in her absence the blind was pulled down. Boldwood augured ill from that sign. She came out.

"My mistress cannot see you Sir," said Liddy.

The farmer instantly went out of the gate. He was unforgiven – that was the issue of it all. He had seen her who was to him simultaneously a delight and a torture, sitting in the room he had shared with her as a peculiarly privileged guest only a little earlier in the summer, and she had denied him an entrance there now.

Boldwood did not hurry homeward. It was ten o'clock at least when, walking deliberately through the lower part of Weatherbury he heard the carrier's spring van entering the village. The van ran to and from a town in a northern direction, and it was owned and driven by a Weatherbury man, at the door of whose house it now pulled up. The lamp fixed to the head of the hood illuminated a scarlet and gilded form, who was the first to alight.

"Aha!" said Boldwood. "Come to see her again!"

Troy entered the carrier's house, which was the place of his lodging on his last visit to his native place. Boldwood seemed moved by a sudden determination. He hastened home. In ten minutes he was back again, and made as if he were going to call upon Troy at the carrier's.

But, as he approached, some one opened the door, and came out. He heard this person say "Good night" to the inmates, and the voice was Troy's. This was strange, coming so immediately after his arrival. Boldwood however, hastened up to him. Troy had what appeared to be a carpet-bag in his hand – the same that he had brought with him. It seemed as if he were going to leave again this very night.

Troy turned up the hill, and quickened his pace. Boldwood stepped forward.

"Sergeant Troy?"

"Yes – I'm Sergeant Troy."

"Just arrived from Melchester, I think."

"Just arrived from Bath."

"I am William Boldwood."

"Indeed."

The tone in which this word was uttered was all that had been wanted to bring Boldwood to the point.

"I wish to speak a word with you," he said.

"What about?"

"About her who lives just ahead there – and about a woman you have wronged."

"I wonder at your impertinence," said Troy, moving on.

"Now look here," said Boldwood, standing in front of him. "Wonder or not, you are going to hold a conversation with me."

Troy heard the dull determination in Boldwood's voice, looked at his stalwart frame, then at the thick cudgel he carried in his hand. He remembered it was past ten o'clock. It seemed worth while to be civil to Boldwood.

"Very well, I'll listen with pleasure," said Troy, placing his bag on the ground. "Only speak low, for somebody or other may overhear us in the farm house there."

"Well, then – I know a good deal concerning your – Fanny Robbin's attachment to you. I may say, too, that I believe I am the only person in the village, excepting one, who does know it. You ought to marry her."

"I suppose I ought. Indeed, I wish to, but I cannot."

"Why?"

Troy was about to utter something hastily: he then checked himself and said, "I am too poor." His voice was changed. Previously it had had a devil-may-care tone. It was the voice of a trickster now.

Boldwood's present mood was not critical enough to notice tones. He continued; "I may as well speak plainly. And understand, I don't wish to enter into the questions of right or wrong, woman's honour and shame, or to express any opinion on your conduct. I intend a business transaction with you."

"I see," said Troy. "Suppose we sit down here."

And old tree trunk lay under the hedge immediately opposite, and they sat down.

"I was engaged to be married to Miss Everdene," said Boldwood; "but you came and – "

"Not engaged," said Troy.

"As good as engaged."

"If I had not turned up she might have become engaged to you."

"D— might."

"Would, then."

"If you had not come I should certainly – yes, *certainly* – have been accepted by this time. If you had not seen her you might have been married to Fanny. Well, there's too much difference between Miss Everdene's station and your own for this flirtation with her ever to benefit you by ending in marriage. So all I ask is, don't molest her any more. Marry Fanny. I'll make it worth your while."

"How will you?"

"I'll pay you well now, I'll settle a sum of money upon her, and I'll see that you don't suffer from poverty in the future. I'll put it clearly. Bathsheba won't have you:[2] give up wasting your time about a great match you'll never make for a moderate and rightful match you may make to-morrow: take up your carpet-bag, turn about, leave Weatherbury now this night, and you shall take fifty pounds with you. Fanny shall have fifty to enable her to prepare for the wedding, when you have told me where she is living, and she shall have five hundred[3] paid down on her wedding-day."

In making this statement Boldwood's voice revealed only too clearly a consciousness of the weakness of his position, his aims, and his method. His manner had lapsed quite from that of the firm and dignified Boldwood of former times, and such a scheme as he had now engaged in he would have condemned as childishly imbecile only a few months ago. We discern a grand force in the lover which he lacks whilst a free man, but there is a breadth of vision in the free man which in the lover we vainly seek. Where there is much bias there must be some narrowness, and love, though added emotion, is subtracted capacity. Boldwood knew nothing of Fanny Robbin's condition[4] or whereabouts, he knew nothing of Troy's possibilities, yet that was what he said.

"I like Fanny best," said Troy; "and if, as you say, Miss Everdene is out of my reach, why I have all to gain by accepting your money, and marrying Fan. But she's only a servant."

"Never mind – do you agree to my arrangement?"

"I do."

"Ah," said Boldwood, in a more elastic voice. "O Troy, if you like her best, why then did you step in here and injure my happiness!"

"I love Fanny best now," said Troy. "But Bathsh – Miss Everdene inflamed me, and displaced Fanny for a time. It is over now."

"Why should it be over so soon? And why then did you come here again?"

"There are weighty reasons. Fifty pounds at once, you said?"

"I did," said Boldwood, "and here they are – fifty sovereigns." He handed Troy a small packet.

"You have everything ready – it seems that you calculated on my accepting them," said the sergeant, taking the packet.

"I thought you might accept them," said Boldwood.

"You've only my word that the programme shall be adhered to, whilst I at any rate have fifty pounds."

"I had thought of that, and I have considered that if I can't appeal to your honour I can trust to your – well, shrewdness we'll call it – not to lose five hundred pounds in prospect and also make a bitter enemy of a man who is willing to be an extremely useful friend."

"Stop – listen!" said Troy in a whisper.

A light pit-pat was audible upon the road just above them.

"By George – 'tis she;" he continued. "I must go on and meet her."

"She – who?"

"Bathsheba."

"Bathsheba – out alone at this time o'night?" said Boldwood in amazement, and starting up. "Why must you meet her?"

"She was expecting me to-night – and I must now speak to her, and wish her good-bye, according to your wish."

"I don't see the necessity of speaking."

"It can do no harm – and she'll be wandering about looking for me if I don't. You shall hear all I say to her. It will help you in your love making when I am gone."

"Your tone is mocking."

"O no. And remember this, if she does not know what has become of me she will think more about me than if I tell her flatly I have come to give her up."

"Will you confine your words – shall I hear every word you say?"

"Every word. Now sit still there, and hold my carpet-bag for me, and mark what you hear."

The light foot-step came closer, halting occasionally, as if the walker listened for a sound. Troy whistled a double note in a soft fluty tone.

"Come to that, is it!" murmured Boldwood uneasily.

"You promised silence," said Troy.

"I promise again."

Troy stepped forward.

"Frank, dearest, is that you?" The tones were Bathsheba's.

"O God!" said Boldwood.

"Yes," said Troy to her.

"How late you are," she continued tenderly. "Did you come by the carrier? I listened and heard his wheels entering the village, but it was some time ago, and I had almost given you up Frank."

"I was sure to come," said Troy. "You knew I should, did you not?"

"Well I thought you would," she said, playfully. "And, Frank, it is so lucky. There's not a soul in my house but me to-night – I've packed them all off, so nobody on earth will know of your visit to your lady's bower. Liddy wanted to go to her grandfather's to tell him about her holiday and I said she might stay with them till to-morrow."

"Capital," said Troy. "But, dear me – I had better go back for my bag – you run home whilst I fetch it – and I'll promise to be in your parlour in ten minutes."

"Yes." She turned and tripped up the hill again.

During the progress of this dialogue there was a nervous twitching of Boldwood's lightly closed lips, and his face became bathed in a clammy dew. He now started forward beside Troy. Troy turned to him and took up the bag.

"Shall I tell her I have come to give her up and cannot marry her?" said the soldier, mockingly.

"No – no – wait a minute – I want to say more to you – more to you," said Boldwood in a hoarse whisper.

"Now," said Troy, "you see my dilemma. Perhaps I am a bad man – the victim of my impulses – led away to do what I ought to leave undone.

I can't, however, marry them both. And I have two reasons for choosing Fanny. First I like her best upon the whole, and second you make it worth my while – "

At the same instant Boldwood sprang upon him, and held him by the neck. Troy felt Boldwood's grasp slowly tightening. The move was absolutely unexpected.

"A moment," he gasped. "You are injuring her you love."

"Well, what do you mean?" said the farmer.

"Give me breath," said Troy.

Boldwood loosened his hand saying, "By Heaven, I've a mind to kill you!"

"And ruin her."

"Save her."

"Oh – how can she be saved now unless I marry her?"

Boldwood groaned. He reluctantly released the soldier and flung him back against the hedge. "Devil – you torture me!" said he.

Troy rebounded like a ball, and was about to make a dash at the farmer. But he checked himself, saying lightly,

"It is not worth while to measure my strength with you. It is a barbarous way of settling a quarrel, – indeed, I shall shortly leave the army because of the same conviction. Now after that revelation of how the land lies, 'twould be a mistake to kill me, would it not?"

"'Twould be a mistake to kill you," repeated Boldwood mechanically, with a bowed head.

"Better kill yourself."

"Far better."

"I'm glad you see it."

"Troy – make her your wife, and don't act upon what I arranged just now. The alternative is dreadful, but take Bathsheba – I give her up. She must love you indeed to sell soul and body to you so utterly as she has done. Wretched woman – deluded woman you are Bathsheba!"

"But about Fanny?"

"Bathsheba is a woman well to do," continued Boldwood in nervous anxiety, "and Troy, she will make a good wife, and indeed, she is worth your hastening on your marriage with her!"

"But she has a will – not to say a temper, and I shall be a mere slave to her. I could do anything with poor Fanny Robbin."

"Troy," said Boldwood imploringly, "I'll do anything for you, only don't desert her – pray don't desert her, Troy."

"Which, poor Fanny?"

"No – Bathsheba Everdene. Love her best! Love her tenderly! How shall I get you to see how advantageous it will be to you to secure her at once."

"I don't wish to secure her in any new way."

Boldwood's arm moved spasmodically towards Troy's person again. He repressed the instinct, and his form drooped as with pain. Troy went on.

"I shall soon purchase my discharge, and then –"

"But I wish you to hasten on this marriage. It will be better for you both – you love each other – and you must let me help you to do it."

"How."

"Why by giving you something more to enable you to marry at once; and I'll settle the five hundred on Bathsheba – no, she wouldn't have it of me: I'll pay it down to you on the wedding day."

"Very well. I agree: I'll marry her and not Fanny. And am I to have the something more now?"[5]

"Yes – if you wish to. But I have not much additional money with me – I did not expect this – but all I have is yours."

Boldwood, more like a somnambulist than a wakeful man pulled out the large canvas bag he carried by way of purse, and searched it.

"I have eleven pounds[6] more with me," he said. "Two notes and a sovereign. But before I leave you I must have a paper signed –"

"Pay me the money, and we'll go straight to her parlour, and make any arrangement you please to secure my compliance with your wishes. But she must know nothing of that fifty-pound business."

"Nothing – nothing," said Boldwood hastily. "Here is the sum – and if you'll come to my house we'll write out the agreement for the remainder, and the terms also."

"First we'll call upon her."

"But why? Come with me to-night, and go with me to-morrow to the surrogate's."

"But she must be consulted – at any rate, informed."

"Very well – go on."

They went up the hill to Bathsheba's house. When they stood at the door Troy said, "Wait here a moment." Opening the door, he glided inside, leaving the door ajar.

Boldwood waited. In two minutes a light appeared in the passage. Boldwood then saw that the chain had been fastened across the door. Troy appeared inside, carrying a bedroom candlestick.

"What, did you think I should break in?" said Boldwood contemptuously.

"O no – it is merely my humour to secure things. Will you read this a moment? I'll hold the light."

Troy handed a folded newspaper through the slit between door and doorpost, and put the candle close. "That's the paragraph," he said, placing his finger on a line.

Boldwood looked and read:

"Marriages"

"On the 17th inst., at St Ambrose's Church, Bath, by the Rev. G. Mincing, B.A., Francis Troy, only son of the late Edward Troy Esq. M.D. of Weatherbury, and Sergeant 11th Dragoon Guards, to Bathsheba, only surviving daughter of the late Mr John Everdene,[7] of Casterbridge."

"This may be called Fort meeting Feeble[8] – hey, Boldwood?" said Troy. A low gurgle of derisive laughter followed the words.

The paper fell from Boldwood's hand. Troy continued:

"Fifty pounds to marry Fanny. Good. Eleven pounds not to marry Fanny, but Bathsheba. Good. Finale: already Bathsheba's husband. Now Boldwood, yours is the ridiculous fate which always attends interference between a man and his wife. And another word. Bad as I am, I am not such a villain as to make the marriage or misery of any woman a matter of huckster and sale. Fanny has long ago left me. I don't know where she is – I have searched everywhere. Another word yet. You say you love Bathsheba. Yet on the merest apparent evidence you instantly believe in her dishonour. A fig for such love. Now that I've taught you a lesson, take your money back again."

"I will not – I will not!" said Boldwood in a hiss.

"Anyhow I won't have it," said Troy contemptuously. He wrapped the packet of gold in the notes, and threw the whole into the road.

Boldwood shook his clenched fist at him. "You juggler of Satan! You black hound! – But I'll punish you yet – mark me – I'll punish you yet!"

Another peal of laughter. Troy then closed the door, and locked himself in.

Throughout the whole of that night Boldwood's dark form might have been seen walking about the hills and downs of Weatherbury like an unhappy Shade in the Mournful Fields by Acheron.[9]

CHAPTER XXXIV

At an upper window.

It was very early the next morning – a time of sun and dew. The confused beginnings of many birds' songs spread into the healthy air, and the wan blue of the heaven was here and there coated with thin webs of incorporeal cloud which were of no effect in obscuring day. All the lights in the scene were yellow as to colour, and all the shadows were attenuated as to form. The creeping plants about the old manor-house were bowed with rows of heavy water-drops, which had upon objects behind them the effect of minute lenses of high magnifying power.

Just before the clock struck five Gabriel Oak and Coggan passed the village cross, and went on together to the fields. They were yet barely in view of their mistress's house when Oak fancied he saw the opening of a casement in one of the upper windows. The two men were at this moment partially screened by an elder bush, now beginning to be enriched with black bunches of fruit, and they paused before emerging from its shade.

A handsome man leaned idly from the lattice. He looked east and then west, in the manner of one who makes a first morning survey. The man was Sergeant Troy. His red coat was loosely thrown on but not buttoned, and he had altogether the unbent look of a soldier taking his ease.

Coggan spoke first, looking quietly at the window.

"She has married him!" he said.

Gabriel had previously looked, and he now stood with his back turned, making no reply.

"I fancied we should know something to-day," continued Coggan. "I heard wheels pass my door just after dark – you were out somewhere." He glanced round upon Gabriel. "Good Heavens above us, Oak, how white your face is; you look like a corpse!"

"Do I?" said Oak, with a faint smile.

"Lean on the gate: I'll wait a bit."

"All right, all right."

They stood by the gate awhile, Gabriel listlessly looking on the ground. His mind sped into the future, and saw there enacted in years of leisure the scenes of repentance that would ensue from this work of haste. That they were married he had instantly decided. Why had it been so mysteriously managed? It was not at all Bathsheba's way of doing things. With all her faults she was candour itself. Could she have been entrapped? The union was not only an unutterable grief to him: it amazed him notwithstanding that he had passed the preceding week in a suspicion that such might be the issue of Troy's meeting her away from home. Her quiet return with Liddy had to some extent dispersed the dread. Just as that imperceptible motion which appears like stillness is infinitely divided in its properties from stillness itself, so had struggling hopes against the imagined deed differentiated it entirely from the thing done.

In a few minutes they moved on again towards the house. The sergeant still looked from the window.

"Morning, comrades!" he shouted in a cheery voice when they came up.

Coggan replied to the greeting. "Baint ye going to answer the man?" he then said to Gabriel. "I'd say Good morning – you needn't spend a hapeth of meaning upon it, and yet keep the man civil."

Gabriel soon decided too that, since the deed was done, to put the best face upon the matter would be the greatest kindness to her he loved.

"Good morning Sergeant Troy," he returned in a ghastly voice.

"A rambling roomy house this," said Troy smiling.

"Why – they *may* not be married!" suggested Coggan. "Perhaps she's not there."

Gabriel shook his head. The soldier turned a little towards the east, and the sun kindled his scarlet coat to an orange glow.

"But it is a nice old house," responded Gabriel.

"Well – I suppose so; but I feel like new wine in an old bottle[1] here. My notion is that sash-windows should be put throughout, and these old wainscoted walls brightened up a bit, or the oak cleared quite away, and the walls papered."

"It would be a pity I think."

"Well, no. A philosopher once said in my hearing that the old builders who worked when art was a living thing had no respect for the work of builders who went before them, but pulled down and altered as they thought fit, and why shouldn't we? 'Creation and preservation don't do well together,' says he, 'and a million of antiquarians can't invent a style.' My mind exactly. I am for making this place more modern that we may be cheerful whilst we can."

The military man turned and surveyed the interior of the room, to assist his ideas of improvement in this direction. Gabriel and Coggan began to move on.[2]

"I shall be down in the fields with you some time this week; but I have a few matters to attend to first. So good day to you. We shall of course keep on just as friendly terms as usual. I'm not a proud man: Nobody is ever able to say that of Sergeant Troy. However, what is must be, and here's half-a-crown to drink my health, men."

Troy threw the coin dexterously across the front plot towards Gabriel, who shunned it in its fall, his face turning to an angry red. Coggan twirled his eye, edged forward, and caught the money in its ricochet upon the grass.

"Very well – you keep it Coggan," said Gabriel with disdain and almost fiercely. "As for me, I'll do without gifts from him."

"Don't show it too much," said Coggan musingly. "For if he's married to her, mark my words, he'll buy his discharge and be our master here. Therefore 'tis well to say 'Friend' outwardly though you say 'Enemy' within."

"Well – perhaps it is best to be silent; but I can't go further than that. I can't flatter, and if my place here is only to be kept by smoothing him down, my place must be lost."

A horseman, whom they had for some time seen in the distance, now appeared close beside them.

"There's Mr Boldwood," said Oak.

Coggan and Oak nodded respectfully to the farmer, just checked their paces to discover if they were wanted, and finding they were not stood back to let him pass on.

The only signs of the terrible sorrow Boldwood had been combating through the night and was combating now were the colourlessness of his well defined face, the enlarged appearance of the veins in his forehead and temples, and the sharper lines about his mouth. The horse bore him away, and the very step of the animal seemed significant of dogged despair. Gabriel, for a minute, rose above his own grief in noticing Boldwood's. He saw the square figure sitting erect upon the horse, the head turned to neither side, the elbows steady by the hips, the brim of the hat level and undisturbed in its onward glide, until the keen edges of Boldwood's figure sank by degrees over the hill. To one who knew the man and his story there was something more striking in this immobility than in a collapse. The clash of discord between mood and matter here was forced painfully home to the heart; and, as in laughter there are more dreadful phases than in tears, so was there in the steadiness of this troubled man an expression deeper than a cry.

CHAPTER XXXV

Wealth in jeopardy: The revel.

One night at the end of August when Bathsheba's experiences as a married woman were still new, and when the weather was yet dry and sultry, a man stood motionless in the stackyard of Weatherbury Upper Farm, looking at the moon and sky.

The night had a sinister aspect. A heated breeze from the south slowly fanned the summits of lofty objects, and in the sky, dashes of buoyant cloud were sailing in a course at right angles to that of another stratum, neither of them in the direction of the breeze below. The moon as seen through these films had a lurid metallic look. The fields were sallow with the impure light, and all were tinged in monochrome, as if beheld through stained glass. That same evening the sheep had trailed homeward head to tail, the behaviour of the rooks had been confused, and the horses had moved with timidity and caution.

Thunder was imminent, and taking some secondary appearances into consideration, it was likely to be followed by one of the lengthened rains which mark the close of dry weather for the season. Before twelve hours had passed, a harvest atmosphere would be a bygone thing.

Oak gazed with misgiving at eight naked and unprotected ricks, massive and heavy with the rich produce of one half the farm for that year. He went on to the barn.

This was the night which had been selected by Sergeant Troy – ruling now in the room of his wife – for giving the harvest-supper and dance. As Oak approached the building the sound of violins and a tambourine, and the regular jigging of many feet, grew more distinct. He came close to the large doors, one of which stood slightly ajar, and looked in.

The central space, together with the whole of one end, was emptied of all encumbrances, and this area, covering about two-thirds of the whole, was appropriated for the gathering, the remaining end, which was piled to the ceiling with oats, being screened off with sail-cloth. Tufts and garlands of green foliage decorated the walls, beams, and extemporized chandeliers, and immediately opposite to Oak a rostrum had been erected, bearing a table and chairs. Here sat three fiddlers, and beside them stood a frantic man with his hair on end, perspiration streaming down his cheeks, and a tambourine quivering in his hand.

The dance ended, and on the black oak floor in the midst a new row of couples immediately formed for another.

"Now ma'am, and no offence I hope, I ask what dance you would like next?" said the first violin.

"Really, it makes no difference," said the clear female voice of Bathsheba, who stood at the inner end of the building observing the scene, behind a table covered with cups and viands. Troy was lolling beside her.

"Then," said the fiddler, "I'll venture to name that the right and proper thing is 'The Soldier's Joy'[1] – there being a gallant soldier married into the farm – hey, my sonnies, and gentlemen all?"

"It shall be 'The Soldier's Joy'," exclaimed a chorus.

"Thanks for the compliment," said the sergeant gaily, taking Bathsheba by the hand and leading her to the top of the dance. "For though I have purchased my discharge from Her Most Gracious Majesty's regiment of Cavalry, the 11th Dragoon Guards, to attend to the new duties awaiting me here, I shall continue a soldier in spirit and feeling as long as I live."

Now as to the merits of 'The Soldier's Joy' there cannot be, and never were, two opinions. It has been observed in the musical circles of

Weatherbury and its vicinity that the 'Soldier's Joy,' at the end of three quarters of an hour of thunderous footing, still possesses more stimulative properties for the heel and toe than the majority of other dances at the first opening. 'The Soldier's Joy' has too an additional charm in being so admirably adapted to the tambourine – in itself no mean instrument in the hands of a performer who understands the proper convulsions, spasms, St Vitus's dances and fearful frenzies necessary in exhibiting the tones of that instrument in their highest perfection.

The immortal tune ended, a final DD rolling forth from the bass-viol with the sonorousness of thunder itself. Gabriel delayed his entry no longer. He avoided Bathsheba, and got as near as possible to the platform, where Sergeant Troy was now seated, drinking brandy and water, though the others drank without exception cider and ale. Gabriel could not easily thrust himself within speaking distance of the sergeant, and he sent a message asking him to come down for a moment. The sergeant said he could not attend.

"Will you tell him then," said Gabriel, "that I only came to say that a heavy rain is sure to fall soon, and that something should be done to protect the ricks?"

"Mr Troy says it will not rain," returned the messenger, "and he cannot stop to talk to you about such fidgets."

In juxtaposition with Troy, Oak had a melancholy tendency to look like a candle beside gas, and ill at ease he went out again, thinking he would go home; for, under the circumstances, he had no heart for the scene in the barn. At the door he paused for a moment: Troy was speaking.

"Friends it is not only the Harvest Home that we are celebrating to-night; but this is also a Wedding Feast. A short time ago I had the happiness to lead to the altar this lady your mistress, and not until now have we been able to give any public flourish to the event in Weatherbury. That it may be thoroughly well done and that every man may go happy to bed, I have ordered to be brought here some bottles of brandy and kettles of hot-water. A treble-strong goblet will be handed round to each guest."

Bathsheba put her hand on his arm and with upturned pale face said imploringly, "No – don't give it to them – pray don't Frank. It will only do them harm: they have had enough of everything."

"Trew – we don't wish for no more, thank ye," said one or two.

"Pooh!" said the sergeant contemptuously, and raised his voice as if lighted up by a new idea. "Friends," he said, "we'll send the women-folk home! 'Tis time they were in bed. Then we cockbirds will have a jolly carouse to ourselves. If any of the men show the white feather, let them look elsewhere for a winter's work."

Bathsheba indignantly left the barn, followed by all the women and children. The musicians, not looking upon themselves as "company", slipped quietly away to their spring waggon and put in the horse. Thus Troy and the men on the farm were left sole occupants of the place. Oak, not to appear unnecessarily disagreeable stayed a little while; then he, too, arose and quietly took his departure, followed by a friendly oath from the sergeant for not staying to a second round of grog.

Gabriel proceeded towards his house. In approaching the door his toe kicked something which felt and sounded soft, leathery, and distended, like a small boxing-glove. It was a large toad humbly travelling across the path. Oak took it up thinking it might be better to kill it to save it from pain, but finding it uninjured he placed it again among the grass. He knew what this direct message from the Great Mother meant. And soon came another.

When he struck a light indoors there gleamed across the table a thin glistening streak, as if a brush of varnish had been lightly dragged across it. Oak's eyes followed the serpentine sheen to the other side, where it led up to a huge brown garden slug, which had come indoors to-night for reasons of its own. It was Nature's second way of hinting to him that he was to prepare for foul weather.

Oak sat down meditating for nearly an hour. During this time two or three black spiders, of the kind common in thatched houses, promenaded the ceiling, ultimately dropping to the floor. This reminded him that if there was one class of manifestation on this matter that he thoroughly understood, it was the instincts of sheep. He left the room, ran across two or three fields towards the flock, got upon a hedge, and looked over upon them.

They were crowded close together on the other side around some furze bushes, and the first peculiarity observable was that on the sudden appearance of Oak's head over the fence they did not stir or run away. They had now a terror of something greater than their terror of man. But this was not the most noticeable feature: they were all grouped in such a way that their tails, without a single exception, were towards that half of the horizon from which the storm threatened. There was an inner circle closely huddled, and outside these they radiated wider apart, the pattern formed by the flock as a whole being not unlike a vandyked lace collar to which the clump of furze bushes stood in the position of a wearer's neck.

This was enough to re-establish him in his original opinion. He knew now that he was right and that Troy was wrong. Every voice in nature was unanimous in bespeaking change. But two distinct translations attached to these dumb expressions. Apparently there was to be a thunderstorm, and afterwards a cold continuous rain. The creeping things seemed to know all about the latter rain, but little of the interpolated thunderstorm; whilst the sheep knew all about the thunderstorm and nothing of the latter rain.

This complication of weathers being uncommon, was all the more to be feared. Oak returned to the stack-yard. All was silent here, and the conical tips of the ricks jutted darkly into the sky. There were five wheat ricks in this yard, and three stacks of barley. The wheat when threshed would average about thirty quarters to each stack, the barley at least forty. Their value to Bathsheba, and indeed to anybody, Oak mentally estimated by the following simple calculation:

$$
\begin{aligned}
5 \times 30 = 150 \text{ quarters} &= 500£ \\
3 \times 40 = 120 \text{ quarters} &= \underline{250£} \\
\text{Total } &\underline{750£}
\end{aligned}
$$

Seven hundred and fifty pounds in the divinest form that money can wear – that of necessary food for man and beast – should the risk be run of deteriorating this bulk of corn to less than half its value because of the instability of a woman? "Never if I can prevent it!" said Gabriel.

Such was the argument that Oak set outwardly before him. But man, even to himself, is a cryptographic page[2] having an ostensible writing, and another between the lines. It is possible that there was this golden legend under the utilitarian one: "I will help to my last breath the woman I have loved so dearly."

He went back to the barn to endeavour to obtain assistance for covering the ricks that very night. All was silent within, and he would have passed on in the belief that the party had broken up had not a dim light, yellow as saffron by contrast with the greenish whiteness outside, streamed through a knot hole in the folding doors.

Gabriel looked in. An offensive picture met his eye.

The candles suspended among the evergreens had burnt down to their sockets, and in some cases the leaves tied about them were scorched. Many of the lights were quite gone out, others smoked and stank, grease dropping from them upon the floor. Here, under the table, and leaning against forms and chairs in every conceivable attitude except the perpendicular, were the wretched persons of all the labourers, the hair of their heads at such low levels being suggestive of mops and brooms. In the midst of them shone red and distinct the figure of Sergeant Troy, leaning back in a chair. Coggan was on his back with his mouth open, buzzing forth snores, as were several others, the united breathings of the horizontal assemblage forming a subdued roar like London from a distance. Joseph Poorgrass was curled round in the fashion of a hedgehog, apparently in attempts to present the least possible portion of his surface to the air; and behind him was dimly visible an unimportant remnant of William Smallbury. The glasses and cups still stood upon the table, a water-jug being overturned, from which a small rill, after tracking its course with marvellous precision down the centre of the long table, fell into the neck of the unconscious Mark Clark in a steady monotonous drip, like the dripping of a stalactite in a cave.

Gabriel glanced hopelessly at the group, which with one or two exceptions composed all the able-bodied men upon the farm. He saw at once that if the ricks were to be saved that night, or even the next morning, he must save them with his own hands.

A faint "ting-ting" resounded from under Coggan's waistcoat. It was Coggan's watch striking the hour of two.

Oak went to the recumbent form of Matthew Moon, who usually undertook the rough thatching of the homestead, and shook him. The shaking was without effect.

Gabriel shouted in his ear, "Where's your thatching beetle, and rick-stick, and spars?"[3]

"Under the staddles," said Moon mechanically, with the unconscious promptness of a medium.

Gabriel let go his head, and it dropped upon the floor like a bowl. He then went to Susan Tall's husband.

"Where's the key of the granary?"

No answer. The question was repeated, with the same result. To be shouted to at night was evidently less of a novelty to Susan Tall's husband than to Matthew Moon. Oak flung down Tall's head into the corner again, and turned away.

To be just, the men were not greatly to blame for this painful and demoralizing termination to the evening's entertainment. Sergeant Troy had so strenuously insisted, glass in hand, that drinking should be the bond of their union, that those who wished to refuse hardly liked to be so unmannerly under the circumstances. Having from their youth up been entirely unaccustomed to any liquor stronger than cider or mild ale, it was no wonder that they had succumbed one and all with extraordinary uniformity after the lapse of about an hour.

Gabriel was greatly depressed. This debauch boded ill for that wilful and fascinating mistress whom the faithful man even now felt within him as the εἴδωλον[4] of all that was sweet and bright and hopeless.

He put out the expiring lights, that the barn might not be endangered, closed the door upon the men in their deep and oblivious sleep, and went again into the lone night. A hot breeze, as if breathed from the parted lips of some dragon about to swallow the globe, fanned him from the south while directly opposite, in the north, hung a body of cloud.[5]

Going on to the village Oak flung a small stone against the window of Laban Tall's bedroom, expecting Susan to open it; but nobody stirred. He went round to the back door which had been left unfastened for Laban's entry, and passed in to the foot of the staircase.

"Mrs Tall, I've come for the key of the granary, to get at the rick-cloths," said Oak in a stentorian voice.

"Is that you?" said Mrs Susan Tall, half awake.

"Yes," said Gabriel.

"Come along to bed do, you drawlatching rogue – keeping a body awake like this!"

"It isn't Laban – 'tis Gabriel Oak. I want the key of the granary."

"Gabriel! What in the name of fortune did you pretend to be Laban for?"

"I didn't. I thought you meant – "

"Yes you did. What do you want here?"

"The key of the granary."

"Take it then. 'Tis on the nail. People coming disturbing virtuous women at this time of night ought...."[6]

Gabriel took the key without waiting to hear the conclusion of the address. Ten minutes later his lonely figure might have been seen dragging four large water-proof coverings across the rick-yard, and soon two of these heaps of treasure in grain were covered snug – two cloths to each. Two hundred pounds were secured. Three wheat stacks remained open, and there were no more cloths. Oak looked under the staddles and found a fork. He mounted the third pile of wealth and began operating, adopting the plan of sloping the upper sheaves one over the other, and, in addition, filling the interstices with the material of some untied sheaves.

So far all was well. By this hurried contrivance Bathsheba's property in wheat was safe for at any rate a week or two, provided always that there was not much wind.

Next came the barley. This it was only possible to protect by systematic thatching. Time went on and the moon vanished not to re-appear. The night had a haggard look like a sick thing, and there came finally an utter expiration of air from the whole heaven in the form of a slow breeze, which might have been likened to a death. And now nothing was heard in the yard but the dull thuds of the beetle which drove in the spars, and the rustle of the thatch in the intervals.

CHAPTER XXXVI
The storm: the two together.

A light flapped over the scene, as if reflected from phosphorescent wings crossing the sky, and a rumble filled the air. It was the first arrow from the approaching storm, and it fell wide.

The second peal was noisy, with comparatively little visible lightning. Gabriel saw a candle shine in Bathsheba's bedroom, and soon a shadow moved to and fro upon the blind.

Then came a third flash. Manoeuvres of a most extraordinary kind were going on in the vast firmamental hollows overhead. The lightning now was the colour of silver, and gleamed in the heavens like a mailed army. Rumbles became rattles. Gabriel from his elevated position could see over the landscape for at least half-a-dozen miles in front. Every hedge, bush, and tree, was distinct as in a line engraving. In a paddock in the same direction was a herd of heifers, and the forms of these were visible at this moment in the act of galloping about in the wildest maddest confusion, flinging their heels and tails high into the air, their heads to earth. A poplar in the immediate foreground was like an ink stroke on burnished tin. Then the picture vanished, leaving a darkness so intense that Gabriel worked entirely by feeling with his hands.

He had stuck his ricking rod, groom, or poignard as it is sometimes called – a long iron lance, sharp at the extremity and polished by handling – into the stack to support the sheaves. A blue light appeared in the zenith and in some indescribable manner flickered down near the top of the rod. It was the fourth of the larger flashes. A moment later and there was a smack, smart, clear, and short. Gabriel felt his position anything but a safe one and he resolved to descend.

Not a drop of rain had fallen as yet. He wiped his weary brow, and looked again at the black forms of the unprotected stacks. Was his life so valuable to him, after all? What were his prospects that he should be so chary of running risk when important and urgent labour could not be carried on without such risk? He resolved to stick to the stack. However, he took a precaution. Under the staddles was a long tethering chain used to prevent the escape of errant horses. This he carried up the ladder, and sticking his rod through the clog at one end allowed the other end of the chain to trail upon the ground. The spike attached to this he drove in. Under the shadow of this extemporized lightning-conductor he felt himself comparatively safe.

Before he had laid his hands upon his tools again out leapt the fifth flash, with the spring of a serpent and the shout of a fiend. It was green as an emerald, and the reverberation was stunning. What was this the light revealed to him? In the open ground before him, as he looked over the ridge of the rick, was a dark and apparently female form. Could it be that of the only venturesome woman in the parish – Bathsheba? The form moved on a step: then he could see no more.

"Is that you ma'am?" said Gabriel to the darkness.

"Who is there?" said the voice of Bathsheba.

"Gabriel. I am on the rick, thatching."

"O Gabriel, and are you! I have come about them. The weather awoke me and I thought of the corn. I am so distressed about it – can we save it anyhow? I cannot find my husband. Is he with you?"

"He is not here."

"Do you know where he is?"

"Asleep in the barn."

"He promised that the stacks should be seen to, and now they are all neglected. Can I do anything to help? Liddy is afraid to come out. Fancy finding you here at such an hour! Surely I can do something?"

"You can bring up some reed-sheaves to me, one by one, ma'am, if you are not afraid to come up the ladder in the dark," said Gabriel. "Every moment is precious now, and that would save a good deal of time. It is not very dark when the lightning has been gone a bit."

"I'll do anything!" she said resolutely. She instantly took a reed-sheaf upon her shoulder, clambered up close to his heels, placed it behind the rod, and descended for another. At her third ascent the rick suddenly brightened like burnished silver – every knot in every straw was visible. On the slope in front of him appeared two human shapes, black as jet. The rick lost its sheen – the shapes vanished. Gabriel turned his head. It had been the sixth flash, which had come from the east behind him, and the two dark forms on the slope had been the shadows of himself and Bathsheba.

Then came the peal. It was hardly credible that such a heavenly light could be the parent of such a Stygian[1] sound.

"How terrible!" she exclaimed, and clutched him by the sleeve. Gabriel turned and steadied her on her aerial perch by holding her arm. At the same moment, while he was still reversed in his attitude, there was more light, and he saw as it were a copy of the tall poplar tree on the hill drawn in black on the wall of the barn. It was the shadow of that tree, thrown across by a secondary flash in the west.

The next flare came. Bathsheba was on the ground now, shouldering another sheaf, and she bore its dazzle without flinching, thunder and all, and again ascended with the load. There was then a silence everywhere for four or five minutes, and the crunch of the spars as Gabriel hastily drove them in could be again distinctly heard. He thought the crisis of the storm had passed. But there came a burst of light.

"Hold on!" said Gabriel, taking the sheaf from her shoulder and grasping her arm again.

Heaven opened then indeed. The flash was almost too novel for its inexpressibly dangerous nature to be at once realised, and Gabriel could only comprehend the magnificence of its beauty. It sprang from east, west, north, south. It was a perfect dance of death. The forms of skeletons appeared in the air, shaped with blue fire for bones – dancing, leaping, striding, racing around, and mingling altogether in unparalleled confusion. With these were intertwined undulating snakes of green. Behind these was a broad mass of lesser light. Simultaneously came from every part of the tumbling sky what may be called a shout, since, though no shout ever came near it, it was more of the nature of a shout than of anything else earthly. In the meantime one of the grisly forms had alighted upon the point of Gabriel's rod, to run invisibly down it, down the chain, and into the earth. Gabriel was almost blinded, and he could feel Bathsheba's warm arm tremble in his hand – a sensation novel and thrilling enough; but love, life, everything human, seemed small and trifling in such close juxtaposition with an infuriated universe.

Oak had hardly time to gather up these impressions into a thought, and to see how strangely the red feather of her hat shone in this light when the tall tree on the hill before-mentioned seemed on fire to a white heat, and a new one among these terrible voices mingled with the last crash of those preceding. It was a smack, harsh and pitiless, and it fell upon their ears in a dead, flat blow, without that reverberation which lends the tones of a drum to more distant thunder. By the lustre reflected from every part of the earth and the wide domical scoop above it, he saw that the tree was sliced down the whole length of its tall straight stem, a huge riband of bark being apparently flung off. The other portion remained erect, and revealed the bared surface as a strip of white down the front. The lightning had struck the tree. A sulphurous smell filled the air: then all was silent, and black as a cave in Hinnom.[2]

"We had a narrow escape," said Gabriel hurriedly. "You had better go down."

Bathsheba said nothing; but he could distinctly hear her rhythmical pants, and the recurrent rustle of the sheaf beside her in response to her frightened pulsation. She descended the ladder, and, on second thoughts he followed her. The darkness was now impenetrable by the sharpest vision. They both stood still at the bottom, side by side. Bathsheba appeared to think only of the weather: Oak thought only of her just then. At last he said,

"The storm seems to have passed."

"I think so too," said Bathsheba. "Though there are multitudes of gleams, look." The sky was now filled with an incessant light, frequent repetition melting into complete continuity as an unbroken sound results from the successive strokes on a gong.

"Nothing serious," said he. "I cannot understand no rain falling. But Heaven be praised, it is all the better for us. I am now going up again."

"Gabriel, you are kinder than I deserve! I will stay and help you yet. O why are not some of the others here!"

"They would have been here if they could," said Oak in a hesitating way.

"O I know it all – all," she said, adding slowly: "They are all asleep in the barn, in a drunken sleep, and my husband among them. That's it, is it not? Don't think I am a timid woman, and can't endure things."

"I am not certain," said Gabriel. "I will go and see."

He crossed to the barn, leaving her there alone. He looked through the chink of the door. All was in total darkness, as he had left it, and there still arose, as at the former time, the steady buzz of many snores.

He felt a zephyr curling about his cheek, and turned. It was Bathsheba's breath: she had followed him, and was looking into the same chink.

He endeavoured to put off the immediate and painful subject of their thoughts by remarking gently, "If you'll come back again, Miss – ma'am, and hand up a few more, it would save much time."

Then Oak went back again, ascended to the top, stepped off the ladder, and went on thatching. She followed, but without a sheaf.

"Gabriel," she said, in a strange and impressive voice.

Oak looked up at her. She had not spoken since he left the barn. The soft and continual shimmer of the dying lightning showed a marble face against the black sky of the opposite quarter. Bathsheba was sitting almost on the apex of the stack, her feet gathered up beneath her, and resting on the top round of the ladder.

"Yes, mistress," he said.

"I suppose you thought that when I galloped away to Bath that night it was on purpose to be married?"

"I did at last – not at first," he answered, somewhat surprised at the abruptness with which this came from her.

"And others thought so too."

"Yes."

"And you blamed me for wantonness?"[3]

"Well – a little."

"I thought so. Now I care a little for your good opinion, and I want to explain something – I have longed to do it ever since I returned, and you looked so gravely at me. For if I were to die – and I may die soon – it would be dreadful that you should always think mistakenly of me. Now listen."

Gabriel ceased his rustling.

"I went to Bath that night in the full intention of breaking off my engagement to Mr Troy. It was owing to circumstances which occurred after I got there that – that we were married. Now do you see the matter in a new light?"

"I do – somewhat."

"I must, I suppose, say more now that I have begun. – And perhaps it's no harm, for you are certainly under no delusion that I ever loved you, or that I can have any object in speaking, more than that object I have mentioned. Well, I was alone in a strange city, and the horse was lame. . . . And at last I didn't know what to do. I saw when it was too late that scandal might seize hold of me for meeting him alone in that way. But I was coming away, when he suddenly said he had that day seen a woman more beautiful than I, and that his constancy could not be counted on unless I at once became his. . . . . And I was grieved and troubled. . . ." She cleared her voice, and waited a moment as if to gather breath. "And then, between jealousy and distraction, I married him!" she whispered, with desperate impetuosity.

Gabriel made no reply.

"He was not to blame, for it was perfectly true about – about his seeing somebody else," she quickly added. "And now I don't wish for a single remark from you upon the subject: – indeed I forbid it. I only wanted you to know that bit of my history, before a time comes when you could never know it. – You want some more sheaves?"

She went down the ladder, and the work proceeded. Gabriel soon perceived a languor in the movements of his mistress up and down, and he said to her gently as a mother,

"I think you had better go indoors now: you are tired. I can finish the rest alone. If the wind does not change the rain is likely to keep off."

"If I am useless I will go," said Bathsheba in a flagging cadence. "But O if the wheat should be lost!"

"You are not useless; but I would rather not tire you longer. You have done well."

"And you better!" she said gratefully. "Thank you for your devotion a thousand times Gabriel! Good night – I know you are doing your very best for me."

She diminished in the gloom, and vanished, and he heard the latch of the gate fall as she passed through. He worked in a reverie now, musing upon her story, and upon the contradictoriness of that feminine heart which had caused her to speak more warmly to him tonight than she ever had done whilst unmarried and free to speak as warmly as she chose.

He was disturbed in his meditation by a grating noise from the coach-house. It was the vane on the roof turning round, and this change in the wind was the signal for a disastrous rain.

CHAPTER XXXVII

Rain: one solitary meets another.

It was now five o'clock, and the dawn was promising to break in hues of drab and ash.

The air changed its temperature and stirred itself more vigorously. Cool elastic breezes coursed in transparent eddies round Oak's face. The wind shifted yet a point or two and blew stronger. In ten minutes every wind of heaven seemed to be roaming at large. Some of the thatching on the wheat-stacks was now whirled fantastically aloft, and had to be replaced and weighted with some rails that lay near at hand. This done, Oak slaved away again at the barley. A huge drop of rain smote his face, the wind snarled round every corner, and the trees rocked to the bases of their trunks. Driving in spars at any point and on any system inch by inch he covered more and more safely from ruin this distracting impersonation of seven hundred pounds. The rain came on in earnest, and Oak soon felt the water to be tracking cold and clammy routes down his back. Ultimately he was reduced well-nigh to a homogeneous sop, and a decoction of his person trickled down and stood in a pool at the foot of the ladder. The rain stretched obliquely through the drab atmosphere in liquid spines, unbroken in continuity between their beginnings in the clouds and their points in him.

Oak, suddenly remembered that eight months before this time he had been fighting against fire in the same spot as desperately as he was fighting against water now – and for a futile love of the same woman. As for her –. But Oak was generous and true, and dismissed his reflections.

It was about seven o'clock in the dark leaden morning when Gabriel came down from the last stack, and thankfully exclaimed "It is done!" He was drenched, weary, and sad; and yet not so sad as drenched and weary, for he was cheered by a sense of success in a good cause.

Faint sounds came from the barn, and he looked that way. Figures came singly and in pairs through the doors – all walking awkwardly, and abashed, save the foremost who wore a red coat, and advanced with his hands in his pockets, whistling. The others shambled after with a conscience-stricken air, the whole procession was not unlike Flaxman's group of the suitors tottering on towards the infernal regions under the conduct of Mercury.[1] The shapes and their leader passed on into the village Troy entering the farm house. Not a single one of them had turned his face to the ricks, or apparently bestowed one thought upon their condition. Soon Oak too went homeward, by a different route from theirs. In front of him, against the wet glazed surface of the lane he saw a gentleman walking yet more slowly than himself under an umbrella. The man turned and apparently started: he was Boldwood.

"How are you this morning Sir?" said Oak.

"Yes, it is a wet day. – O I am well, very well I thank you: quite well."

"I am glad to hear it Sir."

Boldwood seemed to awake by degrees. "You look tired and ill, Oak," he said desultorily.

"I am tired. You look strangely altered Sir."

"I? Not a bit of it: I am well enough. What put that into your head?"

"I thought you didn't look so topping as you used to, that was all."

"Indeed, then, you are mistaken," said Boldwood, shortly. "Nothing hurts me. My constitution is an iron one."

"I've been working hard to get our ricks covered, and was barely in time. Never had such a struggle in my life. . . . Yours of course are safe, Sir?"

"O yes." Boldwood added after an interval of silence, "What did you ask, Oak?"

"Your ricks are all covered before this time."

"No."

"At any rate, the large ones upon the stone staddles?"

"They are not."

"Those under the hedge?"

"No. I forgot to tell the thatcher to set about it."

"Nor the little one by the stile?"

"Nor the little one by the stile. I overlooked the ricks this year."

"Then not a tenth of your corn will come to measure, Sir?"

"Possibly not."

"Overlooked them," repeated Gabriel slowly to himself. It is difficult to describe the intensely dramatic effect that announcement had upon Oak at such a moment. All the night he had been feeling that the neglect he was labouring to repair was abnormal and isolated – the only instance of the kind within the circuit of the county. Yet at this very time, within the same parish, a greater waste had been going on, uncomplained of and disregarded. A few months earlier Boldwood's forgetting his husbandry would have been as preposterous an idea as a sailor forgetting he was in a ship. Oak was just thinking that whatever he himself might have suffered from Bathsheba's marriage, here was a man who had suffered more, when Boldwood spoke, strangely – in the voice of one who yearned to make a confidence and relieve his heart by an outpouring.

"Oak you know as well as I that things have gone wrong with me lately. I may as well own it. I was going to get a little settled in life; but in some way my plan has come to nothing."

"I thought my mistress would have married you," said Gabriel, not knowing enough of the full depth of Boldwood's love to keep silence on the farmer's account, and determined not to evade discipline by doing so on his own. "However it is so sometimes, and nothing happens that we expect," he added with the repose of a man whom misfortune had inured rather than subdued.

"I dare say I am rather a joke about the parish," said Boldwood, as if the subject came irresistibly to his tongue and with a miserable lightness which was meant to express his indifference.

"O no – I don't think that."

"– But the real truth of the matter is that there was not, as some fancy, any jilting on – her part. No engagement ever existed between me and Miss Everdene. People say so, but it is untrue: she never promised me!" Boldwood stood still now and turned his wild face to Oak. "O Gabriel," he continued, "I am weak, and foolish, and I don't know what, and I can't fend off my miserable grief! . . . . God prepared a gourd to shade me, and like the prophet I thanked him and was glad. But the next day he prepared a worm to smite the gourd, and wither it; and I feel it is better to die than to live."[2]

A silence followed. Boldwood aroused himself from the momentary mood of confidence into which he had drifted, and walked on again, resuming his usual reserve.

"No Gabriel," he resumed with a carelessness which was like the smile on the countenance of a skull; "it was made more of by other people than ever it was by us. I do feel a little regret occasionally, but no woman ever had power over me for any length of time. Well, good morning. I can trust you not to mention to others what has passed between us two here."

CHAPTER XXXVIII[1]

Coming home: a cry.

On the turnpike road between Casterbridge and Weatherbury, and about a mile from the latter place, is one of those steep long ascents which pervade the roads of this undulating district.[2] In returning from market it is usual for the farmers and other gig-gentry[3] to alight at the bottom and walk up.

One Saturday evening in the month of October Bathsheba's vehicle was duly creeping up this incline. She was sitting listlessly in the second seat of the gig, whilst walking beside her in a farmer's marketing suit of unusually fashionable cut was an erect well made young man. Though on foot, he held the reins and whip, and occasionally aimed light cuts at the horse's ear with the end of the lash, as a recreation. This man was her husband, formerly Sergeant Troy, who having bought his discharge with Bathsheba's money, was gradually transforming himself into a farmer of a spirited and very modern school. People of unalterable ideas still insisted upon calling him "Sergeant" when they met him, which was in some degree owing to his having still retained the well-shaped moustache of his military days, and the soldierly bearing inseparable from his form.

"Yes, if it hadn't been for that wretched rain I should have cleared two hundred as easy as looking, my love," he was saying. "Don't you see, it altered all the chances? To speak like a book I once read, wet weather is the narrative, and fine days are the episodes, of our country's history – now isn't that true?"

"But the time of year is come for changeable weather."

"Well, yes. The fact is, these Autumn races are the ruin of everybody. Never did I see such a day as 'twas! 'Tis a wild open place, not far from the sands, and a drab sea rolled in towards us like liquid misery. Wind and rain – Good Lord! Dark? Why 'twas as black as my hat before the last race was run. 'Twas five o'clock, and you couldn't see the horses till they were almost in, leave alone colours. The ground was as heavy as lead, and all judgment from a fellow's experience went for nothing. Horses, riders, people, were all blown about like ships at sea. Three booths were blown over, and the wretched folk inside crawled out upon their hands and knees; and in the next field were as many as a dozen hats at one time. Ay, Pimpernel regularly stuck fast when about sixty yards off, and when I saw Policy stepping on, it did knock my heart against the fat of my ribs, I assure you, my love!"

"And you mean, Frank," said Bathsheba, sadly – her voice was painfully lowered from the fulness and vivacity of the previous summer –, "that you have lost more than a hundred pounds in a month by this dreadful horseracing. O Frank – it is cruel – it is foolish of you to take away my money so. We shall have to leave the farm – that will be the end of it!"

"Humbug about cruel. Now there 'tis again – turn on the waterworks – that's just like you."

"But you'll promise me not to go to Budmouth races next week, won't you?" she implored. She was at the full depth for tears, but she kept a dry eye.

"I don't see why I should – in fact, if it turns out to be a fine day I was thinking of taking you."

"Never, never! I'll go a hundred miles the other way first. I hate the very sound of the word!"

"But the question of going to see the race or staying at home has very little to do with the matter. Bets are all booked safely enough before the race begins, you may depend. Whether it is a bad race for me, or a good one, will have very little to do with our going there next Monday."

"But you don't mean to say that you have risked anything on this one, too!" she exclaimed, with an agonised look.

"There now – don't you be a little fool. Wait till you are told. Why Bathsheba, you've lost all the pluck and sauciness you formerly had, and upon my life if I had known what a chicken-hearted creature you were under all your boldness I'd never have – I know what."

A flash of indignation might have been seen in Bathsheba's dark eyes as she looked resolutely ahead after this reply. They moved on without further speech, some early-withered leaves from the beech trees which hooded the road at this spot occasionally spinning downwards across their path to the earth.

A woman appeared on the brow of the hill. The ridge was so abrupt that she was very near the husband and wife before she became visible. Troy had turned himself towards the gig to remount, and whilst putting his foot on the step the woman passed behind him.

Though the overshadowing trees and the approach of eventide enveloped them in gloom, Bathsheba could see plainly enough to discern the extreme poverty of the woman's garb, and the sadness of her face.

"Please Sir, do you know at what time Casterbridge Unionhouse closes at night?" The woman said these words to Troy over his shoulder.

Troy started visibly at the sound of the voice. Yet he seemed to recover presence of mind sufficient to prevent himself from giving way to his impulse to turn suddenly and face her. He said slowly,

"I don't know."

The woman, on hearing him speak, quickly looked up, examined the side of his face, and recognised the soldier under the yeoman's garb. Her face was drawn into an expression which had gladness and agony both among its elements. She uttered a hysterical cry, and fell down.

"O poor thing!" exclaimed Bathsheba, instantly preparing to alight.

"Stay where you are, and attend to the horse!" said Troy, peremptorily, throwing her the reins and the whip. "Walk the horse to the top: I'll see to the woman."

"But I – "

"Do you hear? Clk – Poppet!" The horse, gig, and Bathsheba moved on.

"How on earth did you come here – I thought you were miles away, or dead! – Why didn't you write to me?" said Troy to the woman, in a strangely gentle yet hurried voice, as he lifted her up.

"I feared to."

"Have you any money?"

"None."

"Good God[4] – I wish I had more to give you. Here's – wretched! – only eighteen pence. It's every farthing I have left. I have none but what my wife gives me, you know, and I can't ask her now."

The woman made no answer.

"I have only another moment," continued Troy: "now listen. Where are you going tonight? Casterbridge Union?"

"Yes – I thought to go there."

"You shan't go there – Yet wait. Yes – perhaps for to-night. I can do nothing better for you. Sleep there to-night and stay there to-morrow. Monday is the first free day I have; and on Monday morning at ten exactly meet me on Casterbridge Bridge. I'll bring all the money I can muster – you shan't want – I'll see that Fanny. Then I'll get you a lodging somewhere. Good-bye till then."

After advancing the distance which completed the ascent of the hill, Bathsheba turned her head. The woman was upon her feet, and Bathsheba saw her withdrawing from Troy and going feebly down the hill. Troy then came on towards his wife, stepped into the gig, took the reins from her hand, and without making any observation whipped the horse into a trot. He was rather pale.

"Do you know who that woman was?" said Bathsheba, looking searchingly into his face.

"I do," he said, looking boldly back into hers.

"I thought you did," said she, with angry hauteur, and still regarding him. "Who is she?"

He suddenly seemed to think that frankness would benefit neither of the women.

"Nothing to either of us," he said. "I know her by sight."

"What is her name?"

"How should I know her name?"

"I think you do."

"Think if you will and be. . . ." The sentence was completed by a smart cut of the whip round Poppet's flank, which caused the animal to start forward at a wild pace. No more was said.

CHAPTER XXXIX

On Casterbridge highway.

For a considerable time the woman walked on. Her steps became feebler, and she strained her eyes to look afar upon the naked road, now indistinct in the penumbrae of night. At length her onward walk dwindled to the merest totter, and she opened a gate within which was a haystack. Underneath this she sat down, and presently slept.

When the woman awoke it was to find herself in the depths of a moonless and starless night. A heavy unbroken crust of cloud stretched across the sky, shutting out every speck of heaven; and a distant halo which hung over the town of Casterbridge was visible against the black concave, the luminosity appearing the brighter by its great contrast with the circumscribing darkness. Towards this weak soft glow the woman turned her eyes.

"If I could only get there!" she said. "Meet him the day after to-morrow – God help me! Perhaps I shall be in my grave before then."

A clock from the far depths of shadow struck the hour – one – in entombed small tones. After midnight the voice of a clock seems to lose in breadth as much as in length, and to diminish its sonorousness to a thin falsetto.

Afterwards a light – two lights – arose from the remote shade, and grew larger. A carriage rolled along the road, and passed the gate. It probably contained some late diners-out. The beams from one lamp shone for a moment upon the crouching woman, and threw her face into vivid relief. The face was young in the groundwork, old in the finish: the general contours were soft and childlike but the finer lineaments had begun to be sharp and thin.

She stood up, apparently with a revived determination, and looked around. The road appeared to be familiar to her, and she carefully scanned the fence as she slowly walked along. Presently there became visible a dim white shape; it was a milestone. She drew her fingers across its face to feel the marks,

"Three!" she said.[1]

She leant against the stone as a means of rest for a short interval, then bestirred herself and again pursued her way. For a lengthy distance she bore up bravely, afterwards flagging as before. This was beside a lone hazel copse wherein heaps of white chips strewn upon the dark ground showed that woodmen had been faggoting and making hurdles during the day. Now there was not a man, not a breeze, not the faintest clash of twigs to keep her company. The woman looked over the gate, opened it and went in. Close to the entrance stood a row of faggots bound and unbound, together with stakes of all sizes.

For a few seconds the wayfarer stood with that tense stillness which signifies itself to be not the end but merely the suspension of a previous motion. Her attitude was that of a person who listens – either to the external world of sound, or to the imagined discourse of thought. A close criticism might have detected signs proving that she was intent on the latter alternative. Moreover, as was shown by what followed, she was oddly exercising the faculty of invention upon the speciality of the clever Jacquet Droz,[2] the designer of automatic substitutes for human limbs.

By the aid of the Casterbridge aurora, and by feeling with her hands, the woman selected two sticks from the heaps. These sticks were nearly straight to the height of three or four feet, where each branched into a fork like the letter Y. She sat down, snapped off the small upper twigs, and carried the remainder with her into the road. She placed one of these forks under each arm as a crutch, tested them, timidly threw her whole weight upon them – so little that it was – and swung herself forward. She had made for herself a material aid.

The crutches answered well. The pat of her feet, and the tap of her sticks upon the highway were all the sounds that came from the traveller now. She had passed a second milestone by a good long distance, and began to look wistfully towards the bank as if calculating upon another milestone soon. The crutches, though so very useful, had their limits of power. Mechanism only transmutes labour, being powerless to abstract it, and the quantum of exertion was not cleared away; it was thrown into the body and arms. She was exhausted, and each swing forward became fainter. At last she swayed sideways and fell.

Here she lay, a shapeless heap, for ten minutes and more. The morning wind began to boom dully over the flats, and to move afresh dead leaves which had lain still since yesterday. The woman desperately turned round upon her knees, and next rose to her feet. Steadying herself by the help of one crutch she assayed a step, then another, then a third, using the crutches now as walking-sticks only. Thus she progressed till the beginning of a long rail fence came into view. She staggered across to the first post, clung to it, and looked around. Another milestone was on the opposite side of the way.

The Casterbridge lights were now individually visible. It was getting towards morning, and vehicles might be hoped for if not expected soon. She listened. There was not a sound of life save that acme and sublimation of all dismal sounds – the bark of a fox, its three hollow notes rendered at intervals of a minute with the precision of a funeral bell.

"One mile more," the woman murmured. "No, less," she added, after a pause. "The mile is to the Town Hall, and my resting-place is on this side Casterbridge. Three-quarters of a mile, and there I am!" After an interval she again spoke. "Five or six steps to a yard – six perhaps. I have to go twelve hundred yards. A hundred times six, six hundred. Twelve times that. O pity me Lord!"

Holding to the rails she advanced – thrusting one hand forward upon the rail, then the other, then leaning over it whilst she dragged her feet on beneath.

This woman was not given to soliloquy; but extremity of feeling lessens the individuality of the weak as it increases that of the strong. She said again in the same tone, "I'll believe that the end lies five posts forward, and no further, and so get strength to pass them."

This was a practical application of the principle that a feigned and factitious faith is better than no faith at all.

She passed five posts, and held on to the fifth.

"I'll pass five more by believing my longed-for spot is at the next fifth. I can do it."

She passed five more.

"It lies only five further."

She passed five more.

"But it is five further."

She passed them.

"The end of these railings is the end of my journey," she said, when the end was in view.

She crawled to the end. During the effort each breath of the woman went into the air as if never to return again.

"Now for the truth of the matter," she said, sitting down. "The truth is, that I have less than half a mile." Faith in what she had known all the time to be fable had given her strength to come a quarter of a mile that she would have been powerless to face in the lump. The artifice showed that the woman, by some mysterious intuition, had grasped the great paradoxical truth that blindness may do greater things than prescience, and the short-sighted than the far seeing; that limitation, and not comprehensiveness, is needed for striking a blow.

The half-mile stood now before the sick and weary woman like a stolid Juggernaut. It was an impassive King of her world. The road here ran across a level plateau with only a bank on either side. She surveyed the wide space, the lights, herself, sighed, and lay down on the bank.

Never was ingenuity exercised so sorely as the traveller here exercised hers. Every conceivable aid, method, stratagem, trick, mechanism, by which this last desperate hundred yards could be overpassed by a human being, unperceived, was revolved in her busy brain, and dismissed as impracticable. She thought of sticks, wheels, crawling – she even thought of rolling. But the exertion demanded by either of these latter two was greater than to walk erect. The faculty of contrivance was worn out. Hopelessness had come at last.

"No further!" she whispered, and closed her eyes.

From the strip of shadow on the opposite side of the way a portion of shade seemed to detach itself, and move into isolation upon the pale white of the road. It glided noiselessly towards the recumbent woman.

She became conscious of something touching her hand; it was softness and it was warmth. She opened her eyes, and the substance touched her face. A dog was licking her cheek.

He was a huge heavy and quiet creature, standing darkly against the low horizon, and at least two feet higher than the present position of her eyes. Whether Newfoundland, mastiff, bloodhound, or what not, it was impossible to say. He seemed to be of too strange and mysterious a nature to belong to any variety among those of popular nomenclature. Being thus assignable to no species he was the ideal embodiment of canine greatness – a generalization from what was common to all. Night, in its sad, solemn, and benevolent aspect, apart from its stealthy and cruel side, was personified in this form. Darkness endows the small and ordinary ones among mankind with poetical power, and even the suffering woman threw her idea into figure.

In her reclining position she looked up to him just as in earlier times she had, when standing, looked up to a man. The animal respectfully withdrew a step or two when the woman moved, and seeing that she did not repulse him he licked her hand again.

Her thought moved within her like lightning. "Perhaps I can make use of him – I might do it then!"

She pointed in the direction of Casterbridge, and the dog seemed to misunderstand: he trotted on. Then, finding she could not follow he came back and whined.

The saddest and ultimate singularity of woman's effort and invention was reached when, with a quickened breathing she rose to a stooping posture, and, resting her two little hands upon the shoulders of the dog, bore firmly thereon, and murmured stimulating words. Whilst she sorrowed she cheered with her voice, and what was stranger than that the strong should need encouragement from the weak was that cheerfulness should be so well simulated by such utter dejection. Her friend moved forward slowly, and she with small mincing steps moved forward beside him, half her weight being thrown upon the animal. Sometimes she sank as she had sunk from walking erect, from the crutches, from the rails. The dog, who now thoroughly understood her desire and her incapacity, was frantic in his distress on these occasions: he would tug at her dress and run forward. She always called him back, and it was now to be observed that the woman listened for human sounds only to avoid them. It was evident that she had an object in keeping her presence on the road and her forlorn state unknown.

Their progress was necessarily very slow. They reached the brow of the hill, and the Casterbridge lamps lay beneath them like fallen Pleiads[3] as they walked down the incline. Thus the fifty yards were passed, and the goal was reached. On this much-desired spot outside the town rose a picturesque building. Originally it had been a mere case to hold people. The shell had been so thin, so devoid of excrescence, and so closely drawn over the accommodation granted that the character of what was beneath showed through it, as the shape of a body is visible under a winding sheet.

Then Nature, as if offended, lent a hand. Masses of ivy grew up, completely covering the walls, till the place looked like an abbey; and it was discovered that the view from the front, over the Casterbridge chimneys, was one of the most magnificent in the county. A neighbouring earl once said that he would give up a year's income for the view enjoyed by the inmates – and very probably the inmates would have given up the view for his year's income.

This green edifice consisted of a central mass and two wings, whereon stood as sentinels a few slim chimneys, now gurgling sorrowfully to the slow wind. In the middle was a gate, and by the gate a bell-pull formed of a hanging wire. The woman raised herself as high as possible upon her knees, and could just reach the handle. She moved it and fell forward in a bowed attitude, her face upon her bosom.

It was getting on towards six o'clock, and sounds of movement were to be heard inside the building which was the haven of rest to this wearied soul. A little door in the large one now opened, and a man appeared inside. He saw the panting heap of clothes, went back for a light, and came again. He entered a second time and returned with two women.

These lifted the prostrate figure and assisted her in through the doorway. The man closed the door.

"How did she get here?" said one of the women.

"The Lord knows," said the other.

"There is a dog outside," murmured the overcome traveller. "Where is he gone? He helped me."

"I stoned him away," said the man.

The little procession then moved forward; the man in front bearing the light; the two bony women next, supporting between them the small and flexuous one. Thus they entered the door and disappeared.

CHAPTER XL

Suspicion: Fanny is sent for.

Bathsheba said very little to her husband all that evening of their return from market, and he was not disposed to say much to her. He exhibited the unpleasant combination of a restless condition with a silent tongue. The next day, which was Sunday, passed nearly in the same manner as regarded their taciturnity, Bathsheba going to church both morning and afternoon. This was the day before the Budmouth races. In the evening Troy said suddenly,

"Bathsheba, could you let me have twenty pounds?"

Her countenance instantly sank. "Twenty pounds?" she said.

"The fact is, I want it badly." The anxiety upon Troy's face was unusual and very marked. It was a culmination of the mood he had been in all the day.

"Ah, for those races to-morrow."

Troy for the moment made no reply. Her mistake had its advantages to a man who shrank from having his mind inspected as he did now. "Well, suppose I do want it for races," he said at last.

"O Frank!" Bathsheba replied, and there was such a volume of entreaty in the words. "Only such a few weeks ago you said that I was far sweeter than all your other pleasures put together, and that you would give them all up for me; and now, won't you give up this one, which is more a worry than a pleasure? Do Frank. Come, let me fascinate you by all I can do – by pretty words and pretty looks and everything I can think of – to stay at home. Say yes to your wife – say yes!"

The tenderest and softest phases of Bathsheba's nature more prominent now – advanced impulsively for his acceptance, without any of the disguises and defences which the wariness of her character too frequently threw over them. Few men could have resisted the arch yet dignified entreaty of the beautiful face, thrown a little back and sideways in the well known attitude that expresses more than the words it accompanies, and which seems to have been designed for these special occasions. Had the woman not been his wife Troy would have succumbed instantly: as it was he thought he would not deceive her.

"The money is not wanted for racing debts at all," he said.

"What is it for?" she asked. "You worry me a great deal by these mysterious responsibilities Frank."

Troy hesitated. He did not now love her enough to allow himself to be carried too far by her ways. Yet it was necessary to be civil. "You wrong me by such a suspicious manner," he said. "Such strait-waistcoating as you treat me to is not becoming in you at so early a date."

"I think that I have a right to grumble a little if I pay," she said with features between a laugh and a pout.

"Exactly, and the former being done suppose we proceed to the latter. Bathsheba, fun is all very well, but don't go too far, or you may have cause to regret something."

She reddened. "I do that already," she said quickly.

"What do you regret?"

"That my romance has come to an end."

"They all end at marriage."

"I wish you wouldn't talk like that. You grieve me to my soul by being smart at my expense."

"You are dull enough at mine. I believe you hate me."

"Not you – only your vices. I do hate them."

"'Twould be much more becoming if you set yourself to cure them. Come, let's strike a balance with the twenty pounds and be friends."

She gave a sigh of resignation. "I have about that sum here for household expenses. If you must have it take it."

"Very good. Thank you. I expect I shall have gone away before you are in to breakfast to morrow."

"And must you go? Ah, there was a time Frank when it would have taken a good many promises to other people to drag you away from me. You used to call me Darling then. But it doesn't matter to you how my days are passed now."

"I must go, in spite of sentiment." Troy as he spoke looked at his watch, and, apparently actuated by *non lucendo*[1] principles, opened the case at the back, revealing, snugly stowed within it, a small coil of hair.

Bathsheba's eyes had been accidentally lifted at that moment, and she saw the action, and saw the hair. She flushed in pain and surprise, and some words escaped her before she had thought whether or not it was wise to utter them. "A woman's curl of hair!" she said. "O Frank, whose is that?"

Troy had instantly closed his watch. He carelessly replied, as one who cloaked some feelings that the sight had stirred. "Why yours, of course. Whose should it be? I had quite forgotten that I had it."

"What a dreadful fib, Frank!"

"I tell you, I had forgotten it!" he said loudly.

"I don't mean that – it was yellow hair."

"Nonsense."

"That's insulting me. I know it was yellow. Now, whose was it – I want to know."

"Very well – I'll tell you, so make no more ado. It is the hair of a young woman I was going to marry before I knew you."

"You ought to tell me her name, then."

"I cannot do that."

"Is she married yet?"

"No."

"Is she alive?"

"Yes."

"Is she pretty?"

"Yes."

"It is wonderful how she can be, poor thing, under such an awful affliction."

"Affliction – what affliction?" he enquired quickly.

"Having hair of that dreadful colour."

"O-ho – I like that!" said Troy recovering himself. "Why her hair has been admired by everybody who has seen her since she has worn it loose, which has not been long. It is beautiful hair. People used to turn their heads to look at it, poor girl, whenever she wore it loose."

"Pooh – that's nothing – that's nothing – people looking," she exclaimed. "If I cared for your love as much as I used to I could say they had turned to look at mine."

"Bathsheba, don't be so fitful and jealous. You knew what married life would be like, and shouldn't have entered it if you feared these contingencies."

Troy had by this time driven her almost to tears; her heart was big in her throat, and the ducts to her eyes were painfully full. Ashamed as she was to show emotion at last she burst out, "This is all I get for loving you so well! Ah, when I married you your life was dearer to me than my own. I would have died for you – how truly I can say that I would have died for you. And now you sneer at my foolishness in marrying you. O is it kind to me to throw my mistake in my face? Whatever opinion you may have of my wisdom you should not tell me of it so mercilessly now that I am in your power."

"I can't help how things fall out," said Troy. "Upon my heart, women will be the death of me."

"Well, you shouldn't keep people's hair. You'll burn it, won't you Frank?"

Frank went on as if he had not heard her. "There are considerations even before my consideration for you – reparation to be made – ties you know nothing of. If you repent of marrying, so do I."

Trembling now, she put her hand upon his arm, saying in mingled tones of wretchedness and coaxing, "I only repent if you don't love me better than any other woman in the world. I don't otherwise, Frank. You don't repent because you already love somebody better than you love me, do you?"

"I don't know. Why do you say that?"

"You won't burn that curl. You like the woman who owns that pretty hair: yes, it is pretty – more beautiful than my miserable black mane. Well, it is no use. I can't help being ugly. You must like her best if you will."

"Until to-day, when I took it from a drawer, I have never looked upon that bit of hair for several months. That I am ready to swear."

"But just now you said 'ties'. And then, that woman we met."

"'Twas the meeting with her that reminded me of the hair."

"Is it hers, then?"

"Yes. There now that you have wormed it out of me I hope you are content."

"And what are the ties?"

"O that meant nothing – a mere jest."

"A mere jest!" she said in mournful astonishment. "Can you jest when I am so wretchedly in earnest! Tell me the truth Frank. I am not a fool you know, although I am a woman and have my woman's moments. Come, treat me fairly," she said looking honestly and fearlessly into his face. "I don't want much; bare justice – that's all. Ah, once I felt I could be content with nothing less than the highest homage from the husband I should choose. Now anything short of cruelty will content me. Yes the independent and spirited Bathsheba is come to this!"

"For heaven's sake don't be so desperate," Troy said snappishly, rising as he did so and leaving the room.

Directly he had gone Bathsheba burst into great sobs – dry-eyed sobs which cut as they came, without any softening by tears. But she determined to repress all evidences of feeling. She was conquered, but she would never own it as long as she lived. Her pride was indeed brought low by this despairing perception of spoliation by marriage with a less pure nature than her own. She chafed to and fro in rebelliousness, like a caged leopard, her whole soul was in arms, and the blood fired her face. Until she had met Troy Bathsheba had been proud of her position as a woman; it had been a glory to her to know that her lips had been touched by no man's on earth, that her waist had never been encircled by a lover's arm. She hated herself now. In those earlier days she had always nourished a secret contempt for girls who were the slaves of the first good-looking young fellow who should choose to salute them. She had never taken kindly to the idea of marriage in the abstract as did the majority of women she saw about her. In the turmoil of her anxiety for her lover she had agreed to marry him, but the perception that had accompanied her happiest hours on this account was rather that of self-sacrifice than of promotion and honour. Although she scarcely knew the divinity's name, Diana[2] was the goddess whom Bathsheba instinctively adored. That she had never by look word or sign encouraged a man to approach her, that she had felt herself sufficient to herself, and had in the independence of her girlish heart fancied there was a certain degradation in renouncing the simplicity of a maiden existence to become the humbler half of an indifferent whole, were facts now bitterly remembered. O if she had never stooped to folly of this kind, respectable as it was, and could only stand again as she had stood on the hill at Norcombe, and dare Troy or any other man to pollute a hair of her head by his interference.

The next morning she rose earlier than usual, and had the horse saddled for her ride round the farm in the customary way. When she came in at half past eight, their usual hour for breakfasting, she was informed that her husband had risen, taken his breakfast, and driven off to Casterbridge with the gig and Poppet.

After breakfast she was cool and collected – quite herself in fact, and she rambled to the gate intending to walk to another quarter of the farm, which she still personally superintended as well as her duties in the house would permit, continually however finding herself preceded in forethought by Gabriel Oak, for whom she began to entertain the genuine friendship of a sister. Of course she sometimes thought of him in the light of an old lover, and had momentary imaginings of what life with him as a husband would have been like – also of life with Boldwood under the same conditions. But Bathsheba, though she could feel, was not much given to dreaming, and her musings under this head were short, and entirely confined to the times when Troy's neglect was more than ordinarily evident.

She saw coming up the hill a man like Mr Boldwood. It was Mr Boldwood. Bathsheba blushed painfully, and watched. The farmer stopped when still a long way off, and held up his hand to Gabriel Oak, who was in another part of the field. The two men then approached each other and seemed to engage in earnest conversation. Thus they continued for a long time. Joseph Poorgrass now passed near them wheeling a barrow of apples up the hill to Bathsheba's residence. Boldwood and Gabriel called to him, spoke to him for a few minutes, and then all three parted, Joseph immediately coming up the hill with his barrow.

Bathsheba, who had seen this pantomime with some surprise, experienced great relief when Boldwood turned back again. "Well, what's the message Joseph?" she said.

He set down his barrow, and putting upon himself the refined aspect that a conversation with a lady required, spoke to Bathsheba over the gate.

"You'll never see Fanny Robbin no more – use nor principal,[3] ma'am."

"Why?"

"Because she's dead in the Union."

"Fanny dead – never!"

"Yes, ma'am."

"What did she die from?"

"I don't know for certain, but I should be inclined to think it was from general weakness of constitution. She was such a limber[4] maid that 'a could stand no hardship, even when I knowed her. She was soon gone it seems. She was taken ill in the morning, and being quite feeble and worn out she died in the afternoon. She belongs by law to our parish, and Mr Boldwood is going to send a waggon this afternoon to fetch her home here and bury her."

"Indeed I shall not let Mr Boldwood do any such thing – I shall do it. Fanny was my uncle's servant, and although I only knew her for a couple of days, she belongs to me. How very very sad this is! – the idea of Fanny being in a workhouse." Bathsheba had begun to know what suffering was, and she spoke with deep feeling. . . . "Send across to Mr Boldwood's and say that Mrs Troy will take upon herself the duty of fetching an old servant of her family. . . . . We ought not to put her in a waggon: we'll get a hearse."

"There will hardly be time ma'am, will there?"

"Perhaps not," she said musingly. "When did you say we must be at the door – three o'clock?"

"Three o'clock this afternoon ma'am, so to speak."

"Very well – you go with it. A pretty waggon is better than an ugly hearse, after all. Joseph, have the new spring waggon with the blue body and red wheels, and wash it very clean. – And Joseph."

"Yes ma'am."

"Carry with you some evergreens and flowers to put upon her coffin – indeed, gather a great many, and completely bury her in them. Get some boughs of laurustinus, and variegated box, and yew, and boy's-love: ay, and some bunches of chrysanthemum.[5] And let old Pleasant draw her, because she knew him so well."

"I will ma'am. I ought to have said that the Union in the form of four labouring men will meet me when I gets to our churchyard gate, and take her and bury her according to the rites of the Board of Guardians, as by law ordained."

"Dear me – Casterbridge Union – and is Fanny come to this!" said

Bathsheba musing. "I wish I had known of it sooner. I thought she was far away. How long has she lived there?"

"She has only been there a day or two."

"O – then she has not been staying there as a regular inmate?"

"No. She's been picking up a living at seampstering in Melchester for several months, at the house of a very respectable widow-woman who takes in work of that sort. She only arrived at the Union-house on Sunday morning 'a b'lieve, and 'tis supposed here and there that she had walked every step of the way from Melchester. Why she left her place I can't say, for I don't know, and as to a lie, why, I wouldn't tell it. That's the short of the story ma'am."

"Ah-h!"

No gem ever flashed from a rosy ray to a white one more rapidly than changed the young wife's countenance whilst this word came from her in a long drawn breath. "Did she walk along our turnpike road?" she said in a suddenly restless and eager voice.

"I believe she did. . . . . Ma'am, shall I call Liddy. You baint well, ma'am, surely. You look like a lily – so very pale."

"No – don't call her: it is nothing. When did she pass Weatherbury?"

"Last Saturday night."

"That will do Joseph: now you may go."

"Certainly ma'am."

"Joseph, come hither a moment. What was the colour of Fanny Robbin's hair?"

"Really mistress, now that 'tis put to me promiscuous-like, I can't call to mind, if ye'll believe me."

"Never mind – go on and do what I told you. Stop – well no, go on."

She turned herself away from him, that he might no longer notice the mood which had set its sign so visibly upon her, and went indoors with a distressing sense of faintness and a beating brow. About an hour after she heard the noise of the waggon and went out, still with a painful consciousness of her bewildered and troubled look. Joseph, dressed in his best suit of clothes, was putting in the horse to start. The shrubs and flowers were all piled in the waggon as she had directed. Bathsheba hardly saw them now.

"Died of what? did you say Joseph?"

"I don't know ma'am."

"Are you quite sure?"

"Yes ma'am, quite sure."

"Sure of what?"

"I am sure that all I know is that she arrived in the morning and died in the evening without further parley. What Oak and Mr Boldwood told me was only these few words. 'Little Fanny Robbin is dead, Joseph,' Gabriel said, looking in my face in his steady quiet way. I was very sorry and I said, 'Ah – and how did she come to die?' 'Well, she's dead in Casterbridge Union,' he said; 'and perhaps 'tisn't much matter about how she came to die. She reached the Union early Sunday morning and died in the afternoon – that's clear enough.' Then I asked what she'd been doing lately, and Mr Boldwood turned round to me then, and left off spitting a thistle with the top of his stick. He told me about her having lived by seampstering in Melchester, as I mentioned to you, and that she walked therefrom at the end of last week, passing near here Saturday night in the dusk. They then said I had better just name the fact of her death to you, and away they went. Her death might have been brought on by exposure to the night wind, you know ma'am; for people used to say she'd go off in a decline: she used to cough a good deal in winter time. However, 'tisn't much difference to us about that now, for 'tis all over."

"Have you heard a different story at all?" She looked at him so intently that Joseph's eyes quailed.

"Not a word mistress, I assure you," he said. "Hardly anybody in the parish knows the news yet."

"I wonder why Gabriel didn't bring the message to me himself. He mostly makes a point of seeing me upon the most trifling errand." These words were merely murmured, and she was looking upon the ground.

"Perhaps he was busy ma'am," Joseph suggested. "And sometimes he seems to suffer from things upon his mind connected with the time when he was better off than 'a is now. 'A's rather a curious man, but a very understanding shepherd, and learned in books."

"Did anything seem upon his mind whilst he was speaking to you about this?"

"I cannot but say that there did, ma'am. He was very gloomy, and so was Farmer Boldwood."

"Thank you Joseph. That will do. Go on now, or you'll be late."

Bathsheba, still unhappy, went indoors again. In the course of the afternoon she said to Liddy, who had been informed of the occurrence, "What was the colour of poor Fanny Robbin's hair – Do you know? I cannot recollect – I only saw her for a day or two."

"It was light ma'am – but she wore it rather short and packed away under her cap, so that you would hardly notice it. But I have seen her let it down when she was going to bed, and it looked beautiful then. Real golden hair."

"Her young man was a soldier, was he not?"

"Yes. In the same regiment as Mr Troy. He says he knew him very well."

"What, Mr Troy says so? How came he to say that?"

"One day I just named it to him and asked him if he knew Fanny's young man. He said O yes, he knew the young man as well as he knew himself, and that there wasn't a man in the regiment he liked better."

"A-ha. Said that, did he."

"Yes, and he said there was a strong likeness between himself and the other young man, so that sometimes people mistook them –"

"Liddy for Heaven's sake stop your talking!" said Bathsheba with the nervous petulance that comes from unhappiness.

CHAPTER XLI

Joseph and his burden: "Buck's Head".

A wall bounded the site of Casterbridge Unionhouse except along a portion of the end. Here a high gable stood prominent, and it was covered like the front with a mat of ivy. In this gable was no window, chimney, ornament, or protuberance of any kind. The single feature appertaining to it except the expanse of dark green leaves was a small door.

The situation of the door was peculiar. The sill was three or four feet above the ground, and one was for a moment at a loss for an explanation of this exceptional altitude, till ruts immediately beneath suggested that the door was used solely for the passage of articles and persons to and from the level of a vehicle standing on the outside. Upon the whole, the door bore the expression of a species of Traitor's Gate translated to another element. That entry and exit hereby was only at rare intervals was made apparent by some of the ivy twigs having crept from the doorpost over the door itself.

As the clock from the tower of St George's Church pointed at three minutes to three a blue spring waggon picked out with red, and containing boughs and flowers, turned from the high road and halted on this side of the building. Whilst the chimes were yet stammering out a shattered form of "Malbrook"[1] Joseph Poorgrass rang the bell, and received directions to back his waggon against the high door under the gable. The door then opened and a plain elm coffin was slowly thrust forth, and laid by two men in fustian along the middle of the vehicle.

One of the men then stepped up beside it, took from his pocket a lump of chalk, and wrote upon the cover the name and date in a large scrawling hand (We believe that they do these things more tenderly now, and provide a plate). He covered the whole with a black cloth, threadbare, but decent, the back-board of the waggon was returned to its place, one of the men handed a certificate of registry to Poorgrass, and both entered the door, closing it behind them. Their connection with her, short as it had been, was over for ever.

Joseph then placed the flowers as he had been enjoined, the evergreens around the flowers, till it was difficult to divine what the waggon contained, smacked his whip, and the rather pleasing funeral car crept up the hill, and along the road to Weatherbury.

The afternoon drew on apace, and looking to the left towards the sea as he walked beside the horse, Poorgrass saw rolling over the high hills which girt the landscape in that quarter scrolls and wreaths of mist. They came in yet greater volumes, and indolently crept across the intervening valleys, and around the withered papery flags of the sloughs and river brinks. Then their dank spongy forms closed in upon the sky. It was a sudden overgrowth of atmospheric fungi, which had their roots in the sea, and by the time that horse, man, and corpse entered Yalbury Great Wood these silent workings of an invisible hand reached them, and they were completely enveloped. It was the first arrival of the Autumn fogs, and the first fog of the series.

The air was as an eye suddenly struck blind. The waggon and its load rolled no longer on the horizontal division between clearness and opacity. They were imbedded in an elastic body of a monotonous pallor throughout.

There was no perceptible motion in the air, not a visible drop of water fell upon a leaf of the beeches, birches, and firs composing the wood on either side. The trees stood in an attitude of intentness, as if they waited longingly for a wind to come and rock them. A startling quiet overhung all surrounding things – so completely, that the crackle of the waggon-wheels was as a great noise, and small rustles, which had never obtained a hearing except by night, were distinctly individualized.

Joseph Poorgrass looked round upon his sad burden as it loomed faintly through the flowering laurustinus, then at the unfathomable glooms amid the high trees on each hand, indistinct shadowless and spectre-like in their monochrome of grey. He felt anything but cheerful, and wished he had the company even of a cat or dog. Stopping the horse he listened. Not a footstep or wheel was audible anywhere around, and the dead silence was broken only by a heavy particle falling from a tree through the evergreens and alighting with a smart rap upon the coffin of poor Fanny. The fog had by this time saturated the trees, and this was the first dropping of water from the overbrimming leaves. The hollow echo of its fall reminded the waggoner painfully of "Dust to Dust".[2] Then hard by there was another drop, then two or three. Presently there was a continual tapping of these heavy drops upon the dead leaves, the road, and the travellers. The nearer boughs were beaded with the mist to the greyness of aged men, and the rusty red leaves of the beeches were hung with similar drops, like diamonds on chestnut hair.

Situated by the roadside in the midst of this wood[3] was the old inn called Buck's Head. It was about a mile and a half from Weatherbury, and in the meridional times of stage-coach travelling had been the point at which some of the coaches kept their relays of horses. All the old stabling was now pulled down, and little remained besides the habitable inn itself, which, standing a little way back from the road, signified its existence to people far up and down the highway by a sign which hung from the horizontal bough of an elm on the opposite side of the way.

Travellers – for the variety *tourist* had hardly developed into a distinct species at this date – sometimes said in passing, as they cast their eyes up to the sign-bearing tree, that artists were fond of representing the sign-board hanging thus, but that they themselves had never noticed an actual instance of such an arrangement before. It was near this tree that the waggon was standing into which Gabriel Oak crept on his first journey to Weatherbury, but owing to the darkness the sign and the inn had been unobserved.

The manners of the inn were of the old established type. Indeed, in the minds of its frequenters they existed as unalterable formulae: e.g.

"Rap with the bottom of your pint for more liquor."

"For tobacco, shout."

"In calling for the girl in waiting, say 'Maid!'"

"Ditto for the landlady, say 'Old Soul!' &c, &c."

It was a relief to Joseph's soul when the friendly sign-board came in view, and stopping his horse immediately beneath it he proceeded to fulfil an intention made a long hour before. His spirits were oozing out of him quite. He turned the horse's head to the green bank, and entered the hostel for a mug of ale.

Going down into the kitchen of the inn, the floor of which was a step below the passage, which in its turn was a step below the road outside, what should Joseph see to gladden his eyes but two copper-coloured discs in the form of the countenances of Mr Jan Coggan and Mr Mark Clark. These owners of the two most appreciative throats in the neighbourhood on this side of respectability were now sitting face to face over a three legged circular table, having an iron rim to keep cups and pots from being accidentally elbowed off, and they resembled the setting sun and the full moon shining vis-a-vis across the globe.

"Why, 'tis neighbour Poorgrass!" said Mark Clark. "I'm sure your face don't praise your mistress's table, Joseph."

"I've had a very pale companion for the last five miles," said Joseph, indulging in a shudder toned down by resignation. "And to speak the truth, 'twas beginning to tell upon me. I assure ye I ha'n't seed the colour of victuals or drink since breakfast time this morning, and that was no more than a dew-bit afield."

"Then drink Joseph, and don't restrain yerself," said Coggan, handing him a hooped mug three-quarters full.

Joseph drank for a moderately long time, then for a longer time, saying as he lowered the jug, "'Tis pretty drinking – very pretty drinking, and is more than cheerful on my melancholy errand, so to speak it."

"True, drink is a pleasant delight," said Jan, as one who repeated a truism so familiar to his brain that he hardly noticed its passage over his tongue, and lifting the cup Coggan tilted his head gradually backwards with closed eyes, that his expectant soul might not be diverted for one instant from its bliss by irrelevant surroundings.

"Well, I must be on again," said Poorgrass. "Not but that I should like another nip with ye; but the country might lose confidence in me if I was seen here."

"Where be ye trading o't to to-day then Joseph?"

"Back to Weatherbury. I've got poor little Fanny Robbin in my waggon outside, and I must be at the churchyard gates at a quarter to five with her."

"Ay – I've heard of it. And so she's nailed up in parish boards after all, and nobody to pay the bell shilling and the grave half-crown."[4]

"The parish pays the grave half-crown, but not the bell shilling, because the bell's a luxery; but 'a can hardly do without the grave, poor body. However I expect our mistress will pay all."

"A pretty maid as ever I see! But what's yer hurry, Joseph. The pore woman's dead, and you can't bring her to life, and you may as well sit down comfortable and finish another with us."

"I don't mind taking just the merest thimbleful of imagination more with ye, souls. But only a few minutes because 'tis as 'tis."

"Of course you'll have another drop. A man's twice the man afterwards. You feel so warm and glorious, and you whop and slap at your work without any trouble, and everything goes on like sticks a-breaking. Too much liquor is bad, and leads us to that horned man in the smoky house,[5] but after all, many people haven't the gift of enjoying a tipple, and since we are highly favoured with a power that way we should make the most of it."

"True," said Mark Clark. "'Tis a talent the Lord has mercifully bestowed upon us, and we ought not to neglect it. But what with the parsons and clerks and schoolpeople and serious tea-parties the merry old ways of good life have gone to the dogs – upon my carcase they have."

"Well really I must be onward again now," said Joseph.

"Now, now, Joseph; nonsense! The poor woman is dead, isn't she, and what's your hurry."

"I hope Providence won't be in a way with me for my doings," said Joseph again sitting down. "I've been troubled with weak moments lately. Yes, I've been drinky once this month already, and I didn't go to church a-Sunday, and I dropped a curse or two yesterday, so I don't want to go too far for my safety. Your next world is your next world, and not to be squandered lightly."

"I believe ye to be a dissenter, Joseph. That I do."

"O no no. I don't go so far as that."

"For my part," said Coggan, "I'm staunch Church of England."

"Ay, and faith, so be I," said Mark Clark.

"I won't say much for myself: I don't wish to," Coggan continued with that tendency to talk on principles which is characteristic of the barley corn. "But I've never changed a single doctrine: I've stuck like a plaster to the old faith I was born in. Yes, there's this to be said for the church, a man can belong to the church and bide in his cheerful old inn, and never trouble or worry his mind about doctrines at all. But to be a dissenter you must go to chapel in all winds and weathers, and make yerself as frantic as a skit. Not but that chapel-members be clever chaps enough in their way. They can lift up beautiful prayers out of their own heads, all about their families and shipwracks in the newspaper."

"They can – they can," said Mark Clark, with corroborative feeling; "but we churchmen, you see, must have it all printed aforehand, or, dang it all, we should no more know what to say to a great person like Providence than to the man in the moon."

"Chapel-folk be more hand-in-glove with them above than we," said Joseph thoughtfully.

"Yes," said Coggan. "We know very well that if anybody goes to heaven, they will. They've worked hard for it, and they deserve to have it, such as 'tis. I'm not such a fool as to pretend that we who stick to the church have the same chance as they, because we know we have not. But I hate a feller who'll change his old ancient doctrines for the sake of getting to heaven. I'd as soon turn King's-evidence for the few pounds you get. Why, neighbours, when every one of my potatoes were frosted our Parson Thirdly were the man who gave me a sack for seed, though he hardly had one for his own use, and no money to buy 'em. If it hadn't been for him I shouldn't have had a tatie to put in my garden. D'ye think I'd turn after that? No, I'll stick to my side, and if we be in the wrong, so be it: I'll fall with the fallen."

"The same here," said Mark. "If anything can beat the old martyrs who used to smoke for their principles here upon earth 'tis being willing to smoke for 'em hereafter."

"'Tis the old feeling in a new way," said Coggan.[6]

"Well said – very well said," observed Joseph. "However, folks, I must be moving now: upon my life I must. Parson Thirdly will be waiting at the church gates, and there's the woman a-biding outside in the waggon."

"Joseph Poorgrass, don't be so miserable. Parson Thirdly won't mind. He's a generous man; he's found me in tracts[7] for years, and I've consumed a good many in the course of a long and rather shady life; but he's never been the man to complain of the expense. Sit down."

The longer Joseph Poorgrass remained the less was his spirit troubled by the duties which devolved upon him this afternoon. The minutes glided by uncounted, until the evening shades began perceptibly to deepen, and the eyes of the three were but sparkling points on the surface of darkness. Coggan's watch struck six from his pocket in the usual still small tones.

At that moment hasty steps were heard in the entry, and the door opened to admit the figure of Gabriel Oak, followed by the maid of the inn bearing a candle. He stared sternly at the one lengthy and two round faces of the sitters, which confronted him with the blank aspects of a fiddle and a couple of warming-pans. Joseph Poorgrass blinked, and shrank several inches into the background.

"Upon my soul I'm ashamed of you; 'tis disgraceful, Joseph, disgraceful!" said Gabriel indignantly. "Coggan, you call yourself a man and don't know better than this!"

Coggan looked up indefinitely at Oak, one or other of his eyes occasionally opening and closing of its own accord, as if it were not a member but a dozy individual with a distinct personality.

"Don't take on so, Shepherd!" said Mark Clark, looking reproachfully at the candle which appeared to possess special features of interest for his eyes.

"Nobody can hurt a dead woman," said Coggan, with the precision of a machine. "All that could be done for her is done – she's beyond us; and why should a man put himself in a tearing hurry for lifeless clay that can neither feel nor see, and don't know what you do with her at all? If she'd been alive I would have been the first to help her. If she now wanted victuals and drink I'd pay for it, money down. But she's dead, and no speed of ours will bring her to life. The woman's independent of us – time spent upon her is throwed away: why should we hurry to do what's not required? Drink, Shepherd, or be friends, for to-morrow we may be like her."[8]

"We may," added Mark Clark emphatically, at once drinking himself, to run no further risk of losing his chance by the event alluded to, Jan meanwhile merging, by a slight confusion of ideas, his further thoughts of to-morrow in a song: –

To-mor-row, to-mor-row:
And while peace and plen-ty I find at my board,
With a heart free from sick-ness and sor-row,
With my friends will I share what to-day may af-ford,
And let them spread the ta-ble to-mor-row.
To-mor-row, to-mor –

"Do hold thy horning, Jan!" said Oak; and turning upon Poorgrass, "As for you Joseph, who do your wicked deeds in such confoundedly holy ways, you are as drunk as you can stand."

"No, Shepherd Oak, no! Listen to reason, Shepherd. All that's the matter with me is the affliction called a multiplying eye, and that's how it is I look double to you – I mean, you look double to me."

"A multiplying eye is a very distressing thing," said Mark Clark.

"It always comes on when I have been in a public-house a little time," said Joseph Poorgrass, meekly. "Yes, I see two of every sort, as if I were some holy man living in the times of King Noah[9] and the entering into the ark. . . . . . Y-y-y-yes," he added becoming much affected by the picture of himself as a person thrown away, and shedding tears, "I feel too good for England: I ought to have lived in Genesis by rights, like the other men of sacrifice, and then I shouldn't have b-b-been called a d-d-drunkard in such a way!"

"I wish you'd show yourself a man of spirit, and not sit whining there."

"Show myself a man of spirit? . . . Ah well, let me take the name of drunkard humbly – let me be a man of contrite knees – let it be! I know that I always do say 'Please God' afore I do anything, from my getting up to my going down of the same, and I am willing to take as much disgrace as belongs to that holy act. Hah, yes! . . . But not a man of spirit? Have I ever allowed the toe of pride to be lifted against my person[10] without shouting manfully that I question the right to do so? I enquire that query boldly!"

"We can't say that you have, Joseph Poorgrass."

"Never have I allowed such discipline to pass unquestioned. Yet the shepherd says in the face of that rich testimony that I am not a man of spirit! Well, let it pass by, and death is a kind friend."

Gabriel, seeing that neither of the three was in a fit state to take charge of the waggon for the remainder of the journey, made no reply, but closing the door again upon them went across to where the vehicle stood, now getting indistinct in the fog and gloom of this mildewy time. He pulled the horse's head from the large patch of turf it had eaten bare, re-adjusted the boughs over the coffin, and drove along through the unwholesome night.

It had gradually become rumoured in the village that the body to be brought and buried that day was all that was left of the unfortunate Fanny Robbin who had followed the 11th from Casterbridge to Melchester. But thanks to Boldwood's reticence and Oak's generosity, the lover she had followed had never been individualized as Troy. Gabriel hoped that the whole truth of the matter might not be published till at any rate the girl had been in her grave for a few days, when the interposing barriers of earth and time, and a sense that the events had been somewhat shut into the past, would deaden the sting that revelation and invidious remark would have for Bathsheba just now.

By the time that Gabriel reached the old manor-house, her residence, which lay in his way to the church, it was quite dark. A man came from the gate and said through the fog which hung between them like blown flour,

"Is that Poorgrass with the corpse?"

Gabriel recognized the voice as that of the parson, Mr Thirdly.

"The corpse is here, sir," said Gabriel.

"I have just been to enquire of Mrs Troy if she could tell me the reason of the delay. I am afraid it is too late now for the funeral to be performed with proper decency. Have you the registrar's certificate?"

"No," said Gabriel. "I expect Poorgrass has that; and he's at the Buck's Head. I forgot to ask him for it."

"Then that settles the matter. We'll put off the funeral till to-morrow morning. The body may be brought on to the church, or it may be left here at the farm and fetched by the bearers in the morning. They waited more than an hour, and have now gone home."

Gabriel had his reasons for thinking the latter a most objectionable plan, notwithstanding that Fanny had been an inmate of the farm-house for several years in the lifetime of Bathsheba's uncle. Visions of several unhappy contingencies which might arise from this delay flitted before him. But his will was not law, and he went indoors to enquire of his mistress what were her wishes on the subject. He found her in an unusual mood: her eyes as she looked up to him were suspicious, and perplexed, as with some antecedent thought. Troy had not yet returned. At first Bathsheba assented with a mien of indifference to his proposition that they should go on to the church at once with their burden; but immediately afterwards, following Gabriel to the gate, she swerved to the extreme of solicitousness on Fanny's account, and desired that the girl might be brought into the house. Oak argued upon the convenience of leaving her upon the waggon, just as she lay now with her flowers and green leaves about her, merely wheeling the vehicle into the coach-house till the morning, but to no purpose. "It is unkind and unchristian," she said, "to leave the poor thing in a coach-house all night."

"Very well, then," said the parson. "And I will arrange that the funeral shall take place early to-morrow. Perhaps Mrs Troy is right in feeling that we cannot treat a dead fellow-creature too thoughtfully. We must remember that though she may have erred grievously in leaving her home, she is still our sister; and it is to be believed that God's uncovenanted mercies are extended towards her, and that she is a member of the flock of Christ."

The parson's words spread into the heavy air with a sad yet unperturbed cadence, and Gabriel shed an honest tear. Bathsheba seemed unmoved. Mr Thirdly then left them, and Gabriel lighted a lantern. Fetching three other men to assist him they bore the unconscious truant indoors, placing the coffin on two benches in the middle of a little sitting-room next the hall, as Bathsheba directed.

Every one except Gabriel Oak then left the room. He still indecisively lingered beside the body. He was deeply troubled at the wretchedly ironical aspect that circumstances were putting on with regard to Troy's wife, and at his own powerlessness to counteract them. In spite of his careful manoeuvring all this day, the very worst event that could in any way have happened in connection with this burial had happened now. Oak imagined possibilities resulting from this day's work that might cast over Bathsheba's life a shade which the interposition of many lapsing years might but indifferently lighten, and which nothing at all might altogether remove.

Suddenly, as in a last attempt to save Bathsheba from, at any rate, immediate pain, he looked again as he had looked before at the chalk writing upon the coffin-lid. The scrawl was this simple one: "*Fanny Robbin and child.*" Gabriel took his handkerchief and carefully rubbed out the two latter words. He then left the room, and went out quietly by the front door.

CHAPTER XLII[1]

Fanny's revenge.

"Do you want me any longer ma'am?" enquired Liddy, standing by the door with a bedroom candle in her hand, and addressing Bathsheba who sat cheerless and alone in the large parlour beside the first fire of the season.

"No more to-night Liddy."

"I'll sit up for master if you like, ma'am. I am not at all afraid of Fanny, if I may sit in my own room and have a candle. She was such a childlike innocent thing[2] that her spirit couldn't appear to anybody if it tried, I'm quite sure."

"O no, no. You go to bed. I'll sit up for him myself till twelve o'clock, and if he has not arrived by that time I shall give him up and go to bed too."

"It is half-past ten now."

"O is it. Fanny was *very* consumptive?"

"Well not very – she was rather."

"She has been away from us about eight months. Did anybody say before she left that she hadn't a twelvemonth to live?"

"I never heard anybody say so."

"If she had lived to be an old woman nobody would have been surprised?"

"I don't think they would."

"Have you heard to-day from anybody that she was not at all delicate in her chest?"

"No – have you ma'am?"

"O no no – I merely asked, being interested in Fanny." She murmured then, "People surely can't walk miles and miles the day before they die of consumption, inflammation of the lungs, or anything of the kind."[3]

"Why don't you sit upstairs ma'am?"

"Why don't I?" said Bathsheba desultorily. "It isn't worth while – there's a fire here. – Liddy," she suddenly repeated in an impulsive and excited whisper, "have you heard anything strange said of Fanny?" The words had no sooner escaped her than an expression of unutterable regret crossed her face, and she burst into tears.

"No – not a word!" said Liddy, looking at the weeping woman with astonishment. "What is it makes you cry so, ma'am, has anything hurt you?" She came to Bathsheba's side with a face full of sympathy.

"No Liddy – I don't want you any more. I can hardly say why I have taken so to crying lately: I never used to cry. Good night."

Liddy then left the parlour and closed the door.

Bathsheba was lonely and miserable now; not lonelier actually than she had been before her marriage; but her loneliness then was to that of the present time as the solitude of a mountain is to the solitude of a cave. And within the last day or two had come these disquieting thoughts about her husband's past. Her wayward sentiment that evening concerning Fanny's temporary resting-place had been the result of a strange complication of impulses in Bathsheba's bosom. Perhaps it would be more accurately described as a determined rebellion against her prejudices, a revulsion from a lower instinct of uncharitableness, which would have withheld all sympathy from the dead woman because in life she had preceded Bathsheba in the attentions of a man whom Bathsheba had by no means ceased from loving, though her love was sick to death just now from the gravity of her misgivings.

In five or ten minutes there was another tap at the door. Liddy reappeared and coming in a little way stood hesitating, until at length she said, "Mary-ann has just heard something very strange, but I know it isn't true. And we shall be sure to know the rights of it in a day or two."

"What is it?"

"O nothing connected with you or us, ma'am. It is about Fanny. That same thing you have heard."

"I have heard nothing."

"I mean that a wicked story is got to Weatherbury within this last hour – that – that there's *two of 'em* in there!" Liddy as she spoke, slanted her head in the direction of the hall, delivering the words in a slow low tone.

"Where?"

"In the coffin."

Bathsheba trembled from head to foot.

"I don't believe it!" she said excitedly. "And it is not written on the cover."

"Nor I ma'am. And a good many others don't, but I thought I'd just tell you. We shall be sure to learn the rights of it to-morrow. Oak was heard to say that the story belongs to another poor girl, and I believe him,[4] for we should surely have been told more about it if it had been true – don't you think so ma'am."

"We might or we might not."

Bathsheba turned and looked into the fire that Liddy might not see her face. Finding that her mistress was going to say no more Liddy glided out closed the door softly and went to bed.

Bathsheba's face as she continued looking into the fire that evening might have excited solicitousness on her account even among those who loved her least. The sadness of Fanny Robbin's fate did not make Bathsheba's glorious, although she was the Esther to this poor Vashti[5] and their fates might be supposed to stand in some respects as contrasts to each other. When Liddy came into the room a second time the dark eyes which met hers had worn a listless weary look. When she went out after telling the story they had expressed wretchedness in full activity. This also sank to apathy after a time. But her thoughts, sluggish and confused at first, acquired more life as the minutes passed, and the dull misgiving in her brow and eyes suddenly gave way to the stillness of concentration.[6]

Bathsheba had grounds for conjecturing a connection between her own history and the possible tragedy which may have ended Fanny's life, which Oak and Boldwood never for a moment suspected her of possessing. The meeting with the lonely woman on the previous Saturday night had been unwitnessed and unspoken of. Oak may have had the best of intentions in withholding for as many days as possible the details of what had happened; but had he known that Bathsheba's perceptions had already been exercised in the matter he would have done nothing to lengthen the minutes of suspense she was now undergoing, when the certainty which must terminate it would be the worst fact suspected after all.

She suddenly felt a longing desire to speak to some one stronger than herself, and so get strength to sustain her surmised position with dignity, and her carking doubts with stoicism. Where could she find such a friend? Nowhere in the house. She was by far the coolest of the women under her roof. Patience, and suspension of judgment for a few hours, were what she wanted to learn, and there was nobody to help her.[7] Might she but go to Gabriel Oak! but that could not be. What a way Oak had she thought, of enduring things. Boldwood, who seemed so much deeper, and higher, and stronger in feeling than Gabriel, had not yet learnt any more than she herself the simple lesson which Oak showed a mastery of by every turn and look he gave – that among the multitude of interests by which he was surrounded, those which affected his personal well-being were not the most absorbing and important in his eyes. Oak meditatively looked upon the horizon of circumstances without any special regard to his own standpoint in the midst. That was how she would wish to be. But then Oak was not racked by incertitude upon the inmost matter of his bosom as was she at this moment. Oak knew all that she wished to know – she felt convinced of that. If she were to go to him now at once and say no more than these few words, "What is the truth of the story?" he would feel bound in honour to tell her. It would be an inexpressible relief. No further speech would need to be uttered. He knew her so well that no eccentricity of behaviour in her would alarm him.

She flung a cloak round her, went to the door and opened it. Every blade, every twig was still. The air was yet thick with moisture, though somewhat less dense than during the afternoon, and a steady smack of drops upon the fallen leaves under the boughs was almost musical in its soothing regularity. It seemed better to be out of the house than within it, and Bathsheba closed the door, and walked slowly down the lane till she came opposite to Gabriel's cottage, where he now lived alone, having left Coggan's house through being pinched for room. There was a light in one window only, and that was downstairs. The shutters were not closed, nor was any blind or curtain drawn over the window, neither robbery nor observation being a contingency which could do much injury to the occupant of the domicile. Yes, it was Gabriel himself who was sitting up: he was reading. From her standing-place in the road she could see him plainly, sitting quite still, his light curly head upon his hand, and only occasionally looking up to snuff the candle which stood beside him. At length he pulled out his watch, seemed surprised at the lateness of the hour, closed his book, and arose. He was going to bed, she knew, and if she tapped it must be done at once.

Alas for her resolve – She felt she could not do it. Not for worlds now could she give a hint about her misery to him – much less ask him plainly for information. She must suspect, and guess, and chafe, and bear it all alone.

Like a homeless wanderer she lingered by the bank, as if lulled and fascinated by the atmosphere of content which seemed to spread from that little dwelling, and was so sadly lacking in her own. Gabriel appeared in an upper room, placed his light in the window-bench and then – knelt down to pray. The contrast of the picture with her rebellious and agitated existence at this same time was too much for her to bear to look upon longer. It was not for her to make a truce with trouble by any such means. She must tread her giddy dismal measure to its last note, as she had begun it. With a swollen heart she went again up the lane, and entered her own door.

More fevered now by a reaction from the first feelings which Oak's example had raised in her, she paused in the hall, looking at the door of the room wherein Fanny lay. She locked her fingers, threw back her head, and strained her hot hands rigidly across her forehead, saying with a hysterical sob, "Would to God you would speak and tell me your secret, Fanny!. . . . O I hope, hope it is not true. . . . If I could only look in upon you for one little minute I should know all."

A few moments passed, and she added slowly, "*And I will!*"

Bathsheba in aftertimes could never guage the mood which carried her through the actions following this return to the house on this memorable evening of her life. At the end of a short though undefined time she found herself in the small room, quivering with emotion, a mist before her eyes and an excruciating pulsation in her brain, standing beside the uncovered coffin of the girl whose conjectured end had so entirely engrossed her, and saying to herself in a husky voice as she gazed within:

"It was best to know the worst, and I know it now."

She was conscious of having brought about this situation by a series of actions done as by one in an extravagant dream; of following that idea as to method, which had burst upon her in the hall with glaring obviousness, by searching about the house for something she required for her purpose; then by gliding to the top of the stairs, assuring herself by listening to the heavy breathing of her maids that they were asleep, gliding down again, turning the handle of the door within which the young girl lay, and deliberately setting herself to do what, if she had anticipated any such undertaking, would have frightened her, but which, when done was not so dreadful as was the conclusive proof which came with knowing beyond doubt the last chapter of Fanny's story.[8]

Bathsheba's eager eyes were not directed to the upper end. By the dead girl's side, enclosed by one of her arms, was the object of the search: –

A curious frame of Nature's work,
A flow'ret crushéd in the bud,
A nameless piece of Babyhood,

neatly apparelled in its first and last outfit for earth – a miniature wrapping of white linen – with a face so delicately small in contour and substance that its cheeks and the plump backs of its little fists irresistibly reminded her, excited as she was, of the soft convexity of mushrooms on a dewy morning.

Fanny was framed in by that yellow hair of hers, just as she had slept hundreds of times in this house, with the exception of the fresh colour which had formerly adorned her. There was no longer any room for doubt as to the origin of the curl owned by Troy. She appeared rounder in feature and much younger than she had looked during the latter months of her life. Her hands had acquired a preternatural refinement, and a painter in looking upon them might have fancied that at last he had found the fellows of those marvellous hands and fingers which must have served as originals to Bellini.[9]

The youth and fairness of both the silent ones withdrew from the scene all associations of a repulsive kind – even every unpleasant ray. The mother had been no further advanced in womanliness than had the infant in childhood; they both had stood upon the threshhold of a new stage of existence, and had vanished before they could well be defined as examples of that stage. They struck upon the sense in the aspect of incipiency, not in that of decadence. They seemed failures in creation, by nature interesting, rather than instances of dissolution, by nature frightful.

But what was all this to her who stood there? A thought of a few moments, which pity and a common sex insisted upon introducing. Then Bathsheba was in the real world again, and other than the highly poetical aspects of this scene returned upon her mind. Her head sank upon her bosom, and the breath which had been bated in suspense, curiosity, and interest, was exhaled now in the form of a whispered wail: "Oh-h-h!"

Her tears fell fast beside the unconscious pair – tears of a complicated origin, of a nature indescribable, almost indefinable, except as other than those of simple sorrow. Assuredly their wonted fires must have lived in Fanny's ashes when events were so shaped as to chariot her hither in this natural, unobtrusive yet effectual manner. The one feat alone – that of dying – by which a mean condition could be resolved into a grand one, Fanny had achieved. And to that had destiny subjoined this rencounter to-night, which had, in Bathsheba's wild imagining, turned her companion's failure to success, her humiliation to triumph, her lucklessness to ascendancy; it had thrown over herself a garish light of mockery, and set upon all things about her an ironical smile.[10] But even Bathsheba's heated fancy failed to endow that innocent white countenance with any triumphant[11] consciousness of the pain she was retaliating for her pain with all the merciless rigour of the Mosaic law: "Burning for burning; wound for wound; strife for strife."[12]

Bathsheba indulged in contemplations of escape from her position by the way of death, which, thought she, though it was an inconvenient and awful way, had limits to its inconvenience and awfulness which could not be overpassed; whilst the terrors of life were measureless. Yet even this scheme of extinction by death was but tamely copying her rival's method without the reasons which had glorified it in her rival's case. She glided rapidly up and down the room, as was mostly her habit when excited, her hands hanging clasped in front of her, as she thought and in part expressed in broken words; "O I hate them[13] – yet I don't mean that I hate them, for it is grievous and wicked – and yet I hate them a little! Yes, my flesh insists upon hating them, whether my spirit is willing or no. . . . . If she had only lived I could have been angry and cruel towards her with some justification, but to be vindictive toward a poor dead woman and babe recoils upon myself. O God have mercy – I am miserable at all this!"

Bathsheba became at this moment so terrified at her own state of mind that she looked around for some sort of refuge from herself. The vision of Oak kneeling down that night recurred to her, and with the imitative instinct which animates women she seized upon the idea, resolved to kneel and if possible, pray. Gabriel had prayed; so would she.

She knelt beside the coffin, covered her face with her hands, and for a time the room was silent as a tomb. Whether from a purely mechanical, or from another cause, when Bathsheba arose it was with a quieted spirit, and a regret for the antagonistic instincts which had seized upon her just before.

In her desire to make atonement she took flowers from a vase by the window, and began laying them around the dead girl's head. Bathsheba knew no other way of showing kindness to persons departed than by giving them flowers. She knew not how long she remained engaged thus. She forgot time, life, where she was, what she was doing. A slamming together of the coach-house doors in the yard brought her to herself again. An instant after, the front door opened and closed, steps crossed the hall, and her husband appeared at the entrance to the room, looking in upon her.

He beheld it all by degrees, stared in stupefaction at the scene, as if he thought it an illusion raised by some fiendish incantation. Bathsheba gazed back at him in the same wild way.

So little are instinctive guesses the fruit of a legitimate induction that at this moment as he stood with the door in his hand, Troy never once thought of Fanny in connection with what he saw. His first reasoned idea was that somebody in the house had died.

"Well – what?" said Troy blankly.

"I must go – I must go!" said Bathsheba, to herself more than to him. She came with a dilated eye towards the door, to push past him.

"What's the matter in God's name – who's dead!" said Troy.

"I cannot say – let me go out – I want air!" she continued.

"But no – stay, I insist!" He seized her hand; and then volition seemed to leave her, and she went off into a state of collapse. He, still holding her, came up the room, and thus, hand in hand, Troy and Bathsheba approached the coffin's side.

The candle was standing on a bureau close by them, and the light slanted down, distinctly enkindling the features of the young girl and babe.[14] Troy looked in, dropped his wife's hand, knowledge of it all came over him in a lurid sheen, and he stood still.

So still he remained that he could be imagined to have left in him no motive power whatever. The clashes of feeling in all directions confounded one another, produced a neutrality, and there was motion in none.

"Do you know her?" said Bathsheba, in a small enclosed echo, as from the interior of a cell.

"I do," said Troy.

"Is it she?"

"It is."

He had originally stood perfectly erect. And now, in the well-nigh congealed immobility of his frame could be discerned an incipient movement, as in the darkest night may be discerned light after a while. He was gradually sinking forwards. The lines of his features softened, and dismay modulated to illimitable sadness. Bathsheba was regarding him from the other side, still with parted lips and distracted eyes. Capacity for intense feeling is proportionate to the general intensity of the nature, and in all Fanny's sufferings, much greater relatively to her strength, there never was a time when she suffered in an absolute sense what Bathsheba suffered now.

This is what Troy did. He sank upon his knees with an indefinable union of remorse and reverence upon his face, and, bending over Fanny Robbin, gently kissed her, as one would kiss an infant asleep to avoid awakening it.

At the sight and sound of that, to her, unendurable act, Bathsheba sprang towards him. All the strong feelings which had been scattered over her existence since she knew what feeling was seemed gathered together in one pulsation now. The revulsion from her indignant mood a little earlier, when she had meditated upon compromised honour, forestallment, eclipse by another, was violent and entire. All that was forgotten in the simple and still strong attachment of wife to husband. She had sighed for her self-completeness then, and now she cried aloud against the severance of the union she had deplored. She flung her arms round

Troy's neck, exclaiming wildly from the deepest deep of her heart: –

"Don't – don't kiss them! O Frank, I can't bear it – I can't! I love you better than she did – kiss me too, Frank – kiss me too! *You will Frank kiss me too!*"

There was something so abnormal and startling in the childlike pain and simplicity of this appeal from a woman of Bathsheba's calibre and independence that Troy, loosening her tightly clasped arms from his neck, looked at her in bewilderment. It was such an unexpected revelation of all women being alike at heart, even those so different in their accessories as Fanny and this one beside him, that Troy could hardly seem to believe her to be his proud wife Bathsheba. Fanny's own spirit seemed to be animating her frame. But this was the mood of a few instants only. When the momentary surprise had passed, his expression changed to a silencing imperious gaze.

"I will not kiss you," he said, pushing her away.

Had the wife now but gone no further. – Yet perhaps, under the harrowing circumstances, to speak out was the one wrong act which can be better understood, if not forgiven in her than the right and politic one. She drew all the feeling she had been betrayed into showing back to herself again by a strenuous effort of self-command.

"What have you to say as your reason?" she asked, her bitter voice being strangely low – quite that of another woman now.

"I have to say that I have been a bad, black-hearted man," he answered.

"And that this woman is your victim – and I not less than she."

"Ah! Don't taunt me, madam. This woman is more to me, dead as she is, than ever you were, or are, or can be. If Satan had not tempted me with that face of yours and those coquettish airs I should have married her. I never had another thought till you came in my way. Would to God that I had – but it is all too late! I deserve to live in torment for this." He turned to Fanny then. "But never mind darling," he said; "in the sight of heaven you are my very very own."

At these words there arose from Bathsheba's lips a long low cry of measureless despair and indignation – such a wail of anguish as had never before been heard within those old-inhabited walls. It was the Τετέλεσται[15] of her union with Troy.

"If she's – that, – what – am I?" she added, as a continuation of the same cry, and sobbing brokenly; and the rarity with her of such abandonment only made the condition more terrible.

"You are nothing to me – nothing," said Troy heartlessly. "A ceremony before a priest doesn't make a marriage. I am not morally yours."

A vehement impulse to flee from him, to run from this place, hide, and escape humiliation at any price, not stopping short of death itself, mastered Bathsheba now. She waited not an instant, but turned to the door and ran out.

CHAPTER XLIII

Under a tree: reaction.

Bathsheba went along the dark road neither knowing nor caring about the direction or issue of her flight. The first time that she definitely noticed her position was when she reached a gate leading into a thicket overhung by some large oak and beech trees. On looking into the place it occurred to her that she had seen it by daylight on some previous occasion, and that what appeared like an impassable thicket was in reality a brake of fern, now withering fast. She could think of nothing better to do with her palpitating self than to go in here and hide; and entering she lighted on a spot sheltered from the damp fog by a reclining trunk, where she sank down upon a tangled couch of fronds and stems. She mechanically pulled some armfulls round her to keep off the breezes, and closed her eyes.

Whether she slept or not that night Bathsheba was not clearly aware. But it was with a freshened existence and a cooler brain that a long time afterwards she became conscious of some interesting proceedings that were going on in the trees above her head and around.

A coarse-throated chatter was the first sound.

It was a sparrow just waking.

Next: "Chee-weeze-weeze-weeze!" from another retreat.

It was a finch.

Third: "tink-tink-tink-tink-a-chink!" from the hedge.

It was a robin.

"Chuck-chuck-chuck!" overhead.

A squirrel.

Then, from the road, "With my ra-ta-ta, and my rum-tum-tum!"

It was a ploughboy. Presently he came opposite, and she believed from his voice that he was one of the boys on her own farm. He was followed by a shambling tramp of heavy feet, and looking through the fern Bathsheba could just discern in the wan light of daybreak a team of her own horses. They stopped to drink at a pond on the other side of the way. She watched them flouncing into the pool, drinking, tossing up their heads, drinking again, the water dribbling from their lips in silver threads. There was another flounce and they came out of the pond, and turned back again towards the farm.

She looked further around. Day was just dawning, and beside its cool air and colours, her heated actions and resolves of the night stood out in lurid contrast. She perceived that in her lap, and clinging to her hair, were red and yellow leaves that had come down from the tree and settled silently upon her during her partial sleep. Bathsheba shook her dress to get rid of them, when multitudes of the same family lying round about her rose and fluttered away in the breeze she thus created – "like ghosts from an enchanter fleeing".[1]

There was an opening towards the east, and the glow from the as yet unrisen sun attracted her eyes thither. From her feet, and the beautiful yellowing ferns with their feathery arms, the ground sloped downwards to a hollow, in which was a species of swamp, dotted with fungi. A morning mist hung over it now – a fulsome yet magnificent silvery veil, full of light from the sun, yet semi-opaque – the hedge behind it being in some measure hidden by its hazy luminousness. Up the sides of this depression grew sheaves of the common rush, and here and there a peculiar species of flag, the blades of which glistened in the emerging sun like scythes. But the general aspect of the swamp was malignant. From its moist and poisonous coat seemed to be exhaled the essences of evil things in the earth, and in the waters under the earth. The fungi grew in all manner of positions from rotting leaves and tree stumps, some exhibiting to her listless gaze their clammy tops, others their oozing gills. Some were marked with great splotches, red as arterial blood – others were scabbed[2] – others of a saffron yellow, and others tall and attenuated with thin stems like macaroni. Some were leathery and of richest browns. The hollow seemed a nursery of pestilences small and great, in the immediate neighbourhood of comfort and health, and Bathsheba arose with a tremor at the thought of having passed the night on the brink of so dismal a place.

There were now other footsteps to be heard along the road. Bathsheba crouched down out of sight again, and the pedestrian came into view. He was a schoolboy, with a bag slung over his shoulder containing his dinner, and a book in his hand. He paused by the gate, and without looking up continued murmuring words in tones quite loud enough to reach her ears.

"'O Lord O Lord O Lord O Lord O Lord': That I know. 'Give us give us give us give us give us': That I know. 'Grace that grace that grace that grace that': That I know." Other words followed to the same effect. The boy was of the dunce class apparently: the book was a psalter, and this was his way of learning the collect. In the worst attacks of trouble there appears to be always a superficial film of consciousness which is left disengaged and open to the notice of trifles, and Bathsheba was faintly amused at all this, till he too passed on.

By this time stupor had given place to anxiety, and anxiety began to make room for hunger and thirst. A form now appeared upon the rise on the other side of the swamp, half hidden by the mist, and came towards Bathsheba. The female, for it was a female, approached with her face askance, as if looking earnestly on all sides of her. When she got a little further round to the left, and drew nearer, Bathsheba could see the newcomer's profile against the sunny sky, and knew the wavy sweep from forehead to chin, with neither angle nor decisive line anywhere about it, to be the familiar contour of Liddy Smallbury.

Bathsheba's heart bounded with gratitude in the thought that she was not altogether deserted, and she jumped up. "O Liddy!" she said or attempted to say. The words had only been framed by her lips: there came no sound. She had lost her voice by exposure to the clogged atmosphere all these hours of night.

"O ma'am – I am so glad I have found you!" said the girl as soon as she saw Bathsheba.

"You can't come across," Bathsheba said in a whisper which she vainly endeavoured to make loud enough to reach Liddy's ears. Liddy, not knowing this, stepped down upon the swamp, saying as she did so, "It will bear me up, I think."

Bathsheba never forgot that transient little picture of Liddy crossing the swamp to her there in the morning light. Iridescent bubbles of dank subterranean breath rose from the sweating sod beside the waiting-maid's feet as she trod, hissing as they burst and expanded away to join the vapoury firmament above. Liddy did not sink as Bathsheba had anticipated. She landed safely on the other side, and looked up at the beautiful though pale and weary face of her young mistress.

"Poor thing!" said Liddy with tears in her eyes. "Do hearten up yourself a little ma'am. How ever did –"

"I can't speak above a whisper – my voice is gone for the present," said Bathsheba hurriedly. "I suppose the damp air from that hollow has taken it away. Liddy, don't question me, mind. Who sent you – anybody?"

"Nobody. I thought when I found you were not at home that something cruel had happened. I fancy I heard his voice late last night. And so knowing something was wrong –"

"Is he at home?"

"No – he left just before I came out."

"Is Fanny taken away?"

"Not yet. She will soon be – at nine o'clock."

"We won't go home at present, then. Suppose we walk about in this wood."

Liddy without exactly understanding everything, or anything, in this episode, assented, and they walked together further among the trees.

"But you had better come in ma'am, and have something to eat. You will die of a chill."

"I shall not come indoors yet – perhaps never."

"Shall I get you something to eat, and something else to put over your head besides that little shawl."

"If you will Liddy."

Liddy vanished and at the end of twenty minutes returned with a cloak, hat, some slices of bread and butter, a tea cup, and some hot tea in a little china jug.

"Is Fanny gone?" said Bathsheba, in the same difficult whisper.

"No," said her companion pouring out the tea.

Bathsheba wrapped herself up and eat and drank sparingly. Her voice was then a little clearer, and a trifling colour returned to her face. "Now we'll walk about again," she said.

They wandered about the wood for nearly two hours, Bathsheba replying in monosyllables to Liddy's prattle. Her companion's mind ran on one subject and one only. She interrupted with

"I wonder if Fanny is gone by this time?"

"I will go and see."

She came back with the information that the men were just taking away the corpse; that Bathsheba had been enquired for, that she had replied to the effect that her mistress was unwell and could not be seen.

"Then they think I am in my bedroom?"

"Yes." Liddy then ventured to add: "You said when I first found you that you might never go home again. You didn't mean it, ma'am?"

"No – I've altered my mind. It is only women with no pride in them who run away from their husbands. There is one position worse than that of being found dead in your husband's house from his ill-usage, and that is to be found alive through having run away to the house of somebody else. I've thought of it all this night past, and I've chosen my course. A runaway wife is an encumbrance to everybody, a burden to herself, and a byword – all of which make up a heap of misery greater than any that comes by staying at home, though this may include the trifling items of insult, beating and starvation. Liddy if ever you marry – God forbid that you ever should – you'll find yourself in a fearful situation; but mind this, don't you flinch. Stand your ground and be cut to pieces. That's what I'm going to do."

"O mistress – don't talk so!" said Liddy taking her hand. "But I knew you had too much sense to run away."

In about ten minutes they returned to the house by a circuitous route, entering at the rear. Bathsheba glided up the back stairs to a disused attic, and her companion followed.

"Liddy," she said, "you are to be my confidante for the present – somebody must be, and I choose you. Well, I shall take up my abode here for a while. Will you get a fire lighted, put down a piece of carpet, and help me to make the place comfortable? Afterwards I want you and Mary-ann to bring up that little iron bedstead in the small room, and the bed belonging to it, and a table, and some other things. What shall I do to pass the heavy time away?"[3]

"Hemming handkerchiefs is a very good thing," said Liddy.

"O no no. I hate needlework – I always did."

"Knitting?"

"And that too."

"You might finish your sampler. Only the carnations and peacocks want filling in, and then it could be framed and glazed and hung beside your aunt's, ma'am."

"Samplers are out of date – horribly countrified. No Liddy, I'll read. Bring up some books. Not new ones. I haven't heart to read anything new."

"Some of your uncle's old ones ma'am?"

"Yes: some of those we stowed away in boxes." A faint gleam of humour passed over her face as she said, "Bring Beaumont and Fletcher's *Maid's Tragedy*; and the *Mourning Bride*; and – let me see – *Night Thoughts*, and the *Vanity of Human Wishes*."[4]

"And that story of the black man[5] who murdered his wife Desdemona is a nice dismal one that would suit you, ma'am, don't you think so?" hinted Liddy.

"Now Lidd – you've been looking into my books without telling me! And I said you were not to. How do you know it would suit me? It wouldn't suit me at all."

"But if the others do –"

"No they don't. And I won't read dismal books. Why should I read dismal books indeed? Bring me *Love in a Village*, and *The Maid of the Mill*, and *Doctor Syntax* and some volumes of the *Spectator*."[6]

All that day Bathsheba and Liddy lived in the attic in a state of barricade, a precaution which proved to be needless as against Troy, for he did not appear in the neighourhood or trouble them at all. Bathsheba sat at the window till sunset, sometimes attempting to read, at other times watching every movement outside without much purpose, and listening without much interest to every sound.

The sun went down almost blood-red that night, and a livid cloud received its rays in the east. Up against this dark background the west front of the church tower – the only part of the edifice visible from the farm-house windows – rose distinct and lustrous, the vane upon the pinnacle bristling with rays. Here, about six o'clock, the young men of the village gathered, as was their custom, for a game of fives.[7] The tower had been consecrated to this ancient diversion from time immemorial, the western facade conveniently forming the boundary of the churchyard at that end, where the ground was trodden hard and bare as a pavement by the players. She could see the balls flying upwards almost to the belfry window, and the brown and black heads of the young lads darting about right and left, their white shirt-sleeves gleaming in the sun, whilst occasionally a shout and a peal of hearty laughter varied the stillness of the evening air. They continued playing for a quarter of an hour or so, when the game concluded abruptly, and the players leapt over the wall and vanished round the north side behind a yew tree, which was also half behind a beech, now spreading in one mass of golden foliage, on which the branches traced black lines.

"Why did the fives'-players finish their game so suddenly?" Bathsheba enquired the next time that Liddy entered the room.

"I think 'twas because two men came just then from Casterbridge and began putting up a grand carved tombstone," said Liddy. "The lads went to see whose it was."

"Do you know?" Bathsheba asked.

"I don't," said Liddy.

CHAPTER XLIV

Troy's romanticism.

When Troy's wife had left the house at the previous midnight his first act was to cover the dead from sight. This done he ascended the stairs, and throwing himself down upon the bed, dressed as he was, he waited miserably for the morning.

Fate had dealt grimly with him through the last four and twenty hours. His day had been spent in a way which varied very materially from his intentions regarding it. There is always an inertia to be overcome in striking out a new line of conduct – not more in ourselves, it seems, than in circumscribing events which appear as if leagued together to allow no novelties in the way of amelioration.

Twenty pounds having been secured from Bathsheba he had managed to add to the sum every farthing he could muster on his own account, which had been seven pounds ten. With this money, twenty-seven pounds ten in all, he had hastily driven from the gate that morning to keep his appointment with Fanny Robbin.

On reaching Casterbridge he left the horse and trap at an inn, and at five minutes before ten, went to the bridge at the further end of the town, and sat himself upon the parapet. The clocks struck the hour, and no Fanny appeared. In fact at that moment she was being robed in her grave clothes by two attendants at the Union poorhouse – the first and last tiring women the gentle creature had ever been honoured with. The quarter went, the half hour. A rush of recollection came upon Troy as he waited: this was the second time she had broken a serious engagement with him. In anger he vowed it should be the last, and at eleven o'clock, when he had lingered and watched the stones of the bridge till he knew every lichen upon their faces, and heard the chink of the ripples underneath till they oppressed him, he jumped from his seat, went to the inn for his gig, and in a bitter mood of remorse for the past and indifference as to the future drove on to Budmouth races.

He reached the race-course at two o'clock, and remained either there or in the town till nine. Fanny's image as it had appeared to him in the sombre shadows of that Saturday evening still haunted his mind, backed up by Bathsheba's reproaches. He vowed he would not bet, and he kept his vow, for when he left town at nine o'clock in the evening he had diminished his cash only to the extent of a few shillings.

He trotted slowly homeward, and it was now that he was struck for the first time with a thought that Fanny had been really prevented by illness from keeping her promise. This time she could have made no mistake. He regretted that he had not remained in Casterbridge and made enquiries. Reaching home he quietly unharnessed the horse and came indoors as we have seen.

As soon as it grew light enough to distinguish objects Troy arose from the coverlet of the bed, and in a mood of absolute indifference to Bathsheba's whereabouts, and almost unconscious of her existence, he stalked downstairs and left the house by the back door. His walk was towards the churchyard, entering which he searched around till he found a newly dug unoccupied grave. The position of this having been marked he hastened on to Casterbridge only pausing and musing for a while at the hill whereon he had last seen Fanny alive.

Reaching the town, Troy descended into a side street and entered a pair of gates surmounted by a board bearing the words "Harrison,[1] stone and marble mason." Within were lying about stones of all sizes and designs, inscribed as being sacred to the memory – of unnamed persons who had not yet died.

Troy was so unlike himself now in look word and deed that the want of likeness was perceptible even to his own consciousness. His method of engaging himself in this business of purchasing a tomb was that of an absolutely unpractised man. He could not bring himself to consider, calculate, or economize. He waywardly wished for something, and he set about obtaining it like a child in a nursery. "I want a good tomb," he said to the man who stood in a little office within the yard. "I want as good a one as you can give me for twenty-seven pounds."

It was all the money he possessed.

"That sum to include everything?"

"Everything. Cutting the name, carriage to Weatherbury, and erection. And I want it now, at once."

"We could not get anything special worked this week."

"I must have it now."

"If you would like one of these in stock it could be got ready immediately."

"Very well," said Troy impatiently. "Let's see what you have."

"The best I have in stock is this one," said the stonecutter, going into a shed. "Here's a marble headstone beautifully crocketted, with medallions beneath of typical subjects: here's the footstone after the same pattern, and here's the coping to enclose the grave. The polishing alone of the set cost me eleven pounds – the slabs are the best of their kind, and I can warrant them to resist rain and frost for a hundred years without flying."

"And how much?"

"Well. I could add the name, and put it up at Weatherbury for the sum you mention."

"Get it done today, and I'll pay down the money now."

The man agreed, and wondered at such a mood in a visitor who wore not a shred of mourning. Troy then wrote the words which were to form the inscription, settled the account, and went away. In the afternoon he came back again, and found that the lettering was almost done. He waited in the yard till the tomb was packed, and saw it placed in the cart and starting on its way to Weatherbury, giving directions to the two men who were to accompany it to enquire of the sexton for the grave of the person named in the inscription.

It was quite dark when Troy came out of Casterbridge. He carried rather a heavy basket upon his arm, with which he strode moodily along the road, resting occasionally at bridges and gates, whereon he deposited his burden for a time. Midway on his journey he met in the darkness the men and the waggon which had conveyed the tomb. He merely enquired if the work was done, and, on being assured that it was, passed on again.

Troy entered Weatherbury churchyard about ten o'clock, and went immediately to the corner where he had seen the vacant grave early in the morning. It was on the north side of the tower, screened to a great extent from the view of passers along the road – a spot which until lately had been abandoned to heaps of stones and bushes of alder, but now it was cleared and made orderly for interments, by reason of the rapid filling of the ground elsewhere.

Here now stood the tomb as the men had stated, snow-white and shapely in the gloom, with a head and foot stone, an enclosing border of marblework uniting them. In the midst was mould, suitable for plants.

Troy deposited his basket beside the tomb, and vanished for a few minutes. When he returned he carried a spade and a lantern, the light of which he directed for a few moments upon the tomb, whilst he read the inscription. He hung his lantern on the lowest bough of the yew tree, and took from his basket flower-roots of several varieties. There were bundles of snowdrop, hyacinth and crocus bulbs, violets, and double daisies, which were to bloom in spring, and of carnations, pinks, picotees, lilies of the valley, heartsease, forget-me-not, summer's farewell and others, for the later seasons of the year.

Troy laid these out upon the grass, and with an impassive face set to work to plant them. The snowdrops were arranged in a row on the outside of the coping, the remainder within the enclosure of the grave. The crocuses and hyacinths were to grow in rows: some of the summer flowers he placed over her head and feet; the lilies and forget-me-nots over her heart. The remainder were dispersed in the spaces between these.

Troy, in his prostration at this time, had no perception that in the futility of these romantic doings, dictated by a remorseful reaction from previous indifference, there was any element of absurdity. Deriving his idiosyncrasies from both sides of the Channel, he showed at such junctures as the present both the inelasticity of the Englishman, and the blindness to the line where sentiment verges on mawkishness so characteristic of the French.

It was a cloudy, muggy, and very dark night, and the rays from Troy's lantern spread into the two old yews with a strange illuminating power, flickering, as it seemed, up to the black ceiling of cloud above. He felt a large drop of rain upon the back of his hand; and presently one came and entered the open side of the lantern, whereupon the candle sputtered and went out. Troy was weary, and it being now not far from midnight, and the rain threatening to increase, he resolved to leave the finishing touches of his labour until the day should break. He groped along the wall and over the graves in the dark till he found himself round at the south side. Here he entered the porch, and reclining upon the bench within, fell asleep.

CHAPTER XLV

The gurgoyle: its doings.

The tower of Weatherbury Church was a square erection of fourteenth-century date, having two stone gurgoyles on each of the four faces of its parapet. Of these eight carved protuberances only two at this date continued to serve the purpose of their erection – that of spouting the water from the lead roof within. One mouth in each front had been closed by bygone churchwardens as superfluous and two others were broken away and choked – a matter not of much consequence to the well-being of the tower, for the two mouths which still remained open and active were gaping enough to do all the work.

It has been sometimes argued that there is no truer criterion of the vitality of any given art-period than the power of the master-spirits of that time in grotesque; and certainly in the instance of Gothic art there is no disputing the proposition. Weatherbury tower was a somewhat early instance of the use of an ornamental parapet in parish as distinct from cathedral churches, and the gurgoyles, which are the necessary correlatives of a parapet were exceptionally prominent – of the boldest cut that the hand could shape, and of the most original design that a human brain could conceive. There was that symmetry in their distortion, so to speak, which is less the characteristic of British than of Continental grotesques of the period, though all four were different from each other.[1] A beholder was convinced that nothing on earth could be more hideous than those he saw on the south side – until he went round to the north.[2] Of the two on this latter face, only that at the north-eastern corner concerns the story. It was too human to be called like a dragon, too impish to be like a man, too animal to be like a fiend, and not enough like a bird to be called a griffin. This horrible stone entity was fashioned as if covered with a wrinkled hide, it had short erect ears, eyes starting from their sockets, and its fingers and hands were seizing the corners of its mouth, which they thus seemed to pull open to give freer passage to the water it vomited. The lower row of teeth was quite washed away, though the upper still remained. Here and thus, jutting a couple of feet from the wall against which its feet rested as a support, the creature had for four hundred years laughed at the surrounding landscape voicelessly in dry weather, and, in wet, with a gurgling and snorting sound.[3]

Troy slept on in the porch, and the rain increased outside. Presently from the mouth of the gurgoyle a small stream began to trickle through the seventy feet of aerial space between its head and the ground, which the water-drops smote like duckshot in their accelerated velocity. The stream thickened in substance, and increased in power, – gradually spouting further and yet further from the side of the tower. When the rain fell in a steady and ceaseless torrent, the stream dashed downward in volumes.

We follow its curve to the ground at this point of time. The base of the liquid parabola has come forward from the wall, has advanced over the plinth mouldings, over a heap of stones, over the marble border, into the midst of Fanny Robbin's grave.

The force of the stream had until very lately been received upon some loose stones spread thereabout, which had acted as a shield to the soil under the onset. These during the summer had been cleared from the ground, and there was now nothing to resist the downfall but the bare earth. For several years the stream had not spouted so far from the tower as it was doing on this night, and such a contingency had been overlooked. Sometimes this obscure corner received no inhabitant for the space of two or three years, and then it was usually but a pauper, a poacher, or other sinner of undignified sins.

The persistent torrent from the gurgoyle's jaws directed all its vengeance into the grave. The rich tawny mould was stirred into motion, and boiled like chocolate. The water accumulated and washed deeper down, and the roar of the pool thus formed spread into the night as the head and chief among other noises of the kind formed by the deluging rain. The flowers so carefully planted by Fanny's repentant lover began to move and turn in their bed. The heartsease turned slowly upside down, and became a mere mat of mud. Soon the snowdrop and other bulbs danced in the boiling mass like ingredients in a cauldron. Roots of the tufted species were loosened, rose to the surface, and floated off.

Troy did not wake from his comfortless sleep till it was broad day. Not having been in bed for two nights his shoulders felt stiff, his feet tender, and his head heavy. He remembered his position, arose, shivered, took the spade, and again went out.

The rain had quite ceased, and the sun was shining through the green, brown, and yellow leaves, now sparkling and varnished by the rain drops to the brightness of similar effects in the landscapes of Ruysdael and Hobbema,[4] and full of all those infinite beauties that arise from the union of water and colour with high lights. The air was rendered so transparent by the heavy fall of rain that the autumn hues of the middle distance were as rich as those near at hand, and the distant fields intercepted by the angle of the tower appeared in the same plane as the tower itself.

He entered the gravel path which would take him behind the tower. The path instead of being stony, as it had been the night before, was browned over with a thin coating of mud. At one place in the path he saw a tuft of stringy roots washed white and clean as a bundle of tendons. He picked it up – surely it could not be one of the primroses he had planted? He saw a bulb, another, and another, as he advanced. Beyond doubt they were the crocuses. With a face of perplexed dismay Troy turned the corner and then beheld the wreck the stream had made.

The pool upon the grave had soaked away into the ground, and in its place was a hollow. The disturbed earth was washed over the grass and pathway in the guise of the brown mud he had already seen, and it spotted the marble tombstone with the same hues. Nearly all the flowers were washed clean out of the ground, and they lay, roots upwards, on the spots whither they had been floated by the stream.

Troy's brow became heavily contracted. He set his teeth closely, and his compressed lips moved as those of one in great pain. This trifling accident, by a strange confluence of emotions in him, was felt as the sharpest sting of all. Troy's face was very expressive, and any observer who had seen him now would hardly have believed him to be a man who had laughed, and sung, and poured love-trifles into a woman's ear. To curse his miserable lot was at first his impulse, but even that lowest stage of rebellion needed an activity whose absence was necessarily antecedent to the existence of the sort of misery he now endured. The sight, coming as it did, superimposed upon the other dark scenery of the previous days, formed a sort of climax to the whole panorama; and it was more than he could endure. Sanguine by nature, Troy had a power of eluding grief by simply adjourning it. He could put off the consideration of any particular spectre till the matter had become old and softened by time. The planting of flowers on Fanny's grave had been perhaps but a species of elusion of the primary grief, and now it was as if his intention had been known and circumvented.

Almost for the first time in his life, Troy, as he stood by this dismantled grave, wished himself another man. It is seldom that a person with much animal spirit does not feel that the fact of his life being his own is the one circumstance which singles it out as a more hopeful life than that of others who may actually resemble him in every particular. Troy had felt, in his transient way, hundreds of times, that he could not envy other people their condition, because the possession of that condition would have necessitated a different personality, when he desired no other than his own. He had not minded the peculiarities of his birth, the vicissitudes of his life, the meteor-like uncertainty of all that related to him, because these appertained to the hero of his story, without whom there would have been no story at all; and it seemed to be only in the nature of things that matters would right themselves at some distant date and wind up well for him. This very morning the illusion completed its disappearance, and, as it were all of a sudden, Troy hated himself. The suddenness was probably more apparent than real. A coral reef which just comes short of the ocean surface is no more to the horizon than if it had never been begun, and the mere finishing stroke is what often appears to create an event which has long been potentially an accomplished thing.

He stood and meditated – a miserable man. Whither should he go? "He that is accursed, let him be accursed still", was the text of the sermon[5] written in this spoliated effort of his newborn solicitousness. A man who has spent his primal strength in journeying in one direction has not much strength left for reversing his course. Troy had, since yesterday, faintly reversed his; but the merest opposition had disheartened him. To turn about would have been hard enough under the greatest Providential encouragement; but to find that Providence, far from helping him into a new course, or showing any wish that he might adopt one, actually jeered his first trembling and critical attempt in that kind was more than nature could bear.

He slowly withdrew from the grave. He did not attempt to fill up the hole, replace the flowers, or do anything at all. He simply threw up his cards[6] and forthwith vanished from the churchyard. Shortly afterwards he had gone from the village.[7]

Meanwhile Bathsheba remained a voluntary prisoner in the attic. The door was kept locked except during the entries and exits of Liddy for whom a bed had been arranged in a small adjoining room. The light of Troy's lantern in the churchyard was noticed about ten o'clock by the maidservant who casually looked from the window in that direction whilst taking her supper, and she called Bathsheba's attention to it. They looked curiously at the phenomenon for a time, until Liddy was sent to bed.

Bathsheba did not sleep very heavily that night. When her attendant was unconscious and softly breathing in the next room the mistress of the house was still looking out of the window at the faint gleam spreading from among the trees – not in a steady shine, but blinking like a revolving coast light, though this appearance failed to suggest to her that a person was passing and repassing in front of it. Bathsheba sat here till it began to rain, and the light vanished, when she withdrew to lie restlessly in her bed and re-enact in a worn mind the lurid scene of yesternight. Almost before the first faint sign of dawn appeared she arose again and opened the window to obtain a full breathing of the new morning air, the panes being now wet with trembling tears left by the night rain, each one rounded with a pale lustre caught from primrose-hued slashes through a cloud low down in the awakening sky. From the trees came the sound of steady dripping upon the horny leaves under them, and from the direction of the church she could hear another noise – peculiar, and not intermittent like the rest – the purl of water falling into a pool.

Liddy knocked at eight o'clock, and Bathsheba unlocked the door.

"What a heavy rain we've had in the night ma'am," said Liddy when her enquiries about breakfast had been made.

"Yes: very heavy."

"Did you hear the strange noise from the churchyard?"

"I heard one strange noise. I've been thinking it must have been the water from the tower spouts."

"Well, that's what the shepherd was saying ma'am. He's now gone on to see."

"O – Gabriel has been here this morning?"

"Only just looked in in passing – quite in his old way, which I thought he had left off lately. But the tower spouts used to spatter on the stones, and we are puzzled, for this was like the boiling of a pot."

Not being able to read think or work Bathsheba asked Liddy to stay and breakfast with her. The tongue of the more childish woman still ran upon recent events. "Are you going across to the church ma'am?" she asked.

"Not that I know of," said Bathsheba.

"I thought you might like to go and see where they have put Fanny. The tree hides the place from your window."

Bathsheba had all sorts of dreads about meeting her husband. "Has Mr Troy been in to-night?" she said.

"No, ma'am: I think he's gone to Budmouth."

Budmouth. The sound of the word carried with it a much diminished perspective of him and his deeds: there were fifteen miles interval betwixt them now. She hated questioning Liddy about her husband's movements, and indeed had hitherto sedulously avoided doing so; but now all the house knew that there had been some dreadful disagreement between them, and it was futile to attempt disguise. Bathsheba had reached a stage at which people cease to have any appreciative regard for public opinion.

"What makes you think he has gone there?" she said.

"Laban Tall saw him on the Budmouth road this morning before breakfast."

Bathsheba was momentarily relieved of that wayward heaviness of the past twenty-four hours which had quenched the vitality of youth in her without substituting the philosophy of maturer years, and she resolved to go out and walk a little way. So when breakfast was over she put on her bonnet and took a direction towards the church. It was nine o'clock, and the men having returned to work again from their first meal she was not likely to meet many of them in the road. Knowing that Fanny had been laid in the reprobates' quarter of the graveyard, called in the parish "behind church", which was invisible from the road, it was impossible to resist the impulse to enter and look upon a spot which from nameless feelings she at the same time dreaded to see. She had been unable to overcome an impression that some connection existed between her rival and the light through the trees.

Bathsheba skirted the buttress, and beheld the hole and the tomb, its delicately veined surface splashed and stained just as Troy had seen it and left it two hours earlier. On the other side of the scene stood Gabriel. His eyes too were fixed on the tomb, and her arrival having been noiseless she had not as yet attracted his attention. Bathsheba did not at once perceive that the grand tomb and the disturbed grave were Fanny's, and she looked on both sides and around for some humbler mound, earthed up and clodded in the usual way. Then her eye followed Oak's and she read the words with which the inscription opened: –

"Erected by Francis Troy in memory of Fanny Robbin."

Oak saw her, and his first act was to gaze enquiringly and learn how she received this knowledge of the authorship of the work, which to himself had caused considerable astonishment. But such discoveries did not much affect her now. Emotional convulsions seemed to have become the commonplaces of her history, and she bade him Good morning, and asked him to fill in the hole with the spade which was standing by. Whilst Oak was doing as she desired Bathsheba collected the flowers, and began planting them with that sympathetic manipulation of roots and leaves which is so conspicuous in a woman's gardening, and which flowers seem to understand and thrive upon. She requested Oak to get the churchwardens to turn the leadwork at the mouth of the gurgoyle that hung gaping down upon them, that by this means the stream might be directed sideways, and a repetition of the accident prevented. Finally, with the superfluous magnanimity of a woman whose converse and narrower instincts have brought down bitterness upon her instead of love, she wiped the mud spots from the tomb as if she rather liked its words than otherwise, and went home again with a trembling lip.

CHAPTER XLVI

Adventures by the shore.

Troy wandered along towards the coast. A composite feeling, made up of disgust with the, to him, humdrum tædium of a farmer's life, gloomy images of her who lay in the churchyard, remorse, and a general aversion to his wife's society impelled him to seek a home in any place on earth save Weatherbury. The sad accessories of Fanny's end confronted him as vivid pictures which threatened to be indelible, and made life in Bathsheba's house intolerable. At three in the afternoon he found himself at the foot of a slope more than a mile in length, which ran to the ridge of a range of hills lying parallel with the shore, and forming a monotonous barrier between the basin of cultivated country inland and the wilder scenery of the coast. Up the hill stretched a road perfectly straight and perfectly white, the two sides approaching each other in a gradual taper till they met the sky at the top about two miles off. Throughout the length of this narrow and irksome inclined plane not a sign of life was visible on this garish afternoon. Troy toiled up the road with a languor and depression greater than any he had experienced for many a day and year before. The air was warm and muggy, and the top seemed to recede as he approached.

At last he reached the summit, and a new and novel prospect burst upon him with an effect almost like that of the Pacific upon Balboa's[1] gaze. The broad steely sea, marked only by faint lines which had a semblance of being etched thereon to a degree not deep enough to disturb its general evenness, stretched the whole width of his front and round to the left, where, near the town and port of Budmouth, the sun bristled down upon it and banished all colour to substitute in its place a clear oily polish. Nothing moved in sky, land, or sea, except a frill of milkwhite foam along the nearer angles of the shore, shreds of which licked the contiguous stones like the tongues of so many dogs.

He descended and came to a small basin of sea enclosed by the cliffs. Troy's nature freshened within him: he thought he would rest and bathe here before going further. He undressed and plunged in. Inside the cove the water was uninteresting to a swimmer, being smooth as a pond, and to get a little of the ocean swell Troy presently swam between the two projecting spurs of rock which formed the pillars of Hercules to this miniature Mediterranean.[2] Unfortunately for Troy a current unknown to him existed outside, which, unimportant to craft of any burden, was awkward for a swimmer who might be taken in it unawares. Troy found himself carried to the left and then round in a swoop out to sea.

He now recollected the place and its sinister character. Many bathers had there prayed for a dry death from time to time and like Gonzalo[3] had been unanswered; and Troy began to deem it possible that he might be added to their number. Not a boat of any kind was at present within sight, but far in the distance Budmouth lay upon the sea, as it were quietly regarding his efforts, and beside the town the harbour showed its position by a dim meshwork of ropes and spars. After well-nigh exhausting himself, in attempts to get back to the mouth of the cove, in his weakness swimming several inches deeper than was his wont, keeping up his breathing entirely by his nostrils, turning on his back a dozen times over, swimming *en papillon*, and so on, Troy resolved as a last resource to tread water at a slight incline, and so endeavour to reach the shore at any point, merely giving himself a gentle impetus inwards whilst carried on in the general direction of the tide. This though a slow process he found to be not altogether so difficult, and though there was no choice of a landing place – the objects on shore passing by him in a sad and slow procession – he perceptibly approached the extremity of a spit of land yet further to the left – now well defined against the sunny portion of the horizon. While the swimmer's eyes were fixed upon the spit as his only means of salvation on this side of the Unknown a moving object broke the outline of the extremity, elongating the whole like a pencil propelled from its case, and immediately a ship's boat appeared, manned with several sailor lads, her bows towards the sea.

All Troy's vigour spasmodically revived to prolong the struggle yet a little further. Swimming with his right arm he held up his left to hail them, splashing upon the waves, and shouting with all his might. From the position of the setting sun his white form was distinctly visible upon the now deep hued bosom of the sea to the east of the boat, and the men saw him at once. Backing their oars and putting the boat about they pulled towards him with a will, and in five or six minutes from the time of his first halloo, two of the sailors hauled him in over the stern.

They formed part of a brig's crew and had come ashore for sand.[4] Troy had sunk down exhausted, and it was some time before he could speak connectedly, his deliverers meanwhile lending him what little clothing they could spare among them as a slight protection against the rapidly cooling air. He soon told them his tale, and begged to be put ashore at his bathing place, which he pointed out to them as being about a mile distant. Their boat was somewhat laden, but after a little demuring they agreed to row in the direction signified, and set him down. Troy however had considerably understated the distance, and what with this and keeping wide of the current they rowed more than two miles before the narrow mouth of the cove appeared. By the time that their keel crunched among the stones of the beach within the opening the sun was down, a crescent moon had risen, and solitude reigned around, rendering distinct the gentle slide of the wavelets up the sloping shore and the rustle of the pebbles against each other under the caress of each swell – the brisker ebb and flow outside the bar being audible above the mild repetition of the same motion here within.

Troy anxiously scanned the margin of the cove for the white heap of clothes he had left there. No sign of them apparently remained. He leapt out, searched up and down – behind boulders and under weeds. Beyond all doubt the clothes were gone.

"By jingo," he said to them with blank offhandedness; "all I possess is gone; and I haven't a friend or a penny in the world!"

The seamen took counsel, and one of them said, "If you come aboard with us, perhaps we can find you in a kit. We've been waiting in Budmouth for hands, and are short still. Can't get 'em to join. Captain's glad of anything he can pick up, and might take you."

Troy meditated for a moment. He was so relieved at the recovery of his life at any price that the loss of his clothes and what little he possessed besides did not trouble him very deeply, though it had its inconvenience just at present, in putting him so entirely into the hands of these new friends. It was scarcely probable that they would allow him to leave them, wearing as he did a portion of the garment of three or four. Some sort of repayment would be looked for, and before that could be made it must be earned.

"How long is the voyage to be," he said, in the course of some further remarks.

"Six months – though the old hands have signed up for two years, in case of trading from a foreign port; but 'twould certainly be no more than six months for you. However, come to the ship and read down the articles: we can put ye into Budmouth afterwards right enough."

Troy accepted the invitation, and away they went towards the roadstead. It would be doing Bathsheba a generous turn to leave the country, he thought grimly. His absence would be to her benefit as his presence might be to her ruin – though as she would never give him credit for his considerateness, he was hardly called upon to show it unless the gain was mutual.

And while he thought thus night drooped slowly upon the wide watery levels in front; and at no great distance from them, where the shore line curved round and formed a low riband of shade upon the horizon, a series of points of yellow light began to start into existence, denoting the spot to be the site of Budmouth, where the lamps were being lighted along the parade. The cluck of their oars was the only sound of any magnitude upon the sea, and as they laboured amid the thickening shades the lamplights grew larger, each appearing to send a flaming sword deep down into the waves before it, until there arose among other dim shapes of the kind the form of the vessel for which they were bound.

CHAPTER XLVII[1]

Boldwood again: the clothes.

Bathsheba underwent the enlargement of her husband's absence from hours to days with a slight feeling of surprise, and a slight feeling of relief; yet neither sensation rose at any time far above the level commonly designated as indifference. She belonged to him: the certainties of that position were so well-defined, and the reasonable probabilities of its issue so bounded, that she could not speculate on contingencies. Taking no further interest in herself as a splendid woman she acquired the indifferent feelings of an outsider in contemplating her probable fate as an interesting wretch; for Bathsheba drew herself and her future in colours that no reality could exceed for darkness. Her original vigorous pride of youth had sickened, and with it had declined all her anxieties about coming years; since anxiety recognises a better and a worse alternative, and Bathsheba had made up her mind that alternatives on any noteworthy scale had ceased for her. Soon, or later – and that not very late – her husband would be home again. And then the days of their tenancy of the Upper Farm would be numbered. There had originally been shown by the agent to the estate some mistrust of Bathsheba's tenure as James Everdene's successor, on the score of her sex, and her youth, and her beauty; but the peculiar nature of her uncle's will, his own frequent testimony before his death to her cleverness in such a pursuit, and her vigorous marshalling of the numerous flocks and herds which came suddenly into her hands before negotiations were concluded had won confidence in her powers, and no further objections had been raised. She had latterly been in great doubt as to what the legal effects of her marriage would be upon her position, but no notice had been taken as yet of her change of name, and only one point was clear, that in the event of her own or her husband's inability to meet the agent at the forthcoming January rent-day very little consideration would be shown, and, for that matter, very little would be deserved. Once out of the farm the approach of poverty would be sure.

Hence Bathsheba lived in a perception that her purposes were broken off. She was not a woman who could hope on without good materials for the process, differing thus from the less far-sighted and energetic, though more petted ones of her sex, with whom hope goes on as a sort of clockwork which the merest food and shelter are sufficient to wind up; and perceiving clearly that her mistake had been a fatal one she accepted her position, and waited coldly for the end.

The first Saturday after Troy's departure she went to Casterbridge alone, a journey she had not before taken since her marriage. On this Saturday Bathsheba was passing slowly on foot through the crowd of rural business-men gathered as usual in front of the market-house, and as usual gazed upon by the burghers with feelings that those healthy lives were dearly paid for by the lack of possible aldermanship, when a man who had apparently been following her said some words to another on her left hand. Bathsheba's ears were keen as those of any wild animal, and she distinctly heard what the speaker said, though her back was towards him.

"I am looking for Mrs Troy. Is that she there?"

"Yes: that's the young lady I believe," said the person addressed.

"I have some awkward news to break to her. Her husband is drowned."

As if endowed with the spirit of prophesy, Bathsheba gasped out, "O it is not true: it cannot be true!" Then she said and heard no more. The ice of self-command which had gathered over her was broken, and the currents burst forth again, and overwhelmed her. A darkness came into her eyes, and she fell.

But not to the ground. A gloomy man who had been observing her from under the portico of the old corn-exchange when she passed through the group without, stepped quickly to her side at the moment of her exclamation and caught her in his arms as she sank down.

"What is it?" said Boldwood, looking up at the bringer of the big news as he supported her.

"Her husband was drowned this week while bathing in Carrow Cove. A coastguardsman found his clothes and brought them into Budmouth yesterday."

Thereupon a strange fire lighted up Boldwood's eye and his face flushed with the suppressed excitement of an unutterable thought. Everybody's glance was now centered on him and the unconscious Bathsheba. He lifted her bodily off the ground and smoothed down the folds of her dress as a child might have taken a storm-beaten bird and arranged its ruffled plumes, and bore her along the pavement to the Three Choughs Inn. Here he passed with her under the archway into a private room, and by the time he had deposited – so lothly – the precious burden upon a sofa, Bathsheba had opened her eyes, and remembering all that had occurred murmured "I want to go home!"

Boldwood left the room. He stood for a moment in the passage to recover his senses. The experience had been too much for his consciousness to keep up with, and now that he had grasped it it had gone again. For those few heavenly golden moments she had been in his arms. What did it matter about her not knowing it? – she had been close to his breast; he had been close to hers.

He started onward again and sending a woman to her went out to ascertain all the facts of the case. These appeared to be very limited, and very conclusive. He then ordered her horse to be put into the gig and when all was ready returned to inform her. He found that though still pale and unwell she had in the meantime sent for the Budmouth man who brought the tidings, and learnt from him all there was to know.

Being hardly in a condition to drive home alone as she had driven to town Boldwood with every delicacy of manner and feeling offered to get her a driver, or to give her a seat in his phaeton, which was more comfortable than her own conveyance. These proposals Bathsheba gently declined, and the farmer at once departed. About half an hour later she invigorated herself by an effort and took her seat and the reins as usual – in external appearance much as if nothing had happened. She went out of the town by a tortuous back street and drove slowly along, unconscious of the road and the scene. The first shades of evening were showing themselves when Bathsheba reached home, where, silently alighting and leaving the horse in the hands of the boy, she proceeded at once upstairs. Liddy met her on the landing. The news had preceded Bathsheba to Weatherbury by half an hour, and Liddy looked enquiringly into her mistress's face. Bathsheba had nothing to say.

She entered her bedroom and sat by the window and thought and thought till night enveloped her, and the extreme lines only of her shape were visible. Somebody came to the door knocked, and opened it.

"Well, what is it Liddy?" she said.

"I was thinking there must be something got for you to wear," said Liddy with hesitation.

"What do you mean?"

"Mourning."

"No no no," said Bathsheba hurriedly.

"But I suppose there must be something done for poor –"

"Not at present I think. It is not necessary."

"Why not ma'am?"

"Because he's still alive."

"How do you know that?" said Liddy, amazed.

"I don't know it. But wouldn't it have been different, or shouldn't I have heard more, or wouldn't they have found him Liddy? – or – I don't know how it is, but death would have been different from how this is. I am full of a feeling that he is still alive!"

Bathsheba remained firm in this opinion till Monday, when two circumstances conjoined to shake it. The first was a short paragraph in the local newspaper which, beyond making by a methodizing pen formidable presumptive evidence of Troy's death by drowning contained the important testimony of a young Mr Barker, M. D. of Budmouth, who spoke to being an eyewitness of the accident in a letter to the Editor. In this he stated that he was passing over the cliff on the remoter side of the cove just as the sun was setting. At that time he saw a bather carried along in the current outside the mouth of the cove, and guessed in an instant that there was but a poor chance for him unless he should be possessed of unusual muscular powers. He drifted behind a projection of the coast, and Mr Barker followed along the shore in the same direction. But by the time that he could reach an elevation sufficiently great to command a view of the sea beyond, dusk had set in, and nothing further was to be seen.

The other circumstance was the arrival of his clothes, when it became necessary for her to examine and identify them – though this had virtually been done long before by those who inspected the letters in his pockets. It was so evident to her in the midst of her agitation that Troy had undressed in the full conviction of dressing again almost immediately that the notion that anything but death could have prevented him was never entertained.

Then Bathsheba said to herself that others were assured in their opinion, and why should not she be. A strange reflection occurred to her, causing her face to flush. Troy had left her and followed Fanny into another world. Had he done this intentionally, yet contrived to make his death appear like an accident? Oddly enough this thought of how the apparent might differ from the real – made vivid by her bygone jealousy of Fanny, and the remorse he had shown that night – blinded her to the perception of any other possible difference, less tragic, but to herself far more terrible.

When alone late that evening beside a small fire, and much calmed down Bathsheba took Troy's watch into her hand, which had been restored to her with the rest of the articles belonging to him. She opened the case as he had opened it before her a week ago. There was the little coil of pale hair which had been as the fuze to this great explosion.

"He was hers, and she was his, and they are gone together," she said. "I am nothing to either of them, and why should I keep her hair?" She took it in her hand, and held it over the fire.

"No – I'll not burn it – I'll keep it in memory of her, poor thing!" she added, snatching back her hand.

CHAPTER XLVIII

Oak's advancement: a great hope.

The later autumn and the winter drew on apace, and the leaves lay thick upon the turf of the glades and the mosses of the woods. Bathsheba having previously been living in a state of suspended feeling which was not suspense now lived in a mood of quietude which was not peacefulness. While she had known him to be alive she could have thought of his death with equanimity, but now that she believed she had lost him she regretted that he was not hers still. She kept the farm going, raked in her profits without caring keenly about them, and expended money on ventures because she had done so in bygone days, which though not long gone by seemed infinitely removed from her present. She looked back upon that past over a great gulf, as if she were now a dead person having the faculty of meditation still left in her by means of which, like the mouldering gentlefolk of the poet's story, she could sit and ponder what a gift life used to be.[1]

However, one excellent result of her general apathy was the long-delayed installation of Oak as bailiff; but he having virtually exercised that function for a long time already, the change, beyond the substantial increase of wages it brought, was little more than a nominal one addressed to the outside world.

Boldwood lived secluded and inactive. Much of his wheat and all his barley of that season had been spoilt by the rain. It sprouted, grew into intricate mats, and was ultimately thrown to the pigs in armfuls. The strange neglect which had produced this ruin and waste became the subject of whispered talk among all the people round, and it was elicited from one of Boldwood's men that forgetfulness had nothing to do with it, for he had been reminded of the danger to his corn as many times and as persistently as inferiors dared to do. The sight of the pigs turning in disgust from the rotten ears seemed to arouse Boldwood, and he one evening sent for Oak. Whether it was suggested by Bathsheba's recent act of promotion or not, the farmer proposed at the interview that Gabriel should undertake the superintendence of the Lower Farm as well as of Bathsheba's, because of the necessity Boldwood felt for such aid, and the impossibility of discovering a more trustworthy man. Gabriel's malignant star was assuredly setting fast.

Bathsheba, when she learnt of this proposal – for Oak was obliged to consult her – at first languidly objected. She considered that the two farms together were too extensive for the observation of one man. Boldwood, who was apparently determined by personal rather than commercial reasons, suggested that Oak should be furnished with a horse for his sole use, when the plan would present no difficulty; the two farms lying side by side. Boldwood did not directly communicate with her during these negotiations, only speaking to Oak, who was the go-between throughout. All was harmoniously arranged at last, and we now see Oak mounted on a strong cob, and daily trotting the length and breadth of about two thousand acres in a cheerful spirit of surveillance, as if the crops all belonged to him, the actual mistress of the one half and the master of the other sitting in their respective homes in gloomy and sad seclusion.

Out of this there arose during the spring succeeding, a talk in the parish that Gabriel Oak was feathering his nest fast. "Whatever d'ye think," said Susan Tall, "Gable Oak is coming it quite the dand. He now wears shiny boots with hardly a hob in 'em two or three times a week and a tall hat a-Sundays, and 'a hardly knows the name of smockfrock. When I see people strut enough to be cut up into bantam cocks I stand dormant with wonder and says no more."

It was eventually known that Gabriel, though paid a fixed wage by Bathsheba independent of the fluctuations of agricultural profits, had made an arrangement with Boldwood by which Oak was to receive a share of the receipts – a small share certainly, yet it was money of a higher quality than mere wages, and capable of expansion in a way that wages were not. Some were beginning to consider Oak a near man, for though his condition had thus far improved he lived in no better style than before, occupying the same cottage, paring his own potatoes, mending his stockings, and sometimes even making his bed with his own hands. But as Oak was not only provokingly indifferent to public opinion, but a man who clung persistently to old habits and usages simply because they were old, there was room for doubt as to his motives.

A great hope had latterly germinated in Boldwood, whose unreasoning devotion to Bathsheba could only be characterized as a fond madness which neither time nor circumstance, evil nor good report, could weaken or destroy. This fevered hope had grown up again like a grain of mustard-seed[2] during the quiet which followed the universal belief that Troy was drowned. He nourished it fearfully, and almost shunned the contemplation of it in earnest, lest facts should reveal the wildness of the dream. Bathsheba having at last been persuaded to wear mourning, her appearance as she entered the church in that guise was in itself a weekly addition to his faith that a time was coming – very far off perhaps, yet surely nearing – when his waiting on events should have its reward. How long he might have to wait he had not yet closely considered. What he would try to recognise was that the severe schooling she had been subjected to had made Bathsheba much more considerate than she had formerly been of the feelings of others, and he trusted that should she be willing at any time in the future to marry any man at all, it would be himself. There was a substratum of good feeling in her: her self reproach for the injury she had thoughtlessly done him might be depended upon now to a much greater extent than before her infatuation and disappointment. It would be possible to approach her by the channel of her good nature, and to suggest a friendly business-like compact between them for fulfilment at some future day, keeping the passionate side of his desire entirely out of her sight. Such was Boldwood's hope.

To the eyes of the middle aged, Bathsheba was perhaps additionally charming just now. Her exuberance of spirit was pruned down: the original phantom of delight had shown herself to be not too good for human nature's daily food,[3] and she had been able to enter this second poetical phase without losing much of the first in the process.

Bathsheba's return from a two month's visit to her old aunt at Norcombe afforded the impassioned and yearning farmer a pretext for enquiring directly after her – now presumably in the ninth month of her widowhood

– and endeavouring to get a notion of her state of mind regarding him. This occurred in the middle of the haymaking, and Boldwood contrived to be near Liddy who was assisting in the fields.

"I am glad to see you out of doors Lydia," he said pleasantly.

She simpered, and wondered in her heart why he should speak so frankly to her.

"I hope Mrs Troy is quite well after her long absence," he continued, in a manner expressing that the coldest hearted neighbour could scarcely say less.

"She's quite well sir."

"And cheerful I suppose."

"Yes cheerful."

"Fearful did you say?" Boldwood wished to get more involved in talk without seeming to attempt it.[4]

"O no. I merely said she was cheerful."

He was almost afraid to go further; yet it suddenly occurred to him that if Liddy should notice his drift and report his words no harm would be done.

"Mrs Troy puts much confidence in you Lydia; and very wisely perhaps."

"She does sir. I've been with her all through her troubles and was with her at the time of Mr Troy's death and all. And if she were to marry again I expect I should bide with her."

"She promises that you shall – quite natural," said the strategic lover, throbbing throughout him at the presumption which Liddy's words appeared to warrant – that his darling had thought of re-marriage.

"No – she doesn't promise it exactly. I merely judge on my own account."

"Yes, yes, I understand. When she alludes to the possibility of marrying again you conclude –"

"She never does allude to it Sir," said Liddy, thinking how very stupid Mr Boldwood was getting.

"Of course not," he returned hastily, his hope falling again. – You needn't take quite such long reaches with your rake Lydia – short and quick ones are best. – Well, perhaps as she is absolute mistress again now, it is wise of her to resolve never to give up her freedom."

"My mistress did certainly once say, though not seriously, that she supposed she might marry again at the end of seven years from last year, if she wished."

"Ah – six years from the present time. Said that she might. She might marry at once in every reasonable person's opinion, whatever the lawyers may say to the contrary."

"Have you been to ask then?" said Liddy innocently.

"Not I!" said Boldwood growing red. "Liddy, you needn't stay here a minute later than you wish, so Mr Oak says. I am now going on a little further. Good afternoon."

He went away vexed with himself and ashamed of having for this one time in his life done anything which could be called underhand. Poor Boldwood had no more skill in finesse than a battering-ram, and he was uneasy with a sense of having made himself to appear stupid, and, what was worse, mean. But he had, after all, lighted upon one fact by way of repayment. It was a singularly fresh and fascinating one, and though not without its sadness it was pertinent and real. In little more than six years from this time Bathsheba might certainly marry him. There was something definite in that hope, for admitting that there might have been no deep thought in her words to Liddy about marriage, they showed at least her creed on the matter.

This pleasant notion was now continually in his mind. Six years were a long time, but how much shorter than never, the idea he had for so long been obliged to endure! Jacob had served twice seven years for Rachel:[5] what were six for such a woman as this. He tried to like the notion of waiting for her better than that of winning her at once. Boldwood felt his love to be so deep and strong, and eternal, that it was possible she had never yet known its full volume, and this patience in delay would afford him an opportunity of giving sweet proof on the point. He would annihilate the six years of his life as if they were minutes – so little did he value his time on earth beside her love. He would let her see, all those six years of intangible ethereal courtship, how little care he had for anything but as it bore upon that consummation.

Meanwhile the early and the late summer brought round the week in which Greenhill Fair[6] was held. This fair was frequently attended by the folk of Weatherbury.

CHAPTER XLIX

The sheep fair: Troy holds his wife's hand.

Greenhill was the Nijnii Novgorod[1] of Wessex; and the busiest, merriest, noisiest day of the whole statute number was the day of the sheep-fair. This yearly gathering was upon the summit of a hill which retained in good preservation the remains of an ancient earthwork, consisting of a huge rampart and entrenchment of an oval form encircling the top of the hill, though somewhat broken down here and there. To each of the two chief openings on opposite sides a winding road ascended, and the level green space of twenty or thirty acres enclosed by the bank was the site of the fair. A few permanent erections dotted the spot, but the majority of the visitors patronized canvas alone for resting and feeding under during the day of their sojourn here.

Shepherds who attended with their flocks from long distances started from home two or three days, or even a week, before the fair day, driving their charges a few miles each day – not more than ten or twelve – and resting them at night in hired fields by the wayside at previously chosen points where they fed, having fasted all the day. The shepherd of each flock marched behind, a bundle containing his kit for the week strapped upon his shoulders, and in his hand his crook, which he used as the staff of his pilgrimage. Several of the sheep would get worn and lame, and occasionally a lambing occurred on the road. To meet these contingencies there was frequently provided, to accompany the flocks from the remoter points, a pony waggon into which the weakly ones were taken for the remainder of the journey.

The Weatherbury Farms however were no such long distance from the Hill, and those arrangements were not necessary in their case. But the large united flocks of Bathsheba and Farmer Boldwood formed a valuable and imposing multitude which demanded much attention, and on this account Gabriel, in addition to Boldwood's shepherd and Cain Ball, accompanied them along the way – Old George the dog of course behind them.

When the autumn sun slanted over Greenhill this morning and lighted the dewy flat upon its crest, nebulous clouds of dust were to be seen floating between the pairs of hedges which streaked the wide prospects around in all directions. These gradually converged upon the base of the hill, and the flocks became individually visible, climbing the serpentine ways which led to the top. Thus in a slow procession they entered the openings to which the roads wended, multitude after multitude, horned and hornless – blue flocks and red flocks, buff flocks and brown flocks, even green and salmon-tinted flocks, according to the fancy of the colourist and custom of the farm.[2] Men were shouting, dogs were barking, with greatest animation, but the thronging travellers in so long a journey had grown nearly indifferent to such terrors, though they still bleated piteously at the unwontedness of their experiences, a tall shepherd rising here and there in the midst of them like a gigantic idol amid a crowd of prostrate devotees.

The great mass of sheep in the fair consisted of South Downs and the old Wessex horned breeds: to the latter class Bathsheba's and Farmer Boldwood's mainly belonged. These filed in about nine o'clock, their vermiculated horns lopping gracefully on each side of their cheeks in geometrically perfect spirals, a small pink and white ear nestling under each horn. Before and behind came other varieties, perfect leopards as to the full rich substance of their coats, and only lacking the spots. There were also a few of the Oxfordshire breed, whose wool was beginning to curl like a child's flaxen hair, though surpassed in this respect by the effeminate Leicesters, which were in turn less curly than the Cotswolds. But the most picturesque by far was a small flock of Exmoors[3] which chanced to be there this year. Their pied faces and legs, dark and heavy horns and tresses of wool hanging round their swarthy foreheads, relieved the monotony of the flocks in that quarter. All these bleating, panting, and weary thousands had entered and were penned before the morning had far advanced, the dog belonging to each flock being tied to the corner of the pen containing it. Alleys for pedestrians intersected the pens, which soon became crowded with buyers and sellers from far and near.

In another part of the hill an altogether different scene began to force itself upon the eye towards midday. A circular tent, of exceptional newness and size, was in course of erection here. As the day drew on the flocks began to change hands, lightening the shepherds' responsibilities; and they turned their attention to this tent, and enquired of a man at work there, whose soul seemed concentrated on tying a bothering knot in no time, what was going on.

"The Royal Hippodrome Performance of Turpin's Ride to York and the Death of Black Bess,"[4] replied the man promptly without turning his eyes or leaving off tying.

As soon as the tent was completed the band struck up highly stimulating harmonies, and the announcement was publicly made, Black Bess standing in a conspicuous position on the outside, as a living proof, if proof were wanted, of the truth of the oracular utterances from the stage over which the people were to enter. These were so convinced by such genuine appeals to heart and understanding both that they soon began to crowd in abundantly, among the foremost being visible Jan Coggan and Joseph Poorgrass, who were holiday keeping here to-day.

"That's the great ruffin pushing me!" screamed a woman in front of Jan over her shoulder to him when the rush was at its fiercest.

"How can I help pushing ye when the folk behind push me?" said Coggan in a deprecating tone, turning his head towards the aforesaid folk as far as he could without turning his body which was jammed as in a vice.

There was a silence when the drums and trumpets again sent forth their echoing notes. The crowd was again ecstasied and gave another lurch in which Coggan and Poorgrass were again thrust by those behind upon the woman in front.

"O that helpless feymels should be at the mercy of such ruffins!" exclaimed one of these ladies again as she swayed like a reed shaken by the wind.[5]

"Now," said Coggan, appealing in an earnest voice to his neighbours and the public at large as it stood clustered about his shoulderblades; "did ye ever hear such a unreasonable woman as that? Upon my carcase, neighbours, if I could only get out of this cheesewring the d— women might eat the show for me!"

"Don't ye lose yer temper Jan!" implored Joseph Poorgrass in a whisper. "They might get their men to murder us, for I think by the roll of their eyes that they are a sinful form of womankind."

Jan held his tongue as if he had no objection to be pacified to please a friend, and they gradually got to the foot of the ladder, Poorgrass being flattened like a jumping-jack, and the sixpence for admission, which he had got ready half an hour earlier, having become so reeking hot in the tight squeeze of his excited hand that the woman in spangles, brazen rings set with glass diamonds, and with chalked face and shoulders, who took the money of him, hastily dropped it again from a fear that some trick had been played to burn her fingers. So they all entered, and the sides of the tent, to the eyes of an observer on the outside, became bulged into innumerable pimples such as we observe on a sack of potatoes, caused by the various human heads, backs, and elbows, at high pressure within.

At the back of the large tent there were two small dressing-tents. One of these, allotted to the male performers, was partitioned into halves by a cloth; and in one of the divisions there was sitting on the grass, pulling on a pair of jack-boots, a young man whom we instantly recognise as Sergeant Troy.

Troy's appearance in this position may be briefly accounted for. After embarking on board the brig in Budmouth Roads as a new man with a new name[6] he had worked his passage to the United States, where he made a precarious living in various towns as Professor of Gymnastics, Sword Exercise, Fencing, and Pugilism. A few months were sufficient to give him a distaste for this kind of life. There was a certain animal form of refinement in his nature, and however pleasant a strange condition might be whilst privations were easily warded off, it was disadvantageously coarse when money was short. There was ever present too the idea that he could claim a home and its comforts did he but choose to return to England and Weatherbury Farm. Whether Bathsheba thought him dead was a frequent subject of curious conjecture. To England he did return at last, but the fact of drawing nearer to Weatherbury abstracted its fascinations, and his intention to enter his old groove at that place became modified. It was with gloom he considered on landing at Liverpool that if he were to go home his reception would be of a kind very unpleasant to contemplate; for what Troy had in the way of emotion was an occasional florid fitful sentiment which sometimes caused him as much inconvenience as emotion of a strong and healthy kind. Bathsheba was not a woman to be made a fool of, or set to suffer in silence; and how could he endure existence with a spirited wife to whom at first entering he would be beholden for food and lodging? Moreover it was not at all unlikely that his wife would fail at her farming if she had not already done so; and he would then become liable for her maintenance; and what a life a future of poverty with her would be, the spectre of Fanny constantly between them, harrowing his temper, and embittering her words![7] Thus for reasons touching on distaste, regret, and shame commingled he put off his return from day to day, and would have decided to put it off altogether if he could have found anywhere else the ready made establishment which existed for him there.

At this time – the July preceding the September in which we find him at Greenhill Fair – he fell in with a travelling circus which was performing in the outskirts of a northern town. Troy introduced himself to the manager by taming a restive horse of the troupe, hitting a suspended apple with a pistol-bullet fired from the animal's back when in full gallop, and other feats. For his merits in these – all more or less based upon his experiences as a Dragoon Guardsman – Troy was taken into the company, and the play of Turpin was prepared with a view to his personation of the chief character. Troy was not greatly elated by the appreciative spirit in which he was undoubtedly treated, but he thought the engagement might afford him a few weeks for consideration. It was thus carelessly and without having formed any definite plan for the future that Troy found himself at Greenhill Fair with the rest of the company on this day.

And now the mild autumn sun got lower, and in front of the pavilion the following incident had taken place. Bathsheba – who had been driven to the fair that day by her odd man Poorgrass – had, like everyone else, read or heard the announcement that Mr Francis, the Great Cosmopolite Equestrian and Roughrider would enact the part of Turpin, and she was not yet too old and careworn to be without a little curiosity to see him. This particular show was by far the largest and grandest in the fair, a horde of little shows grouping themselves under its shade like chicken around a hen. The crowd had passed in, and Boldwood, who had been watching all the day for an opportunity of speaking to her, seeing her comparatively isolated, came up to her side.

"I hope the sheep have done well to-day Mrs Troy?" he said nervously.

"O yes, thank you," said Bathsheba, colour springing up in the centre of her cheeks. "I was fortunate enough to sell them all before we got upon the hill, so we hadn't to pen at all."

"And now you are entirely at leisure."

"Yes – except that I have to see one more dealer in two hours' time: otherwise I should be going home. I was looking at this large tent and the announcement. Have you ever seen the play of 'Turpin's Ride to York'? Turpin was a real man, was he not?"

"O yes – perfectly true – all of it. Indeed I think I've heard Jan Coggan say that a relation of his knew Tom King,[8] Turpin's friend, quite well."

"Coggan is rather given to strange stories connected with his relations we must remember. I hope they can all be believed."

"Yes, yes; we know Coggan. But Turpin is true enough. You have never seen it played I suppose?"

"Never. I was not allowed to go into these places when I was young. Hark – what's that prancing? How they shout!"

"Black Bess just starting off I suppose. – Am I right in supposing you would like to see the performance, Mrs Troy? Please excuse my mistake, if it is one; but if you would like to, I'll get a seat for you with pleasure." Perceiving that she hesitated he added, "I myself shall not stay to see it: I've seen it before."

Now Bathsheba did care a little to see the show, and had only withheld her feet from the ladder because she feared to go in alone. She had been hoping that Oak might appear, whose assistance in such cases was always accepted as an inalienable right, but Oak was nowhere to be seen; and hence it was that she said, "Then if you will just look in first, to make sure that there's room, I think I will go in for a minute or two."

And so a short time after this Bathsheba appeared in the tent with Boldwood at her elbow, who taking her to a "reserved" seat again withdrew.

This feature consisted of one raised bench in a very conspicuous part of the circle, covered with red cloth and floored with a piece of carpet, and Bathsheba immediately found to her confusion that she was the single reserved individual in the tent, the rest of the crowd of spectators one and all standing on their legs on the borders of the arena, where they got twice as good a view of the performance for half the money. Hence as many eyes were turned upon her, enthroned alone in this place of honour, against a scarlet background, as upon the ponies and clown who were engaged in preliminary exploits in the centre, Turpin not having yet appeared. Once there, Bathsheba was forced to make the best of it and remain: she sat down, spreading her skirts with some dignity over the unoccupied space on each side of her, and giving a new and feminine aspect to the pavilion. In a few minutes she noticed the fat red nape of

Coggan's neck among those standing just below her, and Joseph Poorgrass's saintly profile a little further on.

The interior was shadowy with a peculiar shade. The strange luminous semi-opacities of fine autumn afternoons and eves, intensified into Rembrandt effects[9] the yellow sunbeams which came through holes and divisions in the canvas, and spirted like jets of gold dust across the dusky blue atmosphere of haze pervading the tent, until they alighted on inner surfaces of cloth opposite and shone like little lamps suspended there.

Troy, on peeping from his dressing tent through a slit for a reconnoitre before entering saw his unconscious wife on high before him as described, sitting as queen of the tournament. He started back in utter confusion, for although his disguise effectually concealed his personality, he instantly felt that she would be sure to recognise his voice. He had several times during the day thought of the possibility of some Weatherbury person or other appearing and recognising him; but he had taken the risk carelessly: "If they see me, let them," he had said. But here was Bathsheba in her own person; and the reality of the scene was so much intenser than any of his prefigurings that he felt he had not half enough considered the point. She looked so charming and fair that his cool mood about Weatherbury people was changed. He had not expected her to exercise this power over him in the twinkling of an eye. Should he go on, and care nothing? He could not bring himself to do that. Beyond a politic wish to remain unknown there suddenly arose in him now a sense of shame at the possibility that his attractive young wife who already despised him should despise him more by discovering him in so mean a condition after so long a time. He actually blushed at the thought, and was vexed beyond measure that his sentiments of dislike towards Weatherbury should have led him to dally about the country in this way. But Troy was never more clever than when absolutely at his wits' end. He hastily thrust aside the curtain dividing his own little dressing space from that of the manager and proprietor, who now appeared as the individual called Tom King as far down as his waist, and the aforesaid respectable manager thence to his toes.

"Here's the devil[10] to pay," said Troy.

"How's that?"

"Why, there's a good-for-nothing scamp in the tent I don't want to see, who'll discover me and nab me as sure as Satan if I open my mouth. What's to be done?"

"You must appear now I think."

"I can't."

"But the play must proceed."

"Do you give out that Turpin has got a bad cold, and can't speak his part; but that he'll perform it just the same without speaking."

The proprietor shook his head.

"Anyhow, play or no play, I won't open my mouth," said Troy firmly.

"Very well, then let me see – I tell you how we'll manage," said the other man, who perhaps felt it would be extremely awkward to offend his leading man just at this time. "I won't tell them anything about your keeping silence; go on with the piece, and say nothing – doing what you can by a judicious wink now and then, and a few indomitable nods in the heroic places, you know. They'll never find out that the speeches are omitted."

This seemed feasible enough, for Turpin's speeches were not many or long, the fascination of the piece lying entirely in the action; and accordingly the play began and at the appointed time Black Bess leapt into the grassy circle amid the plaudits of the spectators. At the turnpike scene, where Bess and Turpin are hotly pursued at midnight by the officers, and the half-awake gate-keeper in his tasselled nightcap denies that any horseman has passed, Coggan uttered a broad-chested "Well done!" which could be heard all over the fair above the bleating, and Poorgrass smiled delightedly with a nice sense of dramatic contrast between our hero who coolly leaps the gate and halting justice in the form of his enemies who must needs pull up cumbersomely and wait to be let through. At the death of Tom King he could not refrain from seizing Coggan by the hand and whispering with excitement, "Of course he's not really shot Jan – only seemingly!" And when the last sad scene came on and the body of gallant and faithful Bess had to be carried out on a shutter by twelve volunteers from among the spectators, nothing could restrain Poorgrass from lending a hand, exclaiming, as he asked Jan to join him "'Twill be something to tell of at Warren's in future years Jan, and hand down to our children." For many a year in Weatherbury Joseph told with the air of a man who had had experiences in his time that he touched with his own hands the hoof of Bess as she lay upon the board upon his shoulder. If, as some thinkers hold, immortality consists in being enshrined in others' memories, then did Black Bess become immortal that day if she never had done so before.

Meanwhile Troy had added a few touches to his ordinary make up for the character, the more effectually to disguise himself, and though he had felt faint qualms on first entering, the metamorphosis effected by judiciously "lining" his face with a wire rendered him safe from the eyes of Bathsheba and her men. Nevertheless, he was relieved when it was got through. There was a second performance in the evening, and the tent was lighted up. Troy had taken his part very quietly this time, venturing to introduce a few speeches on occasion, and was just concluding it, when whilst standing at the edge of the circle contiguous to the first row of spectators he observed within a yard of him the eye of a man darted keenly into his side features. Troy hastily shifted his position after having recognised in the scrutineer the knavish bailiff Pennyways, his wife's sworn enemy, who still hung about the outskirts of Weatherbury.

At first Troy resolved to take no notice and abide by circumstances. That he had been recognised by this man was highly probable; yet there was room for a doubt. Then the great objection he had felt to allowing news of his proximity to precede him to Weatherbury in the event of his return – based on a feeling that knowledge of his present occupation would discredit him still further in his wife's eyes – returned in full force. Moreover should he resolve not to return at all, a tale of his being alive and in the neighbourhood would be awkward; and he was anxious to acquire a knowledge of his wife's temporal affairs before deciding which to do.

In this dilemma Troy at once went out to reconnoitre. It occurred to him that to find Pennyways and make a friend of him if possible would be a very wise act. He had put on a thick beard borrowed from the establishment, and in this he wandered about the fair-field. It was now almost dark, and respectable people were getting their carts and gigs ready to go home.

The largest refreshment booth in the fair was provided by an innkeeper from a neighbouring town. This was considered an unexceptionable place for obtaining the necessary food and rest, Host Trencher (as he was wittily called by the local newspaper) being a substantial man of high repute for catering through all the country round. The tent was divided into first and second class compartments, and at the end of the first class division was a yet further enclosure for the most exclusive, fenced off from the body of the tent by a luncheon bar, behind which the host himself stood bustling about in white apron and shirt sleeves and looking as if he had never lived anywhere but under canvas all his life. In these penetralia were chairs and a table, which on candles being lighted made quite a cosy and luxurious show with an urn, silver tea and coffee pots, china tea cups and plum cakes.

Troy stood at the entrance to the booth, where a gipsy woman was frying pancakes over a little fire of sticks and selling them at a penny a piece, and looked over the heads of the people within. He could see nothing of Pennyways, but he soon discerned Bathsheba through an opening into the reserved space at the further end. Troy thereupon retreated, went round the tent into the darkness and listened. He could hear Bathsheba's voice immediately inside the canvas; she was conversing with a man. A warmth overspread his face: surely she was not so unprincipled as to flirt in a fair! He wondered if, then, she reckoned upon his death as an absolute certainty. To get at the root of the matter Troy took a penknife from his pocket and softly made two little cuts crosswise in the cloth, which, by folding back the corners, left a hole the size of a wafer. Close to this he placed his face, withdrawing it again in a movement of surprise; for his eye had been within twelve inches of the back of Bathsheba's head. It was too near to be convenient. He made another hole a little to one side and lower down, in a shaded place beside her chair, from which it was easy and safe to survey her by looking upwards.

Troy took in the scene completely now. She was leaning back, sipping a cup of tea that she held in her hand, and the owner of the male voice was Boldwood, who had apparently just brought the cup to her. Bathsheba, being in a negligent mood, leant so idly against the canvas that it was pressed to the shape of her shoulder, and she was, in fact, as good as in Troy's arms; and he was obliged to keep his breast carefully backward that she might not feel its warmth through the cloth as he gazed in.

Troy found unexpected chords of feeling to be stirred again within him as earlier in the day. She was handsome as ever, and she was his. It was some minutes before he could counteract his sudden wish to go in and claim her. Then he thought how the proud girl who had always looked down upon him even whilst it was to love him, would hate him on discovering him to be a strolling player. Were he to make himself known, that chapter of his life must at all risks be kept for ever from her and from the Weatherbury people, or his name would be a byword throughout the parish. He would be nicknamed "Turpin" as long as he lived. Assuredly before he could claim her these few past months of his existence must be entirely blotted out.

"Shall I get you another cup before you start ma'am?" said Farmer Boldwood.

"Thank you," said Bathsheba. "But I must be going at once. It was great neglect in that man to keep me waiting here till so late. I should have gone two hours ago if it had not been for him. I had no idea of coming in here; but there's nothing so refreshing as a cup of tea – though I should never have got one if you hadn't helped me."

Troy scrutinized her cheek as lit by the candles, and watched each varying shade thereon, and the white shell-like sinuosities of her little ear. She took out her purse and was insisting to Boldwood on paying for her tea herself, when at this moment Pennyways entered the tent. Troy trembled: here was his scheme for respectability endangered at once. He was about to leave his hole of espial, attempt to follow Pennyways and find out if the ex-bailiff had recognized him, when he was arrested by the conversation – and found he was too late.

"Excuse me ma'am," said Pennyways; "I've some private information for your ear alone."

"I cannot hear it now," she said, coldly. That Bathsheba could not endure this man was evident: in fact, he was continually coming to her with some tale or other by which he might creep into favour at the expense of persons maligned.

"I'll write it down," said Pennyways, confidently. He stooped over the table, pulled a leaf from a warped pocket book, and wrote upon the paper, in a round hand: –

"*Your husband is here. I've seen him. Who's the fool now?*"

This he folded small and handed towards her. Bathsheba would not read it: she would not even put out her hand to take it. Pennyways then with a laugh of derision tossed it into her lap, and turning away, left her.

From the words and action of Pennyways Troy, though he had not been able to see what the bailiff wrote, had not a moment's doubt that the note referred to him. Nothing that he could think of could be done to check the exposure. "Curse my luck!" he whispered, and added imprecations which rustled in the gloom like a pestilent wind. Meanwhile Boldwood said, taking up the note from her lap:

"Don't you wish to read it Mrs Troy? If not, I'll destroy it."

"Oh – well," said Bathsheba carelessly, "perhaps it is unjust not to read it. But I can guess what it is about. He wants me to recommend him, or to tell me of some little detail or another connected with my work people. He's always doing that."

Bathsheba held the note in her right hand. Boldwood handed towards her a plate of cut bread and butter, when, in order to take a slice she put the note into her left hand where she was still holding the purse, and then allowed her hand to drop beside her close to the canvas. The moment had come for saving his game, and Troy impulsively felt that he would play the card. For yet another time he looked at the fair hand, and saw the pink finger-tips, and the blue veins of the wrist, encircled by a bracelet of coral chippings which she wore: how familiar it all was to him! Then, with the lightning action in which he was such an adept, he noiselessly slipped his hand under the bottom of the tent-cloth, which was far from being pinned tightly down, lifted it a little way keeping his eye to the hole, snatched the note from her fingers, dropped the canvas, and ran away in the gloom towards the bank and ditch, smiling at the scream of astonishment which burst from her. Troy then slid down on the outside of the rampart, hastened round in the bottom of the entrenchment to a distance of a hundred yards, ascended again and crossed boldly in a slow walk towards the front entrance of the tent. His object was now to get to Pennyways and prevent a repetition of the announcement until such time as he should choose.

Troy reached the tent door and standing among the groups there gathered looked anxiously for Pennyways, evidently not wishing to make himself prominent by enquiring for him. One or two men were speaking of a daring attempt that had just been made to rob a young lady by lifting the canvas of the tent beside her. It was supposed that the rogue had imagined a slip of paper which she held in her hand to be a bank-note, for he had seized it and made off with it, leaving her purse behind. His chagrin and disappointment at discovering its worthlessness would be a good joke, it was said. However, the occurrence seemed to have become known to few, for it had not interrupted a fiddler who had lately begun playing by the door of the tent, nor the four bowed old men with grim countenances and walking-sticks in hand who were dancing Major Malley's Reel to the tune. Behind these stood Pennyways. Troy glided up to him, beckoned, and whispered a few words; and with a mutual glance of concurrence the two men went into the night together.

CHAPTER L

Bathsheba talks with her outrider: advice.

The arrangement for getting back again to Weatherbury had been that Oak should take the place of Poorgrass in Bathsheba's conveyance and drive her home, it being discovered late in the afternoon that Joseph was suffering from his old complaint, a multiplying eye, and was therefore hardly trustworthy as coachman and protector to a lady. But Oak had found himself so occupied, and was full of so many cares relative to those portions of Boldwood's flocks that were not disposed of, that Bathsheba, without telling Oak or anybody, resolved to drive home herself, as she had many times done from Casterbridge market, and trust to her good angel for performing the journey unmolested. But having fallen in with Farmer Boldwood accidentally (on her part at least) at the refreshment tent, she found it impossible to refuse his offer to ride on horseback beside her as escort. It had grown twilight before she was aware, but Boldwood assured her that there was no cause for uneasiness, as the moon would be up in half an hour.

Immediately after the incident in the tent she had risen to go – now absolutely alarmed and really grateful for her old lover's protection – though regretting Gabriel's absence, whose company she would have much preferred, as being more pleasant as well as more proper, since he was her own managing man and servant. This however could not be helped: she would not on any consideration treat Boldwood harshly having once already ill-used him, and the moon having risen and the gig being ready, she drove across the hill top into the wending ways which led downwards – to oblivious obscurity as it seemed, for the moon and the hill it flooded with light were in appearance on a level, the rest of the world lying as a vast shady concave between them. Boldwood mounted his horse and followed in close attendance behind. Thus they descended into the lowlands, and the sounds of those left on the hill came like voices from the sky, and the lights were as those of a camp in heaven. They soon passed the merry stragglers in the immediate vicinity of the hill, and got upon the high road.

The keen instincts of Bathsheba had perceived that the farmer's helpless devotion to herself was still undiminished, and she sympathized deeply. The sight had quite depressed her this evening; had reminded her of her folly: she wished anew as she had wished many months ago for some means of making reparation for her fault. Hence her pity for the man who so persistently loved on to his own injury and permanent gloom had betrayed Bathsheba into an injudicious considerateness of manner this evening, which appeared almost like tenderness, and gave new vigour to the exquisite dream of a Jacob's seven years' service[1] in poor Boldwood's mind.

He soon found an excuse for advancing from his position in the rear, and rode close by her side. They had gone two or three miles in the moonlight, speaking desultorily across the wheel of her gig concerning the fair, farming, Oak's usefulness to them both, and other indifferent subjects, when Boldwood said suddenly and simply,

"Mrs Troy, will you marry again some day?"

This point-blank query unmistakably confused her, and it was not till a minute or more had elapsed that she said, "I have not seriously thought of any such subject."

"I quite understand that. Yet your late husband has been dead nearly one year, and – "

"You forget that his death was never absolutely proved, and so I suppose I am not legally a widow," she said, catching at the straw of escape that the fact afforded.

"Not absolutely proved perhaps, but it was proved circumstantially. A man saw him drowning, too. No reasonable person has any doubt of his death, nor have you, ma'am, I should imagine."

"I have none now – or I should have acted differently," she said, gently. "I certainly at first had a strange unaccountable feeling that he could not have perished, but I have been able to explain that in several ways since. But though I am fully persuaded that I shall see him no more, I am far from thinking of marriage with another. I should be very contemptible to indulge in such a thought."

They were silent now awhile, and having struck into an unfrequented track across a common the creaks of Boldwood's saddle and her gig were all the sounds to be heard. Boldwood ended the pause.

"Do you remember when I carried you fainting in my arms into the Three Choughs in Casterbridge? Every dog has his day: that was mine."

"I know – I know it all," she said hurriedly.

"I for one shall never cease regretting that events so fell out as to deny you to me."

"I too am very sorry," she said, and then checked herself. "I mean, you know, I am sorry you thought I –"

"I have always this dreary pleasure in thinking over those past times with you – that I was something to you before *he* was anything, and that you belonged *almost* to me. But of course that's nothing. You never liked me."

"I did, and respected you too."

"Do you now?"

"Yes."

"Which?"

"How do you mean, which?"

"Do you like me or do you respect me?"

"I don't know – at least I cannot tell you. It is difficult for a woman to define her feelings in language which is chiefly made by men to express theirs. My treatment of you was thoughtless, inexcusable, wicked. I shall eternally regret it. If there had been anything I could have done to make amends I would most gladly have done it – there was nothing on earth I so longed to do as to repair the error. But that was not possible."

"Don't blame yourself – you were not so far in the wrong as you suppose. Bathsheba, suppose you had real complete proof that you are what in fact you are – a widow – would you repair the old wrong to me by marrying me?"

"I cannot say. I shouldn't yet at any rate."

"But you might at some future time of your life?"

"O yes, I might at some time."

"Well then, do you know that without further proof of any kind you may marry again in about six years from the present – subject to nobody's objection or blame?"

"O yes," she said quickly. "I know all that. But don't talk of it – seven or six years – where may we all be by that time!"

"They will soon glide by: and it will seem an astonishingly short time to look back upon when they are past – much less than to look forward to now."

"Yes, yes: I have found that in my own experience."

"Now listen once more," Boldwood pleaded. "If I wait that time, will you marry me? You own that you owe me amends – let that be your way of making them."

"But Mr Boldwood – six years –"

"Do you want to be the wife of any other man?"

"No indeed! I mean that I don't like to talk about this matter now. Perhaps it is not proper, and I ought not to allow it. Let us drop it for the present, please do!"

"Of course I'll drop the subject if you wish. But propriety has nothing to do with reasons. I am a middleaged man, willing to protect you for the remainder of our lives. On your side at least there is no passion or blamable haste – on mine perhaps there is. But I can't help seeing that if you choose, from a feeling of pity and as you say a wish to make amends, to make a bargain with me for a far-ahead time – an agreement which will set all things right and make me happy, late though it may be – there is no fault to be found with you as a woman. Hadn't I the first place beside you? Haven't you been almost mine once already? Surely you can say to me as much as this, you will have me back again should circumstances permit? Now pray speak. O Bathsheba, promise – it is only a little promise – that if you marry again you will marry me!"

His tone was so excited that she almost feared him at this moment even whilst she sympathized. It was a simple physical fear – the weak of the strong: there was no emotional aversion or inner repugnance. She said with some distress in her voice, for she remembered vividly his outburst on the Yalbury road, and shrank from a repetition of his anger:

"I will never marry another man whilst you wish me to be your wife, whatever comes."

"But let it stand in these simple words – that in six years' time you will be my wife? Unexpected accidents we'll not mention, because those of course must be given way to. Now this time I know you will keep your word."

"That's why I hesitate to give it."

"But do give it! Remember the past, and be kind."

She waited, and then said mournfully: "Consider all this. I don't love you, and I much fear I never shall love you as much as a woman ought to love a husband. If you, sir, know that, and I can yet give you happiness by a mere promise without feeling, and just in friendliness, to marry at the end of six years, it is a great honour to me. And if you value such an act of friendship from a woman who doesn't esteem herself as she did, and has little love left, why I – I will –"

"Promise!"

"– Consider if I cannot promise soon."

"But soon is perhaps never."

"O no it is not. I mean soon. Christmas we'll say."

"Christmas." He said nothing further till he added: "Well, I'll say no more to you about it till that time."

Bathsheba was in a very peculiar state of mind, which showed how entirely the soul is the slave of the body, the ethereal spirit dependent for its quality upon the tangible flesh and blood.[2] It is hardly too much to say that she felt coerced by a force stronger than her own will not only into the act of promising upon this singularly remote and vague matter, but into the emotion of fancying that she ought to promise. When the weeks intervening between the night of this conversation began perceptibly to diminish, her anxiety and perplexity increased.

One day she was led by an accident into an oddly confidential dialogue with Gabriel about her difficulty. It afforded her a little relief – of a dull and cheerless kind. They were auditing accounts and something occurred in the course of their labours which led Oak to say, speaking of Boldwood, "He'll never forget you, ma'am; never."

Then out came her trouble before she was aware; and she told him how she had again got into the toils; what Boldwood had asked her, and how he was expecting her assent. "The most mournful reason of all for my agreeing to it," she said sadly, "and the true reason why I think to do so for good or for evil is this – it is a thing I have not breathed to a living soul as yet – I believe that if I don't give my word he'll go out of his mind."

"Really – do you," said Gabriel gravely.

"I believe this," she continued, with reckless frankness; "and Heaven knows I say it in a spirit the very reverse of vain, for I am grieved and troubled to my soul about it – I believe I hold that poor man's future in my hand. His career depends entirely upon my treatment of him. O Gabriel, I tremble at my responsibility, for it is terrible!"

"Well I think this much, ma'am, as I told you years ago," said Oak, "that his life is a total blank whenever he isn't hoping for you; but I can't suppose – I hope that nothing so dreadful attaches to it as you fancy. His natural manner has always been dark and strange, you know. – But since the case is so sad and peculiar, why don't ye give the conditional promise? I think I would."

"But is it right? Some rash acts of my past life have taught me that a watched woman must have very much circumspection to retain only a very little credit, and I do want and long to be discreet in this. And six years – why we may all be in our graves by that time. Indeed the long time and the uncertainty of the whole thing give a sort of absurdity to the scheme. Now isn't it preposterous, Gabriel? However he came to dream of it I cannot think. But is it wrong? You know – you are older than I."

"Eight years, ma'am."

"Yes, eight years – and it is wrong?"

"Perhaps it would be an uncommon agreement for a man and woman to make: I don't see anything really wrong about it," said Oak, slowly. "In fact the very thing that makes it doubtful if you ought to marry him under any condition, that is, your not caring about him – for I may suppose – "

"Yes, you may suppose that love is wanting," she said shortly. "Love is an utterly bygone, sorry, worn-out, miserable thing with me – for him or anyone else."

"Well, your want of love seems to me the one thing that takes away harm from such an agreement with him. If wild heat had to do with it, making you long to overcome the awkwardness about your husband's death,[3] it might be wrong; but a cold-hearted agreement to oblige a man seems different, somehow. The real sin, ma'am, in my mind lies in thinking of ever wedding with a man you don't love honest and true."

"That I'm willing to pay the penalty of," said Bathsheba, firmly. "You know Gabriel this is what I cannot get off my conscience, that I once seriously injured him in sheer idleness. If I had never played a trick upon him he would never have wanted to marry me. O if I could only pay some heavy damages in money to him for the harm I did, and so get the sin off my soul that way! . . . . Well there's the debt, which can only be discharged in one way, and I believe I am bound to do it if it honestly lies in my power, without any consideration of my own future at all. When a person gambles away his expectations the fact that it is an inconvenient debt doesn't make him the less liable. The single point I ask you is, considering that my own scruples, and the fact that in the eye of the law my husband is only missing, will keep any man from marrying me until seven years have passed, am I free to entertain such an idea, even though 'tis as a sort of penance – for it will be that: I *hate* the act of marriage under such circumstances, and the class of women I should seem to belong to by doing it!"

"It seems to me that all depends upon whether you think, as everybody else does, that your husband is dead."

"Yes – I've long ceased to doubt that.[4] I well know what would have brought him back long before this time if he had lived."

"Well then in a religious sense you must be as free to think of marrying again as any other widow of one year's standing. But why don't you ask Mr Thirdly's advice on how to treat Mr Boldwood?"

"No. When I want a broad-minded opinion for general enlightenment, distinct from special advice, I never go to a man who deals in the subject professionally. So I like the parson's opinion on law, the lawyer's on doctoring, the doctor's on business, and my business-man's – that is, yours – on morals."

"And on love –"

"My own."

"I'm afraid there's a hitch in that argument," said Oak with a grave smile.

She did not reply at once, and then saying, "Good evening, Mr Oak," went away.

She had spoken frankly, and neither asked nor expected any reply from Gabriel more satisfactory than that she had obtained. Yet in the centremost parts of her complicated heart there existed at this minute a little pang of disappointment, for a reason she would not allow herself to recognise. Oak had not once wished her free that he might marry her himself – had not once said, "I could wait for you as well as he." That was the insect sting. Not that she would have listened to any such hypothesis – O no – for wasn't she saying all the time that such thoughts of the future were improper, and wasn't Gabriel far too poor a man to be allowed to speak sentiment to her? Yet he might have just hinted about that old love of his, and asked in a playful off-hand way if he might speak of it. It would have seemed pretty and sweet, if no more; and then she would have shown how kind and inoffensive a woman's "No" can sometimes be. But to give such cool advice – the very advice she had asked for – it ruffled our heroine all the afternoon.

CHAPTER LI[1]

Converging courses.

I

Christmas-eve came, and a party that Boldwood was to give in the evening was the great subject of talk in Weatherbury. It was not that the rarity of Christmas parties in the parish made this one a wonder, but that Boldwood should be the giver. The announcement had had an abnormal and incongruous sound, as if one should hear of croquet playing in a cathedral aisle, or that some much respected judge was going upon the stage. That the party was intended to be a truly jovial one there was no room for doubt. A large bough of mistletoe had been brought from the woods that day and suspended in the hall of the bachelor's home. Holly and ivy had followed in armfuls. From six that morning till past noon the huge wood fire in the kitchen roared and sparkled at its highest, the kettle the saucepan and the three legged pot appearing in the midst of the fire like Shadrach Meshach and Abednego;[2] moreover, roasting and basting operations were continually carried on in front of the genial blaze.

As it grew later the fire was made up in the large long hall into which the staircase descended, and all encumbrances were cleared out for dancing. The log which was to form the back-brand of the evening fire was the uncleft trunk of a tree, so unwieldy that it could be neither brought nor rolled to its place; and accordingly four men were to be observed dragging and heaving it in by chains and levers as the hour of assembly drew near.

In spite of all this the spirit of revelry was wanting in the atmosphere of the house. Such a thing had never been attempted before by its owner, and it was now done as by a wrench. Intended gaieties would insist upon appearing like solemn grandeurs, the organization of the whole effort was carried out coldly by hirelings, and a shadow seemed to move about the rooms saying that the proceedings were unnatural to the place and the lone man who lived there, and therefore not good.

2

Bathsheba was at this time in her room dressing for the event. She had called for candles, and Liddy entered and placed one on each side of her mistress's glass.

"Don't go away Liddy," said Bathsheba, almost timidly. "I am strangely agitated – I cannot tell why. I wish I had not been obliged to go to this dance; but there's no escaping now. I have not spoken to Mr Boldwood since the autumn, when I promised to see him at Christmas on business but I had no idea there was to be anything of this kind."

"But I would go now," said Liddy, who was going with her; for Boldwood had been indiscriminate in his invitations.

"Yes, I shall make my appearance of course," said Bathsheba. "But I am *the cause* of the party; and that upsets me."

"You the cause of it ma'am?"

"Yes, I am the reason for the party – I. If it had not been for me there would never have been one. I can't explain any more – there's no more to be explained. I wish I had never seen Weatherbury."

"That's wicked of you – to wish to be worse off than you are."

"No it isn't. I have never been free from trouble since I have lived here, and this party is likely to bring me more. Now fetch my black silk dress, and see how it sits upon me."

"But you will leave off that, surely ma'am? You have been a widow lady fourteen months, and ought to brighten up a little on such a night as this."

"It is not necessary. I mean to appear as usual, for if I were to wear any light dress people would say things about me, and I should seem to be rejoicing when I am solemn all the time. The party doesn't elevate me a bit; but never mind, stay and help to finish me off."

3

Boldwood was dressing also at this hour. A tailor from Casterbridge was with him, assisting him in the operation of trying on a new coat that had just been brought home.

Never had Boldwood been so fastidious, unreasonable about the fit, and generally difficult to please. The tailor walked round and round him, tugged at the waist, pulled the sleeve, pressed out the collar, and, for the first time in his experience Boldwood was not bored. Times had been when the farmer had exclaimed against all such niceties as childish, but now no philosophic or hasty rebuke whatever was provoked by this man for attaching as much importance to a crease in the coat as to an earthquake in South America. Boldwood at last expressed himself nearly satisfied, and paid the bill, the tailor passing out of the door just as Oak came in to report progress for the day.

"Ah, Oak," said Boldwood, "I shall of course see you here to-night. Make yourself merry. I am determined that neither expense nor trouble shall be spared."

"I'll try to be here, Sir, though perhaps it may not be very early," said Gabriel, quietly. "I am glad indeed to see such a change in you from what it used to be."

"Yes – I must own it – I am bright to-night: cheerful and more than cheerful – so much so that I am almost sad again with the sense that all of it is passing away. And sometimes, when I am excessively hopeful and blithe, a trouble is looming in the distance: so that I often get to look upon gloom in me with content, and to fear a happy mood. Still this may be absurd – I feel that it is absurd. Perhaps my day is dawning at last."

"I hope it will be a long and a fair one."

"Thank you – thank you. Yet perhaps my cheerfulness rests upon a slender hope. And yet I trust my hope. It is faith – not hope. I think this time I reckon with my host. – Oak my hands shake, and I am nervous, and I can't tie this neckerchief properly. The fact is I have not been well lately, you know."

"I am sorry to hear that, sir."

"O it's nothing. – Perhaps you will tie the knot for me. I want it done as well as you can, please. Is there any late knot in fashion, Oak?"

"I don't know, Sir," said Oak. His tone had sunk to sadness.

Boldwood approached Gabriel, and as Oak tied the neckerchief the farmer went on feverishly,

"Does a woman keep her promise, Gabriel?"

"If it is not inconvenient to her she may."

"– Or rather an implied promise."

"I won't answer for her implying," said Oak, with faint bitterness. "That's a word as full of holes as a sieve with them."

"Oak, don't talk like that. You have got quietly cynical lately, – how is it? We seem to have shifted our positions: I have become the young and hopeful man, and you the old and unbelieving one. However, does a woman keep a promise – not to marry, but to enter on an engagement to marry at some time? Now you know women better than I – tell me."

"I am afraid you honour my understanding too much. However she may keep such a promise, if it is made with an honest intention to repair a wrong."

"It has not gone far yet – but I think it will soon – yes, I know it will," he said in a fervent whisper. "I have pressed her upon the subject, and she inclines to be kind to me, and to think of me as a husband at a long future time; and that's enough for me. How can I expect more? She has a notion that a widow should not marry within seven years of her husband's death – that her own self shouldn't, I mean – because his body was not found. It may be merely this legal reason which influences her, or it may be a religious one, but she is reluctant to talk on the point. Yet she has promised – implied – that she will ratify an engagement to-night."

"Seven years," murmured Oak.

"No, no – it is no such thing!" he said with impatience. "Five years, nine months, and a few days. Fifteen months nearly have passed since his death, and is there anything so wonderful in an engagement of little more than five years?"

"It seems long in a forward view. Don't build too much upon such promises, sir. Remember, you have once been deceived. Her intentions may be good; but there – she's young yet."

"Deceived? Never!" said Boldwood, vehemently. "She never promised me at that first time, and hence she did not break her promise. If she promises me she'll marry me. Bathsheba is a woman to her word."

4

Troy was sitting in a small apartment in a small tavern[3] at Casterbridge, smoking and drinking a steaming mixture from a glass. A knock was given upon the door, and Pennyways entered.

"Well, have you seen him?" Troy enquired, pointing to a chair.

"Boldwood?"

"No – Lawyer Long."[4]

"He was not at home. I went there first, too."

"That's a nuisance."

"'Tis rather, I suppose."

"Yet I don't see that because a man appears to be drowned and was not he should be liable for anything. I shan't ask any lawyer – not I."

"But that's not it exactly. If a man by changing his name and so forth takes steps to deceive the world and his own wife, he's a cheat, and that in the eye of the law is ayless a rogue, and that is ayless a vagabond; and that's a punishable word."

"Ha-ha! Well done Pennyways." Troy had laughed, but it was with some anxiety that he said, "Now, what I want to know is this, do you think there's really anything going on between her and Boldwood? Upon my soul I should never have believed it! How she must detest me! Have you found out whether she has encouraged him?"

"I've not been able to learn. There's a deal of feeling on his side seemingly, but I don't answer for her. I didn't know a word about any such thing till yesterday, and all I heard then was that she was going to the party at his house to-night. This is the first time she has ever gone there they say. And they say that she've not so much as spoke to him since they were at Greenhill Fair – but what can folk believe o't? However, she's not fond of him – quite offish and careless, I know."

"I'm not so sure of that. . . . . . She's a handsome woman Pennyways, is she not. Own that you never saw a finer or more splendid creature in your life. Upon my honour when I set eyes upon her that day I wondered what I could have been made of to be able to leave her by herself so long. And then I was hampered with that bothering show, which I'm free of at last, thank the stars." He smoked on awhile and then added, "How did she look when you passed by yesterday?"

"Oh, she took no great heed of me, ye may well fancy; but she looked well enough, far's I know. Just flashed her haughty eyes upon my poor scram body, and then let them go past me to what was yond, much as if I'd been no more than a leafless tree. She had just got off her mare to look at the last wring down of cider for the year; she had been riding and so her colours were up and her breath rather quick, so that her bosom plimmed and fell – plimmed and fell – every time plain to my eye. Ay, and there were the fellers round her wringing down[5] the cheese and bustling about and saying, 'Ware o' the pommy, ma'am: 'twill spoil yer gown.' 'Never mind me,' says she. Then Gabe brought her some of the new cider, and she must needs go drinking it through a strawmote and not in a naterel way at all. 'Liddy,' says she, 'bring indoors a few gallons and I'll make some cider-wine.' Sergeant, I was no more to her than a morsel of scroff in the fuel house."

"I must go and find her out at once – O yes, I see that – I must go. Oak is head man still, isn't he?"

"Yes 'a b'lieve. And at Lower Farm too. He manages everything."

"'Twill puzzle him to manage her, or any other man of his compass."

"I don't know about that. She've a few soft corners to her mind – though I've never been able to get into one, the devil's in't. – But she can't do without him, and knowing it well he's pretty independent."

"Ah, Baily, she's a notch above you, and you must own it: a higher class of animal – a finer tissue. However, stick to me, and neither this haughty goddess, dashing piece of womanhood, Juno-wife of mine (Juno[6] was a goddess you know), nor anybody else shall hurt you. But all this wants looking into I perceive. What with one thing and another I see that my work is well cut out for me."

5

"How do I look to-night Liddy?" said Bathsheba, giving a final adjustment to her dress before leaving the glass.

"I never saw you look so well before. Yes – I'll tell you when you looked like it – that night a year and half ago when you came in so wild-like and scolded us for making remarks about you and Mr Troy."

"Everybody will think that I am setting myself to captivate Mr Boldwood, when goodness knows how I dread the thought. Can't I be toned down a little? I dread going – yet I dread more the risk of wounding him by staying away."

"Anyhow ma'am you can't well be dressed plainer than you are unless you go in sackcloth at once. 'Tis your excitement is what makes your looks so noticeable to-night."

"I don't know what's the matter," she sighed. "I feel wretched at one time, and buoyant at another. I wish I could have continued quite calm as I have been for the last year or so, with no hopes and no fears, and no pleasure and no grief."

"Now just suppose Mr Boldwood should ask you – only just suppose it – to run away with him, what would you do, ma'am?"

"Liddy – none of that," said Bathsheba gravely. "Mind I won't hear joking on any such matter. Do you hear?"

"I beg pardon ma'am. But knowing what rum things we women are I just said – however I won't speak of it again."

"No marrying for me yet for many a year; if ever, 'twill be for reasons very, very different from those you think, or others will believe. Now get my cloak, for it is time to go."

6

"Oak," said Boldwood, "before you go I want to mention what has been passing in my mind lately – that little arrangement we made about your share in the farm I mean. That share is small, too small, considering how little I attend to business now, and how much time and thought you give to it. Well, since the world is brightening for me I want to show my sense of it by increasing your proportion in the partnership. I'll make a memorandum of the arrangement which struck me as likely to be convenient, for I haven't time to talk about it now; and then we'll discuss it at our leisure. My intention is ultimately to retire from the management altogether, and until you can take all the expenditure upon your shoulders I'll be a sleeping partner in the stock. Then, if I marry her – and I hope – I feel I shall, why –"

"Pray don't speak of it sir," said Oak hastily. "We don't know what may happen. So many circumstances arise. There's many a slip, as they say – and I would advise you – I know you'll pardon me this once – not to be *too sure.*"

"I know, I know. But the feeling I have about increasing your share is on account of what I know of you. Oak, I have learnt a little about your secret: your interest in her is more than that of a bailiff for an employer. But you have behaved like a man, and I, as a sort of successful rival – successful partly through your goodness of heart – should like definitely to show my sense of your friendship under what must have been a great pain to you."

"Oh, that's not necessary, thank you," said Oak, offhandedly. "I must get used to such as that: other men have, and so shall I."

Oak then left him. He was uneasy on Boldwood's account, for he saw that this constant passion of the farmer for her had left him not the man he once had been.

As Boldwood continued awhile in his room alone – ready and dressed to receive his company – the mood of anxiety about his appearance seemed to pass away, and to be succeeded by a deep solemnity. He looked out of the window, and regarded the dim outline of the trees upon the sky, and the twilight deepening to darkness.

Then he went to a locked closet, and took from a locked drawer therein a small circular case the size of a pill-box, and was about to put it into his pocket. But he lingered to open the cover and take a momentary glance inside. It contained a woman's finger-ring, set all the way round with small diamonds, and from its appearance had evidently been recently purchased. Boldwood's eyes dwelt upon its many sparkles a long time, though that its material aspect concerned him little was plain from his manner and mien, which were those of a mind following out the presumed thread of that jewel's future history.

The noise of wheels at the front of the house became audible. Boldwood closed the box, stowed it away carefully in his pocket, and went out upon the landing. The old man who was his indoor factotum came at the same moment to the foot of the stairs.

"They be coming sir – lots of 'em – a foot and a driving."

"I was coming down this moment. Those wheels I heard – is it Mrs Troy?"

"No sir – 'tis not she yet."

A reserved and sombre expression had returned to Boldwood's face again, but it poorly cloaked his feelings when he pronounced Bathsheba's name; and his feverish anxiety continued to show its existence by a galloping motion of his fingers upon the side of his thigh as he went down the stairs.

7

"How does this cover me?" said Troy to Pennyways. "Nobody would recognize me now I'm sure."

He was buttoning on a heavy grey overcoat of Noachian cut, with cape and high collar, the latter being erect and rigid, like a girdling wall, and nearly reaching to the verge of the travelling cap which was pulled down over his ears.

Pennyways snuffed the candle, and then looked up and deliberately inspected Troy.

"Ye've made up your mind to go then?" he said.

"Made up my mind? Yes, of course I have."

"Why not write to her? 'Tis a very queer corner that you have got into sergeant. You see all these things will come to light if you go back, and they won't sound well at all. Faith, if I was you I'd even bide as you be – a single man of the name of Francis. A good wife is good, but the best wife is not so good as no wife at all. Now that's my outspoke mind, and I've been called a long-headed feller here and there."

"All nonsense. There she is with plenty of money, and a house and farm, and horses, and comfort, and here am I living from hand to mouth – a needy adventurer. – Besides, it is no use talking now; it is too late, and I am glad of it: I've been seen and recognized here this very afternoon.

I should have gone back to her the day after the fair if it hadn't been for you talking about the law and rubbish about her getting a separation; and I won't put it off any longer. What the deuce put it into my head to run away at all I can't think. Humbugging sentiment – that's what it was. But what man on earth was to know that his wife would be in such a hurry to get rid of his name!"

"I should have known it. She's bad enough for anything."

"Pennyways, mind who you are talking to."

"Well, sergeant, all I say is this, that if I were you I'd go abroad again where I came from – 'tisn't too late to do it now. I wouldn't stir up the business and get a bad name for the sake of living with her – for all that about your play-acting is sure to come out, you know, although you think otherwise. My eyes and limbs, there'll be a racket if you go back just now – in the middle of Boldwood's Christmasing!"

"H'm, yes. I expect I shall not be a very welcome guest if he has her there," said the sergeant with a slight laugh. "A sort of Alonzo the Brave;[7] and when I go in the guests will sit in silence and fear, and all laughter and pleasure will be hushed, and the lights in the chamber burn blue, and the worms – Ugh, horrible! – Ring for some more brandy Pennyways, I felt an awful shudder just then. Well what is there besides? I must have a walking-stick."

Pennyways now felt himself to be in something of a difficulty, for should Bathsheba and Troy become reconciled it would be necessary to regain her good opinion if he would secure the patronage of her husband. "I sometimes think she likes ye yet, and is a good woman at bottom," he said, as a saving sentence. "But there's no telling to a certainty from a body's outside. Well – you'll do as you like about going of course sergeant, and as for me, I'll do as you tell me."

"Now let me see what the time is," said Troy, after emptying his glass in one draught as he stood. "Half past six o'clock. I shall not hurry along the road, and shall be there then before nine."

CHAPTER LII

Momentâ horæ concurritur.[1]

Outside the front of Boldwood's house a group of men stood in the dark with their faces towards the door, which occasionally opened and closed again to admit some guest or servant, when a golden rod of light would stripe the gravel for the moment, and vanish again, leaving nothing outside but the glowworm shine of the pale lamp amid the evergreens over the door.

"He was seen in Casterbridge this afternoon – so the boy said," one of them remarked in a whisper. "And I for one believe it. His body was never found, you know."

"'Tis a strange story," said the next. "You may depend upon it that she knows nothing about it."

"Not a word."

"Perhaps he don't mean that she shall," said another man.

"If he's alive and here in the neighbourhood he means mischief," said the first. "Poor young girl: I do pity her if 'tis true. He'll drag her to the dogs."

"O no – he'll settle down quiet enough," said one disposed to take a more hopeful view of the case.

"What a fool she must have been ever to have had anything to do with the man! She is so self willed and independent too, that one is more inclined to say it serves her right than pity her."

"No, no. I don't hold with ye there. She was no otherwise than a girl mind, and how could she tell what the man was made of. If 'tis really true, 'tis too hard a punishment, and more than she deserves. – Hullo, who's that?" This was to some footsteps that were heard approaching.

"William Smallbury," said a dim figure in the shades, coming up and joining them. "Dark as a hedge, to-night, isn't it. I all but missed the plank over the river ath'art there in the bottom – never did such a thing before in my life. Be ye any of Boldwood's workfolk?" He peered into their faces.

"Yes – all o' us. We met here a few minutes ago."

"O, I hear now – that's Sam Samway: thought I knowed the voice, too. Going in."

"Presently. But I say William," he whispered, "have ye heard this strange tale?"

"What – that about Sergeant Troy being seen, d'ye mean souls?" said Smallbury, also lowering his voice.

"Ay: in Casterbridge."

"Yes, I have. Laban Tall named a hint of it to me but now – but I don't think it. Hark – here Laban comes himself I think." A footstep drew near.

"Laban?"

"Yes, 'tis I," said Tall.

"Have ye heard any more about that?"

"No," said Tall, joining the group. "And I'm inclined to think we'd better keep quiet. If 'tis not true 'twill flurry her and do her much harm to repeat it; and if 'tis true 'twill do no good to forestall her time of trouble. God send that it may be a lie, for though Henery Fray and some of 'em do speak against her, she's never been anything but fair to me. She's hot and hasty, but she's a brave girl who'll never tell a lie however much the truth may harm her, and I've no cause to wish her evil."

"She never do tell women's little lies, that's true; and 'tis a thing that can be said of very few. Ay, all the harm she thinks she says to yer face: there's nothing underhand wi' her."

They stood silent then, every man busied with his own thoughts, during which interval sounds of merriment could be heard within. Then the front door again opened, the rays streamed out, the well-known form of Boldwood was seen in the rectangular area of light, the door closed, and Boldwood walked slowly down the path.

"'Tis master," one of the men whispered as he neared them. "We'd better stand quiet – he'll go in again directly. He would think it ill-mannered of us to be loitering here."

Boldwood came on, and passed by the men without seeing them, they being under the bushes on the grass. He paused, leant over the gate, and breathed a long breath. They heard low words come from him:

"I hope to God she'll come, or all this night will be nothing but misery to me. O my darling, my darling, why do you keep me in suspense like this!"

He said this to himself, and they all distinctly heard it. Boldwood remained silent after that, and only the noise from indoors was to be heard, until, a few minutes later, light wheels could be distinguished coming down the hill. They drew nearer, and ceased at the gate. Boldwood hastened back to the door and opened it; and the light shone upon Bathsheba coming up the path.

Boldwood compressed his emotion to mere welcome: the men heard her light laugh and apology as she met him: he took her into the house; and the door closed again.

"Gracious Heaven – I didn't know it was like that with him!" said one of the men. "I thought that fancy of his was over long ago."

"You don't know much of master if you thought that," said another.

"I wouldn't he should know we heard what he said for the world," remarked a third.

"I wish we had told of the report at once," the first uneasily continued. "More harm may come of this than we know of. Poor Mr Boldwood – it will be hard upon him. I wish Troy was in—: Well, God forgive me for such a wish! A scoundrel to play a poor wife such tricks. Nothing has prospered in Weatherbury since he came here. And now I've no heart to go in. Let's look into Warren's, shall we neighbours?"

Samway, Tall, and Smallbury agreed to, and went out at the gate, the remaining ones entering the house. The three soon drew near the malt-house, approaching it from the adjoining orchard, and not by way of the street. The pane of glass was illuminated as usual. Smallbury was a little in advance of the rest, when, pausing, he turned suddenly to his companions and said, "Hist! See there."

The light from the pane was now perceived to be shining not upon the ivied wall as usual, but upon some object close to the glass. It was a human face.

"Let's come closer," whispered Samway, and they approached on tiptoe. There was no disbelieving the report any longer. Troy's face was almost close to the pane, and he was looking in. Not only was he looking in, but he appeared to have been arrested by a conversation which was in progress in the malt-house, the voices of the interlocutors being those of Oak and the maltster.

"The spree is all in her honour, isn't it – hey?" said the old man. "Although he made believe 'tis only keeping up o' Christmas."

"I cannot say," replied Oak.

"O 'tis true enough, faith. I can't understand Farmer Boldwood being such a fool at his time o' life as to hanker after that woman in the way 'a do, and she not care a bit about en."

The men, after recognizing Troy's features, withdrew across the orchard as silently as they had come. The air was big with Bathsheba's fortunes to-night: every word everywhere concerned her. When they were quite out of earshot all by one instinct paused.

"It gave me quite a turn – his face," said Tall, breathing.

"And so it did me," said Samway. "What's to be done."

"I don't see that it's any business of ours," Smallbury murmured dubiously.

"O yes. 'Tis a thing which is everybody's business," said Samway. "We know very well that master's on a wrong tack, and that she's quite in the dark, and we should let 'em know at once. Laban you know her best – you'd better go and ask to speak to her."

"I'm not fit for any such thing," said Laban nervously. "I should think William ought to if anybody. He's oldest."

"I shall have nothing to do with it," said Smallbury. "'Tis a ticklish business altogether. Why, he'll go on to her himself in a few minutes, ye'll see."

"We don't know that he will. Come Laban."

"Very well, if I must I must I suppose," Tall reluctantly answered. "What must I say?"

"Just ask to see master."

"O no: I shan't speak to Mr Boldwood. If I tell anybody 'twill be mistress."

"Very well," said Samway.

Laban then went to the door. When he opened it the hum of bustle rolled out as a wave upon a still strand – the assemblage being immediately inside the hall – and was deadened to a murmur as he closed it again. The men waited intently, and looked around at the dark tree tops gently rocking against the sky and occasionally shivering in a slight wind, as if they took interest in the scene, which they did not. One of them began walking up and down, and then came to where he started from and stopped again, with a sense that walking was a thing not worth doing.

"I should think Laban must have seen mistress by this time," said

Smallbury breaking the silence. "Perhaps she won't come and speak to him."

The door opened. Tall appeared, and joined them.

"Well?" said both, and suspended breath.

"I didn't like to ask for her after all," Laban faltered out. "They were all in such a stir, trying to put a little spirit into the party. Somehow the fun seems to hang fire, though everything's there that a heart can desire, and I couldn't for my soul interfere and throw damp upon it – if 'twas to save my life I couldn't."

"I suppose we had better all go in together," said Samway gloomily. "Perhaps I may have a chance of saying a word to master."

So the men entered the hall, which was the room selected and arranged for the gathering because of its size. The younger men and maids were at last just beginning to dance. Bathsheba had been perplexed how to act, for she was no more than a slim young maid herself, and the weight of stateliness sat heavy upon her. Sometimes she thought she ought not to have come under any circumstances: then she considered what cold unkindness that would have been: and finally resolved upon the middle course of coming for about an hour only, and gliding off unobserved. From the first Bathsheba made up her mind that she could on no account dance, sing, or take any active part in the proceedings.

Her allotted hour having been passed in chatting, and looking on, Bathsheba told Liddy not to hurry herself and went to the small parlour to prepare for departure, which like the hall was decorated with holly and ivy, and well lighted up.

Nobody was in the room, but she had hardly been there a moment when the master of the house entered.

"Mrs Troy – you are not going?" he said. "We've hardly begun."

"If you'll excuse me, I should like to go now." Her manner was restive, for she remembered her promise, and imagined what he was about to say. "But as it is not late," she added, "I can walk home, and leave my man and Liddy to come when they choose."

"I've been trying to get an opportunity of speaking to you," said Boldwood. "You know perhaps what I long to say?"

Bathsheba silently looked on the floor.

"You do give it?" he said eagerly.

"What?" she whispered.

"Now, that's evasion! Why, the promise. I don't want to intrude upon you at all, or to let it become known to anybody. But do give your word! A mere business compact, you know, between two people who are beyond the influence of passion." Boldwood knew how false this picture was as regarded himself; but it was the only tone in which she would allow him to approach her. "A promise to marry me at the end of five years and three-quarters. You owe it to me!"

"I feel that I do," said Bathsheba: "that is, if you demand it. But I am a changed woman – an unhappy woman – and not – not –"

"You are a very beautiful woman," said Boldwood. Honesty and pure conviction suggested the remark, unaccompanied by any perception that it might have been adopted by blunt flattery to soothe and win her.

However, it had not much effect now, for she said, in a passionless murmur which was in itself a proof of her words: "I have no feeling in the matter at all. And I don't at all know what is right to do in my difficult position – and I have nobody to advise me. But I give my promise, if I must. I give it as the rendering of a debt."[2]

"You'll marry me between five and six years hence."

"Don't press me too hard. I'll marry nobody else."

"But surely you will name the time, or there's nothing in the promise at all."

"O I don't know – pray let me go!" she said, her bosom rising in her distress. "I am afraid what to do – I want to be just to you, and to be that seems to be wronging myself, and perhaps it is breaking the commandments.[3] There is a shadow of doubt of his death, and then it is dreadful – let me ask a solicitor Mr Boldwood, if I ought or no!"

"Say the words dear one, and the subject shall be dismissed – a blissful loving intimacy of six years, and then, marriage – O Bathsheba – say them!" he begged in a husky voice, unable to sustain the forms of mere friendship any longer. "Promise yourself to me – I deserve it, indeed I do, for I have loved you more than anybody in the world. And if I said hasty words and showed uncalled for heat of manner towards you, believe me, dear, I did not mean to distress you: I was in agony Bathsheba, and I didn't know what I said. You wouldn't let a dog suffer what I have suffered, could you but know it! Sometimes I shrink from your knowing what I have felt for you, and sometimes I am distressed that all of it you never will know. Be gracious, and give up a little to me when I would give up my life for you!"

The trimmings of her dress as they quivered against the light showed how agitated she was, and at last she burst out crying. "And you'll not – press me – about anything more – if I say in five or six years?" she sobbed when she had power to frame the words.

"Yes, then I'll leave it to time."

"Very well. I'll marry you in six years from this day if we both live," she said solemnly.

"And you'll take this as a token from me?"

Boldwood had come close to her side, and now he clasped one of her hands in both his own, and lifted it to his breast.

"What is it? O I cannot wear a ring!" she exclaimed on seeing what he held besides. "I wouldn't have a soul know that it's an engagement. – Perhaps it is improper – Besides we are not engaged in the usual sense are we? Don't insist Mr Boldwood – don't!" In her trouble at not being able to get her hand away from him at once, she stamped passionately on the floor with one foot and tears crowded to her eyes again.

"It means simply a pledge – no sentiment – the seal of a practical compact," he said more quietly, but still retaining her hand in his firm grasp. "Come, now!" And Boldwood slipped the ring on her finger.

"I cannot wear it," she said weeping as if her heart would break. "You frighten me – almost. So wild a scheme. Please let me go home!"

"Only to-night: wear it just to-night to please me."

Bathsheba sat down in a chair, and buried her face in her handkerchief, shaking with an occasional sob. At length she said in a sort of hopeless whisper,

"Very well then – I will to-night, if you wish it so earnestly. Now loosen my hand – I will, indeed I will wear it to-night."

"And it shall be the beginning of a pleasant secret courtship of six years, with a wedding at the end?"

"It must be I suppose, since you will have it so!" she said fairly beaten into non-resistance.

Boldwood pressed her hand, and allowed it to drop into her lap. "I am happy now," he said. "God bless you!"

He left the room, and when he thought she might be sufficiently composed sent one of the maids to her. Bathsheba cloaked the effects of the late scene as she best could, followed the girl, and in a few minutes came downstairs with her hat and cloak on, ready to go. To get to the door it was necessary to pass through the hall, and before doing so she paused on the bottom of the staircase which descended in one corner, to take a last look at the gathering.

There was no music or dancing in progress just now. At the lower end, which had been arranged for the workfolk, specially, a group conversed in whispers, and with clouded looks. Boldwood was standing by the fireplace, and he too, though so absorbed in visions arising from her promise that he scarcely saw anything, seemed at that moment to have observed their peculiar manner and their looks askance.

"What is it you are in doubt about, men?" he said.

One of them turned and replied uneasily: "It was something Laban heard of, that's all, Sir."

"News? Anybody married, or engaged, born or dead?" enquired the farmer gaily. "Tell it to us, Tall. One would think from your looks and mysterious ways that it was something very dreadful indeed."

"O no Sir – nobody is dead," said Tall.

"I wish somebody was," said Samway in a whisper.

"What do you say Samway?" asked Boldwood, somewhat sharply. "If you have anything to say, speak out. If not, get up another dance."

"Mrs Troy has come downstairs," said Samway to Tall. "If you want to tell her you had better do it now."

"Do you know what they mean?" the farmer asked of Bathsheba across the room.

"I don't in the least," said Bathsheba.

There was a smart rapping at the door. One of the men opened it instantly, and went outside.

"Mrs Troy is wanted," he said, on returning.

"Quite ready," said Bathsheba. "I didn't tell them to send."

"It is a stranger ma'am," said the man by the door.

"A stranger?" she said.

"Ask him to come in," said Boldwood.

The message was given, and Troy, wrapped up to his eyes as we have seen him, stood in the doorway.

There was an unearthly silence, all looking towards the newcomer. Those who had just learnt that he was in the neighbourhood recognized him instantly: those who did not were perplexed. Nobody noted Bathsheba. She was leaning on the stairs. Her brow had heavily contracted; her whole face was pallid, her lips apart, her eyes rigidly staring at their visitor.

Boldwood was among those who did not notice that he was Troy. "Come in, come in!" he repeated cheerfully, "and drain a Christmas beaker with us, stranger!"

Troy next advanced into the middle of the room, took off his cap, turned down his coat-collar, and looked Boldwood in the face. Even then Boldwood did not recognise him.[4] Troy began to laugh a mechanical laugh; and Boldwood recognised him now.

Troy turned to Bathsheba. The poor girl's wretchedness at this time was beyond all fancy or narration. She had sunk down on the lowest stair, and there she sat, her mouth blue and dry, and her dark eyes fixed vacantly upon him, as if she wondered whether it were not all a terrible illusion.

Then Troy spoke. "Bathsheba, I come here for you."

She made no reply.

"Come home with me: come."

Bathsheba moved her feet a little, but did not rise. Troy went across to her.

"Come madam, do you hear what I say?" he said peremptorily.

A strange voice came from the fireplace – a voice sounding far off and confined, as if from a dungeon. Hardly a soul in the assembly recognised the thin tones to be those of Boldwood.

"Bathsheba, go with your husband!"

Nevertheless, she did not move. The truth was that Bathsheba was beyond the pale of activity – and yet not in a swoon. She was in a state of mental *gutta serena*; her mind was for the minute totally deprived of light at the same time that no obscuration was apparent from without.

Troy stretched out his hand to pull her towards him, when she quickly shrank back. This visible dread of him seemed to irritate Troy, and he seized her arm and pulled it sharply. Whether his grasp pinched her, or whether his mere touch was the cause, was never known, but at the moment of his seizure she writhed, and gave a quick low scream.

The scream had been heard but a few seconds when it was followed by a sudden deafening report that echoed through the room and stupefied them all. The oak partition shook with the concussion, and the place was filled with grey smoke.

In bewilderment they turned their eyes to Boldwood. At his back, as he stood before the fireplace was a gun-rack, as is usual in farm houses, constructed to hold two guns. When Bathsheba had cried out in her husband's grasp Boldwood's face of gnashing despair had changed. The veins had swollen and a frenzied look had gleamed in his eye. He had turned quickly, taken one of the guns, cocked it, and at once discharged it at Troy.

Troy fell. The distance apart of the two men was so small that the charge of shot did not spread in the least, but passed like a bullet into his body. He uttered a long guttural sigh – there was a contraction – an extension – then his muscles relaxed, and he lay still.

Boldwood was seen through the smoke to be now again engaged with the gun. It was double-barrelled, and he had meanwhile in some way fastened his handkerchief to the trigger, and with his foot on the other end was in the act of turning the second barrel upon himself. Samway, his man, was the first to see this, and in the midst of the general horror darted up to him. Boldwood had already twitched the handkerchief and the gun exploded a second time, sending its contents, by a timely blow from Samway, into the beam which crossed the ceiling.

"Well, it makes no difference." Boldwood gasped. "There is another way for me to die."

Then he broke from Samway, crossed the room to Bathsheba and kissed her hand. He put on his hat, opened the door, and went into the darkness, nobody thinking of preventing him.

CHAPTER LIII

After the shock.

Boldwood passed into the high road, and turned in the direction of Casterbridge. Here he walked at an even steady pace by Buck's Head, along the dead level beyond, mounted Casterbridge hill, and between eleven and twelve o'clock descended into the town. The streets were nearly deserted now, and the waving lamp-flames only lighted up rows of grey shop shutters, and strips of white paving upon which his step echoed as he passed along. He turned to the left, and halted before an archway of old brown brick, which was closed by an iron-studded pair of doors. This was the entrance to the gaol, and over it a lamp was fixed, the light enabling the wretched traveller to find a bell pull.

The small wicket at last opened and a porter appeared. Boldwood stepped forward and said something in a low tone, when, after a delay, another man came. Then Boldwood entered and the door was closed behind him, and he walked the world no more.

Long before this time Weatherbury had been thoroughly aroused, and the wild deed which had terminated Boldwood's merrymaking became known to all. Of those out of the house Oak was one of the first to hear of the catastrophe, and when he entered the room, which was about five minutes after Boldwood's exit, the scene was terrible. All the female guests were huddled aghast against the walls like sheep in a storm – and the men were bewildered as to what to do. As for Bathsheba, she had changed. She was sitting on the floor beside the body of Troy, his head pillowed in her lap where she had herself lifted it. With one hand she held her handkerchief to his breast and covered the wound, though scarcely a single drop of blood had flowed, and with the other she tightly clasped one of his. The household convulsion had made her herself again. The temporary coma had ceased, and activity had come with the necessity for it. Deeds of endurance which seem ordinary in philosophy are rare in conduct: and Bathsheba was astonishing all around her now, for her philosophy was her conduct, and she seldom thought practicable what she did not practise. She was of the stuff of which great men's mothers are made. She was indispensable to high generation, feared at tea-parties, hated in shops, and loved at crises. Troy in his recumbent wife's lap formed now the sole spectacle in the middle of the spacious room.

"Gabriel," she said automatically, when he entered, turning up a face of which only the well known lines remained to tell him it was hers, all else in the picture having faded quite. "Ride to Casterbridge instantly for a surgeon. It is, I believe useless, but go. Mr Boldwood has shot my husband."

Her statement of the fact in such quiet and simple words came with more force than a tragic declamation, and had somewhat the effect of setting the distorted images in each mind present into proper focus. Oak, almost before he had comprehended anything beyond the briefest abstract of the event, hurried out of the room, saddled a horse and rode away. Not till he had ridden more than a mile did it occur to him that he would have done better by sending some other man on this errand, remaining himself in the house. What had become of Boldwood? – he should have been looked after. Was he mad – had there been a quarrel? Then how had Troy got here – where had he come from – how did this remarkable reappearance come to pass when he was supposed to be at the bottom of the sea. Oak had in some slight measure been prepared for the presence of Troy by hearing a rumour of his return just before entering Boldwood's house; but before he had weighed that information this fatal event had been superimposed. However it was too late now to think of sending another messenger, and he rode on – in the excitement of these self enquiries not discerning when about three miles from Casterbridge a square figured pedestrian passing along under the dark hedge in the same direction as his own.

The miles necessary to be traversed, and other hindrances incidental to the lateness of the hour and the darkness of the night delayed the arrival of Mr Granthead the surgeon; and more than three hours passed between the time at which the shot was fired and that of his entering the house. Oak was additionally detained in Casterbridge through having to give notice to the authorities of what had happened; and he then found that Boldwood had also entered the town and delivered himself up.

In the meantime the surgeon, having hastened into the hall at Boldwood's, found it in darkness and quite deserted. He went on to the back of the house, where he discovered in the kitchen an old man of whom he made enquiries.

"She's had him took away to her own house, Sir," said his informant.

"Who has?" said the doctor.

"Mrs Troy. 'A was quite dead, sir."

This was astonishing information. "She had no right to do that," said the doctor. "There will have to be an inquest, and she should have waited to know what to do."

"Yes sir: it was hinted to her that she had better wait till the law was known. But she said law was nothing to her, and she wouldn't let her dear husband's corpse bide neglected for folks to stare at for all the crowners in England."

Mr Granthead drove at once back again up the hill to Bathsheba's. The first person he met was poor Liddy, who seemed literally to have dwindled smaller in these few latter hours. "What has been done?" he said.

"I don't know sir," said Liddy with suspended breath. "My mistress has done it all."

"Where is she?"

"Upstairs with him, sir. When he was brought home and taken upstairs she said she wanted no further help from the men. And then she called me, and made me fill the bath, and after that told me I had better go and lie down because I looked so ill. Then she locked herself into the room alone with him, and wouldn't let a nurse come in or anybody at all. But I thought I'd wait in the next room in case she should want me. I heard her moving about inside for more than an hour, but she only came out once, and that was for more candles because hers had burnt down into the socket. She said we were to let her know when you or Mr Thirdly came Sir."

Oak entered with the parson at this moment, and they all went upstairs together, preceded by Liddy Smallbury. Everything was silent as the grave when they paused on the landing. Liddy knocked; and Bathsheba's dress was heard rustling towards the door, the key turned in the lock, and she opened it. Her looks were calm and nearly rigid, like a slightly animated bust of Melpomene.[1]

"Oh – Mr Granthead – you have come at last," she murmured from her lips merely, and threw back the door. "Ah – and Mr Thirdly. Well, all is done, and anybody in the world may see him now." She then passed by them, crossed the landing, and entered another room.

Looking into the chamber of death she had vacated they saw by the light of the candles which were on the drawers a tall straight shape lying at the further end of the bedroom, wrapped in white. Everything around was quite orderly. The doctor went in, and after a few minutes returned to the landing again, where Oak and the parson still waited.

"It is all done indeed, as she says," remarked Mr Granthead. "The body has been undressed and properly laid out in grave clothes. Gracious Heaven – this mere girl! She must have the nerve of a stoic!"

"The solicitude of a wife merely," floated in a whisper about the ears of the three, and turning they saw Bathsheba in the midst of them. Then as if at that instant to prove that her fortitude had been more of will than of spontaneity she silently sank down between them and was a shapeless heap of drapery on the floor. The simple consciousness that superhuman strain was no longer required had at once put a period to her power to continue it.

They took her away into a further room, and the medical attendance which had been useless in Troy's case was invaluable in Bathsheba's, who fell into a series of fainting-fits that had a serious aspect for a time. The sufferer was got to bed, and Oak, finding from the bulletins that nothing really dreadful was to be apprehended on her score, left the house. Liddy kept watch in Bathsheba's chamber, where she heard her mistress moaning through the dull slow hours of that wretched night: "O it is my fault – how can I live! O Heaven, how can I live!"

CHAPTER LIV

The March following: "Bathsheba Boldwood".

We pass rapidly on into the month of March, to a breezy day without sunshine frost or dew. On Yalbury Hill, about midway between Weatherbury and Casterbridge, where the turnpike road passes over the crest, a numerous concourse of people had gathered the eyes of the greater number being frequently stretched afar in a northerly direction. The groups consisted of a throng of idlers, a party of javelin-men, and two trumpeters, and in the midst were carriages, one of which contained the high sheriff.[1] Among the idlers – many of whom had mounted to the top of a cutting formed for the road – were several Weatherbury men and boys – among others Poorgrass, Coggan and Cain Ball.

After waiting half an hour a faint dust was seen in the expected quarter, and shortly after a travelling carriage bringing one of the two judges on that circuit[2] came up the hill and halted on the top. The judge changed carriages whilst a flourish was blown by the big-cheeked trumpeters, and a procession being formed of the carriages and javelin-men they all proceeded towards the town, excepting the Weatherbury men who, as soon as they had seen the judge move off returned home again to their work.

"Joseph, I seed you squeezing close to the carriage," said Coggan, as they walked. "Did ye notice my lord judge's face?"

"I did," said Poorgrass. "I looked hard at him, as if I would read his very soul; and there was mercy in his eyes – or to speak with the exact truth required of us at this solemn time, in the eye that was towards me."

"Well, I hope for the best," said Coggan, "though bad that must be. However, I shan't go to the trial, and I'd advise the rest of ye that baint wanted to bide away. 'Twill disturb his mind more than anything to see us there staring at him as if he were a show."

"The very thing I said this morning," observed Joseph. "'Justice is come to weigh him in the balance,' I said in my reflectious way, 'and if he's found wanting so be it unto him;'[3] and a learned stranger said 'Hear, hear: A man who can talk like that ought to be heard.' But I don't like dwelling upon it, for my few words are my few words, and not much; though the speech of some men is rumoured abroad as though by nature formed for such."

"So 'tis Joseph. And now neighbours, as I said, every man bide at home."

The resolution was adhered to; and all waited anxiously for the news next day. Their suspense was diverted however by a discovery which was made in the afternoon throwing more light on Boldwood's conduct and condition than any details which had preceded it.

That he had been from the time of Greenhill Fair until the fatal Christmas eve in excited and unusual moods was known to those who had been intimate with him; but nobody had imagined that there had been shown unequivocal symptoms of the mental derangement which Bathsheba and Troy[4] alone of all others, and at different times had momentarily suspected. In a locked closet was now discovered an extraordinary collection of articles. There were several sets of lady's dresses in the piece, of sundry expensive materials; silks and satins, poplins and serges, all of colours which from Bathsheba's style of dress might have been judged to be her favourites. There were two muffs, sable and ermine. Above all there was a case of jewellery containing four heavy gold bracelets and several lockets and rings, all of good quality and manufacture. These things had been bought in Bath and other towns from time to time, and brought home by stealth. They were all carefully packed in paper, and each package was labelled "Bathsheba Boldwood", a date being subjoined six years in advance in every instance.

These somewhat pathetic evidences of a mind crazed with care and love were the subject of discourse in Warren's Malthouse when Oak entered from Casterbridge with tidings of the sentence. He came in the afternoon, and his face as the kiln glow shone upon it told the tale sufficiently well. Boldwood, as every one supposed he would do, had pleaded Guilty, and had been sentenced to death.

The conviction that Boldwood had not been morally responsible for his later acts now became general. Facts elicited previous to the trial had pointed strongly in the same direction, but they had not been of sufficient weight to lead to an order for an examination into the state of Boldwood's mind. It was astonishing now that a genuine presumption of insanity was raised how many collateral circumstances were remembered, to which a condition of mental disease afforded the only explanation – among others, the unprecedented neglect of his corn-stacks in the previous summer.

A petition was addressed to the Home Secretary, advancing the circumstances which appeared to justify a request for a reconsideration of the sentence. It was not "numerously signed" by the inhabitants of Casterbridge, as is usual in such cases, for Boldwood had never made many friends over the counter. The shops thought it very natural that a man who, by importing direct from the producer, had daringly set aside the first great principle of existence, namely, that God made country villages to supply customers to country towns, should have confused ideas about the second, the decalogue.[5] The promoters were a few thoughtful men who had carefully considered the facts latterly unearthed, and the result was that evidence was taken which it was hoped might remove the crime, in a moral point of view, out of the category of wilful murder, and lead it to be regarded as a sheer outcome of madness.

The upshot of the petition was waited for in Weatherbury with solicitous interest. The execution had been fixed for eight o'clock on a Saturday morning about a fortnight after the sentence was passed, and up to Friday afternoon no answer had been received. At that time Gabriel came from Casterbridge Gaol, whither he had been to wish Boldwood Good-bye, and turned up a by-street to avoid the town. When past the last house he heard a hammering, and lifting his bowed head he looked back for a moment. Over the chimneys he could see the upper part of the gaol entrance, rich and glowing in the afternoon sun, and some moving figures were there. They were carpenters lifting a post into a vertical position within the parapet. He withdrew his eyes quickly and hastened on.

It was dark when he reached home, and half the village was out to meet him.

"No tidings," Gabriel said wearily. "And I'm afraid there's no hope. I've been with him more than two hours, and his mind seems quite a wreck. However, that we can talk of another time. Has there been any change in mistress this afternoon?"[6]

"None at all."

"Is she downstairs?"

"No. And getting on so nicely as she was too. She's but very little better now again than she was a-Christmas. She keeps on asking if you be come, and if there's news, till one's wearied out wi' answering her. Shall I go and say you've come?"

"No," said Oak. "There's a chance yet; but I couldn't stay in town any longer – after seeing him too. So Laban – Laban is here, isn't he?"

"Yes," said Tall.

"What I've arranged is that you shall ride to town the last thing to-night: leave here about nine, and wait a while there, getting home about twelve. If nothing has been received by eleven to-night they say there's no chance at all."

"I do so hope his life will be spared," said Liddy. "If it is not, she'll go out of her mind too. Poor thing: her sufferings have been dreadful; she deserves anybody's pity."

"Is she altered much?" said Coggan.

"If you haven't seen poor mistress since Christmas you wouldn't know her," said Liddy. "Her eyes are so miserable that she's not the same woman. Only two years ago she was a romping girl, and now she's this."

Laban departed as directed, and at eleven o'clock that night several of the villagers strolled along the road to Casterbridge and awaited his arrival – among them Oak, and nearly all the rest of Bathsheba's men. Gabriel's anxiety was so great that he paced up and down, pausing at every turn and straining his ears for a sound.[7] At last, when they all were weary, the tramp of a horse was heard in the distance:

First dead, as if on turf it trode,
Then clattering on the village road
In other pace than forth he yode.[8]

"We shall soon know now, one way or t'other," said Coggan, and they all stepped down from the bank on which they had been standing into the road, and the rider pranced into the midst of them.

"Is that you Laban?" said Gabriel.

"Yes – 'tis come. He's not to die. 'Tis confinement during her Majesty's pleasure."

"Hurrah!" said Coggan, with a swelling heart. "God's above the devil yet."

CHAPTER LV
Beauty in loneliness: After all.

Bathsheba revived with the spring. The utter prostration which had followed the low fever from which she had suffered diminished perceptibly when all uncertainty upon every subject had come to an end.

But she remained alone now for the greater part of her time, and stayed in the house, or at furthest went into the garden. She shunned every one, even Liddy, and could be brought to make no confidences, and to ask for no sympathy.

As the summer drew on she passed more of her time in the open air, and began to examine into farming matters from sheer necessity, though she never rode out or personally superintended as at former times. One Friday evening in August she walked a little way along the road and entered the orchard for the first time since the sombre event of the preceding Christmas. None of the old colour had as yet come back to her cheek, and its absolute paleness was heightened by the jet black of her dress till it appeared preternatural. When she reached the gate at the other end of the orchard, which opened nearly opposite to the churchyard, Bathsheba heard singing inside the church, and she knew that the singers were practising. She opened the gate, crossed the road and entered the graveyard, the high sills of the church windows effectually screening her from the eyes of those gathered within. Her stealthy walk was to the nook wherein Troy had worked at planting flowers upon Fanny Robbin's grave, and she came to the marble tombstone.

A motion of satisfaction enlivened her face as she read the complete inscription. First came the words of Troy himself: –

Erected by Francis Troy
In memory of
Fanny Robbin
Who died October 9th 18—
Aged 20 years.[1]

Underneath this was now inscribed in new letters; –

In the same grave lie
The remains of the aforesaid
Francis Troy
Who died December 24th 18—
Aged 26 years.

Whilst she stood and read and meditated the tones of the organ began again in the church and she went with the same light step round to the porch and listened. The door was closed, and the choir was learning a new hymn. Bathsheba was stirred by emotions which latterly she had assumed to be altogether dead within her. The little attenuated voices of the children brought to her ear in distinct utterance the words they sang without thought or comprehension –

Lead kindly Light, amid the encircling gloom
Lead Thou me on.[2]

Bathsheba's feeling was always to some extent dependent upon her will, as is the case with many other women. Something big came into her throat and an uprising to her eyes – and she thought that she would allow the imminent tears to come if they wished. They did come and plenteously, and one fell upon the stone bench beside her. Once that she had begun to cry for she hardly knew what she could not leave off for crowding thoughts she knew too well. She would have given anything in the world to be as those children were, unconcerned at the meaning of their words because too innocent to feel the necessity for any such expression. All the impassioned scenes of her brief experience seemed to revive with added emotion at that moment, and those scenes which had been without emotion during enactment had emotion then. Yet grief came to her rather as a luxury than as the scourge of former times.

Owing to Bathsheba's face being buried in her hands she did not notice a form which came quietly into the porch, and on seeing her moved as if to retreat, then paused and regarded her. Bathsheba did not raise her head for some time, and when she looked round her face was wet, and her eyes drowned and dim. "Mr Oak," exclaimed she, disconcerted. "How long have you been here?"

"A few minutes ma'am," said Oak respectfully.

"Are you going in?" said Bathsheba.

(I loved the garish day; and spite of fears
Pride ruled my will: remember not past years)

came from inside as from a prompter.

"I was," said Gabriel. "I am one of the bass singers, you know. I have sung bass for several months."

"Indeed: I wasn't aware of that. I'll leave you then."

(Which I have loved long since, and lost awhile)

"Don't let me drive you away, mistress. I think I won't go in to-night."

"O no – you don't drive me away."

Then they stood in a state of some embarrassment, Bathsheba trying to wipe her dreadfully drenched and inflamed face without his noticing her. At length Oak said, "I've not seen you – I mean spoken to you – since ever so long, have I." But he feared to bring distressing memories back, and interrupted himself with: "Were you going into church?"

"No," she said. "I came to see the tombstone privately – to see if they had cut the inscription as I wished. Mr Oak, you needn't mind speaking to me, if you wish to, on the matter which is in both our minds at this moment."

"And have they done it as you wished?" said Oak.

"Yes. Come and see it, if you have not already."

So together they went and read the tomb. "Eight months ago!" Gabriel murmured when he saw the date. "It seems like yesterday to me."

"And to me as if it were years ago – long years, and I had been dead between. And now I am going home, Mr Oak."

Oak walked after her. "I wanted to name a small matter to you, as soon as I could," he said with hesitation. "Merely about business, and I think I may just mention it now if you'll allow me."

"O yes, certainly."

"It is that I may soon have to give up the management of your farm, Mrs Troy. The fact is, I am thinking of leaving England – not yet you know: next spring."

"Leaving England!" she said in surprise, and genuine disappointment. "Why Gabriel, what are you going to do that for?"

"Well, I've thought it best," Oak stammered out. "California[3] is the spot I've had in my mind to try."

"But it is understood everywhere that you are going to take the Lower Farm on your own account."

"I've had the refusal of it, 'tis true; but nothing is settled yet, and I have reasons for declining. I shall finish out my year there as manager for the trustees, but no more."

"And what shall I do without you? O Gabriel, I don't think you ought to go away! You've been with me so long – through bright times and dark times – such old friends as we are – that it seems unkind almost. I had fancied that if you leased the other farm as master you might still give a helping look across at mine. And now going away!"

"I would have willingly."

"Yet now that I am more helpless than ever you go away."

"Yes, that's the ill fortune of it," said Gabriel, in a distressed tone. "And it is because of that very helplessness that I feel obliged to go. – Good afternoon, ma'am." He concluded in evident anxiety to get away, and at once went out of the churchyard by a path she could follow on no pretence whatever.

Bathsheba went home, her mind occupied with a new trouble, which being rather harassing than deadly was calculated to do good by diverting her from the chronic gloom of her life. She was set thinking a great deal about Oak, and of his wish to shun her; and there occurred to Bathsheba several incidents of her latter intercourse with him, which, trivial when singly viewed, amounted together to a perceptible disinclination for her society. It broke upon her at length as a great pain that her last old disciple was about to forsake her and flee.[4] He who had believed in her and argued on her side when all the rest of the world was against her had at last like the others become weary, and neglectful of the old cause, and was leaving her to fight her battles alone.

The weeks went on, and more evidence of his want of interest in her was forthcoming. She noticed that instead of entering the small parlour or office where the farm accounts were kept, and waiting, or leaving a memorandum as he had hitherto done during her seclusion, Oak never came at all when she was likely to be there, only entering at unseasonable hours when her presence in that part of the house was least to be expected. Whenever he wanted directions he sent a message, or note with neither heading nor signature, to which she was obliged to reply in the same off hand style. Poor Bathsheba began to suffer now from the most torturing sting of all – a sensation that she was despised.

The autumn wore away gloomily enough amid these melancholy conjectures, and Christmas day came, completing a year of her legal widowhood, and two years and a quarter of her life alone. On examining her heart it appeared beyond measure strange that the subject of which the season might have been supposed suggestive – the event in the hall at Boldwood's – was not agitating her at all, but instead, an agonizing conviction that everybody abjured her – for what she could not tell – and that Oak was the ringleader of the recusants. Coming out of church that day she looked round in the hope that Oak, whose bass voice she had heard rolling out from the gallery overhead in a most unconcerned manner, might chance to linger in her path in the old way. There he was as usual, coming up the path behind her, but on seeing Bathsheba turn he looked aside, and as soon as he got beyond the gate, and there was the barest excuse for a divergence, he made one, and vanished.

The next morning brought the culminating stroke – she had been expecting it long. It was a formal notice by letter from him that he should not renew his engagement with her for the following Lady Day.

Bathsheba actually sat and cried over this letter most bitterly. She was aggrieved and wounded that the possession of hopeless love from Gabriel, which she had grown to regard as her inalienable right for life, should have been withdrawn just at his own pleasure in this way. She was bewildered too by the prospect of having to rely on her own resources again: it seemed to herself that she never could again acquire energy sufficient to go to market, barter, and sell. Since Troy's death Oak had attended all sales and fairs for her, transacting her business at the same time with his own. What should she do now! Her life was becoming a desolation.

So desolate was Bathsheba this evening, that in an absolute hunger for pity and sympathy, and miserable in that she appeared to have outlived the only true friendship she had ever owned she put on her bonnet and cloak and went down to Oak's house just after sunset, guided on her way by the pale primrose rays of a crescent moon a few days old.

A dancing firelight shone from the window, but nobody was visible in the room. She tapped nervously, and then thought it doubtful if it were right for a single woman to call upon a bachelor who lived alone, although he was her manager and she might be supposed to call on business without any real impropriety. Gabriel opened the door, and the moon shone upon his forehead.

"Mr Oak," said Bathsheba faintly.

"Yes, I am Mr Oak," said Gabriel. "Who have I the honour – O how stupid of me – not to know you, mistress!"

"I shall not be your mistress much longer, shall I Gabriel?" she said in pathetic tones.

"Well, no – I suppose – But come in ma'am. Oh – and I'll get a light," Oak replied, with some awkwardness.

"No – not on my account."

"It is so seldom that I get a lady visitor that I'm afraid I haven't proper accommodation. Will you sit down please. Here's a chair, and there's one, too. I am sorry that my chairs all have wood seats, and are rather hard, but I was thinking of getting some new ones." Oak placed two or three for her.

"They are quite easy enough for me."

So down she sat, and down sat he, the fire dancing in their faces, and upon

> The few worn-out traps, all a-sheenen
> With long years of handlen[5]

that formed Oak's array of household possessions, which sent back a dancing reflection in reply. It was very odd to these two persons who knew each other passing well that the mere circumstance of their meeting in a new place and in a new way should make them so awkward and constrained. In the fields, or at her house, there had never been any embarrassment: but now that Oak had become the entertainer their lives seemed to be moved back again to the days when they were strangers.

"You'll think it strange that I have come, but –"

"O no – not at all."

"– But I thought – Gabriel, I have been uneasy in the belief that I have offended you, and that you are going away on that account. It grieved me very much, and I couldn't help coming."

"Offended me! As if you could do that Bathsheba."

"Haven't I?" she asked gladly. "But what are you going away for else?"

"I am not going to emigrate, you know: I wasn't aware that you would wish me not to when I told you, or I shouldn't have thought of doing it," he said simply. "I have arranged for the Lower Farm, and shall have it in my own hands at Lady Day. You know I've had a share in it for some time. Still, that wouldn't prevent my attending to your business as before, hadn't it been that things have been said about us."

"What?" said Bathsheba in surprise. "Things said about you and me – what are they?"

"I cannot tell you."

"It would be wiser if you were to, I think. You have played the part of mentor to me many times, and I don't see why you should fear to do it now."

"It is nothing that you have done this time. It amounts to this, that I am sniffing about here, and waiting for poor Boldwood's farm, with the idea of getting you some day."

"Getting me – what does that mean?"

"Marrying you, in plain British. – You asked me to tell, so you mustn't blame me."

Bathsheba did not look quite so alarmed as if a cannon had been discharged by her ear, which was what Oak had expected. "Marrying me – I didn't know it was that you meant," she said quietly. "Such a thing as that is too absur – too soon – to think of by far."

"Yes, of course it is too absurd. I don't desire any such thing – I should think that was visible enough by this time. You are, necessarily, the last person in the world I think of marrying. It is too absurd, as you say."

"Too s-s-soon were the words I used."

"I must beg your pardon for correcting you, but you said, too absurd, and so do I."

"I beg your pardon too!" she returned with tears in her eyes. "Too soon was all I said. But it doesn't matter a bit – not at all – but I only said too soon. Indeed I didn't, Mr Oak, and you must believe me!"

Gabriel looked her long in the face, but the fire light being faint there was not much to be seen. "Bathsheba," he said tenderly and in surprise, and coming closer: "If I only knew one thing – whether you would allow me to love you and win you and marry you after all – if I only knew that!"

"But you never will know," she murmured.

"Why?"

"Because you never ask!"

"O – O!" said Gabriel, with a low laugh of joyousness. "My own dear –"

"You ought not to have sent me that harsh letter this morning!" she interrupted. "It shows you didn't care a bit about me, and were ready to desert me like all the rest of them. It was very cruel of you considering I was the first sweetheart that you ever had, and you were the first I ever had, and I shall not forget it!"

"Now Bathsheba, was ever anybody so provoking," he said laughing. "You know it was purely that I as an unmarried man carrying on a business for you as a marriageable young woman had a very difficult part to play – more particularly that people knew I had a sort of feeling for you; and I fancied from the way we were mentioned together that it might injure your good name. Nobody knows the uneasiness I have been caused by it."

"And was that all?"

"All."

"O how glad I am I came!" she exclaimed thankfully as she rose from her seat. "I have thought so much more of you since I fancied you did not want ever to see me again. But I must be going now, or I shall be missed. Why Gabriel," she said with a slight laugh as they went to the door; "it seems exactly as if I had come courting you – how dreadful."

"And quite right too," said Oak. "I've danced attendance on you, my beautiful Bathsheba, for many a long mile, and many a long day, and it is hard to begrudge me this one visit."

He accompanied her up the hill, explaining to her the details of his forthcoming tenure of the Lower Farm. They spoke very little of their mutual feelings: pretty phrases and warm attentions being probably unnecessary between such tried friends. Theirs was that substantial affection which arises (if any arises at all) when the two who are thrown together begin first by knowing the rougher sides of each other's character, and not the best till further on, the romance growing up in the interstices of a mass of hard prosaic reality. This good-fellowship – *camaraderie*, usually occurring through similarity of pursuits, is unfortunately seldom superadded to love between the sexes, because they associate not in their labours but in their pleasures merely. Where however happy circumstance permits its development the compounded feeling proves itself to be the only love which is strong as death – that love which many waters cannot quench, nor the floods drown,[6] beside which the passion usually called by the name is evanescent as steam.

CHAPTER LVI

A foggy night and morning: Conclusion.

"The most private, secret, plainest wedding that it's possible to have".

Those had been Bathsheba's words to Oak one evening some time after the event of the preceding chapter, and he meditated a full hour by the clock upon how to carry out her wishes to the letter.

"A licence – O yes, it must be a licence," he said to himself at last. "Very well then: first, a licence."

On a dark night several days later Oak came with mysterious steps from the surrogate's door in Casterbridge. On the way home he heard a heavy tread in front of him, and overtaking the man found him to be Coggan. They walked together into the village till they came to a little lane behind the church, leading down to the cottage of Laban Tall, who had lately been installed as clerk of the parish and was yet in mortal terror when he heard his lone voice among certain hard words of the Psalms whither no man ventured to follow him.

"Well, good-night Coggan," said Oak, "I'm going down this way."

"Oh!" said Coggan, surprised. "What's going on to-night then, make so bold, Mr Oak."

It seemed rather ungenerous not to tell Coggan under the circumstances, for Coggan had been true as steel all through the time of Gabriel's unhappiness about Bathsheba, and Gabriel said, "You can keep a secret, Coggan?"

"You've proved me, and you know."

"Yes, I have; and I do know. Well then, mistress and I mean to get married to-morrow morning."

"Heaven's high tower. – And yet I've thought of such a thing from time to time: true, I have. But keeping it so close! Well, there, 'tis no business of mine, and I wish ye joy o' her."

"Thank you Coggan. But I assure you that this secrecy is not what I wished for at all – or what either of us would have wished if it hadn't been for certain things that would make a gay wedding seem hardly the thing. Bathsheba has a great wish that all the parish shall not be in Church looking at her – she's ridiculously nervous about it in fact – so I'm doing this to humour her."

"Ay I see – quite right, too, I suppose I must say. And you be now going down to the clerk."

"Yes. You may as well come with me."

"I am afeard your labour in keeping it close will be all thrown away," said Coggan as they walked along. "Labe Tall's old woman will spread it all over parish in half an hour."

"So she will, upon my life: I never thought of that," said Oak pausing. "Yet I must tell him to-night I suppose, for he's working so far off, and leaves early.

"I'll tell ye how we could manage," said Coggan. "I'll knock and ask to speak to Laban outside the door – you standing in the background. Then he'll come out, and you can tell yer tale. She'll never guess what I want him for; and I'll make up a few words about the farm work as a blind."

This scheme was considered feasible; and Coggan advanced boldly and rapped at Mrs Tall's door. Mrs Tall herself opened it.

"I wanted to have a word with Laban."

"He's not at home, and won't be this side of eleven o'clock. He've been forced to go to Yalbury since leaving work. I shall do quite as well."

"I hardly think you will. Stop a moment." And Coggan stepped round the corner of the porch to consult Oak.

"Who's t'other man then?" said Mrs Tall.

"Only a friend," said Coggan.

"Say he's wanted to meet mistress near church hatch to-morrow morning at ten," said Oak in a whisper. "That he must come without fail, and wear his best clothes."

"The clothes will floor us as safe as houses!" said Coggan.

"It can't be helped," said Oak. "Tell her."

So Coggan delivered the message. "Mind wet or dry, blow or snow, he must come," added Jan. "'Tis very particular indeed. The fact is 'tis to witness her sign an agreement about taking shares wi' another farmer for a long term o' years. There that's what 'tis, and now I've told ye mother Tall, in a way I shouldn't ha' done if I hadn't loved ye so hopeless well."

Coggan retired before she could ask any further, and then they called at the vicar's in a way which excited no curiosity at all. Then Gabriel went home and prepared for the morrow.

"Liddy," said Bathsheba on going to bed that night. "I want you to call me at seven o'clock to-morrow in case I shouldn't wake."

"But you always do wake afore then, ma'am."

"Yes, but I have something important to do, which I'll tell you of when the time comes, and it's best to make sure."

Bathsheba however awoke voluntarily at four, nor could she by any contrivance get to sleep again. About six, being quite positive that her watch had stopped during the night she could wait no longer: she went and tapped at Liddy's door and after some labour awoke her.

"But I thought it was I who had to call you?" said the bewildered Liddy. "And it isn't six yet."

"Indeed it is – how can you tell such a story Liddy. I know it must be ever so much past seven. Come to my room as soon as you can: I want you to give my hair a good brushing."

When Liddy came to Bathsheba's room her mistress was already waiting. Liddy could not understand this extraordinary promptness. "Whatever *is* going on ma'am?" she said.

"Well, I'll tell you," said Bathsheba, with a mischievous smile in her bright eyes. "Farmer Oak is coming here to dine with me to-day."

"Farmer Oak – and nobody else? – you two alone?"

"Yes."

"But is it safe ma'am?" said her companion dubiously. "A woman's good name is such a perishable article that – "

Bathsheba laughed with a flushed cheek, and whispered in Liddy's ear, although there was nobody present. Then Liddy stared and exclaimed, "Souls alive, what news! It makes my heart go quite bumpity-bump!"

"It makes mine rather furious too," said Bathsheba. "However, there's no getting out of it now."

It was a damp disagreeable morning when, at twenty minutes to ten o'clock, Oak came out of his house and

Went up the hill side
With that sort of stride
A man puts out when walking in search of a bride,[1]

and knocked at Bathsheba's door. Ten minutes later two large umbrellas might have been seen moving from the same door and through the mist along the road to the church. The distance was not more than a hundred yards,[2] and these two sensible persons deemed it unnecessary to drive. An observer must have been very close indeed to discover that the forms under the umbrellas were those of Oak and Bathsheba, arm in arm for the first time in their lives – Oak in a great coat extending to his knees, and Bathsheba in a cloak that reached her clogs. Yet though so plainly dressed there was a certain rejuvenated appearance about her: –

As though a rose should shut and be a bud again.[3]

Repose had again incarnadined her cheeks; and having by Gabriel's request arranged her hair this morning as she had worn it years ago on Norcombe Hill she seemed in his eyes remarkably like the girl of that first fascinating dream, which considering that she was now only three or four and twenty was perhaps not very wonderful. In the church were Tall,

Liddy and the parson, and in a remarkably short space of time the deed was done.

The two sat down very quietly to tea in Bathsheba's parlour in the evening of the same day, for it had been arranged that Farmer Oak should go there to live, since he had as yet neither money, house, nor furniture worthy of the name, though he was on a sure way towards them, whilst Bathsheba was, comparatively, in a plethora of all three. Just as Bathsheba was pouring out a cup of tea their ears were greeted by the firing of a cannon followed by what seemed like a tremendous blowing of trumpets in the front of the house.

"There!" said Oak laughing, "I knew those fellows were up to something by the look of their faces."

Oak took up the light and went into the porch, followed by Bathsheba with a shawl over her head. The rays fell upon a group of male figures gathered upon the gravel in front, who, when they saw the newly married couple in the porch, set up a loud Hurrah, and at the same moment bang again went the cannon in the background, followed by a hideous clang of music from a drum, tambourine, clarionet, serpent, hautboy, tenor-viol, and double-bass – the only remaining relics of the true and original Weatherbury band – venerable worm-eaten instruments which had celebrated in their own persons the victories of Marlborough,[4] under the fingers of the forefathers of those who played them now. The performers came forward and marched up to the front.

"Those bright boys Mark Clark and Jan are at the bottom of all this," said Oak. "Come in souls, and have something to eat and drink with me and my wife."

"Not to-night," said Mr Clark, with evident self-denial. "Thank ye all the same, but we'll call at a more convenient time. However, we couldn't think of letting the day pass without a note of admiration of some sort. If ye could send a drop of anything down to Warren's, why so it is. Here's long life and happiness to Neighbour Oak and his comely bride!"

"Thank you – thank you all," said Gabriel. "A bit and a drop shall be sent to Warren's for ye at once. I had a thought that we might very likely get a salute of some sort from our old friends, and I was saying so to my wife but now."

"Faith," said Coggan in a critical tone and turning to his companions, "The man has learnt to say 'my wife' in a wonderful naterel way, considering how very youthful he is in wedlock as yet – hey, neighbours all?"

"I never heerd a skilful old married feller of twenty years standing pipe 'my wife' in a more used note than 'a did," said Jacob Smallbury. "It might have been a little more naterel if 't had been a little chillier, but that couldn't be expected yet."

"That improvement will come with time," said Jan.

Then Oak laughed, and Bathsheba smiled, for she never laughed readily now; and their friends turned to go.

"Yes, I suppose that's the size o't," said Joseph Poorgrass with a cheerful sigh; "and I wish him joy o' her; though I were once or twice upon saying to-day with holy Hosea in my scripture manner which is my second nature, 'Ephraim is joined to idols: let him alone.'[5] But since 'tis as 'tis, why it might have been worse, and I feel my thanks accordingly."

THE END

NOTES

All textual points raised in the Notes are more fully discussed in:

Rosemarie Morgan, *Cancelled Words: Rediscovering Thomas Hardy* (London and New York: Routledge, 1992).

The following sources have been helpful in tracing some of the more obscure identifications:

Brewer, Cobham E., *The Dictionary of Phrase and Fable*, Classic edition (New York: Avenue Books, 1978).
The King James (Authorized) version of the Holy Bible (Tennessee: The Gideons International, 1965).
Saxelby, Outwin F., *A Thomas Hardy Dictionary* (London: Routledge & Sons, 1911).
Schweik, Robert C. (ed.) *Far from the Madding Crowd* (New York: W. W. Norton & Co., Inc., 1986).

Editions of *Far From the Madding Crowd*, excepting the Smith, Elder 1874 edition which adopts the *Cornhill* text virtually unamended, are identified as follows:

ms	Holograph manuscript used for the *Cornhill* serial
C	*Cornhill* magazine, 1874
1875	Smith, Elder 1875 edition
Harper 1901	Sixpenny edition
1895	Osgood, McIlvaine 1895 edition (in Hardy's first Collected Works)
1912	Macmillan 1912, Wessex Edition

CHAPTER I

1. *Gabriel*: this name has many associations. In Christian mythology it is Gabriel who announces to Zacharias the future birth of John the Baptist, and to Mary, at the Annunciation, her conception of Jesus (Luke 1). The trumpeter of the Last Judgment, Gabriel also means 'power of God', and in *Paradise Lost* Milton makes him chief of the angelic guards placed over Paradise. Although critical focus has stressed the 'angelic', Hardy's allusions to Milton in this novel are

frequently subversive or ironic: Gabriel Oak's self-appointed role as Bathsheba's moral judge is, for example, severely compromised by his espial role in which Hardy aligns him with Milton's Satan. In Jewish mythology, Gabriel is the angel of death and prince of fire and thunder; in the Old Testament he is said to have explained visions to Daniel (Daniel 8–9); in Islam he reveals the Koran to Muhammad.

2. *Laodicean*: a person who is lukewarm, especially in religion or politics. St John the Divine rebuked the people of Laodicea for being 'neither hot nor cold', and therefore 'I will spue thee out of my mouth' (Revelation 3:16).

3. *Sacrament*: refers to the sacramental rites of the Church. Hardy uses the word here as a synecdoche referring to regular (as opposed to irregular) churchgoers. *1912* has 'Communion people'.

4. *Nicene*: of Nicaea in Bithynia. The Nicene Creed is a formal statement of Christian belief based on that adopted at the first Nicene Council in A.D. 325.

5. *Doctor Johnson's*: in Boswell's *Journal of a Tour to the Hebrides* (1785), Dr Johnson wears 'a very wide brown cloth great coat with pockets which might have almost held the two volumes of his folio dictionary'. And in his *Life of Samuel Johnson* (1791), Boswell describes Johnson's morning dress as 'uncouth', and his 'brown suit of cloaths looked very rusty' (entry for 24 May 1763).

6. *vestal*: in Greek mythology, a maiden dedicated to celibacy and to serving the goddess Vesta – custodian of the sacred fire brought by Aeneas from Troy – who kept the temple fire constantly burning, both day and night. Hardy's reference to 'curtailing their dimensions' may refer to the *Vade in pacem* (Go into peace) practice of 'immuring': Vestal virgins (and Roman Catholic nuns who broke their vows of chastity) were 'immured' by burial in a niche only large enough to contain their body and a small pittance of bread and water.

7. *C*: 'Through a spur of this hill ran the highway'. *1912* omits 'sunk in a deep cutting' and has: '. . . highway between Emminster and Chalk-Newton'. These are Hardy's fictional names for Beaminster and Maiden Newton, and, as late revisions, impose a topographical unity upon the Wessex landscape. *Norcombe Hill* corresponds to a hill near Eggardon, between Dorchester and Bridport.

8. *wages*: farm labourers earned, during the 1870s and 1880s, approximately 7–8 shillings for a six-day working week. Bathsheba pays more, approximately 9–10 shillings; harvesters in summer, and shepherds at lambing time, earned extra in season.

9. *Saint John . . . Judas Iscariot*: aesthetic convention and Christian ideology dictate that beauty is equated with goodness and ugliness with evil: the portrayal of St John as a devoted disciple of Jesus is, therefore, 'beautiful', and that of Judas Iscariot, as the betrayer of Jesus, 'ugly'.

CHAPTER II

1. *St Thomas*: patron saint of masons and architects. St Thomas's day is 21 December, when the poor go 'Thomasing' for gifts of food, etc., from the farmers.

2. *1912*: '. . . had remained till this very mid-winter time on the twigs which bore them'.

3. *north star . . . fiery red*: also known as the Pole Star, in Little Bear (Ursa Minor), a creamy supergiant which marks the north celestial pole; *Bear* (Ursa Major), also known as the Big Dipper (USA), or the Plough; *Sirius*, also known as the Dog Star, in Canis Major, is the biggest and brightest star in the heavens; *Capella*, a yellow star in Auriga, is the seventh brightest star in the heavens (fifth brightest visible from England); *Aldebaran* is the brightest in Taurus, and *Betelgueux* is a red supergiant, the brightest in Orion.

4. *Ark*: cf. Genesis 8:4: 'And the Ark rested . . . upon the mountains of Ararat.' Hardy's allusion is lightly parodic. Oak's 'Ark' rests not upon a mountain range but 'on two small wheels which raised its floor about a foot from the ground'.

5. *bailiff*: originally an officer under a sheriff executing writs, distraints and arrests; more recently an overseer or farm manager occupied in rent collection.

6. *mercurial*: quick, lighthearted, sprightly. Astrological notion: ingenious – like those born under the white-hot planet, Mercury (nearest the sun); chemical notion: volatile – like the white, liquid metal otherwise known as quicksilver; mythological notion: deft – like Mercury, Roman god of eloquence, skill, thieving, and winged messenger of the gods.

7. *Dog-star*: a common name for Sirius. *Pleiades*: otherwise known as the Seven Sisters or 'sailing stars' – the Greeks considered navigation safe when the Pleiades were visible. In Greek mythology, the Pleiades were the seven daughters of Pleione and Atlas; after their deaths they were transformed into a cluster of twinkling stars, hence 'restless'.

8. *Orion*: also known as the Hunter, in a constellation near Gemini and Taurus, Orion is an equatorial constellation which includes Betelgeuse and Rigel (previously alluded to by Hardy), which dominates the winter sky. Orion, in Greek mythology, was renowned for his 'gorgeous' beauty; he was blinded by Enopion but had his sight restored by exposing his eyes to the sun. Slain by Diana, Orion became a star whose brightness (burning 'vividly') in the night sky is supposed to indicate stormy weather. The only weather indication Hardy gives here is that the wind is forceful enough to blow Bathsheba's hat off.

9. *Castor and Pollux . . . Cassiopeia's Chair*: the two brightest stars in Gemini; also associated with stormy weather. *Pegasus*: the winged horse on which Bellerophon rode against the Chimera, forms a constellation with few stars

visible within it, hence 'barren and gloomy'. *Vega*: 'sparkles' a brilliant blue-white in Lyra; *Cassiopeia*: in Greek mythology she boasted that the beauty of her daughter, Andromeda, surpassed that of the sea-nymphs and was banished to the stars for punishment; the northern circumpolar constellation of Cassiopeia forms, from its five brightest stars, the 'daintily poised' 'Cassiopeia's Chair'.

10. *Satan first saw Paradise*: in book 4, lines 179–96, of Milton's *Paradise Lost*, Satan perches in the Tree of Life 'like a Cormorant' to look down on Paradise below. *1912* has 'Milton's Satan'.

11. *Lucina*: Roman goddess of childbirth.

12. *side saddle*: a saddle enabling women to sit with both legs on the same side of the horse. It was deemed unladylike for women to ride astride like men.

CHAPTER III

1. *1912*: 'Soon soft spirts alternating with loud spirts came . . . shed, the obvious sounds of a person milking a cow.'

2. *eight heads*: in true classical form human body proportions are measured, aesthetically, in 'heads' – an ideal height being eight times the length of the head.

3. *Nymphean*: a nymph is one of a class of (Greek) mythological semi-divine beautiful maidens inhabiting sea, rivers, fountains, woods. *Without throwing*: purporting not to draw comparisons between the divinely beautiful nymph and her ordinary human counterpart but, inferentially, doing precisely that.

4. *Maiden's Blush . . . Provence . . . Crimson Tuscany*: names of roses ranging in hue from pink to deepest red.

5. *Samson*: in Judges 16–20 Samson awakens from sleeping in Delilah's lap and says, 'I will go out as at other times before, and shake myself.' He then discovers his hair has been shorn and his strength gone. In true subversive fashion Hardy not only reverses the Samson legend but also the role of the shearer: it is Oak who ultimately strips the beloved of 'strength' by persistently cutting down her self-assurance, self-esteem, emotional energy and power.

CHAPTER IV

1. *C*: 'The only superiority in women that is tolerable to the rival sex . . .' *1912* has 'possibilities of capture' instead of 'possibilities of impropriation'.

2. *Full of sound and fury / Signifying nothing*: quoted from Shakespeare's *Macbeth*, V, v, 24–8, in which, following the death of his wife, the anguished Macbeth

bemoans his life as a 'tale/ Told by an idiot, full of sound and fury,/ Signifying nothing.' Hardy's touch is mock-heroic here (see also Introduction).

3. *Bathsheba*: in II Samuel 11–12, King David espies, while walking out on his roof, a beautiful woman innocently bathing. It is Bathsheba; she is summoned to him and subsequently conceives his child. Determined to have her as his wife, David orders her husband, Uriah, into the thick of battle to die. But, for his unlawful appropriation of Bathsheba and the killing of her husband, David is punished by God: his newborn son sickens; anguished prayers and fasting avail nothing; the infant dies seven days later. Bathsheba later bears another son who becomes the great and wise King Solomon.

The analogue is loose in Hardy: there is Bathsheba's powerful beauty and the attempts by three desirous men to subdue her into submission, and the espial motif by which Oak invades her privacy and renders her body a public object.

4. *tracasseries*: petty quarrels, annoyances, fusses. *1912* has 'scandal and rumour to be no less the staple topic . . .'

5. *commination-service*: an Ash Wednesday morning service including a recital of divine curses against sinners intended to rouse them to 'walk more warily in these dangerous days'. *1912* omits 'liturgical'.

6. *peony*: a plant with large, luscious, globular red, pink or white flowers. In *Tess* Hardy reinvokes the peony but in this instance to emphasize the soft fullness of Tess's expressive mouth.

7. *Ecclesiastes*: 'Then I looked on all the works that my hands had wrought, and on the labour that I had laboured to do: and, behold, all was vanity and vexation of spirit, and there was no profit under the sun' (Ecclesiastes 2: 11). Ecclesiastes is something of a book of doom; the allusion humorously melodramatizes Oak's disappointment.

CHAPTER V

1. *Turner's*: Joseph Mallord William Turner (1775–1851), foremost English romantic painter – a favourite of Hardy's – famous for his large iridescent landscapes and abstract portrayal of light, space and elemental forces of nature. *Indigo*: a deep blue but unstable pigment that tends to fade when used in paintings.

2. *ovey*: short for ovine (of or like sheep), from Latin *ovis*. Hardy added this note to later editions: 'It is somewhat singular – possibly a survival from the Roman occupation of Britain – that shepherds of this region should call to their sheep in Latin.'

3. *Hylas on the Mysian shore*: in Greek mythology, Hylas, a beautiful boy beloved by Hercules, was carried off by nymphs while drawing water from a fountain in Mysia. Hercules and his sailors called for him in vain. Hardy's allusion is mock-heroic.

4. *Napoleon at St Helena*: Napoleon, in enforced exile on the Atlantic island of St Helena (1815), was depicted in numerous cartoons and pictures as an immobilized, brooding figure silhouetted against the sky.
5. *morning star*: a planet, usually Venus, visible in the eastern sky before sunrise.

CHAPTER VI

1. Chapter VI begins the February instalment.
2. *yearly statute or hiring fair*: a day set by statute, attended by workers seeking employment. Hiring fairs were often held on Candlemas (2 February) with employment to begin on Lady Day (25 March).
3. *C*: 'but there was left to him a dignified calm ...' *1912* cuts the section beginning 'He had lost' and ending 'from which he had started', and substitutes: 'He had sunk from his modest elevation as pastoral king into the very slime-pits of Siddim; but there was left to him ...' In Genesis 14:3–10, the vale of Siddim, on the shores of the Dead Sea, is described as 'full of slime pits'.
4. *C*: 'then ... war' omitted. Although Hardy describes this novel as contemporary in setting he (or Stephen) may have cut the 'war' in proof revision to avoid too close an historical specificity. The British, in the early 1870s, had been uneasy about the outcome of the Franco-Prussian war, and the fragility of the League of the Three Emperors (Germany, Austria-Hungary and Russia).
5. *"Jocky to the Fair"*: a 'Jocky' (boy) is a little 'Jack' (common man). In this eighteenth-century song, two youngsters, Jocky and Jenny, run away together to a fair. This and other songs mentioned in *Far From the Madding Crowd* are contained in manuscript music books once belonging to the Hardy family, now held in the Dorset County Museum.
6. *Arcadian*: Arcadia, a legendary region of Greece, idyllically pastoral, where the god Pan entranced his listeners with beautiful melodies played on his pan-pipe (a flute with seven reeds).
7. *C*: 'and in half an hour had earned in pence what was a small fortune to a destitute man.' *Coppers*: pennies; twelve to one shilling; Oak's flute-playing earns him more than a full day's wage.
8. *C* does not follow the ms from 'field of enquiry' to 'village in question', but substitutes: 'enquiry, because it lay in the Weatherbury quarter. Moreover, the Weatherbury folk were by no means uninteresting intrinsically. If report spoke truly they were as hardy, merry, thriving, wicked a set as any in the whole county. Oak resolved to sleep at Weatherbury that night on his way to Shottsford, and struck out at once into the high road which had been recommended as the direct route to the village in question.

The road stretched through ...'

9. *Charles's Wain*: the most prominent part of Ursa Major, also known as the Plough or Big Dipper (USA).
10. *C*: 'be concerned. But that's only the skin of the woman, and these dandy cattle be as proud as a lucifer in their insides.' *Dandy cattle*: good-looking people. *Proud as a lucifer*: proverbial phrase as in Milton's characterization of the proud Lucifer (Satan) in *Paradise Lost* – having the pride of the devil.
11. *C*: 'This was . . . he spoke' omitted.
12. *C*: 'Master Poorgrass.' Hardy's many alterations to forms of address indicate his attempts to accentuate forms of social deference and class division. As such they remain vitally important to our understanding of his artistic endeavour.
13. *C*: 'every bank in Casterbridge'.
14. *pitch-halfpenny*: a game in which players toss coins at a line, the nearest being the winner. Bathsheba is not shown by Hardy either to flaunt her wealth or to gamble, and with a sovereign equal to 480 halfpence these gambling stakes would be very high indeed.

CHAPTER VII

1. *C*: 'All was practical again now. A summer eve and loneliness . . .'
2. *Ashtoreth*: in I Kings 11:3–5, King Solomon's 700 wives, who practise a variety of different religions, persuade him to worship 'many strange women' including Ashtoreth (or Ashtaroth), the Sidonian goddess of sex and fertility.
3. *loving his neighbour as himself*: 'Thou shalt love thy neighbour as thyself' appears several times in the Bible, e.g. in Matthew 19:19.

CHAPTER VIII

1. *Elymas-the-sorcerer*: in Acts 13:6–12, Elymas the sorcerer is struck blind as a punishment for influencing people against learning the Christian faith. He 'went about seeking someone to lead him by the hand'. Oak, here, is groping with his hands.
2. *Her Majesty's Servants*: a theatre company.
3. *milestone*: a stone set beside a road (on a bank) to mark distance in miles between towns. Figuratively, a milestone marks a significant point in life, progress, etc. Milestones were often whitewashed to make them prominent on the roadside and visible in the dark; hence the comical comparison with Jacob's 'one tooth in the left centre of his upper jaw'.
4. *Purification Day*: William Smallbury is recalling the (previous year's) Church Feast of the Purification on 2 February when Andrew's family was last seen 'to

traypse up to the Vestry' to collect the charity-money ('use-money': see note 5 below) distributed on that day. Purification Day commemorates not only the ritual cleansing of women after childbirth, enjoined by Jewish law, but also the presentation of Jesus in the Temple in Jerusalem on completion of Mary's purification (see Luke 2:22–35).

5. *use-money*: after 'usury' – the annual interest on funds (invested to endow charities) which is donated to 'second best poor folk' or paupers.

6. *C*: 'whom to meet anywhere in your travels was to know, to know was to drink with, and to drink with was, unfortunately, to pay for.'

7. *Saint-Simonian notions*: Claude Henri de Rouvroy, comte de Saint-Simon, French Socialist (1760–1825), advocated a scientific division of labour; in this sense Hardy's allusion is humorous, the inference being that the (effortful) 'division' of a drink is akin to a division of labour.

8. *jerry-go-nimble show*: a tumbling, equestrian performance; a circus. *Greenhill Fair* – where Troy will later perform on horseback – is Hardy's fictional name for Woodbury Hill, overlooking Bere Regis, where an annual fair was held every September. 'Kingsbere' and environs also feature in *The Trumpet-Major* (1880), *The Mayor of Casterbridge* (1886) and *Tess of the D'Urbervilles* (1891).

9. *Woman's Skittle Alley*: in skittles, like ninepins or bowling, 'pins' are set up in a frame at the end of an 'alley' to be knocked down by a ball or wooden disk. Special alleys were reserved for women but gained a reputation for attracting people of ill-repute. Hence Poorgrass's experience of 'a horrible gross situation'. The *Tailor's Arms* was the name of a local inn. Like *Buck's Head* later, Hardy is here alluding to actual places – *Weatherbury*, however, is a fictional name corresponding to Puddletown, about five miles north-east of Dorchester, and Yalbury Wood/Bottom/Hill corresponds to Yellowham Wood/Bottom/Hill.

10. *C*: 'feel my few poor gratitudes.' This is one of many such instances of Hardy's experimentation with the language of indecorum, as indicated by his revisions: *1912* has 'sinful' for 'gross', 'ba'dy' (bawdy) for 'wicked'.

11. *1912* omits 'as to whether . . . the word.' This hindsight revision suggests that the liberalism of the original (irreligious) idea undermined the more ennobled Oak that Hardy was trying to stress in later years.

12. *1912* omits 'and forcing out . . . trepidation any more.' See note 11 above: Oak's identification with the weak-minded Poorgrass is inexpedient here.

13. *Keeper Day's*: (keeper of Yalbury Wood) also appears as the father of Fancy Day in *Under the Greenwood Tree* (1872).

14. *Farmer Everdene*: is also one of Michael Henchard's creditors in *The Mayor of Casterbridge* (1886).

15. *C*: 'his wife'. This seemingly minor revision of 'her' to 'wife' would have been typical of Stephen who pounced on any suggestion of sexual ambiguity:

Coggan *could* be still contemplating the 'sweetheart' frolics; an inserted 'wife' judiciously assigns all bedroom activity to matrimonial business.

16. *committing the seventh*: breaking the seventh of the biblical commandments: 'Thou shalt not commit adultery' (Deuteronomy 5:18). This passage caused Stephen some trouble. According to the *Life* he was upbraided by three respectable ladies for allowing such an improper passage into publication. Hardy later confronted him with a *Times* review which 'quoted in a commendatory review the very passage that had offended' (*Life*, 95–101).

17. *C*: 'ungodly'. This revision alters Poorgrass's stance entirely, and repositions him as internal censor, or moralizer, for the reader's edification.

18. *Let Your Light so Shine*: recited from Matthew 5:16 by Anglican clergymen at the beginning of the Offertory of the Communion Service during which the 'money-plate' is passed among the congregation for donations. This manner of ostentatious piety raises the question as to whether this 'ficklest' of husbands was, in truth, something more than 'godfather' to all those little 'come-by-chance' (out-of-wedlock) children.

19. *Parson Thirdly*: also appears in Hardy's poem, 'Channel Firing' (1914).

20. *as the d— said of the owl*: *1912* amends this phrase to 'like the Devil's head in a cowl', which Hardy annotates with an explanatory note claiming that 'This phrase is a conjectural emendation of the unintelligible expression, "as the Devil said to the Owl", used by the natives.'

21. *1912* has 'ba'dy' for 'loose' and 'loose low man' for 'lewd low' – see note 10 above, on indecorum.

22. *Dame Durden*: a folksong about a notable housewife who kept five serving women for milking and five serving men for digging and flailing (hand-threshing), and the five men loved the five women.

23. *Minerva*: in classical mythology, the goddess of wisdom and the arts who invented the flute but discarded it because it contorted her features. This 'private' moment of male conceit recalls Bathsheba's in the looking-glass scene when Oak had judged *her* vanity to be an innate fault in women.

24. *new's bell*: ringing in the ears supposedly signifying ill-tidings. Hardy's rustics communicate their fears and anxieties vividly and expressively through a common language of superstitions and omens. See notes to XXV.

25. *magpie all alone*: in folk tradition a magpie (a crow with a long tail and black-and-white plumage) heralds a change in fortunes. According to one ancient chant: 'One's sorrow, two's mirth/Three's a wedding, four's a birth,' etc.

26. *Robbin*: this is Hardy's original spelling. See A Note on the History of the Text.

27. *library*: Oak's library contains mainly standard works widely read in the nineteenth century. Self-help books, such as *The Young Man's Best Companion*, by George Fisher, would contain both housekeeping advice (wine-making, laundering) and health care as well as, say, the rudiments of book-keeping and carpentry. *The Farrier's Sure Guide* and *The Veterinary Surgeon* follow the same principle, but applied to husbandry; Walkingame's *Arithmetic* (1751) and John Ash's *Dictionary* (1775) would offer a guide to numbers and words respectively; John Milton's *Paradise Lost* (1667) was an extremely popular epic poem based on the creation story in Genesis; John Bunyan's *Pilgrim's Progress* (1678–84) provides an allegory of Christian pathways to salvation; and Daniel Defoe's *Robinson Crusoe* (1719) is a novel (purportedly the first English novel) about shipwreck and survival on an uninhabited island.

CHAPTER IX

1. Chapter IX begins the March instalment.
2. *Classic Renaissance*: *Jacobean*, of the reign of James I (1603–25), an early phase of English Renaissance architecture and decoration, blending Gothic and Renaissance styles introduced by Inigo Jones, favouring round-arch arcades, *fluted pilasters* (vertically grooved, rectangular columns projecting from a wall), *gables* (triangular canopied upper parts of walls at ends of ridged roofs), and featuring interiors of heavy, dark oak.
3. *Terburg or a Gerard Douw*: Gerard Terburgh or Terborch (1617–81), a Dutch Baroque painter known for his use of subtle gradations of colour to enhance distinct surface textures. Gerard Douw (1613–75), a Dutch Baroque painter, student of Rembrandt, noted for his handling of chiaroscuro.
4. *Boldwood*: is also a peripheral character in Hardy's *The Mayor of Casterbridge* (1886), described as 'a silent and reserved young man' in Chapter XXX. With his age set at forty-one in the present 1874 novel, which Hardy describes as contemporary in setting, and with the internal action of *The Mayor of Casterbridge* set in the late 1840s, Boldwood would then have been a youth in his mid-teens.
5. *C*: 'stern-looking – and rich' – one of many revisions accentuating class difference.
6. *pucker*: a needlework term meaning to gather into folds or (unintentionally) into a wrinkle or bulge. Bathsheba suggests a twisted situation.
7. *pelican in the wilderness*: from Psalms 102:6: 'I am like a pelican in the wilderness' – meaning in the wrong place.
8. *C*: 'was irresistible by aspiring virginity, in spite of her spleen at having been published as old' – an erroneous revision: 'old' has already been changed to 'staid' in proofs for *C*.
9. *Philistines*: a biblical tribe that repeatedly harassed the Israelites; in common parlance, a vulgar person lacking cultured interests. Liddy, who is clearly one of the workfolk herself, is lightly mocking her own kind in Judges 16:9, 'The

Philistines be upon thee', which are Delilah's words when, as a spy for the Philistines, she pretends to warn Samson of their approaching attack.

CHAPTER X

1. *C*: 'iniquities, to the squire' – a revision clarifying class-separation. See note 5 to IX.
2. *thinking 'twas Abel killed Cain*: in Genesis 4:1–15, Abel is killed by his jealous brother, Cain, eldest son of Adam and Eve. *1912* has (instead of 'She didn't . . . godmother'), 'The parson put it right, but 'twas too late, for the name could never be got rid of in the parish.'
3. *sins of the parents . . . upon the children*: in Deuteronomy 5:9, God demands exclusive allegiance of the Israelites: 'I the Lord thy God am a jealous God, visiting the iniquity of the fathers upon the children unto the third or fourth generation of them that hate me.' Henery's allusion to God's curse upon the Israelites shows his grasp of the issue but comically exaggerates it.
4. *Jove . . . Olympus*: Jove, otherwise Jupiter – Latin for Zeus. In much early classical Greek poetry (Homer, Euripides), the gods inhabit Mount Olympus (the highest mountain peak in Greece, at Macedonia and Thessaly), and Jove held his fabulous court there; but by the third century B.C. the gods have been elevated to the heavens – thus 'into the wide sky'. See also Introduction.
5. *thief in the night*: in 1 Thessalonians 5:2, St Paul advises sobriety, preparedness and piety, 'For yourselves know perfectly that the day of the Lord so cometh as a thief in the night.' See also Introduction.
6. *C*: 'any war.' See note 4 to VI.
7. *C*: 'hall'. According to the niceties of Victorian class distinction Bathsheba would more properly perform her payroll duties in the manorial hall – the kitchen being the workplace of servants and lacking the dignity necessary for the role-enforcement of class separation.

CHAPTER XI

1. *Sergeant Troy*: Frank Troy is ambiguously named: he is 'frank' in the sense of being open and outspoken in sexual preening, seductive admiration and captivation but not in the sense of being candid and guileless. Similarly, whereas 'Troy' may invoke the Trojan city renowned for its courageous fighters (as Frank Troy will shortly display his fighting skills with the sword), 'Troy' also connotes a maze, labyrinth or twisted path (from Welsh and Anglo-Saxon usages), which aptly mirrors his twisting-and-turning unreliability and instability.

CHAPTER XII

1. *little Jove*: according to Greek mythology the Titans made war against Jove (otherwise Jupiter/Zeus), and tried to dethrone him. Analogously, the triumphant Bathsheba holds her own in this challenging male stronghold, and she 'walks as a queen among these gods'.
2. *C*: 'He was a gentlemanly man, with full . . .' – a revision accentuating class.
3. *C*: 'A low carriage, bowling along . . . behind a horse of unimpeachable breed . . .' – a revision accentuating class. Bathsheba's gig is a light two-wheeled one-horse carriage; Boldwood's carriage – the more luxurious chaise(?) – sports a thoroughbred horse.

CHAPTER XIII

1. *Sortes Sanctorum*: Latin for 'the oracles of the writings'. This kind of concatenation is highly characteristic of Hardy's subversive style of aligning belief systems and superstition, holy writ and folklore: the biblical/valentine 'oracle'.
2. *Bible and Key*: here the idea is to think of possible marriage partners and then to insert a large key into the Bible at the book of Ruth, tie the book shut with the handle of the key protruding, and then wait for the Bible to turn when the verse is spoken. Then it depends upon *to* whom the book swings and *of* whom the recipient is thinking at the time, for the future marriage partner to be foretold. The verse to be uttered from the book of Ruth is generally held to be 1:16: "whither thou goest, I will go; and where thou lodgest, I will lodge: thy people shall be my people, and thy God my God'.
3. *His pew*: special pews, facing each other across the transept end of the nave, were reserved for the gentry. The remainder of the congregation sat in rows in the main body of the nave facing the altar.
4. *C*: upgrades his class, 'Rich and gentlemanly, what does he care?' See note 5 to IX.
5. *Daniel*: in Daniel 6:10–16, the chief president under King Darius, Daniel, refuses to observe a new decree outlawing certain religious practices such as kneeling towards Jerusalem in prayer. The suggestion here is that Boldwood's refusal to observe the social niceties seems, to Bathsheba, provokingly absurd; at the same time the narrative point of view suggests that she shares this sense of the absurd in holding such a view.

CHAPTER XIV

1. *C*: 'St. Valentine's Day'. Hardy's world assimilates much Christian tradition to folk-culture – for example, Christmas to Yuletide, and May Day (St Mary-the-Virgin's Day) to pagan fertility rites, as in maypole dancing. However, *C* restores the (sacred) 'Saint' to the (more profane) 'Valentine' whose day of celebration (14 February) is supposed to occur at the peak of the mating season, at bird-pairing time, and whose name is actually a corruption of *galantin* (a lover, a dangler), a gallant.
2. *C* has 'by a beaming fire of aged logs', emphasizing gentlemanly luxury and leisure.
3. *C*: 'Here the bachelor's gaze . . . red seal became as a blot of blood on the retina . . .' 'Blood' is prophetic: intimations of distorted vision and organic breakdown.
4. *Puritan Sunday*: this would involve the strictest abstinence from pleasure, entertainment, and stimulants of all kinds – including laughter. Puritans were originally seceders from the Protestant Reformed Church under Elizabeth I, and sought to abolish all showy ceremonials, permissive practices and leniency in religion and morality.
5. *Columbus*: on Christopher Columbus's first voyage to the New World in 1492, the sighting of floating strands of seaweed gave hope that land was nearby. Analogously, Boldwood is 'grabbing at straws'.

CHAPTER XV

1. Chapter XV begins the April instalment.
2. *C*: 'hyperbolic' – Leslie Stephen's alteration.
3. *C*: the long segment from 'four o'clock' to 'without a baily?' is omitted. Stephen possibly felt it lacked the necessary pace for opening a new instalment. This and later cuts to the Malthouse dialogues (see notes below) shortened the chapter considerably. Hardy then inserted a plot 'accelerator' – the 'All Saints' ' segment.
4. *Joey Iscariot*: Henery's name for Judas Iscariot, the disciple who betrayed Christ.
5. *C*: 'and rear . . . notice' to the segment beginning 'A headstrong maid' is omitted. *A man ready . . . race* alludes to Tennyson's poem, 'Locksley Hall' (1842), whose speaker dreams of escaping his life and duties in England, '. . . to burst all links of habit – there to wander far away,/On from island unto island at the gateways of the day . . ./I will take some savage woman, she shall rear my dusky race' (ll. 157–8, 168).

6. *putting the bellows . . . stinging her*: *put the bellows on the table*: a superstition portending a quarrel. Many such portentous signs, now obscure in origin, once signified subtle behavioural or atmospheric changes requiring attention or preventive action. Sally's misplacement of the bellows portends Troy's rash incitement to revelry when all implements of work are thrown aside on the night of the thunderstorm. Heated quarrels then ensue with Bathsheba. *A white cat come in to me*: a superstition portending bad luck. From ancient Egyptian tradition to the Renaissance and beyond, cats – black and white – have been both venerated and feared as manifesting all manner of forms and omens: 'Some . . . are mad if they behold a cat' (*Merchant of Venice*, IV, i). *Coffin-handle . . . candle*: a superstition predicting death. The 'coffin-handle' might take shape from the dripping tallow, or may appear as a separate flame. On his last visit to his deeply loved friend, Horace Moule, Hardy saw just such an omen: 'Moule . . . pointed unconsciously at a candle whose wax was "shaping to a shroud"' (*Biography*, 154). Three months later Moule cut his throat. *Seed the new moon . . . through glass*: a superstition heralding the breaking of glass; customarily 'glass-breakers' – hard drinkers – either cracked the bottle or broke the stem of their glass to impel swallowing the contents in one gulp. *Dreamed of bees stinging her*: traditionally an ill-omen which Freudians might interpret as a sign of repressed desire for (or fear of) sexual penetration.

7. *travel*: 'travail' – 'hard labour'. Henery is misapplying Jesus's words of comfort to his disciples at the last hour: 'A woman when she is in her travail hath sorrow, because her hour is come: but as soon as she is delivered of the child, she remembereth no more the anguish' (John 16:21).

8. *Thor*: in Norse mythology the striking of the god Thor's hammer produces thunder.

9. *1912*: 'this town.' This late change more precisely identifies Fanny's location to be in Melchester (in 'this town'). It was common knowledge, locally, that the Dragoon Guards were currently stationed in Melchester, as evidenced by Billy Smallbury's immediate departure to search for Fanny and her soldier at Melchester barracks (IX). 'This town' also better explains why Boldwood, in learning of Fanny's movements, deplores her as a 'silly girl' of 'lost reputation': he evidently fears she has turned camp-follower.

10. *C*: adds 'indeed, a nobleman by blood', upgrading his class.

11. *C*: The segment beginning 'Strange to say' and ending 'at a lawyer's in Casterbridge' is altered in *C* to read: 'A slight romance attaches to him, too. His mother, a French governess, was married to a poor medical man, and while money was forthcoming all went on well. Unfortunately for the boy, his best friends died; and he got then a situation as second clerk at a lawyer's in Casterbridge.' *1912* reads: 'A slight romance attaches to him. His mother was a French governess, and it seems that a secret attachment existed between her and the late Lord Severn. She was married to a poor medical man, and soon after an infant was born; and while money was forthcoming all went on well. Unfortunately for her boy, his best friends died; and he got then a situation as second clerk at a lawyer's . . .' The aspect of illegitimacy is clarified in later revisions.

12. *C* omits 'She has now lost . . . what will she do?' – one of many such instances of censorship.

CHAPTER XVI

1. *Adam . . . Eve*: 'God caused a deep sleep to fall upon Adam . . . and he took one of his ribs . . . [and] . . . made he a woman' (Genesis 2:21–2).

2. *injured lover's hell*: jealousy – an allusion to Milton's *Paradise Lost*, v. 449–50: 'Love unlibidinous reigned, nor jealousy/Was understood, the injured lover's hell.'

CHAPTER XVII

1. *C*: 'backs and tails'. See note 12 to XV (censorship).

2. *almonry and cloister*: an almonry was used for the official distribution of alms; in hospitals, the place designated for the aftercare of patients – in Boldwood's case, for the care 'of his four-footed dependents'. Hardy evidently enjoys the incongruity of aligning a barnyard with cloisters – a conventual/monastic prayer-path.

3. *C*: 'Spiritually' – one of several such instances of a cancelled neologism. See also Introduction.

4. *1912* omits the segment beginning 'Emotionally and mentally' and ending 'not structural at all.' See notes 11 and 12 to VIII.

5. *1912* omits 'Boldwood . . . cold' and 'The shallows . . . bottomless.'

6. *C*: 'spirited'. *1912*: 'wild'. See note 3 above.

7. *the uncertain glory of an April day*: an allusion to Shakespeare's *Two Gentlemen of Verona*, I, iii: 'Oh! how this spring of love resembleth/The uncertain glory of an April day,/Which now shows all the beauty of the sun,/And by and by a cloud takes all away!'

CHAPTER XVIII

1. *Cyclops' eye*: *cyclops* is Greek for 'circular eye'. 'One of a group of giants with only one eye, and that in the centre of their forehead, whose business it was to forge iron for Vulcan. They were probably Pelasgians, who worked in quarries, and attached a lantern to their forehead to give them light underground. The lantern was their *one eye as big as the full moon*' (Brewer, p. 323; my italics).
2. *C*: 'chaise' – a pleasure or travelling carriage, open, for one or two persons; *gig*: a light two-wheeled, one-horse carriage; 'chaise' upgrades Boldwood's social status.

CHAPTER XIX

1. *C*: 'possession'. *1912* has: 'ordinary men take wives . . . ordinary women accept . . .' – thus particularizing Hardy's view of sexual relationships: men 'take' wives, women 'accept' husbands.
2. *C*: 'brain'. *Elizabeth. . . Mary Stuart*: the distinction is one of head and heart. Queen Elizabeth I (1533–1603) is held to be astute, shrewd, strongminded; Queen Mary Stuart (1542–1587) excitable, courageous, passionate.
3. *Eros*: in Greek mythology, boy-god of love. See Introduction.
4. *Ixion's punishment*: in Greek mythology King Ixion is punished for his arrogance in trying to imitate the fire (thunder) of heaven by being chained to a revolving wheel of fire. Prison inmates in the nineteenth century were forced to endure pointless hard labour by turning the handle of a crank machine to pull ladles through sand (treadmills were often referred to as 'Ixion's wheel'), which could be leavened by the turn of a screw ('screw' – the nickname for prison warders). Hence Hardy's reference to 'the history of gaols'.
5. *Danby sunset*: the landscape painter James Francis Danby (1816–75) was noted for the brilliant colours of his sunsets; likewise his father, Francis Danby (1793–1861).
6. *C* omits 'previous . . . Egypt.' An allusion to Exodus 10:28–9: 'And Pharaoh said unto him, Get thee from me . . . see my face no more; for in *that* day thou seest my face thou shalt die.

And Moses said, Thou hast spoken well, I will see thy face again no more.'

As the story goes, Moses' complacency arises from the fact that he has God on his side.

CHAPTER XX

1. Chapter XX begins the May instalment.
2. *Ephesians . . . Thessalonians*: Ephesians is one of the shorter epistles of Paul the Apostle, set between Corinthians and Thessalonians, and is easily overlooked when thumbing through the New Testament. In Ephesians, the imprisoned Paul utters inspiriting blessings in a softly comforting extended prayer for love, peace, faith and spiritual repose. Ironically, Joseph Poorgrass's irritation increases to swearing point in trying to find it.
3. *C*: 'numskulls' (numb skull); *stumpoles* – 'stum' ('stom') meaning 'dumb', and 'pole' meaning 'wooden shaft' – probably struck Leslie Stephen as too vulgar for ladylike utterance, especially since, idiomatically, it scoffs not at the skull but the phallus.
4. *Swoln . . . drew*: in Milton's *Lycidas* (1637), 'The hungry sheep look up, and are not fed, But swoln with wind, and the rank mist they draw,/Rot inwardly, and foul contagion spread' (ll. 125–7).
5. *Oriental*: to 'orient' oneself is to find one's bearings; originally from turning to the east (Orient) for meditation and prayer. Christian churches are built with the chancel end facing eastward (to the Orient). Hardy's touch here is gently ironic: Henery is not 'reflective' but brainless.
6. *Morton's . . . Shrewsbury*: in Shakespeare's *2 Henry IV* (I, i), Morton announces the death of Hotspur with a face 'so spiritless,/So dull, so dead in look, so woebegone' (ll. 70–71).
7. *lettre-de-cachet*: French, literally 'a sealed letter', signifying a warrant from a high-ranking noble (identified by the seal), containing an order for imprisonment without trial – therefore, a letter that must be obeyed. In *C*, the phrase is italicized; Hardy customarily reserves italics for stress-placement only, not for highlighting naturalized imported usages.
8. *beggars . . . choosers*: beggars must take what is given to them; they cannot dictate their choice to the giver. Oak, deliberately insulting Bathsheba, implies that she, as beggar, cannot ask one favour when she has just rejected another – his advice/criticism.
9. *ease . . . time*: in Edmund Burke's 'Theory of Delight' he makes 'use of the word Delight to express the sensation which accompanies the removal of pain or danger' (*Philosophical Enquiry*, 1757, I, iv).

CHAPTER XXI

1. *spring tides . . . could not*: spring tides are those at their fullest and highest and neap tides are lowest, occurring shortly after the first and third quarters of the moon. The analogy, in Oak's case, is that if he cannot 'float off' (from his attachment) at 'high water' (when the time is right), how will he ever do so?
2. *Flossy catkins . . . time*: *catkins*: the cylindrical flower clusters of willow, hazel, etc., usually drooping and silky; *fern-fronds like bishops' crosiers*: young curling fern-fronds resembling the hooked staff (crosier) which symbolizes the pastoral office of bishops; *moschatelle*: a small shade-loving plant with pale-green flowers and musky smell; *cuckoo-pint*: wild arum, a plant with an elongated flower cluster sheathed by a bract (leaf-scale), also known as 'Lords and Ladies' – the plant that, in *Tess* (1891), during the Talbothays idyll, Tess sensuously rubs down between her fingers while a self-absorbed Angel thinks of teaching her history; *malachite*: bright green mineral taking a high polish and used for ornament; *lady's smocks*: also known as 'cuckoo flower', a meadow flower with pale lavender flowers in spring; *toothwort*: a fleshy-looking parasitic plant with tooth-like root-scales; *enchanter's nightshade*: a white-flowered plant with black poisonous berries, of the genus *Circaea*, traditionally associated with witchcraft; *doleful-bells*: a plant with drooping, dark-coloured flowers.
3. *C*: 'back' – see note 12 to XV (censorship).
4. *Guildenstern . . . happy*: paraphrase from Shakespeare's *Hamlet* (II, ii).
5. *Aphrodite . . . foam*: in Greek mythology, Cronus, urged by his mother Gaeia, castrates his father Uranus and throws his genitals into the sea. Aphrodite, goddess of love, springs from the foam (Greek *aphros*, foam), and is later adulated by the assembly of the Immortals for her bewitching beauty. In Botticelli's painting on this theme, Aphrodite arises from the foam in a soft cloud of cascading tresses, and also looks 'startled and shy'.
6. *shorn skin*: in the first ms writing Hardy has 'sheep'; the revision to 'shorn skin' accentuates the defloration imagery in this scene.
7. *ovine criticism*: analysis of sheep.
8. *St John Long's death . . . disease*: John St John Long (1798–1834) claimed to heal tuberculosis (consumption) by liniments and friction. Put on trial twice for the death of his consumptive patients, he did not attempt to use his own treatment when he himself became fatally ill with the disease. Likewise Boldwood's frigid treatment of the opposite sex does not save him now from the ills of infatuation.
9. *better wed . . . moor*: a mixen, otherwise 'midden' (Scottish), is a domestic rubbish heap. Better to seek a wife from your own back yard than from foreign parts.
10. *Pharisaical . . . matter*: 'The Pharisee stood and prayed thus with himself, God

I thank thee that I am not as other men are' (Luke 18:11). Gabriel, too, is smugly self-righteous.

11. *close with*: Henery boasts that he could gibe and spar with Oak on an equal level.

12. *Nicholas Poussin's*: Poussin (1594–1665), French painter and notable pictorial classicist of the Baroque period, was admired by Hardy as one of the 'inventors of the Grand Historical Landscape'.

13. *I find more bitter . . . nets*: the preacher, Ecclesiastes, says: 'And I find more bitter than death the woman whose heart is snares and nets' (7:26). These castigating words aptly reflect Gabriel Oak's tendency to blame the female for his own male desire.

14. *gospel . . . speak it*: a paraphrase of St John's Gospel, 3:15: 'That whosoever believeth in him should not perish . . .' Nicodemus is asking Jesus how man can be 'born again' if he cannot re-enter his mother's womb. Jesus replies by 'rebirth' of the spirit. Poorgrass, inevitably, misapplies the phrase.

CHAPTER XXII

1. *ballet . . . composure*: Joseph's *ballet* (ballad) is not, in fact, his 'composure' but a seventeenth-century ballad, 'The Seeds of Love', attributed to Mrs Fleetwood Habergam.

2. *Silenus . . . Chromis . . . Mnasylus*: in Greek mythology the music-lover and prophet Silenus (foster father of Bacchus) was much given to debauch; in Virgil's 6th *Eclogue* he is found by Chromis and Mnasylus drunk and asleep; they bind him with his own garlands until he will sing them a prophetic song; this turns out to be 'a ballad [both] inclusive and interminable', being a very long account of Greek myths.

3. *The Banks of Allan Water*: a ballad by M. G. (Monk) Lewis in which a beautiful maiden loses her heart to a soldier in springtime, grieves over the falsity of his 'winning tongue' in summertime, 'smil'd no more' in autumn, and by wintertime is lying in her grave. The theme and seasonal pattern of the ballad parallels Bathsheba's misfortunes with Troy but with a reversal of deathbeds.

4. *a too happy happiness*: an allusion to John Keats's 'Ode to a Nightingale' (1819–20), in which the speaker describes a 'drowsy numbness' caused not 'through envy of thy happy lot,/But being too happy in thine happiness' (ll. 5–6). In late revisions Hardy tended to name the origin of his allusions (as in *1912*) instead of infusing them (as here) into his text.

5. *a fearful joy*: an allusion to Thomas Gray's 'Ode on a Distant Prospect of Eton College' (1747): 'Still as they run they look behind,/They hear a voice in every wind,/And snatch a fearful joy.' This idea corresponds to Edmund Burke's theory of sublime agony (see note 9 to XX). It also coheres with more recent theories that fear and desire are both stimulated by the same hormone: adrenalin.

CHAPTER XXIII

1. *ninth . . . Egypt*: in Exodus 10:21–3, the Lord, having called up grievous plagues on Egypt while hardening Pharaoh's heart against the 'children of Israel', tells Moses: 'Stretch out thine hand . . . that there may be darkness over the land.' And there was 'a thick darkness in all the land of Egypt three days'. Bathsheba, too, has her fair share of 'plagues'.
2. *lilliputian musketry*: in Jonathan Swift's *Gulliver's Travels* (1726), Gulliver is shipwrecked on an island, Lilliput, whose inhabitants are only 6 inches (15 cm) tall, so their musket-shots (from an infantry soldier's light gun) would sound like tiny clicks.
3. *C* inserts: 'And then, her appearance with half a skirt gone!' – a revision which enhances the erotic suggestiveness of this episode.
4. *knot . . . untying*: the bond of marriage. In the song by Thomas Campbell (1777–1844), 'How Delicious is the Winning', the last verse goes: 'Can you keep the bee from ranging,/Or the ringdove's neck from changing?/No! nor fettered love from dying/In the knot there's no untying'. Part of the marriage service used to involve the *nodus Herculeus* which required the bridegroom to loosen the bride's girdle, thus to untie the knot which was then 're-tied' by the marriage bond.
5. *C* omits 'a walking ruin . . . say' – see note 12 to XV (censorship).
6. *dand*: a dandy: a man unduly concerned with smart clothes. *C* adds:

   'He's a doctor's son by name, which is a great deal; and he's an earl's son by nature!'

   'Which is a great deal more. Fancy! Is it true?'

   'Yes, And he was brought up so well, and sent to . . .'

   See note 5 to IX (class upgrade).

CHAPTER XXIV

1. Chapter XXIV begins the June instalment.
2. *lied like a Cretan*: Hardy is playing with the paradox created by the Cretan poet Epimenides, who stated that 'All Cretans are liars.'
3. *sacrifices . . . groves*: the suggestion is that in surrendering to erotic pleasure Troy 'sacrifices' himself to Venus, the goddess of love.
4. *C* omits 'and regrater' – literally a middleman who buys market produce at

a low price and re-sells at a profit. This was formerly considered offensive practice but had probably gained acceptability by the 1870s as the growth of capitalism, industrialization and corporate enterprise eroded the ethics, principles and customs of traditional commercial practices. 'Regrater' has now disappeared entirely from common usage.

5. *Corinthian*: an allusion to the citizens of Corinth, notorious for their immorality and libertinism – as illustrated in Horace's *Odes* (notably I, vii), and Walter Pater's *Marius the Epicurean* (1885).

6. *passados*: a fencing term for a forward sword thrust while advancing one foot.

7. *tilt bonnets . . . nankeen*: Hardy provided the *OED* with this definition: 'a woman's or girl's bonnet in the form of a wagon-tilt, made by bending a piece of pasteboard into a half-cylinder, and covering it with linen or calico, a drawing-string holding it in shape, the material being extended to cover the crown and form a curtain'. Nankeen, a sturdy yellow cotton cloth, originally came from Nanking, China.

8. *knight-service*: a knight, originally a 'boy' employed in feudal times as a servant; those of distinguished families bore arms for the king (thus 'knight' as a title of honour and nobility). Tenure of land could be gained by military service (knight-service) – but in this instance the intended 'gain' is upon Bathsheba's heart.

CHAPTER XXV

1. *C*: 'intolerable': *infernal* meaning 'hellish', one of many such instances of (excised) profane language.

2. *plain blunt man*: Mark Antony in Shakespeare's *Julius Caesar* (III, ii, 216–17): 'I am no orator, as Brutus is,/But, as you know me all, a plain blunt man.' Troy, not in the least unaware of his own eloquence, is being facetious.

3. *C*: 'by —'. See note 1 above.

4. *third . . . ninth*: the third of the ten Commandments forbids taking the name of the Lord in vain. Because *C* has muted Troy's curse, Bathsheba's 'profane' seems an over-reaction – see note 3 above. The ninth forbids lying (Deuteronomy 5:7–21).

5. *Tophet*: see 2 Kings 23:10; Tophet was a hell-valley near Jerusalem (also called Gehinnom, Hinnom, Gehenna) where children were made to 'pass through the fire to Moloch', their shrieks being drowned by beating drums.

6. *seriate changes*: changes in orderly sequence; as in serial progression.

7. *John Knox's . . . queen*: zealous Scottish religious reformer (1514?–72), founder of Scottish Presbyterianism (Protestant), who vociferously attacked the rebellious

Mary, Queen of Scots (Catholic). Troy is being roguish and Hardy's inapt allusion to the puritanical John Knox teases out the mischief.

8. *C* inserts '(my mother was a Parisienne)'.

9. *ewe-lamb*: a cherished beloved. In 2 Samuel 12:2–4:

'The rich man had exceeding many flocks and herds:

But the poor man had nothing, save one little ewe lamb, which he had bought and nourished up: and it grew up together with him, and with his children; it did eat of his own meat, and drank of his own cup, and lay in his bosom, and was unto him as a daughter.

And there came a traveller unto the rich man . . . [who] took the poor man's lamb . . .'

Unlike the rustics, Troy knows and understands his biblical sources and does not use them idly or pretentiously.

10. *C* omits 'It was my poor father's . . . all the fortune he left me', and reads, instead:

'That watch has a history. Press the spring and open the back.'

She did so.

'What do you see?'

'A crest and a motto.'

'A coronet with five points, and beneath, *Cedit amor rebus* – "Love yields to circumstance." It's the motto of the Earls of Severn. That watch belonged to the last lord, and was given to my mother's husband, a medical man, for his use till I came of age, when it was to be given to me. It was all the fortune that I ever inherited. That watch has regulated imperial interests in its time – the stately ceremonial, the courtly assignation, pompous travels, and lordly sleeps. Now it is yours.'

The motto *Cedit amor rebus* (wittily apt) is from Ovid's *Remedia Amoris*, I, 144.

11. *C*: 'A more plebeian one' – see note 5 to IX (class upgrade).

12. *C* adds, 'for it is my one poor patent of nobility' – see note 5 to IX (class upgrade).

CHAPTER XXVI

1. *alleged formations of the universe*: probably refers to the theories of the French astronomer Pierre Simon, Marquis de Laplace (1748–1827), who held that stars and planets were formed by the gradual convergence of matter originally distributed in a gaseous nebula.

CHAPTER XXVII

1. *C*: 'diaphanous' – 'succulent' being too overtly sensuous.
2. In this and following sentences, *cuts* are hits made with the sword's edge, *thrusts* and *points* with the sword's point, and *guards* are defensive positions. Hardy owned two military manuals: *Instructions for the Sword ... For the Use of Cavalry*, and *Infantry Sword Exercises*.
3. *aurora militaris*: (Latin, 'military radiance'). The legend goes that when the activist James, Earl of Derwentwater was beheaded for rebellion in 1716, the northern lights flashed with unnatural brilliance on that night.
4. *Moses in Horeb*: alludes to Exodus 17:6. See Introduction.

CHAPTER XXVIII

1. *lymph ... Eros*: see Introduction.
2. *reck'd not her own rede*: not taking (not *reck*oning) her own counsel (*rede*). Ophelia cautions her brother Laertes in Shakespeare's *Hamlet*: 'Do not, as some ungracious pastors do,/Show me the steep and thorny way to heaven,/Whiles, like a puff'd and reckless libertine,/Himself the primrose path of dalliance treads,/And recks not his own rede' (I, iii).
3. *Hippocrates ... physical pains*: the Greek empiricist-physician, Hippocrates, says in *Aphorisms* (2, no. 46): 'When two pains occur simultaneously but not in the same place, the more violent obscures the other' (*c*. 460–370 B.C.).

CHAPTER XXIX

1. Chapter XXIX begins the July instalment.
2. *C*: 'simpleton' – 'fool' being unladylike.
3. In the first ms writing Hardy has 'hussy' (unladylike).
4. *Union*: see note 6 to Preface (Appendix I). The irony here is that Troy's lover is doomed to the Union – but that lover is not Bathsheba.
5. *Amazonian*: a legendary nation of warrior women in Africa who defended their race by either killing (or sending to its father) every new-born male, and by removing their own right breast at puberty to improve their skills in archery and the spear. Hence 'almighty womanish', fierce and indomitable.
6. *maid*: in ms, Hardy first wrote 'maid's virtue'; 'virtue' was an implicit reference to female sexual desire.

CHAPTER XXX

1. *C*: 'femininity' – see note 3 to XVII (neologisms). Whereas *feminality* implies a biological/hormonal influence (overwhelming 'unbidden emotions' in the female faced with the brute force of the male), 'femininity' applies to gender – a cultural construct – and alters Hardy's meaning.

CHAPTER XXXI

1. *C*: 'disjointed' – see note 3 to XVII (neologisms). *Unjointed* is more apt.
2. *C*: 'stupids' – *fools* too vulgar to be attributed to the lady of the house.
3. *C*: 'villains' – *devils* too profane; see note 1 to XXV (censorship).
4. Stephen's pencil has gone through most of Hardy's footprint diagrams in this episode (see illustrations). Instead, *C* has descriptive accounts such as: 'they were in equidistant pairs, three or four feet apart, the right and left foot of each pair being exactly opposite one another.'
5. *1912*: 'Coggan carried an old pinchbeck repeater which he had inherited from some genius in his family; and it now struck one.' (See A Note on the History of the Text.) *Pinchbeck*: named after Christopher Pinchbeck, an eighteenth-century London watchmaker; an imitation gold alloy (five parts copper, one part zinc) used for watchcases and the like; *repeater*, an hour-striking pocket-watch.
6. *1912* inserts: 'She won't be in Bath by no daylight!' – one of many such late revisions adjusting distances between sites. See Introduction.

CHAPTER XXXII

1. *Gilpin's rig*: alludes to William Cowper's humorous ballad, 'The Diverting History of John Gilpin' (1782). *Rig*: outfit; a person's (or object's) appearance, as determined by clothes or equipment – in this instance, Bathsheba's equipage.
2. *under your bushel . . . you*: modestly, discreetly. In Matthew 5:15, Jesus says, 'Neither do men light a candle and put it under a bushel, but on a candlestick: and it giveth light unto all that are in the house' – meaning, share/show your gifts. A bushel is a measure of capacity (= 8 gallons/32 quarts). Because it is socially unacceptable to boast of one's merits Poorgrass affects to chastise himself ('under your bushel, Joseph!').
3. *Sermon on the Mount . . . therein*: in Matthew 5:3–11, Jesus's Sermon on the Mount names nine qualities of the blessed, including: 'Blessed are the meek: for

they shall inherit the earth.' Ironically, because meekness cannot name itself without a loss of meekness, Joseph's hint that he may be named among the meek loses him the right to that particular state of blessedness.
4. *water . . . boiled for use*: Bath is situated in an extinct volcano and is famous, from Roman times, for its hot springs. Hardy visited Bath with Emma Gifford, his fiancée, in June 1873; in the July instalment Bathsheba flies off by night to meet her lover in Bath.
5. *Club-walking*: an annual group walk (as in *Tess*) through towns and countryside by the members of a parish benefit club or 'friendly society' usually providing welfare, sick allowances, etc. *White Tuesday*: otherwise Whit-Tuesday, the first Tuesday after Whit-Sunday, the second Sunday after the feast of the Ascension – generally known as Whitsuntide, a traditional time for club-walkings.
6. *Moses . . . Aaron . . . children of Israel*: Aaron and his brother Moses – the Old Testament prophet who led his tribe, the children of Israel, out of Egypt – are customarily represented in artwork as bearded, venerable figures of authority, although, according to Exodus, only in their early forties.
7. *wish her cake dough*: proverbially, to 'wish my cake were dough again' is to 'wish I had never married'.
8. *little rascals*: Stephen's pencil has scored through 'little rascals!' in the ms. 'Rascal', applied to a woman, implied camp-follower.
9. *Matthew . . . powder*: 'And whosoever shall fall on this stone shall be broken: but on whomsoever it shall fall, it will grind him to powder' (Matthew 21:44). Jesus is pointing to the unbelieving Pharisees (not to oath-taking), warning that he, as prophet, is the cornerstone of the Kingdom of God and will break them.
10. *Shimei . . . came*: alludes to 2 Samuel 16:5–8, in which King David is stoned and cursed by Shimei: 'he came forth, and cursed still as he came'. Poorgrass's sense of melodrama is getting the better of him here.

CHAPTER XXXIII

1. Chapter XXXIII begins the August instalment.
2. *C*: 'Bathsheba is only playing with you: you are too poor for her, as I said' – a revision demonstrating a gentlemanly awareness of social status.
3. *five hundred*: five hundred pounds was then equivalent to an average middle-class annual income.
4. *C*: 'circumstances' – *condition* is too suggestive of Fanny's pregnancy.
5. *C*: 'Troy paused in secret amazement at Boldwood's wild and purblind infatuation. He carelessly said, "And am I to have anything now?"' – one of many such instances of a revision stressing Boldwood's latent psychosis.

6. *C*: 'twenty-one pounds' – this may better represent the amount of cash a gentleman would carry on his person.
7. *John Everdene*: his name was Levi Everdene in Chapter VIII.
8. *Fort . . . Feeble*: the stronger part of the sword-blade, near the hilt (Fort), fending off the weaker tip (Feeble) of an opponent's blade.
9. *unhappy Shade . . . Acheron*: in Greek mythology, when the dead (Shades) arrived in Hades (underworld), they had to pay the boatman, Charon, to ferry them across Acheron – the 'River of Sorrows', one of the five rivers of the infernal regions. If unable to pay the fee (or if the dead were unburied), the unhappy souls were condemned to wander the fields of Acheron for ever.

CHAPTER XXXIV

1. *new wine . . . old bottle*: alludes to Mark 2:22, where Jesus says, 'And no man putteth new wine into old bottles: else the new wine doth burst the bottles.' Troy feels unsettled and restless in this stately old home.
2. *C* inserts:

'O, Coggan,' said Troy, as if inspired by a recollection, 'do you know if insanity has ever appeared in Mr Boldwood's family?'

Jan reflected for a moment.

'I once heard that an uncle of his was queer in his head, but I don't know the rights o't,' he said.

'It is of no importance,' said Troy lightly. 'Well, I shall be down in the fields . . .'

See note 5 to XXXIII (psychosis).

CHAPTER XXXV

1. *'The Soldier's Joy'*: a lively dance tune, no. 24 in the second of three Hardy manuscript music books now in the Thomas Hardy Collection, Dorset County Museum.
2. *1912*: 'palimpsest' – material upon which the original writing has been effaced to make room for a second writing. *Cryptographic page*: written in cipher, or secret writing. Thus, consciously, Oak sees himself motivated by the 'instability of a woman' while unconsciously he is motivated by love.
3. *thatching beetle . . . rick-stick . . . spars*: in thatching, first the straw or grain is combed with a toothed device called a rick-stick, then fastened down with U-shaped spars with pointed ends which are driven into the thatch with a wooden mallet called a beetle.

4. *C*: 'embodiment'.
5. *C* adds: '... in the north rose a grim misshapen body of cloud, in the very teeth of the wind. So unnaturally did it rise that one could fancy it to be lifted by machinery from below. Meanwhile the faint cloudlets had flown back into the south-east corner of the sky, as if in terror of the large cloud, like a young brood gazed in upon by some monster.'
6. Stephen's pencil has gone through 'virtuous' – see note 12 to XV (censorship).

CHAPTER XXXVI

1. *Stygian*: the mythic Styx – river of Hell.
2. *Hinnom*: a metaphor for Hell. See note 5 to XXV.
3. *C*: 'it'. Stephen's pencil has gone through '*wantonness*'. See note 12 to XV (censorship).

CHAPTER XXXVII

1. *Flaxman's ... Mercury*: alludes to the sculptor and artist, John Flaxman (1775–1826). See Introduction.
2. *he prepared... live*: an allusion to Jonah 4:6–8, which Boldwood cites almost verbatim.

CHAPTER XXXVIII

1. Chapter XXXVIII begins the September instalment.
2. *1912*: 'about three miles from the former place, is Yalbury Hill, one of those steep long ascents which pervade the highways of this undulating part of South Wessex.' One of several topographical changes in this chapter. See Introduction.
3. *gig-gentry*: an ironic reference to 'elite' farmworkers who can afford a gig. Oak had earlier promised Bathsheba a 'ten-pound gig for market' (IV).
4. *C*: 'Good Heaven' – see note 1 to XXV (profanity).

CHAPTER XXXIX

1. *1912*: '"Two more!" she said' – one of several topographical revisions to this chapter.
2. *Jacquet Droz*: Pierre Jacquet-Droz (1721–90), famous Swiss clockmaker and

designer of automatons which could be activated to write, play musical instruments, etc.

3. *Pleiads*: the Pleiades are a cluster in the constellation Taurus. See note 7 to II.

CHAPTER XL

1. *non lucendo*: from the Latin phrase, *lucus a non lucendo* – a proverbial example of illogicality and irrationality: it is said a struggling scholar once tried to deduce *lucus* (grove) from *non lucendo* (not shining), arguing that the deduction is valid because groves do not shine.

2. *Diana*: Roman goddess of hunting and chastity.

3. *use nor principal*: in monetary terms, 'principal' is the money invested and 'use' is the interest paid on it. Idiomatically, the phrase means 'never at all'.

4. *limber*: lithe, pliant, soft, impressible – not tough. In the first writing (cancelled) Hardy has Poorgrass say, 'I believe it was from inflammation of the lungs, though some say she broke her heart.' Clearly this would not be the official statement issued to and from Boldwood: 'weakness of constitution' reflects both his kind of tactful phrasing as well as Poorgrass's manner of parroting his superiors.

5. *laurustinus... chrysanthemum*: *laurustinus*: a wild laurel, evergreen winter-flowering shrub; *variegated box*: evergreen shrub with dark/light-green leathery leaves, much used in garden borders; *yew*: dark-leaved evergreen coniferous tree; *boy's-love*: southernwood, a plant with fine, aromatic leaves; *chrysanthemum*: autumn-blooming composite plant with sturdy red or yellow flowers. Victorian readers would have been keenly attentive to Hardy's botanical selection. See also note 2 to XXI.

CHAPTER XLI

1. *'Malbrook'*: an eighteenth-century French lullaby, sung to the tune of 'For He's a Jolly Good Fellow', 'Malbrouck s'en va-t-en guerre'. Focusing, as so often in death-scenes, on the bizarre and incongruous, Hardy here brings out the coffin to the musical chimes of jollification.

2. *Dust to Dust*: from the Christian funeral ceremony: 'Ashes to ashes and dust to dust.'

3. *1912*: 'at the roadside hamlet called Roy-Town' – Hardy's 'Wessex' name corresponding to Troy Town, a small hamlet (a village without a church) once situated on the road from Dorchester to Puddletown.

4. *parish boards ... half-crown*: a cheap board coffin supplied by the parish;

bell-shilling: shilling/twelve pence paid to a bell-ringer to toll the church bell at funerals; *grave half-crown*: two-shillings and sixpence/thirty pence, the cost of a pauper's grave.

5. *horned. . . smoky house*: the devil in Hell. Coggan feels more comfortable with euphemisms – not naming the devil outright.

6. Stephen's pencil has scored through this entire section, from Mark Clark's comment on smoking martyrs to Coggan's assent. See note 12 to XV (censorship), and note 1 to XXV (profanity).

7. *found me in tracts*: supplied with religious pamphlets (tracts).

8. *Drink. . . her*: paraphrase of Isaiah 22:13 and Corinthians 15:32: 'let us eat and drink; for tomorrow we shall die'.

9. *King Noah*: Noah, who 'found grace in the eyes of the Lord', was chosen to save two of every kind of animal in his ark when the 'world' was flooded (Genesis 6:8). Poorgrass (wrongly) crowns Noah king!

10. In the first ms writing Hardy has: 'to be lifted against my hinder parts' which is restored in *1912* – a rare instance of a late revision actually matching the original ms. See note 10 to VIII (indecorum).

CHAPTER XLII

1. Chapter XLII begins the October instalment.

2. *childlike innocent thing: C* has 'childlike nesh young thing' – the idea of an innocent fallen woman was heretical. But because current ghostlore held that only guilty souls wandered the earth after death, Liddy's meaning – she is assured of Fanny's innocence and thus not afeared of her ghost – is entirely lost with 'nesh' (gentle, delicate).

3. *C* cuts the section 'Fanny was *very* consumptive . . . anything of the kind' – the reference to Fanny's absence of eight months draws (indecorous) attention to her death in the ninth month under unmentionable circumstances.

4. *C* cuts the segment 'but I thought I'd just tell you . . . believe him', which shows Oak to be a liar. See notes 11 and 12, VIII, and Introduction.

5. *Esther . . . Vashti*: the Book of Esther, 1–2, tells of King Ahasuerus, whose queen, Vashti, repeatedly 'refused to come at the king's commandment'. In his wrath he calls for 'fair young virgins' and gives Vashti's estates and entitlements to the maiden of his choice – the beautiful Esther, a Jewish orphan in captivity, who is humble, obedient and dutiful. See also Introduction.

6. *1912* replaces 'This also sank . . . stillness of concentration' with 'Her simple country nature, fed on old-fashioned principles, was troubled by that which would have troubled a woman of the world very little, both Fanny and her child, if she had one, being dead.' This late revision is inapt: Bathsheba is town-bred, her 'principles' are not 'old-fashioned' but noticeably contemporary, and she is not struggling with the morality of the situation but with her own tortured feelings.

7. *C*: 'there was nobody to teach her.' See notes 11 and 12, VIII.

8. The 'Babyhood' section was not, as is commonly supposed, revised by Hardy for publication at Stephen's request but silently cut and censored by the latter – from 'Bathsheba's eager eyes' down to 'returned upon her mind' in the third paragraph following.

9. *Bellini*: Giovanni Bellini (1430–1516), of the illustrious Venetian family of Renaissance painters, was noted for the serenity, majesty and luminous colours of his paintings which include many mythological themes. Hardy writes: 'My art is to intensify the expression of things, as is done by . . . Bellini . . . so that the heart and inner meaning is made vividly visible' (*Life*, 183).

10. *C* here inserts a portion of the censored section: from 'Fanny's face' to 'by Troy.'

11. *C*: 'In Bathsheba's heated fancy the innocent white countenance expressed a dim triumphant . . .' This reverses Hardy's meaning entirely but was probably enforced by the expurgated version's newly-distorted focus.

12. *Mosaic law . . . strife*: promulgated by God through Moses, the law sets a maximum for punishment – that it should simply match the crime. In Exodus 21 these punishments are spelled out in detail: 'Eye for eye, tooth for tooth, hand for hand, foot for foot,/Burning for burning, wound for wound, stripe for stripe' (24–5).

13. *C*, after eliminating all direct references to the illegitimate baby, replaces each plural pronoun with the singular (i.e. 'them' with 'her'). See note 12 to XV (censorship).

14. *C*: 'the cold features within' – Hardy tries to reinstate portions of the original ms later in *1912*, and has 'the cold features of both mother and babe'.

15. Τετέλεσται: Greek for 'it is finished'; it alludes to the last words of Christ on the cross (John 19:30).

CHAPTER XLIII

1. *like ghosts . . . fleeing*: alludes to Shelley's 'Ode to the West Wind' (1820). See Appendix II.

2. Stephen has struck out 'others . . . scabbed'.

3. In the first ms writing (cancelled) Bathsheba goes to the window and hears the distant sound of musketry, suggesting that Troy was to have left with the troops.

4. *Beaumont . . . Human Wishes*: Beaumont and Fletcher's *The Maid's Tragedy*

(*c.* 1610), a sensational play featuring several suicides and murders; William Congreve's *The Mourning Bride* (1677), a tragedy of a woman whose father opposes her marriage to one of his enemies – the play contains the famous lines, 'Heaven hath no rage, like love to hatred turned,/Nor hell a fury, like a woman scorned'; Edward Young's *Night Thoughts on Life, Death, and Immortality* (1742–6), a long, solemn, didactic poem exhorting repudiation of worldliness and preparation for death, the last judgment and eternity; Samuel Johnson's *The Vanity of Human Wishes* (1749), a poetic meditation on human aspirations and delusions urging resignation to God's will.

5. *black man*: Liddy means Shakespeare's *Othello* (1604).

6. *Love . . . Spectator*: Isaac Bickerstaff's *Love in a Village* (1762) and *The Maid of the Mill* (1765) were comic operas; William Combe's *Doctor Syntax* (1809–21) is a series of comic verses accompanying Thomas Rowland's caricatures of a clergyman 'in search of the picturesque'; the *Spectator*, a periodical edited by Addison and Steele in 1711–12 (Addison alone in 1714), featured lively comic essays and character sketches.

7. *1912* has 'a game of Prisoner's base. The spot had been consecrated . . . the old stocks conveniently forming a base facing the boundary . . .' Prisoner's base is chiefly played by boys who form two groups each occupying a base; the aim is to touch (capture) players running from the other base. *Stocks*: a timber frame with holes for feet (occasionally for hands) in which petty offenders were confined in public, though not in churchyards.

CHAPTER XLIV

1. *1912*: 'Lester'. This late revision coincides with the onset, for Hardy, of a valued, lifelong friendship with Frederic Harrison, the widely esteemed leading English positivist.

CHAPTER XLV

1. *C*: 'all the eight were different from each other.' 'Four' in the ms refers to paired heads.

2. *1912* reverses 'north' and 'south' – one of several directional changes made to this episode.

3. Hardy notes: 'The local tower and churchyard [St Mary's, Puddletown] assumed to be those of "Weatherbury" do not answer precisely to the foregoing description.'

4. *Ruysdael and Hobbema*: Jacob van Ruysdael (1628–82) and his pupil Meindert

Hobbema (1638–1709) were Dutch Baroque landscape painters. 'The method,' wrote Hardy, 'of Hobbema, in his view of a road with formal lopped trees and flat tame scenery – is that of infusing emotion into the baldest external objects either by the presence of a human figure among them, or by mark of some human connection with them' (*Works*, 123–4).

5. *the text of the sermon*: seems to be St Paul's, who claims the only true teaching is his own: 'if any man preach any other gospel unto you . . . let him be accursed' (Galatians 1:8–9).

6. Between 'cards' and 'churchyard' *C* substitutes: 'and forswore his game for that time and always. Going out of the churchyard silently and unobserved – none of the villagers having yet risen – he passed down some fields at the back, and emerged just as secretly upon the high road.'

7. The ms shows that Hardy originally intended Chapter XLV to end here.

CHAPTER XLVI

1. *Balboa's*: Vasco Nunez de Balboa (*c.* 1475–1519), Spanish conquistador. Fleeing Hispaniola in 1510, he stowed away in explorer Enciso's ship, bound for Panama, which he then seized; crossing the isthmus with the help of native Americans he sighted the Pacific in 1513 – the first European to set eyes upon it – which he claimed for Spain.

2. *pillars of Hercules . . . Mediterranean*: the gigantic rocks, Calpe at the southernmost tip of Spain, and Abyla at Ceuta on the African side of the Straits of Gibraltar, were reputedly torn asunder by the fabled Greek hero, Hercules, so that the waters of the Atlantic and Mediterranean could connect. It was held that they marked the outermost limits of the habitable world – Hardy's Pillars of Hercules mark the outermost limits of South Wessex.

3. *Gonzalo*: in Shakespeare's *The Tempest*, Gonzalo, fearing shipwreck, cries: 'Now would I give a thousand furlongs of sea for an acre of barren ground. . . . I would fain die a dry death' (I, i, 65–8).

4. *C* omits the long section: 'Troy had sunk . . . night drooped slowly', and substitutes:

'Lending him what little clothing they could spare among them as a slight protection against the rapidly cooling air, they agreed to land him in the morning; and without further delay, for it was growing late, they made again towards the roadstead where their vessel lay.

And now night drooped . . .'

There is no indication in the ms or elsewhere, apart from his small portion struck through in ink, that Hardy authorized this substantial cut which he subsequently tried to restore, in fragments, elsewhere in the text – see, for example, note 7 to XLIX.

CHAPTER XLVII

1. Chapter XLVII begins the November instalment. *C* has the title 'Doubts Arise: Doubts Vanish'; *1912* has 'Linger' in place of 'Vanish' – two of many such instances pertaining to Hardy's hindsight stress on Bathsheba's denial of Troy's death. See A Note on the History of the Text.

CHAPTER XLVIII

1. *sit and ponder what a gift life used to be*: alludes to Robert Browning's poem 'The Statue and the Bust' (ll. 218–19), 'they sit and ponder/ What a gift life was, ages ago'. Just before her marriage to another, a beautiful woman catches sight of the young Great-Duke Ferdinand; so constant and strong is their attraction to each other that when they grow old she has a figure of her younger self made and set in the window from which she has gazed down on him over the years, while he sets a statue of his younger self in the square below.

2. *mustard-seed*: alludes to Christ's parable in Mark 4:30–32, in which a mustard-seed, 'when it is sown in the earth, is less than all the seeds. . . . But . . . it groweth up, and becometh greater than all herbs.' Boldwood's hopes are disproportionately large, in light of the facts.

3. *phantom of delight . . . daily food*: alludes to William Wordsworth's poem, 'She Was a Phantom of Delight' (1807), 'A creature not too bright or good/For human nature's daily food.'

4. *C* omits 'Boldwood wished . . . attempt it' and 'He was almost afraid . . . no harm would be done', and substitutes:

'Tells you all her affairs?'
'No, sir.'
'Some of them?'
'Yes, sir.'

See note 5 to XXXIII (psychosis).

5. *Jacob . . . Rachel*: alludes to Genesis 29. Custom decreed that the firstborn daughter, Leah, should be married before her sister, Rachel – chosen by Jacob, who undertook seven years' service to win her only to find himself presented with Leah. So he 'fulfilled her week' and then undertook an additional seven years' service to secure Rachel.

6. *Greenhill Fair*: an annual fair held at Woodbury Hill (Greenhill) every September.

CHAPTER XLIX

1. *Nijnii Novgorod*: a city in Russia once famous for its large annual fairs attracting visitors from both Europe and Asia.
2. *colourist . . . farm*: flocks were identified by colour-branding/stamping the owner's initials upon the sheep's skin after shearing (see XXI).
3. *South Downs . . . Exmoors*: *South Downs* are a breed of small sheep with short, fine wool; *Wessex horned breeds* (Dorset Horn) have large curled horns and fine-textured, short wool; *Oxfordshires* are hornless with thick curly fleece; *Leicesters*, hornless and long-woolled; *Cotswolds*, hornless, with heavy long-woolled fleeces; *Exmoors*, horned, hardy sheep with thick fleeces. The name of the breed originates from the area in which sheep were first bred.
4. *Turpin's Ride . . . Black Bess*: Dick Turpin was an infamous eighteenth-century highwayman, famed for his twelve-hour ride between York and London on his magnificent horse, Black Bess.
5. *a reed . . . wind*: alludes to Matthew 11:7/Luke 7:24, in which Jesus reminds the multitude that they have not come to see 'a reed shaken with the wind', but the great prophet, John the Baptist. Hardy is, however, using the term in its literal sense of being shaken.
6. *C* omits the section 'After embarking. . . . with a new name' and replaces it with 'The brig aboard which he was taken in Budmouth Roads was about to start on a voyage, though somewhat short of hands. Troy had read the articles and joined, and, before they sailed, a boat was despatched across the bay to Carrow Cove; but as he had half expected, his clothes were gone. He ultimately worked his passage . . .' This revised section in *C* was necessitated by the cuts to Chapter XLVI (see note 4 to that chapter).
7. The section 'Moreover. . . . her words!' is inserted in the ms at 'food and lodging' with a caret from a postscriptive entry on the verso of the previous ms page. This section was initially intended for the 'Adventures by the shore' episode. See note 4, to XLVI.
8. *Tom King*: a highwayman accidentally killed by Turpin on his flight from London to York.
9. *Rembrandt effects*: Rembrandt Harmenszoon van Rijn (1606–69), Dutch painter famous for his dramatic use of light and shadow (chiaroscuro); Hardy particularly admired the profound humanity of his art.
10. *C*: 'd—'; see note 1 to XXV (profanity).

CHAPTER L

1. *Jacob's . . . service*: see note 5 to XLVIII.
2. These epiphenomenalist ideas were familiar to Hardy from his readings in Comte, the Positivists, and the philosopher T. H. Huxley, for whom the causal influence of mind over body was likened to 'the steam above the factory' (see Huxley's *Lectures and Essays*, London and New York: 1903).
3. *1912*: 'vanishing' – this late revision does not fully cohere with Oak's next assertion that 'everybody' except Bathsheba believes Troy to be dead.
4. *1912* omits 'Yes . . . that' and substitutes 'I shall get to, I suppose, because I cannot help feeling what would have brought him back . . .' This is one of six late revisions in this chapter – see note 1 to XLVII – which problematizes Oak's role. See A Note on the History of the Text.

CHAPTER LI

1. Chapter LI begins the December (final) instalment.
2. *Shadrach Meshach and Abednego*: in Daniel 3:8–30, these three Hebrew captives of King Nebuchadnezzar refuse to worship a golden idol and are thrown into a fiery furnace where their faith in the Hebrew god miraculously saves them from harm.
3. *1912*: 'in a corner of The White Hart tavern' – one of several changes naming existing taverns (e.g., *The Three Choughs Inn* becomes the *King's Arms* – the name of a real hotel in Dorchester: XLVII). *The White Hart* stood at the eastern end of High Street, Dorchester, where a newer version stands today.
4. *Lawyer Long*: Long also appears in *The Mayor of Casterbridge* at a Council meeting (XXXVII).
5. *wringing down*: part of the cider-making process by which the crushed apples, called *pommy* (after pomace), are squeezed in a cider press leaving a compressed, cheese-like apple pulp. *Cider-wine* is fermented from apple-juice.
6. *Juno*: queen of Heaven, sister and wife of Jupiter; imposing, severe and powerful.
7. *Alonzo the Brave*: alludes to Matthew Gregory (Monk) Lewis's ballad, 'Alonzo the Brave and Fair Imogine' (1795), in which the ghost of the dead knight, Alonzo, appears at the wedding-feast of his beloved, Imogine, who had vowed not to remarry. Troy's somewhat prophetic words parallel the lines: 'The guests sat in silence and fear . . . All pleasure and laughter were hush'd at his sight; The dogs, as they eyed him drew back in affright; The lights in the chamber burnt blue!' (ll. 44–8).

CHAPTER LII

1. *C*: 'Concurritur: Horae Momento' – from Horace's Satires (I, i, ll. 7–8): 'Concurritur: horae momento cita mors venit aut victoria laeta' ('The battle commences: in an instant comes swift death or joyful victory').
2. *1912* adds: 'conditionally, of course, on my being a widow' – one of many such revisions accentuating Bathsheba's doubts about Troy's death. See note 1 to XLVII and A Note on the History of the Text.
3. *commandments*: see note 16 to VIII (adultery). Bathsheba is prevaricating.
4. *C* inserts: '. . . Boldwood did not recognize that the impersonator of Heaven's persistent irony towards him, who had once before broken in upon his bliss, scourged him, and snatched his delight away, had come to do these things a second time.'

CHAPTER LIII

1. *Melpomene*: in Greek mythology, the daughter of Zeus, one of the nine Muses, patron of tragedy and lyre-playing, represented in the arts with tragic mask and club of Heracles. Like the well-known statue of Melpomene in the Louvre in Paris, Bathsheba appears rigidly calm.

CHAPTER LIV

1. *javelin-men . . . trumpeters . . . sheriff*: as part of the paraphernalia of high office in the Justice department, a group of men carrying light spears (javelin-men) formed the official escort of judges and sheriffs to the regional assizes (trials in session); the full retinue included trumpeters for the heralding of arrivals and departures. Hardy, in true iconoclastic form, evokes the atmosphere of a travelling circus.
2. *circuit*: judges were assigned to trials periodically held at major towns on specific circuits. *1912* has 'Western Circuit', thus creating a link with Hardy's short story, 'On the Western Circuit' (*Life's Little Ironies*, 1894).
3. *Justice . . . unto him*: alludes to Daniel 5:27, in which Daniel is summoned by Chaldean King Belshazzar to interpret mysterious writings made by a ghostly hand upon the wall of his palace. Having deciphered the message as a castigation by God of Belshazzar's immoral conduct and abuse of kingship, Daniel is then proclaimed third ruler of the Chaldean kingdom and Belshazzar is slain.

Poorgrass's pretentiousness partially mitigates Hardy's satirical juxtaposition of the two systems of justice, one of which comes (to Belshazzar) by occult means.

4. *1912* substitutes 'Oak' for Troy – an anomaly, since Troy had been the first to suspect derangement (XXXIII), and Oak not only argues otherwise (LI) but now, contradicting himself, would seem monstrous if actually advising Bathsheba to marry a deranged man!

5. *decalogue*: Ten Commandments; see note 16 to VIII. Boldwood breaks the sixth: 'Thou shalt not kill'. 'Importing direct from the producer' has not been supported by textual evidence; see also note 4 to XXIV.

6. *C* cuts 'and his mind seems quite a wreck', and substitutes:

'Do ye think he *really* was out of his mind when he did it?' said Smallbury.

'I can't honestly say that I do,' Oak replied. 'However . . .'

See note 4 above (anomaly).

7. *C* cuts 'that he paced . . . sound,' and substitutes: 'that Boldwood might be saved even though in his conscience he felt that he ought to die; for there had been qualities in the farmer which Oak loved.'

8. *First dead . . . yode*: from Sir Walter Scott's *Marmion* (1808), canto 3, stanza 31, which describes the 'foot-tramp of a flying steed'. 'Yode' means 'went'.

CHAPTER LV

1. Hardy wrote marginal instructions for his publisher that the tombstone inscriptions and the brief extracts from the hymn should be printed in small type.

2. *Lead kindly Light . . . on*: this and the following two quotations are from a poem by (Cardinal) John Henry Newman (1801–90), 'The Pillar of Cloud' (1833), set to music as a hymn in 1861 by John Bacchus Dykes (1823–76).

3. *California*: Hardy has British Columbia (cancelled) in the first ms writing.

4. *last old disciple . . . flee*: alludes to Matthew 26:56/Mark 14:50, in which all Jesus's disciples 'forsook him and fled'. Bathsheba does not customarily utter herself in biblical terms.

5. *The few worn-out traps . . . handlen*: by 'W. Barnes' (Hardy's note), from his poem 'Woak Hill'. The poet and philologist William Barnes (1801–86), much admired by Hardy, kept a school next door to the architect's office in Dorchester where Hardy worked from 1856 to 1860. The poem tells of the enduring love of a husband for his wife who hopes, after her death, that her spirit will stay with him in his new abode. Hardy quotes, slightly inaccurately, from the second stanza of 'Woak Hill'; the correct version reads:

I pack'd up my traps, all a-sheenēn
Wi' long years o' handlēn,
On dowsty red wheels or a waggon,
To ride at Woak Hill.

Select Poems of William Barnes, edited by Thomas Hardy, was published in 1908.
6. *love . . . drown*: alludes to the Song of Solomon 8:6–7: 'For love is as strong as death . . . Many waters cannot quench love, neither can the floods drown it . . .' See Introduction.

CHAPTER LVI

1. *Went . . . bride*: quoted from 'Patty Morgan the Milkmaid's Story' in the first series of R. H. Barham's collection of narrative poems, *The Ingoldsby Legends* (1840–47).
2. *1912*: 'a quarter of a mile' – one of many such topographical revisions. See A Note on the History of the Text.
3. *As . . . again*: quoted from John Keats's poem 'The Eve of St Agnes' (1820), l. 243. The romantic medievalism of Keats's poem sharply contrasts this sadder-but-wiser marriage.
4. *victories of Marlborough*: the first Duke of Marlborough, General John Churchill (1650–1722), led victorious British troops against the French under Louis XIV at Blenheim (1704), Ramillies (1706), and Oudenaarde (1708).
5. *Hosea . . . alone*: Hosea 4–5 tells of God's threat to destroy all the 'children of Israel' if they do not obey him – including Ephraim: 'Ephraim is joined to idols' and possesses 'the spirit of whoredoms', he will therefore be 'oppressed and broken'. See Introduction.

R.M.

APPENDIX I

Preface

From 1912 Wessex Edition (Macmillan), Vol. II.

In reprinting this story for a new edition[1] I am reminded that it was in the chapters of "Far from the Madding Crowd,"[2] as they appeared month by month in a popular magazine,[3] that I first ventured to adopt the word "Wessex"[4] from the pages of early English history, and give it a fictitious significance as the existing name of the district once included in that extinct kingdom. The series of novels I projected being mainly of the kind called local, they seemed to require a territorial definition of some sort to lend unity to their scene. Finding that the area of a single county did not afford a canvas large enough for this purpose, and that there were objections to an invented name, I disinterred the old one. The region designated was known but vaguely, and I was often asked even by educated people where it lay. However, the press and the public were kind enough to welcome the fanciful plan, and willingly joined me in the anachronism of imagining a Wessex population living under Queen Victoria; – a modern Wessex of railways, the penny post,[5] mowing and reaping machines, union workhouses,[6] lucifer matches,[7] labourers who could read and write, and National school children.[8] But I believe I am correct in stating that, until the existence of this contemporaneous Wessex in place of the usual counties was announced in the present story, in 1874, it had never been heard of in fiction and current speech, if at all, and that the expression, "a Wessex peasant", or "a Wessex custom", would theretofore have been taken to refer to nothing later in date than the Norman Conquest.

I did not anticipate that this application of the word to modern story would extend outside the chapters of these particular chronicles. But it was soon taken up elsewhere, the first to adopt it being the now defunct *Examiner*, which, in the impression bearing date July 15, 1876, entitled one of its articles "The Wessex Labourer",[9] the article turning out to be no dissertation on farming during the Heptarchy,[10] but on the modern peasant of the south-west counties.

Since then the appellation which I had thought to reserve to the horizons and landscapes of a partly real, partly dream-country, has become more and more popular as a practical provincial definition; and the dream-country has, by degrees, solidified into a utilitarian region which people can go to, take a house in, and write to the papers from. But I ask all good and idealistic readers to forget this, and to refuse steadfastly to believe that there are any inhabitants of a Victorian Wessex outside these volumes in which their lives and conversations are detailed.

Moreover, the village called Weatherbury,[11] wherein the scenes of the present story of the series are for the most part laid, would perhaps be hardly discernible by the explorer, without help, in any existing place nowadays; though at the time, comparatively recent, at which the tale was written, a sufficient reality to meet the descriptions, both of backgrounds and personages, might have been traced easily enough. The church remains, by great good fortune, unrestored and intact,[12] and a few of the old houses; but the ancient malt-house, which was formerly so characteristic of the parish, has been pulled down these twenty years; also most of the thatched and dormered cottages that were once lifeholds. The heroine's fine old Jacobean house would be found in the story to have taken a witch's ride of a mile or more from its actual position; though with that difference its features are described as they still show themselves to the sun and moonlight. The game of prisoner's-base,[13] which not so long ago seemed to enjoy a perennial vitality in front of the worn-out stocks, may, so far as I can say, be entirely unknown to the rising generation of schoolboys there. The practice of divination by Bible and key, the regarding of valentines as things of serious import, the shearing-supper, the long smock-frocks, and the harvest-home, have, too, nearly disappeared in the wake of the old houses; and with them has gone, it is said, much of that love of fuddling to which the village at one time was notoriously prone. The change at the root of this has been the recent supplanting of the class of stationary cottagers, who carried on the local traditions and humours, by a population of more or less migratory labourers, which has led to a break of continuity in local history, more fatal than any other thing to the preservation of legend, folk-lore, close inter-social relations, and eccentric individualities. For these the indispensable conditions of existence are attachment to the soil of one particular spot by generation after generation.

T. H.

1895–1902

NOTES

1. *new edition*: in *1895*, but this version comes from *1912*.
2. *Far from the Madding Crowd*: Hardy's title alludes to the following lines from Thomas Gray's 'Elegy Written in a Country Churchyard' (1751):

> Far from the madding crowd's ignoble strife,
> Their sober wishes never learned to stray;
> Along the cool sequestered vale of life
> They kept the noiseless tenor of their way.

Hardy's allusion is ironic: his microcosmic world is no less subject to 'ignoble strife' than any other. See also *Literary Notebooks* on Gray's influence on Hardy.
3. *popular magazine*: the London *Cornhill* magazine, one of the most eminent literary journals of the day, in which *Far From the Madding Crowd* was serialized monthly from January to December 1874.
4. *Wessex*: from 'West Saxon' – one of the kingdoms of Anglo-Saxon England (*c*. 494–927), which included much of south-west England including Dorset. The rulers of Wessex became the rulers of England.
5. *penny post*: 1840 saw the introduction of postage stamps and uniform postal rates based on weight; previously the recipient of mail paid all charges.
6. *union workhouses*: the New Poor Law of 1834 obliged adjacent parishes to erect joint workhouses to which paupers were required to go for relief. This was done to assist in the transference of labour from the land, where it was redundant, to the industrial market. Hardy points to the inhumanity of this institution in his depiction of the stoning of the one and only 'humanitarian' assistant in evidence – a Newfoundland dog! (XLIX), and in the attitudes of cold-blooded mechanistic utilitarianism apparent in the incarceration and disposal of Fanny's body as it is delivered forth from an institution itself likened to a corpse, itself an 'offence' to 'Nature'.
7. *lucifer matches*: the first practical friction matches invented by John Walter in 1826.
8. *National school children*: originated by Andrew Bell, *c*. 1811, an elementary school system under the auspices of the Anglican Church which by 1851 extended to

some 3,400 National Schools. As Hardy was in the process of writing *Far From the Madding Crowd*, the implementation of the 1870 Education Bill, introduced by William Edward Forster, M.P., was already under way, inaugurating a network of national, standardized, compulsory elementary schools for all (not free until 1880).

9. *Examiner* . . . "*The Wessex Labourer*": from which Hardy probably quoted in his Preface, but with significant amendments concerning the education and working conditions of his 'Wessex' labourer. The *Examiner* states that 'Dorset was the very last county in England whose sacred soil was broken by a railroad, and those which now traverse it leave the very heart of the shire untouched . . . Time in Dorset has stood still; advancing civilisation has given the labourer only lucifer-matches and the penny post' (p. 793).

10. *Heptarchy*: the seven kingdoms, with seven rulers, of Angles and Saxons in Britain in the 7th–8th centuries: Kent, Essex, Sussex, Wessex, East Anglia, Mercia, Northumbria.

11. *Weatherbury*: 'partly real' evocation of Puddletown, near Dorchester, one of the many places cited in *Far From the Madding Crowd* loosely based on real locales in the Dorset region, the centre of Hardy's Wessex. See the map provided with this edition.

12. *unrestored and intact*: Hardy notes (1912), 'This is no longer the case.'

13. *prisoner's-base*: see note 7 to XLIII.

APPENDIX II

The Surviving Draft-Fragments of Far From the Madding Crowd

Both of the two draft fragments are headed: 'Far from the Madding Crowd.' The first continues 'Some pages of the first Draft – afterwards revised. T.H.' The lower inscription is marked in red ink and '1873' is added in pencil on the last sheet. The second has a later note in red ink: 'Some pages of 1st Draft – (Details of Sheep-rot – omitted from MS. when revised) T.H.' In 1915 Hardy had the two draft-fragments bound together and gave them to his second wife, Florence.[1]

I

The first of the two draft-fragments, written on seven leaves, is numbered 2–18 to 2–24 and has the chapter number, 'XXIII', written in pencil. The measurements of these leaves differ significantly from those of the ms, indicating that the fragment itself probably formed one of the occasional set pieces Hardy submitted to his editor, Leslie Stephen, for appraisal before settling upon the text proper. He carried around a notebook for just such a purpose – as much for making detailed observations of the sights, sounds, events and conversations of everyday life as for re-creating these details in literary form. In fact, according to Hardy's own chronicle, *Far From the Madding Crowd* was composed 'sometimes indoors, sometimes out – when he would occasionally find himself without a scrap of paper at the very moment that he felt volumes. In such circumstances he would use large dead leaves . . .'[2]

Whereas both the chapter number and story-line of this particular draft-fragment cohere with the ms account of the shearing supper, this episode ultimately went through many changes and many titles in the composition process from 'A merry time: a second declaration' to 'Eventide: A Second Declaration', before settling on 'A pleasant time: a second declaration'. In the process only a few passages from the draft-fragment were retained for the ms version and, consequently, for publication in the *Cornhill*.

As to the date of composition, one thing is certain: it was written after serialization had begun in 1874, not before in 1873 – as Hardy quite reasonably but quite forgetfully dates it with hindsight. He had not at that time – December 1873 – yet completed Chapters XX–XXIII for the May number, nor had he, as yet, adopted the *Cornhill* spelling of Fanny 'Robin'. This appeared, unauthorized by him, in the first published instalment of *Far From the Madding Crowd*, which he came across quite by chance while travelling on New Year's Eve, 1873–4. At this point he was still writing 'Robbin' in his ms (Chapters VIII–XIV – March number), which he had sent off to Stephen late in December 1873 before seeing the first instalment in print.[3] But, of course, once 'Robin' was visibly in print there was nothing to be done except to follow suit.[4] Thus the shearing episode saw the first of Hardy's adopted *Cornhill* spellings of 'Robin'.

He was, then, in the process of completing this episode during the earlier part of February 1874, shortly after spending much time and care making radical alterations to earlier issues to accommodate Stephen's cuts, his imposition of alternative chapter divisions and what he judged, in his editorial wisdom, to be 'a better break'[5] between instalments. Now nervously anxious about his May chapters, Hardy awaited Stephen's verdict. On 17 February it arrived. Please would Hardy 'omit the chapter headed the "shearing supper" and add a few paragraphs to the succeeding or preceding, just explaining that there has been a supper'?

Hardy must have been devastated. Framed in artistic terms, that the shearing episode 'rather delays the action unnecessarily', Stephen's request to omit the chapter pointed not at all, at this juncture, to the issue of censorship, but quite simply at pertinence: 'I don't know whether anything turns on the bailiff's story: but I don't think it necessary.' The 'bailiff's story' was Stephen's delicate way of speaking of Fanny Robbin's illicit-sex story. Naturally enough, at this nerve-racking point on the eve of publication, Hardy threw it out!

In this, his early struggle to circumvent Mrs Grundy – or Leslie Stephen – Hardy must have felt his integrity had been severely compromised, the more so for the fact that in the same 'prudery' letter and with the same daintiness of mind Stephen goes on to 'suggest that Troy's seduction of the young woman will require to be treated in a gingerly fashion'. Still unable to utter Fanny's name Stephen does not, in the end, 'suggest' so much as command. Censorship was the order of the day. Nevertheless, despite these enforcements Hardy had succeeded in producing – for the shearing episode – two set-pieces which had genuinely delighted his editor: the segments entitled the 'Great Barn' and 'A Merry Mist'. And these he incorporated into two newly-reduced, newly-divided chapters (XXI and XXII) treating with the barn-shearing and merrymaking supper respectively. Thus, judiciously negotiating Stephen's request to 'add a few paragraphs . . . just explaining that there has been a supper', he recreated a shearing supper episode after all.

The fragment has been transcribed exactly, except ampersands have been expanded silently. (The square brackets are Hardy's.)

THE FIRST DRAFT-FRAGMENT

The shearing-supper.

For the shearing-supper a long table was placed on the grass-plot beside the farm house, the end of the table being thrust over the sill of the wide parlour-window, and a foot or two into the room, whence with its white cloth it protruded as a sort of jetty mantled in new fallen snow. The outward extremity stretched under the trees, the flexible boughs having been pruned by cattle to the greatest height attainable by their extended necks and nibbling mouths, forming, to sitters at that end of the board, a roof coloured with young green of untanned diaphanous hue.

Bathsheba and Liddy were to be seen sitting inside the window and facing down the table: Bathsheba was thus at the head, without mingling with the men. Mutton-pies and beef, apple and rhubarb pudding, cider and ale in five large God-forgive-me mugs, were the chief furniture of the board, which was speedily environed by the shearers, the wives of two or three assisting as waiters.

This evening Bathsheba was unusually excited, her red cheeks and lips contrasting lustrously with the mazy skeins of her shadowy hair. She seemed to expect assistance, and the seat at the bottom of the table was left vacant by her request until after they had begun the meal. She then asked Gabriel to take the place and the duties appertaining to that end, which he did with great readiness.

Just at this moment Farmer Boldwood came in at the gate, and crossed the green to Bathsheba at the window. He apologised for his lateness: his arrival was evidently by arrangement.

Gabriel, said she, will you move again, please, and let Mr Boldwood come there? Gabriel moved in silence back to his original seat.

The farmer appeared dressed in cheerful style, in a new coat and a light modern summer waistcoat, quite in contrast to his usual suits of sober brown and grey, and, like the rest of the assembly, he was further brightened up by the sun, which stretched vivid lines through the leaves to his shoulders and decorated him with argus spots.[6] Inwardly too he was blithe, and consequently chatty to an exceptional degree; so also was Bathsheba now that he had come. Boldwood being at the remote end of the table she made it her pleasure to talk to Mr Jan Coggan.

I see one person here I don't know, Coggan, she said. Who is he – that man in velveteen?

Mistress, said the shearer, you know the old portions of him well enough – 'tis his new part you don't know. 'Tis Baily Pennyways, in the array of a beard, which he's been growing ever since he left you.

He has no business here! she said her face flaming with displeasure.

He is come to tell ye news of Fanny Robin, replied Coggan.

Ah! said Bathsheba, interested now, and raising her voice to reach the stranger. And what do you know of Fanny?

I see her in Melchester, ma'am, said the man of beard and velveteen.

O – did you.

Yes, I see her in Melchester, ma'am, the ex-bailiff continued, who seemed anxious to make a very little knowledge of Fanny Robin last as long as a very large quantity of the food he was at that time consuming.

And what do you know about her? Did she speak to you?

No. That was a point she did not do.

Did you speak to her?

I did not. That's one of the things I was going to name as not having accomplished to the full extent.

Then you know nothing about her at all?

Ma'am, how can you! said the bailiff reproachfully and still eating on.

Yes indeed more than nothing at all – much more. 'Twas the eye that I used, as regards her dress.

What did you see?

That she was too well-off to be anything but a ruined woman.

Why did you bring such an uncouth and shuffling man here? Bathsheba said to Coggan.

I didn't in particular, Mistress, he apologised. And if I had known his tale was going to be such a bruckle hit as that I wouldn't have let him come on no account. Still, I assure ye he's a very nice feller, and can sing a song as heartily as any martel man can wish. All that can be said against poor Pennyways is that he can't keep himself from a curious habit of thieving and telling lies, but he'll do his duty like a saint as a member of good company. He's only been in prison a very few times since he left us. Never been transported in his life. O no, no: we'd never ask a convict to our table – 'twould be too low. You'll let him finish his meal, ma'am?

O yes: let him stay if you wish it, but just see that he doesn't steal anything. His knowledge of Fanny is all sham.

Ay, ay, ma'am.

Dear me – 'tis time to fetch the clean plates for the puddens! said Maryann Money suddenly.

Not at all – not at all, said Mr Coggan, answering Maryann, but looking at Bathsheba and then the whole company. No such trouble desired ma'am. 'Tis the greatest extravagance in the world, neighbours, to set people running about for plates when ye've got one warm and clane ready to hand – hey, Master Poorgrass?

True – considerably true, neighbour Coggan: quite true, as I may say.

Then the head-shearer took his plate by its edges, shovelled off his knife and fork upon the cloth and turned the plate bottom upwards. Master Poorgrass followed suit with slavish closeness of imitation, and he was followed unconcernedly by the majority of the company.

Pudden for you Joseph? said Mrs Coggan from a distance.

– A tiny bit – the smallest crumb of imagination, Mrs Coggan.

And a bit about the size of a horse's toe-nail will be quite enough for me, said Jan.

The genius displayed in this remark seized so forcibly upon the fancy of one of the juvenile Coggans who was present, and the enigma it contained filled him with such unqualified delight, that it was treasured up, and repeated to friends and enemies half a dozen times a day for the space of a week.

When I was at my sister-law's at Casterbridge t'other day, continued Jan, and turned my plate as I do now, and as I always do at meals, as did my father afore me, and yours too, neighbours all [the neighbours nodded their heads in assent] my wife made quite a noise about it. 'Why Jane,' I said, 'how canst be so extravagant? There's two clane sides to yer plate always, and ye never use but one of them'. . . . Why, neighbour Oak, pudding wouldn't have had the right taste to my father and yours if they hadn't had it off the bottom of their trenchers? [Coggan threw a strenuous gaze of demand on the shepherd, who expressed similarity of opinion by the minor muscles]. Ah there's my wife listening to what I've got to say [turning to Mrs Coggan, who was wiping knives and forks in the rear]. Bless her dear old heart! Jane you be like a good fiddle – the older and more battered you get, the sweeter you grow. Ah, she've presented me with five youngsters, and I fancy I can see another in that twinkling eye of hers!

Don't be such a noddy, Jan! said Mrs Coggan indignantly, and blushing with confusion.

Well – there – time will tell – 'tis the only proof for prophets, said Jan lowering his spirits. Joseph Poorgrass, in some surprise at the words, privately surveyed Mrs Coggan and thereupon coloured more than had Mrs Coggan herself. Jacob Smallbury, to the great relief of that matron, then started a new subject.

Now if there's one sort of sallet I like at the springtime of the year, 'tis watercress, he said, putting a little heap of salt upon the tablecloth, and folding together a tuft of the cress into the form of a bow.

As for myself, I can always chaw in a head of lettuce in its naterel state, said Susan Tall's husband, helping himself to a complete plant that had been rinsed without mutilation, rolling it round like an umbrella, and then reaching over Joseph Poorgrass's shoulders and probing a distant salt-cellar with the base of the stalk in a fencing attitude, till a satisfactory quantity of salt had adhered. What with a mouthful of rawmil' cheese, and another shard of cider[7] 'tis as neat a stopper down as – The remainder of the statement was lost in a noise slightly resembling the crackling of thorns under a pot, produced by the action of Mr Tall's teeth upon the lettuce-leaves and stem, as the flourishing plant gradually disappeared from daylight, like a plume of feathers vanishing down a conjuror's throat.

II

The second of the two draft-fragments is simply headed 'Chapter.', and consists of 11 leaves of blue paper (with revisions on 3 versos), measuring five and seven-eighths by eight inches and foliated 106a–k. All physical indications suggest that this fragment is an anomaly – probably one of the roughest outline-sketches made for Stephen who no doubt saw the potential in it. But it was never part of the holograph ms: the different leaf measurements, different blue paper and different mode of foliation bear no relation to the ms sheets which are ivory-tinted, measure six and a half by eight and three-eighths inches, and bear a numerical foliation which is both haphazard and frequently overwritten but not alphabetical. These indications, together with the uncharacteristic pencil-markings and roughness of composition – its heavy alterations, unfilled gaps, unamended interlinear revisions, word abbreviations and careless handwriting – bear out Hardy's claim that he often drafted snippets for *Far From the Madding Crowd* if not always on dead leaves at any rate on whatever notebook he had to hand, as he roamed the highways and byways of his Wessex or crossed its wider boundaries by rail.

The extraneous nature of this draft-fragment is also consistent with his practice of self-borrowing. Just as he chose to infuse his published prose with measures of his unpublished verse, or with lost threads of his unpublished novel, *The Poor Man and the Lady* (1868), so the ms version of *Far From the Madding Crowd* acquires choice remnants of the 'Sheep-rot' segment which, with its statistical focus coupled with its ramshackle prose structure, appears to have been primarily a referential piece on pestilential footrot.

The most remarkable of these self-borrowings is that of the 'noxious vapoury' swamp. Elaborated and embedded in Chapter XLIII of the ms, into the scene of Bathsheba's night retreat after her conflict with Troy, this transferred segment now ingeniously provides an apt correlation to the treacherous domestic 'terrain' within: figuratively, an exteriorization of what Bathsheba inwardly experiences as the 'pollution' of her person by marriage.

By contrast there is the less artistically noteworthy self-borrowing of Troy's words to Gabriel after their skirmish: 'Now . . . remember that I am her husband, & injuring me is injuring her: & if you go now it will be injuring . . . me.' Adapted for the ms these now become Troy's self-preserving words in his skirmish with *Boldwood*: 'A moment,' he gasped. 'You are injuring her you love. . . . How can she be saved now unless I marry her?' (XXXIII).

Since Hardy was writing under great pressure, against the clock – many chapters remaining unfinished right up to the last few weeks before publication date – expediency was, no doubt, a significant factor in these self-borrowings. Hence, the transfer of certain segments from the draft-fragment to the ms which may have been handy rather than matchless. The skirmish scene is just such a segment – not only in its transference of the 'injury' idea to Chapter XXXIII in the ms, but also in its infusion into Chapter XIX of Gabriel's firing by Troy after the sheep-rot episode, which is adapted (in the ms) into his firing by Bathsheba before the sheep-blasting episode.

Art and not expediency, though, surely prompted the transfer of Gabriel's 'glowing autumn sunset'. This finds Hardy struggling for apt words and vivid images in the draft-fragment. But by the time it has found its way into the ms and into Bathsheba's sunrise (XLIII), also to round out her hours of desolate repose as it settles into her sundown, the artistic struggle is over: the configuration of the solar orbit enacts an artistic completion of a kind that simultaneously renders the erstwhile fragment poetically whole.

It happens thus. Whereas, in the draft-fragment, Gabriel is set in an incoherent photosphere alternately pausing to contemplate a glowing sunset, 'bristling with a thousand spines of light, which stuck & tormented his eyes', and then turning aside to look down on 'a Valley of the Shadow of Death', Bathsheba, by contrast, is set, in *her* moment of contemplation (at the selfsame swamp), in a coherent firmament in which all elements unite, evoking a slow awakening of both her hazy consciousness and the softly radiating sun. Accordingly, in place of the allusion to the twenty-third Psalm and the 'Valley of the Shadow of Death', Hardy now more appropriately cites (in the ms) Shelley's 'Ode to the West Wind', which he links with Bathsheba's 'creation' of the breezes that shake off the unseen presences of the dead.[8] Equally, as the 'fiery mist' rises, in the draft-fragment, to the accompaniment of a rather inappropriate allusion to

Hamlet's 'god kissing carrion' so in the ms the same mist more poetically provides 'a fulsome yet magnificent silvery veil, full of light from the sun' to illumine the dawning of Bathsheba's outer and inner world. And ultimately, as the haze clears and the new day begins – a lustral day for Bathsheba – and as this, in turn, completes its solemn course at eventide, so too the sun goes 'down almost blood-red' over her domain, striking not with a 'thousand spines of light' upon 'tormented eyes' as in the draft-fragment, but upon the soaring church spire, which 'rose distinct and lustrous . . . bristling with rays' – as the lonely woman watching at her window awaits the dark night, and the black days of mourning to come.

In addition to the conventions for transcribing the first fragment, 'wd' has been expanded to 'would'. Omitted full stops and commas have been added in square brackets. When Hardy failed to delete his original wording, only the revised wording is transcribed.

Chapter.

Troy soon began to make himself busy about the farm.

Bathsheba's flock always fell naturally into two great divisions, the store sheep, and the fatting sheep. At this time of the year the latter could be subdivided, with different shades of distinctness into several grades of fatness, each group of which at due intervals of time follow to market the one preceeding it.

It now happened that Oak was absent from Weatherbury for two or three days on account of two great-markets and one fair which he had attended with some young rams, and he had taken the opportunity of spending a day at Norcombe on his way back. On his return he did not go near the forward fatting wethers for two or three days in addition, so it was about a week from the time of his departure that one evening at dusk he again set eyes on them.

He was amazed at the change in their appearance. Could his eyes deceive him – he went round them pushed them felt them: no, there was no mistake – they had increased beyond all anticipation. When Oak was at home that night, he suddenly thought of something in connection with the sheep and looked concerned. It is impossible he said to himself. However he was uneasy.

Next morning, he went straight to these promising creatures hooked one of them by the leg, held it between his legs and examined the gland in the corner of its eye.

It was yellow.

Oak turned pale, and murmured one word.

Rot!

Now to an honest shepherd or farmer symptoms of Rot are as an alarm of fire to a householder or panic to a capitalist – It is a ruinous catastrophe: the most fearful visitation of the sheep walk, and generally speaking incurable. So destructive is this pestilence that not one sheep in a hundred, when once tainted ever recovers. The animal, after a certain stage, wastes to a skeleton, and at the end of two or three months it dies. It has been calculated by those who collect statistics of this subject – that more than a million sheep and lambs die in Great Britain every year from this disease alone.

We have here regarded rot entirely in its ultimate result, and given it the complexion it naturally wears in the mind of conscientious owners of flocks. But the most remarkable feature of this remarkable malady remains to be pointed out. It has an antecedent feature which is abnormal and surprising, and on account of this to sheep owners not over scrupulous the word has another meaning altogether. It is an opportunity. The disease is a remedy: the blight of what is owned is the enrichment of the owner. It is a means to an end which can be reached so quickly by no other route[.] The end is readiness of stock for market, and consequent early profits from sales.

The explanation, which also embodies an explanation of the wonderful appearance of Bathsheba's fatting ewes just at this time, is briefly this. At the beginning of the attack the bile absorbed into the system operates apparently as a stimulant. It forces on the animal at a rate which is simply astounding. Its appetite is increased, all its nutritive organs seem strengthened, and fat and flesh accumulate with marvellous rapidity upon the most meagre frames. The fatting processes which would naturally occupy two or three months complete themselves by the demoniac aid of this pestilence in half that time. Then comes the re-action, and the poor creatures literally melt away.

The trick is or was, to take the flock to market at the climax of that first stage of the disease, immediately before the skin becomes yellow, and when the animal is plump, sleek and round, and none but an experienced eye can distinguish between its condition and that of the carefully fattened animal.

It was a practice which Oak in common with a few honest farmers of the vicinity resolutely set his face against, and his perplexity now was of a peculiar kind. On examination he found that the limits of the rot in his flock were marked in a very definite and singular manner. The sheep affected were precisely those which were first wanted for market. All the others were as usual. In other words it seemed as if in his absence somebody had been operating upon the sheep for purposes before mentioned.

Gabriel made up his mind at once. Whether the result were that of accident or design, he would have nothing to do with such a scheme, and would do his utmost to counteract it. He took them away from all green food, substituted hay – and gave them each plenty of rock salt to lick, which was the best antidote then in his power. Next morning the salt was gone. The sheep could not have consumed it. Oak had his suspicions.[9]

That day Troy came and said

These shall go off on Saturday I think Oak. Is not there something wonderful in their advance lately. Did you ever see sheep fatten so.

Never, except when they have been rotted, as these are, said Oak, looking Troy full in the face.

O no – nonsense – said Troy. They are not rotted.

Oak did not trouble to reply just then, for his knowledge of the events which had transpired in his absence was limited and he wanted proofs. The damage must have been done some time before he left W. though its effects were not visible till his return[.] The sheep were sent away on the Saturday as Troy had desired.

How the sheep became rotted seemed likely to continue a mystery, and the matter gradually passed into the vast list of unknown causes or undiscovered crimes.

The next batch intended to be fattened were at this time feeding by themselves as usual in a portion of the Great Ewelease.[10] It was in the main a high dry and altogether desirable declivity for the purpose. One end however ran down to a fenny nook at the level of the springs, and was one of the spots on the farm, and the most likely spot, for engendering the disease. To guard against any such contingency Oak had railed off this spot by iron hurdles, which were only removed in winter frosts, when sheep can with perfect impunity depasture upon land at other times fatal. This corner of the land could be flooded by raising a hatch in a small weir at the upper end.

Gabriel finding no other traces of the pestilence in his flock might possibly have ignored the suspicion altogether had not a new incident deepened it. One evening after having been at the other end of the farm for the greater part of the day he passed this corner of the meadow, and paused to look at one of the most glowing of autumn sunsets which shone upon him across the swamp. The effect was indeed, beautiful, and one of which description though it has been exercised for centuries, in every variety of sun[,] somehow seems never to become stale and wearisome. The yellow sun, bristling with a thousand spines of light, which stuck into and tormented his eyes . . . . . . Gabriel had poetical ideas, but they were all discreetly diluted with the practical. He admired the red and the gold and the bristling rays, and then looked lower upon the little swamp. He looked upon a Valley of the Shadow of Death to any ovine entity under the sky. But it was indeed beautiful to look upon. The air about it, looking thus towards the sun, had a substance and a surface visible to the eye. It was a magnificent aureate mist or veil; fiery, yet semi-opaque – the hedge behind in being in some measure hidden by its golden brilliancy.

The presence of the fiery mist was caused by the effect of the hot sun's rays upon the swamp that afternoon – . . "god kissing carrion" etc – its colour, of course, by the reflection and refraction of the suns rays.[11]

Oak's thought was that this was a spot which would indeed rot a sheep, or a thousand sheep, in a very short time, and he thought that if those rotted the other day had only got in there, the cause would be accounted for. The corner was a nuisance – a nursery of pestilences small and great – and it was to be drained. The attempt to convert it into a small water-meadow by introducing a running stream had been virtually a failure[.]

He went closer to see if any old sheep tracks were visible there, which would be an explanation. Iridescent bubbles full of dank subterranean breath rose beside his feet as he trod and hissed as they burst and expanded away to join the vapoury[12] firmament above[.] Oak then noticed that very lately water had been artificially admitted to the swamp by drawing the hatch above, and allowing the water to trickle down the course in the centre, formed for irrigation in winter and spring time. This was strange, for such a procedure was useless and unusual at that time of the year and condition of the pasture.

On this account any old sheep tracks would naturally be washed out. But to his surprise he saw new ones, of less than a day's standing, and more recent than the admission of water appeared to have been.

How could the sheep have got in? He went to the iron hurdles, and looked carefully along their length. In the corner one had been removed – a crowd of tracks were visible under it. Among them were the footprints of a man. Oak knelt down and examined the quality of impression. The boot was a light and well shaped one, with only a few small nails round the heel. The single male person on the farm whose boots were not hobnailed, and queued and tipped with iron, was Troy.

Oak felt himself on the track of a discovery. He resolved to lurk about the place. The trick might be repeated through a possibility of failure the first time.

After supper he took a sheepskin from a nail behind his door[,] rolled it under his arms, and crossed Great Ewelease almost – down to the lower corner. Here he rolled himself up in the sheepskin and lay down under the hedge. Troy was a bird of night, he knew.

Presently the moon peeped over the hill and raked the long incline with its rays. Then, as if the light had been waited for, a man came down the hill, and went to the upper corner of the swamp where the weir was fixed. Then Oak heard the soft rush of water and in a few minutes the shady channel in the middle of the swamp brightened like the streak of a match. The sheen widened and leapt into detached holes and depressions over the surface of the ground, spotting the swamp with dancing reflections of the moon. The spot was flooded.

Then he heard the latch lowered with a sudden jolt, and the rush of water ceased. Everything was silent. Oak slid through the hedge – crept onwards – and looked toward the hatch. This standing in a nook, was sheltered by a belt of pollard willows, and was obscure. A red spot of fire increasing and diminishing in regular pulsations was visible among the shades. Immediately underneath was a small whitish patch, triangular in shape. The triangle of white was [the] visible portion of the strangers shirt-front over his waistcoat. The red spot was the fire of a cigar. The man who had irrigated the meadow after turning off the water again was apparently sitting on the rail, smoking[.] Oak retreated to his nook again.

The water partially drained away. Then the effect became visible. The stagnant hollow deprived of every cooling breeze by its position had been highly heated that afternoon by a clear sun. The faint mist which had been previously rising was increased till it assumed the definite form of steam.

Judging from the time which passed it was when the cigar was finished that the man at the weir went up the hill. Oak heard a muffled trotting, without any accompanying tinkle. The wethers (?) about to be fatted had no bell. The flock appeared – the man, whom Oak now distinctly recognised as Troy, removed one of the iron hurdles, and the sheep were admitted. An instant noise of munching began – Every one of the simple creatures was momentarily and inevitably sucking in disease, death – and an antecedent fatness.

Oak jumped up and ran round them. In two minutes they were again outside the rails.

Troy started round, and came forward. Who the devil are you? he said. Why 'tis Oak – what do you do here.

What do *you*, said Oak. I came here to save the sheep. 'Twas you then who rotted them last time.

Well – suppose it was. Every man can do what he likes with his own.

Not if he poisons other people by doing it.

Pooh – it is no use your being such a pattern of virtue as all that, Oak. You know very well that these things must be done. There's nothing new in my rotting sheep to force their fattening. Every body does it.

Do they. I don't, and Farmer Boldwood don't.

Then you must learn to if you stay here. As to a rotted sheep being poison – it's all nonsense. Besides we send 'em to market, and the dealers send 'em to London – and the people who eat them are nothing to us.

'Tis as much harm to hurt people you don't know as people you do.

Not at all – And Londoners have a taste for such things. They deliberately choose the diseased livers of poultry as delicacies and call them pâtès de foie gras, with watering mouths.

Oh –

And woodcock's entrails

Oh[.]

And newborn pigs like bladders of babies' drool which are not healthy enough to rear.

Yes.

And putrid deer and hide bound oxen, And any far gone animal that's killed to save its life

"So I've heard."

Well then, now let us turn in the sheep again.

Not whilst I am here, said Oak firmly, putting himself before the opening.

O – Who says so?

I know so

We'll see. Once for all, are you going to stand aside

I am not.

Take that then!

Troy sprang forward and, as he intended flung himself against Oak's shoulder on the principle of a battering ram, to turn him round on his centre, and so dislodge him. Oak being quite unprepared received the full force of the butt, and recovering himself flung his arms over Troy's, hugged him, flung him against the rails, and pinned him there.

Where are you now, said Oak quietly.

Look here Oak, said Troy. I am the cleverest at this farm, but you are the strongest. So suppose we effect a compromise.

With all my heart said Oak.

Then, loosen my arms.

Suppose we hear the compromise first –

Very well. Here's the treaty. I agree to give up the idea of putting the sheep in the mead to night. You on your part will leave your post as shepherd here to morrow morning.

'Tisn't a treaty at all. I can't help leaving because you discharge me: for my last agreement was only by the week. You can't put the sheep in to night, at any rate because I shant let you. Though you will, doubtless to morrow. There's no choice either side. However let it be. There you are loose.

Now I shall toddle homeward. To morrow morning you shall be paid up and I shall expect you not to trouble me again[.]

Troy went on. Oak replaced the hurdle and followed him.

To Oaks surprise he met Troy just as he left his door the next morning.

Well Oak – how do you feel, said Troy grimly.

A little stiffness in the shoulder – that's all. How do you?

A slight pain in the back where the iron of the railing came. But look here. My wife says – and, privately between us, she has a bit of the wilful in her constitution you know – that I had no right to say anything last night about your leaving us. So, to cut the matter short, what do you say to going on as if nothing had occurred.

Not if any of those tricks with the sheep are to be tried.

Never mind them – you may as well stay. My wife is a favourite of yours I know – and you wouldn't like to see her in difficulty. Now remember that I am her husband, and injuring me is injuring her: and if you go now it will be injuring me. I own candidly that we can't very well do without you, at least so Bathsheba says.

I'll stay till Candlemas fair[13] if you agree not to interfere with the sheep, and I have my own way with them entirely. That's my offer. And if it wasn't for my old mistress's sake I wouldn't make that.

Troy agreed and the subject dropped. Though the rotting system would have saved a clear month and more in the fatting of each sheep the possible loss by having to entrust an untried shepherd with the approaching fall of lambs more than outweighed the certain gain.

Notes

1. The draft-fragments are held in the Thomas Hardy Memorial Collection at the Dorset County Museum, Dorchester, England.
2. *Life*, 96.
3. See A Note on the History of the Text.
4. I am deeply indebted to the excellent scholarly research undertaken by Lilian Swindall, on my behalf, at the Dorset County Museum. She adds, regarding the 'Shearing Supper' fragment, that 'it is possible to detect a slight alteration in the writing of "Robin"; as if a second "b" was commenced but changed to the "i" with the implication that Hardy from previous usage was about to write "Robbin", but was now conforming to the *Cornhill* usage of "Robin".'
5. All references to letters from Stephen to Hardy are taken from *Purdy*, 336–9.
6. *argus spots*: Given his fascination with light and chiaroscuro effects, Hardy is probably referring to the Argus butterfly which has ocellated wings – wings spotted with orbs of colour surrounded by rings of another colour. Diffuse or refracted light falling upon an object frequently reflects back in ocellated patterns.

Argos was a mythical figure with a hundred eyes; to be Argus-eyed is to be vigilant. By way of extending the metaphor, it is clear that, in the social context, there are 'a hundred eyes' on Boldwood at this particular moment.

7. *Rawmil' cheese . . . cider*: 'Rawmil' is a contraction of 'raw milk' – probably referring to the soft, unripened cheeses (cottage or curd cheeses), often made from skimmed milk and produced for immediate consumption, as distinct from matured or cured hard cheeses made from high-quality milk, such as cheddar. On the other hand, unpasteurized milk, which is still referred to as 'raw milk' in New England to distinguish it from pasteurized milk, could explain Tall's reference were it not for the fact that although pasteurization was introduced into English dairy farming in the 1860s the process was not yet universal. Hardy's dairy farming world seems untouched by it. *Shard* may be either a worn or decayed object or, if the misusage is also intended to be vulgar, a 'dungheap' or 'cowdung' of a drink (of cider).

8. Shelley's lines: 'Thou, from whose unseen presence the leaves dead/Are driven, like ghosts from an enchanter fleeing' (ll. 2–3).

9. Lilian Swindall notes that it may not have been 'safe' to publish details of contaminated mutton; moreover footrot appears not to be an authentic contaminant.

10. *Great Ewelease*: this place does not exist in the ms.

11. On the verso of the preceding leaf Hardy has: 'Descr. these fungi thus. Then there was the ____ with its bloody skin and ____ spots. which . . . There was also'

12. *vapoury*: Hardy first wrote 'fulsome'; then 'steaming' above the line; and 'noxious' below – and 'vapoury' below it. The choice of reading is rather arbitrary.

13. The internal dating of this draft-fragment fails, in all respects, to cohere with that of the story proper.

APPENDIX III

Chapter XVI in the Cornhill *magazine*

This two-page chapter, the second in the April 1874 instalment, is taken directly from *Cornhill*. See A Note on the History of the Text.

CHAPTER XVI

All Saints' and All Souls'.

On a week-day morning a small congregation, consisting mainly of women and girls, rose from its knees in the mouldy nave of All Saints' Church, Melchester, at the end of a service without a sermon. They were about to disperse, when a smart footstep, entering the porch and coming up the central passage, arrested their attention. The step echoed with a ring unusual in a church; it was the clink of spurs. Everybody looked. A young cavalry soldier in a red uniform, with three chevrons of a sergeant upon his sleeve, strode up the aisle, with an embarrassment which was only the more accented by the intense vigour of his step, and by the determination upon his face to show none. A slight flush had mounted his cheek by the time he had run the gauntlet between these females; but, passing on through the chancel arch, he never paused till he came close to the altar railing. Here for a moment he stood alone.

The officiating curate, who had not yet doffed his surplice, perceived the new-comer and followed him to the communion-space. He whispered to the soldier, and then beckoned to the clerk, who in his turn whispered to an elderly woman, apparently his wife, and they also went up the chancel steps.

"'Tis a wedding!" murmured some of the women, brightening. "Let's wait!"

The majority again sat down.

There was a creaking of machinery behind, and some of the young ones turned their heads. From the interior face of the west wall of the tower projected a little canopy with a quarter-jack and small bell beneath it, the automaton being driven by the same machinery that struck the large bell in the tower. Between the tower and the church was a close screen, the door of which was kept shut during services, hiding this grotesque clockwork from sight. At present, however, the door was open, and the egress of the jack, the blows on the bell, and the mannikin's retreat into the nook again, were visible to many, and audible throughout the church.

The jack had struck half-past eleven.

"Where's the woman?" whispered some of the spectators.

The young sergeant stood still with the abnormal rigidity of the old pillars around. He faced the south-east, and was as silent as he was still.

The silence grew to be a noticeable thing as the minutes went on, and nobody else appeared, and not a soul moved. The rattle of the quarter-jack again from its niche, its blows for three-quarters, its fussy retreat, were almost painfully abrupt, and caused many of the congregation to start palpably.

"I wonder where the woman is!" a voice whispered again.

There began now that slight shifting of feet, that artificial coughing among several, which betrays a nervous suspense. At length there was a titter. But the soldier never moved. There he stood, his face to the south-east, upright as a column, his cap in his hand.

The clock ticked on. The women threw off their nervousness, and titters and gigglings became more frequent. Then came a dead silence. Everyone was waiting for the end. Some persons may have noticed how extraordinarily the striking of quarters seems to quicken the flight of time. It was hardly credible that the jack had not got wrong with the minutes when the rattle began again, the puppet emerged, and the four quarters were struck fitfully as before. One could almost be positive that there was a malicious leer upon the hideous creature's face, and a mischievous delight in its twitchings. Then followed the dull and remote resonance of the twelve heavy strokes in the tower above. The women were impressed, and there was no giggle this time.

The clergyman glided into the vestry, and the clerk vanished. The sergeant had not yet turned; every woman in the church was waiting to see his face, and he appeared to know it. At last he did turn, and stalked resolutely down the nave, braving them all, with a compressed lip. Two bowed and toothless old almsmen then looked at each other and chuckled, innocently enough; but the sound had a weird effect in that place.

Opposite to the church was a paved square, around which several overhanging wood buildings of old time cast a picturesque shade. The young man on leaving the door went to cross the square, when, in the middle, he met a little woman. The expression of her face, which had been one of intense anxiety, sank at the sight of his nearly to terror.

"Well?" he said, in a suppressed passion, without looking at her.

"O, Frank – I made a mistake! I thought the church with the spire was All Saints', and I was at the door at half-past eleven to a minute, as you said. I waited till a quarter to twelve, and found then that I was in All Souls'. But I wasn't much frightened, for I thought it could be to-morrow as well."

"You fool, for so fooling me! But say no more."

"Shall it be to-morrow, Frank?" she asked blankly.

"To-morrow!" and he gave vent to a hoarse laugh. "I don't go through that experience again for some time, I warrant you!"

"But after all," she expostulated in a trembling voice, "the mistake was not such a terrible thing! Now, dear Frank, when shall it be?"

"Ah, when? God knows!" he said, with a light irony, and turning from her walked rapidly away.

APPENDIX IV

A Note on the First Illustrator of *Far From the Madding Crowd*: Helen Paterson

Helen Paterson had already illustrated several monthly instalments of *Far From the Madding Crowd* when she first met Hardy in 1874. It was springtime, she was young, talented, strongminded, free-spirited, vital – and he was enchanted.

Some months earlier, before the first *Cornhill* instalment had appeared on the bookstalls, Hardy had

expressed with regard to any illustrations, in a letter of October 1873, 'a hope that the rustics, although *quaint*, may be made to appear intelligent, and not boorish at all'; adding in a later letter: 'In reference to the illustrations, I have sketched in my note-book during the past summer a few correct outlines of smockfrocks, gaiters, sheep-crooks, rick-"staddles", a sheep-washing pool, one of the old-fashioned malt-houses, and some other out-of-the-way things that might have to be shown. These I could send you if they would be of any use to the artist, but if he is a sensitive man and you think he would rather not be interfered with, I would not do so.'[1]

'Man' the illustrator was not, as Hardy discovered shortly afterwards when the first instalment of *Far From the Madding Crowd* appeared in print at the end of December. 'Sensitive' she may well have been, although Hardy was to have no cause for concern in that area. An enthusiastic follower of the Idyllists, Helen Paterson had a profound love for the way of life of the English countryside and a sharp eye for rustic detail. Indeed, in many respects she seems to have been Hardy's very counterpart in so far as her keen powers of observation fully complemented those of the 'man who used to notice such things', as he liked to speak of himself. Seeking out the informal, intimate, and often humorous characteristics of a scene – a figure set in familiar surroundings, the relationship between human forms and their environment – Paterson's affinity with Hardy's aesthetic values and artistic vision could scarcely have been closer. And although her woodcut illustrations to *Far From the Madding Crowd* are limited to black-and-white visual representations of a decorative nature (rather than explanatory), her watercolour paintings elsewhere of rustic scenes are remarkable for their clarity of detail and observation, conveying the accuracy with which she studied landscape and architecture.

Like Hardy's detailed literary renditions, Paterson's watercolours stand as a historical record of the lost appearance and way of life of the English countryside. Frequently delineating the subtle relationship between natural-world objects and mankind's imprint upon them, she also possessed Hardy's lifelong fascination with tracing the timeworn marks of humanity upon the face of timeless nature – in his case, such timeworn marks as the sheep-washing pool, 'the circular basin of brickwork in the meadows' in *Far From the Madding Crowd*, whose glassy surface appears to birds on the wing 'as a glistening Cyclops' eye in a green face' (XVIII), or the ancient dry white track overlaying the Roman vicinal way, in *The Return of the Native*, which bisects the surface of the heath 'like a parting-line on a head of black hair' (II), or even, at a more homely level, the old stone floor in 'The Self-Unseeing' which has shaped itself, over the years, and by innumerable tracks, to something resembling the disfigured surface of the speaker's memory which has itself become sculpted by time and circumstance – 'footworn and hollowed and thin'.

When Paterson was introduced to Hardy in May 1874 she was already a well-established professional artist working for the *Graphic*. Born in Burton-on-Trent some twenty-six years earlier, in 1848, she was a former student of John Everett Millais and Frederick Leighton, and had attended the Birmingham School of Design and Royal Academy Schools in 1867. This was followed by a short sketching tour of Italy in 1868. By the time author and illustrator met in London *Far From the Madding Crowd* was, in fact, well advanced and Paterson had almost completed her artwork for the *Cornhill*, but this did not, apparently, lessen Hardy's interest in her:

> It was no doubt at his instigation that Miss Thackeray wrote from Southwell Gardens to invite Miss Paterson to dine with Hardy and herself at the Pall Mall Café: they could meet at the restaurant itself, she suggested, or 'if you liked better to come here & go with us we wd take gt care of you'.[2]

But the friendship was nipped in the bud: three months later Paterson married the fifty-year-old Irish poet, William Allingham, and Hardy concluded his long engagement to Emma Lavinia also with an August wedding.

Marriage to Allingham now gave the gifted young artist sufficient financial independence to concentrate on her watercolour paintings. The year after she met Hardy she was elected an Associate of the Royal Society of Painters in Water Colours in 1875 and moved to Witley, Surrey, in 1881 – close to her friend and mentor Birket Foster and within walking distance of some of her favourite painting haunts. In the meantime Ruskin, a strong admirer of her work, had praised her representations of 'the gesture, character and humour of charming children in country landscapes' (*Art of England*, 1884), while Hardy, having been asked to find a first-class illustrator for his novel-in-progress, *A Laodicean*, promptly wrote to her only to be instantly disappointed: she replied by return of post to say that she had now given up book illustration altogether.

Returning to live in London in 1890, Helen Paterson (Allingham) now became a commuter in reverse, taking off from her Hampstead home with fellow-artist, Kate Greenaway, into the Middlesex countryside on painting expeditions:

> During the summer . . . we continued our outdoor work together, generally taking an early train from Finchley Road to Pinner, for the day. She [Greenaway] was always scrupulously thoughtful for the convenience and feelings of the owners of the farm or cottage we wished to paint, with the consequence that *we* were made welcome to sit in the garden or orchard where *others* were refused admittance.[3]

Occasionally working from the black-and-white illustrations she had previously made for book publication, Helen Paterson (Allingham) produced vivid paintings of children that were essentially literary in origin. 'Young Customers', for example, which was exhibited in 1875, was based on her illustrations for a book called *A Flat Iron for a Farthing*. This features two tiny pink-bonneted little girls sitting on high stools in a toy store pondering their findings, and although the work clearly follows the 'angelic childhood' theme of Victorian painting, the representation is quite beautifully casual despite the doll-like quality attributed to the young innocents. One silken shoe, for instance, has been kicked off one tiny rebellious foot and lies discarded on the dusty floor in defiance of middle-class decorum.

Of greater relevance to the Hardyan theme is Paterson's painting entitled 'South Country Cottage'. This shows a low thatched cottage flanked by luxuriant flowers amid which a young woman stands with a child in her arms, gazing dreamily out of the garden at a fruiting apple tree bathed in soft summer sunshine. Although there is no record that Paterson ever visited Hardy's birthplace, the thatched cottage bears an uncanny resemblance to his maternal home at Bockhampton in Dorset. More important, the tone and mood of the painting most aptly matches Hardy's cinematic evocation of apple-gathering on a summertime morning in *Under the Greenwood Tree*, where Fancy Day and her friend Susan Dewey are 'pulling down a bough laden with early apples':

It was a morning of the latter summer-time; a morning of lingering dews, when the grass is never dry in the shade. Fuchsias and dahlias were laden till eleven o'clock with small drops and dashes of water, changing the colour of their sparkle at every movement of the air. . . . In the dry and sunny places, dozens of long-legged crane-flies whizzed off the grass at every step the passer took. (Part the Third: III)

The connection between Paterson and Hardy was, in truth, all too brief and, for him, all too sadly perceived as yet another lost opportunity. Some thirty years after their Maytime meeting in London, and some sixteen years after William Allingham had died in 1889, Hardy wrote to his friend and fellow-writer, Edmund Gosse, in answer to an enquiry:

The illustrator of *Far From the Madding Crowd* began as a charming young lady, Miss Helen Paterson, & ended as a married woman, – charms unknown – wife of Allingham the poet. I have never set eyes on her since she was the former & I met her & corresponded with her about the pictures to the story. She was the best illustrator I ever had. She & I were married about the same time in the progress in our mutual work, but not to each other, which I fear rather spoils the information. Though I have never thought of her for the last 20 years your enquiry makes me feel 'quite romantical' about her (as they say here) & as she is a London artist, well known as Mrs A, you might hunt her up, & tell me what she looks like as an elderly widow woman. If you do, please give her my kind regards; but you must not add that those two simultaneous weddings would have been one but for a stupid blunder of God Almighty.[4]

The words are immoderate and 'God Almighty' is a blundering idiot. And that Hardy dwells, with purposeful ambiguity, not only upon the simultaneity of the two marriages but also upon the 'charms unknown' of the 'married woman' of thirty years ago, does not entirely pass the reader's understanding given that the first ten years (following their Maytime encounter) are excluded in the decades of purported oblivion.

'Oblivion' takes a slightly different turn in stanza three of Hardy's poem dedicated to Helen Paterson as follows:

The Opportunity
(For H.P.)

Forty springs back, I recall,
We met at this phase of the Maytime:
We might have clung close through all,
But we parted when died that daytime.

We parted with smallest regret;
Perhaps should have cared but slightly,
Just then, if we never had met:
Strange, strange that we lived so lightly!

Had we mused a little space
At that critical date in the Maytime,
One life had been ours, one place,
Perhaps, till our long cold claytime.

This is a bitter thing
For thee, O man: what ails it?
The tide of chance may bring
Its offer; but nought avails it!

Hardy is notorious for his 'lost-prize' poems. Many are lyrical obituaries of a kind, but not in the case of Helen Paterson. And here the loss seems to be recalled not from over twenty years ago, or thirty years, but forty – presumably a decade after writing to Gosse, *c.* 1914 (although poems have a way of mulling over long periods of time). Paterson was still very much alive in 1914 so this is in no sense a lyrical obituary but an address to a living person. And I would hazard a guess – especially given that the poem is dedicated to 'H.P.' and not to 'H.A.' – that the retrospective dating of 'forty springs back' is, in fact, a late addition, a postdating, and that the lines were originally addressed to a Helen Paterson of but a few 'springs back', at a time when desire was still quick and alive, when longing was still deep and heartfelt, when the error was still seen as quintessentially human, and when bitter regret was more painfully introjected than hopelessly and angrily projected on to an external cause – on to a blundering 'God Almighty'.

Helen Paterson Allingham died in 1926, two years before Hardy's 'cold claytime' in 1928. And he was right to sense the irony in their diverging courses. For as artists they had an unusual amount in common, quite apart from their mutual love of the English countryside, of landscape and architecture, of figures and timeworn objects set in their own familiar surroundings. Paterson's humorous touches and the pleasure she took in elements both incongruous and absurd bring her even closer to Hardy, as also to that generation of pre-Modernists to which they both belonged for whom the more subjective approach of epiphenomenalism and a keen interest in the patterns and conjunctions of form would ultimately serve as the foundation of the modern aesthetic.

Notes

1. *Life*, 97.
2. *Biography*, 159.
3. M. H. Spielmann and G. S. Layard, *Kate Greenaway* (1905).
4. Quoted in *Seymour-Smith*, 190–91.

R.M.

GLOSSARY

Abbreviations

a.	adjective
advb.	adverb
cp.	assimilated to common parlance from French
pr.p.	present participle
pron.	pronoun
sb.	substantive
sb.pl.	substantive plural
vb.	verb

Abraded, vb.	worn away by time and weather
All Fours, phrase	a two-player card game having four main terms – 'High', 'Low', 'Jack', and 'Game'
Amaranthine, a.	lustrous deep purple
Ayless, sb.	phonetic for alias
Baint, vb.	be not; aren't
Baking trendle, sb.	large tub for mixing dough
Banns or licence, sb.	Anglican church regulations require that banns – notice of forthcoming marriages – be announced publicly on three successive Sundays in the parishes of both parties. Alternatively, a licence may be obtained from the bishop of the diocese or his designate (surrogate), which is speedier but more costly
Barley corn, sb.	*barley*: cereal used in making malt liquors; *corn*: its grain. Hence, meaning alcohol
Batty-cake, sb.	small cake
Belief, The, phrase	Credo: the simplest and probably earliest form of Christian creed, ascribed to the Apostles – a formal statement of Christian belief beginning: 'I believe in God the Father Almighty'

Biffins, sb.pl.	deep-red cooking apple
Bit and drop, sb.	a snack or light meal. See also *Drap of sommit*
Blasted, a.	ovine condition: blown-up stomach; bloated with gas/wind from eating too much clover
Board of Guardians, sb.	administrators of the Union workhouse. See also *Union*
Bobbin, sb.	small bar and string for raising a door-latch
Boots hobbed, phrase	studded with broad-headed nails to reinforce heavy-duty boot-soles and heels
Brake of fern, phrase	fern brushwood; *brake*: an abbreviation of bracken
Brandise, sb.	iron tripod used to support pots or kettles over a fire
Bruckle, a.	dirty
Buttresses, sb.pl.	supports built against a wall to help carry the thrust of the roof-vaulting
Carking, a.	burdensome
Chain Salpae, sb.	marine animals that reproduce by forming a tube beneath their bodies that links their embryos in a chainlike formation
Chamfers, sb.pl.	symmetrically bevelled corners
Chancel, sb.	enclosed part of a church near the altar, reserved for clergy and choir
Chaw, vb.	chew
Cheesewring, sb.	a press used to wring the whey from the curds in the making of cheese
Chevrons, sb.pl.	V-shaped insignia of a sergeant
Chiel, sb.	child
Chinchilla, sb.	small South American rodent with very soft pearly-grey fur
Christening, sb.	baptismal ceremony; admission to the Christian Church by name-giving
Cob, sb.	sturdy short-legged riding horse
Cocks and windrows, sb.pl.	hay would first be raked into rows (*windrows*) and then piled into small stacks (*cocks*) for collection
Collars, sb.pl.	horizontal beams connecting two rafters in an A-frame truss

Collect, sb. — short prayer of Anglican or Catholic Church, usually assigned to a particular day or season

Come-by-chance, phrase — born out of wedlock

Communion-space, sb. — between the front row of pews and the altar rail, where wedding ceremonies are held

Contretemps, sb.cp. — mischance

Conventual, a. — pertaining to a convent or to the less strict branch of Franciscans living in large convents

Coping, sb. — stone edging to define the sides of graves, etc.

Copper-plate, sb. — fine printing – achieved by engraving or etching on to polished copper-plate which is then inked and printed

Copse, sb. — otherwise 'coppice' – a thicket of small trees, grown for periodical cutting

Costard, sb. — variety of apple tree

Creeping up, phrase — growing up

Crib-maker, sb. — person who builds cattle pens (cribs) and portable frames made of sticks for temporary pens (hurdles)

Crocketted, adj. — with stonework ornamentation, usually of buds and curled leaves

Crook, sb. — hooked staff for pulling (hooking) sheep

Crowner, sb. — coroner

Dandle-smack-and-coddle, vb. — kiss-and-hug. *Dandle* means petting

Dearly beloved brethren, phrase — the opening of the exhortation to general confession of sin that is read to the congregation as part of Morning and Evening Prayer in the Anglican Church

Devon breed, sb. — beef cattle from Devonshire in south-west England

Dew-bit, sb. — light snack before breakfast

Dibble, sb. — pointed stick for making holes in the ground for planting

Dissenter, sb. — otherwise *chapel-member*. Both describe members of splinter groups of the established national or orthodox church; separated from the Church of

	England by a difference of opinion; otherwise known as *meetinger* or nonconformist – i.e. Methodist. Hardy rings the changes
Down, sb.	open high land, especially treeless undulating chalk uplands of southern England used for pasture
Drabbet, sb.	light ochre-brown twilled linen used for smock-frocks and similar work-garments
Dragoon Guards, sb.pl.	cavalry, originally so named because their muskets seemed to breathe fire like a dragon
Drap of sommit, phrase	a drop of something (*sommit/sommat*) to drink
Drawlatching, a.	sneak-thief, waster – equivalent to shoplifter
Dryads, sb.pl.	in Greek mythology, wood nymphs inhabiting trees
Dutchman, sb.	'I'm a . . .'/'If I'm a . . .' – form of asseveration; statement of abomination rendering the previous statement strongly emphatic; stemming from wars between England and Holland, 'Dutch' became synonymous with all that was abhorrent
Early Ball, sb.	variety of apple
Early Flourballs, sb.	variety of potato
En, pron.	all-purpose pronoun serving for 'him', 'her', 'it'
En papillon, phrase	French: butterfly stroke
Entr'acte, sb.cp.	interval between the acts of a play
Espalier, sb.cp.	tree trained to grow flat upon lattice-work
Ewe-lease, sb.	land set aside for grazing sheep
Faggoting, vb.	binding bundles of sticks together for fuel
Felon, sb.	whitlow, inflamed sore
Fives, sb.	ball-game similar to handball, played with gloved hands (or bat) and requiring three or four walls
Flags, sb.pl.	iris – tall flowering plant with long slender-bladed leaf, growing on moist ground
Flitch, sb.	a side of pork salted and cured
Flying, a.	in stonemasonry: crumbling, flaking
Fob, sb.	a watch pocket just below the waistband of the

	trousers
Fork, sb.	pitchfork, a long-handled fork with two prongs for pitching hay
Froward, a.	perverse
Fuddling, vb.	getting drunk
Fustian, sb.	thick twilled short-napped cotton, usually dyed dark (taken from *Fostat*, a suburb of Cairo)
Gage, sb.	pledge, or token of security
Gaiters, sb.pl.	leather or cloth covering for the lower leg
Gape and swaller, phrase	to open one's mouth wide and gulp down a drink
Gawkhammer mortel, phrase	brainless or empty-headed person (mortal).
Genius loci, sb.	Latin: the spirit of place – from Roman mythology, the guardian spirit of a particular place
Gig, sb.	compact, light, two-wheeled one-horse carriage
Gimp, sb.	flat trimming made of cotton, silk, or other material, often stiffened with wire
Gin, sb.	snare, net, trap
Great Mother, sb.	the earth. In consulting the Oracle at Delphi to ask who would succeed Tarquin, Junius Brutus was told 'He who first kisses his mother,' whereupon he flung himself to the ground, exclaiming, 'Thus, then, I kiss thee, Great Mother Earth,' and was later elected Consul
Guano, sb.	whitish excrement of sea-fowl (or artificial manure made from fish), which is used as fertilizer
Gurgoyle, sb.	otherwise *gargoyle*; grotesque spout, usually resembling human or animal mouth, head or body, projecting from gutter of Gothic building to carry water clear of parapet
Gutta serena, sb.	Latin for 'a clear drop of fluid'; otherwise amaurosis, or blindness unaccompanied by any apparent change in the eye itself
Haggling, vb.	bargaining. See also *higgling* (in *1912*)
Hang fire, phrase	to be slow in going off, as with a firearm's delayed reaction

Hapeth, sb.	half-pennyworth
Hautboy, sb.	otherwise oboe, a wooden double-reed wind instrument of treble pitch and plaintive incisive tone
Haybonds, sb.pl.	cords of hay. See also *wimbling*
Hob, sb.	hobnail; short nail used to reinforce heavy boots
Home Secretary, sb.	Secretary of State for Home Affairs, dealing with law and order, immigration, etc., in England and Wales; has discretionary power, like the President of the USA, to remit the death sentence as it then existed
Horning, vb.	trumpeting, bellowing
Hurdles, sb.pl.	portable fences woven from saplings
Hustings, sb.	temporary platform upon which parliamentary candidates stand to address their constituents
In a taking, phrase	in a fit, a state of excitement
Indian red, a.	copper-coloured, as in 'Red Indian': Native American with deep copper-red skin
Juggernaut, sb.	Hindu god, Vishnu, from Sanscrit *jagannatha* ('lord of the world'), shaped like a seven-headed serpent with winged flaps on each cheek. Juggernaut has, however, come to mean the *car of the Juggernaut*: an enormous wooden machine said to contain the bride of the god, mounted on sixteen wheels and dragged annually by fifty men to the temple in Orissa. Sometimes onlookers would be caught under its wheels
Jumping-jack, sb.	jack-in-a-box, child's toy which consists of a spring-propelled figure held under compression in a box until coil is released
Kerseymere great-coat, sb.	made of a heavy twilled woollen cloth
Lady Day, sb.	25 March, commemorating the Feast of the Annunciation (when it was announced to Mary by the angel Gabriel that she would conceive the Christ-child); also the day when yearly farm labourers' contracts were made and renewed, and quarterly rents became due

Lammas sky, sb.	dry, white-hot midsummer sky; from *Lammas*, the old English *hlafmaesse*, 'loaf-mass' – a harvest festival mass celebrating the first ripe-grain loaves, around 1 August
Lanceolate, a.	shaped like a lance-head, tapering to each end
Lancet, sb.	narrow arched window with pointed head
Leicesters, sb.pl.	a shaggy, hornless breed of sheep native to Leicestershire
Licence, sb.	marriage by special licence. See also *Banns*
Lief as not, phrase	as gladly or willingly do one thing as another
Linsey, sb.	a coarse or inferior wool woven on cotton warp
Long hundreds, phrase	generally a large number (specifically, six score: 120)
Loose-box, sb.	stall in a stable in which an animal can move about
Lord's Prayer, phrase	the 'Our Father' prayer taught by Christ to his disciples (Matthew 6:9–13)
Louvre-boards, sb.pl.	overlapping, sloping boards designed for excluding rain but allowing for ventilation of the fermenting fumes within the malthouse (or similar building)
Mace, sb.	crinkly, dried outer covering of nutmeg, used as spice
Malthouse, sb.	a building where moist grain such as barley or wheat would be spread on the floor and regularly turned over with a shovel until almost germinating, whereupon the maltster would roast the grain in a large fire-heated oven called a 'kiln', eventually to produce the malt used for brewing beer or ale
Meetinger, sb.	See *Dissenter*
Metheglin, sb.	a form of mead, an alcoholic drink made from fermented honey and spices
Moorish arch, sb.	an arch that narrows at the bottom – horseshoe-shaped
Nave, sb.	body of a church up to the chancel, where the altar is located

Near, a.	close-fisted, stingy
Nebula, sb.	a luminous haze or bright area due to a galaxy or large cloud of distant stars
Neck and crop, phrase	entirely, completely. The *crop* is the gorge of a bird
Nits, sb.pl.	eggs of lice or parasitic insect. The practice of regular delousing gives rise to the phrase 'dead as nits'
Noachian, a.	an allusion to the biblical Noah – in common parlance, oversized or cumbrous, as in Noah's Ark, reputedly as big as a medium-sized church
Noddy, sb.	fool, simpleton
Odd man, sb.	handyman; a man who does odd jobs
Offertory plate, sb.	the plate on which money is collected from the congregation during religious services
Orientation of the axis, phrase	the compass direction in which a building is aligned
Ovine, a.	pertaining to sheep
Palter, vb.	to haggle, equivocate
Parabola, sb.	curved path of a trajectory under action of gravity
Parapet, sb.	low wall at edge of roof, balcony, bridge, etc.
Parley, vb.cp.	debating of a point, proviso
Pattens, sb.pl.	footwear like clogs, easily slipped into, and worn to keep feet or shoes out of mud and water; usually consisting of a wooden sole above a projecting metal ring
Penetralia, sb.	innermost recesses of a building, temple, or shrine
Penneth, sb.	short for pennyworth
Phaeton, sb.	light, open four-wheeled carriage usually drawn by a pair of horses; named after the Greek Phaethon, son of Helios the sun god, and noted for his careless driving of the sun-chariot
Pipkin, sb.	small earthenware pot
Pippin, sb.	red and yellow dessert apple. Also slang for an excellent person or thing

Plimmed, vb.	swelled, heaved
Plinth mouldings, sb.pl.	projecting part of wall immediately above ground – e.g. at the base of a church tower
Pony carriage, sb.	carriage with an underslung axle and lengthwise seats
Portcullis, sb.	fortress entrance-grating, sliding up and down in vertical grooves, lowered to block gateway
Promiscuous, a.	irregular, out-of-order, overly casual
Psalter, sb.	book of psalms – sacred songs
Punctilio, sb.	a delicate point of ceremony, formality or the etiquette of conduct
Put in the horse, phrase	put the horse into harness and waggon
Quarrington, sb.	variety of apple tree (in *1912*: 'Quarrenden')
Quarter-jack, sb.	figure of a man who strikes the clock's bell at quarter-hour intervals
R.A., sb.	Royal Academician – member of the British Royal Academy of Arts; presumably a reliable judge of conventional beauty
Rake, sb.	a dissipated or immoral individual of fashion
Rathe Ripe, sb.	variety of apple
Reed-drawing, vb.	combing straw through a frame to prepare it for thatching
Rick-cloths, sb.pl.	tarpaulins
Ricks, sb.pl.	'stacks' of straw, hay, corn, etc., but more often regularly built and thatched for durable storage
Roman cement, sb.	a mixture of chalk or clay, sand, lime, and water
Rooted, a.	short for 'uprooted'
Route, The, sb.	a specific route designated by military order
Rowel, sb.	spiked revolving disc at the end of a spur
Ruck, sb.	the majority, the general run
Ruined woman, phrase	indicating a ruined reputation, this 'unmentionable' condition carried a heavy social stigma which Hardy, throughout his entire literary career, struggled to ameliorate, most notably in *Tess of the d'Urbervilles* (1891). A ruined woman was a sexually active unmarried woman: according to the prevailing ideology and moral law, in

	having lost her virginity she could not be taken as a man's lawful wife for fear of illegitimate offspring and threat to the patriarchal blood-line. Thus, not only of ruined moral reputation but also economically ruined because unable to secure her right to a husband and financial support for herself and children
Rumen, sb.	first of a sheep's four stomach compartments
Russia duck, sb.	plain-woven linen canvas used to make tents, sails, and work-clothing
Sackcloth, sb.	sacking, a coarse fabric of flax or hemp; garment worn as an act of penitence or mourning
Sampler, sb.	piece of artwork embroidery worked in various stitches to show skill – for display
Saying after me, phrase	concluding words to *Dearly beloved brethren* (see above)
Scram, a.	puny, withered
Scroff, sb.	refuse for burning
Seampstering, sb.	work as a seamstress, sewing-woman
Sengreen, sb.	herb with pink flowers often found growing on walls and roofs of houses
Serpent, sb.	wind instrument made of an eight-foot-long leather-covered wooden tube shaped in several snake-like curves, giving a powerful deep-bass note
Sexajessamine, sb.	Sexagesima – the second Sunday before Lent – refers to the sixtieth day after Christmas
Show the white feather, phrase	to show cowardice. A gaming term: no gamecock has a white feather so if this is displayed it indicates a cross-breed and not a true game bird – not a true fighter
Skit, sb.	skittish young horse
Smith's shop, sb.	metal-worker's shop
Smockfrocks, sb.pl.	field-labourers' former outer linen garment of shirt-like shape and with the upper part closely gathered; a similar garment was worn by artists

Snapper, sb.	a sudden spell (snap) of frosty or cold weather
Speak with closed doors, phrase	to speak confidentially
Spear-bed, sb.	reed-bed
Spoliated, vb.	plundered
Spreading-board, sb.	board upon which a sheep is laid for shearing
Spring waggon, sb.	a waggon mounted on springs to cushion the ride
Staddles, sb.pl.	platform, pillars or framework supporting a hay-rick on posts, to raise ricks and granaries from the earth, keeping rats out
Stales, sb.pl.	baked goods left over from the previous day
Staple, sb.	fibre of wool used for determining length
Stile, sb.	steps or rungs arranged to allow people entry through a fence or hedge, but excluding livestock
Strait-waistcoating, sb.	strong garment put on a violent person to confine the arms; figuratively, restrictive measures
Straw-mote, sb.	particle of (straw) dust
Stun-poll, sb.	literally, stunned head (*poll*): blockhead
Surrogate, sb.	notariser – a bishop's deputy authorized to grant marriage licences without calling banns. See also *Banns*
Ten Commandments, sb.	the ten rules for worshipping God that, according to the Old Testament, were given to Moses on Mount Sinai, engraved on tablets of stone
Tergiversation, sb.	turning one's back on something, equivocating
Thesmothete, sb.	the name given to certain judges in ancient Athens
Thompson's Wonderfuls, sb.pl.	variety of potato
Three-double, a.	bent over or doubled over in three parts
Tined, vb.	shut
Tipple, sb.	a pleasantly intoxicating drinking bout
To pen, phrase	ovine culture: to put into safety and shelter in sheep enclosure
Tom Putt, sb.	variety of apple
Toper, sb.	habitual drinker

Topping, a.	excellent; pre-eminent in rank
Trading o't to, phrase	an abbreviation of 'trading out to'
Traitor's Gate, sb.	river gate on the Thames through which traitors and other state prisoners entered the Tower of London
Transepts, sb.pl.	lateral arms of a cruciform church
Trencher, sb.	serving dish, plate
Tressy oat-ears, phrase	like silky locks of hair; oat-ears, or corn-ears, are the seedheads of the grain
Trochar, sb.	a sharply pointed lance that projects from within a hollow tube
Turn king's evidence, phrase	when an accomplice to a crime testifies for the prosecution, usually for a reward
Turnpike, sb.	road where a toll has to be paid
Tything, sb.	in close affiliation – an old rural cooperative system involving the unification of a group of ten householders
Union, sb.	a system of workhouses introduced by the Poor Law of 1834: adjacent parishes were obliged to unite in the construction and support of local Unions in order to provide relief for paupers (see also note 6 to Preface)
Vandyked lace collar, sb.	a wide collar with deeply scalloped pointed borders, common in portraits by Van Dyck, Flemish painter (1599–1641)
Vermiculations, sb.pl.	worm-like grooves and ridges
Vetches, sb.pl.	plant of the pea family cultivated for forage
Vitus's (St) dance, sb.	a nervous disorder otherwise known as Sydenham's chorea characterized by involuntary muscular spasms, twitches and jerks
Wafer, sb.	small, thin, disk-shaped object
White Monday, sb.	otherwise Whit Monday, the day after Whit Sunday or Pentecost (the second Sunday after Ascension Day) in the ecclesiastical year, which commemorates the descent of the Holy Spirit upon the disciples. White Monday is followed by White Tuesday (Whit Tuesday), the traditional

	day for clubwalking
Whitlow, sb.	infected sore
Whop and slap, phrase	*Whop*: to defeat, overcome, thrash; *slap*: cheerfully casual – hence a happy-go-lucky approach to work
Wimbling, vb.	twisting hay into cords with an auger (wimble)
Winding-sheet, sb.	burial cloth for a corpse
Yeaning, pr.p./sb.	birthing
Zephyr, sb.	soft breeze; from Greek mythology – Zephuros, god of the west wind

R.M.

THE STORY OF PENGUIN CLASSICS

THE STORY OF PENGUIN CLASSICS

Before 1946 ...'Classics' are mainly the domain of academics and students, without readable editions for everyone else. This all changes when a little-known classicist, E. V. Rieu, presents Penguin founder Allen Lane with the translation of Homer's *Odyssey* that he has been working on and reading to his wife Nelly in his spare time.

1946 *The Odyssey* becomes the first Penguin Classic published, and promptly sells three million copies. Suddenly, classic books are no longer for the privileged few.

1950s Rieu, now series editor, turns to professional writers for the best modern, readable translations, including Dorothy L. Sayers's *Inferno* and Robert Graves's *The Twelve Caesars*, which revives the salacious original.

1960s The Classics are given the distinctive black jackets that have remained a constant throughout the series's various looks. Rieu retires in 1964, hailing the Penguin Classics list as 'the greatest educative force of the 20th century'.

1970s A new generation of translators arrives to swell the Penguin Classics ranks, and the list grows to encompass more philosophy, religion, science, history and politics.

1980s The Penguin American Library joins the Classics stable, with titles such as *The Last of the Mohicans* safeguarded. Penguin Classics now offers the most comprehensive library of world literature available.

1990s The launch of Penguin Audiobooks brings the classics to a listening audience for the first time, and in 1999 the launch of the Penguin Classics website takes them online to a larger global readership than ever before.

The 21st Century Penguin Classics are rejacketed for the first time in nearly twenty years. This world famous series now consists of more than 1300 titles, making the widest range of the best books ever written available to millions – and constantly redefining the meaning of what makes a 'classic'.

The Odyssey continues ...